EL DORADO COUNTY LIBRARY
3 1738 00379 4961

D0962193

BOOK THREE OF *THE TAMULI*

THE HIDDEN CITY

By David Eddings
Published by Ballantine Books:

THE BELGARIAD

Book One: *Pawn of Prophecy*
Book Two: *Queen of Sorcery*
Book Three: *Magician's Gambit*
Book Four: *Castle of Wizardry*
Book Five: *Enchanters' End Game*

THE MALLOREON

Book One: *Guardians of the West*
Book Two: *King of the Murgos*
Book Three: *Demon Lord of Karanda*
Book Four: *Sorceress of Darshiva*
Book Five: *The Seeress of Kell*

THE ELENIUM

Book One: *The Diamond Throne*
Book Two: *The Ruby Knight*
Book Three: *The Sapphire Rose*

High Hunt

The Losers

THE TAMULI

Book One: *Domes of Fire*
Book Two: *The Shining Ones*
Book Three: *The Hidden City*

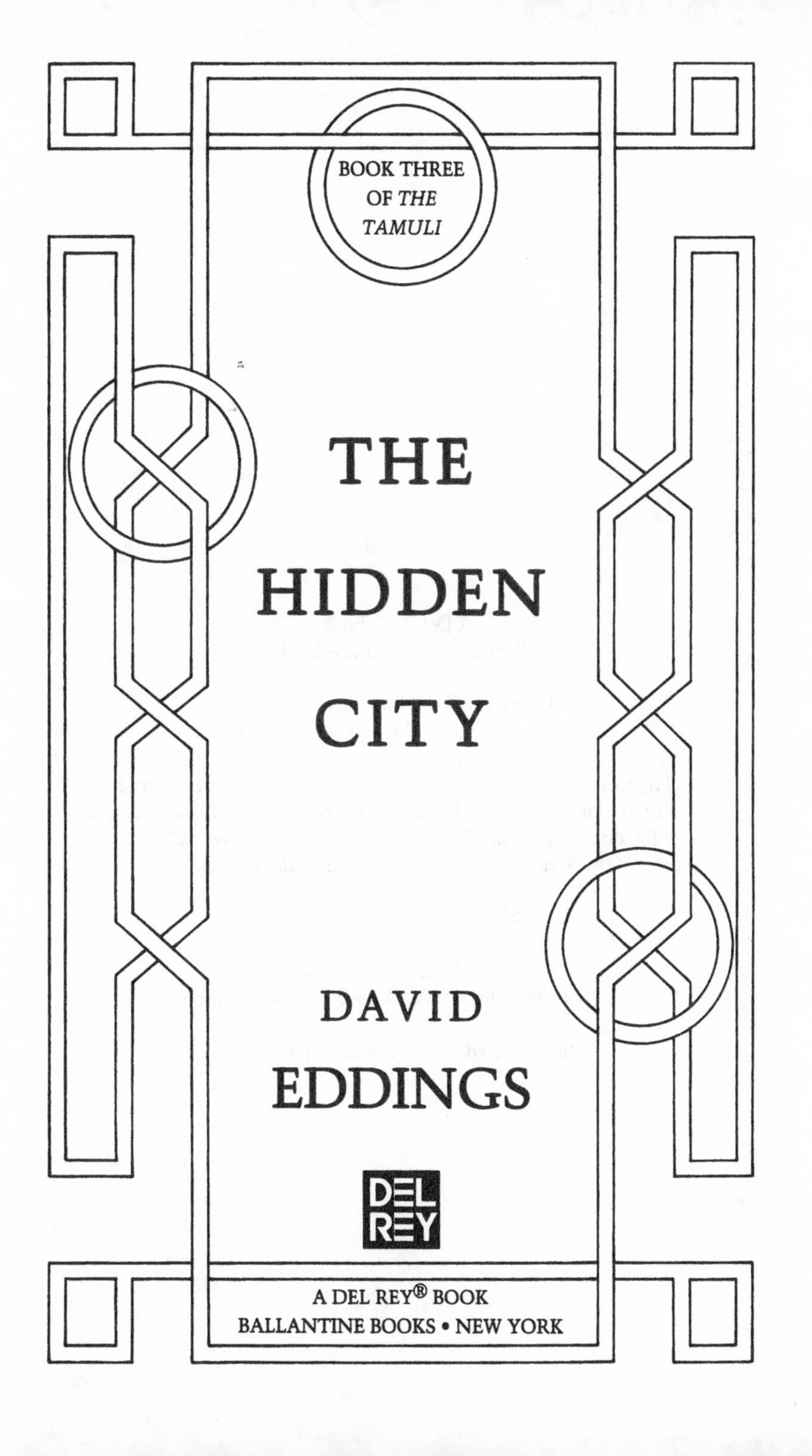

BOOK THREE OF *THE TAMULI*

THE HIDDEN CITY

DAVID EDDINGS

DEL REY

A DEL REY® BOOK
BALLANTINE BOOKS • NEW YORK

A Del Rey® Book
Published by Ballantine Books

ISBN 0-345-37323-5

Text design by Holly Johnson

Manufactured in the United States of America

For Dr. Bruce Gray—

For his enthusiasm and his technical advice—and for keeping our favorite author (and wife) alive—

and for Nancy Gray, R.N.,

who takes care of everybody else,
and neglects to take care of herself.

Shape up, Nancy.

BOOK THREE OF *THE TAMULI*

THE HIDDEN CITY

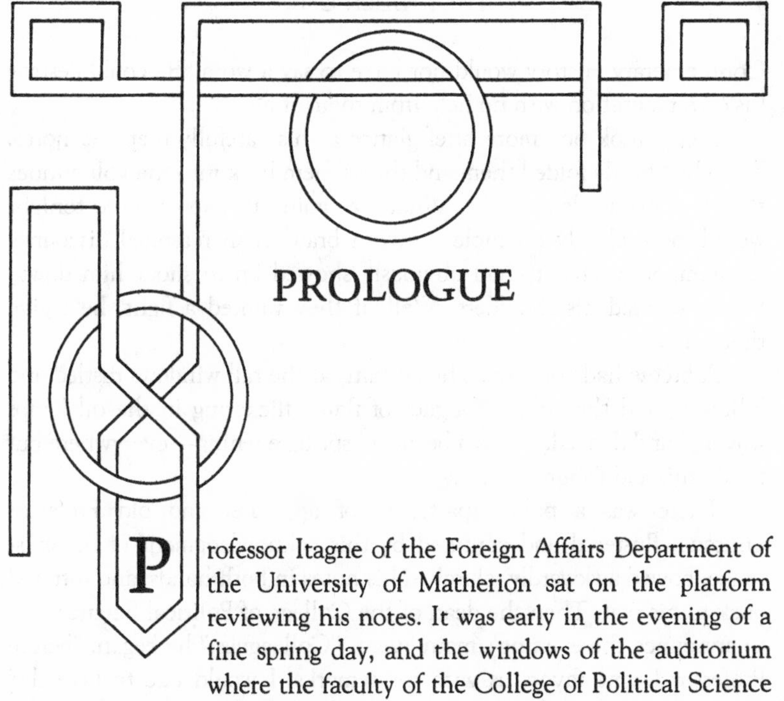

PROLOGUE

Professor Itagne of the Foreign Affairs Department of the University of Matherion sat on the platform reviewing his notes. It was early in the evening of a fine spring day, and the windows of the auditorium where the faculty of the College of Political Science had gathered were open to admit the smell of flowers and grass and the faintly distracting sound of birdsong.

Professor Emeritus Gintana of the International Trade Department stood at the lectern droning on interminably about twenty-seventh-century tariff regulations. Gintana was a wispy, white-haired, and slightly vague academic customarily referred to as "that dear old man." Itagne was not really listening to him.

This was not going to go well, he concluded wryly, crumpling up and discarding yet another sheet of notes. Word of his subject had been broadcast across the campus, and academics from as far away as Applied Mathematics and Contemporary Alchemy packed the hall, their eyes bright with anticipation. The entire faculty of the Contemporary History Department filled the front rows, their black academic robes making them look like a flock of crows. Contemporary History was here in force to ensure all the fireworks anyone could hope for.

Itagne idly considered a feigned collapse. How in the name of God—any God—was he going to get through the next hour without making a total ass of himself? He had all the facts, of course, but what rational man would *believe* the facts? A straightforward account of what had really happened during the recent turmoil would sound like the ravings of a lunatic. If he stuck to straight truth, the hacks from

Contemporary History would not have to say a word. He could destroy his own reputation with no help from them at all.

Itagne took one more brief glance at his carefully prepared notes. Then he bleakly folded them and thrust them back into the voluminous sleeve of his academic robe. What was going to happen here tonight would more closely resemble a tavern brawl than reasoned discourse. Contemporary History had obviously showed up to shout him down. Itagne squared his shoulders. Well, if they wanted a fight, he'd give them one.

A breeze had come up. The curtains at the tall windows rustled and billowed, and the golden tongues of flame flickering in the oil lamps wavered and danced. It was a beautiful spring evening—everywhere but inside this auditorium.

There was a polite spattering of applause, and old Professor Gintana, flustered and confused by this acknowledgment of his existence, bowed awkwardly, clutched his notes in both hands, and tottered back to his seat. Then the dean of the College of Political Science rose to announce the evening's main event. "Colleagues," he began, "before Professor Itagne favors us with his remarks, I would like to take this opportunity to introduce some visitors of note. I'm sure you will all join with me in welcoming Patriarch Emban, First Secretary of the Church of Chyrellos; Sir Bevier, the Cyrinic Knight from Arcium; and Sir Ulath of the Genidian Order located in Thalesia."

There was more polite applause as a pale, gawky student ushered the Elene visitors onto the stage and Itagne hurried across the platform to greet his friends. "Thank God you're here," he said fervently. "The whole Contemporary History Department's turned out—except for the few who are probably outside boiling the tar and bringing up bags of feathers."

"You didn't think your brother was going to hang you out to dry, did you, Itagne?" Emban smiled, settling onto a bench beneath the window. "He thought you might get lonesome here, so he sent us to keep you company."

Itagne felt better as he returned to his seat. If nothing else, Bevier and Ulath could head off any *physical* attacks.

"And now, colleagues and distinguished guests," the dean continued, "Professor Itagne of the Foreign Affairs Department will respond to a recent paper published by the Department of Contemporary History under the title, 'The Cyrga Affair: An Examination of the Recent Crisis.' Professor Itagne."

Itagne rose, strode purposefully to the lectern, and assumed his most offensively civilized expression. "Dean Altus, distinguished colleagues, faculty wives, honored guests . . ." He paused. "Did I leave anybody out?"

There was a titter of nervous laughter. Tension was high in the hall.

"I'm particularly pleased to see so many of our colleagues from Contemporary History here with us this evening," Itagne continued, throwing the first punch. "Since I'll be discussing something near and dear to their hearts, it's much better that they're present to hear what I say with their own ears rather than being forced to rely on garbled secondhand accounts." He smiled benignly down at the scowling hacks in the front row. "Can you hear me, gentlemen?" he asked. "Am I going too fast for any of you?"

"This is outrageous!" a portly, sweating professor protested loudly.

"It's going to get worse, Quinsal," Itagne told him. "If the truth bothers you, you'd better leave now." He looked out over the assemblage. "It's been said that the quest for truth is the noblest occupation of man, but there be dragons lurking in the dark forests of ignorance. And the names of these dragons are 'Incompetence' and 'Political Bias' and 'Deliberate Distortion' and 'Sheer, Wrongheaded Stupidity.' Our gallant friends here in Contemporary History bravely sallied forth to do battle with these dragons in their recently published 'Cyrga Affair.' It is with the deepest regret that I must inform you that the dragons won."

There was more laughter, and dark scowls from the front row.

"It's never been any secret at this institution that the Contemporary History Department is a political entity rather than an academic one," Itagne continued. "It has been sponsored from its very inception by the prime minister, and its only reasons for existence have been to gloss over his blunders and to conceal as best they might his absolute incompetence. To be sure, Prime Minister Subat and his accomplice, Interior Minister Kolata, have never been interested in honesty, but *please*, gentlemen, this is a university. Shouldn't we at least *pretend* to be telling the truth?"

"Rubbish!" a burly academic in the front row bellowed.

"Yes," Itagne replied, holding up a yellow-bound copy of "The Cyrga Affair," "but if you knew it was rubbish, Professor Pessalt, why did you publish it?"

The laughter in the hall was even louder this time, and it drowned out Pessalt's spluttered attempt to answer.

"Let us push on with this great work that we are in," Itagne suggested. "We all know Pondia Subat for a scheming incompetent, but the thing that baffles me about your 'Cyrga Affair' is its consistent attempt to elevate the Styric renegade Zalasta to near sainthood. How in the name of God could *anyone*—even someone as severely limited as the prime minister—revere this scoundrel?"

"How *dare* you speak so of the greatest man of this century?" one of the hacks screamed at him.

"If Zalasta's the best this century can manage, colleague, I think we're in deep trouble. But we digress. The crisis which Contemporary History chooses to call 'The Cyrga Affair' has been brewing for several years."

"Yes," someone shouted with heavy sarcasm, "we noticed that!"

"I'm so happy for you," Itagne murmured, drawing another loud laugh from the audience. "To whom did our idiot prime minister turn for aid? To Zalasta, of course. And what was Zalasta's answer to the crisis? He urged us to send for the Pandion Knight, Prince Sparhawk of Elenia. Why would the name of an Elene nobleman leap to Zalasta's lips in answer to the question—almost before it was asked—*particularly* in view of the sorry record of the Elenes in their relations with the Styrics? To be sure, Prince Sparhawk's exploits are legendary, but what was it about the man that made Zalasta pine for his company? And why was it that Zalasta neglected to tell us that Sparhawk is Anakha, the instrument of the Bhelliom? Did the fact somehow slip his mind? Did he think that the spirit which creates whole universes was somehow irrelevant? I find no mention at all about Bhelliom in this recently published heap of bird droppings. Did you omit the most momentous event of the past eon deliberately? Were you so caught up in trying to give your adored Pondia Subat credit for policy decisions he had no part in that you decided not to mention Bhelliom at all?"

"Balderdash!" a deep voice roared.

"I'm pleased to meet you, Professor Balderdash. My name's Itagne. It was good of you to introduce yourself. Thanks awfully, old boy."

The laughter was tumultuous this time.

"Fast on his feet, isn't he?" Itagne heard Ulath murmur to Bevier.

Itagne looked up. "Colleagues," he said, "I submit that it was *not* Prince Sparhawk that Zalasta so yearned for, but the Bhelliom. Bhelliom is the source of ultimate power, and Zalasta has been trying to get his hands on it for three centuries—for reasons too disgusting to mention. He has been willing to go to any lengths. He has betrayed his faith, his people, and his personal integrity—such as it was—to gain what the Trolls call 'the flower-gem.' "

"That tears it!" the corpulent Quinsal declared, rising to his feet. "This man is mad! Now he's talking about Trolls! This is an academic affair, Itagne, not the children's hour. You've picked the wrong forum for fairy tales and ghost stories."

"Why don't you let me do this, Itagne?" Ulath said, rising to his feet and coming to the podium. "I can settle this question in just a moment or two."

"Feel free," Itagne said gratefully.

Ulath set one huge hand on each side of the lectern. "Professor Itagne has requested me to brief you gentlemen on a few matters," he said. "I take it that you're having some difficulties with the notion of Trolls."

"None at all, Sir Knight." Quinsal retorted. "Trolls are an Elene myth and nothing else. There's no difficulty in that at all."

"What an amazing thing. I spent five years compiling a Trollish grammar. Are you saying that I was wasting my time?"

"I think you're as mad as Itagne is."

"Then you probably shouldn't irritate me, should you? Particularly in view of the fact that I'm so much bigger than you are." Ulath squinted at the ceiling. "Logic tells us that no one can prove a negative. Are you sure you wouldn't like to amend your statement?"

"No, Sir Ulath. I'll stand by what I just said. There's no such thing as a Troll."

"Did you hear that, Bhlokw?" Ulath raised his voice slightly. "This fellow says that you don't exist."

There was a hideous roar in the corridor outside the auditorium, and the double doors at the rear splintered and crashed inward.

"Stay calm!" Bevier hissed as Itagne jumped. "It's an illusion. Ulath's amusing himself."

"Would you like to turn around and tell me what you see at the back of the hall, Quinsal?" Ulath asked. "Exactly what would you call my friend Bhlokw there?"

The creature hulking in the doorway was huge, and its bestial face was contorted with rage. It stretched its paws forth hungrily. "Who has said this, U-lat?" it demanded in a hideous voice. "I will cause hurt to it! I will rip it to pieces and eat it!"

"Can that Troll actually speak Tamul?" Itagne whispered.

"Of course not," Bevier smiled. "Ulath's getting carried away."

The hideous apparition in the doorway bellowed a horribly graphic description of its plans for the faculty of the Contemporary History Department. "Were there any other questions about Trolls?" Ulath asked mildly, but none of the assembled academics heard him over all the shouts, screams, and the tipping over of chairs.

It took the better part of a quarter of an hour to restore order once Ulath had dismissed his illusion; and when Itagne reapproached the lectern, the entire audience was huddled closely together near the front of the auditorium. "I'm touched by your eagerness to hear my every word, gentlemen—" Itagne smiled. "—but I can speak loudly enough to be heard at the back of the hall, so you needn't draw so close. I trust that the visit of Sir Ulath's friend has cleared up the little misunderstanding about Trolls?" He looked at Quinsal, who was still cowering on the floor, gibbering in terror. "Splendid," Itagne said. "Briefly then, Prince Sparhawk came to Tamuli. Elenes are sometimes a devious people, so Sparhawk's wife, Queen Ehlana, proposed a state visit to Matherion and concealed her husband and his friends in her entourage. Upon their arrival, they almost immediately uncovered some facts which we had somehow overlooked. First, Emperor Sarabian actually has a mind; and second, the government led by Pondia Subat was in league with our enemies."

"Treason!" a thin, balding professor shrieked, leaping to his feet.

"Really, Dalash?" Itagne asked. "Against whom?"

"Why—uh—" Dalash floundered.

"You still don't understand, do you, gentlemen?" Itagne asked the faculty of Contemporary History. "The previous government has been overthrown—by the emperor himself. Tamuli is now an Elene-style monarchy, and Emperor Sarabian rules by decree. The previous government—and its prime minister—are no longer relevant."

"The prime minister cannot be removed from office!" Dalash screamed. "He holds his position for life!"

"Even if that were true, it suggests a rather simple solution to the problem, doesn't it?"

"You wouldn't *dare*!"

"Not me, old boy. That's the emperor's decision. Don't cross him, gentlemen. If you do, he'll decorate the city gates with your heads. But let's press on here; I'd like to cover a bit more ground before our customary recess. It was the aborted coup attempt that finally brought things to a head. Pondia Subat was a party to the entire conspiracy and he fully intended to stand around wringing his hands while the drunken mob murdered all of his political enemies, evidently including the emperor himself. If Professor Dalash wants to scream 'treason' he might take a look at that. We discovered much in the aftermath of that failed coup, not only concerning the treason of the prime minister, but of the minister of the interior as well. Most important, however, was the discovery that it had been *Zalasta* who had engineered the entire plot, *and* that he was secretly allied with Ekatas, High Priest of Cyrgon, the God of the supposedly extinct Cyrgai.

"At this point Prince Sparhawk had no choice but to retrieve Bhelliom from its hiding place and to send to Chyrellos for reinforcements. He enlisted other allies as well, not the least of which were the Delphae—who *do* in fact exist in all their glowing horror."

"This is absurd!" Contemporary History's reigning bullyboy, the crude and muscular Professor Pessalt, sneered. "Are we supposed to believe this nonsense?"

"You've already seen a Troll this evening, Pessalt," Itagne reminded him. "Would you like a personal visitation by a Shining One as well? I can arrange it, if you'd like—but outside, please. We'd never get rid of the stink if you were dissolved into a puddle of slime right here in front of the platform."

Dean Altus cleared his throat meaningfully.

"Yes sir," Itagne assured him. "I'll just be a few more minutes." He turned back to the audience. "Now then," he continued quickly, "since the subject of the Trolls has come up again, we might as well clear it away once and for all. As you've noticed, the Trolls are real. They were lured to Tamuli from their home range in northern Thalesia by Cyrgon, who posed as one of their Gods. The *real* Troll-Gods have been imprisoned for eons, and Prince Sparhawk offered them an exchange—their freedom in return for their aid. He then led a sizable force to northern Atan, where the misguided Trolls had been stirring up turmoil in hopes of forcing the Atans to return to defend their homeland—which would have left us effectively defenseless, since the Atans comprise the bulk of our army. Sparhawk's move *seemed* to play right into the hands of our enemies, but when Cyrgon and Zalasta unleashed the Trolls, Sparhawk called forth their Gods to reclaim them. In desperation, Cyrgon reached back in time and produced a huge army of his Cyrgai—and the Trolls, true to their nature, ate them."

"You don't really expect us to swallow this, do you, Itagne?" Professor Sarafawn, chairman of the Department of Contemporary History and brother-in-law of the prime minister, demanded scornfully.

"Was that supposed to be a pun, Sarafawn?" Itagne asked. "No matter. The short answer is that you might as well," Itagne told him. "Your wife's brother isn't dictating official history anymore. From now on, the emperor wants us to give our students the plain, unvarnished truth. I'll be publishing a factual account in the next month or so. You'd better reserve a copy, Sarafawn, because you're going to be required to teach it to all your students in the future—assuming that you *have* a future at this institution. Next year's budget's going to be a little tight, I understand, so a number of departments will probably have to be dropped." He paused. "Are you any good with tools, Sarafawn? There's a very nice little vocational school at Jura, I hear. You'd just *love* Daconia."

The dean cleared his throat again, a bit more urgently this time.

"Sorry, Dean Altus," Itagne apologized. "I'm running past time, gentlemen, so I'll just briefly sum up one more development. Despite their crushing defeat, Cyrgon and Zalasta were by no means powerless. In a bold stroke, Zalasta's natural son, one Scarpa, crept into the imperial compound and abducted Queen Ehlana, leaving behind a demand that Sparhawk give up the Bhelliom in exchange for the safe return of his wife.

"Following the recess Dean Altus has been so patiently awaiting, I will take up Prince Sparhawk's reaction to *that* development."

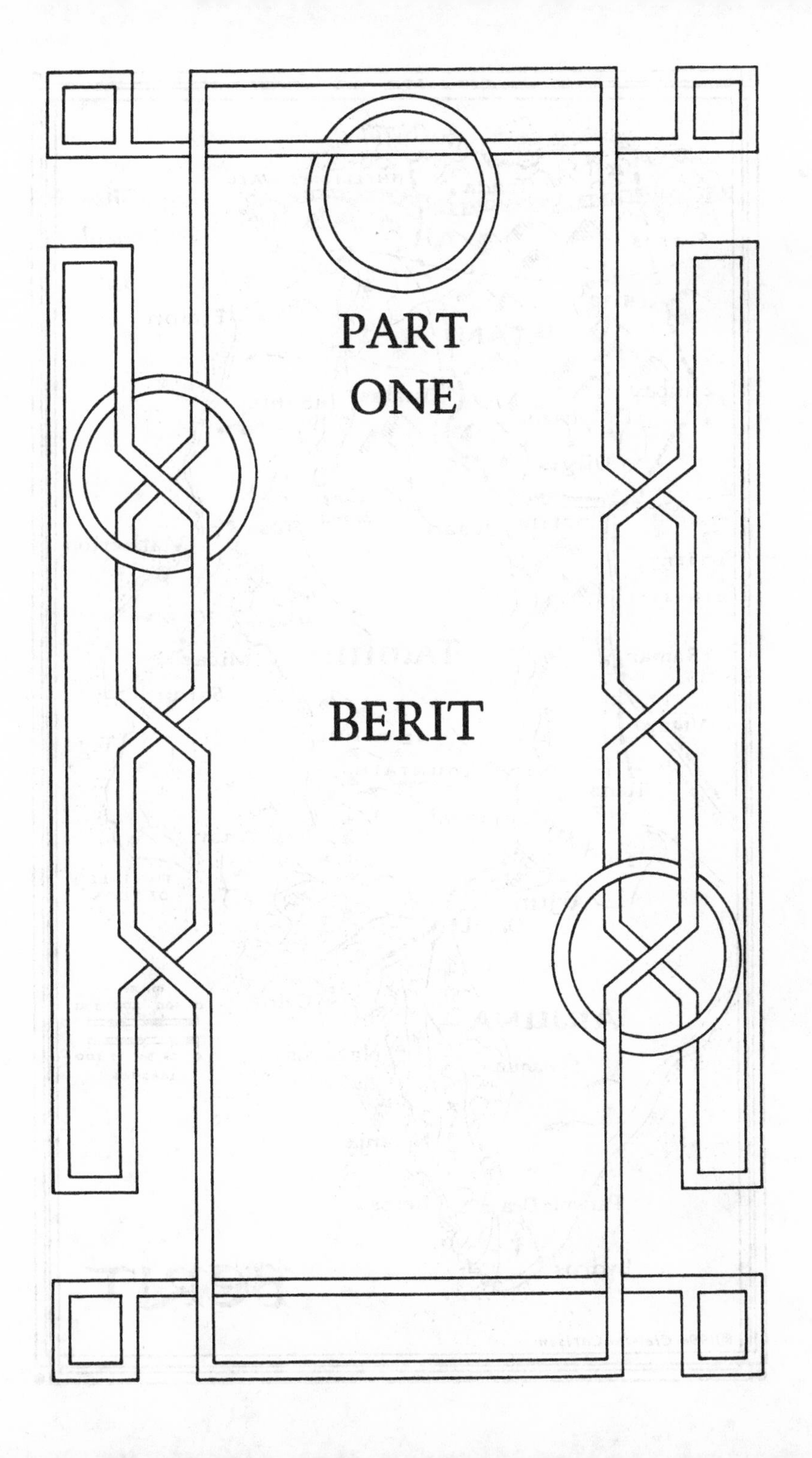

PART ONE

BERIT

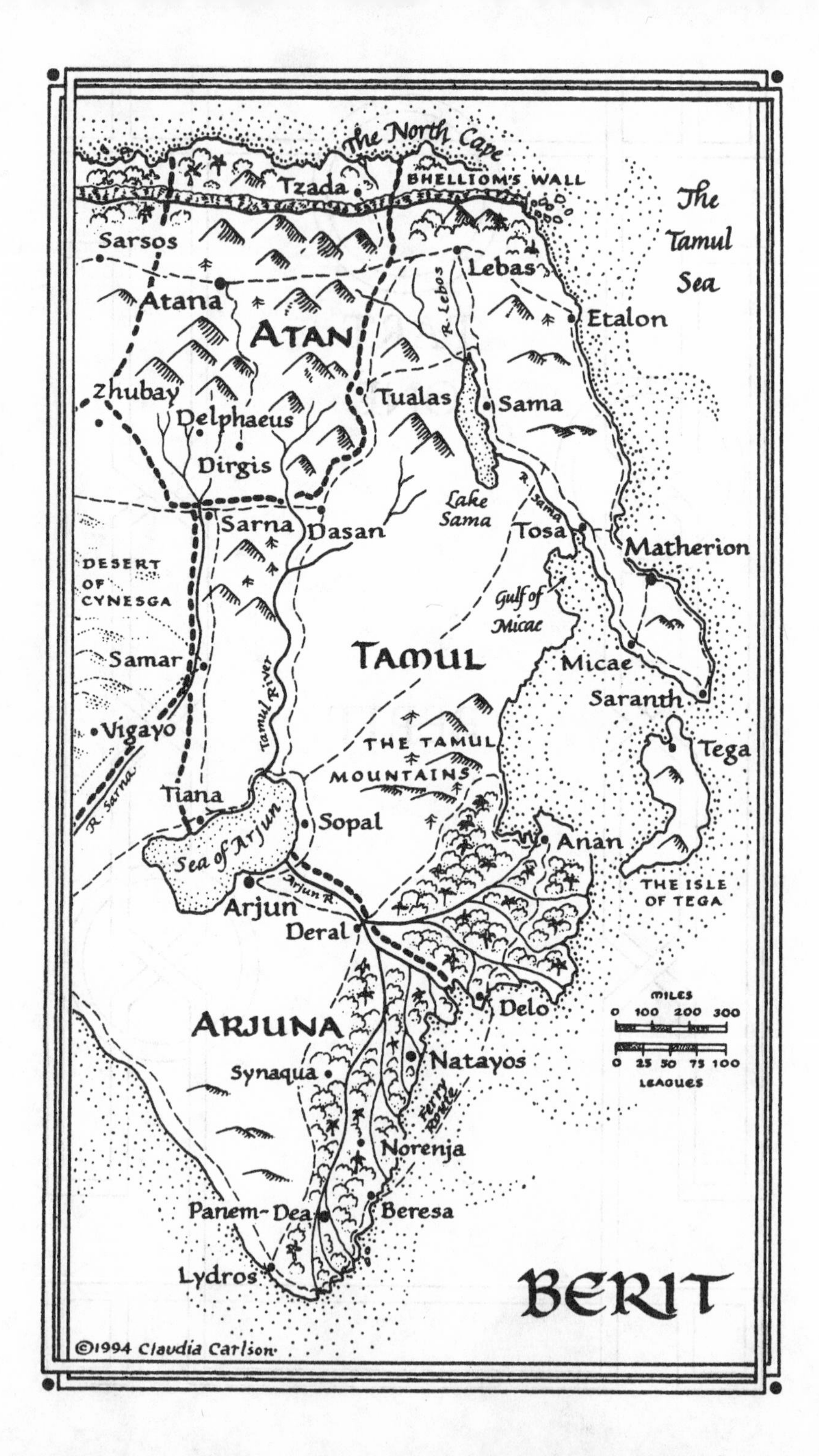

The North Cape
Tzada
BHELLTOM'S WALL
The Tamul Sea
Sarsos
Lebas
Atana
R. Lebos
Etalon
ATAN
Zhubay
Tualas
Sama
Delphaeus
Dirgis
Lake Sama
R. Sama
Sarna
Dasan
Tosa
Matherion
DESERT OF CYNESGA
Gulf of Micae
TAMUL
Micae
Samar
Tamul River
Saranth
Vigayo
THE TAMUL MOUNTAINS
Tega
R. Sarna
Tiana
Sopal
Sea of Arjun
Anan
Arjun R.
Arjun
THE ISLE OF TEGA
Deral
Delo
MILES
0 100 200 300
0 25 50 75 100
LEAGUES
ARJUNA
Natayos
Synaqua
Ferry route
Norenja
Beresa
Panem-Dea
Lydros
BERIT
©1994 Claudia Carlson

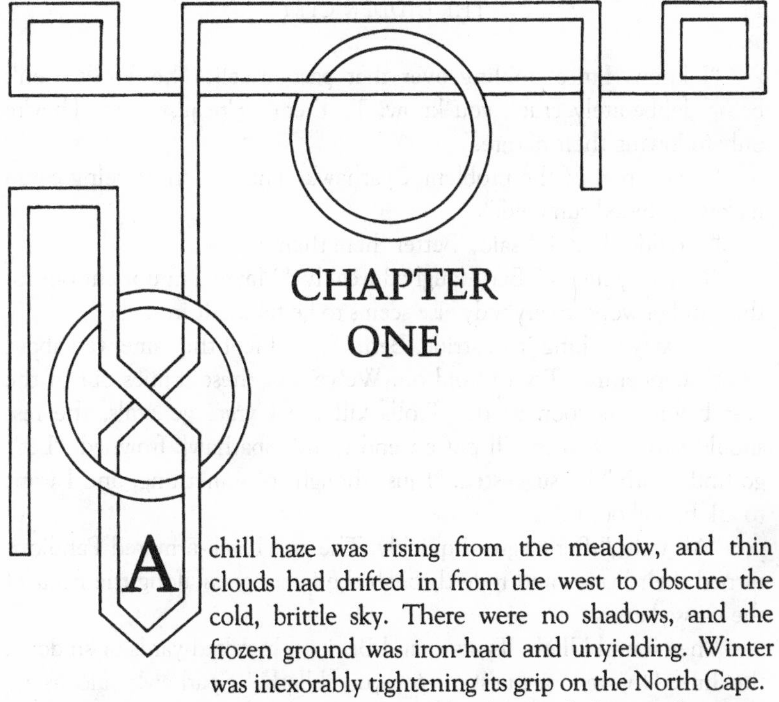

CHAPTER ONE

A chill haze was rising from the meadow, and thin clouds had drifted in from the west to obscure the cold, brittle sky. There were no shadows, and the frozen ground was iron-hard and unyielding. Winter was inexorably tightening its grip on the North Cape.

Sparhawk's army, girt in steel and leather and thousands strong, was lined up along a broad front in the frost-covered grass of the meadow near the ruins of Tzada. Sir Berit sat his horse in the center of the bulky, armored Church Knights watching the ghastly feast taking place a few hundred yards to the front. Berit was a young and idealistic knight, and he was having some difficulty with the behavior of their new allies.

The screams were remote, mere rumors of agony, and those who were screaming were not actually people—not really. They were no more than shades, the scarce-remembered reflections of long-dead men. Besides, they were enemies—members of a cruel and savage race that worshipped an unspeakable God.

But they steamed. That was the part of the horror Sir Berit could not shrug off. Though he told himself that these Cyrgai were dead—phantoms raised by Cyrgon's magic—the fact that steam rose from their eviscerated bodies as the ravening Trolls fed on them brought all of Berit's defenses crashing down around his ears.

"Trouble?" Sparhawk asked sympathetically. Sparhawk's black armor was frost-touched, and his battered face was bleak.

Berit felt a sudden embarrassment. "It's nothing, Sir Sparhawk," he lied quickly. "It's just—" He groped for a word.

"I know. I'm stumbling over that part myself. The Trolls aren't being deliberately cruel, you know. To them we're just food. They're only following their nature."

"That's part of the problem, Sparhawk. The notion of being eaten makes my blood run cold."

"Would it help if I said, 'Better them than us'?"

"Not very much." Berit laughed weakly. "Maybe I'm not cut out for this kind of work. Everybody else seems to be taking it in stride."

"*Nobody's* taking it in stride, Berit. We all feel the same way about what's happening. Try to hold on. We've met these armies out of the past before. As soon as the Trolls kill the Cyrgai generals, the rest should vanish, and that'll put an end to it." Sparhawk frowned. "Let's go find Ulath," he suggested. "I just thought of something, and I want to ask him about it."

"All right," Berit agreed quickly. The two black-armored Pandions turned their horses and rode through the frosty grass along the front of the massed army.

They found Ulath, Tynian, and Bevier a hundred yards or so down the line. "I've got a question for you, Ulath," Sparhawk said as he reined Faran in.

"For *me*? Oh, Sparhawk, you shouldn't have!" Ulath removed his conical helmet and absently polished the glossy black Ogre-horns on the sleeve of his green surcoat. "What's the problem?"

"Every time we've come up against these antiques before, the dead all shriveled up after we killed the leaders. How are the Trolls going to react to that?"

"How should I know?"

"You're supposed to be the expert on Trolls."

"Be reasonable, Sparhawk. It's never happened before. Nobody can predict what's going to happen in a totally new situation."

"Make a guess," Sparhawk snapped irritably.

The two of them glared at each other.

"Why badger Ulath about it, Sparhawk?" Bevier suggested gently. "Why not just warn the Troll-Gods that it's going to happen, and let *them* deal with the problem?"

Sparhawk rubbed reflectively at the side of his face, his hand making a kind of sandy sound on his unshaven cheek. "Sorry, Ulath," he apologized. "The noise from the banquet hall out there's distracting me."

"I know just how you feel," Ulath replied wryly. "I'm glad you brought it up, though. The Trolls won't be satisfied with dried rations when there's all this fresh meat no more than a quarter-mile away." He put his Ogre-horned helmet back on. "The Troll-Gods will honor their commitment to Aphrael, but I think we'd better warn them about this. I definitely want them to have a firm grip on their Trolls when supper turns stale. I'd hate to end up being the dessert course."

"*Ehlana?*" Sephrenia gasped.

"Keep your voice down!" Aphrael muttered. She looked around. They were some distance to the rear of the army, but they were not alone. She reached out and touched Ch'iel's bowed white neck, and Sephrenia's palfrey obediently ambled off a little way from Kalten and Xanetia to crop at the frozen grass. "I can't get too many details," the Child-Goddess said. "Melidere's been badly hurt, and Mirtai's so enraged that they've had to chain her up."

"Who did it?"

"I don't *know*, Sephrenia! Nobody's talking to Danae. All I can get is the word *hostage*. Somebody's managed to get into the castle, seize Ehlana and Alean, and spirit them out. Sarabian's beside himself. He's flooded the halls with guards, so Danae can't get out of her room to find out what's really happening."

"We must tell Sparhawk!"

"Absolutely not! Sparhawk bursts into flames when Ehlana's in danger. He's got to get his army safely back to Matherion before we can let him catch on fire."

"But—"

"No, Sephrenia. He'll find out soon enough, but let's get everyone to safety before he does. We've only got a week or so left until the sun goes down permanently and everything—and everyone—up here turns to solid ice."

"You're probably right," Sephrenia conceded. She thought a moment, staring off at the frost-silvered forest beyond the meadow. "That word *hostage* explains everything, I think. Is there any way you can pinpoint your mother's exact location?"

Aphrael shook her head. "Not without putting her in danger. If I start moving around and poking my nose into things, Cyrgon will feel me nudging at the edges of his scheme, and he might do something to Mother before he stops to think. Our main concern right now is keeping Sparhawk from going crazy when he finds out what's happened." She suddenly gasped and her dark eyes went very wide.

"What is it?" Sephrenia asked in alarm. "What's happening?"

"I don't *know*!" Aphrael cried. "It's something monstrous!" She cast her eyes about wildly for a moment and then steadied herself, her pale brow furrowing in concentration. Then her eyes narrowed in anger. "Somebody's using one of the forbidden spells, Sephrenia," she said in a voice that was as hard as the frozen ground.

"Are you sure?"

"Absolutely. The very air stinks of it."

Djarian the necromancer was a cadaverous-looking Styric with sunken eyes, a thin, almost skeletal frame, and a stale, mildewed odor about him. Like the other Styric captives, he was in chains and under the close watch of Church Knights well-versed in countering Styric spells.

A cold, oppressive twilight was settling over the encampment near the ruins of Tzada when Sparhawk and the others finally got around to questioning the prisoners. The Troll-Gods had taken their creatures firmly in hand when the feeding orgy had come suddenly to an end, and the Trolls were now gathered around a huge bonfire several miles out in the meadow, holding what appeared to be religious observances of some sort.

"Just go through the motions, Bevier," Sparhawk quietly advised the olive-skinned Cyrinic Knight as Djarian was dragged before them. "Keep asking him irrelevant questions until Xanetia signals that she's picked him clean."

Bevier nodded. "I can drag it out for as long as you want, Sparhawk. Let's get started."

Sir Bevier's gleaming white surcoat, made ruddy by the flickering firelight, gave him a decidedly ecclesiastical appearance, and he prefaced his interrogation with a lengthy prayer. Then he got down to business.

Djarian replied to the questions tersely in a hollow voice that seemed almost to come echoing up out of a vault. Bevier appeared to take no note of the prisoner's sullen behavior. His whole manner seemed excessively correct, even fussy, and he heightened that impression by wearing fingerless wool gloves such as scribes and scholars wear in cold weather. He doubled back frequently, rephrasing questions he had previously asked and then triumphantly pointing out inconsistencies in the prisoner's replies.

The one exception to Djarian's terse brevity was a sudden outburst of vituperation, a lengthy denunciation of Zalasta—and Cyrgon—for abandoning him here on this inhospitable field.

"Bevier sounds exactly like a lawyer," Kalten muttered quietly to Sparhawk. "I *hate* lawyers."

"He's doing it on purpose," Sparhawk replied. "Lawyers like to spring trick questions on people, and Djarian knows it. Bevier's forcing him to think very hard about the things he's supposed to conceal, and that's all Xanetia really needs. We always seem to underestimate Bevier."

"It's all that praying," Kalten said sagely. "It's hard to take a man seriously when he's praying all the time."

"We're Knights of the Church, Kalten—members of religious orders."

"What's that got to do with it?"

"In his own mind he is more dead than alive," Xanetia reported later when they had gathered around one of the large fires the Atans had built to hold back the bitter chill. The Anarae's face reflected the glow of the fire, as did her unbleached wool robe.

"Were we right?" Tynian asked her. "Is Cyrgon augmenting Djarian's spells so that he can raise whole armies?"

"He is," she replied.

"Was that outburst against Zalasta genuine?" Vanion asked her.

"Indeed, my Lord. Djarian and his fellows are increasingly discontent with the leadership of Zalasta. They have all come to expect no true comradeship from their leader. There is no longer common cause among them, and each doth seek to wring best advantage to himself from their dubious alliance. Overlaying all is the secret desire of each to gain sole possession of Bhelliom."

"Dissention among your enemies is always good," Vanion noted, "but I don't think we should discount the possibility that they'll all fall in line again after what happened here today. Could you get anything specific about what they might try next, Anarae?"

"Nay, Lord Vanion. They were in no wise prepared for what hath come to pass. One thing did stand out in the mind of this Djarian, however, and it doth perhaps pose some danger. The outcasts who surround Zalasta do all fear Cyzada of Esos, for he alone is versed in Zemoch magic, and he alone doth plunge his hand through that door to the netherworld which Azash opened. Horrors beyond imagining lie within his reach. It is Djarian's thought that since all their plans have thus far gone awry, Cyrgon in desperation might command Cyzada to use his unspeakable art to raise creatures of darkness to confront and confound us."

Vanion nodded gravely.

"How did Stragen's plan affect them?" Talen asked curiously.

"They are discomfited out of all measure," Xanetia replied. "They did rely heavily on those who now are dead."

"Stragen will be happy to hear that. What were they going to do with all those spies and informers?"

"Since they had no force capable of facing the Atans, Zalasta and his cohorts thought to use the hidden employees of the Ministry of the Interior to assassinate diverse Tamul officials in the subject kingdoms of the empire, hoping thereby to disrupt the governments."

"You might want to make a note of that, Sparhawk," Kalten said.

"Oh?"

"Emperor Sarabian had some qualms when he approved Stragen's plan. He'll probably feel much better when he finds out that all Stragen really did was beat our enemies to the well. They'd have killed our people if Stragen hadn't killed theirs first."

"That's very shaky moral ground, Kalten," Bevier said disapprovingly.

"I know," Kalten admitted. "That's why you have to run across the top of it so fast."

The sky was overcast the following morning; thick, roiling clouds steamed in from the west, all seethe and confusion. Because it was late autumn and they were far to the north, it seemed almost that the sun was rising in the south, turning the sky above Bhelliom's escarpment a fiery orange and reaching feebly out with ruddy, low-lying light to paint the surging underbellies of the swift-scudding cloud with a brush of flame.

The campfires seemed wan and weak and very tiny against the overpowering chill here on the roof of the world, and the knights and their friends all wore fur cloaks and huddled close to the fires.

There were low rumbles off to the south, and flickers of pale, ghastly light.

"Thunder?" Kalten asked Ulath incredulously. "Isn't it the wrong time of the year for thunderstorms?"

"It happens." Ulath shrugged. "I was in a thunderstorm north of Heid once that touched off a blizzard. That's a very unusual sort of experience."

"Whose turn is it to do the cooking?" Kalten asked him absently.

"Yours," Ulath replied promptly.

"You're not paying attention, Kalten." Tynian laughed. "You know better than to ask that question."

Kalten grumbled and started to stir up the fire.

"I think we'd better get back to the coast today, Sparhawk," Vanion said gravely. "The weather's held off so far, but I don't think we'll be able to count on that much longer."

Sparhawk nodded.

The thunder grew louder, and the fire-red clouds overhead blanched with shuddering flickers of lightning.

Then there was a sudden, rhythmic booming sound.

"Is it another earthquake?" Kring cried out in alarm.

"No," Khalad replied. "It's too regular. It sounds almost like somebody beating a very big drum." He stared at the top of Bhelliom's wall. "What's that?" he asked, pointing.

It was like a hilltop rearing up out of the forest beyond the knifelike edge of the top of the cliff—very much like a hilltop, except that it was moving.

The sun was behind it, so they could not see any details, but as it rose higher and higher they could make out the fact that it was a kind of flattened dome with two pointed protuberances flaring out from either side like huge wings. And still it swelled upward. As they could see more of it, they realized that it was not a dome. It seemed to be some enormous, inverted triangle instead, wide at the top, pointed at the bottom, and with those odd winglike protuberances jutting out from its sides. The pointed bottom seemed to be set in some massive column. Since the light was behind it, it was as black as night, and it rose and swelled like some vast darkness.

Then it stopped.

And then its eyes opened.

Like two thin, fiery gashes at first, the blazing eyes opened wider and wider, cruelly slanted like cat's eyes and all ablaze with fire more incandescent than the sun itself. The imagination shuddered back from the realization of the enormity of the thing. What had appeared to be huge wings were the creature's ears.

And then it opened its mouth and roared, and they knew that what they had heard before had not been thunder.

It roared again, and its fangs were flickers of lightning that dripped flame like blood.

"Klæl!" Aphrael shrieked.

And then, like two rounded, bulky mountains, the shoulders rose above the sharp line of the cliff, and, fanning out from the shoulders like black sails, two jointed, batlike wings.

"What is it?" Talen cried.

"It's Klæl!" Aphrael shrieked again.

"What's a Klæl?"

"Not *what*, you dolt. *Who!* Azash and the other Elder Gods cast him out! Some idiot has returned him!"

The enormity atop the escarpment continued to rise, revealing vast arms with many-fingered hands. The trunk was huge, and flashes of lightning seethed beneath its skin, illuminating ghastly details with their surging flickers.

And then that monstrous presence rose to its full height, towering eighty, a hundred feet above the top of the escarpment.

Sparhawk's spirit shriveled. How could they possibly—? "Blue-Rose!" he said sharply. "Do something!"

"There is no need, Anakha." Vanion's usurped voice was very calm as Bhelliom once again spoke through his lips. "Klæl hath but momentarily escaped Cyrgon's grasp. Cyrgon will not risk his creature in a direct confrontation with me."

"That thing belongs to Cyrgon?"

"For the moment. In time that will change, and Cyrgon will belong to Klæl."

"What is it *doing?*" Betuana cried.

The monstrosity atop the cliff had raised one huge fist and was striking at the ground with incandescent fire, hammering at the earth with lightning. The face of the escarpment shuddered and began to crack away, falling, tumbling, roaring down to smash into the forest at the foot of the cliff. More and more of the sheer face crumbled and sheared away and fell in a huge thundering landslide.

"Klæl was never uncertain of the strength of his wings," Bhelliom observed calmly. "He would come to join battle with me, but he fears the height of the wall. Thus he prepares a stair for himself."

Then with a booming like that of the earthquake which had spawned it, a mile or more of the escarpment toppled ponderously outward and crashed into the forest, piling rubble higher and higher against the foot of the cliff.

The enormous being continued to savage the top of the cliff, spilling more and more rubble down to form a steep causeway reaching up and up to the top of the wall.

And then the thing called Klæl vanished, and a shrieking wind swept the face of the escarpment, whipping away the boiling clouds of dust the landslide had raised.

There was another sound as well. Sparhawk turned quickly. The Trolls had fallen to their faces, moaning in terror.

"We've always known about him," Aphrael said pensively. "We used to frighten ourselves by telling stories about him. There's a certain perverse pleasure in making one's own flesh crawl. I don't think I ever really admitted to myself that he actually existed."

"Exactly what is he?" Bevier asked her.

"Evil." She shrugged. "We're supposed to be the essence of good—at least that's what we tell ourselves. Klæl is the opposite. He's our way of explaining the existence of evil. If we didn't have Klæl, we'd have to accept the responsibility for evil ourselves, and we're a little too fond of ourselves to do that."

"Then this Klæl is the King of Hell?" Bevier asked.

"Well, sort of. Hell isn't a place, though. It's a state of mind. The story has it that when the Elder Gods—Azash and the others—emerged, they found Klæl already here. They wanted the world for themselves, and he was in their way. After several of them had tried individually to get rid of him and got themselves obliterated, they banded together and cast him out."

"Where did he come from? Originally, I mean?" Bevier pressed. Bevier was very much caught up in first causes.

"How in the world should I know? I wasn't there. Ask Bhelliom."

"I'm not so much interested in where this Klæl came from as I am in what kinds of things it can do," Sparhawk said. He took Bhelliom out of the pouch at his waist. "Blue-Rose," he said, "I do think we must talk concerning Klæl."

"It might be well, Anakha," the jewel responded, once again taking control of Vanion.

"Where did he—or it—originate?"

"Klæl did not originate, Anakha. Even as I, Klæl hath always been."

"What is it—he?"

"Necessary. I would not offend thee, Anakha, but the necessity of Klæl is beyond thine ability to comprehend. The Child-Goddess hath explained Klæl sufficiently—within her capabilities."

"Well, *really*!" Aphrael spluttered.

A faint smile touched Vanion's lips. "Be not wroth with me,

Aphrael. I do love thee still—despite thy limitations. Thou art young, and age shall bring thee wisdom and understanding."

"This is not going well, Blue-Rose," Sephrenia warned the stone.

"Ah, well," Bhelliom sighed. "Let us then to work. Klæl *was*, in fact, cast out by the Elder Gods, as Aphrael hath told thee—although the spirit of Klæl, even as my spirit, doth linger in the very rocks of this world—as in all others which I have made. Moreover, what the Elder Gods could do, they could also undo, and the spell which hath returned Klæl was implicit in the spell which did cast Klæl out. Clearly, some mortal conversant with the spells of the Elder Gods hath reversed the spell of casting out, and Klæl hath returned."

"Can he—or it—be destroyed?"

"It is not 'he' of which we speak, nor do we speak of some 'it.' We speak of Klæl. But nay, Anakha, Klæl cannot be destroyed—no more than can I. Klæl is eternal."

Sparhawk's heart sank. "I think we're in trouble," he muttered to his friends.

"The fault is in some measure mine. So caught up was I in the birth of this latest child of mine that mine attention did stray from needful duties. It is my wont to cast Klæl out at a certain point in the making of a new world. This particular child did so delight me, however, that I delayed the casting out. Then it was that I did encounter the red dust which did imprison me, and the duty to cast Klæl out did devolve upon the Elder Gods. The casting-out was made imperfect by reason of *their* imperfection, and thus it was possible for Klæl to be returned."

"By Cyrgon?" Sparhawk asked bleakly.

"The spell of casting out—and returning—is Styric. Cyrgon could not utter it."

"Cyzada, then," Sephrenia guessed. "He might very well have known the spell. I don't think he'd have used it willingly, though."

"Cyrgon probably forced him to use it, little mother," Kalten said. "Things haven't been going very well for Cyrgon and Zalasta lately."

"But to call Klæl!" Aphrael shuddered.

"Desperate people do desperate things." Kalten shrugged. "So do desperate Gods, I suppose."

"What do we do, Blue-Rose?" Sparhawk asked. "About Klæl, I mean to say?"

"Thou canst do nothing, Anakha. Thou didst well when thou didst meet Azash, and doubtless will do well again in thy dispute with Cyrgon. Thou wouldst be powerless against Klæl, however."

"We're doomed, then." Sparhawk suddenly felt totally crushed.

"Doomed? Of course thou art not doomed. Why art thou so easily downcast and made disconsolate, my friend? I did not make thee to confront Klæl. That is *my* duty. Klæl will trouble us in some measure, as is Klæl's wont. Then, as is our custom, Klæl and I will meet."

"And thou wilt once more banish him?"

"That is never certain, Anakha. I do assure thee, however, that I will strive to mine utmost to cast Klæl out—even as Klæl will strive to cast *me* out. The contest between us doth lie in the future, and as I have oft told thee, the future is concealed. I will approach the contest with confidence, however, for doubt doth weaken resolve, and timorous uncertainty doth weigh down the spirit. Battle should be joined with a light heart and joyous demeanor."

"You can be very sententious sometimes, World-Maker," Aphrael said with just a hint of spitefulness.

"Be nice," Bhelliom chided mildly.

"Anakha!" It was Ghworg, the God of Kill. The huge presence came across the frosty meadow, plowing a dark path through the silver-sheathed grass.

"I will hear the words of Ghworg," Sparhawk replied.

"Have *you* summoned Klæl? Is it your thought that Klæl will aid us in causing hurt to Cyrgon? It is not good if you have. Let Klæl go back."

"It was not my doing, Ghworg. Neither was it the flower-gem's doing. It is our thought that it was Cyrgon who summoned Klæl to cause hurt to us."

"Can the flower-gem cause hurt to Klæl?"

"That is not certain. The might of Klæl is even as the might of the flower-gem."

The God of Kill squatted on the frozen turf, scratching at his shaggy face with one huge paw. "Cyrgon is as nothing, Anakha," he rumbled in an almost colloquial form of speech. "We can cause hurt to Cyrgon tomorrow—or some time by-and-by. We must cause hurt to Klæl now. We cannot wait for by-and-by."

Sparhawk dropped to one knee on the frozen turf. "Your words are wise, Ghworg."

Ghworg's lips pulled back in a hideous approximation of a grin. "The word you use is not common among us, Anakha. If Khwaj said, 'Ghworg is wise,' I would cause hurt to him."

"I did not say it to cause you anger, Ghworg."

"You are not a Troll, Anakha. You do not know our ways. We must cause hurt to Klæl so that he will go away. How can we do this?"

"We cannot cause hurt to him. Only the flower-gem can make him go away."

Ghworg smashed his fist against the frozen ground with a hideous snarl.

Sparhawk held up one hand. "Cyrgon has called Klæl," he said. "Klæl has joined Cyrgon to cause hurt to us. Let us cause hurt to Cyrgon now, not by-and-by. If we cause hurt to Cyrgon, he will fear to aid Klæl when the flower-gem goes to cause hurt to Klæl and make him go away."

Ghworg puzzled his way through that. "Your words are good, Anakha," he said finally. "How might we best cause hurt to Cyrgon now?"

Sparhawk considered it. "The mind of Cyrgon is not like your mind, Ghworg, nor is it like mine. Our minds are direct. Cyrgon's is guileful. He threw your children against our friends here in the lands of winter to make us come here to fight them. But your children were not his main force. Cyrgon's main force will come from the lands of the sun to attack our friends in the city that shines."

"I have seen that place. The Child-Goddess spoke first with us there."

Sparhawk frowned, trying to remember the details of Vanion's map. "There are high places here and to the south," he said.

Ghworg nodded.

"Then, even farther south, the high places grow low and then they become flat."

"I see it," Ghworg said. "You describe it well, Anakha." That startled Sparhawk. Evidently Ghworg could visualize the entire continent.

"In the middle of that flat place is another high place that the man-things call the Tamul Mountains."

Ghworg nodded in agreement.

"The main force of Cyrgon's children will pass that high place to reach the city that shines. The high place will be cool, so your children will not suffer from the sun there."

"I see which way your thought goes, Anakha," Ghworg said. "We will take our children to that high place and wait there for Cyrgon's children. Our children will not eat Aphrael's children. They will eat Cyrgon's children instead."

"That will cause hurt to Cyrgon and his servants, Ghworg."

"Then we will do it." Ghwrog turned and pointed toward the landslide. "Our children will climb Klæl's stairway. Then Ghnomb will make time stop. Our children will be in the high place before the sun goes to sleep this night." He stood up abruptly. "Good hunting," he growled, turned, and went back to join his fellows and the still-terrified Trolls.

"We have to proceed as if things were normal," Vanion told them as they gathered near the fire a couple of hours past noon. The sun, Sparhawk noted, was already going down. "Klæl can probably appear at any time and any place. We can't plan for him—any more than we can plan for a blizzard or a hurricane. If you can't plan for something, about the only thing you can do is take a few precautions and then ignore it."

"Well spoken," Queen Betuana approved. Betuana and Vanion were getting along well.

"What do we do then, friend Vanion?" Tikume asked.

"We're soldiers, friend Tikume," Vanion replied. "We do what soldiers do. We get ready to fight armies, not Gods. Scarpa's coming up out of the jungles of Arjuna, and I'd expect another thrust to come out of Cynesga. The Trolls will probably hamper Scarpa, but they can only move out a short way from those mountains in southern Tamul proper because of the climate. After the initial shock of encountering Trolls, Scarpa will probably try to go around them." Vanion consulted his map. "We'll have to have forces in place to respond either to Scarpa or to an army coming out of Cynesga. I'd say that Samar would be the best location."

"Sarna," Betuana disagreed.

"Both," Ulath countered. "Forces in Samar could cover everything from the southern edge of the Atan Mountains to the Sea of Arjuna *and* be in position to strike eastward to the southern Tamul Mountains if Scarpa evades the Trolls. Forces in Sarna could block the invasion route through the Atan Mountains."

"His point's well taken," Bevier said. "It divides our forces, but we don't have much choice."

"We could put the knights and the Peloi in Samar and the Atan infantry in Sarna," Tynian added. "The lower valley of the River Sarna's ideal for mounted operations, and the mountains around Sarna itself are natural for Atans."

"Both positions are defensive," Engessa objected. "Wars aren't won from defensive positions."

Sparhawk and Vanion exchanged a long look. "Invade Cynesga?" Sparhawk asked dubiously.

"Not yet," Vanion decided. "Let's wait until the Church Knights get here from Eosia before we do that. When Komier and the others cross into Cynesga from the west, *that's* when we'll want to come at the place from the east. We'll put Cyrgon in a vise. With that sort of force coming at him from both sides, he can raise every Cyrgai who's ever lived, and he'll still lose."

"Right up until the moment he unleashes Klæl," Aphrael added moodily.

"No, Divine One," Sparhawk told her. "Bhelliom *wants* Cyrgon to send Klæl against us. If we do it this way, we'll force the issue in a place and time that *we* choose. We'll pick the spot, Cyrgon will unleash Klæl, and I'll unleash Bhelliom. Then all we have to do is sit back and watch."

"We'll go to the top of the wall the same way the Trolls went, Vanion-Preceptor," Engessa said the following morning. "We can climb as well as they can."

"It might take *us* a little longer," Tikume added. "We'll have to push boulders out of the way to get our horses up that slope."

"We will help you, Tikume-Domi," Engessa promised.

"That's it, then," Tynian summed up. "The Atans and the Peloi will go south from here to take up positions in Sarna and Samar. We'll take the knights back to the coast, and Sorgi will ferry us back to Matherion. We'll go overland from there."

"It's the ferrying that concerns me," Sparhawk said. "Sorgi's going to have to make at least a half-dozen trips."

Khalad sighed and rolled his eyes upward.

"I gather you're going to embarrass me in public again," Sparhawk said. "What am I overlooking?"

"The rafts, Sparhawk," Khalad said in a weary voice. "Sorgi's gathering up the rafts to take them south to the timber markets. He's going to lash them all together into a long log boom. Put the knights in the ships, the horses on the boom, and we can all make it to Matherion in one trip."

"I forgot about the rafts," Sparhawk admitted sheepishly.

"That log boom won't move very fast," Ulath pointed out.

Xanetia had been listening to their plans intently. She looked at

Khalad and spoke diffidently, almost shyly. "Might a steady wind behind thy logs assist thee, young Master?" Xanetia asked Khalad.

"It would indeed, Anarae," Khalad said enthusiastically. "We can weave rough sails out of tree limbs."

"Won't Cyrgon—or Klæl—feel you raising a breeze, dear sister?" Sephrenia asked.

"Cyrgon cannot detect Delphaeic magic, Sephrenia," Xanetia replied. "Anakha can ask Bhelliom whether Klæl is similarly unaware."

"How did you manage that?" Aphrael asked curiously.

Xanetia looked slightly embarrassed. "It was to hide from thee and thy kindred, Divine Aphrael. When Edaemus did curse us, he did so arrange his curse that our magic would be hidden from our enemies—for thus did we view thee at that time. Doth that offend thee, Divine One?"

"Not under *these* circumstances, Anarae," Flute replied, swarming up into Xanetia's arms and kissing her soundly.

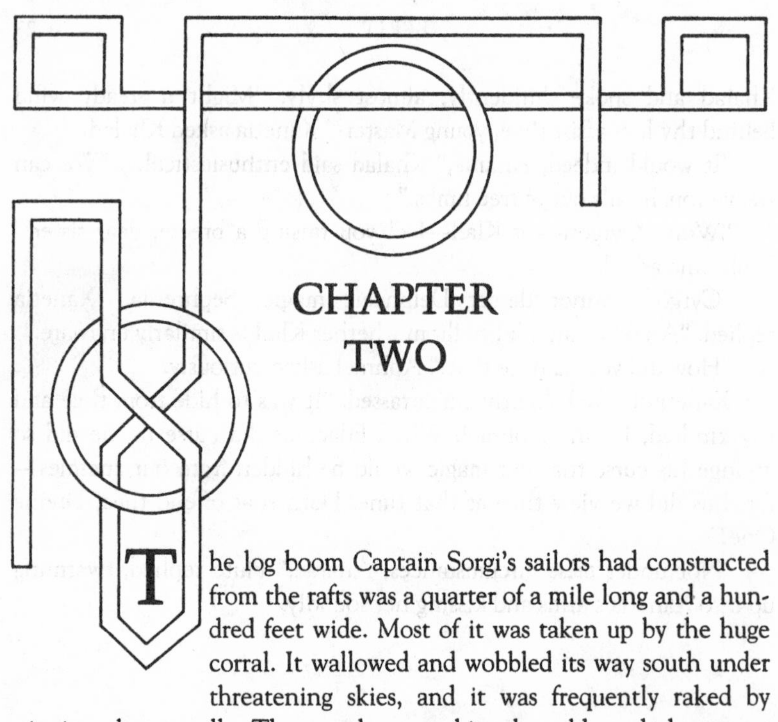

CHAPTER TWO

The log boom Captain Sorgi's sailors had constructed from the rafts was a quarter of a mile long and a hundred feet wide. Most of it was taken up by the huge corral. It wallowed and wobbled its way south under threatening skies, and it was frequently raked by stinging sleet-squalls. The weather was bitterly cold, and the young knights who manned the raft were bundled to the ears in furs and spent most of their time huddled in the dubious shelter of the flapping tents.

"It's all in attention to detail, Berit," Khalad said as he tied off the rope holding the starboard end of one of their makeshift sails in place. "That's all that work really is—details." He squinted along the ice-covered line of what was really much more like a snow fence than a sail. "Sparhawk looks at the grand plan and leaves the details to others. It's a good thing, really, because he's a hopeless incompetent when it comes to little things and real work."

"Khalad!" Berit was actually shocked.

"Have you ever seen him try to use tools? That was something our father used to tell us over and over: 'Don't *ever* let Sparhawk pick up a tool.' Kalten's fairly good with his hands, but Sparhawk's hopeless. If you hand him anything associated with honest work, he'll hurt himself with it." Khalad's head came up sharply, and he swore.

"What's wrong?"

"Didn't you feel it? The port-side towropes just went slack. Let's go wake up those sailors. We don't want this big cow turning broadside on us again." The two fur-clad young men started across the icy collection of lashed-together rafts, skirting the huge corral where the horses huddled together in the bitterly cold breeze coming from astern.

The idea of making a log boom out of the rafts was very good in theory, but the problems of steering proved to be far more complex than either Sorgi or Khalad had anticipated. Khalad's thickly woven fences of evergreen boughs acted well enough as sails, moving the sheer deadweight of the boom steadily southward ahead of Xanetia's breeze. But Sorgi's ships were supposed to provide steerageway by towing the boom, and that was where the problems cropped up. No two ships ever move at exactly the same rate of speed, even when propelled by the same wind. Thus, the fifty ships ahead and the twenty-five strung out along each side of the boom had to be almost constantly fine-tuned to keep the huge raft moving in the right general direction. As long as everybody paid very close attention, all went well. Two days south of Bhelliom's wall, however, a number of things had gone wrong all at once, and the log boom had swung around sideways. No amount of effort had been able to straighten it out, and so they had been obliged to take it apart and reassemble it—back-breaking labor in the bitter cold. Nobody wanted to go through that again.

When they reached the port side of the boom, Berit took a dented brass horn out from under his fur cape and blew a flat, off-key blat at the port-side towboats while Khalad picked up a yellow flag and began to wave it vigorously. The prearranged signals were simple. The yellow flag told the ships to crowd on more sail to keep the towing hawsers taut; the blue flag told them to put out the sea anchors to slack off on the ropes; and the red flag told them to cast off all lines and get out of the way.

The towropes went tight again as Khalad's crisp signal trickled down through the ranks to the sailors who actually did the work aboard the ships.

"How do you keep track of everything?" Berit asked his friend. "And how do you know so quickly that something's wrong?"

"Pain," Khalad replied wryly. "I don't really want to spend several days taking this beast apart and putting it back together again with the spray freezing on me, so I'm paying very close attention to the things my body's telling me. You can feel things change in your legs and the soles of your feet. When one of the hawsers goes slack, it changes the feel of how the boom moves."

"Is there *anything* you don't know how to do?"

"I don't dance very well." Khalad squinted up into the first stinging pellets of another sleet-squall. "It's time to feed and water the horses," he said. "Let's go tell the novices to stop sitting around admiring their titles and get to work."

"You really dislike the aristocracy, don't you?" Berit asked as they started forward along the edge of the corral toward the wind-whipped tents of the apprentice knights.

"No, I don't dislike them. I just don't have any patience with them, and I can't understand how they can be so blind to what's going on around them. A title must be a very heavy thing to carry if the weight makes you ignore everything else."

"You're going to be a knight yourself, you know."

"It wasn't my idea. Sparhawk gets silly sometimes. He thinks that making knights of my brothers and me is a way of honoring our father. I'm sure that Father's laughing at him right now."

They reached the tents, and Khalad raised his voice. "All right, gentlemen!" he shouted. "It's time to feed and water the animals! Let's get at it!" Then he critically surveyed the corral. Five thousand horses leave a great deal of evidence that they have been present. "I think it's time for another lesson in the virtue of humility for our novices," he said quietly to Berit. Then he raised his voice again. "And after you've finished with that, you'd better break out the scoop shovels and wheelbarrows again. We wouldn't want to let the work pile up on us, would we, gentlemen?"

Berit was not yet fully adept at some of the subtler forms of magic. That part of the Pandion training was the study of a lifetime. He *was* far enough along, however, to recognize "tampering" when he encountered it. The log boom *seemed* to be lumbering southward at a crawl, but the turning of the seasons was giving some things away. It should have taken them much longer to escape the bitter cold of the far north, for one thing; and the days should not have become so much longer in such a short time, for another.

However it was managed, and whoever managed it, they arrived at a sandy beach a few miles north of Matherion late one golden autumn afternoon, long before they should have, and began wading the horses ashore from the wobbly collection of rafts.

"Short trip," Khalad observed laconically as the two watched the novices unloading the horses.

"You noticed." Berit laughed.

"They weren't particularly subtle about it. When the spray stopped freezing in my beard between one minute and the next, I started having suspicions." He paused. "Is magic very hard to learn?" he asked.

"The magic itself isn't too hard. The hard part is learning the Styric language. Styric doesn't have any regular verbs. They're *all* irregular—and there are nine tenses."

"Berit, please speak plain Elenic."

"You know what a verb is, don't you?"

"Sort of, but what's a tense?"

Somehow that made Berit feel better. Khalad did *not* know everything. "We'll work on it," he assured his friend. "Maybe Sephrenia can make some suggestions."

The sun was going down in a blaze of color when they rode through the opalescent gates into fire-domed Matherion, and it was dusk when they reached the imperial compound.

"What's wrong with everybody?" Khalad muttered as they rode through the gate.

"I didn't follow that," Berit confessed.

"Use your eyes, man! Those gate guards were looking at Sparhawk as if they expected him to explode—or maybe turn into a dragon. Something's going on, Berit."

The main body of Church Knights rode off across the twilight-dim lawn to their barracks while the rest of the party clattered across the drawbridge into Ehlana's castle. They dismounted in the torchlit courtyard and trooped inside.

"It's even worse here," Khalad murmured. "Let's stay close to Sparhawk in case we have to restrain him. The knights at the drawbridge seemed to be actually afraid of him."

They went up the stairs to the royal apartment. Mirtai was not in her customary place at the door, and that made Berit even more edgy. Khalad was right. Something here was definitely not the way it should be.

Emperor Sarabian, dressed in his favorite purple doublet and hose, was nervously pacing the blue-carpeted floor of the sitting room as they entered, and he seemed to shrink back as Sparhawk and Vanion approached him.

"Your Majesty," Sparhawk greeted him, inclining his head. "It's good to see you again." He looked around. "Where's Ehlana?" he asked, laying his helmet on the table.

"Uh—in a minute, Sparhawk. How did things go on the North Cape?"

"More or less the way we'd planned. Cyrgon doesn't command the Trolls anymore, but we've got another problem that might be even worse."

"Oh?"

"We'll tell you about it when Ehlana joins us. It's not such a pretty story that we'd want to go through it twice."

The emperor gave Foreign Minister Oscagne a helpless look.

"Let's go speak with Baroness Melidere, Prince Sparhawk," Oscagne suggested. "Something's happened here. She was present, so she'll be able to answer your questions better than we would."

"All right." Sparhawk's gaze was level, and his voice was steady, despite the fact that Sarabian's nervousness and Oscagne's evasive answer fairly screamed out the fact that something was terribly wrong.

Baroness Melidere sat propped up in her bed. She wore a fetching blue dressing gown, but the sizable bandage on her left shoulder was a clear indication that something serious had happened. Her face was pale, but her eyes were cool and rock-steady. Stragen sat at her bedside in his white satin doublet, his face filled with concern.

"Well," Melidere said, "finally." Her voice was crisp and businesslike. She flicked a withering glance at the emperor and his advisers. "I see that these brave gentlemen have decided to let *me* tell you about what happened here, Prince Sparhawk. I'll try to be brief. One night a couple of weeks ago, the queen, Alean, and I were getting ready for bed. There was a knock on the door, and four men we thought were Peloi came in. Their heads were shaved and they wore Peloi clothing, but they weren't Peloi. One of them was Krager. The other three were Elron, Baron Parok, and Scarpa."

Sparhawk did not move, and his face did not change expression. "And?" he asked, his voice still unemotional.

"You've decided to be sensible, I see," Melidere said coolly. "Good. We exchanged a few insults, and then Scarpa told Elron to kill me—just to prove to the queen that he was serious. Elron lunged at me, and I deflected his thrust with my wrist. I fell down and smeared the blood around to make it appear that I'd been killed. Ehlana threw herself over me, pretending to be hysterical, but she'd seen what I'd done." The baroness took a ruby ring out from under her pillow. "This is for you, Prince Sparhawk. Your wife hid it in my bodice. She also said, 'Tell Sparhawk that I'm all right, and tell him that I forbid him to give up

Bhelliom, no matter what they threaten to do to me.' Those were her exact words. Then she covered me with a blanket."

Sparhawk took the ring and slipped it onto his finger. "I see," he said in a calm voice. "What happened then, Baroness?"

"Scarpa told your wife that he and his friends were taking her and Alean as hostages. He said that you were so foolishly attached to her that you'd give him anything for her safe return. He obviously intends to exchange her for the Bhelliom. Krager had a note already prepared. He cut off a lock of Ehlana's hair to include in the note. I gather that there'll be other notes, and each one will have some of her hair in it to prove that it's authentic. Then they took Ehlana and Alean and left."

"Thank you, Baroness," Sparhawk said, his voice still steady. "You've shown amazing courage in this unfortunate business. May I have the note?"

Melidere reached under her pillow again, took out a folded and sealed piece of parchment, and handed it to him.

Berit had loved his queen from the moment he had first seen her sitting on her throne encased in crystal, although he had never mentioned the fact to her. There would be other loves in his life, of course, but she would always be the first. So it was that when Sparhawk broke the seal, unfolded the parchment, and gently removed the thick lock of pale blonde hair, Berit's mind suddenly filled with flames. His grip tightened around the haft of his war ax.

Khalad took him by the arm, and Berit was dimly startled by just how strong his friend's grip was. "That's not going to do anybody any good at all, Berit," he said in a crisp voice. "Now why don't you just give me the ax before you do something foolish with it?"

Berit drew in a deep, trembling breath, pushing away his sudden, irrational fury. "Sorry, Khalad," he said. "I sort of lost my grip there for a moment. I'll be all right now." He looked at his friend. "Sparhawk's going to let you kill Krager, isn't he?"

"So he says."

"Would you like some help?"

Khalad flashed him a quick grin. "It's always nice to have company when you're doing something that takes several days," he said.

Sparhawk quickly read the note, his free hand still gently holding the lock of Ehlana's pale hair. Berit could see the muscles rippling along his friend's jaw as he read. He handed the note to Vanion. "You'd better read this to them," he said bleakly.

Vanion nodded and took the note. He cleared his throat.

" 'Well, now, Sparhawk,' " he read aloud. " 'I gather that your temper tantrum's over. I hope you didn't kill *too* many of the people who were supposed to be guarding your wife.

" 'The situation here is painfully obvious, I'm afraid. We've taken Ehlana hostage. You *will* behave yourself, won't you, old boy? The tiresomely obvious part of all of this is that you can have her back in exchange for Bhelliom and the rings. We'll give you a few days to rant and rave and try to find some way out of this. Then, when you've come to your senses and realize that you have no choice but to do exactly as you're told, I'll drop you another note with some rather precise instructions. Do be a good boy and follow the instructions to the letter. I'd really rather not be forced to kill your wife, so don't try to be creative.

" 'Be well, Sparhawk, and keep an eye out for my next note. You'll know it's from me because I'll decorate it with another lock of Ehlana's hair. Pay very close attention, because if our correspondence continues for *too* long, your wife will run out of hair, and I'll have to start using fingers.'

"And it's signed 'Krager,' " Vanion concluded.

Kalten smashed his fist into the wall, his face rigid with fury.

"That's enough of that!" Vanion snapped.

"What are we going to do?" Kalten demanded. "We have to do *something*!"

"We're *not* going to jump eight feet into the air and come down running, for a start," Vanion told him.

"Where's Mirtai?" Kring's voice had a note of sudden alarm.

"She's perfectly all right, Domi," Sarabian assured him. "She was a little upset when she found out what happened."

"A *little*?" Oscagne murmured. "It took twelve men to subdue her. She's in her room, Domi Kring—chained to the bed, actually. There are some guards there as well to keep her from doing herself any injury."

Kring abruptly turned and left Melidere's bedroom.

"We're tiring you, aren't we, Baroness?" Sarabian said then.

"Not in the least, your Majesty," she replied in a cool voice. She looked around at them. "It's a bit cramped in here. Why don't we adjourn to the sitting room? I'd imagine we'll be most of the night at this, so we might as well be comfortable." She threw back her blankets and started to get out of bed.

Stragen gently restrained her. Then he picked her up.

"I can walk, Stragen," she protested.

"Not while I'm around, you can't." Stragen's customary expression of civilized urbanity was gone as he looked around at the others, and it had been replaced with one of cold, tightly suppressed rage. "One thing, gentlemen," he told them. "When we catch up with these people, Elron's mine. I'll be very put out with anybody who accidently kills him."

Baroness Melidere's eyes were quite content, and there was a faint smile on her face as she laid her head on Stragen's shoulder.

Caalador was waiting for them in the sitting room. His knees and elbows were muddy, and there were cobwebs in his hair. "I found it, your Majesty," he reported to the emperor. "It comes out in the basement of that barracks the Church Knights have been using." He looked appraisingly at Sparhawk. "I'd heard you were back," he said. "We've managed to pick up a little information for you."

"I appreciate that, Caalador," Sparhawk replied quietly. The big Pandion's almost inhuman calm had them all more than a little on edge.

"Stragen was a bit distracted after what happened to the baroness here," Caalador reported, "so I was left more or less to my own devices. I took some fairly direct steps. The ideas were all mine, so don't blame him for them."

"You don't have to do that, Caalador," Stragen said, carefully tucking a blanket around Melidere's shoulders. "You didn't do anything I didn't approve of."

"I take it that there were a few atrocities," Ulath surmised.

"Let me start at the beginning," Caalador said, brushing his hands through his hair, trying to dislodge the cobwebs. "One of the men we'd been planning to kill during the Harvest Festival managed to evade my cutthroats, and he sent me a message offering to exchange information for his life. I agreed to that, and he told me something I didn't know about. We knew that there were tunnels under the lawns here in the imperial compound, but what we *didn't* know is that the ground under the whole city's honeycombed with more tunnels. That's how Krager and his friends got into the imperial grounds, and that's how they took the queen and her maid out."

"Prithee, good Master Caalador, stay a moment," Xanetia said. "I have seen into the memories of the minister of the interior, and he had no knowledge of such tunnels."

"That wouldn't be hard to explain, Anarae," Patriarch Emban told her. "Ambitious underlings quite often conceal things from their superiors. Teovin, Director of the Secret Police, probably had his eye on Kolata's position."

"That's most likely it, your Grace," Caalador agreed. "Anyway, my informant knew the location of *some* of the tunnels, and I put men down there to look around for more while I questioned various members of the Secret Police who were in custody. My methods were fairly direct, and the ones who survived the questioning were more than happy to cooperate.

"The tunnels were very busy on the night the queen was abducted. The diplomats who were forted up in the Cynesgan embassy knew about the scheme, and they realized that we'd kick down their walls as soon as we found out that the queen was gone. They tried to escape through the tunnels, but I already had men down in those ratholes. There were a number of noisy encounters, and we either rounded up or killed just about the entire embassy staff. The ambassador himself survived, and I let him watch while I interrogated several undersecretaries. I'm very fond of Queen Ehlana, so I was quite firm with them." He looked at Sephrenia. "I don't think I need to go into too much detail," he added.

"Thank you," Sephrenia murmured.

"The ambassador didn't really know all that much," Caalador continued apologetically, "but he *did* tell me that Scarpa and his friends were going south from here—which may or may not have been a ruse. His Majesty ordered the ports of Micae and Saranth sealed, and he put Atan patrols on the road from Tosa to the coast, just to be on the safe side. Nothing's turned up yet, so Scarpa either got way ahead of us, or he's gone down a hole someplace nearby."

The door opened, and Kring rejoined them, his face gloomy.

"Did you unchain her?" Tynian asked him.

"That wouldn't be a good idea right now, friend Tynian. She feels personally responsible for the queen's abduction. She wants to kill herself. I took everything with any kind of sharp edge out of the room, but I don't think it's really safe to unshackle her just yet."

"Did you get that spoon of hers away from her?" Talen asked.

Kring's eyes went wide. "Oh, God!" he exclaimed, bolting for the door.

"If he'd only yell at us or bang his fist against the wall or something," Berit murmured to Khalad the next morning when they gathered once again in the blue-draped sitting room. "All he does is sit there."

"Sparhawk keeps his feelings to himself," Khalad replied.

"It's his *wife* we're talking about, Khalad! He sits there like a lump. Doesn't he have any feelings at all?"

"Of course he does, but he's not going to take them out and wave them around for us to look at. Right now it's more important for him to think than to feel. He's listening and putting things together. He's saving up his feelings for when he gets his hands on Scarpa."

Sparhawk sat in his chair with his daughter in his lap. He seemed to be studying the floor, and he was absently stroking Princess Danae's cat.

Lord Vanion was telling the emperor and the others about Klæl and about their strategic disposition of forces: the Trolls to the Tamul Mountains in south-central Tamul proper, the Atans to Sarna, and Tikume's Peloi to Samar.

Flute was sitting quietly on Sephrenia's lap. Berit noticed something that hadn't occurred to him before. He glanced first at Princess Danae and then at the Child-Goddess. They appeared to be about the same age, and their bearing and manner seemed very much alike for some reason.

The presence of the Child-Goddess was having a peculiar effect on Emperor Sarabian. The brilliant, erratic ruler of the continent seemed dumbfounded by her presence and he sat gazing wide-eyed at her. His face was pale, and he was obviously not hearing a word Lord Vanion was saying.

Aphrael finally twisted around and returned his gaze. Then she slowly crossed her eyes at him.

The emperor stared back violently.

"Didn't your mother ever tell you that it's not polite to stare, Sarabian?" she asked him.

"Mind your manners," Sephrenia chided.

"He's supposed to be listening. If I want adoration, I'll get myself a puppy."

"Forgive me, Goddess Aphrael," the emperor apologized. "I seldom have divine visitors." He looked at her rather closely. "I hope you don't mind my saying so, but you rather resemble Prince Sparhawk's daughter. Have you ever met her Royal Highness?"

Sparhawk's head came up sharply, and there was a strange, almost wild look in his eyes.

"Now that you mention it, I don't think I have," Flute said. She looked across the room at the princess. Berit noticed that Sephrenia's eyes were also just a bit wild as Flute slid down out of her lap and went across the room to Sparhawk's chair. "Hullo, Danae," the Child-Goddess said in an offhand sort of way.

"Hullo, Aphrael," the princess replied in almost exactly the same tone. "Are you going to do something to get my mother back home?"

"I'm working on it. Try to keep your father from getting too excited about this. He's no good to any of us when he flies all to pieces and we have to gather him up and put him back together again."

"I know. I'll do what I can with him. Would you like to hold my cat?"

Flute glanced at Mmrr, whose eyes were filled with a look of absolute horror. "I don't think she likes me," she declined.

"I'll take care of my father," Danae assured the little Goddess. "You deal with these others."

"All right." Aphrael paused. "I think we'll get on well together," she said. "You wouldn't mind if I stopped by from time to time, would you?"

"Any time, Aphrael."

Something very peculiar was going on. Berit saw nothing unusual in the conversation between the two little girls, but Sparhawk's face—and Sephrenia's—clearly showed that they were both very disturbed. Berit kept his expression casual and looked around. Everyone else had faintly indulgent smiles on their faces as they watched the exchange—all except Lord Vanion and Anarae Xanetia. *Their* faces were no less strained than Sparhawk's and Sephrenia's. Evidently something titanic had just happened, but for the life of him, Berit could not fathom out what it might have been.

"I don't think we should discount the possibility," Oscagne said gravely. "Baroness Melidere has demonstrated again and again the fact that she has a very penetrating mind."

"Thank you, your Excellency," Melidere said sweetly.

"I wasn't really being complimentary, Baroness," he replied coolly. "Your intelligence is a resource to be exploited in this situation. You've seen Scarpa and we haven't. Do you really believe he's mad?"

"Yes, your Excellency, quite mad. It wasn't only *his* behavior that convinced me of it. Krager and the others treated him the way you'd treat a live cobra. They're terrified of him."

"That dovetails rather neatly with some of the reports I got from the thieves of Arjuna," Caalador agreed. "There's always a certain amount of exaggeration involved when people talk about madmen, but every report that came in mentioned it."

"If you're trying to make Sparhawk and me feel better, you're going at it in a strange way, Caalador," Kalten accused. "You're suggesting that the women we love are the prisoners of a crazy man. He could do *anything*."

"It might not be as bad as it looks, Sir Kalten," Oscagne said. "If Scarpa's mad, couldn't this abduction have been *his* idea alone? If that's the case, our solution becomes almost too simple. Prince Sparhawk simply follows the instructions he receives to the letter, and when Scarpa appears with Queen Ehlana and Alean, his Highness simply hands over the Bhelliom. We all know what'll happen to Scarpa as soon as he touches it."

"You're equating insanity with feeblemindedness, Oscagne," Sarabian disagreed, "and that's simply not the way it works. Zalasta knows that the rings would protect him if he ever managed to get his hands on Bhelliom, and if he knows, then we have to assume that Scarpa does, too. He'll demand the rings before he even tries to touch the jewel."

"We have three possibilities then," Patriarch Emban summed up. "Either Cyrgon instructed Zalasta to arrange for the abduction, or Zalasta came up with the notion on his own, or Scarpa's so crazy that he thinks he can just pick up Bhelliom and start giving it commands with no instruction or preparation at all."

"There's one more possibility, your Grace," Ulath said. "Klæl could already be in charge, and this could be his way to force Bhelliom to come to *him* for their customary contest."

"What difference does it make at this point?" Sparhawk asked suddenly. "We won't know whose idea it is until we see who shows up to make the exchange."

"We *should* have some plans in place, Prince Sparhawk," Oscagne pointed out. "We should try to think our way through each situation so that we'll know what to do."

"I already know what I'm going to do, your Excellency," Sparhawk told him bleakly.

"At the moment, we can't do anything," Vanion said, moving in rather quickly. "All we can do is wait for Krager's next note."

"Truly," Ulath agreed. "Krager's going to give Sparhawk instructions. Those instructions might give us some clues about whose idea this *really* is."

"You noticed it, too, didn't you?" Berit said to Khalad that evening when the two of them were getting ready for bed.

"Noticed what?"

"Don't play the innocent with me, Khalad. You see everything that's going on around you. *Nothing* gets by you. Sparhawk and Sephrenia were behaving very peculiarly when Flute and Danae were talking to each other."

"Yes," Khalad admitted calmly. "So what?"

"Aren't you curious about why?"

"Has it occurred to you that 'why' might not be any of our business?"

Berit stepped around that. "Did you notice how much the two little girls resemble each other?"

Khalad shrugged. "You're the expert on girls."

Berit suddenly blushed and silently cursed himself for blushing.

"It isn't a secret, you know," Khalad told him. "Empress Elysoun's fairly obvious. She doesn't hide her feelings any more than she hides—well, you know."

"She's a good girl," Berit quickly came to her defense. "It's just that her people don't pay any attention to our kind of morality. They can't even comprehend the notion of fidelity."

"I'm not throwing rocks at her. If the way she behaves doesn't bother her husband, it certainly doesn't bother me. I'm a country boy, remember? We're more realistic about things like that. I just wouldn't get *too* attached to her, Berit. Her attention may wander in time."

"It already has," Berit replied. "She doesn't want to discontinue *our* friendship, though. She wants to be friendly to me *and* to him—and to the half-dozen or so others she neglected to mention earlier."

"The world needs more friendliness, Berit." Khalad grinned. "There wouldn't be so many wars if people were friendlier."

Krager's next note arrived two days later, and it was authenticated by another lock of Ehlana's hair. The thought of the sodden drunkard violating his queen's pale blonde hair enraged Berit for some obscure reason. Vanion once again read the note to them while Sparhawk sat somewhat apart, gently holding the lock of his wife's hair in his fingers.

" 'Sparhawk, old boy,' " the note began. " 'You don't mind if I call you that, do you? I always admired the way Martel sort of tossed that off when everything was going his way. It was pretty much the *only* thing about him that I admired.

" 'Enough of these fond reminiscences. You're going to be making a trip, Sparhawk. We want you to take your squire and travel by the customary overland route to Beresa in southeastern Arjuna. You'll be watched, so don't take any side trips, don't have Kalten and the other baboons trailing along behind you, don't have Sephrenia disguised as a mouse or a flea hidden in your pocket, and most *definitely* don't use Bhelliom for anything at all—not even for building campfires. I know we can depend on your absolute cooperation, old boy, since you'll never see Ehlana alive again if you misbehave.

" 'It's always a pleasure to talk with you, Sparhawk, particularly in view of the fact that it's *your* hands that are chained *this* time. Now stop wasting time. Take Khalad and the Bhelliom and go to Beresa. You'll receive further instructions there.

" 'Fondly, Krager.' "

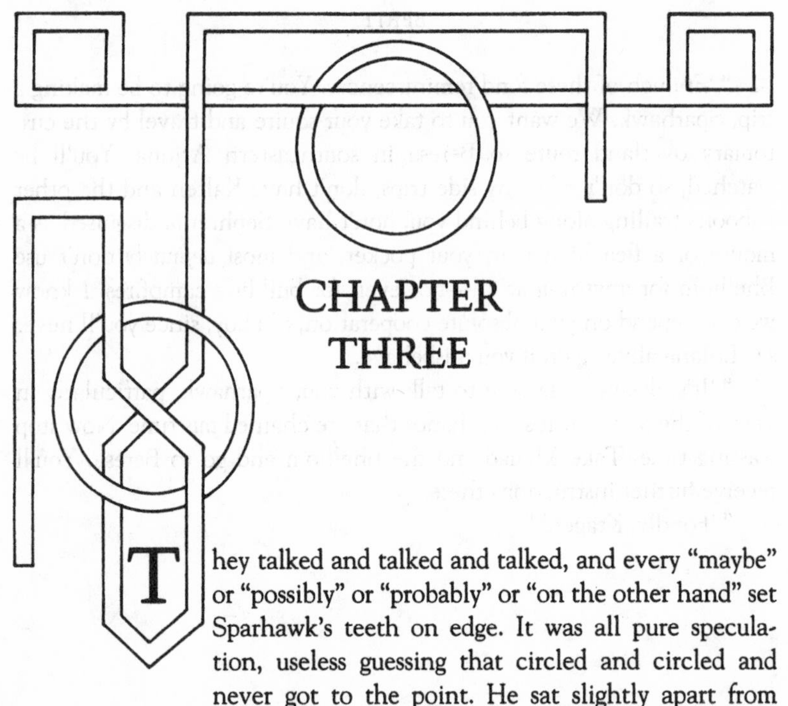

CHAPTER THREE

They talked and talked and talked, and every "maybe" or "possibly" or "probably" or "on the other hand" set Sparhawk's teeth on edge. It was all pure speculation, useless guessing that circled and circled and never got to the point. He sat slightly apart from them holding the lock of pale hair. The hair felt strangely alive, coiling around his fingers in a soft caress.

It was his fault, of course. He should never have permitted Ehlana to come to Tamuli. It went further than that, though. Ehlana had been in danger all her life, and it had all been because of him—because of the fact that he was Anakha. Xanetia had said that Anakha was invincible, but she was wrong. Anakha was as vulnerable as *any* married man. By marrying Ehlana, he had immediately put her at risk, a risk that would last for as long as she lived.

He should never have married her. He loved her, of course, but was it an act of love to put her in danger? He silently cursed the weakness that had led him even to consider the ridiculous notion when she had first raised it. He was a soldier, and soldiers should never marry—particularly not scarred, battered old veterans with too many years and too many battles behind them and too many enemies still about. Was he some selfish old fool?—some disgusting, half-senile lecher eager to take advantage of a foolish young girl's infatuation? Ehlana had extravagantly declared that she would die if he refused her, but he knew better than that. People die from a sword in the belly, or from old age, but they do not die from love. He should have laughed in her face and rejected her absurd command. Then he could have arranged a proper marriage for her, a marriage to some handsome young nobleman with good manners and a safe occupation. If he had, she would still be safely back in Cimmura instead of in the hands of madmen, degenerate sorcerers, and alien Gods to whom her life meant nothing at all.

And still they talked on and on. Why were they wasting all their breath? There wasn't any choice in the matter. Sparhawk would obey the instructions because Ehlana's life depended on it. The others were certain to argue with him about it, and the arguments would only irritate him. The best thing would probably be just to take the Bhelliom and Khalad and slip out of Matherion without giving them the chance to drive him mad with their meaningless babble.

It was the touch of a springlike breeze on his cheek and a soft nuzzling on his hand that roused him from his gloomy reverie.

"It was not mine intent to disturb thy thought, Sir Knight," the white deer apologized, "but my mistress would have words with thee."

Sparhawk jerked his head around in astonishment. He no longer sat in the blue-draped room in Matherion, and the voices of the others had faded away to be replaced by the sound of the gentle lapping of waves upon a golden strand. His chair now sat on the marble floor of Aphrael's temple on the small verdant island that rose gemlike from the sea. The breeze was soft under the rainbow-colored sky, and the ancient oaks around the alabaster temple rustled softly.

"Thou hast forgotten me," the gentle white hind reproached him, her liquid eyes touched with sorrow.

"Never," he replied. "I shall remember thee always, dear creature, for I do love thee, even as I did when first we met." The extravagant expression came to his lips unbidden.

The white deer sighed happily and laid her snowy head in his lap. He stroked her arched white neck and looked around.

The Child-Goddess Aphrael, gowned in white and surrounded by a glowing nimbus, sat calmly on a branch of one of the nearby oaks. She lifted her many-chambered pipes and blew an almost mocking little trill.

"What are you up to now, Aphrael?" he called up to her, deliberately forcing away the flowery words that jumped to his lips.

"I thought you might want to talk," she replied, lowering the pipes. "Did you want some more time for self-mortification? Would you like a whip so that you can flog yourself with it? Take as much time as you want, Father. This particular instant will last for as long as I want it to." She reached out with one grass-stained little foot, placed it on nothing at all, and calmly walked down a nonexistent stairway to the alabaster floor of her temple. She sank down on it, crossed her feet at the ankles, and lifted her pipes again. "Will it disturb your sour musings if I play?"

"Just what do you think you're doing?" he demanded.

She shrugged. "You seem to have this obscure need for penance of some kind, and there's no time for it. I wouldn't be much of a Goddess if I couldn't satisfy both needs at the same time, now would I?" She raised her pipes. "Do you have any favorites you'd like to hear?"

"You're actually serious, aren't you?"

"Yes." She breathed another little trill into the pipes.

He glared at her for a moment, and then he gave up. "Can we talk about this?" he asked her.

"You've come to your senses? Already? Amazing."

He looked around at the island. "Where is this place?" he asked curiously.

The Child-Goddess shrugged. "Wherever I want it to be. I carry it with me everyplace I go. Were you serious about what you were just thinking, Sparhawk? Were you really going to snatch up Bhelliom, grab Khalad by the scruff of the neck, leap onto Faran's back, and try to ride off in three directions at the same time?"

"All Vanion and the others are doing is talking, Aphrael, and the talk isn't going anywhere."

"Did you speak with Bhelliom about this notion of yours?"

"The decision is *mine*, Aphrael. Ehlana's *my* wife."

"How brave you are, Sparhawk. You're making a decision that involves the Bhelliom without even consulting it. Don't be misled by its seeming politeness, Father. That's just a reflection of its archaic speech. It *won't* do something it knows is wrong, no matter how sorry you're feeling for yourself, and if you grow *too* insistent, it might just decide to create a new sun—about six inches from your heart."

"I have the rings, Aphrael. I'm still the one giving the orders."

She laughed at him. "Do you *really* think the rings mean anything, Sparhawk? They have no control over Bhelliom at all. That was just a subterfuge that concealed the fact that it has an awareness—and a will and purpose of its own. It can ignore the rings anytime it wants to."

"Then why did it need me?"

"Because you're a necessity, Sparhawk—like wind or tide or rain. You're as necessary as Klæl is—or Bhelliom—or me, for that matter. Someday we'll have to come back here and have a long talk about necessity, but we're a little pressed for time right now."

"And was that little virtuoso performance of yours yesterday another necessity as well? Would the world have come to an end if you hadn't held that public conversation with yourself?"

"What I did yesterday was useful, Father, not necessary. I am who I am, and I can't change that. When I'm going through one of these transitions, there are usually people around who know both of the little girls, and they start noticing the similarities. I always make it a point to have the girls meet each other in public. It puts off tiresome questions and lays unwanted suspicions to rest."

"You terrified Mmrr, you know."

She nodded. "I'll make it up to her. That's always been a problem. Animals can see right through my disguises. They don't look at us in the way that we look at each other."

He sighed. "What am I going to do, Aphrael?"

"I was hoping that a visit here would bring you back to your senses. A stopover in reality usually has that effect."

He looked up at her private, rainbow-colored sky. "*This* is your notion of reality?"

"Don't you like my reality?"

"It's lovely," he told her, absently stroking the white deer's neck, "but it's a dream."

"Are you really sure about that, Sparhawk? Are you so certain that *this* isn't reality and that other place isn't the dream?"

"Don't do that. It makes my head hurt. What should I do?"

"I'd say that your first step ought to be to have a long conversation with Bhelliom. All of your moping around and contemplating arbitrary decisions has it more than a little worried."

"All right. Then what?"

"I haven't gotten that far yet." She grinned at him. "I'm a-workin' on it, though, Dorlin'," she added.

"They're going to be all right, Kalten," Sparhawk said, gently laying his hand on his suffering friend's shoulder.

Kalten looked up, his eyes filled with hopeless misery. "Are you sure, Sparhawk?"

"They will be if we can just keep our heads. Ehlana was in much more danger when I came back from Rendor, and we took care of that, didn't we?"

"I suppose you're right." Kalten straightened up in his chair and jerked down his blue doublet. His face was bleak. "I think I'm going to find some people and hurt them," he declared.

"Would you mind if I came along?"

"You can help if you like." Kalten rubbed at the side of his face. "I've been thinking," he said. "You know that if you follow those orders in Krager's note, he'll be able to keep you plodding from one end of Tamuli to the other for the next year or more, don't you?"

"Do I have any choice? They're going to be watching me."

"Let them. Do you remember how we met Berit?"

"He was a novice in the chapterhouse in Cimmura," Sparhawk shrugged.

"Not when *I* first saw him, he wasn't. I was coming back from exile in Lamorkand, and I stopped at a roadside tavern outside of Cimmura. Berit was there with Kurik, and he was wearing your armor. I've known you since we were children, and even *I* couldn't tell that he wasn't you. If *I* couldn't tell, Krager's spies certainly won't be able to. If somebody has to plod around Tamuli, let Berit do it. You and I have better things to do."

Sparhawk was startled. "That's the best idea I've heard yet." He looked around at the others. "Could I have your attention, please?" he said.

They all looked sharply at him, their faces apprehensive.

"It's time to get to work," he told them. "Kalten here just reminded me that we've used Sir Berit as a decoy in the past. Berit and I are nearly the same size, and my armor fits him—more or less—and with his visor down, nobody can really tell that he isn't me. If we can prevail on him to masquerade as a broken-down old campaigner again, we might just be able to prepare a few surprises for Krager and his friends."

"You don't even have to ask, Sparhawk," Berit said.

"Get some details before you volunteer like that, Berit," Khalad told his friend in a pained voice.

"Your father used to say almost exactly the same thing," Berit recalled.

"Why didn't you listen to him?"

"It's an interesting plan, Prince Sparhawk," Oscagne said a bit dubiously, "but isn't it extremely dangerous?"

"I'm not afraid, your Excellency," Berit protested.

"I wasn't talking about *your* danger, young sir. I'm talking about the danger to Queen Ehlana. The moment someone penetrates your disguise—well . . ." Oscagne spread his hands.

"Then we'll just have to make sure that his disguise is foolproof," Sephrenia said.

"He can't keep his visor down forever, Sephrenia," Sarabian objected.

"I don't think he'll have to," Sephrenia replied. She looked speculatively at Xanetia. "Do we trust each other enough to cooperate, Anarae?" she asked. "I'm talking about something a little deeper than we've gone so far."

"I will listen most attentively to thy proposal, my sister."

"Delphaeic magic is directed primarily inward, isn't it?"

Xanetia nodded.

"That's probably why no one can hear or feel it. Styric magic is just the reverse. We alter things around us, so our magic reaches out. Neither form will work by itself in this particular situation, but if we were to combine them . . ." She left it hanging in the air between them.

"Interesting notion," Aphrael mused.

"I'm not sure I follow," Vanion said.

"The Anarae and I are going to have to experiment a bit," Sephrenia told him, "but if what I've got in mind works, we'll be able to make Berit look so much like Sparhawk that they'll be able to use each other for shaving mirrors."

"As long as each of us knows exactly what the other's doing, it's not too difficult, Sparhawk," Sephrenia assured him later when he and Berit joined her, Vanion, and the Anarae in the room she shared with Vanion.

"Will it really work?" he asked her dubiously.

"They haven't actually tried it yet, Sparhawk," Vanion told him, "so we're not entirely positive."

"That doesn't sound too promising. This isn't much of a face, but it's the only one I've got."

"There will be no danger to thee or to young Sir Berit, Anakha," Xanetia said. "In times past it hath oft been necessary for my people to leave our valley and to go abroad amongst others. This hath been our means of disguising our true identity."

"It works sort of like this, Sparhawk," Sephrenia explained. "Xanetia casts a Delphaeic spell that would normally imprint your features on her own face, but just as she releases *her* spell, *I* release a Styric one that deflects the spell to Berit instead."

"Won't every Styric in Matherion feel it when you release your spell?" Sparhawk asked.

"That's the beauty of it, Sparhawk," Aphrael told him. "The spell itself originates with Xanetia, and others can't feel or hear a Delphaeic spell. Cyrgon himself could be in the next room and he wouldn't hear a thing."

"You're sure it's going to work?"

"There's one way to find out."

Sparhawk, of course, did not feel a thing. He *was* only the model, after all. It was a bit disconcerting to watch Berit's appearance gradually change, however.

When the combined spell had been completed, Sparhawk carefully inspected his young friend. "Do I really look like that from the side?" he asked Vanion, feeling a bit deflated.

"I can't tell the two of you apart."

"That nose is really crooked, isn't it?"

"We thought you knew."

"I've never looked at myself from the side this way before." Sparhawk looked critically at Berit's eyes. "You should probably try to squint just a little," he suggested. "My eyes aren't as good as they used to be. That's one of the things you have to look forward to as you get older."

"I'll try to remember that." Even Berit's voice was different.

"Do I really sound like that?" Sparhawk was crestfallen.

Vanion nodded.

Sparhawk shook his head. "Seeing and hearing yourself as others do definitely lowers your opinion of yourself," he admitted. He looked at Berit again. "I didn't feel anything, did you?"

Berit nodded, swallowing hard.

"What was it like?"

"I'd really rather not talk about it." Berit gently explored his new face with cringing fingertips, wincing as he did.

"I *still* can't tell them apart," Kalten marveled, staring first at Berit and then at Sparhawk.

"That was sort of the idea," Sparhawk told him.

"Which one are you?"

"Try to be serious, Kalten."

"Now that we know how it's done, we can make some other changes as well," Sephrenia told them. "We'll give you all different faces so that you'll be able to move around freely—*and* we'll put men wearing *your* faces here in the palace. I think we can all expect to be watched, even after the Harvest Festival, and this should nullify that particular problem."

"We can make more detailed plans later," Vanion said. "Let's get Berit and Khalad on their way first. What's the customary route when someone wants to go overland from here to Beresa?" He unrolled a map and spread it out on the table.

"Most travelers go by sea," Oscagne replied, "but those who don't usually cross the peninsula to Micae and then take a ship across the gulf to the mainland."

"There don't seem to be any roads over there." Vanion frowned, looking at the map.

"It's a relatively uninhabited region, Lord Vanion—" Oscagne shrugged. "—salt marshes and the like. What few tracks there are wouldn't show up on the map."

"Do the best you can," Vanion told the two young men. "Once you get past the Tamul Mountains, you'll hit that road that skirts the western side of the jungle."

"I'd make a special point of staying out of those mountains, Berit," Ulath advised. "There are Trolls there now."

Berit nodded.

"You'd better have a talk with Faran, Sparhawk," Khalad suggested. "I don't think he'll be fooled just because Berit's wearing your face, and Berit's going to have to ride him if this is going to be convincing."

"I'd forgotten that," Sparhawk admitted.

"I thought you might have."

"All right, then," Vanion continued his instructions to the two young men, "follow that road down to Lydros, then take the road around the southern tip of Arjuna to Beresa. That's the logical route, and they'll probably be expecting you to go that way."

"That's going to take quite a while, Lord Vanion," Khalad said.

"I know. Evidently Krager and his friends want it to. If they were in a hurry, they'd have instructed Sparhawk to go by sea."

"Give Berit your wife's ring, Sparhawk," Flute instructed.

"What?"

"Zalasta can sense the ring, and if he can, Cyrgon can, too—and Klæl will *definitely* feel it. If you don't give Berit the ring, changing his face was just a waste of time."

"You're putting Berit and Khalad in a great deal of danger," Sephrenia said critically.

"That's what we get paid for, little mother." Khalad shrugged.

"I'll watch over them," Aphrael assured her sister. She looked critically at Berit. "Call me," she told him.

"Ma'am?"

"Use the spell, Berit," she explained with exaggerated patience. "I want to be sure you're doing it right."

"Oh." Berit carefully enunciated the spell of summoning, his hands moving in the intricate accompanying gestures.

"You mispronounced '*kajerasticon*,' " she corrected him.

Sephrenia was trying without much success to suppress a laugh.

"What's so funny?" Talen asked her.

"Sir Berit's pronunciations raised some questions about his meaning," Stragen explained.

"What did he say?" Talen asked curiously.

"Just never mind what he said," Flute told him primly. "We're not here to repeat off-color jokes about the differences between boys and girls. Practice on that one, Berit. Now try the secret summoning."

"What's that?" Itagne murmured to Vanion.

"It's used to pass messages, your Excellency," Vanion replied. "It summons the awareness of the Child-Goddess, but not her presence. We can give her a message to carry to someone else by using that spell."

"Isn't that just a little demeaning for the Child-Goddess? Do you really make her run errands and carry messages that way?"

"I'm not offended, Itagne." Aphrael smiled. "After all, we live only to serve those we love, don't we?"

Berit's pronunciation of the second spell raised no objections.

"You'll probably want to use that one most of the time anyway, Berit," Vanion instructed. "Krager warned Sparhawk about using magic, so don't be too obvious about things. If you get any further instructions along the road, make some show of following them, but pass the word on to Aphrael."

"There's no real point in decking him out in Sparhawk's armor now, is there, Lord Vanion?" Khalad asked.

"Good point," Vanion agreed. "A mail shirt should do, Berit. We *want* them to see your face now."

"Yes, my Lord."

"Now you'd better get some sleep," Vanion continued. "You'll be starting early tomorrow morning."

"Not *too* early, though," Caalador amended. "We surely wouldn't want th' spies t' oversleep therselfs an' miss seein' y' leave. Gittin' a new face don't mean shucks iffn y' don't git no chance t' show it off, now does it?"

It was chill and damp in the courtyard the following morning, and a thin autumn mist lay over the gleaming city. Sparhawk led Faran out of the stables. "Just be careful," he cautioned the two young men in chain-mail shirts and travelers' cloaks.

"You've said that already, my Lord," Khalad reminded him. "Berit and I aren't deaf, you know."

"You'd better forget that name, Khalad," Sparhawk said critically. "Start thinking of your young friend here as me. A slip of the tongue in the wrong place could give this all away."

"I'll keep that in mind."

"Do you need money?"

"I thought you'd never ask."

"You're as bad as your father was," Sparhawk pulled a purse from under his belt and handed it to his squire. Then he firmly took Faran by the chin and looked straight into the big roan's eyes. "I want you to go with Berit, Faran," he said. "Behave exactly as you would if he were me."

Faran flicked his ears and looked away.

"Pay attention," Sparhawk said sharply. "This is important."

Faran sighed.

"He knows what you're talking about, Sparhawk," Khalad said. "He's not stupid—just bad-tempered."

Sparhawk handed the reins to Berit. Then he remembered something. "We'll need a password," he said. "The rest of us are going to have different faces, so you won't recognize us if we have to contact you. Pick something ordinary."

They all considered it.

"How about *ramshorn*?" Berit suggested. "It shouldn't be too hard to work it into an ordinary conversation, and we've used it before."

Sparhawk suddenly remembered Ulesim, most-favored-disciple-of-holy-Arasham, standing atop a pile of rubble with Kurik's crossbow bolt sticking out of his forehead and the word *ramshorn* still on his lips. "Very good, Berit—ah—Sir Sparhawk, that is. It's a word we all remember. You'd better get started."

They nodded and swung up into their saddles.

"Good luck," Sparhawk said.

"You, too, my Lord," Khalad replied. And then the pair turned and rode slowly toward the drawbridge.

"All we've really got to work with is the name *Beresa*," Sarabian mused, somewhat later. "Krager's note said that Sparhawk would receive further instructions there."

"That could be a ruse, your Majesty," Itagne pointed out. "Actually, the exchange could take place at any time—and any place. That *might* have been the reason for the instructions to go overland."

"That's true," Caalador agreed. "Scarpa and Zalasta might just be waiting on the beach on the west side of the Gulf of Micae wanting to make the trade right there, for all we know."

"We're going to an awful lot of trouble here," Talen said. "Why doesn't Sparhawk just have Bhelliom go rescue the queen? It could pick her up and have her back here before Scarpa even knew she was gone."

"No," Aphrael said, shaking her head. "Bhelliom can't do that any more than I can."

"Why not?"

"Because we don't know where she *is*—and we can't go looking for her, because they'll be able to sense us moving around."

"Oh. I didn't know that."

Aphrael rolled her eyes upward. "Men!" She sighed.

"It was very resourceful of Ehlana to slip her ring to Melidere," Sephrenia said, "but locating her would be much easier if she still had it with her."

"I sort of doubt that, dear," Vanion disagreed. "Zalasta of all people knows that the rings can be traced. If Ehlana had still been wearing it, the first thing Scarpa would have done would have been to send Krager or Elron off in the opposite direction with it."

"You're assuming that Zalasta's involved in this," she disagreed. "There *is* the possibility that Scarpa's acting on his own, you know."

"It's always better to assume the worst." He shrugged. "Our situation is much more perilous if Zalasta and Cyrgon are involved. If it's only Scarpa, he'll be relatively easy to dispose of."

"But *only* after Ehlana and Alean are safe," Sparhawk amended.

"That goes without saying, Sparhawk," Vanion said.

"Everything hinges on the moment of the exchange, then, doesn't it?" Sarabian noted. "We can make some preparations, but we won't be able to do anything at all significant until the moment that Scarpa actually produces Ehlana."

"And that means that we have to stay close to Berit and Khalad." Tynian added.

"No." Aphrael was shaking her head. "You'll give everything away if you all start hovering over those two. Let *me* do the staying close. I don't wear armor, so no one will be able to smell me from a thousand paces off. Itagne's right. The exchange could come at any time. I'll let Sparhawk know the very instant Scarpa shows up with Ehlana and Alean. Then Bhelliom can set him down—with knife—right on top of them. We'll have the ladies back, and we'll be more or less in charge of things again."

"And that brings us right back to a purely military situation," Patriarch Emban mused. "I think we'll want to send word to Komier and Bergsten. We're going to need the Church Knights in Cynesga and Arjuna, not in Edom or Astel—or here in Matherion. Let's have them ride southeast after they come down out of the mountains of Zemoch. We'll have the Atans in Sarna, the eastern Peloi and the Church Knights we've already got in Samar, the Trolls in the Tamul Mountains and Komier and Bergsten on the western side of the Desert of Cynesga. We'll be able to squeeze the land of the Cyrgai like a lemon at that point."

"And see what kind of seeds come popping out," Kalten added bleakly.

Patriarch Emban, First Secretary of the Church of Chyrellos, was a man who absolutely adored lists. The fat little churchman automatically drew up a list when any subject was being discussed. There is a certain point in most discussions when things have all been settled and the participants start going back over the various points. Inevitably, that was the point at which Emban pulled out his list. "All right, then," he said in a tone that clearly said that he was summing up, "Sparhawk will take ship for Beresa, along with Milord Stragen and young master Talen, right?"

"It puts him in place in case Berit and Khalad do, in fact, have to ride all the way down there, your Grace," Vanion said. "And Stragen and Talen have contacts in Beresa, so they'll probably be able to find out just who else is in town."

Emban checked that off his list. "Next: Sir Kalten, Sir Bevier, and Master Caalador will sail south on a different ship and go into the jungles of Arjuna."

Caalador nodded. "I've got a friend in the Delo who has contacts with the robber bands in those jungles," he said. "We'll join one of those bands, so we'll be able to keep an eye on Natayos and pass the word if Scarpa's army starts to move."

"Right." Emban checked *that* off. "Next. Sir Ulath and Sir Tynian will go to the Tamul Mountains to stay in touch with the Trolls." He frowned. "Why is Tynian going there?" he asked. "He doesn't speak Trollish."

"Tynian and I get along well," Ulath rumbled, "and I'll get terribly lonely if there's no one around to talk with but Trolls. You have no idea how depressing it is to be alone with Trolls, your Grace."

"Whatever makes you happy, Sir Ulath." Emban shrugged. "Now then, Sephrenia and Anarae Xanetia will go to Delphaeus to advise Anari Cedon about all these recent developments and to explain what we're doing."

"*And* to see what we can do to make peace between Styricum and the Delphae," Sephrenia added.

Emban checked off another item. He said, "Lord Vanion, Queen Betuana, Ambassador Itagne, and Domi Kring will take the five thousand knights and go to western Tamul proper to join with the forces they have in place in Sarna and Samar."

"Where *is* Domi Kring?" Betuana asked, looking around for the little man.

"He's standing guard over Mirtai," Princess Danae said. "He's still about half-afraid she might try to kill herself."

"We might have a problem there," Bevier observed. "Under those circumstances, Kring might not be willing to leave Matherion."

"We can get along without him if we have to," Vanion said. "I can deal with Tikume directly. Having Kring around would make it easier, but I can make do without him if he really thinks that Mirtai might do something foolish."

Emban nodded. "Emperor Sarabian, Foreign Minister Oscagne, and I will stay here in Matherion to hold down the fort, and the Child-Goddess will keep us all in touch with each other. Have I left anything out?"

"What do you want me to do, Emban?" Danae asked sweetly.

"You'll stay here in Matherion with us, your Royal Highness," Emban replied, "to brighten our gloomy days and nights with the sunshine of your smile."

"Are you making fun of me, your Grace?"

"Of course not, Princess."

To say that Mirtai was unhappy would have been the grossest of understatements. She was in chains when Kring brought her into the council chamber with a hopeless look on his face. "Nothing I say reaches her," the Domi told them. "I think she's even forgotten that we're betrothed."

The golden Atan giantess would not look at any of them, but sank instead to the floor in abject misery.

"She has failed her owner." Betuana shrugged. "She must either avenge her or die."

"Not quite, your Majesty," Sparhawk's daughter said firmly. She slipped down from the chair in the corner from which she had been watching the proceedings. She deposited Rollo in one corner of the chair and Mmrr in the other and crossed the room to Mirtai with a businesslike look on her small face. "Atana Mirtai," she said crisply, "get up off the floor."

Mirtai looked sullenly at her, then slowly rose, her chains clinking.

"In my mother's absence, I am the queen," Danae declared.

Sparhawk blinked.

"You're not Ehlana," Mirtai said.

"I'm not pretending to be. I'm stating a legal fact. Sarabian, isn't that the way it works? Isn't my mother's power mine while she's away?"

"Well—technically, I suppose."

"Technically, my foot. I'm Queen Ehlana's heir. I'm assuming her position until she returns. That means that I temporarily own everything that's hers—her throne, her crown, her jewels, *and* her personal slave."

"I'd hate to have to argue against her in a court of law," Emban admitted.

"Thank you, your Grace," Danae said. "All right, Atana Mirtai, you heard them. You're *my* property now."

Mirtai scowled at her.

"Don't do that," Danae snapped. "Pay attention. I am your owner, and I forbid you to kill yourself. I *also* forbid you to run off. I need you here. You're going to stay here with Melidere and me, and you're going to guard us. You failed my mother. Don't fail me."

Mirtai stiffened, and then she broke her chains with an angry wrench of her arms. "It shall be as you say, Majesty," she snapped, her eyes blazing.

Danae looked around at the rest of them with a smug little smile. "See," she said. "Now that wasn't so hard, was it?"

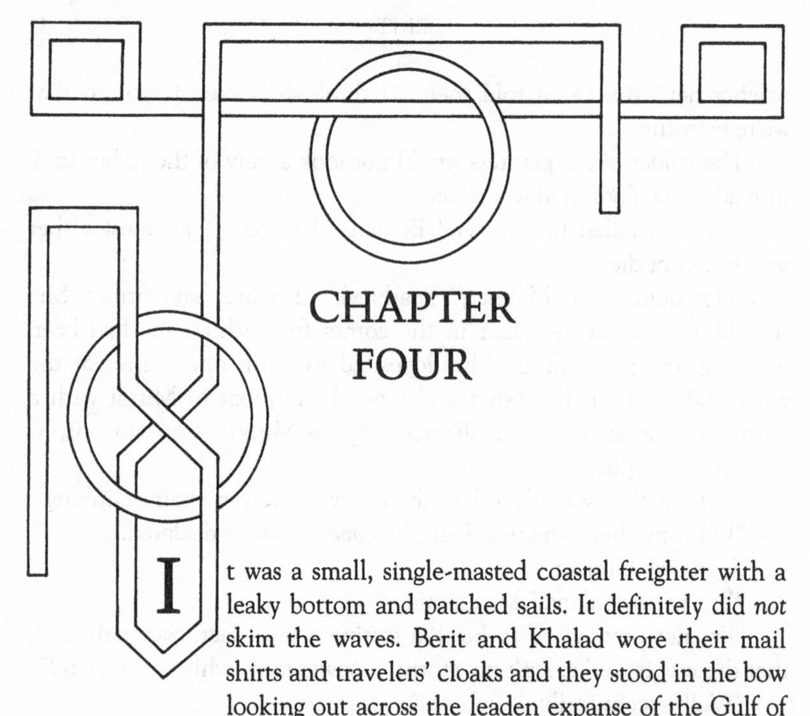

CHAPTER FOUR

It was a small, single-masted coastal freighter with a leaky bottom and patched sails. It definitely did *not* skim the waves. Berit and Khalad wore their mail shirts and travelers' cloaks and they stood in the bow looking out across the leaden expanse of the Gulf of Micae as the wretched vessel wallowed along. "Is that the coast up ahead?" Berit asked hopefully.

Khalad looked out across the choppy water. "No, just a cloud bank. We're not moving very fast, my Lord. We won't make the coast today, I'm afraid." He looked aft and lowered his voice. "Stay alert after the sun goes down," he instructed. "The crew of this tub is made up of waterfront sweepings, and the captain isn't much better. I think we should take turns sleeping tonight."

Berit glanced back along the deck at the assortment of ruffians loitering on deck. "I wish I had my ax," he muttered.

"Don't say things like that out loud, Berit," Khalad muttered. "*Sparhawk* doesn't use a war ax. Krager knows that, and one of these sailors may be working for him."

"Still? After the Harvest Festival?"

"Nobody's ever figured out a way to kill *all* the rats, my Lord, and it only takes one. Let's both behave as if we're being watched and every word we say is being overheard—just to be on the safe side."

"I'll be a lot happier once we get ashore. Did we really have to make this leg of the trip by sea?"

"It's the custom," Khalad shrugged. "Don't worry. We can hold off these sailors if we have to."

"That's not what's bothering me, Khalad. This scow waddles through the water like a whale with a sprained back. It's making me queasy."

"Eat a piece of dry bread."

"I'd rather not. This is *really* miserable, Khalad."

"But we're having an *adventure*, my Lord," Khalad said brightly. "Doesn't the excitement make up for the discomfort?"

"No. Not really."

"You're the one who wanted to be a knight."

"Yes, I know—and right now I'm trying to remember why."

Patriarch Emban was very displeased. "This is really outrageous, Vanion," he protested as he waddled along with the others toward the chapel in the west wing. "If Dolmant ever finds out that I've permitted the practice of witchcraft in a consecrated place of worship, he'll have me defrocked."

"It's the safest place, Emban," Vanion replied. "The pretense of 'sacred rites' gives us an excuse to chase all the Tamuls out of the west wing. Besides, the chapel's probably never really been consecrated anyway. This is an imitation castle built to make Elenes feel at home. The people who built it couldn't have known the rite of consecration."

"You don't *know* that it hasn't been consecrated."

"And you don't know that it has. If it bothers you all that much, Emban, you can reconsecrate it after we finish."

Emban's face blanched. "Do you know what's involved in that, Vanion?" he protested. "The hours of praying—the prostration before the altar—the fasting?" His chubby face went pale. "Good God, the fasting!"

Sephrenia, Flute, and Xanetia had slipped into the chapel several hours earlier, and they were sitting unobtrusively in one corner listening to a choir of Church Knights singing hymns.

Emban and Vanion were still arguing when they joined the ladies. "What's the problem?" Sephrenia asked.

"Patriarch Emban and Lord Vanion are having a disagreement about whether or not the chapel's been consecrated, little mother," Kalten explained.

"It hasn't," Flute told him with a little shrug.

"How can you tell?" Emban demanded.

She gave him a long-suffering look. "Who am I, your Grace?" she asked him.

He blinked. "Oh. I keep forgetting that for some reason. Is there actually a way you can tell whether or not a place has been consecrated?"

"Well of *course* there is. Believe me, Emban, this chapel's never been consecrated to your Elene God." She paused. "There *was* a spot not far from here that was consecrated to a tree about eighteen thousand years ago, though."

"A *tree*?"

"It was a very nice tree—an oak. It's always an oak for some reason. Nobody ever seems to want to worship an elm. Lots of people used to worship trees. They're predictable, for one thing."

"How could anybody in his right mind worship a tree?"

"Whoever said that religious people were in their right minds? Sometimes you humans confuse us a great deal, you know."

Since there was an exchange of features involved in most cases here, Sephrenia and Xanetia had experimented a bit to alter the spell that had imprinted Sparhawk's face on Berit. No exchange was necessary for Sparhawk, however, so they modified him first. He sat beside his old friend, Sir Endrik, a veteran with whom he, Kalten, and Martel had endured their novitiates. Xanetia approached them with the color draining from her features and that soft radiance suffusing her face. She examined Endrik meticulously, and then her voice rose as she began to intone the Delphaeic spell in her oddly accented, archaic Tamul. Sephrenia stood at her side simultaneously casting the Styric spell.

Sparhawk felt nothing whatsoever as Xanetia released her spell. Then at the crucial instant, Sephrenia extended her hand, interposing it between Sir Endrik's face and Xanetia's and simultaneously releasing the Styric spell. Sparhawk *definitely* felt that. His features seemed to somehow soften like melting wax, and he could actually feel his face changing, almost as wet clay is changed and molded by the potter's hand. The straightening of his broken nose was a bit painful, and the lengthening of his jaw made his teeth ache as they shifted in the bone.

"What do you think?" Sephrenia asked Vanion when the process had been completed.

"I don't think you could get them any closer," Vanion replied, examining the two men closely. "How does it feel to be twins, Endrik?"

"I didn't feel a thing, my Lord," Endrik replied, staring curiously at Sparhawk.

"*I* did," Sparhawk told him, gingerly touching his reshaped nose. "Does the ache go away eventually, Anarae?" he asked.

"Thou wilt notice it less as time doth accustom thee to the alteration, Anakha. I did warn thee that some discomfort is involved, did I not?"

"You did indeed." Sparhawk shrugged. "It's not unbearable."

"Do I really look like that?" Endrik asked.

"Yes," Vanion replied.

"I should take better care of myself. The years aren't being good to me."

"Nobody stays young and beautiful forever, Endrik." Kalten laughed.

"Is that all that needs to be done to these two, Anarae?" Vanion asked.

"The process is complete, Lord Vanion," Xanetia replied.

"We need to talk, Sparhawk," the Preceptor said. "Let's go into the vestry where we'll be out of the way while the ladies modify the others."

Sparhawk nodded, stood up, and followed his friend to the small door to the left of the altar.

Vanion led the way inside and closed the door behind them. "You've made all the arrangements with Sorgi?" he asked.

Sparhawk sat down. "I talked with him yesterday," he replied. "I told him that I had some friends that had to go to Beresa without attracting attention. He's had the usual desertions, so he's holding three berths open. Stragen, Talen, and I'll merge with the crew. We should be able to slip into Beresa without being noticed."

"I imagine that cost you. Sorgi's prices are a little steep sometimes."

Sparhawk massaged the side of his aching jaw. "It wasn't all that bad," he said. "Sorgi owes me a couple of favors, and I gave him time to pick up a cargo to cover most of the cost."

"You'll be going directly to the harbor from here?"

Sparhawk nodded. "We'll use that tunnel Caalador found under the barracks. I told Sorgi that his three new crew members would report to him about midnight."

"You'll sail tomorrow, then?"

Sparhawk shook his head. "The day after. We have to load Sorgi's cargo tomorrow."

"Honest work, Sparhawk?" Vanion smiled.

"You're starting to sound like Khalad."

"He *does* have opinions, doesn't he?"

"So did his father."

"Quit rubbing your face like that, Sparhawk. You'll make your skin raw." Vanion paused. "What was it like?"

"Very strange."

"Painful?"

"The nose was. It feels almost as if somebody broke it again. Be glad you don't have to go through it."

"There wouldn't be much point in that. I won't be sneaking down alleys the way the rest of you will." Vanion looked sympathetically at his friend. "We'll get her back, Sparhawk," he said.

"Of course. Was that all?" Sparhawk's tone was deliberately unemotional. The important thing here was *not* to feel.

"Just be careful, and try to keep a handle on your temper."

Sparhawk nodded. "Let's go see how the others are coming."

The alterations were confusing; there was no question about that. It was hard to tell exactly who was talking, and sometimes Sparhawk was startled by just who answered his questions. They said their good-byes and quietly left the chapel with the main body of the Church Knights. They went out into the torchlit courtyard, crossed the drawbridge, and proceeded across the night-shrouded lawn to the barracks of the knights, where Sparhawk, Stragen, and Talen changed into tar-smeared sailor's smocks while the others also donned the mismatched clothing of commoners. Then they all went down to the cellar.

Caalador, who now wore the blocky face of a middle-aged Deiran knight, led the way into a damp, cobweb-draped tunnel with a smoky torch. When they had gone about a mile, he stopped and raised the torch. "This yere's yer exit, Sparhawk," he said, pointing at a steep, narrow stairway. "You'll come out in an alley—which it is ez don't smell none too sweet, but is good an' dork." He paused. "Sorry, Stragen," he apologized. "I wanted to give you something to remember me by."

"You're too kind." Stragen murmured.

"Good luck, Sparhawk," Caalador said then.

"Thanks, Caalador." The two shook hands, and then Caalador lifted his torch and led the rest of the party down the musty-smelling passageway toward their assorted destinations, leaving Sparhawk, Talen, and Stragen alone in the dark.

"They won't be in any danger, Vanion," Flute assured the preceptor as the ladies were packing. "I'll be going along, after all, and I can take care of them."

"*Ten* knights, then," he amended his suggestion downward.

"They'd just be in our way, love," Sephrenia told him. "I do want *you* to be careful, though. A body of armed men is far more likely to be attacked than a small party of travelers."

"But it isn't safe for ladies to travel alone," he protested. "There are always robbers and the like lurking in the forest."

"We won't be in one place long enough to attract robbers or anybody else," Flute told him. "We'll be in Delphaeus in two days. I could do it in one, but I'll have to stop and have a long talk with Edaemus before I go into his valley. He might just take a bit of convincing."

"When art thou leaving Matherion, Lord Vanion?" Xanetia asked.

"About the end of the week, Anarae," he replied. "We've got to spend some time on our equipment, and there's always the business of organizing the supply train."

"Take warm clothing," Sephrenia instructed. "The weather could change at any time."

"Yes, love. How long will you be at Delphaeus?"

"We can't be sure. Aphrael will keep you advised. We have a great deal to discuss with Anari Cedon. The fact that Cyrgon has summoned Klæl complicates matters."

"Truly," Xanetia agreed. "We may be obliged to entreat Edaemus to return."

"Would he do that?"

Flute smiled roguishly. "I'll coax him, Vanion," she said, "and you know how good I am at that. If I really want something, I almost always get it."

"You there! Look lively!" Sorgi's bull-necked bo'sun bellowed, popping his whip at Stragen's heels.

Stragen, who now wore the braids and sweeping mustaches of a blond Genidian Knight, dropped the bale he was carrying across the deck and reached for his dagger.

"No!" Sparhawk elbowed him. "Pick up that bale!"

Stragen glared at him for a moment, then bent and lifted the bale again. "This wasn't part of the agreement," he muttered.

"He's not really going to hit you with that whip," Talen assured the fuming Thalesian. "Sailors all complain about it, but the whip's just for show. A bo'sun who really hits his men with his whip usually gets thrown over the side some night during the voyage."

"Maybe," Stragen growled darkly, "but I'll tell you this right now. If that cretin so much as *touches* me with that whip of his, he won't live long enough to go swimming. I'll have his guts in a pile on the deck before he can even blink."

"You new men!" the bo'sun shouted. "Do your talking on your own time! You're here to work, not to discuss the weather!" And he cracked his whip again.

"She *could* do it, Khalad," Berit insisted.

"I think you've been out in the sun too long," Khalad replied. They were riding south along a lonely beach under an overcast sky. The beach was backed by an uninviting salt marsh where dry reeds clattered against each other in the stiff onshore breeze. Khalad rose in his stirrups and looked around. Then he settled back in his saddle again. "It's a ridiculous idea, my Lord."

"Try to keep an open mind, Khalad. Aphrael's a Goddess. She can do *anything*."

"I'm sure she can, but why would she *want* to?"

"Well—" Berit struggled with it. "She *could* have a reason, couldn't she? Something that you and I wouldn't even understand?"

"Is this what all that Styric training does to a man? You're starting to see Gods under every bush. It was only a coincidence. The two of them look a little bit alike, but that's all."

"You can be as skeptical as you want, Khalad, but I still think that something very strange is going on."

"And *I* think that what you're suggesting is an absurdity."

"Absurd or not, their mannerisms are the same, their expressions are identical, and they've both got that same air of smug superiority about them."

"Of course they do. Aphrael's a Goddess, and Danae's a Crown Princess. They *are* superior—at least in their own minds—and I think you're overlooking the fact that we saw them both in the same room and at the same time. They even *talked* to each other, for God's sake."

"Khalad, that doesn't mean anything. Aphrael's a Goddess. She can probably be in a dozen different places all at the same time if she really wants to be."

"That still brings us right back to the question of why? What would be the purpose of it? Not even a God does things without any reason."

"We don't *know* that, Khalad. Maybe she's doing it just to amuse herself."

"Are you really all that desperate to witness miracles, Berit?"

"She *could* do it," Berit insisted.

"All right. So what?"

"Aren't you the least bit curious about it?"

"Not particularly." Khalad shrugged.

Ulath and Tynian wore bits and pieces of the uniforms of one of the few units of the Tamul army that accepted volunteers from the Elene kingdoms of western Daresia. The faces they had borrowed were those of grizzled, middle-aged knights, the faces of hard-bitten veterans. The vessel aboard which they sailed was one of those battered, ill-maintained ships that ply coastal waters. The small amount of money they had paid for their passage bought them exactly that—passage, and nothing else. They had brought their own food and drink and their patched blankets, and they ate and slept on the deck. Their destination was a small coastal village some twenty-five leagues east of the foothills of the Tamul Mountains. They lounged on the deck in the daytime, drinking cheap wine and rolling dice for pennies.

The sky was overcast when the ship's longboat deposited them on the rickety wharf of the village. The day was cool, and the Tamul Mountains were little more than a low smudge on the horizon.

"What was that horse trader's name again?" Tynian asked.

"Sablis," Ulath grunted.

"I hope Oscagne was right," Tynian said. "If this Sablis has gone out of business, we'll have to walk to those mountains."

Ulath stepped across the wharf to speak to a pinch-faced fellow who was mending a fishnet. "Tell me, friend," he said politely in Tamul, "where can we find Sablis the horse trader?"

"What if I don't feel like telling you?" the scrawny net-mender replied in a whining, nasal voice that identified him as one of those mean-spirited men who would rather die than be helpful, or even polite.

Tynian had encountered his kind before: small men, usually, with an inflated notion of their own worth, men who delighted in irritating others just for the fun of it. "Let me," he murmured, laying one gently restraining hand on his Thalesian companion's arm. Ulath's bunched muscles clearly spoke of impending violence.

"Nice net," Tynian noted casually, picking up one edge of it. Then he drew his dagger and began cutting the strings.

"What are you *doing*?" the pinch-faced fisherman screamed.

"I'm showing you what," Tynian explained. "You said, 'What if I don't feel like telling you?' *This* is what. Think it over. My friend and I aren't in any hurry, so take your time." He took a fistful of net and sawed through it with his knife.

"*Stop!*" the fellow shrieked in horror.

"Ah—where was it you said we might find Sablis?" Ulath asked innocently.

"His corrals are on the eastern edge of town." The words came tumbling out. Then the scrawny fellow gathered up his net in both arms and held it to his chest, almost like a mother shielding a child from harm.

"Have a pleasant day, neighbor," Tynian said, sheathing his dagger. "I can't *begin* to tell you how much we've appreciated your help." And the two knights turned and walked along the wharf toward the shabby-looking village.

Their camp was neat and orderly with a place for everything and everything exactly where it belonged. Berit had noticed that Khalad always set up camp in exactly the same way. He seemed to have some concept of the ideal camp etched in his mind and, since it was perfect, he never altered it. Khalad was very rigid in some ways.

"How far did we come today?" Berit asked as they washed up their supper dishes.

"Ten leagues—" Khalad shrugged. "—the same as always. Ten leagues is standard on level terrain."

"This is going to take *forever*," Berit complained.

"No. It might seem like it, though." Khalad looked around and then lowered his voice until it was hardly more than a whisper. "We're not really in any hurry, Berit," he said. "We might even want to slow down a bit."

"What?"

"Keep your voice down. Sparhawk and the others have a long way to go, and we want to be sure they're in place before Krager—or whoever it is—makes contact with us. We don't know when or where that's going to happen, so the best way to delay it is to slow down." Khalad looked out into the darkness beyond the circle of firelight. "How good are you at magic?"

"Not very," Berit admitted, scrubbing diligently. "I've still got a lot to learn. What did you want me to do?"

"Could you make one of our horses limp—without actually hurting him?"

Berit probed through his memory. Then he shook his head. "I don't think I know any spells that would do that."

"That's too bad. A lame horse would give us a good reason to slow down."

It came without warning: a cold, prickling kind of sensation that seemed to be centered at the back of Berit's neck. "That's good enough," he said in a louder voice. "I'm not getting paid enough to scrub holes in tin plates." He rinsed off the dish he'd been washing, shook most of the water off it, and stowed it back into the pack.

"You felt it, too?" Khalad's whisper came out from between motionless lips. That startled Berit. How could Khalad have known?

Berit buckled the straps on the pack and gave his friend a curt nod. "Let's build up the fire a bit and then get some sleep." He said it loudly enough to be heard out beyond the circle of firelight. The two of them walked toward their pile of firewood. Berit was murmuring the spell and concealing the movements of his hands at the same time.

"Who is it?" Again, Khalad's lips did not move.

"I'm still working on that," Berit whispered back. He released the spell so slowly that it seemed almost to dribble out of the ends of his fingers.

The sense of it came washing back to him. It was something on the order of recognizing an accent—except that it was done when nobody was talking. "It's a Styric," he said quietly.

"Zalasta?"

"No, I don't believe so. I think I'd recognize him. It's somebody I've never been around before."

"Not too much wood, my Lord," Khalad said aloud. "This pile has to get us through breakfast, too, you know."

"Good thinking," Berit approved. He reached out again, very cautiously. "He's moving away," he muttered. "How did you know we were being watched?"

"I could feel it." Khalad shrugged. "I always know when somebody's watching me. How noisy is it when you get in touch with Aphrael?"

"That's one of the good spells. It doesn't make a sound."

"You'd better tell her about this. Let her know that we *are* being watched and that it's a Styric who's doing the watching." Khalad knelt and began carefully to stack his armload of broken-off limbs on their campfire. "Your disguise seems to be working," he noted.

"How did you arrive at that?"

"They wouldn't waste a Styric on us if they knew who you really were."

"Unless they don't have anybody left *except* Styrics. Stragen's celebration of the Harvest Festival might have been more effective than we thought."

"We could probably argue about that all night. Just tell Aphrael about our visitor out there. She'll pass it on to the others, and we'll let *them* get the headache from trying to sort it out with logic."

"Aren't you curious about it?"

"Not so curious that I'm going to lose any sleep over it. That's one of the advantages of being a peasant, my Lord. We're not *required* to come up with the answers to these earth-shaking questions. You aristocrats get the pleasure of doing that."

"Thanks," Berit said sourly.

"No charge, my Lord." Khalad grinned.

Sparhawk had never actually worked for a living before and he discovered that he did not like it very much. He quickly grew to hate Captain Sorgi's thick-necked bo'sun. The man was crude, stupid, and spitefully cruel. He fawned outrageously whenever Sorgi appeared on the quarterdeck, but when the captain returned below decks, the bo'sun's natural character reasserted itself. He seemed to take particular delight in tormenting the newest members of the crew, assigning them the most tedious, exhausting, and demeaning tasks aboard ship. Sparhawk found himself quite suddenly in full agreement with Khalad's class prejudices, and sometimes at night he found himself contemplating murder.

"Every man hates his employer, Fron," Stragen told him, using Sparhawk's assumed name. "It's a very natural part of the scheme of things."

"I could stand him if he didn't deliberately go out of his way to be offensive," Sparhawk growled, scrubbing at the deck with his block of pumice-stone.

"He's *paid* to be offensive, my friend. Angry men work harder. Part of your problem is that you always look him right in the eye. He wouldn't single you out the way he does if you'd keep your eyes lowered. If you don't, this is going to be a very long voyage for you."

"Or a short one for him," Sparhawk said darkly.

He considered it that night as he tried, without much success, to sleep in his hammock. He fervently wished that he could get his hands on the idiot who had decided that humans could sleep in hammocks.

The roll of the ship made it swing from side to side, and Sparhawk continually felt that he was right on the verge of being thrown out.

Anakha. The voice was only a whisper in his mind.

Sparhawk was stunned. "Blue-Rose?" he said.

Prithee, Anakha, do not speak aloud. Thy voice is as the thunder in mine ears. Speak silently in the halls of thine awareness. I will hear thee.

How is this possible? Sparhawk framed the thought. *Thou art confined.*

Who hath power to confine me, *Anakha? When thou art alone and thy mind is clear of other distraction, we may speak thus.*

I did not know that.

Until now, it was not needful for thee to know.

I see. But now it is?

Yes.

How dost thou penetrate the barrier of the gold?

It is no barrier to me, Anakha. Others may not sense me *within the confines of thine excellent receptacle. I, however, may reach out to thee in this manner. This is particularly true when we are so close.*

Sparhawk laid his hand on the leather pouch hanging on a thong about his neck and felt the square outline of the box. *And should it prove needful, may I speak so with thee?*

Even as thou dost now, Anakha.

This is good to know.

I sense thy disquiet, Anakha, and I share thine anxiety for the safety of thy mate.

Thou art kind to say so, Blue-Rose.

Expend thou all thine efforts to securing thy queen's release, Anakha. I *will keep watch over our enemies whilst thou art so occupied.* The jewel under Sparhawk's hand paused. *Hear me well, my friend,* Bhelliom continued, *should it come to pass that no other course be open to thee, fear not to surrender me up to obtain thy mate's freedom.*

That I will not do—for she hath forbidden it.

Do not be untranquil if it should come to pass, Anakha. I *will not submit to Cyrgon, even though mine own child, whom I love even as thou lovest thine, be endangered by my refusal. Be comforted in the knowledge that I will not permit my child—nor thee and all thy kind—to be enslaved by Cyrgon—or worse yet, by Klæl. Thou hast my promise that this will never happen. Should it appear that our task doth verge on failure, I give thee my solemn vow that I shall destroy this child of mine and all who dwell here to prevent such mischance.*

Is that supposed to make me feel better?

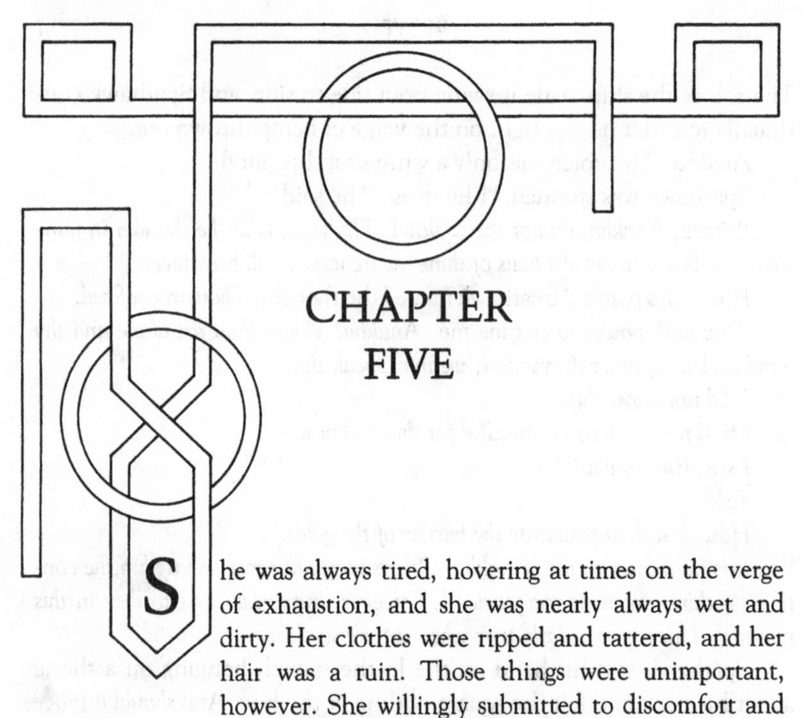

CHAPTER FIVE

She was always tired, hovering at times on the verge of exhaustion, and she was nearly always wet and dirty. Her clothes were ripped and tattered, and her hair was a ruin. Those things were unimportant, however. She willingly submitted to discomfort and indignities to keep the madman who was their captor from hurting the terrified Alean.

The realization that Scarpa was mad had come to her slowly. She had known from the first moment she had seen him that he was ruthless and driven, but the evidence of his insanity had become gradually more and more overwhelming as the endless days of her captivity ground on.

He was cruel, but Ehlana had encountered cruel men before. After she and Alean had been hurried through the dank tunnels under the streets of Matherion to the outskirts of the city, they had been roughly shoved into the saddles of waiting horses, bound securely in place, and literally dragged at breakneck speed down the road leading to the port of Micae on the southwestern coast of the peninsula, seventy-five leagues away. A normal man does not mistreat the animals upon which he is totally dependent. That was the first evidence of Scarpa's madness. He drove the horses, flogging them savagely until the poor beasts were staggering with exhaustion, and his only words during those dreadful four days were, "Faster! Faster!"

Ehlana shuddered as she recalled the horror of that endless ride. They had—

Her horse stumbled in the muddy path, and she was jolted forward, bringing her attention back into the immediate present. The cord that tightly bound her wrists to the saddlebow dug into her flesh, and the bleeding started again. She tried to ease into a different position so that the cord would no longer cut into the already open wounds.

"What are you doing?" Scarpa demanded. His voice was harsh, and it came out almost as a scream. Scarpa almost always screamed when he was talking to her.

"I'm just trying to keep the cord from cutting deeper into my wrists, Lord Scarpa," she replied meekly. She had been instructed early in her captivity to address him so and she had quickly found that failure to do so resulted in savage mistreatment of Alean *and* the withholding of food and water.

"You're not here to be comfortable, woman!" he raged at her. "You're here to obey! I see what you're doing there! If you don't stop trying to loosen those cords, I'll use wire!" His eyes bulged, and she saw again that strange, bluish cast to the whites of those eyes and the abnormally large pupils.

"Yes, Lord Scarpa," she said in her most submissive tone.

He glared at her, his face filled with suspicion and his mad eyes looking hungrily for some excuse to punish or humiliate his prisoners further.

She lowered her gaze to stare fixedly at the rough, muddy track that wound deeper and deeper into the rank, vine-choked forest of the southeast coast of Daresia.

The ship they had boarded at the port of Micae had been a sleek, black-hulled corsair that could not have been built for any honest purpose. She and Alean had been unceremoniously dragged belowdecks and confined in a cramped compartment that smelled of the bilges and was totally dark. After they had been two hours at sea, the compartment door had opened and Krager had entered with two swarthy sailors, one carrying what appeared to be a decent meal, and the other, two pails of hot water, some soap, and a wad of rags for use as towels. Ehlana had resisted an impulse to embrace the fellow.

"I'm really sorry about all this, Ehlana," Krager had apologized, squinting at her nearsightedly, "but I have no control of the situation. Be very careful of what you say to Scarpa. You've probably noticed that he's not entirely rational." He had looked around nervously, then laid a handful of cheap tallow candles on the rough table and left, chaining the door shut behind him.

They had been five days at sea and had reached Anan, a port city on the edge of the jungles of the southeast coast, some time after midnight. Then she and Alean had been hustled into a closed carriage with the pouchy-eyed Baron Parok at the reins. During the transfer from the ship to the carriage, Ehlana had discreetly looked at each of her captors, seeking some weakness. Krager, despite his habitual drunkenness, was too shrewd, and Parok was Scarpa's longtime confederate, a man evidently untroubled by his friend's madness. Then she had coolly appraised Elron. She had noticed that under no circumstances would the foppish Astellian poet look her in the eye. His apparent murder of Melidere had evidently filled him with remorse. Elron was a poseur rather than a man of action, and he clearly had no stomach for blood. She had recalled, moreover, how vain he had been about his long curls when she had first met him and had wondered what form of duress Scarpa had used to force him to shave his head in order to pose as one of Kring's Peloi. She had surmised that the violation of his hair had raised certain strong resentments in him. Elron was clearly reluctant to participate in this affair, and that made *him* the weak link. She kept that fact firmly in mind now. The time might come when she could use it to her advantage.

The carriage had carried them from the waterfront to a large house on the outskirts of Anan. It had been there that Scarpa had spoken with a gaunt Styric with the lumpy features characteristic of the men of his race. The Styric's name was Keska, and his eyes had the look of one hopelessly damned.

"I don't *care* about the discomfort!" Scarpa had half shouted to the gaunt man at one point. "*Time* is important, Keska, time! Just do it! As long as it doesn't kill us, we can endure it!"

The next morning the significance of that command had become all too obvious. Keska was evidently one of those outcast Styric magicians, but not a very good one. He could, with a great deal of clearly exhausting effort, compress the miles that lay between them and Scarpa's intended destination, but only a few miles each time, and the compression was accompanied by a horrid kind of wrenching agony. It seemed almost as if the clumsy magician were jerking them up and hurling them blindly forward with every ounce of his strength, and Ehlana could never be certain after each hideous, bruising jump that she was still intact. She felt torn and battered, but did what she could to conceal her pain from Alean. The gentle girl with the large eyes wept almost continuously now, overcome by her pain and fear and the misery of their circumstances.

Ehlana drew her mind into the present and looked about warily. It was approaching evening again. The overcast sky was gradually darkening, and the time of day Ehlana dreaded the most would soon be upon them.

Scarpa looked with some scorn at Keska, who slumped in his saddle like a wilted flower, obviously near exhaustion. "This is far enough," he said. "Set up some kind of camp and get the women down off those horses." His brittle eyes grew bright as he looked Ehlana full in the face. "It's time for the bedraggled Queen of the Elenes to beg for her supper again. I *do* hope she'll be more convincing this time. It really distresses me to have to refuse her when her pleas aren't sufficiently sincere."

"Ehlana," Krager whispered, touching her shoulder. The fire had died down to embers, and Ehlana could hear the sound of snores coming from the other side of their rude camp.

"What?" she replied shortly.

"Keep your voice down." He was still wearing the black leather Peloi jerkin, his shaved head was sparsely stubbled, and his wine-reeking breath was nearly overpowering. "I'm doing you a favor. Don't put me in danger. I assume you realize by now that Scarpa's completely insane?"

"Really?" she replied sardonically. "What an amazing thing."

"Please don't make this any more difficult. I seem to have made a small error in judgment here. If I'd fully realized how deranged that half-Styric bastard is, I'd have never agreed to take part in this ridiculous adventure."

"What *is* this strange fascination you have with lunatics, Krager?"

He shrugged. "Maybe it's a character defect. Scarpa actually believes that he can outwit his father—and even Cyrgon. He doesn't really believe that Sparhawk will surrender Bhelliom in exchange for your return, and he's managed to about half convince the others. I'm sure you realize by now how he feels about women."

"He's demonstrated it often enough," she said bitterly. "Does he share Baron Harparin's fondness for little boys instead?"

"Scarpa isn't fond of anything except himself. *He* is his only passion. I've seen him spend hours trimming that beard of his. It gives him the opportunity to adore his reflection in the mirror. You haven't seen his delightful personality in full flower. The details of this trip are keeping what he chooses to call his mind occupied. Wait until we get to Natayos and you hear him start raving. He makes Martel and Annias seem like the very souls of sanity by comparison. I don't dare stay too long, so listen closely. Scarpa believes that Sparhawk will bring

Bhelliom with him when he comes, right enough, but he *doesn't* believe he'll bring it to trade for you. Scarpa's absolutely certain that your husband's coming in order to have it out with Cyrgon, *and* he believes that they'll destroy each other in the course of the argument."

"Sparhawk has Bhelliom, you fool, and Bhelliom eats Gods for breakfast."

"I'm not here to argue about that. Maybe Sparhawk will win, and maybe he won't. That's really beside the point. What's important to us is what Scarpa believes. He's convinced himself that Sparhawk and Cyrgon will fight a war of mutual extinction. Then he thinks that Bhelliom will be left lying around free for the taking."

"What about Zalasta?"

"I get the strong feeling that Scarpa doesn't expect Zalasta to be around when the fight's over. Scarpa's more than willing to kill anybody who gets in his way."

"He'd kill his own father?"

Krager shrugged. "Blood ties don't mean anything to Scarpa. When he was younger, he decided that his mother and his half-sisters knew things about him that he didn't want them to share with the authorities, so he killed them. He hated them anyway, so that may not mean all that much. If Sparhawk and Cyrgon *do* kill each other, and if Zalasta's broken out in a sudden rash of mortality during the festivities, Scarpa *might* just be the only one left around to take possession of the Bhelliom. He's got an army in these jungles and, if he has the Bhelliom as well, he might be able to pull it off. He'll march on Matherion, take the city, and slaughter the government. Then he'll crown himself emperor. I'm personally betting against it, though, so for God's sake keep your temper under control. You're not really important to *his* plans, but you're vital to Zalasta's—and mine. If you do anything at all to set Scarpa off, he'll kill you as quickly as he ordered Elron to kill your lady-in-waiting. Zalasta and I believe that Sparhawk *will* trade Bhelliom for you, but only if you're alive. Don't enrage that maniac. If he kills you, all our plans will collapse."

"Why are you telling me this, Krager? There's something else, too, isn't there?"

"Of course. If things go against us, I'd like to have you available to speak out in my behalf when the trials start."

"That wouldn't do any good, I'm afraid," she told him sweetly. "There won't be any trial for you, Krager. Sparhawk's already given you to Khalad, and Khalad's already made up his mind."

"Khalad?" Krager's voice sounded a little weak.

"Kurik's oldest son. He seems to feel that you had some part in his father's death and he feels obliged to do something about it. I suppose you could try to talk him out of it, but I'd advise you to talk fast if you do. Khalad's an abrupt young man, and he'll probably have you hanging from a meat hook before you can get out three words."

Krager didn't answer, but slipped away instead, his shaved scalp pale in the darkness. It wasn't much of a victory, Ehlana privately conceded, but in her situation victories of any kind were very hard to come by.

"They actually do that?" Scarpa's harsh voice was hungry.

"It's an old custom, Lord Scarpa," Ehlana replied in a meek voice, keeping her eyes downcast as they plodded along the muddy path. "Emperor Sarabian is planning to discontinue the practice, however."

"It will be reinstituted immediately following my coronation." Scarpa's eyes were very bright. "It is a proper form of respect." Scarpa had an old purple velvet cloak, shiny with wear, that he had dramatically pulled over one shoulder in a grotesque imitation of an imperial mantle, and he struck absurd poses with each pronouncement.

"As you say, Lord Scarpa." It was tedious to go over the same things again and again, but it kept Scarpa's mind occupied, and when his attention was firmly fixed on the ceremonies and practices of the imperial court in Matherion he was not thinking of ways to make life unbearable for his captives.

"Describe it again," he commanded. "I'll need to know precisely how it's supposed to be done—so that I can punish those who fail to perform it properly."

Ehlana sighed. "At the approach of the imperial person, the members of the court kneel—"

"On both knees?"

"Yes, Lord Scarpa."

"Excellent! Excellent!" His face was exalted. "Go on."

"Then, as the emperor passes, they lean forward, put the palms of their hands on the floor, and touch their foreheads to the tiles."

"Capital!" He suddenly giggled, a high-pitched, almost girlish sound that startled her. She gave him a quick, sidelong glance. His face was grotesquely distorted into an expression of unholy exaltation. And then his eyes grew wide and his expression became one of near-religious ecstasy. "And the Tamuls who rule the world shall be ruled by me!" He intoned in a resonant, declamatory voice. "All power shall be mine!

The governance of the world shall be in *my* hands, and disobedience will be death!"

Ehlana shuddered as he raved on.

And he came to her again as humid night settled over their muddy forest encampment, drawn to her by a hunger, a greed that was beyond his ability to control. It was revolting, but Ehlana realized that her knowledge of the particulars of traditional court ceremonies gave her an enormous power over him. His hunger was insatiable, and only she could satisfy it. She grasped that power firmly, drawing strength and confidence from it, actually relishing it even as Krager and the others withdrew with expressions of frightening revulsion.

"Nine wives, you say!" Scarpa's voice was almost pleading. "Why not ninety? Why not nine hundred?"

"It is the custom, Lord Scarpa. The reason for it should be obvious."

"Oh, of course, of course." He brooded darkly over it. "*I* shall have nine thousand!" he proclaimed. "And each shall be more desirable than the last! And when I have finished with them, they shall be given to my loyal soldiers! Let no woman dare to believe that my favor in any way empowers her! All women are only whores! I shall *buy* them and throw them away when I tire of them!" His mad eyes bulged, and he stared into the campfire. The flickering flames reflected in those eyes seemed to seethe like the madness that lay behind them.

He leaned toward her, laying a confiding hand on her arm. "I have seen that which others are too stupid to see," he told her. "Others look, but they do not see—but *I* see. Oh, yes, I see very well. They are all in it together, you know—all of them. They watch me. They have always watched me. I can never get away from their eyes—watching, watching, watching—and talking, talking behind their hands, breathing their cinnamon-scented breath into each other's faces. All foul and corrupt—scheming, plotting against me, trying to bring me down. Their eyes—all soft and hidden and veiled with the lashes that hide the daggers of their hatred, watching, watching." His voice sank lower and lower. "And talking, talking behind their hands so that I can't hear what they're saying. Whispering. I hear it always. I hear the hissing susurration of their endless whispering. Their eyes following me wherever I go—and their laughing and whispering. I hear the hiss, hiss of their whispering—endless whisper—always my name—Ssscar-pa, Ssscar-pa, Ssscar-pa, again and, again, hissing in my ears. Flaunting their rounded limbs and rolling their soot-lined eyes. Plotting, scheming with the endless hissing whispers, always seeking ways to hurt me.

Ssscar-pa, Ssscar-pa, trying to humiliate me." His blue-tinged eyeballs were starting from his face, and his lips and beard were flecked with foam. "I was nothing. They made me nothing. They called me Selga's bastard and gave me pennies to lead them to the beds of my mother and my sisters and cuffed me and spat on me and laughed at me when I cried and they lusted after my mother and my sisters and all around me the hissing in my ears—and I smell the sound—that sweet cloying sound of rotten flesh and stale lust all purple and writhing with the liquid hiss of their whispers and—"

Then his mad eyes filled with terror, and he cringed back from her and fell, groveling in the mud. "Please, Mother!" he wailed. "I didn't do it! Silbie did it! Pleasepleaseplease don't lock me in there again! Please not in the dark! Pleasepleaseplease not in the dark! Not in the dark!" And he scrambled to his feet and fled back into the forest with his "Pleasepleaseplease" echoing back in a long, dying fall.

Ehlana was suddenly overcome with a wrenching, unbearable pity, and she bowed her head and wept.

Zalasta was waiting for them in Natayos. The sixteenth and early seventeenth centuries had seen a flowering of Arjuni civilization, a flowering financed largely by the burgeoning slave trade. An ill-advised slave raid into southern Atan, however, coupled with a number of gross policy blunders by the Tamul administrators of that region, had unleashed an uncontrolled Atan punitive expedition. Natayos had been a virtual gem of a city with stately buildings and broad avenues. It was now a forgotten ruin buried in the jungle, its tumbled buildings snarled in ropelike vines, its stately halls now the home of chattering monkeys and brightly colored tropical birds, and its darker recesses inhabited by snakes and the scurrying rats which were their prey.

But now humans had returned to Natayos. Scarpa's army was quartered there, and Arjunis, Cynesgans, and ragtag battalions of Elenes had cleared the quarter near the ancient city's northern gate of vines, trees, monkeys, and reptiles in order to make it semihabitable.

Zalasta stood leaning on his staff at the half-fallen gate, his silvery-bearded face drawn with fatigue and a look of hopeless pain in his eyes. His first reaction when his son arrived with the captives was one of rage. He snarled at Scarpa in Styric, a language that seemed eminently suited for reprimand and one which Ehlana did not understand. She took no small measure of satisfaction, however, in the look of sullen apprehension that crossed Scarpa's face. For all his bluster and airs of preeminent superiority, Scarpa still appeared to stand in a certain awe and fear of the ancient Styric who had incidentally sired him.

Once and only once, apparently stung by something Zalasta said to him in a tone loaded with contempt, Scarpa drew himself up and snarled a reply. Zalasta's reaction was immediate and savage. He sent his son reeling with a heavy blow of his staff, then leveled its polished length at him, muttered a few words, and unleashed a fiery spot of light from the tip of the staff. The burning spot struck the still-staggering Scarpa in the belly, and he doubled over sharply, clawing at his stomach and shrieking in agony. He fell onto the muddy earth, kicking and convulsing as Zalasta's spell burned into him. His father, the deadly staff still leveled, watched his writhing son coldly for several endless minutes.

"*Now* do you understand?" he demanded in a deadly voice, speaking in Tamul this time.

"Yes! Yes! Father!" Scarpa shrieked. "Stop! I beg you!"

Zalasta let him writhe and squirm for a while longer. Then he lifted the staff. "You are *not* master here," he declared. "You are no more than a brain-sick incompetent. Any one of a dozen others here could command this army, so do not try my patience further. Next time, son or no son, I will let the spell follow its natural course. Pain is like a disease, Scarpa. After a few days—or weeks—the body begins to deteriorate. A man can die from pain. Don't force me to prove that to you." And he turned his back on his pale-faced, sweating son. "My apologies, your Majesty," he said to Ehlana. "This was *not* what I intended."

"And what *did* you intend, Zalasta?" she asked coldly.

"The dispute is between your husband and myself, Ehlana. It was never in my mind to cause you such discomfort. This cretin I must unfortunately acknowledge took it upon himself to mistreat you. I promise you that he will not live to see the sunset of the day in which he does it again."

"I see. The humiliation and pain were not your idea, but the captivity was. Where's the difference, Zalasta?"

He sighed and passed a weary hand over his eyes. "It is necessary," he told her.

"For what reason? Sephrenia will never submit to you, you know. Even if Bhelliom and the rings fall into your hands, you cannot compel her love."

"There are other considerations as well, Queen Ehlana," he said sorrowfully. "Please bring your maid and come with me. I'll see you to your quarters."

"Some dungeon, I suppose?"

He sighed. "No, Ehlana, the quarters are clean and comfortable. I've seen to that myself. Your ordeal is at an end, I promise you."

"My ordeal, as you call it, will not be at an end until I'm reunited with my husband and my daughter."

"That, we may pray, will be very soon. It is, however, in the hands of Prince Sparhawk. All he must do is follow instructions. Your quarters are not far. Follow me, please." He led them to a nearby building and unlocked the door.

Their prison was very nearly luxurious, an apartment of sorts, complete with several bedrooms, a dining hall, a large sitting room, and even a kitchen. The building had evidently been the palace of some nobleman, and, although the upper stories had long since collapsed, the ground-floor rooms, their ceilings supported by great arches, were still intact. The furnishings were ornate, though mismatched, and there were rugs on the floors and drapes to cover the windows—windows, Ehlana noticed, that had recently been fitted with stout iron bars.

The fireplaces were cavernous, and they were all filled with blazing logs, not so much to ward off the minimal chill of the Arjuni winter but to dry out rooms saturated with over a millennium of dank humidity. There were beds and fresh linen and clothing of an Arjuni cut, but most important of all, there was a fair-sized room with a large marble bathtub set into the floor. Ehlana's eyes fixed longingly on that ultimate luxury. It so completely seized her attention that she scarcely heard Zalasta's apologies. After a few vague replies from her, the Styric realized that his continued presence was no longer appreciated, so he politely excused himself and left.

"Alean, dear," Ehlana said in an almost dreamy voice, "that's quite a large tub—certainly large enough for the two of us, wouldn't you say?"

Alean was also gazing at the tub with undisguised longing. "Easily, your Majesty," she replied.

"How long do you think it might take us to heat enough water to fill it?"

"There are plenty of large pots and kettles in that kitchen, my Queen," the gentle girl said, "and all the fireplaces are going. It shouldn't take very long at all."

"Wonderful," Ehlana said enthusiastically. "Why don't we get started?"

"Just exactly who is this Klæl, Zalasta?" Ehlana asked the Styric several days later when he came to call. Zalasta came to their prison often, as if his visits in some way lessened his guilt, and he always talked: long, rambling, sometimes disconnected converse that often revealed far more than he probably intended for her to know.

"Klæl is an eternal being," he replied. Ehlana noted almost absently that the heavily accented Elenic which had so irritated her when they had first met in Sarsos was gone now. Another of his ruses, she concluded. "Klæl is far more eternal than the Gods of this world," he continued. "He's in some way connected to Bhelliom. They're contending principles, or something along those lines. I was a bit distraught when Cyrgon explained the relationship to me, so I didn't fully understand."

"Yes, I can imagine," she murmured. Her relationship with Zalasta was peculiar. The circumstances made ranting and denunciation largely a waste of time, so Ehlana was civil to him. He appeared to be grateful for that, and his gratitude made him more open with her. That civility, which cost her nothing, enabled her to pick up much information from the Styric's rambling conversation.

"Anyway," Zalasta continued, "Cyzada was terrified when Cyrgon commanded him to summon Klæl, and he tried very hard to talk the God out of the notion. Cyrgon was implacable, though, and he was filled with rage when Sparhawk neatly plucked the Trolls right out of his grasp. We'd never even considered the possibility that Sparhawk might release the Troll-Gods from their confinement."

"That was Sir Ulath's idea," Ehlana told him. "Ulath knows a great deal about Trolls."

"Evidently so. At any rate, Cyrgon forced Cyzada to summon Klæl, but Klæl no sooner appeared than he went in search of Bhelliom. That took Cyrgon aback. It had been his intention to hold Klæl in reserve—hiding, so to speak—and to unleash him by surprise. That went out the window when Klæl rushed off to the North Cape to confront Bhelliom. Sparhawk knows that Klæl is here now—although I have no idea what he can do about it. That was what made the summoning of Klæl such idiocy in the first place. Klæl can't be controlled. I tried to explain that to Cyrgon, but he wouldn't listen. Our goal is to gain possession of Bhelliom, and Klæl and Bhelliom are eternal enemies. As soon as Cyrgon takes Bhelliom in his hands, Klæl will attack *him*, and I'm fairly certain that Klæl is infinitely more powerful than he is." Zalasta glanced around cautiously. "The Cyrgai are in many ways a reflection of their God, I'm afraid. Cyrgon abhors any kind of intelligence. He's frighteningly stupid sometimes."

"I hate to point this out, Zalasta," she said insincerely, "but you have this tendency to ally yourself with defectives. Annias was clever enough, I suppose, but his obsession with the Archprelacy distorted his judgment; and Martel's drive for revenge made *his* thinking just as distorted. From what I gather, Otha was as stupid as a stump, and Azash was so elemental that all he had on his mind were his desires. Coherent thought was beyond him."

"You know everything, don't you, Ehlana?" he said. "How on earth did you find all of this out?"

"I'm not really at liberty to discuss it," she replied.

"No matter, I suppose," he said absently. A sudden hunger crossed his face. "How is Sephrenia?" he asked.

"Well enough. She was very upset when she first found out about you, though—and your attempt on Aphrael's life was really ill-conceived, you know. That was the one thing that convinced her of your treachery."

"I lost my head," he confessed. "That cursed Delphaeic woman destroyed three hundred years of patient labor with a toss of her head."

"I suppose it's none of my business, but why didn't you just accept the fact that Sephrenia was wholly committed to Aphrael and let it go at that? There's no way you can compete with the Child-Goddess, you know."

"Could *you* have ever accepted the idea that Sparhawk was committed to another, Ehlana?" His tone was accusing.

"No," she admitted, "I suppose I couldn't have. We do strange things for love, don't we, Zalasta? I was at least direct about it, though. Things might have worked out differently for you if you hadn't tried deceit and deception. Aphrael's not completely unreasonable, you know."

"Perhaps not," he replied. Then he sighed deeply. "But we'll never know, will we?"

"No. It's far too late now."

"The glazier cracked the pane when he was setting it into the frame, my Queen," Alean said quietly, pointing at the defective triangle of bubbled glass in the lower corner of the window. "He was very clumsy."

"How did you come to know so much about this, Alean?" Ehlana asked her.

"My father was apprenticed to a glazier when he was young," the doe-eyed girl replied. "He used to repair windows in our village." She touched the tip of the glowing poker to the bead of lead that held the cracked pane in place. "I'll have to be very careful," she said, frowning in concentration, "but if I do it right, I can fix it so that we can take out this little section of glass and put it back in again. That way, we'll be able to hear what they're talking about out there in the street, and then we'll be able to put the glass back in again so that they'll never know what we've done. I thought you might want to be able to listen to them, and they always seem to gather just outside this window."

"You're an absolute treasure, Alean!" Ehlana exclaimed, impulsively embracing the girl.

"Be careful, my Lady!" Alean cried in alarm. "The hot iron!"

Alean was right. The window with the small defective pane was at the corner of the building, and Zalasta, Scarpa, and the others were quartered in the attached structure. It appeared that whenever they wanted to discuss something out of the hearing of the soldiers, they habitually drifted to the walled-in cul-de-sac just outside the window. The small panes of cheap glass leaded into the windowframe were only semitransparent at best, and so, with minimal caution, Alean's modification of the cracked pane permitted Ehlana to listen and even marginally observe without being seen.

On the day following her conversation with Zalasta, she saw the white-robed Styric approaching with a look of bleakest melancholy on his face and with Scarpa and Krager close behind him. "You've got to snap out of this, Father," Scarpa said urgently. "The soldiers are beginning to notice."

"Let them," Zalasta replied shortly.

"No, Father," Scarpa said in his rich, theatrical voice, "we can't do that. These men are animals. They function below the level of thought. If you walk around through these streets with the face of a little boy whose dog just died, they're going to think that something's wrong and they'll start deserting by the regiment. I've spent too much time and effort gathering this army to have you drive them away by feeling sorry for yourself."

"You'd never understand, Scarpa," Zalasta retorted. "You can't even begin to comprehend the meaning of love. You don't love anything."

"Oh, yes I do, Zalasta," Scarpa snapped. "I love *me*. That's the only kind of love that makes any sense."

Ehlana just happened to be watching Krager. The drunkard's eyes were narrowed, shrewd. He casually moved his ever-present tankard around behind him and poured most of the wine out. Then he raised the tankard and drank off the dregs noisily. Then he belched.

"Parn'me," he slurred, reaching out his hand to the wall to steady himself as he weaved back and forth on his feet.

Scarpa gave him a quick, irritated glance, obviously dismissing him. Ehlana, however, rather quickly reassessed Krager. He was not always nearly as drunk as he appeared to be.

"It's all been for nothing, Scarpa," Zalasta groaned. "I've allied myself with the diseased, the degenerate, and the insane for nothing. I had thought that once Aphrael was gone, Sephrenia might turn to me. But she won't. She'd die before she'll have anything to do with me."

Scarpa's eyes narrowed. "Let her die, then," he said bluntly. "Can't you get it through your head that one woman's the same as any other? Women are a commodity—like bales of hay or barrels of wine. Look at Krager here. How much affection do you think he has for an empty wine barrel? It's the new ones, the full ones, that he loves, right, Krager?"

Krager smirked at him owlishly and then belched again. "Parn'me," he said.

"I can't really see any reason for this obsession of yours anyway," Scarpa continued to grind on his father's most sensitive spot. "Sephrenia's only damaged goods now. Vanion's had her—dozens of times. Are you so poor-spirited that you'd take the leavings of an Elene?"

Zalasta suddenly smashed his fist against the stone wall with a snarl of frustration.

"He's probably so used to having her that he doesn't even waste his time murmuring endearments to her any more," Scarpa went on. "He just takes what he wants from her, rolls over, and starts to snore. You know how Elenes are when they're in a rut. And she's probably no better. He's made an Elene out of her, Father. She's not a Styric anymore. She's become an Elene—or even worse, a mongrel. I'm really surprised to see you wasting all this pure emotion on a mongrel." He sneered. "She's no better than my mother or my sisters, and you know what *they* were."

Zalasta's face twisted, and he threw back his head and actually howled. "I'd rather see her dead!"

Scarpa's pale, bearded face grew sly. "Why don't you kill her, then, Father?" he asked in an insinuating whisper. "Once a decent woman's been bedded by an Elene, she can never be trusted again, you know. Even if you *did* persuade her to marry you, she'd never be faithful." He laid an insincere hand on his father's arm. "Kill her, Father," he advised. "At least your memories of her will be pure; *she* never will be."

Zalasta howled again and clawed at his beard with his long fingernails. Then he turned quickly and ran off down the street.

Krager straightened, and his seeming drunkenness slid away. "You took an awful chance there, you know," he said in a cautious tone.

Scarpa looked sharply at him. "Very good, Krager," he murmured. "You played the part of a drunkard almost to perfection."

"I've had lots of practice." Krager shrugged. "You're lucky he didn't obliterate you, Scarpa—or tie your guts in knots again."

"He couldn't." Scarpa smirked. "I'm a fair magician myself, you know, and I'm skilled enough to know that you have to have a clear head to work the spells. I kept him in a state of rage. He couldn't have worked up enough magic to break a spiderweb. Let's hope that he *does* kill Sephrenia. That should *really* scatter Sparhawk's wits, not to mention the fact that as soon as the desire of his life is no more than a pile of dead meat, Zalasta's very likely to cut his own throat."

"You really hate him, don't you?"

"Wouldn't you, Krager? He could have taken me with him when I was a child, but he'd come to visit for a while, and he'd show me what it meant to be a Styric, and then he'd go off alone, leaving me behind to be tormented by whores. If he doesn't have the stomach to cut his own throat, I'd be more than happy to lend him a hand." Scarpa's eyes were very bright, and he was smiling broadly. "Where's your wine barrel, Krager?" he asked. "Right now I feel like getting drunk." And he began to laugh, a cackling, insane laugh empty of any mirth or humanity.

"It's no use!" Ehlana said, flinging the comb across the room. "Look at what they've done to my hair!" She buried her face in her hands and wept.

"It's not hopeless, my Lady," Alean said in her soft voice. "There's a style they wear in Cammoria." She lifted the mass of blonde hair on the right side of Ehlana's head and brought it over across the top. "You see," she said. "It covers all the bare places, and it really looks quite chic."

Ehlana looked hopefully into her mirror. "It doesn't look *too* bad, does it?" she conceded.

"And if we set a flower just behind your right ear, it would really look very stunning."

"Alean, you're wonderful!" the queen exclaimed happily. "What would I ever do without you?"

It took them the better part of an hour, but at last the unsightly bare places were covered, and Ehlana felt that some measure of her dignity had been restored.

That evening, however, Krager came to call. He stood swaying in the doorway, his eyes bleary and a drunken smirk on his face. "Harvest time again, Ehlana," he announced, drawing his dagger. "It seems that I'll need just a bit more of your hair."

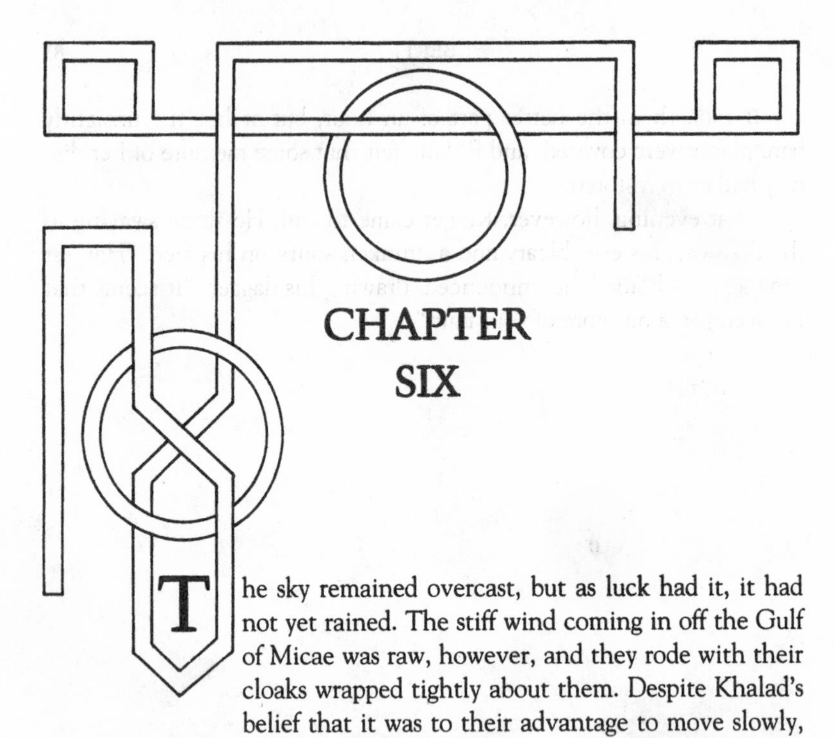

CHAPTER SIX

The sky remained overcast, but as luck had it, it had not yet rained. The stiff wind coming in off the Gulf of Micae was raw, however, and they rode with their cloaks wrapped tightly about them. Despite Khalad's belief that it was to their advantage to move slowly, Berit was consumed with impatience. He knew that what they were doing was only a small part of the overall strategy, but the confrontation they all knew was coming loomed ahead, and he desperately wanted to get on with it. "How can you be so patient?" he asked Khalad about midafternoon one day when the onshore wind was particularly chill and damp.

"I'm a farmer, Sparhawk," Khalad replied, scratching at his short black beard. "Waiting for things to grow teaches you not to expect changes overnight."

"I suppose I've never really thought about what it must be like just sitting still waiting for things to sprout."

"There's not much sitting still when you're a farmer," Khalad told him. "There are always more things to do than there are hours in the day, and if you get bored, you can always keep a close watch on the sky. A whole year's work can be lost in a dry spell or a sudden hailstorm."

"I hadn't thought about that, either." Berit mulled it over. "That's what makes you so good at predicting the weather, isn't it?"

"It helps."

"There's more to it than that, though. You always seem to know about everything that's going on around you. When we were on that log boom, you knew instantly when there was the slightest change in the way it was moving."

"It's called 'paying attention,' my Lord. The world around you is screaming at you all the time, but most people can't seem to hear it. That really baffles me. I can't understand how you can miss so many things."

Berit was just slightly offended by that. "All right, what's the world screaming at you right now that I can't hear?"

"It's telling me that we're going to need some fairly substantial shelter tonight. We've got bad weather coming."

"How did you arrive at that?"

Khalad pointed. "You see those seagulls?" he asked.

"Yes. What's that got to do with it?"

Khalad sighed. "What do seagulls eat, my Lord?"

"Just about everything—fish mostly, I suppose."

"Then why are they flying inland? They aren't going to find very many fish on dry land, are they? They've seen something they don't like out there in the gulf and they're running away from it. Just about the only thing that frightens a seagull is wind—and the high seas that go with it. There's a storm out to sea, and it's coming this way. *That's* what the world's screaming at me right now."

"It's just common sense then, isn't it?"

"Most things are, Sparhawk—common sense and experience." Khalad smiled slightly. "I can still feel Krager's Styric out there watching us. If he isn't paying any more attention than you were just now, he's probably going to spend a very miserable night."

Berit grinned just a bit viciously. "Somehow that information fails to disquiet me," he said.

It was more than a village, but not quite a town. It had three streets, for one thing, and at least six buildings of more than one story, for another. The streets were muddy, and pigs roamed freely. The buildings were made primarily of wood and they were roofed with thatch. There was an inn on what purported to be the main street. It was a substantial-looking building, and there were a pair of rickety wagons with dispirited mules in their traces out front. Ulath reined in the weary old horse he had bought in the fishing village. "What do you think?" he said to his friend.

"I thought you'd never ask," Tynian replied.

"Let's go ahead and take a room as well," Ulath suggested. "The afternoon's wearing on anyway, and I'm getting tired of sleeping on the ground. Besides, I'm a little overdue for a bath."

Tynian looked toward the starkly outlined peaks of the Tamul Mountains lying some leagues to the west. "I'd really hate to keep the Trolls waiting, Ulath," he said with mock seriousness.

"It's not as if we had a definite appointment with them. Trolls wouldn't notice anyway. They've got a very imprecise notion of time."

They rode on into the innyard, tied their horses to a rail outside the stable, and went into the inn.

"We need a room," Ulath told the innkeeper in heavily accented Tamul.

The innkeeper was a small, furtive-looking man. He gave them a quick, appraising glance, noting the bits and pieces of army uniform that made up most of their dress. His expression hardened with distaste. Soldiers were frequently unwelcome in rural communities for any number of very good reasons. "Well," he replied in a whining, singsong sort of voice. "I don't know. It's our busy season—"

"Late autumn?" Tynian broke in skeptically. "*That*'s your busy season?"

"Well—there are all the wagoneers who can come by at any time, you know."

Ulath looked beyond the innkeeper's shoulder into the low, smoky tap room. "I count three," he said flatly.

"There are bound to be more along shortly," the fellow replied just a bit too quickly.

"Of *course* there are," Tynian said sarcastically. "But we're here *now*, and we've got money. Are you going to gamble a sure thing against the remote possibility that some wagon might stop here along about midnight?"

"He doesn't want to do business with a couple of pensioned-off veterans, Corporal," Ulath said. "Let's go talk with the local commissioner. I'm sure he'll be interested in the way this fellow treats his Imperial Majesty's soldiers."

"I'm his Imperial Majesty's loyal subject," the innkeeper said quickly, "and I'll be honored to have brave veterans of his army under my roof."

"How much?" Tynian cut him off.

"A half crown?"

"He doesn't seem very certain, does he, Sergeant?" Tynian asked his friend. "I think you misunderstood," he said then to the nervous innkeeper. "We don't want to *buy* the room. We just want to rent it for one night."

Ulath was staring hard at the now-frightened little Tamul. "Eight pence," he countered with a note of finality.

"*Eight?*" the innkeeper objected in a shrill voice.

"Take it or leave it—and don't be all day about it. We'll need a little daylight to find the commissioner."

"You're a hard man, Sergeant."

"Nobody ever promised you that life would be easy, did they?" Ulath counted out some coins and jingled them in his hand. "Do you want these or not?"

After a moment of agonized indecision, the innkeeper reluctantly took the coins.

"You took all the fun out of that, you know," Tynian complained as the two went back out to the stable to see to their horses.

"I'm thirsty." Ulath shrugged. "Besides, a couple of ex-soldiers would know in advance exactly how much they were willing to pay, wouldn't they?" He scratched at his face. "I wonder if Sir Gerda would mind if I shaved off his beard," he mused. "This thing itches."

"It's not *really* his face, Ulath. It's still yours. You've just been modified to look like him."

"Yes, but when the ladies switch our faces back, they'll use *this* one as a model for Gerda, and when they're done, he'll be standing there with a naked face. He might object."

They unsaddled their horses, put them into stalls, and went back into the taproom. Tamul drinking establishments were arranged differently from those owned by Elenes. The tables were much lower, for one thing, and here the room was heated by a porcelain stove rather than a fireplace. The stove smoked as badly as a fireplace, though. Wine was served in delicate little cups and ale in cheap tin tankards. The smell was much the same, however.

They were just starting on their second tankard of ale when an officious-looking Tamul in a food-spotted wool mantle came into the room and walked directly to their table. "I'll have a look at your release papers, if you don't mind," he told them in a loftily superior tone.

"And if we do?" Ulath asked.

The official blinked. "What?"

"You said if we don't mind. What if we *do* mind?"

"I have the authority to demand to see those documents."

"Why did you ask, then?" Ulath reached inside his red uniform jacket and took out a dog-eared sheet of paper. "In our old regiment, men in authority never asked."

The Tamul read through the documents Oscagne had provided them as a part of their disguise. "These seem to be in order," he said in a more conciliatory tone. "Sorry I was so abrupt. We've been told to keep our eyes out for deserters—all the turmoil, you understand. I guess the army looks a lot less attractive when there's fighting in the wind." He looked at them a bit wistfully. "I see you were stationed in Matherion."

Tynian nodded. "It was good duty—a lot of inspections and polishing, though. Sit down, Commissioner."

The Tamul smiled faintly. "Deputy-Commissioner, I'm afraid, Corporal. This backwater doesn't rate a full commissioner." He slid into a chair. "Where are you men bound?"

"Home," Ulath said, "back to Verel in Daconia."

"You'll forgive my saying so, Sergeant, but you don't look all that much like a Dacite."

Ulath shrugged. "I take after my mother's family. She was an Astel before she married my father. Tell me, Deputy-Commissioner, would we save very much time if we went straight on across the Tamul Mountains to reach Sopal? We thought we'd catch a ferry or some trading ship there, go across the Sea of Arjun to Tiana, and then ride on down to Saras. It's only a short way from there to Verel."

"I'd advise staying out of the Tamul Mountains, my friends."

"Bad weather?" Tynian asked him.

"That's always possible at this time of year, Corporal, but there have been some disturbing reports coming out of those mountains. It seems that the bears up there have been breeding like rabbits. Every traveler who's come through here in the past few weeks reports sighting the brutes. Fortunately they all run away."

"Bears, you say?"

The Tamul smiled. "I'm translating. The ignorant peasants around here use the word *monster*, but we all know what a large, shaggy creature who lives alone in the mountains is, don't we?"

"Peasants are an excitable lot, aren't they?" Ulath laughed, draining his tankard. "We were out on a training exercise once, and this peasant came running up to us claiming that he was being chased by a pack of wolves. When we went out to take a look, it turned out to be one lone fox. The size and number of any wild animal a peasant sees seem to grow with each passing hour."

"Or each tankard of ale," Tynian added.

They talked with the now-polite official for a while longer, and then the man wished them a good journey and left.

"Well, it's nice to know that the Trolls made it this far south," Ulath said. "I'd hate to have to go looking for them."

"Their Gods were guiding them, Ulath," Tynian pointed out.

"You've never talked with the Troll-Gods, I see." Ulath laughed. "Their sense of direction is a little vague—probably because their compass only has two directions on it."

"Oh?"

"North and not-north. It makes finding places a little difficult."

The storm was one of those short, savage gales that seem to come out of nowhere in the late autumn. Khalad had dismissed the possibility of finding any kind of shelter in the salt marshes and had turned instead to the beach. At the head of a shallow inlet he had found the mountain of driftwood he'd been seeking. A couple of hours of fairly intense labor had produced a snug, even cozy little shelter on the leeward side of the pile.

The gale struck just as the last light was fading. The wind screamed through the huge pile of driftwood. The surf crashed and thundered against the beach, and the rain sheeted horizontally across the ground in the driving wind.

Khalad and Berit, however, were warm and dry. They sat with their backs against the huge, bleached-white log that formed the rear wall of their shelter and their feet stretched out toward their crackling fire.

"You always amaze me, Khalad," Berit said. "How did you know that there'd be boards mixed in amongst all this driftwood?"

"There always are." Khalad shrugged. "Any time you find one of these big heaps of driftwood, you're going to find sawed lumber as well. Men make ships out of boards, and ships get wrecked. The boards float around until the wind and currents and tides push them to the same sheltered places where the sticks and the logs have been accumulating." He reached up and patted the ceiling. "Finding this hatch cover all in one piece was a stroke of luck, though, I'll grant you that." He rose to his feet and went to the front of the shelter. "It's really blowing out there," he noted. He extended his hands toward the fire. "Cold, too. The rain's probably going to turn to sleet before midnight."

"Yes," Berit agreed pleasantly. "I certainly pity anybody caught out in the open on a night like this." He grinned.

"Me, too." Khalad grinned back. He lowered his voice, although there was no real need. "Can you get any sense of what he's thinking?"

"Nothing specific," Berit replied. "He's seriously uncomfortable, though."

"What a shame."

"There's something else, though. He's going to come and talk with us. He has a message of some kind for us."

"Is he likely to come in here tonight?"

Berit shook his head. "He has orders not to make contact until tomorrow morning. He's very much afraid of whoever told him what to do and when to do it, so he'll obey those orders to the letter. How's that ham coming?"

Khalad drew his dagger and used its point to lift the lid of the iron pot half-buried in embers at the edge of the fire. The steam that came boiling out smelled positively delicious. "It's ready. As soon as the beans are done, we can eat."

"If our friend out there is downwind of us, that smell should add to his misery just a bit." Berit chuckled.

"I sort of doubt it, Sparhawk. He's a Styric, and he's not allowed to eat pork."

"Oh, yes. I'd forgotten about that. He's a renegade, though. Maybe he's discarded his dietary prejudices."

"We'll find out in the morning. When he comes to us tomorrow, I'll offer him a piece. Why don't you saw off a few slices of that loaf of bread? I'll toast them on the pot lid here."

The wind had abated somewhat the following morning, and the rain had slacked off to a few fitful spatters stuttering on the hatch-cover roof. They had more of the ham and beans for breakfast and began to get things ready to pack. "What do you think?" Berit asked.

"Let's make him come to us. Sitting tight until the last of the rain passes wouldn't be all that unusual." Khalad looked speculatively at his friend. "Would you be offended by a bit of advice, my Lord?" he asked.

"Of course not."

"You *look* like Sparhawk, but you don't *sound* very much like him, and your mannerisms aren't quite right. When the Styric comes, make your face colder and harder. Keep your eyes narrow. Sparhawk squints. You'll also want to keep your voice low and level. Sparhawk's voice gets very quiet when he's angry—and he calls people 'neighbor' a lot. He can put all sorts of meaning into that one word."

"That's right, he does call just about everybody 'neighbor,' doesn't he? I'd almost forgotten that. You've got my permission to correct me any time I start to lose my grip on the real Sparhawk, Khalad."

"Permission?"

"Poor choice of words there, I suppose."

"You might say that, yes."

"The climate got a little too warm for us back in Matherion," Caalador said, leaning back in his chair. He looked directly at the hard-faced man seated across from him. "I'm sure you take my meaning, Orden."

The hard-faced man laughed. "Oh, yes," he replied. "I've left a few places about one jump ahead of the law a time or two myself." Orden was an Elene from Vardenaise who ran a seedy tavern on the waterfront in Delo. He was a burly ruffian who prospered here because Elene criminals felt comfortable in the familiar surroundings of an Elene tavern *and* because Orden was willing to buy things from them—at about a tenth of their real value—without asking questions.

"What we really need is a new line of work." Caalador gestured at Kalten and Bevier, disguised with new faces and rough, mismatched clothing. "A fairly high personage in the Ministry of the Interior was in charge of the group of policemen who stopped by to ask us some embarrassing questions." He grinned at Bevier, who wore the face of one of his brother Cyrinics, an evil-looking knight who had lost an eye in a skirmish in Rendor and covered the empty socket with a black patch. "My one-eyed friend there didn't care for the fellow's attitude, so he lopped his head off with that funny-looking hatchet of his."

Orden looked at the weapon Bevier had laid on the table beside his ale tankard. "That's a lochaber ax, isn't it?" he asked.

Bevier grunted. Kalten felt that Bevier's flair for dramatics was pushing him a little far. The black eye patch was probably enough, but Bevier's participation in amateur theatricals as a student made him seem to want to go to extremes. His intent was obviously to appear dangerously competent. What he was achieving, however, was the appearance of a homicidal maniac.

"Doesn't a lochaber usually have a longer handle?" Orden asked.

"It wouldn't fit under my tunic," Bevier growled, "so I sawed a couple of feet off the handle. It works well enough—if you keep chopping with it. The screaming and the blood don't bother me all that much, so it suits me just fine."

Orden shuddered and looked slightly sick. "That's the meanest-looking weapon I've ever seen," he confessed.

"Maybe that's why I like it so much," Bevier told him.

Orden looked at Caalador. "What line were you and your friends thinking of taking up, Ezek?" he asked.

"We thought we might try our hand at highway robbery or something along those lines," Caalador said. "You know, fresh air, exercise, wholesome food, no policemen in the neighborhood—that sort of thing. We've got some fairly substantial prices on our heads, and now that the emperor's disbanded Interior, all the policing is being done by the Atans. Did you know that you can't bribe an Atan?"

Orden nodded glumly. "Oh, yes," he said. "It's shocking." He squinted speculatively at "Ezek," who appeared to be a middle-aged Deiran. "Why don't you describe Caalador to me, Ezek? I'm not doubting your word, mind. It's just that things are a little topsy-turvy right now, what with all the policemen we used to bribe either in jail or dead, so we *all* have to be careful."

"No offense taken at all, Orden," Caalador assured him. "I wouldn't trust a man who wasn't careful these days. Caalador's a Cammorian, and he's got curly hair and a red face. He's sort of blocky—you know, big shoulders, thick neck, and a little stout around the middle."

Orden's eyes narrowed shrewdly. "What did he tell you? Repeat his exact words."

"Wal, sir," Caalador replied, exaggerating the dialect just a bit, "Ol' Caalador, he tole us t' come down yere t' Delo an' look up a feller name o' Orden—on accounta this yere Orden, he's th' one ez knows whut's whut in the shadowy world o' crime herebouts."

Orden relaxed and laughed. "That's Caalador, all right," he said. "I knew you were telling me the truth before you'd said three words."

"He certainly mangles the language," Caalador agreed. "He's not as stupid as he sounds, though."

Kalten covered a smile with his hand.

"Not by a dang sight, he ain't," Orden agreed, imitating the dialect. "I think you'll find that highway robbery isn't very profitable around here, Ezek, mainly because there aren't that many highways. It's *safe* enough out in the jungle—not even the Atans can find anybody in all that underbrush—but pickings are slim. Three men alone in the bush won't be able to make ends meet. I think you'll have to join one of the bands out there. They make a fair living robbing isolated estates and raiding various towns and villages. That takes quite a number of men, so there are always job openings." He sat back and tapped one finger thoughtfully against his chin. "Do you want to go a *long* way from town?" he asked.

"The farther out the better," Caalador replied.

"Narstil's operating down by the ruins of Natayos. I can *guarantee* that the police won't bother you *there*. A fellow named Scarpa's got an army stationed in the ruins. He's a crazy revolutionary who wants to overthrow the Tamul government. Narstil has quite a few dealings with him. There's some risk involved, but there's a lot of profit to be made in that neighborhood."

"I think you've found just what we're looking for, Orden," Caalador said eagerly.

Kalten carefully let out a long sigh of relief. Without even being prompted, Orden had come up with the exact answer they'd been looking for. If they joined this particular band of robbers, they'd be close enough to Natayos to smell the smoke from the chimneys, and that was a better stroke of luck than they'd even dared to hope for.

"I'll tell you what, Ezek," Orden said, "why don't I write a letter to Narstil introducing you and your friends?"

"We'd definitely appreciate it, Orden."

"But before I waste all that ink and paper, why don't we have a talk about how much you're going to pay me to write that letter?"

The Styric was wet and muddy and very nearly blue with the cold. He was shivering so violently that his voice quavered as he hailed their camp. "I have a message for you," he called. "Don't get excited and do something foolish." He spoke in Elenic, and that made Berit quite thankful, since his own Styric was not all that good. It was the one major flaw in his disguise.

"Come on in, neighbor," he called out to the miserable-looking fellow at the upper end of the beach. "Just keep your hands out in plain sight."

"Don't order me around, Elene," the Styric snapped. "I'm the one who's giving the orders here."

"Then deliver your message from right there, neighbor," Berit said coldly. "Take your time, if you want. I'm warm and dry in here, so waiting while you make up your mind won't be all that unpleasant for me."

"It's a *written* message," the man said in Styric. At least Berit *thought* that was what he said.

"Friend," Khalad said, stepping in quickly, "we've got a slightly touchy situation here. There are all sorts of chances for misunderstandings, so don't make me nervous by talking in a language I don't understand. Sir Sparhawk here understands Styric, but *I* don't, and *my* knife in your belly will kill you just as quick as his will. I'll be very sorry afterward, of course, but you'll still be dead."

"Can I come in?" the Styric asked, speaking in Elenic.

"Come ahead, neighbor," Berit told him.

The lumpy-faced messenger approached the front of their shelter, looking longingly at the fire.

"You *really* look uncomfortable, old boy," Berit noted. "Couldn't you think of a spell to keep the rain off?"

The Styric ignored that. "I'm instructed to give you this," he said, reaching inside his homespun smock and drawing out an oilskin-covered packet.

"Tell me what you're going to do before you stick your hand inside your clothes like that, neighbor," Berit cautioned him in a low voice, and squinting at him as he said it. "As my friend just pointed out, we've got some wonderful opportunities for misunderstandings here. Startling me when I'm this close to you isn't a good way to keep your guts on the inside."

The Styric swallowed hard and stepped back as soon as Berit took the packet.

"Would you care for a slice of ham while my Lord Sparhawk reads his mail, friend?" Khalad offered. "It's nice and greasy, so it'll lubricate your innards."

The Styric shuddered, and his face took on a faintly nauseated look.

"There's nothing quite like a few gobs of oozy pork fat to slick up a man's gullet," Khalad told him cheerfully. "It must come from all the garbage and half-rotten swill that pigs eat."

The Styric made a retching sound.

"You've delivered your message, neighbor," Berit said coldly. "I'm sure you have someplace important to go, and we certainly wouldn't want to keep you."

"Are you sure you understand the message?"

"I've read it. Elenes read very well. We're not illiterates like you Styrics. The message didn't make me very happy, so it's not going to pay you to stay around."

The Styric messenger backed away, his face apprehensive. Then he turned and fled.

"What does it say?" Khalad asked.

Berit gently held the identifying lock of the queen's hair in his hand. "It says that there's been a change of plans. We're supposed to go down past the Tamul Mountains and then turn west. They want us to go to Sopal now."

"You'd better get word to Aphrael."

There was a sudden, familiar little trill of pipes. The two young men spun around quickly.

The Child-Goddess sat cross-legged on Khalad's blankets, breathing a plaintive Styric melody into her many-chambered pipes. "Why are you staring at me?" she asked them. "I *told* you I was going to look after you, didn't I?"

"Is this really wise, Divine One?" Berit asked her. "That Styric's no more than a few hundred yards away, you know, and he can probably sense your presence."

"Not right now, he can't," Aphrael smiled. "Right now he's too busy concentrating on keeping his stomach from turning inside out. All that talk about pork fat was really cruel, Khalad."

"Yes. I know."

"Did you have to be so graphic?"

"I didn't know you were around. What do you want us to do?"

"Go to Sopal the way they told you to. I'll get word to the others." She paused. "What *did* you do to that ham, Khalad?" she asked curiously. "You've actually managed to make it smell almost edible."

"It's probably the cloves." He shrugged. "Nobody's really all that fond of the taste of pork, when you get right down to it, but my mother taught me that almost anything can be made edible—if you use enough spices. You might want to keep that in mind the next time you're thinking about serving up a goat."

She stuck her tongue out at him, and then she vanished.

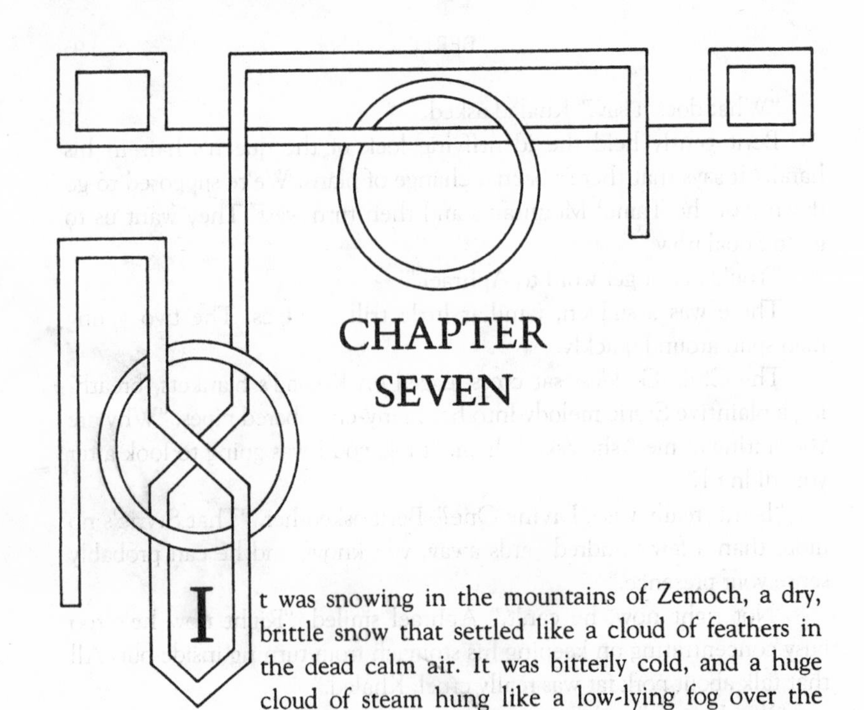

CHAPTER SEVEN

It was snowing in the mountains of Zemoch, a dry, brittle snow that settled like a cloud of feathers in the dead calm air. It was bitterly cold, and a huge cloud of steam hung like a low-lying fog over the horses of the army of the Knights of the Church as they plodded forward, their hooves sending the powdery snow swirling into the air again. The preceptors of the militant orders rode in the lead, dressed in full armor and bundled in furs. Preceptor Abriel of the Cyrinic Knights, still vigorous despite his advanced age, rode with Darellon, the Alcione preceptor, and with Sir Heldin, a scarred old veteran who was filling in as leader of the Pandions during Sparhawk's absence. Patriarch Bergsten rode somewhat apart. The huge churchman was muffled to the ears in fur, and his Ogre-horned helmet made him look very warlike, an appearance offset to some degree by the small, black-bound prayer book he was reading. Preceptor Komier of the Genidians was off ahead with the scouts.

"I don't think I'll ever be warm again," Abriel groaned, pulling his fur cloak tighter about him. "Old age thins the blood. Don't ever get old, Darellon."

"The alternative isn't very attractive, Lord Abriel." Darellon was a slender Deiran who appeared to have been swallowed up by his massive armor. He lowered his voice. "You didn't really have to come along, my friend," he said. "Sarathi would have understood."

"Oh, no, Darellon. This is probably my last campaign. I wouldn't miss it for the world." Abriel peered ahead. "What's Komier doing out there?"

"Lord Komier said that he wanted to take a look at the ruins of Zemoch," Sir Heldin replied in his rumbling basso. "I guess Thalesians take a certain pleasure in viewing the wreckage after a war's over."

"They're a barbaric people," Abriel muttered sourly. He glanced quickly at Bergsten, who seemed totally immersed in his prayer book. "You don't necessarily have to repeat that, gentlemen," he said to Darellon and Heldin.

"I wouldn't dream of it, Abriel," Bergsten said, not looking up from his prayer book.

"You've got unwholesomely sharp ears, your Grace."

"It comes from listening to confessions. People tend to shout the sins of others from the rooftops, but you can barely hear them when they're describing their own." Bergsten looked up and pointed. "Komier's coming back."

The Preceptor of the Genidian Knights was in high spirits as he reined in his horse, swirling up a huge billow of the dustlike snow. "Sparhawk doesn't leave very much standing when he destroys a place," he announced cheerfully. "I didn't entirely believe Ulath when he told me that our broken-nosed friend blew the lid off the Temple of Azash, but I do now. You've never *seen* such a wreck. I doubt if there's a habitable building left in the whole city."

"You really enjoy that sort of thing, don't you, Komier?" Abriel accused.

"That's enough of that, gentlemen!" Bergsten cut in quickly. "We're not going to resurrect *that* worn-out old dispute again. We make war in different ways. Arcians like to build forts and castles, and Thalesians like to knock them down. It's all part of making war, and that's what we get paid for."

"*We*, your Grace?" Heldin rumbled mildly.

"You know what I mean, Heldin. I don't personally get involved in that any more, of course, but—"

"Why did you bring your ax along, then, Bergsten?" Komier asked him.

Bergsten gave him a flat stare. "For old times' sake—*and* because you Thalesian brigands pay closer attention to a man who's got an ax in his hands."

"Knights, your Grace," Komier mildly corrected his countryman. "We're called knights now. We *used* to be brigands, but now we're behaving ourselves."

"The Church appreciates your efforts to mend your ways, my son, even though she knows that you're lying through your teeth."

Abriel carefully covered a smile. Bergsten was a former Genidian Knight himself, and sometimes his cassock slipped a bit. "Who's got the map?" he asked, more to head off the impending argument than out of any real curiosity.

Heldin unbuckled one of his saddlebags, his black armor clinking. "What did you want to know, my Lord?" he asked, taking out his map.

"The usual. How far? How long? What sort of unpleasantness up ahead?"

"It's just over a hundred leagues to the Astellian border, my Lord," Heldin replied, consulting his map, "and nine hundred leagues from there to Matherion."

"A hundred days at least," Bergsten grunted sourly.

"That's if we don't run into any trouble, your Grace," Darellon added.

"Take a look back over your shoulder, Darellon. There are a hundred thousand Church Knights behind us. There's *no* trouble that we can't deal with. What sort of terrain's up ahead, Heldin?"

"There's some sort of divide about three days east of here, your Grace. All the rivers on this side of it run down into the Gulf of Merjuk. On the other side, they run off into the Astel Marshes. I'd imagine that we'll be going downhill after we cross that divide—unless Otha fixed it so that water runs uphill here in Zemoch."

A Genidian Knight rode forward. "A messenger from Emsat just caught up with us, Lord Komier," he reported. "He says he has important news for you."

Komier nodded, wheeled his horse, and rode back toward the army.

The rest of them pushed on as it started to snow a little harder.

Komier was laughing uproariously when he returned with the travel-stained messenger who had chased them down.

"What's so funny?" Bergsten asked him.

"We have good news from home, your Grace," Komier said gaily. "Tell our beloved Patriarch what you just told me," he instructed the messenger.

"Yes, my Lord," the blond-braided Thalesian said. "It happened a few weeks back, your Grace. One morning the palace servants couldn't find a trace of the Prince Regent anywhere at all. The guards tore the place apart for two straight days, but the little weasel seemed to have vanished entirely."

"Mind your manners, man," Bergsten snapped. "Avin's the Prince Regent, after all—even if he *is* a little weasel."

"Sorry, your Grace. Anyway, the whole capital was mystified. Avin Wargunsson never went anywhere without taking a brass band along to blow fanfares announcing his coming. Then one of the servants happened to notice a full wine barrel in Avin's study. That seemed odd, because Avin didn't have much stomach for wine, so they got to looking at the barrel a little more closely. It was clear that it had been opened, because quite a bit of wine had been spilled on the floor. Well, your Grace, they'd all worked up quite a thirst looking for Avin, so they decided to open the barrel, but when they tried to pry it open, they found out that it had been nailed shut. Now *nobody* nails a wine barrel shut in Thalesia, so everybody got suspicious right away. They took some pliers and pulled out the nails and lifted the lid—and there was Avin, stone dead and floating facedown in the barrel."

"You're not serious!"

"Yes, your Grace. Somebody in Emsat's got a very warped sense of humor, I guess. He went to all the trouble of rolling that wine barrel into Avin's study just so that he could stuff him in and nail down the lid. Avin seems to have struggled a bit. He had splinters under his fingernails, and there were claw marks on the underside of the lid. It made an awful mess. I guess the wine drained out of him for a half an hour after they fished him out of the barrel. The palace servants tried to clean him up for the funeral, but you know how hard winestains are to get out. He was very purple when they laid him out on the bier in the Cathedral of Emsat for his funeral." The messenger rubbed at the side of his face reflectively. "It was the strangest funeral I've ever attended. The Primate of Emsat kept trying to keep from laughing while he was reading the burial service, but he wasn't having much luck, and that got the whole congregation to laughing, too. There was Avin lying on that bier, no bigger than a half-grown goat and as purple as a ripe plum, and there was the whole congregation, roaring with laughter."

"At least everybody noticed him," Komier said. "That was always important to Avin."

"Oh, they noticed him all right, Lord Komier. Every eye in the cathedral was on him. Then, after they put him in the royal crypt, the whole city had a huge party, and we all drank toasts to the memory of Avin Wargunsson. It's hard to find something to laugh about in Thalesia when winter's coming on, but Avin managed to brighten up the whole season."

"What kind of wine was it?" Patriarch Bergsten asked gravely.

"Arcian red, your Grace."

"Any idea of what year?"

"Year before last, I believe it was."

"A vintage year," Bergsten sighed. "There was no way to save it, I suppose?"

"Not after Avin had been soaking in it for two days, your Grace."

Bergsten sighed again. "What a waste," he mourned. And then he collapsed over his saddlebow, howling with laughter.

It was cold in the Tamul Mountains as Ulath and Tynian rode up into the foothills. The Tamul Mountains were one of those geographic anomalies which crop up here and there, a cluster of worn-down, weary-looking peaks with no evident connection to neighboring and more jagged peaks forested by fir and spruce and pine. The gentler slopes of the Tamul Mountains were covered with hardwoods which had been stripped of their leaves by the onset of winter.

The two knights rode carefully, staying in the open and making enough noise to announce their presence. "It's very unwise to startle a Troll," Ulath explained.

"Are you sure they're out there?" Tynian asked as they wound deeper into the mountains.

Ulath nodded. "I've seen tracks—or places where they've tried to brush out their traces—and fresh dirt where they've buried their droppings. Trolls take pains to conceal their presence from humans. It's easier to catch supper if it doesn't know you're around."

"The Troll-Gods promised Aphrael that their creatures wouldn't eat humans anymore."

"It may take a few generations for that notion to sift down into the minds of some of the stupider Trolls—and a Troll can be fearfully stupid when he sets his mind to it. We'd better stay alert. As soon as we get up out of these foothills, I'll perform the ceremony that calls the Troll-Gods. We should be safe after that. It's these foothills that are dangerous."

"Why not just perform the ceremony now?"

Ulath shook his head. "Bad manners. You're not supposed to call on the Troll-Gods until you're up higher—up in *real* Troll country."

"This isn't Troll country, Ulath."

"It is now. Let's find a place to camp for the night."

They built their camp on a kind of stair-stepped bench so that they had a solid cliff to their backs and a steep drop to the front. They took turns standing watch, and as the first faint light of dawn began to wash the darkness out of the overcast sky, Tynian shook Ulath awake.

"There's something moving around in the brush at the foot of the cliff," he whispered.

Ulath sat up, his hand going to his ax. He cocked his head to listen. "Troll," he said shortly after a moment.

"How can you tell?"

"Whatever's making all the noise is doing it on purpose. A deer wouldn't crash around like that, and the bears have all denned up for the winter. The Troll wants us to know he's there."

"What do we do?"

"Let's build up the fire a bit—let him know that we're awake. And let's not move too fast." He pushed his blankets aside and rose to his feet as Tynian piled more limbs on the fire.

"Should we invite him in to get warm?" Tynian asked.

"He isn't cold."

"It's freezing, Ulath."

"That's why he's got fur. Trolls build fires for light, not heat. Why don't you go ahead and get started with breakfast? He's not going to do anything until full daylight."

"It's not my turn."

"I have to keep watch."

"I can keep watch as well as you can."

"You wouldn't know what to look for, Tynian." Ulath's tone was reasonable. It usually was when he was talking his way out of doing the cooking.

The light grew gradually stronger. It was a process that was always strange. A man could be looking directly at a dark patch in the surrounding forest and suddenly realize that he could see trees and rocks and bushes where there had been only darkness before.

Tynian brought Ulath a plate of steaming ham and a chunk of leathery-crusted bread. "Leave the ham on the spit," Ulath told him.

Tynian grunted, picked up his own plate, and joined his friend at the front edge of the rocky shelf. They sat and kept watch on the birch forest that ran down the steep slope beneath them as they ate. "There he is," Ulath said gravely, "right beside that big rock."

"Oh, yes," Tynian replied. "I see him now. He blends right in, doesn't he?"

"That's what being a Troll is all about, Tynian. He's a part of the forest."

"Sephrenia says that we're distantly related to them."

"She's probably right. There aren't really all that many differences between us and the Trolls. They're bigger and they have a different diet is about all."

"How long is this likely to take?"

"I have no idea. As far as I know, this has never happened before."

"What'll he do next?"

"As soon as he's sure we know he's there, he'll probably try to communicate in some way."

"Does he know that you speak Trollish?"

"He might. The Troll-Gods are acquainted with me and they know that I run in the same pack with Sparhawk."

"That's an odd way to put it."

"I'm trying to think like a Troll. If I can get it right, I might be able to anticipate what he's going to do next."

Then the Troll shouted up the hill to them.

"What did he say?" Tynian asked nervously.

"He wants to know what he's supposed to do. He's very confused."

"*He's* confused? What about *me*?"

"He's been told to meet us and take us to the Troll-Gods. He doesn't have any idea of our customs or the proper courtesies. We'll have to guide him through this. Put your sword back in its sheath. Let's not make things any worse than they already are." Ulath stood up, being careful not to move too fast. He raised his voice and called to the creature below in Trollish. "Come to this child of Khwaj which we have made. We will take eat together and talk of what we must do."

"What did you tell him?"

"I invited him to join us for breakfast."

"You did *what*? You want a Troll that's no more than a few feet from you to start eating?"

"It's a precaution. It would be discourteous of him to kill us after he's taken food from us."

"Discourteous? That's a *Troll* out there, Ulath."

"Just because he's a Troll doesn't mean that he has bad manners. Oh, I almost forgot. When he comes into camp, he'll want to sniff us. It's polite to sniff him as well. He won't smell very nice, but do it anyway. Trolls do that so that they'll recognize each other if they ever meet again."

"I think you're losing your mind."

"Just follow my lead, and let me do the talking."

"What else *can* I do, you clot? I don't speak Trollish, remember?"

"You *don't*? What an amazing thing. I thought every educated man spoke Trollish."

The Troll approached cautiously, moving smoothly up through the birch forest. He used his arms a great deal as he moved, grasping trees to pull himself along, moving with his whole body. He was about eight and a half feet tall and had glossy brown fur. His face was simian to a degree, though he did not have the protruding muzzle of most apes, and there was a glimmer of intelligence in his deep-sunk eyes. He came up onto the bench where the camp lay, then squatted, resting his forearms on his knees and keeping his paws in plain sight. "I have no club," he half growled.

Ulath made some show of setting his ax aside and held out his empty hands. "I have no club," he repeated the customary greeting. "Undo your sword belt, Tynian," he muttered. "Lay it aside."

Tynian started to object, but decided against it.

"The Child of Khwaj you have made is good," the Troll said, pointing at their fire. "Khwaj will be pleased."

"It is good to please the Gods," Ulath replied.

The Troll suddenly banged his fist on the ground. "This is not how it should be!" he declared in an unhappy voice.

"No," Ulath agreed, dropping down into a squat much like the Troll's, "it is not. The Gods have their reasons for it, though. They have said we must not kill each other. They have also said we must not eat each other."

"I have heard them say it. Could we have misunderstood them?"

"I think we have not."

"Could it be that their minds are sick?"

"It is possible. We must still do as they tell us, though."

"What are you two talking about?" Tynian asked nervously.

"We're discussing philosophy." Ulath shrugged.

Tynian stared at him.

"It's fairly complex. It has to do with whether or not we're morally obliged to obey the Gods if they've gone crazy. I'm saying that we are. Of course my position's a little tainted by self-interest in this particular situation."

"Can it not speak?" the Troll asked, pointing at Tynian. "Are those bird noises the only sounds it can make?"

"The bird noises pass for speech among those of our kind. Will you take some of our eat with us?"

The Troll looked appraisingly at their horses. "Those?" he asked.

"No." Ulath shook his head. "Those are the beasts which carry us."

"Are your legs sick? Is that why you are so short?"

"No. The beasts can run faster than we can. They carry us when we want to go fast."

"What kind of eat do you take?"

"Pig."

"Pig is good. Deer is better."

"Yes."

"Where is the pig? Is it dead? If it is still alive, I will kill it."

"It is dead."

The Troll looked around. "I do not see it."

"We have only brought part of it." Ulath pointed at the large ham spitted over the fire.

"Do you share your eat with the Child of Khwaj?"

Ulath decided not to explain the concept of cooking at that particular moment. "Yes," he said. "It is our custom."

"Does it please Khwaj that you share your eat with his child?"

"It is our thought that it does." Ulath drew his dagger, lifted the spit from off the fire, and sawed off a chunk of ham weighing perhaps three pounds.

"Are your teeth sick?" The Troll even sounded sympathetic. "I had a sick tooth once. It caused me much hurt."

"Our kind does not have sharp teeth," Ulath told him. "Will you take some of our eat?"

"I will." The Troll rose to his feet and came to the fire, towering over them.

"The eat has been near the Child of Khwaj," Ulath warned. "It is hot. It may cause hurt to your mouth."

"I am called Bhlokw," the Troll introduced himself.

"I am called Ulath."

"U-lat? That is a strange thing to be called." Bhlokw pointed at Tynian. "What is it called?"

"Tynian," Ulath replied.

"Tin-in. That is stranger than U-lat."

"The bird noises of our speech make what we are called sound strange."

The Troll leaned forward and snuffled at the top of Ulath's head. Ulath suppressed a strong urge to shriek and run for the nearest tree. He politely sniffed at Bhlokw's fur. The Troll actually didn't smell too bad.

Then the monster and Tynian exchanged sniffs. "Now I know you," Bhlokw said.

"It is good that you do." Ulath held out the chunk of steaming ham.

Bhlokw took it from him and stuffed it into his mouth. Then he quickly spat it back out into his hand. "Hot," he explained a little sheepishly.

"We blow on it to make it cool so that we can eat it without causing hurt to our mouths," Ulath instructed.

Bhlokw blew noisily on the piece of ham for a while. Then he crammed it back into his mouth. He chewed reflectively for a moment. Then he swallowed. "It is different," he said diplomatically. Then he sighed. "I do not like this, U-lat," he confided unhappily. "This is not how things should be."

"No," Ulath agreed, "it is not."

"We should be killing each other. I have killed and eaten you man-things since you first came to the Troll-range. *That* is how things should be. It is my thought that the Gods are sick in their minds to make us do this." He sighed a hurricane sort of sigh. "Your thought is right, though. We must do as they tell us to do. Someday their minds will get well. Then they will let us kill and eat each other again." He stood up abruptly. "They want to see you. I will take you to them."

"We will go with you."

They followed Bhlokw up into the mountains all that day and half of the next, and he led them finally to a snow-covered clearing where a fire burned in a large pit. The Troll-Gods were waiting for them there.

"Aphrael came to us," the enormity that was Ghworg told them.

"She said that she would do this," Ulath replied. "She said that when things happened that we should know about, she would come to us and tell us."

"She put her mouth on our faces." Ghworg seemed puzzled.

"She does this. It gives her pleasure."

"It was not painful," Ghworg conceded a bit dubiously, touching the cheek where Aphrael had kissed him.

"What did he say?" Tynian asked quietly.

"Aphrael came here and talked with them," Ulath replied. "She even kissed them a few times. You know Aphrael."

"She actually *kissed* the Troll-Gods?" Tynian's face grew pale.

"What did it say?" Ghworg demanded.

"It wanted me to say what you had said."

"This is not good, Ulath-from-Thalesia. It should not talk to you in words we do not understand. What is its name?"

"It is called Tynian-from-Deira."

"I will make it so that Tynian-from-Deira knows our speech."

"Brace yourself," Ulath warned his friend.

"What? What's happening, Ulath?"

"Ghworg's going to teach you Trollish."

"Now, wait a minute—" Then Tynian suddenly clapped his hands to the sides of his head, cried out, and fell writhing into the snow. The paroxysm passed quickly, but Tynian was pale and shaking as he sat up, and his eyes were wild.

"You are Tynian-from-Deira?" Ghworg demanded in Trollish.

"Y-yes." Tynian's voice trembled as he replied.

"Do you understand my words?"

"They are clear to me."

"It is good. Do not speak the other kind of talk when you are near us. When you do, you make it so that we do not trust you."

"I will remember that."

"It is good that you will. Aphrael came to us. She told us that the one called Berit has been told not to go to the place Beresa. He has been told to go to the place Sopal instead. She said that you would understand what this means." He paused, frowning. "Do you?" he asked.

"Do we?" Tynian asked Ulath, speaking in Trollish.

"I am not sure." Ulath rose, went to his horse, and took a map out of his saddlebag. Then he returned to the fire. "This is a picture of the ground," he explained to the enormous presences. "We make these pictures so that we will know where we are going."

Schlee looked briefly at the map. "The ground does not look like that," he told them. He squatted and thrust his huge fingers down through the snow into the dirt. "*This* is how the ground looks."

Ulath jumped back as the earth under his feet shuddered slightly. Then he stared down. It was not so much a map as it was a miniaturized version of the continent itself. "This is a *very* good picture of the ground," he marveled.

Schlee shrugged. "I put my hand into the ground and felt its shape. *This* is how it looks."

"Where is Beresa?" Tynian asked Ulath, staring in wonderment at hair-thin little trees bristling like a two-day growth of beard on the sides of tiny mountains.

Ulath checked his map and walked several yards south to a shimmering surface covered with minuscule waves. His feet even sank slightly into Schlee's re-creation of the southern Tamul sea. "It is right here," he replied in Trollish, bending and putting his finger on a spot on the coastline.

"That is where the ones who took Anakha's mate away told him to go," Tynian explained to the Troll-Gods.

"We do not understand," Khwaj said bluntly.

"Anakha is fond of his mate."

"That is how it should be."

"He grows angry when his mate is in danger. The ones who took his mate away know this. They said that they will not give her back to him unless he gives them the flower-gem."

The Troll-Gods all frowned, puzzling their way through it. Then Khwaj suddenly roared, belching out a great, billowing cloud of fire and melting the snow for fifty yards in every direction. "That is wickedness!" he thundered. "It is not right to do this! Their quarrel was with Anakha, not with his mate! I will find these wicked ones! I will turn them into fires that will never go out! They will cry out with hurt forever!"

Tynian shuddered at the enormity of that idea. Then, with a great deal of help from Ulath, he explained their disguises and the subterfuges those disguises made possible.

"Do you in truth look different from how you looked before, Ulath-from-Thalesia?" Ghworg asked, peering curiously at Ulath.

"Much different, Ghworg."

"That is strange. You seem the same to me." The God considered it. "Perhaps it is not so strange," he amended. "Your kind all look the same to me." He clenched his huge fists. "Khwaj is right," he said. "We must cause hurt to the wicked ones. Show us where the one called Berit has been told to go."

Ulath consulted his map again and crossed the miniature world to the edge of the large lake known as the Sea of Arjun. "It is here, Ghworg," he said, bending again and putting his finger to a spot on the coast. Then he bent lower and stared at the shoreline. "It really *is* there!" he gasped. "I can see the tiny little buildings! That is Sopal!"

"Of course," Schlee said as if it were of no particular moment. "It would not be a good picture if I had left things out."

"We have been tricked," Tynian said. "It was our thought that our enemies were in the place Beresa. They are not. They are in the place Sopal instead. The one called Berit does not have the flower-gem. Anakha has the flower-gem. Anakha takes it to Beresa. If the wicked ones meet with Berit in the place Sopal, he will not have the flower-gem with him to give to the wicked ones. They will be angry, and they may cause hurt to Anakha's mate."

"It may be that I taught it too well," Ghworg muttered. "It talks much now."

Schlee, however, had been listening carefully to Tynian's oration. "It has spoken truly, however. Anakha's mate will be in danger. Those who have taken her away may even kill her." The skin on his enormous shoulders flickered, absently shaking off the snowflakes which continually fell on him, and his face twisted as he concentrated. "It is my thought that this will anger Anakha. He may be so angry that he will raise up the flower-gem and make the world go away. We must keep the wicked ones from causing hurt to her."

"Tynian-from-Deira and I will go to the place Sopal," Ulath said. "The wicked ones will not know us because our faces have been changed. We will be nearby when the wicked ones tell the one called Berit that they will give him Anakha's mate if he will give them the flower-gem. We will kill them and take Anakha's mate back when they do this."

"It speaks well," Zoka told the other Troll-Gods. "Its thought is good. Let us help it and the other one—but let us not permit it to kill the wicked ones. Killing them is not enough. The thought of Khwaj is better. Let Khwaj make them into fires that will never go out. Let them burn always. That will be better."

"I will put these man-things into the time which does not move," Ghnomb said. "We will watch them in Schlee's picture of the ground while they go to the place Sopal while the world stands still."

"Can you truly see something as small as a man-thing in Schlee's picture of the ground?" Ulath asked the God of Eat with some surprise.

"Can *you* not?" Ghnomb seemed even more surprised. "We will send Bhlokw with you to help you, and we will watch you in Schlee's picture of the ground. Then, when the wicked ones show Anakha's mate to the one called Berit, to prove to him that they truly have her, you and Tynian-from-Deira will step out of the time which does not move and take her away from them."

"Then *I* will reach into Schlee's picture of the ground and take them up in my hands," Khwaj added grimly. "I will bring them here and make them into fires that will never go out."

"Can you truly reach into Schlee's picture of the ground and pick the wicked ones out of the real world?" Ulath asked in astonishment.

"It is easy." Khwaj shrugged.

Tynian was shaking his head vigorously.

"What?" Schlee demanded.

"The one called Zalasta can also come into the time which does not move. We have seen him do this."

"It will not matter," Khwaj told him. "The one called Zalasta is one of the wicked ones. I will make him into a fire which will never go out as well. I will let him burn forever in the time which does not move. The fire will be just as hot there as it will be here."

The snow was heavier—and wetter—after they crossed the rocky spine that divided the rivers flowing west from those that flowed east. The huge cloud of humid air that hung perpetually above the Astel Marshes lapped against the eastern slopes of the Mountains of Zemoch, unloosing phenomenal snowfalls that buried the forests and clogged the passes. The Church Knights grimly forced their way through sodden drifts as they followed the valley of the south fork on the River Esos toward the Zemoch town of Basne.

Patriarch Abriel of the Cyrinic Knights had begun this campaign with a certain sense of well-being. His health was good, and a lifetime of military training had kept him in peak physical condition. He *was*, however, fast approaching his seventieth year and he found that starting out each morning was growing harder and harder, though he would never have admitted that.

About midmorning on a snowy day, one of the scouting parties ranging ahead returned with three goatskin-clad Zemochs. The men were thin and dirty, and they had terrified expressions on their faces. Patriarch Bergsten rode ahead to question them. When the rest of the main force caught up to the gigantic churchman, he was having a rather heated discussion with an Arcian Knight.

"But they're Zemochs, your Grace," the knight protested.

"Our quarrel was with Otha, Sir Knight," Bergsten said coldly, "not with these poor, superstitious devils. Give them some food and warm clothing and let them go."

"But—"

"We're not going to have trouble about this, are we, Sir Knight?" Bergsten asked in an ominous tone, swelling even larger.

The knight seemed to consider his situation. He backed up a few paces. "Ah—no, your Grace," he replied, "I don't believe so."

"Our Holy Mother appreciates your obedience, my son," Bergsten told him.

"Did those three have anything useful for us?" Komier asked.

"Not much," Bergsten replied, hauling himself back up into his saddle. "There's an army of some kind moving into place somewhere to the east of Argoch. There was a lot of superstition mixed up in what they told me, so I couldn't get anything very accurate out of them."

"A fight then," Komier said, rubbing his hands together in anticipation.

"I sort of doubt that," Bergsten disagreed. "As closely as I could make out from all the gibberish, the force up ahead is composed largely of irregulars—religious fanatics of some kind. Our Holy Mother in Chyrellos didn't make many friends in this part of the world when she tried to reassimilate the branches of Elene faith in western Daresia during the ninth century."

"That was almost two thousand years ago, Bergsten," Komier objected. "That's a long time to hold a grudge."

Bergsten shrugged. "The old ones are the best. Send your scouts out a little farther, Komier. Let's see if we can get some kind of coherent report on the welcoming committee. A few prisoners might be useful."

"I know how to do this, Bergsten."

"Do it, then. Don't just sit there talking about it."

They passed Argoch, and Komier's scouts brought in several prisoners. Patriarch Bergsten interrogated the poorly clad and ignorant Elene captives briefly, and then he ordered them released.

"Your Grace," Darellon protested, "that was very unwise. Those men will run back to their commanders and report everything they've seen."

"Yes," Bergsten replied, "I know. I *want* them to do that. I *also* want them to tell all their friends that they've seen a hundred thousand Church Knights coming down out of the mountains. I'm encouraging defections, Darellon. We don't want to kill those poor misguided heretics, we just want them to get out of our way."

"I still think it's strategically unsound, your Grace."

"You're entitled to your opinion, my son," Bergsten said. "This isn't an article of the faith, so our Holy Mother encourages disagreement and discussion."

"There isn't much point to discussion after you've already let them go, your Grace."

"You know, that very same thought occurred to me."

They encountered the opposing force in the broad valley of the River Esos just to the south of the Zemoch town of Basne thirty leagues or so to the west of the Astellian border. The reports of the scouts and the information gleaned from the captives proved to be accurate. What faced them was not so much an army as it was a mob, poorly armed and undisciplined.

The preceptors of the four orders gathered around Patriarch Bergsten to consider options. "They're members of our own faith," Bergsten told them. "Our disagreements with them lie in the area of church government, not in the substance of our common beliefs. Those matters aren't settled on the battlefield, so I don't want too many of those people killed."

"I don't see much danger of that, your Grace," Preceptor Abriel said.

"They outnumber us about two to one, Lord Abriel," Sir Heldin pointed out.

"One charge should even things out, Heldin," Abriel replied. "Those people are amateurs, enthusiastic but untrained, and about half of them are only armed with pitchforks. If we all drop our visors, level our lances, and charge them en masse, most of them will still be running a week from now."

And that was the last mistake the venerable Lord Abriel was ever to make. The mounted knights fanned out with crisp precision to form up on a broad front stretching across the entire valley. Rank after rank of Cyrinics, Pandions, Genidians, and Alciones, all clad in steel and mounted on belligerent horses, lined up in what was probably one of the more intimidating displays of organized unfriendliness in the known world.

The preceptors waited in the very center of the front rank as their subalterns formed up the rear ranks and the messengers galloped forward to declare that all was in readiness.

"That should be enough," Komier said impatiently. "I don't think the supply wagons will have to charge, too." He looked around at his friends. "Shall we get started, gentlemen? Let's show that rabble out there how *real* soldiers mount an attack." He made a curt signal to a hulking Genidian Knight, and the huge blond man blew a shattering blast on his Ogre-horn trumpet.

The front rank of the knights clapped down their visors and spurred their horses forward. The perfectly disciplined knights and horses galloped forward in an absolutely straight line like a moving wall of steel.

Midway through the charge the forest of upraised lances came down like a breaking wave, and the defections in the opposing army began. The ill-trained serfs and peasants broke and ran, throwing away their weapons and squealing in terror. Here and there were some better-trained units that held their ground, but the flight of their allies from either side left their flanks dangerously exposed.

The knights struck those few units with a great, resounding crash. Once more Abriel felt the old exulting satisfaction of battle. His lance shattered against a hastily raised shield, and he discarded the broken weapon and drew his sword. He looked around and saw that there were other forces massed behind the wall of peasants that had concealed them from view, and *that* army was like none Abriel had ever seen before. The soldiers were huge, larger than even the Thalesians. They wore breastplates and mail, but their cuirasses were more closely molded to their bodies than was normal. Every muscle seemed starkly outlined under the gleaming steel. Their helmets were exotic steel re-creations of the heads of improbable beasts, and they did not have visors as such but steel masks instead, masks that had been sculpted to bear individualized features—the features, Abriel thought, of the warriors who wore them. The Cyrinic Preceptor was suddenly chilled. The features the masks revealed were not human.

There was a strange domed leather tent in the center of that inhuman army, a ribbed, glossy black tent of gigantic dimensions.

But then it moved, opening, spreading wide—two great wings, curved and batlike. And then, rising up from under the shelter of those wings, was a being huge beyond imagining, a creature of total darkness with a head shaped like an inverted wedge and with flaring, pointed ears. Two slitted eyes blazed in that awful absence of a face, and two enormous arms stretched forth hungrily. Lightning seethed beneath the glossy black skin, and the earth upon which the creature stood smoked and burned.

Abriel was strangely calm. He lifted his visor to look full into the face of Hell. "At last," he murmured, "a fitting opponent." And then he clapped his visor down again, drew his warlike shield before his body, and raised the sword he had carried with honor for over half a century. His unpalsied hand brandished the sword at the enormity still rising before him. "For God and Arcium!" he roared his defiance, set himself, and charged directly into obliteration.

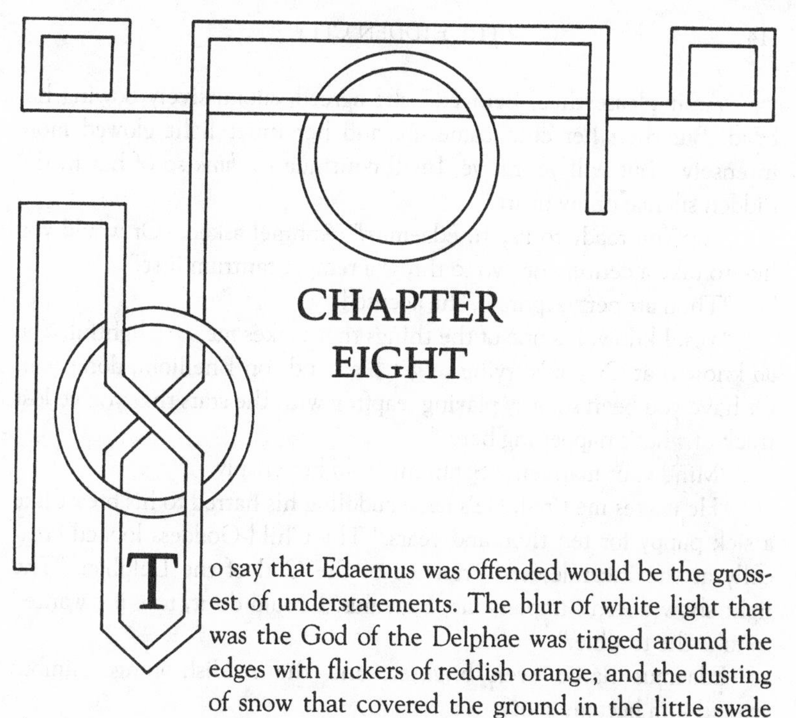

CHAPTER EIGHT

To say that Edaemus was offended would be the grossest of understatements. The blur of white light that was the God of the Delphae was tinged around the edges with flickers of reddish orange, and the dusting of snow that covered the ground in the little swale above the valley of the Delphae fumed tendrils of steam as it melted in the heat of his displeasure. "No!" he said adamantly. "Absolutely not!"

"Oh, be reasonable, cousin," Aphrael coaxed. "The situation has changed. You're holding on to something that no longer has any meaning. There might have been some justification for 'eternal enmity' before. I'll grant you that my family didn't behave very well during the war with the Cyrgai, but that was a long time ago. Clinging to your injured sensibilities now is pure childishness."

"How *couldst* thou, Xanetia?" Edaemus demanded accusingly. "How *couldst* thou do this thing?"

"It was in furtherance of our design, Belovèd," she replied. Sephrenia was more than a little startled by the intensely personal relationship Xanetia had with her God. "Thou didst command me to render assistance unto Anakha, and by reason of his love for Sephrenia, I was obliged to reach accommodation with her. Once she and I did breach the wall of enmity which did stand between us and did learn to trust each other, respect and common purpose did soften our customary despite, and all unbidden, love did gently creep in to replace it. In my heart she is now my dear sister."

"That is an abomination! Thou shalt *not* speak so of this Styric in my presence again!"

"As it please thee, Belovèd," she agreed, submissively bowing her head. But then her chin came up, and her inner light glowed more intensely. "But will ye, nil ye, I will continue to *think* so of her in the hidden silence of my heart."

"Are you ready to listen, Edaemus?" Aphrael asked. "Or would you like to take a century or two to throw a temper tantrum first?"

"Thou art pert, Aphrael," he accused.

"Yes, I know. It's one of the things that makes me so delightful. You *do* know that Cyrgon's trying to get his hands on Bhelliom, don't you? Or have you been so busy playing leapfrog with the stars that you've lost track of what's happening here?"

"Mind your manners," Sephrenia told her crisply.

"He makes me tired. He's been cuddling his hatred to his breast like a sick puppy for ten thousand years." The Child-Goddess looked critically at the incandescent presence of the God of the Delphae. "The light show doesn't impress me, Edaemus. I could do it, too, if I wanted to take the trouble."

Edaemus flared even brighter, and the reddish-orange nimbus around him became sooty.

"How tiresome," Aphrael sighed. "I'm sorry, Xanetia, but we're wasting our time here. Bhelliom and I are going to have to deal with Klæl on our own. Your tedious God wouldn't be any help anyway."

"*Klæl!*" Edaemus gasped.

"Got your attention, didn't I?" She smirked. "Are you ready to listen now?"

"Who hath done this? Who hath unloosed Klæl again upon the earth?"

"Well, it certainly wasn't *me*. Cyrgon had everything going his way, and then Anakha turned things around on him. You know how much Cyrgon hates to lose, so he started breaking the rules. Did you want to help us with this—or would you rather sit around and pout for another hundred eons or so? Quickly, quickly, Edaemus," she said, snapping her fingers at him. "Make up your mind. I don't have all day, you know."

"What makes you think I need any more men?" Narstil demanded. Narstil was a lean, almost cadaverous Arjuni with stringy arms and hollow cheeks. He sat at a table set under a spreading tree in the center of his encampment deep in the jungles of Arjuna.

"You're in a risky kind of business." Caalador shrugged, looking around at the cluttered camp. "You steal furniture and carpets and tapestries. That means that you've been raiding villages and mounting attacks on isolated estates. People fight back when you try that, and that means casualties. About half of your men are wearing bandages right now, and you probably leave a few dead behind you every time you try to steal things. A leader in your line *always* needs more men."

"I don't have any vacancies just now."

"I can arrange some," Bevier told him in a menacing voice, melodramatically drawing his thumb across the edge of his lochaber.

"Look, Narstil," Caalador said in a somewhat less abrasive tone, "we've seen your men. Be honest now. You've gathered up a bunch of local bad-boys who got into trouble for stealing chickens or running off somebody else's goats. You're very light on professionals, and that's what we're offering you—professionalism. Your bad-boys bluster and try to impress each other by looking mean and nasty, but real killing isn't in their nature, and that's why they get hurt when the fighting starts. Killing doesn't bother *us*. We're used to it. Your young bravos have to prove things to each other, but we don't. Orden knows who we are. He wouldn't have sent you that letter otherwise." His eyes narrowed slightly. "Believe me, Narstil, life will be much easier for all of us if we're working *with* you rather than setting up shop across the street."

Narstil looked a little less certain of himself. "I'll think about it," he said.

"Do that. And don't get any ideas about trying to eliminate potential competition in advance. Your bad-boys wouldn't be up to it, and my friends and I would sort of be obliged to take it personally."

"Stop that," Sephrenia chided her sister as the four of them moved through the corridorlike streets of Delphaeus toward the home of Cedon, the Anari of Xanetia's people.

"Edaemus is doing it," Aphrael countered.

"It's his city, and these are his people. It's not polite to do that when you're a guest."

Xanetia gave them a puzzled look.

"My sister's showing off," Sephrenia explained.

"Am not," Aphrael retorted.

"Yes you are, too, Aphrael, and you and I both know it. We've had this argument before. Now stop it."

"I do not understand," Xanetia confessed.

"That's because you've grown accustomed to the sense of her presence, sister," Sephrenia explained wearily. "She's not supposed to flaunt her divinity this way when she's around the worshippers of other Gods. It's the worst form of bad manners, and she knows it. She's only doing it to irritate Edaemus. I'm surprised she hasn't flattened the whole city or set fire to the thatching on the roofs with all that divine personality."

"That's a spiteful thing to say, Sephrenia," Aphrael accused.

"Behave yourself, then."

"I won't unless Edaemus does."

Sephrenia sighed, rolling her eyes upward.

They entered the southern wing of the extended city-building that was Delphaeus and proceeded down a dim hallway to Cedon's door. The Anari was waiting for them, his ancient face filled with wonder. He fell to his knees as the light that was Edaemus approached, but his God dimmed, assumed a human form, and reached out gently to raise him to his feet again. "That is not needful, my old friend," he said.

"Why, Edaemus," Aphrael said, "you're really quite handsome. You shouldn't hide from us in all that light the way you do."

A faint smile touched the ageless face of the Delphaeic God. "Seek not to beguile me with flattery, Aphrael. I know thee, and I know thy ways. Thou shalt not so easily ensnare me."

"Oh, really? Thou art ensnared already, Edaemus. I do but toy with thee now. My hand is already about thine heart. In time, I shall close it and make thee mine." And she laughed a silvery little peal of laughter. "But that's between you and me, cousin. Right now we have other things to do."

Xanetia fondly embraced the ancient Cedon. "As thou canst readily perceive, my dear old friend, momentous changes are afoot. The dire peril which we face doth reshape our entire world. Let us consider that peril first, and then at our leisure may we pause to marvel at how all about us is alterèd."

Cedon led them down the three worn stone steps into his low-ceilinged chamber with its inwardly curving, white plastered walls, its comfortable furniture, and its cheery fire.

"Tell them what's been going on, Xanetia," Aphrael suggested, climbing up into Sephrenia's lap. "That may explain why it was necessary for me to violate all the rules and come here." She gave Edaemus an arch look. "Regardless of what you may think, cousin, I *do* have good manners, but we've got an emergency on our hands."

Sephrenia leaned back in her chair as Xanetia began her account of the events of the past several months. There was a sense of peace, an unruffled calm about Delphaeus that Sephrenia had not perceived during her last visit. At that time, her mind had been so filled with obsessive hatred that she had scarcely taken note of her surroundings. The Delphae had appealed to Sparhawk to seal their valley away from the rest of the world, but that seemed somehow unnecessary. They were already separate—so separate that they no longer seemed even human. In a peculiar way, Sephrenia envied them.

"Infuriating, aren't they?" the Child-Goddess murmured. "And the word you're looking for is 'serenity.' "

"And you're doing everything in your power to disturb that, aren't you?"

"They're still a part of this world, Sephrenia—for a little while longer, anyway. All I'm doing is reminding them that the rest of us are still out here."

"You're behaving very badly toward Edaemus."

"I'm trying to jerk him back to reality. He's been off by himself for the past hundred centuries and he's forgotten what it's like having the rest of us around. I'm reminding him. Actually, it's good for him. He was starting to get complacent." She slipped down from her sister's lap. "Excuse me," she said. "It's time for me to give him another lesson." She crossed the room and stood directly in front of Edaemus, looking pleadingly into his face with her large, dark eyes.

The God of the Delphae was so engrossed in Xanetia's account that he scarcely noticed Aphrael and, when she held out her arms to him, he absently picked her up and settled her into his lap.

Sephrenia smiled.

"And most recently," Xanetia concluded her report, "young Sir Berit hath been given further instruction. He is to turn aside and go to the town of Sopal on the coast of the Sea of Arjun. He hath advised the Child-Goddess of this alteration of direction, and she in turn hath made the rest of us aware of it. It is the intent of the Troll-Gods to transport Sir Ulath and Sir Tynian to Sopal and to conceal them there in what they call 'No-Time.' It is their thought that when our enemies produce Queen Ehlana to exchange her for Bhelliom, they might leap from their concealment and rescue her."

"No-Time?" Cedon asked, his face puzzled.

"Suspended duration," Aphrael explained. "Trolls are hunters, and their Gods have found a new place of concealment for them so that they're able to stalk their prey unseen. It's clever, but it has its drawbacks."

Edaemus asked her something in that language Sephrenia had tried several times to learn but had never really been able to grasp. Aphrael replied, speaking rapidly in a rather dry, technical tone and making intricate gestures with her hands.

"Ah," he said finally, lapsing back into Tamul and with an expression of comprehension flooding his face. "It is a peculiar notion."

"You know how the Troll-Gods are." She made a little face.

"Didst thou in truth wring acceptance of thine outrageous demands from them?"

"I had something they wanted." She shrugged. "They've been trying to think up some way to escape from Bhelliom for three hundred centuries now. They didn't *like* my conditions very much, but they didn't have much choice."

"Thou are cruel, Aphrael."

"Not really. I was driven by necessity, and necessity's neither cruel nor kindly. It just *is*. I kissed them a few times when I stopped by a couple of days ago, and that made them feel better—it did once they realized that I wasn't going to take a bite out of them, anyway."

"Thou didst *not*!" He seemed aghast.

"They aren't so bad," she defended her action. "I suppose I could have scratched them behind the ears instead, but that might have insulted them, so I kissed them instead." She smiled. "A few more kisses and I'd have had them licking my fingers like puppies."

He straightened, then suddenly blinked as if realizing for the first time where she was sitting.

She gave him another of those mysterious little smiles and patted his cheek. "That's all right, cousin," she told him. "You'll come around eventually. They always do." And she slipped down from his lap and walked back across the room to rejoin her sister.

"That's *my* place!" a burly fellow of indeterminate race asserted threateningly as Kalten dropped his saddlebags and bedroll on a clear spot under a large tree.

"It *was*," Kalten grunted.

"You can't just walk in here and steal a man's place like this."

"Oh? Is it against the law or something?" Kalten straightened. He was at least a head taller than the other man, and he bulked large in his mail shirt. "My friends and I are going to be staying right here," he stated flatly, "so pick up your bed and all this other trash and go someplace else."

"I'm not in the habit of taking orders from Elenes!"

"That's too bad. Now move away. I've got work to do." Kalten was not in a good humor. Alean's peril gnawed at him constantly, and even slight irritations rubbed his temper raw. Some of that must have showed on his face. The other man backed off a few steps.

"Farther," Kalten told him.

"I'll be back," the man blustered, retreating a few more steps. "I'll be back with all my friends."

"I can hardly wait." Kalten deliberately turned his back on the man he had just dispossessed.

Caalador and Bevier joined him. "Trouble?" Caalador asked.

"I wouldn't call it that." Kalten shrugged. "I was just establishing some rank, is all. Any time you come into a new situation, you have to push a few people around to make everybody else understand that you're not going to put up with any foolishness. Let's get settled in."

They had erected their tent and were gathering leaves and moss for beds when Narstil stopped by. "I see you're getting set up, Ezek," he said to Caalador. His tone was conciliatory, though not quite cordial.

"A few finishing touches are about all that's left," Caalador replied.

"You men make a good camp," Narstil noted. "Tidy."

"A cluttered camp is the sign of a cluttered mind," Caalador declared. "I'm glad you stopped by, Narstil. We hear that there's an army camped out not far from here. Do they cause you any problems?"

"We've got an agreement with them," Narstil replied. "We don't steal from them, and they leave us alone. That's not a real army in Natayos, though. It's more like a large band of rebels. They want to overthrow the government."

"Doesn't everybody?"

Narstil laughed. "Actually, having that mob in Natayos is very good for *my* business. The fact that they're all there keeps the police out of this part of the jungle, and one of the reasons they tolerate *us* is because we rob travelers, and that keeps people from snooping around Natayos. We do a fairly brisk business with them. They're a ready market for just about everything we steal."

"How far is this Natayos place from here?"

"About ten miles. It's an old ruin. Scarpa—he's the one in charge over there—moved in with his rebels a couple of years back. He's fortified it, and he's bringing in more of his followers every day. I don't care much for him, but business is business."

"What's he like?"

"He's crazy. Some days he's so crazy that he bays at the moon. He's convinced that he'll be emperor one day, and I expect it won't be long until he marches his rabble out of those ruins. He's fairly safe in this jungle, but just as soon as he gets out into open country, the Atans will grind him into dog meat right on the spot."

"Are we supposed to care about that?" Bevier asked.

"I personally couldn't care less," Narstil assured the apparently one-eyed ruffian. "It's the loss of his business that concerns me."

"Can just anybody walk in and out of Natayos anytime he feels like it?" Kalten asked as if only mildly curious.

"If you're leading a mule loaded down with food or drink, they'll welcome you with open arms. I send an oxcart loaded down with barrels of ale every few days. You know how soldiers like their ale."

"Oh, yes," Kalten agreed. "I've know a few soldiers in my time, and their whole world stops when somebody opens an ale-barrel."

"It doth derive from our ability to control the light which doth emanate from us," Cedon explained. "What we call sight is profoundly influenced by light. The subterfuge is not perfect. Some faint shimmers do appear, and we must be wary lest our shadows reveal our presence, but with a certain care, we can be unobserved."

"Now *there* are some interesting contrasts," Aphrael said. "The Troll-Gods tamper with time, you tamper with light, and I tamper with the attention of the people I want to hide from, but it's all an attempt to achieve some measure of invisibility."

"Knowest thou of any who can be *truly* invisible, Divine One?" Xanetia asked.

"*I* don't. Do you, cousin?"

Edaemus shook his head.

"We can come close, though," the Child-Goddess said. "The real thing would probably have drawbacks. It's a very good idea, Anari Cedon, but I don't want Xanetia to put herself in any kind of danger. I love her too much for that."

Xanetia flushed slightly, and then she gave Edaemus an almost guilty look. Sephrenia laughed. "I must in honesty warn thee, Edaemus," she said. "Guard well thy worshippers. My Goddess is a notorious thief." She frowned thoughtfully. "If Xanetia could go unobserved into Sopal, it could be very useful. Her ability to reach into the thoughts of others would enable her to discover in short order whether Ehlana's there or not. If she is, we can take steps. If not, we'll know that Sopal's just another diversion."

Cedon looked at Edaemus. "I think, Beloved One, that we must extend our involvement in the world around us farther than we had earlier planned. Anakha's concern for the safety of his wife doth take precedence in his mind o'er all else, and his promise to us doth stand in peril until she be returned to him safe and whole."

Edaemus sighed. "It may be e'en as thou sayeth, my Anari. Though it doth make me unquiet, it would appear that we must set aside our repugnance and join in the search for Anakha's wife, lending such aid as is within our power."

"Are you *really* sure you want to become involved in this, Edaemus?" Aphrael asked him. "Really, *really* sure?"

"I have said it, Aphrael."

"Aren't you the least bit interested in why I'm so concerned with the fate of a pair of Elenes? Elenes *do* have their own God, you know. Why do you imagine that *I'd* be so interested in them?"

"Why is it ever thy wont to speak circuitously, Aphrael?"

"Because I love to surprise people," she replied sweetly. "I really *do* want to thank you for your concern about the well-being of my mother and father, cousin. You've touched me to the very heart."

He stared at her in stunned astonishment. "*Thou didst not!*" he gasped.

"*Somebody* had to do it." She shrugged. "One of us has to keep an eye on Bhelliom. Anakha is Bhelliom's creature, but as long as I have my hand around his heart, I can more or less control the things he does."

"But they're *Elenes*!"

"Oh, grow up, Edaemus. Elene, Styric, Delphae—what difference does it make? You can love all of them if your heart's not closed."

"But they eat *pigs*!"

"I know." She shuddered. "Believe me, I know. It's one of the things I've been working on."

Senga was a good-natured brigand whose racial origins were so mixed that no one could really tell *what* he was. He grinned a great deal, and he was loud and boisterous and had an infectious laugh. Kalten liked him, and Senga appeared to have found a kindred spirit in the Elene outlaw he knew as Col. He was laughing as he came across Narstil's cluttered compound where furniture and other household goods were stacked in large, untidy heaps on the bare ground. "Ho, Col," he shouted as he approached the tree where Kalten, Caalador, and Bevier had pitched their tent. "You should have come along. An oxcart load of ale opens every door in Natayos."

"Armies make me nervous, Senga," Kalten replied. "The officers are always trying to enlist you—usually at swordpoint—and generals as a group tend to be overly moralistic for my taste. The term *martial law* makes my blood run cold for some reason."

"Scarpa grew up in a tavern, my friend," Senga assured him, "and his mother was a whore, so he's accustomed to the seamier side of human nature."

"How did you make out?" Kalten asked.

Senga grinned, rolled his eyes, and jingled a heavy purse. "Well enough to make me consider giving up crime and opening my own brewery. The only problem with that is the fact that our friends at Natayos probably won't be there all that much longer. If I set up shop as a brewer and my customers all marched off to get killed by the Atans, I'd probably have to drink all that ale by myself, and nobody's *that* thirsty."

"Oh? What makes you think those rebels are getting ready to leave?"

"Nothing very specific," Senga said, sprawling out on the ground and offering Kalten his wineskin. "Scarpa's been gone for the past several weeks. He and two or three Elenes left Natayos last month, and nobody I talked with knew where he was going or why."

Kalten carefully kept his expression disinterested. "I hear that he's crazy. Crazy men don't need reasons for the things they do or the places they go."

"Scarpa's crazy enough, all right, but he can certainly whip those rebels of his into a frenzy. When he decides to make a speech, you'd better find a comfortable place to sit, because you're going to be there for six hours at least. Anyway, he went off a while back, and his army was getting settled in for the winter. That's all changed now that he's back."

Kalten became very alert. "He's come back?"

"That he has, my friend. Here, give us a drink." Senga took the wineskin and tipped it up, squirting a long stream of wine into his mouth. Then he wiped his chin on the back of his hand. "He and those Elene friends of his came riding into Natayos not four days ago. They had a couple of women with them, I hear."

Kalten sank down on the ground and made some show of adjusting his sword belt to cover his sudden excitement. "I though Scarpa hated women," he said, trying to keep his voice casual.

"Oh, *that* he does, my friend, but from what I hear, these two women weren't just some playthings he picked up along the way. They had their hands tied, for one thing, and the fellow I talked with said that they were a little bedraggled, but they didn't look like tavern wenches. He didn't get a very good look at them, because Scarpa hustled them into a house that seems to have been fixed up for somebody a little special—fancy furniture and rugs on the floor and all that."

"Was there anything unusual about them?" Kalten almost held his breath.

Senga shrugged and took another drink. "Just the fact that they weren't treated like ordinary camp followers, I suppose." He scratched his head. "There *was* something else the fellow told me," he said. "What was it now?"

Kalten *did* hold his breath this time.

"Oh, yes," Senga said, "now I remember. The fellow said that these two women Scarpa took all the trouble to invite to Natayos were Elenes. Isn't *that* odd?"

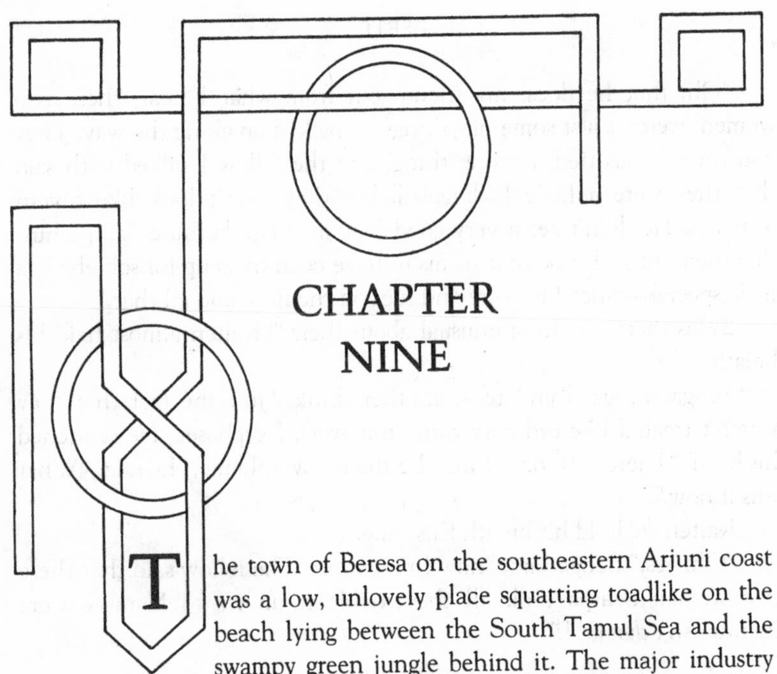

CHAPTER NINE

The town of Beresa on the southeastern Arjuni coast was a low, unlovely place squatting toadlike on the beach lying between the South Tamul Sea and the swampy green jungle behind it. The major industry of the region was the production of charcoal, and acrid smoke hung in the humid air over Beresa like a curse.

Captain Sorgi dropped his anchor some distance out from the wharves and went ashore to consult with the harbormaster.

Sparhawk, Stragen, and Talen, wearing their canvas smocks, leaned on the port rail staring across the smelly water toward their destination. "I have an absolutely splendid idea, Fron," Stragen said to Sparhawk.

"Oh?" Sparhawk replied.

"Why don't we jump ship?"

"Nice try, Vymer." Talen laughed. They were all more or less at ease with the assumed names by now.

Sparhawk looked around carefully to make sure that none of the rest of the crew was near. "An ordinary sailor wouldn't leave without collecting his pay. Let's not do anything to attract attention. All that's really left to do is the unloading of the cargo."

"Under the threat of the bo'sun's whip," Stragen added glumly. "That man *really* tests my self-control. Just the sight of him makes me want to kill him."

"We can endure him this one last time," Sparhawk told him. "This town's going to be full of unfriendly eyes. Krager's bound to have people here to make sure I'm not trying to sneak in reinforcements behind his back."

"That might just be the flaw in this whole plan, Fron," Stragen said. "Sorgi knows that we're not ordinary sailors. Is he the kind to let things slip?"

Sparhawk shook his head. "Sorgi knows how to keep his mouth shut. He was paid to get us to Beresa unnoticed, and Sorgi always does what he's paid to do."

The captain returned late that afternoon, and they raised anchor and eased up to one of the long wharves protruding out into the harbor. They unloaded the cargo the next morning. The bo'sun cracked his whip only sparingly, and the unloading proceeded rapidly.

Then, when the cargo holds were all emptied, the sailors lined up and filed along the quarterdeck where Sorgi sat at a small table with his account book and his stacks of coins. The captain gave each sailor a little speech as he paid him. The speeches varied slightly, but the general message was the same: "Stay out of trouble, and get back to the ship on time. I won't wait for you when the time comes to sail." He did not alter the speech when he paid Sparhawk and his friends, and his face did not in any way betray the fact they were anything other than ordinary crew members.

Sparhawk and his two friends went down the gangway with their seabags on their shoulders and with a certain amount of anticipation. "Now I see why sailors are so rowdy when they reach port," Sparhawk said. "That wasn't really much of a voyage, and I still feel a powerful urge to kick over the traces."

"Where to?" Talen asked when they reached the street.

"There's an inn called the Seaman's Rest," Stragen replied. "It's supposed to be a clean, quiet place out beyond the main battle zone here along the waterfront. It should give us a base of operations to work from."

The sun was just going down as they passed through the noisy, reeking streets of Beresa. The buildings were constructed for the most part of squared-off logs, since stone was rare here on the vast, soggy delta of the Arjun River, and the logs appeared to have been attacked by damp rot almost before they were in place. Moss and fungus grew everywhere, and the air was thick with the chill damp and the acrid wood smoke from the charcoal yards outside of town. The Arjunis in the streets were noticeably more swarthy than their Tamul cousins of the north; their eyes were shifty; and even their most casual gait through the muddy streets of their unlovely town seemed somehow furtive.

Sparhawk muttered the spell under his breath as they passed along the shabby street, and he released it carefully to avoid alerting the watchers he was sure were there.

"Well?" Talen asked. Talen had been around Sparhawk long enough to know the signs that the big Pandion was using magic.

"They're out there," Sparhawk replied. "Three of them that I can pick up."

"Are they concentrating on us?" Stragen asked tensely.

Sparhawk shook his head. "Their attention's sort of generalized. They aren't Styrics, so they won't know I've gone looking for them. Let's just move along. If they start to follow us, I'll let you know."

The Seaman's Rest was a square, tidy inn festooned with fishnets and other nautical decorations. It was run by a burly retired sea captain and his equally burly wife. They brooked no nonsense under their roof and they recited a long list of house rules to each prospective tenant before they would accept his money. Sparhawk had not even heard of some of the things that were prohibited.

"Where to now?" Talen asked after they had stowed their seabags in their room and come back out into the muddy street.

"Back to the waterfront," Stragen replied. "The chief of the local thieves is a man named Estokin. He deals extensively with smugglers and with sailors who pilfer things from cargo holds. I've got a letter from Caalador. Ostensibly, we're here to make sure that he got his money's worth during the Harvest Festival. Arjunis aren't generally trusted, so Estokin won't be too surprised to see us."

Estokin the Arjuni was a man who had clearly been destined for a life of crime from the day he was born. He had what was perhaps the most evil face Sparhawk had ever seen. His left eye peered perpetually off in a northeasterly direction, and he had a pronounced squint. His beard was sparse and straggly, and his skin was blotched with a scaly disease. He scratched at his face almost continually, showering white flakes as if from a winter sky. His high-pitched, nasal voice was very much like the whine of a hungry mosquito, and he reeked of garlic, cheap wine, and pickled herring. "Is Caalador accusing me of cheating him, Vymer?" he demanded with some show of indignation.

"Of course not." Stragen leaned back in the rickety chair in the back room of the smelly waterfront dive. "If he thought that, you'd already be dead. He wants to know if we missed anybody, that's all. Were any local people particularly upset when the bodies started to turn up?"

Estokin squinted at Stragen with his good eye. "What's it worth to him?" he haggled.

"We've been instructed to let you live if you cooperate," Stragen countered in a cool voice.

"You can't threaten me like that, Vymer," Estokin blustered.

"I wasn't threatening you, old boy. I was just letting you know how things stand. Let's get to the point here. Who got excited here in Beresa after the killings?"

"Not very many, really." Stragen's chilly manner had evidently persuaded Estokin to behave himself. "There was a Styric here who was fairly free with his money before the Harvest Festival."

"What was he buying?"

"Information, mostly. He was on the list Caalador gave me, but he managed to get away—rode off into the jungle. I've got a couple of local cutthroats on his trail."

"I'd sort of like to talk with him before they put him to sleep."

"Not much chance, Vymer. They're a long way out in the bush by now." Estokin scratched at his forehead, stirring up another snow flurry. "I'm not sure why Caalador wanted all those people killed," he said, "and I don't really want to know, but I'm getting a whiff or two of politics, and here in Arjuna that means Scarpa. You might want to warn Caalador to be very careful. I've talked with a few deserters from that rebel army in the jungle. We've all heard stories about how crazy Scarpa is, but let me tell you, my friend, the stories don't even come close. If only half of what I've heard is true, Scarpa's the craziest man who ever lived."

Sparhawk's stomach gave a lurch, and then it settled into a cold knot.

Father?

Sparhawk sat up in bed quickly.

Are you awake? the Child-Goddess asked, her voice roaring in his mind.

"Of course. Please lower your voice a bit. You're jarring my teeth."

I wanted to be sure I had your attention. Some things have happened. Berit and Khalad got some new instructions from Krager. They're supposed to go to Sopal now instead of coming here to Beresa.

Sparhawk swore.

Please don't use that kind of language, Father. I am *just a little girl, you know.*

He ignored that. *Is the trade going to take place in Sopal?*

It's hard to say. Bevier's been in touch with me, too. Kalten talked with an outlaw who's been selling beer to the soldiers in Natayos, and he says that Scarpa's gone back there. Then the outlaw told Kalten that Scarpa had two Elene women with him when he returned.

Sparhawk's heart leapt. *Was he sure?*

Kalten thinks so. The fellow didn't have any reason to lie about it. Of course, Kalten's beer merchant didn't actually see them for himself, so don't get your hopes up too much. It could be a very carefully planted story. Zalasta's in Natayos, and he could be trying to lure you there or trying to trick you into giving away any secrets you might have tucked up your sleeve. He knows you well enough to know that you'll try to do something he doesn't expect.

Is there any way you could find out for sure if your mother's in Natayos?

I'm afraid not. I could slip around Scarpa easily enough, but Zalasta would sense me immediately. It's too risky.

What else is going on?

Ulath and Tynian have reached the Troll-Gods. Ghnomb's going to take them to Sopal in that frozen time he's so fond of, and they'll be there when Berit and Khalad arrive. Ghnomb knows another way to play around with time, so he's going to skip Ulath and Tynian from moment to moment. It's a little complicated, but they'll be there and watching and nobody will be able to see them. If Scarpa and Zalasta try to make the trade in Sopal, Tynian and Ulath will be right on top of them to rescue Mother and Alean.

Zalasta can follow them into that frozen moment, you know.

That wouldn't really pay him, Father. Khwaj was outraged when he heard about Mother, so he's going to be lurking in No-Time. If Zalasta tries to follow Ulath and Tynian, Khwaj will set him on fire—and the fire won't ever go out.

I could learn to grow fond of Khwaj.

Sephrenia and Xanetia are in Delphaeus, Aphrael continued. *Edaemus is being tiresome, but the news about Klæl shook his tree, so I'll probably be able to coax him down out of the branches. He knows that Mother's captivity puts the arrangement you have with Cedon at risk, so he's agreed to help us rescue her. I'll keep working on him. If I can push him just a little farther, he might agree to let the Delphae come out of their valley. They could be enormously helpful to us.*

Why didn't you tell me about all of this earlier?

What would you have done if I had, Sparhawk? Jumped over the side of Sorgi's ship and swum ashore?

I need to know these things when they happen, Aphrael.

Why? Let me take care of the fretting and worrying, Sparhawk. All it does is make you foul-tempered.

He let that pass. *I'll tell this to Bhelliom.*

Absolutely not! We don't dare open that box. Cyrgon or Klæl will feel Bhelliom instantly if we do.

Didn't you know? he asked her mildly. *I don't have to open the box to speak with Bhelliom. We can talk with each other right through the gold.*

Why didn't you tell me?

What would you have done if I had? Jumped into the sea and come swimming after Sorgi's ship?

There was a long moment of silence. *You really enjoy turning my own words around and throwing them back in my teeth like that, don't you, Sparhawk?*

Naturally. Was there anything else you'd like to share with me, Divine One?

But the sense of her presence was gone, leaving only a slightly huffy silence behind.

"Where's—ah—Vymer?" Sparhawk asked Talen as the boy entered the room a few minutes later.

"He's out attending to something," Talen replied evasively.

"Attending to what?"

"He asked me not to tell you."

"All right. *I'm* asking you to ignore him—and I'm right here where I can get my hands on you."

"That's a crude way to put it."

"Nobody's perfect. What's he up to?"

Talen sighed. "One of Estokin's men stopped by—just after you came up to go to bed. He said that there are three Elenes in town who are letting it be known they'll pay good money for information about any strangers who seem to be settling in for a long stay. Vymer decided to look them up." Talen glanced meaningfully at the walls of their small room. "I'd guess that he probably wants to find out just exactly what they mean by 'good money.' You know Vymer when there's some profit to be made."

"He should have told me," Sparhawk said cautiously. "I'm not any more allergic to a quick profit than he is."

"Sharing isn't one of Vymer's strong points, Fron." Talen touched his ear and then laid a finger to his lips. "Why don't we go out and see if we can find him?"

"Good idea." Sparhawk quickly pulled on his clothes, and the two of them clattered down the stairs and out into the street.

"I just had a religious experience," Sparhawk murmured as they walked into the noisy area near the docks.

"Oh?"

"One of those Divine visitations."

"Ah. What did your Divine visitor have to say?"

"A broken-nosed friend of ours got another one of those notes. He's been told to go to Sopal instead of coming here."

Talen muttered a fairly vile oath.

"My feelings exactly. Isn't that Vymer coming up the street?" Sparhawk pointed at a blond man in a tar-smeared smock who was lurching unsteadily toward them.

Talen peered at the fellow. "I think you're right." He made a face. "The ladies who changed things around may have gone a little far. He doesn't even walk the same anymore."

"What are you two doing out this late?" Stragen asked as he joined them.

"We got lonesome," Sparhawk replied in a flat tone of voice.

"For me? I'm touched. Let's go for a walk on the beach, my friends. I find myself yearning for the smell of saltwater—and the nice loud sound of waves crashing on the sand."

They walked on past the last of the wharves and then out onto the sand. The clouds had blown off, and there was a bright moon. They reached the water's edge and stood looking out at the long combers rolling in off the South Tamul Sea to hammer noisily on the wet sand.

"What have you been up to, Stragen?" Sparhawk demanded bluntly.

"Business, old boy. I just enlisted us in the intelligence service of the other side."

"You did *what?*"

"The three you sensed when we first got here needed a few good men. I volunteered our services."

"Are you out of your mind?"

"Of course not. Think about it, Sparhawk. What better way is there to gather information? Our celebration of the Harvest Festival thinned their ranks drastically, so they can't afford to be choosy. I paid Estokin to vouch for us, and then I told them a few lies. They're expecting a certain Sir Sparhawk to flood the town with sharp-eyed people. We're supposed to report anybody we see who's acting a little suspicious. I provided them with a prime suspect."

"Oh? Who was that?"

"Captain Sorgi's bo'sun—you know, the fellow with the whip."

Sparhawk suddenly laughed. "That was a truly vicious thing to do, Stragen."

"I rather liked it, myself."

"Aphrael came by to call," Talen said. "She told Sparhawk that Berit and my brother have been ordered to change direction. Now they're supposed to go to Sopal on the coast of the Sea of Arjun."

Stragen swore.

"I already said that," Talen told him.

"We probably should have expected it," Sparhawk said. "Krager's working for the other side and he knows us well enough to anticipate some of the things we might try to do." He suddenly banged his fist into the palm of his hand. "I *wish* I could talk with Sephrenia!" he burst out.

"You *can*, as I recall," Stragen said. "Didn't Aphrael fix it once so that you and Sephrenia talked when she was in Sarsos and you were in Cimmura?"

Sparhawk suddenly felt more than a little foolish. "I'd forgotten about that," he admitted.

"That's all right, old boy," Stragen excused him. "You've got a lot on your mind. Why don't you have a word with her Divine little Whimsicality and see if she can arrange a council of war someplace? I think it might be time for a good, old-fashioned get-together."

Sparhawk knew where he was before he even opened his eyes. The fragrance of wildflowers and tree blossoms immediately identified the eternal spring of Aphrael's own private reality.

"Art thou now awake, Anakha?" the white deer asked him, touching his hand with her nose.

"Yea, gentle creature," he replied, opening his eyes and touching the side of her face. He was in the pavilion again and he looked out through the open flap at the flower-studded meadow, the sparkling azure sea, and the rainbow-colored sky above.

"The others do await thy coming on the eyot," the hind advised him.

"We must hasten, then," he said, rising from his bed. He followed her from the pavilion out into the meadow where the white tigress indulgently watched the awkward play of her large-footed cubs. He rather idly wondered if these were the same cubs she had been tending when he had first visited this enchanted realm a half-dozen years ago.

Well, of course *they are, Sparhawk,* Aphrael's voice murmured in his ear. *Nothing ever changes here.*

He smiled.

The white deer led him to that beautiful, impractical boat, a swan-necked craft with sails like wings, elaborate embellishment, and so much of its main structure above the waterline that a sneeze would have capsized it, had it existed in the real world.

Critic, Aphrael's voice accused him.

It's your dream, Divine One. You can put any impossibility in it that you want.

Oh, thank *you, Sparhawk!* she said with effusive irony.

The emerald green eyot, crowned with ancient oaks and Aphrael's alabaster temple, nestled in the sapphire sea, and the swan-necked boat touched the golden beach in only minutes. Sparhawk looked around as he stepped out onto the sand. The disguises most of them wore in the real world had been discarded, and they all had their own features here in this eternal dream. Some of them had been here before. Those who had not had expressions of bemused wonderment as they all lounged in the lush grass that blanketed the slopes of the enchanted isle.

The Child-Goddess and Sephrenia sat side by side on an alabaster bench in the temple. Aphrael's expression was pensive, and she was playing a complex Styric melody in a minor key on her many-chambered pipes. "What kept you, Sparhawk?" she asked, lowering the rude instrument.

"The person in charge of my travel arrangements took me on a little side trip," he replied. "Are we all here?"

"Everybody who's supposed to be. Come up here, all of you, and let's get started."

They climbed up the slope to the temple.

"Where is this place?" Sarabian asked in an awed voice.

"Aphrael carries it in her mind, your Majesty," Vanion replied. "She invites us here from time to time. She likes to show it off."

"Don't be insulting, Vanion," the Child-Goddess told him.

"Well, don't you?"

"Of course, but it's not nice to come right out and say it like that."

"I feel different here, for some reason," Caalador noted. "Better, somehow."

Vanion smiled. "It's a very healthy place, my friend." he said. "I was seriously ill at the end of the Zemoch war—dying, actually. Aphrael brought me here for a month or so, and I was disgustingly healthy by the time I left."

They all reached the little temple and took seats on the marble benches lining the columned perimeter. Sparhawk looked around, frowning. "Where's Emban?" he asked their hostess.

"It wouldn't have been appropriate for him to be here, Sparhawk. Your Elene God makes exceptions in the case of the Church Knights, but he'd probably throw a fit if I brought one of the Patriarchs of his Church here. I didn't invite the Atans either—or the Peloi." She smiled. "Neither group is comfortable with the idea of religious diversity, and this place would probably confuse them." She rolled her eyes upward. "You wouldn't *believe* how long it took me to persuade Edaemus to permit Xanetia to come. He doesn't approve of me. He thinks I'm frivolous."

"You?" Sparhawk feigned some surprise. "How could he possibly believe something like that?"

"Let's get at this," Sephrenia said. "Why don't you start, Berit? We know generally what happened, but we don't have any details."

"Yes, Lady Sephrenia," the young knight replied. "Khalad and I were coming down the coast, and we'd been watched from almost the moment we came ashore. I used the spell and identified the watcher as a Styric. He came to us after several days and gave us another one of those notes from Krager. This one told us to continue down the coast, but once we get past the Tamul Mountains, we're supposed to cut across-country to Sopal instead of continuing south. We're to get further instructions there. It was definitely from Krager: it had another lock of Queen Ehlana's hair in it."

"I'm going to talk with Krager about that when I catch up with him," Khalad said in a bleak tone of voice. "I want to be sure he understands just how much we resent his touching the queen's hair. Trust me, Sparhawk. Before I'm done with him, he's going to regret it—profoundly."

"I've got enormous confidence in you, Khalad," Sparhawk replied.

"Oh," Khalad said then, "there's something I almost forgot. Does anybody know of a way to make one of our horses limp—without actually hurting him? I think Berit and I might want to be able to slow down from time to time without causing suspicion. An intermittently lame horse should explain it to the people who are watching us."

"I'll talk with Faran," Aphrael promised.

"You won't need to limp on your way to Sopal," Ulath told Khalad. "Ghnomb's going to see to it that Tynian and I are there long before you arrive. You might be able to see us when you get there, but you might not. I'm having a little trouble explaining some things to the Troll-Gods. We'll be able to see you, though. If I can't make Ghnomb understand, I'll slip a note in your pocket."

"If we *do* come out in the open, you'll just *love* our traveling companion." Tynian laughed.

Berit gave him a puzzled look. "Who's that, Sir Tynian?"

"Bhlokw. He's a Troll."

"It's Ghnomb's idea," Ulath explained. "I have to go through a little ceremony before I can talk with the Troll-Gods. Bhlokw doesn't, so having him along speeds up communication. Anyway, we'll be there and out of sight. If Scarpa and Zalasta try to make the trade in Sopal, we'll step out of No-Time, grab the lot of you, and disappear again."

"That's assuming that they're taking Queen Ehlana to Sopal to make the exchange," Itagne said. "We've got some things that don't match up, though. Sir Kalten picked up a rumor that Scarpa's holding the queen and her maid in Natayos."

"I wouldn't want to wager the farm on it, your Excellency," Kalten said. "It's secondhand information at best. The fellow I talked with probably isn't bright enough to make up stories, and he didn't have any reason to lie to me. But he got *his* information from somebody else, so that makes the whole thing a little wormy."

"You've put your finger on the problem, Sir Kalten," Sarabian said. "Soldiers gossip worse than old women." He tugged at one earlobe and looked up at the rainbow-colored sky. "The other side knows that I wasn't entirely dependent on the Ministry of the Interior for information, so they'll expect me to have ears in Natayos. This story Sir Kalten heard could have been planted for our benefit. Prince Sparhawk, is there any way at all you could use Bhelliom to confirm the rumor?"

"It's too dangerous," Sephrenia said flatly. "Zalasta would know immediately if Sparhawk did that."

"I'm not so sure, little mother," Sparhawk disagreed. "It was just recently that we found out that the gold box doesn't totally isolate Bhelliom. I'm getting a strong feeling that a great deal of what we *think* we know about Bhelliom is pure misdirection. The rings evidently don't really mean anything at all—except possibly as a means of communication, and the gold box doesn't appear to be relevant either. It *could* be an idea Bhelliom planted to keep us from enclosing it in iron. I'm guessing, but I'd say that the touch of iron is still painful to it, but whether it's painful enough to actually confine it isn't all that certain."

"He's right, you know," Aphrael told her sister. "A great deal of what we think we know about Bhelliom came from Ghwerig, and Bhelliom had absolute control of Ghwerig. Our mistake was believing that Ghwerig knew what he was talking about."

"That still doesn't answer the question about using Bhelliom to investigate things in Natayos," Sparhawk said, "and it's not the sort of thing I'd want to experiment with."

"I will go to Natayos," Xanetia said quietly. "It had been mine intent to go unseen to Sopal, but Sir Tynian and Sir Ulath will be there already, and well able to determine if the queen be truly there. I will go to Natayos and seek her there instead."

"Absolutely not!" Sarabian said. "I forbid it."

"I am not subject to thee, Sarabian of Tamuli," she reminded him. "But fear not. There is no peril involved for me. None will know that I am there, and I can reach out to those who are about me and share their thoughts. I will soon be able to determine whether or no the queen and her maidservant are in Natayos. This is precisely the kind of service we offered when we concluded our pact with Anakha."

"It's too dangerous," he said stubbornly.

"It seemeth me that thou hast forgot mine *other* gift, Sarabian of Tamuli," she told him quite firmly. "The curse of Edaemus is still upon me, and my touch is still death, an I choose it so. Fear not for me, Sarabian, for should necessity compel me to it, I can spread death and terror through Natayos. Though it doth cause me pain to confess it, I can make Natayos once more a waste, a weed-choked ruin populated only by the dead."

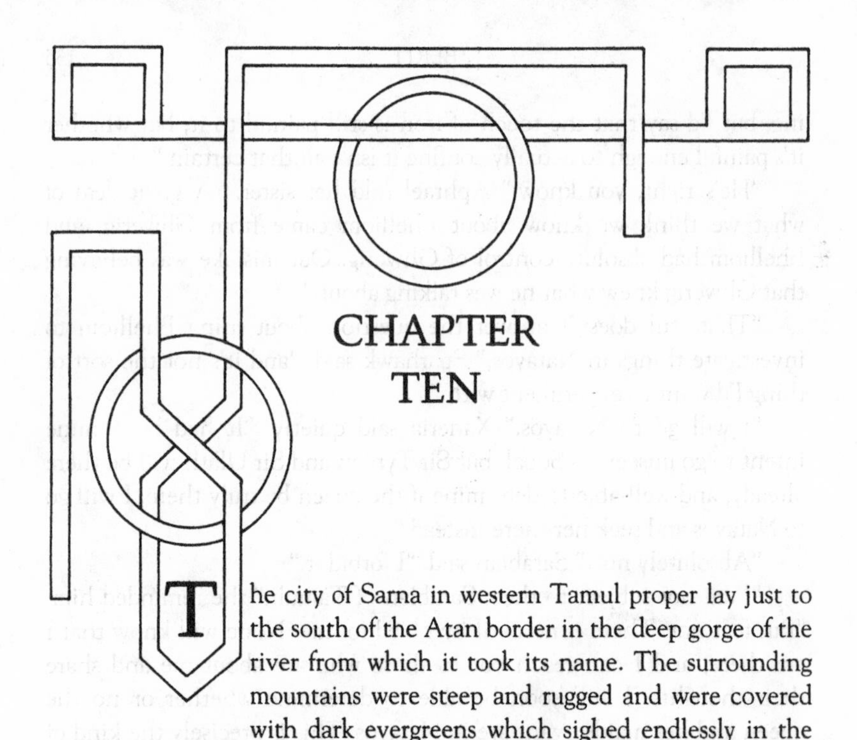

CHAPTER TEN

The city of Sarna in western Tamul proper lay just to the south of the Atan border in the deep gorge of the river from which it took its name. The surrounding mountains were steep and rugged and were covered with dark evergreens which sighed endlessly in the prevailing wind sweeping down out of the wilderness to the north. The weather was cold, and the leaden sky spat stinging pellets of snow as Vanion's army of Church Knights slowly descended the long, steep road leading down into the gorge. Vanion and Itagne, muffled in their heavy cloaks, rode at the head of the column.

"I'd have much preferred to stay on Aphrael's island," Itagne said, shivering and pulling his cloak tighter. "I've never been particularly fond of this time of year."

"We're almost there, your Excellency," Vanion replied.

"Is it customary to campaign in the wintertime, Lord Vanion?" Itagne asked. "In Eosia, I mean?"

"We try to avoid it, your Excellency," Vanion replied. "The Lamorks attack each other in the winter, but the rest of us usually have better sense."

"It's a miserable time to go to war."

Vanion smiled faintly. "That it is, my friend, but that's not why we avoid it. It's a question of economics, really. It's more expensive to campaign in winter because you have to buy hay for the horses. It's the expense that keeps Elene kings peaceful when there's snow on the ground." Vanion stood up in his stirrups to peer ahead. "Betuana's waiting," he said. "We'd better ride down to meet her."

Itagne nodded, and they pushed their horses into a jolting trot.

The Queen of Atan had left them behind at Dasan on the eastern edge of the mountains, determined to come on ahead. She had several very good reasons, of course, but Vanion privately suspected that her decision had been influenced more by impatience than necessity. Betuana was too polite to speak of it, but she clearly had little use for horses, and she seldom missed an opportunity to outrun them. She and Engessa, both garbed in otter skins, waited at the roadside about a mile outside the city.

"Was there any trouble?" the Atan queen asked.

"No, your Majesty," Vanion replied, his black armor clinking as he swung down out of his saddle. "We were watched, but there's nothing unusual about that. Has anything been happening in Cynesga?"

"They're moving up to the border, Vanion-Preceptor," Engessa replied quietly. "They aren't being very subtle about it. We've been disrupting their supply lines and ambushing their scouting parties just to keep them off-balance, but it's fairly obvious that they plan to come across the line in force."

Vanion nodded. "It's more or less what we expected, then. If it's all right with you, your Majesty, I'd like to get my men settled in before we get too involved in discussions. I can always think better after I've seen to all the details."

"Of course," Betuana agreed. "Engessa-Atan and I have arranged quarters for them. When will you be leaving for Samar?"

"Tomorrow or the next day, Betuana-Queen. Tikome's Peloi are probably spread a little thin down there. He has a lot of ground to cover."

"He sent back to Pela for more men, Vanion-Lord," Engessa advised. "You'll have a sizable force in Samar in a week or so."

"Good. Let me go back and hurry the knights along. We have much to discuss."

Night settled early at the bottom of the gorge of the River Sarna, and it was fully dark by the time Vanion joined the others in the headquarters of the city's Atan garrison. Like all Atan structures, the building was severely utilitarian and devoid of any embellishment. The lone exception in the conference room in which they gathered was a very large map covering one entire wall. The map was brightly colored and dotted here and there with fanciful illustrations. Vanion had bathed hurriedly and now wore plain clothing. The years had taught him that armor was impressive and even useful at times, but that no one had yet devised a way to make it comfortable or to eliminate its characteristic smell.

"Are the quarters satisfactory?" Betuana inquired politely.

"Most satisfactory, your Majesty," he replied, settling into a chair. "Have you been advised of the details of our meeting with the Child-Goddess?"

She nodded. "Itagne-Ambassador gave me a report," she replied. She paused. "One is curious to know why one was excluded," she added.

"Theological considerations, your Majesty," Vanion explained. "As I understand it, the Gods have an exquisitely complex etiquette in these situations. Aphrael didn't want to offend your God by inviting his children to her island. There were some other rather conspicuous absences as well. Emperor Sarabian was there and Ambassador Itagne, but Foreign Minister Oscagne wasn't."

Itagne frowned slightly. "The emperor and I are skeptics—agnostics, I suppose you could call us—but Oscagne's an out-and-out atheist. Would that account for it?"

"It might. I'll ask Aphrael the next time I talk with her."

Engessa looked around. "I didn't see Kring-Domi when we met you, Vanion-Preceptor," he noted.

"Kring took his men and veered off toward Samar not long after you and her Majesty left. He thought he'd be more useful there than he would here in Sarna—and you know how the western Peloi feel about mountains and forests. Have the Cynesgans made any forays across the border as yet?"

"No, Vanion-Preceptor," Engessa replied. "They're massing in staging areas and bringing up supplies." He rose and went to the map. "A large force moved out of Cynestra a while back," he said, pointing at the Cynesgan capital. "They're positioned near the border more or less opposite us here. Another force has taken up a similar position just across the line from Samar."

Vanion nodded. "Cyrgon's more like a general than a God in most ways. He's not going to leave fortified positions to his rear. He'll have to neutralize Samar and Sarna before he can strike any deeper into Tamul proper. I'd say that the force you're facing here has been ordered to take Sarna, seal the southern border of Atan, and then swing northeast toward Tualas. I'm sure they'd rather not have the entire Atan nation come swarming down out of these mountains."

"There aren't enough Cynesgans living to keep my people hemmed in," Betuana told him.

"I'm sure of it, your Majesty, but there probably *are* enough to slow you down, and Cyrgon can recruit armies from the past to hinder you all the more." He studied the map, his lips pursed. "I think I see where he's going," he said. "Matherion's on a peninsula, and that narrow neck of land at Tosa is the key to that. If I had to wager anything on it, I'd say that the main battle's going to take place there. Scarpa will move north out of Natayos. Probably the southern Cynesgans are planning to capture Samar and then swing around the north shore of the Sea of Arjun to join him somewhere in the vicinity of the Tamul Mountains. From there the combined army can march up the west shore of the Gulf of Micae to Tosa." He smiled faintly. "Of course, there's a very nasty surprise waiting for them in the Tamul Mountains. I'd imagine that before this is over, Cyrgon will wish that he'd never *heard* of the Trolls."

"I will send an army out of northern Atan to Tosa, Vanion-Preceptor," Betuana said, "but I'll leave enough of my people along the southern and eastern borders to tie up half of the Cynesgans."

"In the meantime I think we can disrupt their preparations," Engessa added. "Raids in force across that border will delay their main attack."

"And that's all we really need," Vanion chuckled. "If we can delay them long enough, Cyrgon's going to have a hundred thousand Church Knights swarming across his western frontier. I think he'll forget about Tosa at that point."

"Don't worry about him, Fron," Stragen told Sparhawk. "He can take care of himself."

"I think we sometimes forget that he's only a boy, Vymer. He doesn't even shave regularly yet."

"Reldin stopped being a boy before his voice started to change." Stragen leaned back on his bed reflectively. "Those of us in our particular line of work tend to lose our childhoods," he said. "It might have been nice to roll hoops and catch polliwogs, but . . ." He shrugged.

"What are you going to do when this is all over?" Sparhawk asked him. "Assuming that we survive?"

"There's a certain lady of our acquaintance who proposed marriage to me a while back. It's part of a business arrangement that's very attractive. The notion of marriage never really appealed to me, but the business proposition's just too good to pass up."

"There's more, too, isn't there?"

"Yes," Stragen admitted. "After what she did back in Matherion that night, I'm not about to let her get away from me. She's one of the coolest and most courageous people I've ever met."

"Pretty, too."

"You noticed." Stragen sighed. "I'm afraid I'm going to end up being at least semi-respectable, my friend."

"Shocking."

"Isn't it? First, though, there's this other little matter I want to deal with. I think I'll present my beloved with the head of a certain Astellian poet of our acquaintance. If I can find a good taxidermist, I may even have it stuffed and mounted for her."

"It's the kind of wedding present every girl dreams of."

"Maybe not *every* girl—" Stragen grinned. "—but I'm in love with a very special lady."

"But there are so *many* of them, U-lat," Bhlokw said plaintively. "They would not miss just one, would they?"

"I am certain they would, Bhlokw," Ulath told the huge, brown-furred Troll. "The man-things are not like the deer. They pay very close attention to the other members of the herd. If you eat one of them, they will know that we are here. Catch and eat one of their dogs instead."

"Is dog good-to-eat?"

"I am not sure. Eat one and tell me if it is good."

Bhlokw grumbled and squatted down on his haunches.

The process Ghnomb had called "breaking the moments in two pieces" produced some rather strange effects. The brightness of noon was dimmed to twilight, for one thing, and the citizens of Sopal seemed to walk about their town with a fast, jerky kind of movement, for another. The God of Eat had assured them that because they were present in only a small part of each instant, they had been rendered effectively invisible. Ulath could see a rather large logical flaw in the explanation, but the spell did work.

Tynian came back up the street shaking his head. "It's impossible to understand them," he reported. "I can pick up a word or two now and then, but the rest is pure gibberish."

"It is talking in bird-noises again," Bhlokw complained.

"You'd better speak in Trollish, Tynian," Ulath said. "You're making Bhlokw nervous."

"I forgot," Tynian admitted, reverting to the hideous language of the Trolls. "I am—" he groped. "What is the word that means that you want it that you had not done something?" he asked their shaggy companion.

"There is no such word, Tin-in," Bhlokw replied.

"Can you ask Ghnomb to make it so that we can understand what the man-things are saying?" Ulath asked.

"Why? What does it matter?" Bhlokw's face was puzzled.

"If we can know what they are saying, we will know which ones of the herd we should follow," Tynian explained. "They will be the ones who will know about the wicked ones."

"They do not *all* know?" Bhlokw asked with some amazement.

"No. Only some know."

"The man-things are very strange. I will talk with Ghnomb. He may understand this." He rose to his feet, towering over them. "I will do it as soon as I come back."

"Where are you going?" Tynian asked politely.

"I am hungry. I will go eat a dog. Then I will come back and talk with Ghnomb." He paused. "I can bring a dog back for you as well, if you are also hungry."

"Ah—no, Bhlokw," Tynian replied. "I do not think I am hungry right now. It was good of you to ask, though."

"We are pack-mates now." Bhlokw shrugged. "It is right to do this." And he shambled off down the street.

"It's not really all that far," Aphrael told her sister as they rode with Xanetia out of the valley of Delphaeus toward the town of Dirgis in southern Atan, "but Edaemus is still reluctant to help us, so I think I'd better mind my manners. He might be offended if I start 'tampering' in the home of his children."

"You've never used that word to describe it before," Sephrenia noted.

"Sparhawk's influence, I guess," the Child-Goddess replied. "It's a useful sort of term: it glosses over things that we don't want to discuss in front of strangers. After we get to Dirgis, we'll be well clear of the home of the Delphae. Then I'll be able to tamper to my heart's content."

"How long dost thou think it will take us to reach Natayos, Goddess?" Xanetia asked. She had once again altered her coloration and suppressed her inner radiance to conceal her racial characteristics.

"No more than a few hours—in real time." Aphrael shrugged. "I can't *quite* jump us around the way Bhelliom does, but I can cover a lot of ground in a hurry when there's an emergency. If things were really desperate, I could fly us there."

Sephrenia shuddered. "It's not *that* desperate, Aphrael."

Xanetia gave her Styric sister a puzzled look.

"It makes her queasy," Aphrael explained.

"No, Aphrael," Sephrenia corrected, "not queasy—terrified. It's a horrible experience, Xanetia. She's done it to me about five times in the past three hundred years. I'm an absolute wreck for weeks afterward."

"I keep telling you not to look down, Sephrenia," Aphrael told her. "If you'd just look at the clouds instead of down at the ground, it wouldn't bother you so much."

"I can't help myself, Aphrael," Sephrenia told her.

"Is it truly so disturbing, sister mine?" Xanetia asked.

"You couldn't even begin to imagine it, Xanetia. You skim along with nothing but about five thousand feet of empty air between you and the ground. It's *awful*!"

"We'll do it the other way," Aphrael assured her.

"I'll start composing a prayer of thanksgiving immediately."

"We'll stay the night in Dirgis," Aphrael told them, "and then tomorrow morning we'll run down to Natayos. Sephrenia and I'll stay out in the woods, Xanetia, and you can go into town and have a look around. If Mother's really being held there, we should be able to bring this little crisis to an end in short order. Once Sparhawk knows exactly where she is, he'll fall on Scarpa and his father like a vengeful mountain. Natayos won't even be a ruin anymore when he's done. It'll just be a big hole in the ground."

"He actually saw them," Talen reported. "He described them too well to have just been making it up." The young thief had just returned from his foray into the seamier parts of Beresa.

"What sort of fellow was he?" Sparhawk asked. "This is too important for us to be taken in by random gossip."

"He's a Dacite," Talen replied, "a guttersnipe from Jura. His politics go about as far as his purse. His main reason for joining Scarpa's army in the first place was his enthusiasm for the idea of taking part in the looting of Matherion. We're not talking about a man with high ideals here. When he got to Natayos and found out that there might be actual fighting involved, he started to lose interest. Anyway, I found him in one of the shabbiest taverns I've ever seen, and he was roaring drunk. Believe me, Fron, he was in no condition to lie to me. I told him that I was thinking of joining Scarpa's army, and he turned all fatherly on me—'Don' even *shink* about it, boy. It's tur'ble there'—that sort of thing. He said that Scarpa's a raving lunatic with delusions of invincibility who thinks he can just blow on the Atans and make them go away. He said he'd just about decided to desert anyway, and then Scarpa came back to Natayos—along with Krager, Elron, and Baron Parok. They had the queen and Alean with them, and Zalasta met them at the gate. The Dacite happened to be nearby, so he could hear what they were saying. Evidently, Zalasta's still got a *few* good manners, so he wasn't very happy about the way Scarpa had been treating his prisoners. The two of them had an argument about it, and Zalasta tied his son into a very complicated knot with magic. I guess Scarpa was squirming around like a worm on a hot rock for a while. Then Zalasta took the ladies to a large house that had been fixed up for them. From what my deserter said, the house comes fairly close to being luxurious—if you discount the bars on the windows."

"He could have been coached," Sparhawk fretted. "Maybe he wasn't as drunk as he appeared to be."

"Believe me, Fron, he was drunk," Talen assured him. "I cut a purse on my way to that tavern—just to keep in practice—so I had plenty of money. I poured enough strong drink into him to stun a regiment."

"I think he's right, Fron," Stragen said. "There are just too many details for this to be a contrived story."

"And if this deserter had been sent to spin cobwebs for *our* benefit, why would he waste time and effort entertaining a young pickpocket?" Talen added. "None of us look the way we did the last time Zalasta saw us, and I doubt that even *he* could have guessed how Sephrenia and Xanetia put their heads together to modify us."

"I still think we should hold off," Sparhawk said. "Aphrael's going to put Xanetia into Natayos in a day or so, and Xanetia can find out for sure if it's really Ehlana who's locked up in that house."

"We could at least get closer," Stragen said.

"Why? Distance doesn't mean anything to my blue friend here." Sparhawk touched the bulge under the front of his tunic. "Just as soon as I know for certain that Ehlana's there, we'll go pay Zalasta and his bastard a call. I might even invite Khwaj to come along. He has some plans for them that sort of interest me."

The light was suddenly very bright, and the citizens of Sopal suddenly stopped jerking around like marionettes on strings and started to walk like normal humans. It had taken a half a day to explain to Ghnomb why it was necessary for them to return to real time, and the God of Eat still had some serious reservations about the whole idea.

"I'll wait in that tavern just up the street," Tynian said to Ulath as the two of them stepped out of the narrow alley. "Do you remember the password?"

Ulath grunted. "I shouldn't be long," he said. He walked across the street toward the pair of travelers who had just come into town. "That's an interesting looking saddlebow you've got there, neighbor," he said to one of them, a broken-nosed man on a roan horse. "What's it made of? Ramshorn?"

Berit gave him a startled look, then glanced quickly around the narrow street near the east gate of Sopal. "I didn't think to ask the saddlemaker, Sergeant," he replied, noticing the blond Elene's tattered-looking uniform jacket. "Ah—maybe you could give my young friend and me some advice."

"Advice is free. Go ahead and ask."

"Do you happen to know of a good inn here in Sopal?"

"The one my friend and I are staying at isn't too bad. It's about three streets over." Ulath pointed. "It's got the sign of a boar hanging out front—although the picture doesn't look very much like any boar *I've* ever seen."

"We'll look into it."

"Maybe my friend and I'll see you there. We're usually in the taproom after supper."

"We'll stop by—if we decide to stay there."

Ulath nodded and walked up the street to a tavern and went inside, where he joined Tynian at a table near the fire. "What did you do with our shaggy friend?" he asked.

"He went out looking for another dog," Tynian replied. "You might have made a mistake there, Sergeant. He seems to be developing a taste for them. There won't be a dog left in the whole town if we stay much longer."

Ulath sat down and leaned back. "Ran into an Elene fellow out there in the street," he said, loudly enough to be heard by the other tavern patrons.

"Oh?" Tynian said casually. "Astellian or Edomish?"

"It was sort of hard to say. He'd had his nose broken at one time or another, so it was a little hard to determine his race. He was looking for a good inn, so I recommended the one where we're staying. We might see him there. It's good to hear somebody talking Elenic for a change. I get tired of listening to people babbling at me in Tamul. If you're about finished here, why don't we drift on down to the harbor and see if we can find somebody to ferry us on across the lake to Tiana."

Tynian drained his tankard. "Let's go," he said, standing up.

The two of them left the tavern and strolled back to their inn, talking casually and moving at the leisurely pace of men with nothing really pressing to do.

"I want to have a look at that shoe on my horse's left forehoof," Ulath said when they arrived. "Go on ahead. I'll meet you in the taproom."

"Where else?" Tynian laughed.

Khalad was in the stable as Ulath had expected. He was making some show of currying Faran. "I see that you and your friend decided to stay here," the big Thalesian said in a casual tone.

"It was handy." Khalad shrugged.

"Listen carefully," Ulath said in a voice hardly more than a whisper. "We were able to pick up some information. Nothing's going to happen here. You'll get another one of those messages."

Khalad nodded.

"It's going to tell you to go on across the lake to Tiana. Be careful of what you say on the boat, because there'll be a fellow on board who's working for the other side—an Arjuni with a long scar on his cheek."

"I'll keep an eye out for him," Khalad said.

"You'll get another message in Tiana," Ulath continued. "You'll be told to go on around the lake to Arjun."

"That's the long way around," Khalad objected. "We could take the road from here and be in Arjun in less than half the time."

"Evidently they don't want you to get there that soon. They've probably got some other irons in the fire. I won't swear to this, but I *think* they'll send you on to Derel from Arjun. If Kalten's right and Ehlana's being held in Natayos, that would be the next logical step."

Khalad nodded again. "I'll tell Berit. I think we'd better stay out of that taproom. I'm sure we're being watched, and if we start talking with other Elenes, we'll just put the other side on their guard."

The horses in the stable suddenly began to squeal and kick at the sides of their stalls.

"What's wrong with the horses?" Khalad demanded. "And what's that odd smell?"

Ulath muttered an oath. Then he raised his voice and spoke in Trollish. "Bhlokw, it is not good that you come into the dens of the man-things this way. You have been eating dog, and the man-things and their beasts can smell you."

There was an injured silence as Ulath's unseen traveling companion withdrew from the stable.

Betuana and Engessa, dressed in sleek otterskins, accompanied Vanion and the knights south from Sarna. At Engessa's suggestion they proceeded due west to come down out of the mountains in eastern Cynesga.

"We've been watching them, Vanion-Preceptor," the towering Atan said as he loped along beside Vanion's horse. "Their main supply dump is about five leagues west of the frontier."

"Did you have anything pressing to attend to, your Majesty?" Vanion asked Betuana, who was running along on the other side.

"Nothing that can't wait. What did you have in mind?"

"Since we're here anyway, we might as well swing over and burn their supply dump. My knights are getting restless, and a little exercise might do them some good."

"It is rather chilly," she observed with just the hint of a smile. "A fire *would* be nice."

"Shall we, then?"

"Why don't we?"

The Cynesgan supply dump covered about five acres. It lay in a rocky, treeless basin, and it was defended by a regiment of Cynesgan troops in flowing robes. As the column of armored knights approached, the defenders galloped forth to meet them. That particular maneuver might best be described as a tactical blunder. The gravel-covered floor of the Desert of Cynesga was flat and clear of obstructions, so the charge of the Church Knights was unimpeded. There was an enormous crash as the two forces collided, and the knights, after only a momentary hesitation, rode on, trampling the bodies of the wounded and slain under the steel-shod hooves of their mounts while the squealing horses of the Cynesgans fled in terror.

"Impressive," Betuana conceded as she ran along beside Vanion's mount. "But isn't it tedious to endure the weight—and the smell—of the armor for months on end for the sake of two minutes of entertainment?"

"There are drawbacks to any style of warfare, your Majesty," Vanion said, raising his visor. "A part of the idea behind armored charges is to persuade others to avoid confrontations. It holds down the casualties in the long run."

"A reputation for extreme severity *is* a good weapon, Vanion-Preceptor," she agreed.

"We like it." He smiled. "Let's go build that bonfire so that your Majesty can warm her toes."

"That would be nice." She smiled.

There was a dust-covered hill directly ahead, rising like a slightly rounded pyramid to block the way to the supply dump. With simple arm gestures, Vanion directed his knights to diverge and sweep around both sides of the hill to swarm over the accumulated supplies of Cyrgon's army. They galloped forward with that vast, steely, clinking thunder that proclaims implacable invincibility.

And then the hill moved. The dust which had covered it shuddered away in a great billowing cloud, and the two enormous wings unfurled their glossy blackness to reveal the wedge-shaped face of Klæl. The beast of ultimate darkness roared, and the fangs of lightning, jagged and flickering, emerged from behind snarling lips.

And out from beneath the shelter of those two great wings came an army like no army Vanion had ever seen.

They were as tall as the Atans and more bulky. Their bare arms were huge, and their steel breastplates fit them like a second skin, revealing every knotted muscle. Their helmets bore exotic-looking embellishments—horns or antlers or stiff steel wings—and, like their breastplates, their visors fit tightly over their faces, exactly duplicating the features of each individual warrior. There was no humanity in those polished faces. The brows were impossibly wide, and, like the face of Klæl himself, they narrowed down to almost delicately pointed chins. The eye-slits blazed, and there were twin holes in place of noses. The mouths of those masks were open, and they were filled with cruelly pointed teeth.

They swarmed out from beneath Klæl's wings with his lightning playing around them. They brandished weapons that appeared to be part mace and part ax—steel atrocities dredged from a nightmare.

They were too close to permit any kind of orderly withdrawal, and the knights, still moving at a thunderous gallop, were committed before they could fully comprehend the nature of the enemy.

The impact as the two armies came together shook the earth, and that solid, steely crash shattered into a chaos of sound—blows, shrieks, the agonized squeals of horses, and the tearing of metal.

"Sound a withdrawal!" Vanion bellowed to the leader of the Genidians. "Blow your heart into that Ogre-horn, man! Get our people clear!"

The carnage was ghastly. Horses and men were being ripped to pieces by Klæl's inhuman army. Vanion drove his spurs home, and his horse leapt forward. The Pandion Preceptor drove his lance through the steel breastplate of one of the aliens and saw blood—at least he thought it might be blood, thick yellow blood—gushing from the steel-lipped mask. The creature fell back, but still swung its cruel weapon. Vanion pulled his hand clear of the butt of the lance, leaving the beast transfixed, skewered, as it were, and drew his sword.

It took a long time. The thing absorbed blows that would have dismembered a human. Eventually, however, Vanion chopped it down—almost like a peasant chopping at a tough, stringy thornbush.

"Engessa!" Betuana's shriek of rage and despair rang out above the other sounds of the battle.

Vanion wheeled his horse and saw the Atan queen rushing to the aid of her stricken general. Even the monstrous creatures Klæl had unleashed quailed in the face of her fury as she cut her way to Engessa's side.

Vanion smashed his way through to her, his sword flickering in the chill light, spraying yellow blood in gushing fountains. "Can you carry him?" he shouted to Betuana.

She bent and with no apparent effort lifted her fallen friend in her arms.

"Pull back!" Vanion shouted. "I'll cover you!" And he hurled his horse into the path of the monsters who were rushing to attack her.

There was no hope in Betuana's face as she ran toward the rear, cradling Engessa's limp body in her arms, and her eyes were streaming tears.

Vanion ground his teeth together, raised his sword, and charged.

Sephrenia was very tired when they reached Dirgis. "I'm not really hungry," she told Xanetia and Aphrael after they had taken a room in a respectable inn near the center of the city. "All I want is a nice hot bath and about twelve hours of sleep."

"Art thou unwell, sister mine?" Xanetia's voice was concerned.

Sephrenia smiled wearily. "No, dear," she said, laying one hand on the Anarae's arm, "just a little tired. All this rushing around is starting to wear on me. You two go ahead and have some supper. Just ask someone to bring a small pot of tea up to the room. That'll be enough for right now. I'll make up for it at breakfast time. Just don't make too much noise when you come up to bed."

She spent a pleasant half hour immersed to her ears in steaming water in the bathhouse and returned to their room tightly wrapped in her Styric robe and carrying a candle to light her way.

Their room was not large, but it was warm and cozy, heated by one of the porcelain stoves common in Tamuli. Sephrenia rather liked the concept of a stove, since it kept the ashes and cinders off the floor. She drew a chair close to the fire and began to brush her long, black hair.

"Vanity, Sephrenia? After all these years?"

She started half to her feet at the sound of the familiar voice. Zalasta scarcely looked the same. He no longer wore his Styric robe, but rather a leather jerkin of an Arjuni cut, stout canvas trousers, and thick-soled boots. He had even so far discarded his heritage that he wore a short sword at his waist. His white hair and beard were tangled, and his face was haggard. "Please don't make a scene, love," he told her. His voice was weary and devoid of any emotion beyond a kind of profound regret. He sighed. "Where did we go wrong, Sephrenia?" he asked sadly. "What tore us apart and brought us to this sorry state?"

"You don't really want me to tell you, do you, Zalasta?" she replied. "Why couldn't you just let it go? I *did* love you—not *that* way, of course, but it *was* love. Couldn't you accept that and forget about the other?"

"Evidently not. It didn't even occur to me."

"Sparhawk's going to kill you, you know."

"Perhaps. To be honest with you, though, I no longer really care."

"What's the point of this, then? Why have you come here?"

"I wanted to see you one last time—hear the sound of your voice." He rose from the chair in the corner where he had been sitting. "It all could have been so different—if it hadn't been for Aphrael. *She* was the one who took you into the lands of the Elenes and corrupted you. You're Styric, Sephrenia. We Styrics have no business consorting with the Elene barbarians."

"You're wrong, Zalasta. Anakha's an Elene. *That's* our business with them. You'd better leave. Aphrael's downstairs eating supper right now. If she finds you here, she'll have your heart for dessert."

"In a moment. There's something I have to do first. After that, she can do anything to me she wants to do." His face suddenly twisted into an expression of anguish. "Why, Sephrenia? Why? How could you *bear* the unclean touch of that Elene savage?"

"Vanion? You wouldn't understand. You couldn't even begin to comprehend it." She stood, her face defiant. "Do whatever it is you have to do and leave. The very sight of you sickens me."

"Very well." His face was suddenly as cold as stone.

She was not really surprised when he drew a long bronze dagger out from under his jerkin. In spite of everything, he was still Styric enough to loathe the touch of steel. "You have no idea of how much I regret this," he told her as he came closer.

She tried to struggle, clawing at his face and eyes as she called out for help. She even felt a momentary sense of triumph when she seized his beard and saw him wince with pain. She jerked at his beard, sawing his face this way and that, but then he jerked free, roughly shoving her back from him. She stumbled back and half fell over a chair, and that was what ultimately defeated her. Even as she struggled to regain her feet, he caught her by the hair, and she knew that she was lost. Despairing, she drew Vanion's face from her memory, filling her eyes and heart with his features even as she attempted again to claw at Zalasta's eyes.

And then he drove the dagger directly into her breast and wrenched it free again.

She cried out, falling back and clutching at the wound, feeling the blood spurting out between her fingers.

He caught her in his arms. "I love you, Sephrenia," he said in a broken voice as the light faded from her eyes.

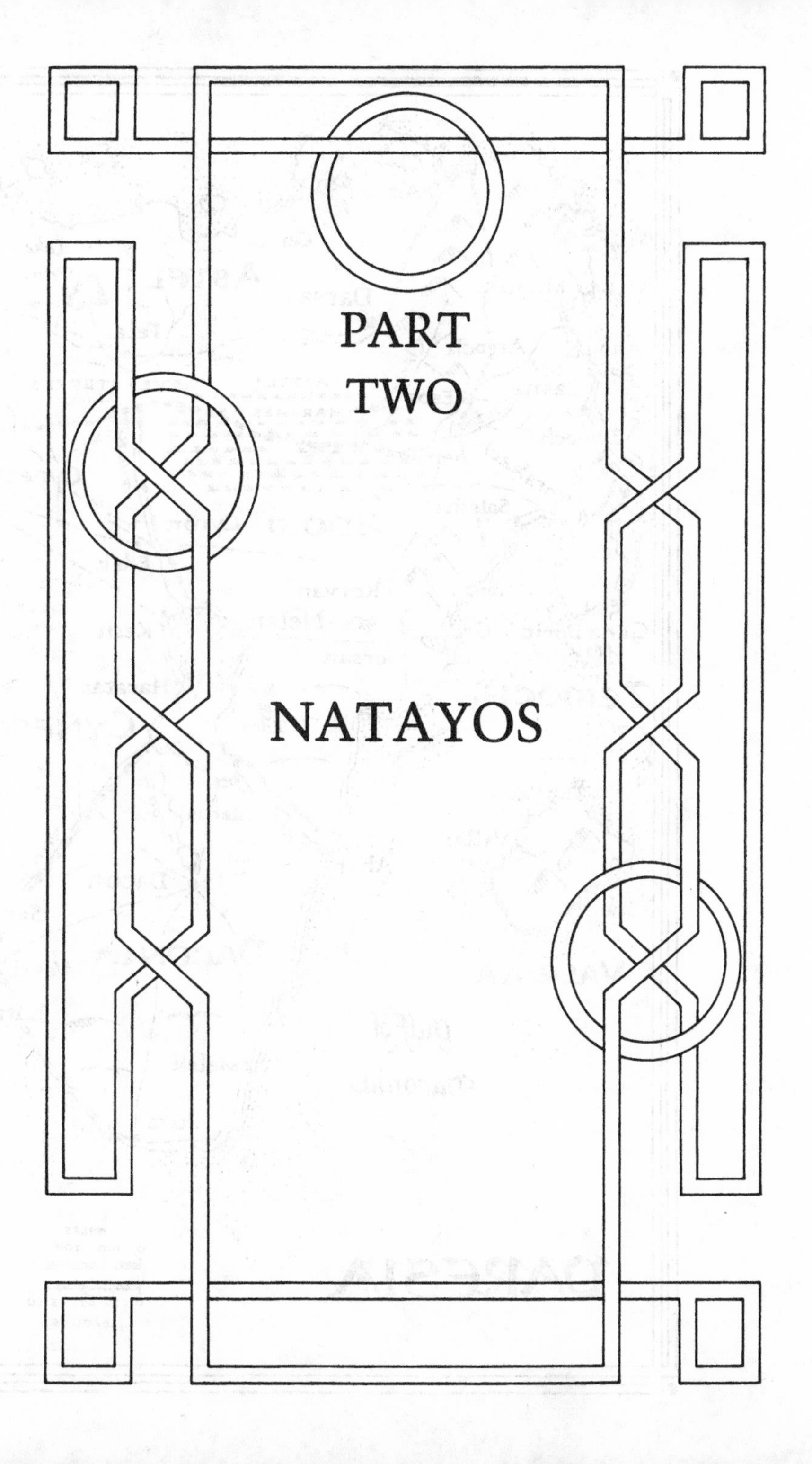

PART TWO

NATAYOS

Aleric
Cenae
ASTEL
Lake Pela
Merjuk
Darsas
Pela
Aka
Argoch
R. Antun
Basne
Esos
ASTEL MARSHES
THE STEPPES
R. Esos
Zemoch
Korakach
Pela R.
Cynestra
R. Edek
Salesha
EDOM
Cyron
Edek
Korvan
DESERT O
Nelan
Kesh
Gana Dorit
Jorsan
Harata
Sea of Edom
ZEMOCH
CYNESGA
Ederus
Dacon R.
Verel R.
Valles
R. Ahar
Ahar
Dacon
Saras
DACONIA
Verel
VALESIA
Kaftal
Gulf of Daconia
Melek
Jura
MILES
0 100 200 300
0 25 50 75 100
LEAGUES
DARESIA

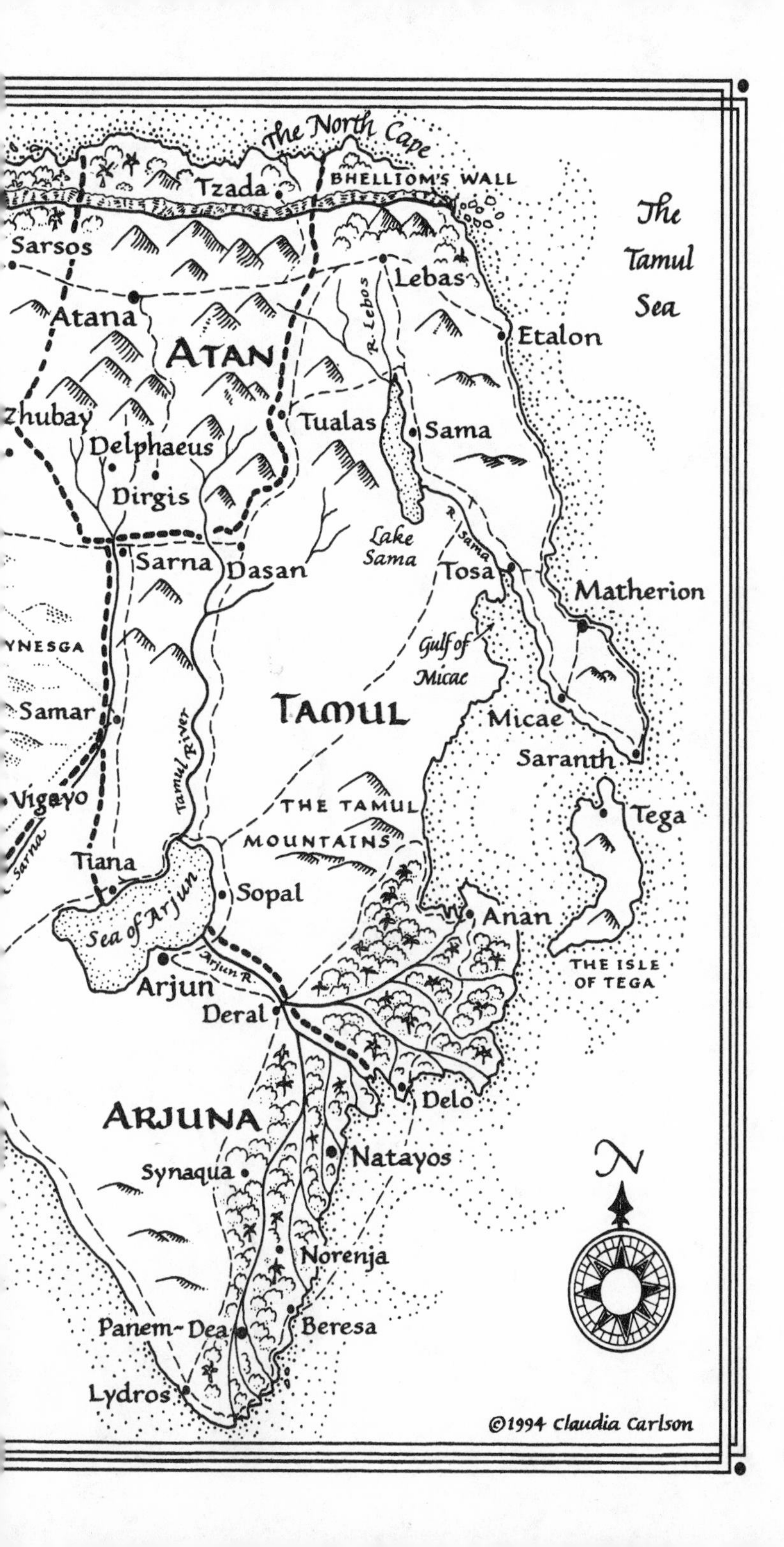
The North Cape
BHELLIOM'S WALL
Tzada
The Tamul Sea
Sarsos
Lebas
R. Lebos
Atana
Etalon
ATAN
Zhubay
Tualas
Sama
Delphaeus
Dirgis
Lake Sama
R. Sama
Sarna
Dasan
Tosa
Matherion
YNESGA
Gulf of Micae
TAMUL
Samar
Micae
Tamul River
Saranth
Vigayo
THE TAMUL MOUNTAINS
Tega
Sarna
Tiana
Sopal
Sea of Arjun
Anan
Arjun R.
THE ISLE OF TEGA
Arjun
Deral
Delo
ARJUNA
Natayos
Synaqua
N
Norenja
Panem-Dea
Beresa
Lydros
©1994 Claudia Carlson

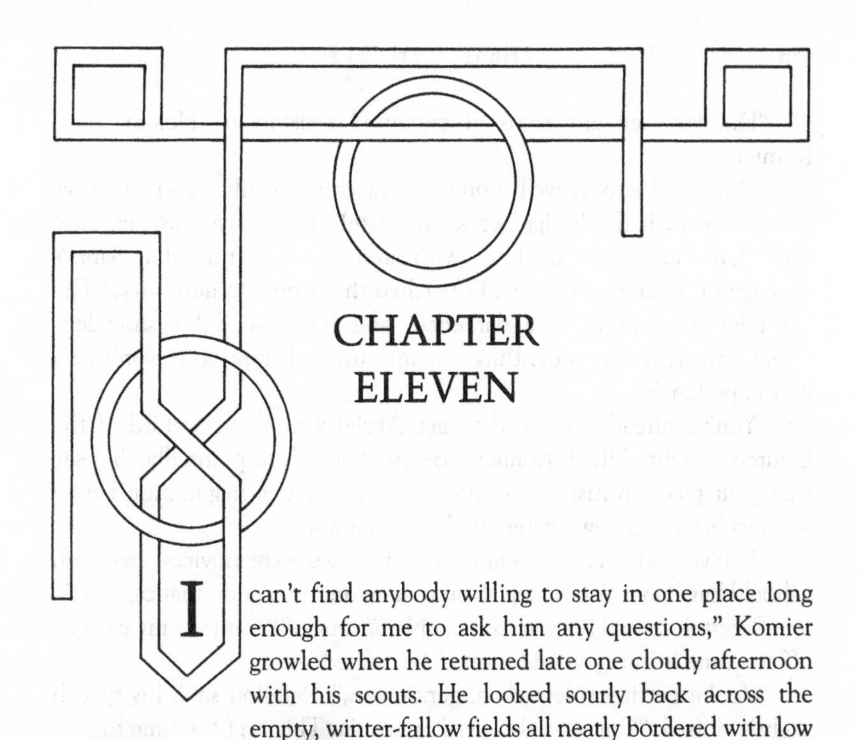

CHAPTER ELEVEN

I can't find anybody willing to stay in one place long enough for me to ask him any questions," Komier growled when he returned late one cloudy afternoon with his scouts. He looked sourly back across the empty, winter-fallow fields all neatly bordered with low stone walls, carefully shifting his broken right arm. "These Astellian serfs all take one look at us and bolt for the woods like frightened deer."

"What's ahead?" Darellon asked him. Darellon's helmet hung from his saddlebow, one side so crushed in that it no longer fit his bandaged head. His eyes were unfocused, and his bandage was bloodsoaked.

Komier took out his map and studied it. "We're coming to the River Astel," he replied. "We saw a city over on the other side—Darsas, most likely. I couldn't catch anybody to tell me for sure, though. I'm not the prettiest fellow in the world, but I've never had people flee from me in terror like this before."

"Emban warned us about that," Bergsten said. "The countryside's crawling with agitators. They're telling the serfs that we've all got horns and tails and that we're coming here to burn down their churches and ram assorted heresies down their throats at swordpoint. This fellow called Sabre seems to be the one behind it all."

"He's the one I want," Komier muttered darkly. "I think I'll run him down and set him up as the centerpiece in a bonfire."

"Let's not stir up the locals any more than they already are, Komier," Darellon cautioned. "We're not in any condition for confrontations at the moment." He glanced back at the battered column and the long string of wagons bearing the gravely wounded.

"Did you see any signs of organized resistance?" Heldin asked Komier.

"Not yet. I expect we'll find out how things really stand when we get to Darsas. If the bridge across the Astel's been torn down and the tops of the city walls are lined with archers, we'll know that Sabre's message of peace and good will's reached the people in authority." The Genidian Preceptor's face darkened, and he squared his shoulders. "That's all right. I've fought my way into towns before, so it won't be a new experience."

"You've already managed to get Abriel and about a third of the Church Knights killed, Komier," Bergsten told him pointedly. "I'd say that your place in history's secure. Let's try a bit of negotiation before we start battering down gates and burning houses."

"You've had a clever mouth ever since we were novices, Bergsten. I should have done something about that before you put on that cassock."

Bergsten hefted his war ax a couple of times. "I can take my cassock off any time it suits you, old friend," he offered.

"You're getting sidetracked, gentlemen," Darellon said, his speech slightly slurred. "Our wounded need attention. This isn't the time to pick fights—either with the local population or with each other. I think the four of us should ride on ahead under a flag of truce and find out which way the wind's blowing before we start building siege engines."

"Am I hearing the voice of reason here?" Heldin rumbled mildly.

They tied a gleaming white Cyrinic cape to Sir Heldin's lance and rode ahead through the cheerless afternoon to the west bank of the River Astel.

The city beyond the river was clearly Elene, an ancient town with soaring towers and spires. It stood proudly and solidly on the far shore of the river under its snapping pennons of red and blue and gold proclaiming, or so it seemed, that it had always been there and always would be. It had high, thick walls and massive, closed gates. The bridge across the Astel was blocked by towering, bronze-faced warriors wearing minimal armor and carrying very unpleasant looking weapons. "Atans," Sir Heldin identified them. "We definitely don't want to fight those people."

The ranks of bleak-faced infantry parted, and an ancient, wrinkled Tamul in a gold-colored mantle came forward to meet them flanked by a vastly bearded Astellian clergyman all in black. "Well met, Sir Knights," the hairless old Tamul greeted the armored men in a dry, dusty voice. "King Alberen's a trifle curious as to your intentions. We don't see Church Knights in this part of the world very often."

"You would be Ambassador Fontan," Bergsten said. "Emban described you very well."

"I thought he had better manners," Fontan murmured.

Bergsten flashed him a brief smile. "You might want to send word back to the city, your Excellency. Assure his Majesty that our intentions are entirely peaceful."

"I'm sure he'll be happy to hear that."

"Emban and Sir Tynian came back to Chyrellos a couple of months ago," Bergsten continued. "Sparhawk sent word that things were getting out of hand here. Dolmant dispatched us to help restore order." The huge patriarch made a sour face. "We didn't get off to a very good start, I'm afraid. We had an unfortunate encounter near Basne and we have many wounded in need of medical attention."

"I'll send word to the nearby monasteries, Sir Knight," the bearded clergyman standing at Fontan's elbow offered.

"Bergsten's not a knight any more, your Reverence," Komier corrected him. "He *used* to be, but God had other plans for him. He's a Patriarch of the Church now. He prays well enough, I suppose, but we haven't been able to get his ax away from him yet."

"My manners must be slipping," Fontan apologized. "My friend here is Archimandrite Monsel, the duly anointed head of the Church of Astel."

"Your Grace." Bergsten inclined his head politely.

"Your Grace," Monsel replied, looking curiously at the warlike clergyman. "Your friend Emban and I had some very stimulating discussions about our doctrinal differences. You and I might want to continue those, but let's see to your wounded first. How many injured men do you have?"

"Roughly twenty thousand, your Grace," Komier answered bleakly. "It's a little hard to keep an exact count. A few score die on us every hour or so."

"What in God's name did you encounter up in those mountains?" Monsel gasped.

"The King of Hell, as closely as we can determine, your Grace," Darellon replied. "We left thirty thousand dead on the field—mostly Cyrinics. Lord Abriel, their preceptor, led the charge, and his knights followed close behind him. They were fully engaged before they realized what they were up against." He sighed. "Abriel was nearing seventy, and he seemed to think he was leading his last charge."

"He was right about that," Komier grunted sourly. "There wasn't enough of him left to bury."

"He died well, though," Heldin added. "Do you have any fast messengers available, your Excellency? Sparhawk and Vanion are counting on us to reach Matherion as soon as possible, so we'd probably better let them know that we're going to be delayed."

"His name's Valash," Stragen told Sparhawk and Talen as the three of them, still wearing their tar-smeared sailor's smocks, stepped out of the noisy torchlit street into a dark, foul-smelling alley. "He and his two friends are Dacites from Verel."

"Have you been able to find out who they're working for?" Sparhawk asked him as they stopped to let their eyes adjust to the darkness and their noses to the smell. The alleys of Beresa were particularly unpleasant.

"I heard one of them mention Ogerajin," Stragen replied. "It makes sense, I guess. Ogerajin and Zalasta seem to be old friends."

"I thought Ogerajin's brains were rotting out," Talen objected.

"Maybe he has lucid moments. It doesn't really matter who sent them, though. While they're here, they're reporting to Krager. As near as I can make out, they've been sent to assess the damage we did to them during the Harvest Festival and to pick up any bits of information that fall to hand. They've got money, but they don't want to turn much of it loose. They're in this strictly for gain—and for the chance to seem important."

"Does Krager come here to get their reports?" Sparhawk asked.

"He hasn't recently. Valash communicates with him by messenger. These three Dacites are seriously out of their depth here. They want to hold on to as much of the money Ogerajin gave them as they can, but they don't want to miss anything important. They aren't professionals by any stretch of the imagination. They spend most of their time trying to figure out some way to get information without paying for it."

"A swindler's dream," Talen noted. "What did they do for a living back in Verel?"

"They sold children to people whose tastes run in that direction," Stragen replied in a disgusted tone. "As I understand it, Ogerajin used to be one of their best customers."

"That puts them right at the bottom, doesn't it?"

"Probably even lower than that." Stragen glanced around to make sure they were alone. "Valash wants to meet you two." Stragen pointed toward the end of the alley. "He's just up those stairs. He's renting a corner in the loft from a fellow who deals in stolen goods."

Talen smiled a rather nasty little smile. "If these Dacites just happened to pass too much erroneous information and false rumors on to Krager, he might just decide that they've outlived their usefulness, wouldn't you say?"

"Probably." Stragen shrugged.

"That sort of stirs my creativity."

"Oh? Why's that?"

"I don't like people who sell children. It's a personal sort of thing. Let's go meet this Valash. I'd like to find out if he's as gullible as you say."

They climbed a rickety outside stairway to a door that was flimsy and patched and showed some signs of having been kicked in a few times. The loft beyond the door was incredibly cluttered with all manner of worn clothing, battered furniture, and dented kitchen utensils. There were even broken farm tools gathering dust in the corners. "Some people will steal anything," Talen sniffed.

A lone candle guttered on the far side of the room, and a bony Elene sat drowsing at a table by its uncertain light. He wore a short green brocade jacket of a Daconian cut, and his sparse mud-colored hair stood almost straight up, looking much like a thin, dirty halo around his gaunt head. As they crossed the loft toward him, he stirred himself and quickly picked up some papers and began to shuffle them in a self-important manner. He looked up with feigned impatience as they approached. "You're late, Vymer," he accused in a high-pitched, nasal voice.

"Sorry, Master Valash," Stragen apologized in a servile tone. "Fron and I were busy extricating young Reldin here from a tense situation. Reldin's very good, but he overextends himself sometimes. Anyway, you wanted to meet my associates." He laid one hand on Sparhawk's shoulder. "This is Fron. He's a tavern brawler, so we let him deal with any situation that can be settled with a few quick punches or a kick in the belly. The boy there is Reldin, the nimblest sneak thief I've ever known. He can wriggle through mouseholes, and his ears are sharp enough to hear ants crossing the street on the other side of town."

"I just want to hire him, Vymer," Valash said. "I don't want to buy him." He giggled at his own joke. He smirked at them, clearly expecting them to join in his laughter. Talen, however, did not laugh. His eyes took on an icy glitter.

Valash seemed a bit abashed by their reception of his feeble joke. "Why are you all dressed as sailors?" he asked, more for something to say than out of any real curiosity.

Stragen shrugged. "It's a port city, Master Valash. The streets are crawling with sailors, so three more won't attract any particular attention."

Valash grunted. "Have you anything for me that I might find worth my while?" he asked in a superior, bored tone of voice.

Talen snatched off his cap. "You'll have to decide that for yourself, Master Valash," he whined, as he bowed awkwardly. "I *did* come across something, if you'd care to hear it."

"Go on," Valash told him.

"Well, sir, there's this rich Tamul merchant who owns a big house over in the fancy part of town. He's got a tapestry on the wall of his study that I've had my eye on for quite some time now. It's a very good one—lots of tiny stitches, and the color hasn't faded very much. The only trouble is that it covers the whole wall. You can get a fortune for really good tapestry, but only if you can get it all out in one piece. It's not worth much if you have to cut it up to carry it out. Anyway, I went into his house the other night to try and come up with some way to get it out without butchering it. The merchant was in the study, though, and he had a friend with him—some noble from the imperial court at Matherion. I listened at the door, and the noble was telling the merchant about some of the rumors running around the imperial palace. Everybody's saying that the emperor's very unhappy with these people from Eosia. That attempt to overthrow the government last fall really frightened him, and he'd like to come to some kind of agreement with his enemies, but this Sparhawk person won't let him. Sarabian's convinced that they're going to lose, so he's secretly outfitted a fleet of ships all loaded down with treasure and as soon as trouble shows up on the horizon, he's going to make a run for it. The courtiers all know about his plans, so they're secretly making arrangements for their own escapes when the fighting starts. Some morning very soon this Sparhawk's going to wake up and find an unfriendly army at his gates and nobody around to help hold them off." He paused. "Was that the sort of information you wanted?"

The Dacite made some effort to conceal his excited interest. He put on a deprecating expression. "It's nothing we haven't heard before. About all it does is help to confirm what we've already picked up." He tentatively pushed a couple of small silver coins across the table. "I'll pass it on to Panem-Dea and see what they think about it."

Talen looked at the coins and then at Valash. Then he crammed his cap back on. "I'll be leaving now, Vymer," he said in a flat tone, "and don't waste my time on this cheapskate again."

"Don't be in such a rush," Stragen said placatingly. "Let me talk with him first."

"You're making a mistake, Valash," Sparhawk told the Dacite. "You've got a heavy purse hanging off your belt. If you try to cheat Reldin, he'll come back some night and slice open the bottom of it. He won't leave you enough to buy breakfast."

Valash put his hand protectively over his purse. Then he opened it with what appeared to be extreme reluctance.

"I thought Lord Scarpa was at Natayos," Stragen said casually. "Has he moved his operations to Panem-Dea?"

Valash was sweating as he counted out coins, his fingers lingering on each one as if he were parting with an old friend. "There are a lot of things you don't know about our operation, Vymer," he replied. He gave Talen a pleading look as he tentatively pushed the money across the table.

Talen made no move to accept the coins.

Valash made a whimpering sound and added more coins.

"That's a little better," Talen told him, scooping up the money.

"Then Scarpa's moved?" Stragen asked.

"Of course not," Valash retorted. "You didn't think his *whole* army's at Natayos, did you?"

"That's what I'd heard. He has other strongholds as well, I take it?"

"Of course. Only a fool puts his entire force in one place, and Scarpa's far from being a fool, I'll tell the world. He's been recruiting men in the Elene kingdoms of western Tamuli for years now, and he sends them all to Lydros and then on to Panem-Dea for training. After that, they go on to either Synaqua or Norenja. Only his crack troops are at Natayos. His army's at least five times larger than most people believe. These jungles positively seethe with his men."

Sparhawk carefully concealed a smile. Valash obviously had a great need to appear important, and that need made him reveal things he shouldn't be talking about.

"I didn't know Scarpa's army was so big," Stragen admitted. "It makes me feel better. It might be nice to be on the winning side for a change."

"It's about time," Sparhawk growled. "I'm getting a little tired of being chased out of every town we visit before I've even had the time to unpack my seabag." He squinted at Valash. "As long as the subject's come up anyway, could we expect Scarpa's people out there in the brush to take us in if things turn sour and we make a run for it?"

"What could possibly go wrong?"

"Have you ever taken a good look at an Atan, Valash? They're as tall as trees and they've got shoulders like bulls. They do unpleasant things to people, so I want a friendly place to come down if I suddenly have to take flight. Are there any other safe places out there in the woods?"

Valash's expression grew wary as if he had suddenly realized that he'd said too much already.

"Ah—I think we know what we need to, Fron," Stragen interposed smoothly. "There *are* safe places out there if we really need to find them. I'm sure there are many things Master Valash knows that he's not supposed to talk about."

Valash puffed himself up slightly, and his expression took on a knowing, secretive cast. "You understand the situation perfectly Vymer," he said. "It wouldn't be proper for me to reveal things Lord Scarpa's told me in strictest confidence." He pointedly picked up his papers again.

"We won't keep you from important matters, Master Valash," Stragen said, backing away. "We'll nose around town some more and let you know if we find out anything else."

"I'd appreciate that, Vymer," Valash replied, shuffling his papers as his visitors departed.

"What an ass," Talen muttered as the three of them carefully descended the rickety staircase to the alley again.

"Where did you learn so much about tapestry?" Sparhawk asked him.

"I don't know anything about tapestry."

"You were talking as if you did."

"I talk about a lot of things I don't know anything about. It fills in the gaps when you're trying to peddle something that's worthless. I could tell by the way Valash's eyes glazed over when I mentioned the word *tapestry* that he didn't know any more about it than I did. He was too busy trying to make us think that he's important to pay any real attention. I could get rich from that one. I could sell him blue butter."

Sparhawk gave him a puzzled look.

"It's a swindler's term," Stragen explained. "The meaning's a little obscure."

"I'm sure it is."

"Did you want me to explain it?"

"Not particularly, no,"

"Is it a family custom? Or just a way to honor your father?" Berit asked Khalad as the two of them, wearing mail shirts and grey cloaks, lounged against the forward rail of the scruffy lake freighter plodding across the Sea of Arjun from Sopal to Tiana.

Khalad shrugged. "No, it's nothing like that. It's just that the men in our family all have heavy beards—except for Talen. If I decided not to wear a beard, I'd have to shave twice a day. I clip it close with scissors once a week and let it go at that. It saves time."

Berit rubbed at his altered cheek. "I wonder what Sparhawk would do if I let his beard grow," he mused.

"*He* might not do anything, but Queen Ehlana would probably peel you like an apple. She likes his face just the way it is. She's even fond of that crooked nose."

"It looks as if we've got weather up ahead." Berit pointed toward the west.

Khalad frowned. "Where did *that* come from? The sky was clear just a minute ago. It's funny I didn't smell it coming."

The cloud bank hovering low on the western horizon was purplish black, and it roiled ominously, swelling upward with surprising speed. There were flickers of lightning deep inside the cloud, and the sullen rumble of thunder came to them across the dark, choppy waters of the lake.

"I hope these sailors know what they're doing," Berit said. "That has the earmarks of a very nasty squall."

They continued to watch the inky cloud as it boiled higher and higher, covering more and more of the western sky.

"That's not a natural storm, Berit," Khalad said tensely. "It's building too fast."

Then there was a shocking crash of thunder, and the cloud blanched and shuddered as the lightning seethed within it. Both the young men saw the shadowy shape in the instant that the bluish lightning thrust back the darkness to reveal what lay hidden in the cloud. "Klæl!" Berit gasped, staring at the monstrous, winged shape half-concealed in the churning stormfront.

The next crash of thunder ripped the sky, and the shabby vessel shuddered in the overwhelming sound. The inverted wedge of Klæl's face seemed to ripple and change in the midst of its veiling cloud, and the slitted eyes flamed in sudden rage. The great, batlike wings began to claw at the approaching storm, and the awful mouth opened to roar forth the thunder of Klæl's frustration. He howled in vast fury, and his enormous arms stretched up into the murky air, reaching hungrily to clutch at something that was not there.

And then the thing was gone, and the unnatural cloud tattered and streamed harmlessly off to the southeast to become no more than a dirty smudge on the horizon. The air, however, was filled with a sulfurous reek.

"You'd better pass the word to Aphrael," Khalad said grimly. "Klæl's loose again. He was looking for something, and he didn't find it. God knows where he'll look next."

"Komier's arm is broken in three places," Sir Heldin rumbled when he joined the mail-shirted Patriarch Bergsten, Ambassador Fontan, and Archimandrite Monsel in Monsel's book-littered study in the east wing of the palace, "and Darellon's still seeing two of everything. Komier can travel if he has to, but I think we'd better leave Darellon here until he recovers."

"How many knights are fit to ride?" Bergsten asked.

"Forty thousand at most, your Grace."

"We'll just have to make do with what we've got. Emban knew that we'd probably come this way; he's been sending messengers by the platoon. Things are coming to a head in southeastern Tamuli. Sparhawk's wife has been taken hostage, and our enemies are offering to trade her for Bhelliom. There's a rebel army in the Arjuni jungles preparing to march on Matherion, and two more armies massing on the eastern frontier of Cynesga. If those armies all join up, the game's over. Emban wants us to ride east across the steppes until we're past the Astel Marshes and then turn south and lay siege to the Cynesgan capital. He needs a diversion of some kind to pull those armies back from the border."

Sir Heldin pulled out his map. "It's workable," he said after a moment's study, "but we're going to be a little light for that kind of job."

"We'll get by. Vanion's in the field, but he's badly outnumbered along that Cynesgan frontier. If we don't create enough of a disturbance to relieve some of the pressure on him, he'll be swarmed under."

Heldin looked speculatively at the huge Thalesian patriarch. "You're not going to like this, your Grace," he said, "but there's not much choice in the matter."

"Go ahead," Bergsten told him.

"You're going to have to lay your cassock aside and take command. Abriel's been killed, Darellon's incapacitated, and if Komier gets into a fight, the weight of his ax will cripple him."

"*You're* still here, Heldin. You can take charge."

Heldin shook his head. "I'm not a preceptor, your Grace, and everybody in the army knows it. I'm also a Pandion, and the other orders have strong feelings about us. We haven't made very many friends in the past couple of centuries. The other orders won't accept me as commander. You're a patriarch, and you speak for Sarathi—and the Church. They'll accept you with no argument."

"It's out of the question."

"Then we'll have to sit here until Dolmant sends us a new commander."

"We *can't* wait!"

"My point exactly. Do I have your permission to tell the knights that you're taking command?"

"I can't, Heldin. You know that I'm forbidden to use magic."

"We can work our way around that, your Grace. There are plenty of accomplished magicians in the ranks. Just tell us what you want done, and we'll see to it."

"I've taken an oath."

"You took another one earlier, Lord Bergsten. You promised to defend the Church. *That* oath takes precedence in this situation."

The hugely bearded and black-robed Archimandrite Monsel looked speculatively at the reluctant Thalesian. Then he spoke in a neutral sort of way. "Would you like an independent opinion, Bergsten?"

Bergsten scowled at him.

"You're going to get it anyway," the Astellian churchman said with unruffled calm. "Given the nature of our opponent, we're face to face with a 'Crisis of the Faith,' and that suspends all the other rules. God needs your ax, Bergsten, not your theology." He squinted at the Thalesian Patriarch. "You don't seem convinced," he said.

"I'm not trying to be offensive, Monsel, but 'Crisis of the Faith' can't just be pulled out and dusted off whenever we want to bend some rules."

"All right, let's try this one, then. This is Astel, and your Church at Chyrellos recognizes *my* authority here. As long as we're in Astel, *I* speak for God."

Bergsten pulled off his helmet and absently polished the glossy black Ogre-horns on his sleeve. "Technically, I suppose," he conceded.

"Technicalities are the very soul of doctrine, your Grace." Monsel's huge beard bristled with disputational fervor. "Do you agree that I speak for God here in Astel?"

"All right, for the sake of argument, yes."

"I'm glad you agree; I'd hate to have to excommunicate you. Now then, I speak for God here, and God wants you to take command of the Church Knights. Go forth and smite God's enemies, my son, and may heaven strengthen your arm."

Bergsten squinted out the window at the dirty-looking sky for a long moment, mulling the clearly specious argument over in his mind. "You take full responsibility, Monsel?" he asked.

"I do."

"That's good enough for me, then." Bergsten crammed his helmet back on his head. "Sir Heldin, go tell the knights that I'm assuming command of the four orders. Instruct them to make all the necessary preparations. We march first thing in the morning."

"At once, General Bergsten," Heldin replied, coming to attention.

Anakha, Bhelliom's voice echoed in the vaults of Sparhawk's mind, *thou must awaken.*

Even before he opened his eyes, Sparhawk could feel a light touch on the thong about his neck. He caught the little hand and opened his eyes. "What do you think you're doing?" he demanded of the Child-Goddess.

"I *have* to have the Bhelliom, Sparhawk!" Her voice was desperate, and her eyes were streaming tears.

"What's going on, Aphrael? Calm down and tell me what's happened."

"Sephrenia's been stabbed! She's dying! Please, Sparhawk! Give me the Bhelliom!"

He came to his feet all in one motion. "Where did this happen?"

"In Dirgis. She was getting ready for bed, and Zalasta came into her room. He stabbed her in the *heart*, Sparhawk! Please, Father, give me the Bhelliom! I've got to have it to save her!"

"She's still alive?"

"Yes, but I don't know for how long! Xanetia's with her. She's using a Delphaeic spell to keep her breathing, but she's dying, my sister's dying!" She wailed and hurled herself into his arms, weeping uncontrollably.

"Stop that, Aphrael! This isn't helping. When did this happen?"

"A couple of hours ago. Please, Sparhawk! Only Bhelliom can save her!"

"We *can't*, Aphrael! If we take Bhelliom out of that box, Cyrgon will know immediately that we're trying to trick him, and Scarpa will kill your mother!"

The Child-Goddess clung to him, sobbing uncontrollably. "I *know!*" she wailed. "What are we going to do, Father? We *can't* just let her die!"

"Can't *you* do something?"

"The knife touched her heart, Sparhawk! I can't reverse that! Only Bhelliom has that kind of power!"

Sparhawk's soul seemed to shrivel, and he smashed at the wall with his fist. He lifted his face. "What can I do?" he hurled his voice upward. "What in God's name can I do?"

Compose thyself, Anakha! Bhelliom's voice was sharp in his mind. *Thou wilt serve neither Sephrenia nor thy mate by this unseemly display!*

We have to do something, Blue-Rose!

Thou art not at this moment fit to decide. Thou must therefore be ruled by me. Go at once and do as the Child-Goddess doth entreat thee.

Thou wilt condemn my wife!

That is not certain, Anakha. Sephrenia, however, doth linger on the brink of death. That much is certain. It is her *need that is most pressing.*

No! I can't do that!

Thou wilt obey me, Anakha! Thou art my *creature, and therefore subject to* my *will! Go thou and do as I have commanded thee!*

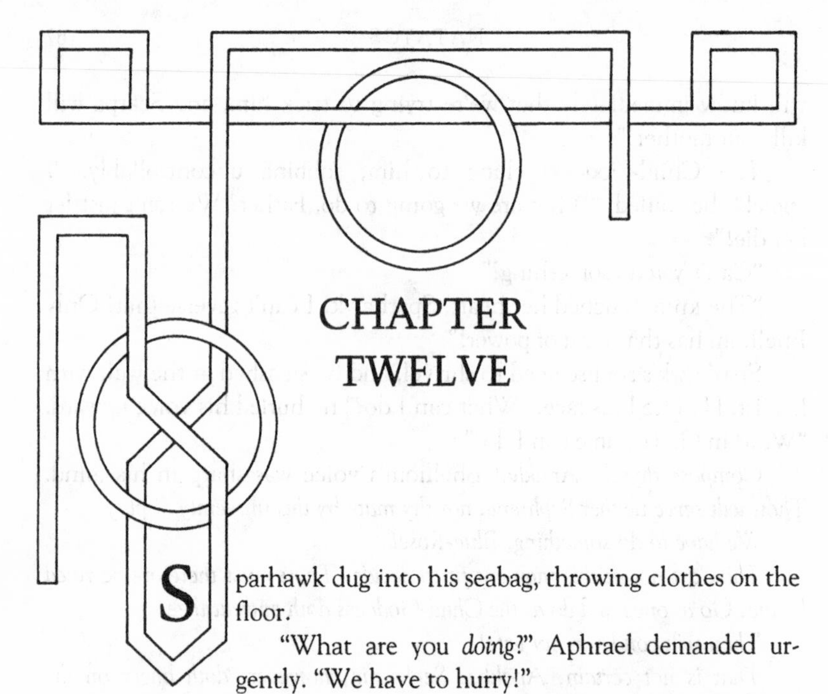

CHAPTER TWELVE

Sparhawk dug into his seabag, throwing clothes on the floor.

"What are you *doing*?" Aphrael demanded urgently. "We have to hurry!"

"I've got to leave a note for Stragen, but I can't find any paper."

"Here." She held out her hand, and a sheet of parchment appeared in it.

"Thank you." He took the parchment and continued to rummage in the bag.

"Get *on* with it, Sparhawk."

"I need something to write with."

She muttered something in Styric and handed him a quill and a small inkpot.

Vymer, Sparhawk scribbled, *something's come up, and I'll be gone for a while. Keep Reldin out of trouble*. And he signed it, *Fron*. Then he laid it in the center of Stragen's bed.

"*Now* can we go?" she asked impatiently.

"How are you going to do this?" He picked up his cloak.

"We have to get out of town first. I don't want anybody to see us. What's the quickest way to the woods?"

"East. It's about a mile to the edge of the forest."

"Let's go."

They left the room, hurrying down the stairs and out into the street. Sparhawk picked her up and half enfolded her in his cloak.

"I can walk," she protested.

"Not without attracting attention, you can't. You're a Styric, and people would notice that." He started off down the street, carrying her in his arms.

"Can't you go any faster?"

"Just let me handle this part of it, Aphrael. If I start running, people will think I've stolen you." He looked around to make sure no one on the muddy street was close enough to hear. "How are you going to manage this?" he asked her. "There *are* people out there who can feel it when you tamper with things, you know. We don't want to attract attention."

She frowned. "I'm not sure. I was upset when I came here."

"Are you *trying* to get your mother killed?"

"That's a hateful thing to say." She pursed her little mouth in thought. "There's always a certain amount of noise," she mused.

"I didn't quite follow that."

"It's one of the disadvantages of having our two worlds overlap the way they do. The sounds of one spill over into the other. Most humans can't hear us—or feel us—when we move around, but *we* can definitely hear and feel each other."

Sparhawk crossed the street to avoid a noisy brawl that had just erupted from a sailors' tavern. "If the others can hear you, how are you going to hide what you're doing?"

"You didn't let me finish, Sparhawk. We're not alone here. There are others all around us—my family, the Tamul Gods, your Elene God, various spirits and ghosts, and the air's positively littered with the Powerless Ones. Sometimes they flock up like migrating birds."

He stopped and stepped back to let a rickety charcoal wagon creak past. "Who are these 'Powerless Ones'?" he asked her. "Are they dangerous?"

"Hardly. They don't even really exist any more. They're nothing but memories—old myths and legends."

"Are they real? Could I see them?"

"Not unless you believe in them. They were Gods once, but their worshippers either died out or were converted to the worship of other Gods. They wail and flutter around the edges of reality without substance or even thought. All they have is need." She sighed. "We go out of fashion, Sparhawk—like last year's gowns or old shoes and hats. The Powerless Ones are discarded Gods who shrink and shrink as the years go by until they're finally nothing at all but a kind of anguished wailing." She sighed again. "Anyway," she went on, "there's all this noise in the background, and it sometimes makes it hard to concentrate or pick out specifics."

They passed another smelly tavern loud with drunken song. "Is this noise something like that?" Sparhawk asked, jerking his head toward the singing, "meaningless sound that fills up your ears and keeps you from hearing what you're really listening for?"

"More or less. We have a couple of senses that you don't, though, so we know when others are around, for one thing, and we know when they're doing things—tampering, if you want to call it that—for another. Maybe I can hide what I'm doing in all that other noise. How much farther do we have to go?"

He turned a corner into a quiet street. "We're coming to the edge of town now." He shifted her in his arms and continued on up the street, walking a little faster now. The houses here on the outskirts of Beresa were more substantial, and they were set back from the streets in aloof, self-important pride. "After we go through the charcoal yards, we'll come to the woods," he told her. "Are you *sure* this noise that I can't hear will be loud enough to hide your spells?"

"I'll see if I can get some help. I just thought of something. Cyrgon doesn't know exactly where I am, and it'll take him a little while to identify me and pinpoint my exact location. I'll ask some of the others to come here and have a party or something. If they're loud enough, and if I move fast enough, he won't even know that I've been here."

There were only a few workmen tending the sullen fires in the charcoal yards that ringed Beresa, incurious men, blackened by their tasks and far gone with drink, who lurched around the smoky flames like hellish imps dancing on eternal coals. Sparhawk walked even faster now, carrying the distraught Child-Goddess toward the shadowy edge of the tangled forest.

"I'll need to be able to see the sky," she told him. "I don't want any tree limbs in my way." She paused. "Are you afraid of heights?" she asked.

"Not particularly, why?"

"Just asking. Don't get excited when we start. I won't let anything happen to you. You'll be perfectly safe as long as I'm holding your hand." She paused again. "Oh, dear," she murmured. "I just remembered something."

"What?" He pushed aside a branch and slipped past it into the darkness of the forest.

"I have to be real when I do this."

"What do you mean 'real'? You're real now, aren't you?"

"Not exactly. Don't ask questions, Sparhawk. Just find me a patch of open sky and don't bother me for a while. I have to appeal for some help—if I can find them."

He pushed through the tangled brush, a cold knot in his stomach and his heart like a stone in his chest. The hideous dilemma they faced tore at him, seeming almost to rip him apart. Sephrenia was dying, but he must endanger Ehlana in order to save her life. It was only the force of Bhelliom's will that kept him moving at all. His own will was paralyzed by the conflicting needs of the two he loved most in all the world. He pushed at the tangle surrounding him in a kind of hopeless frustration.

Then he broke through the screen of brush into a small clearing carpeted by deep moss where a pool of water fed by a gurgling spring winked back at the stars strewn like bright grain across the velvet night. It was a quiet place, almost enchanted, but his eyes refused to accept its beauty. He stopped and set Aphrael down. Her small face was devoid of expression, and her eyes were blank, unseeing. Sparhawk waited tensely.

"Well, *finally*!" she said at last in an exasperated tone of voice. "It's so hard to explain anything to them. They never stop babbling long enough to listen."

"Who's this we're talking about?"

"The Tamul Gods. Now I can see why Oscagne's an atheist. I finally persuaded them to come *here* to do their playing. That should help to hide you and me from Cyrgon."

"Playing?"

"They're children, Sparhawk, babies who run and play and squeal and chase each other for months on end. Cyrgon absolutely hates them, so he won't go anywhere near them. That should help. They'll be here in a few minutes, and then we'll be able to start. Turn your back, Father. I don't like having people watch me change."

"I've seen you before—your reflection, anyway."

"That part doesn't bother me. The process of the changeover's a little degrading, though. Just turn your back, Father. You wouldn't understand."

He obediently turned and gazed up at the night sky. Several familiar constellations were either missing or in the wrong places.

"All right, Father, you can turn around now." Her voice was richer and more vibrant.

He turned. "Would you *please* put some clothes on?"

"Why?"

"Just do it, Aphrael. Humor my quirks."

"This is so tedious." She reached out and took hold of a gauzy kind of veil she had spun out of nothing and wrapped herself in it. "Better?" she asked.

"Not much. Can we leave now?"

"I'll check." Her eyes went distant for a moment. "They're coming," she reported. "They got sidetracked. It doesn't take much to distract them. Now, listen very carefully. Try to stay calm when we do this. Just keep the fact firmly in mind that I'm not going to let you get hurt. You won't fall."

"Fall? Fall from where? What are you talking about?"

"You'll see. I'd do it differently, but we *have* to get to Dirgis in a hurry, and I don't want Cyrgon to have time to locate me. We'll take it in easy stages at first, so you'll have time to get used to the idea." She turned her head slightly. "They're here," she said. "We can start now."

Sparhawk cocked his head slightly. He seemed to hear the distant sound of childish laughter, though it might have been only the sound of an errant breeze rustling the leaves in the treetops.

"Give me your hand," she instructed.

He reached out and took her by the hand. It seemed very warm and somehow comforting.

"Just look up at the sky, Sparhawk," the heartbreakingly beautiful young woman instructed.

He raised his face and saw the upper edge of the moon come creeping pale and luminous up above the treetops.

"You can look down now."

They were standing some ten feet above the rippled waters of the pool. Sparhawk's muscles tensed.

"Don't do that!" she said sharply. "Just relax. You'll slow us down if I have to drag you through the air like a waterlogged canoe."

He tried, but he didn't have much success. He was certain that his eyes were lying to him, though. He could *feel* solidity under his feet. He stamped on it, and it was as firm as earth ought to be.

"That's just for now," the Goddess told him. "In a little while you won't need it any more. I always have to put something solid down for Sephrenia—" Her voice broke off with a strange little sob. "*Please* get control of yourself, Sparhawk," she pleaded. "We *must* hurry. Look at the sky again. We're going a little higher."

He felt nothing at all, no rush of air, no sinking in the pit of his stomach, but when he looked down again, the clearing and its enchanted pool had shrunken to a dot. The tiny lights of Beresa twinkled from minuscule windows, and the moon had laid a long, glowing path out across the Tamul Sea.

"Are you all right?" Her inflections were still Aphrael's, but her voice, and most definitely her appearance, were totally different. Her face peculiarly combined Flute's features with Danae's, making her the adult who had somehow been both little girls. Sparhawk didn't answer, but stood instead stamping one foot on the solid nothing under him.

"I won't be able to keep that there when we start," she warned. "We'll be going too fast. Just hold onto my hand, but don't get excited and break my fingers."

"Don't do anything to surprise me, then. Are you going to sprout wings?"

"What an absurd idea. I'm not a bird, Sparhawk. Wings would only get in my way. Just lean back and relax." She looked intently at him. "You're really handling this well. Sephrenia's usually in hysterics at this point. Would you be more at ease if you sat down?"

"On what?"

"Never mind. Maybe we'd better stand. Take a couple of deep breaths, and let's get started."

He found that looking up helped. When he was looking at the stars and the newly risen moon, he could not see the awful emptiness under him.

There was no sense of movement, no whistle of the wind in his ears, no flapping of his cloak. He stood holding Aphrael's hand and looking intently at the moon as it receded ponderously southward.

Then there was a pale luminosity coming up from beneath.

"Oh, bother," the Goddess said.

"What's wrong?" His voice was a little shrill.

"Clouds."

He looked down and saw a fairy-tale world under them. Tumbled white cloud, glowing in the moonlight, stretched out as if forever. Mountains of airy mist swelled up from a folded, insubstantial plain, and pillars and castles of curded cloud stood sentinellike between. Sparhawk's mind filled with wonder as the soft, moonlit cloudscape flowed smoothly back below them. "Beautiful," he murmured.

"Maybe, but I can't see the ground."

"I think I prefer it that way."

"I need reference points, Sparhawk. I can't see where I am, so I can't tell where I'm going. Bhelliom can find a place with nothing but a name to work with, but I can't. I need landmarks, and I can't see them with all these clouds in the way."

"Why don't you use the stars?"

"What?"

"That's what sailors do when they're out at sea. The stars don't move, so the sailors pick out a certain star or constellation and steer toward it."

There was a long silence while the swiftly receding rush of cloud beneath them slowed and finally stopped. "Sometimes you're so clever that I can't stand you, Sparhawk," the Goddess holding his hand said tartly.

"Do you mean you've never even thought of it?" he asked her incredulously.

"I don't fly at night very often." Her tone was defensive. "We're going down. I have to find a landmark."

They sank downward, the clouds rushing up to meet them, and then they were immersed in a dense, clinging mist. "They're made out of fog, aren't they? Clouds, I mean." Sparhawk was surprised.

"What did you think they were?"

"I don't know. I've never thought of it before. It just seems strange for some reason."

They broke out of the underside of the cloud—clouds no longer bathed in moonglow, now hanging close over their heads like a dirty ceiling that closed off the light. The earth beneath them was enveloped in almost total darkness. They drifted along, standing in air and veering this way and that, peering down and searching for something recognizable.

"Over there." Sparhawk pointed. "It must be a fair-sized town. There's quite a lot of light."

They moved in that direction, drawn toward the light like mindless insects. There was a sense of unreality as Sparhawk looked down. The town lying beneath them seemed tiny. It huddled like some child's toy on the edge of a large body of water. Sparhawk scratched at his cheek, trying to remember the details of his map. "It's probably Sopal," he said. "That lake almost has to be the Sea of Arjun." He stopped, his mind suddenly reeling. "That's over three hundred leagues from where we started, Aphrael!" he exclaimed. "Almost a thousand miles!"

"Yes—if that town really *is* Sopal."

"It has to be. The Sea of Arjun's the only large body of water on this part of the continent, and Sopal's on the east side of it. Arjun's on the south side, and Tiana's on the west." He stared at her incredulously. "A thousand miles! And we only left Beresa a half an hour ago! Just how fast are we going?"

"What difference does it make? We got here. That's all that matters." The young woman holding his hand looked speculatively down at the miniature town on the lakeshore. "Dirgis is off to the west a little way, so we won't want to go straight north." She shifted them around in midair until they were facing in a slightly northwesterly direction. "That should be fairly close. Don't move your head, Sparhawk. Keep looking in that direction. We'll go back up, and you pick out a star."

They rose swiftly through the clouds, and Sparhawk saw the familiar constellation of the wolf lying above the misty horizon ahead. "There," he pointed. "The five stars clustered in the shape of a dog's head."

"It doesn't look like any dog *I've* ever seen."

"You have to use your imagination. How is it you've never thought of steering by the stars before?"

She shrugged. "Probably because I can see farther than you can. You see the sky as a surface—a kind of overturned bowl with the stars painted on it all at the same distance from you. That's why you can see that cluster of stars as a dog's head. I can't, because I can see the difference in distances. Keep an eye on your dog, Sparhawk. Let me know if we start to drift off-course."

The moon-bathed cloud beneath them began to flow smoothly back again, and they flew on in silence for a while. "This isn't so bad," Sparhawk said, "at least not when you get used to it."

"It's better than walking," the gauze-clad Goddess replied.

"It made my hair stand on end right at first, though."

"Sephrenia's never gotten past that stage. She starts gibbering in panic as soon as her feet come up off the ground."

Sparhawk remembered something. "Wait a minute," he objected. "When we killed Ghwerig and stole the Bhelliom, you came floating up out of that chasm in his cave, and she walked out across the air to meet you. She wasn't gibbering in panic then."

"No. It was probably the bravest thing she's ever done. I was so proud of her that I almost burst."

"Was she conscious at all? When you found her, I mean?"

"Off and on. She was able to tell us who'd attacked her. I managed to slow her heartbeat and take away the pain. She's very calm now." Aphrael's voice quavered. "She expects to die, Sparhawk. She can feel the wound in her heart, and she knows what that means. She was giving Xanetia a last message for Vanion when I left." The young Goddess choked back a sob. "Can we talk about something else?"

"Of course." Sparhawk's eyes flickered away from the constellation in the night sky. "There are mountains sticking up out of the clouds just ahead."

"We're almost there, then. Dirgis is in the big basin lying beyond that first ridge."

Their rapid flight began to slow. They passed over the snowy peaks of the southernmost expanse of the mountains of Atan, peaks that rose out of the clouds like frozen islands, and found that there was only thin cloud-cover over the basin lying beyond.

They descended, drifting down like dandelion puffs toward the forest-covered hills and valleys of the basin, a landscape sharply etched in the moonlight that leeched out all color. There was another cluster of lights some distance to the left—ruddy torches in narrow streets and golden candlelight in little windows. "That's Dirgis," Aphrael said. "We'll set down outside of town. I should probably change back before we go on in."

"Either that or put on some more clothes."

"That really bothers you, doesn't it, Sparhawk? Am I ugly or something?"

"No. Quite the opposite—and that bothers me all the more. I can't think while you're standing around naked, Aphrael."

"I'm not really a woman, Sparhawk—not in the sense that seems to bother you so much, anyway. Can't you think of me as a mare—or a doe?"

"No, I can't. Just do whatever you have to do, Aphrael. I don't really think we need to talk about how I think of you."

"Are you blushing, Sparhawk?"

"Yes, as a matter of fact, I am. Now can we drop it?"

"That's really rather sweet, you know?"

"Will you stop?"

They came down in a secluded little glen about a half mile from the outskirts of Dirgis, and Sparhawk turned his back while the Child-Goddess once again assumed the more familiar form of the Styric waif they all knew as Flute. "Better?" she asked when he turned around.

"Much." He picked her up and started toward town, his long legs stretching out in a rapid stride. He concentrated on that. It seemed to help him avoid thinking.

They went directly into town, made one turn off the main street, and came to a large, two-story building. "This is it," Aphrael said. "We'll just go in and up the stairs. I'll make the innkeeper look the other way."

Sparhawk pushed open the door, crossed the common room on the main floor, and went up the stairs.

They found Xanetia all aglow and cradling Sephrenia in her arms. The two women were on a narrow bed in a small room with roughly squared-off log walls. It was one of those snug, comfortable rooms such as one finds in mountain inns the world over. It had a porcelain stove, a couple of chairs, and a nightstand beside each bed. A pair of candles cast a golden light on the pair on the bed. The front of Sephrenia's robe was covered with blood, and her face was deathly pale, tinged slightly with that fatal grey. Sparhawk looked at her, and his mind suddenly filled with flames. "I will cause hurt to Zalasta for this," he growled in Trollish.

Aphrael gave him a startled look. Then she also spoke in the guttural language of the Trolls. "Your thought is good, Anakha," she agreed fiercely. "Cause much hurt to him." The rending sound of the Trollish word for *hurt* seemed very satisfying to both of them. "His heart still belongs to me, though," she added. "Has there been any change?" she asked Xanetia, lapsing into Tamul.

"None, Divine One," Xanetia replied in a voice near to exhaustion. "I am lending our dear sister of mine own strength to sustain her, but I am nearly spent. Soon both she and I will die."

"Nay, gentle Xanetia," Aphrael said. "I will *not* lose you both. Fear not, however. Anakha hath come with Bhelliom to restore ye both."

"But that must not be," Xanetia protested. "To do so would put the life of Anakha's queen in peril. Better that thy sister and I both perish than that."

"Don't be noble, Xanetia," Aphrael told her tartly. "It makes my hair hurt. Talk to Bhelliom, Sparhawk. Find out how we're supposed to do this."

"Blue-Rose," Sparhawk said, touching his fingers to the bulge under his smock.

I hear thee, Anakha. The voice in Sparhawk's mind was a whisper.

"We have come unto the place where Sephrenia lies stricken."

Yes.

"What must we now do? I implore thee, Blue-Rose, do not increase the peril of my mate."

Thine admonition is unseemly, Anakha. It doth bespeak a lack of trust.

Let us proceed. Surrender thy will to me. It is through thy *lips that I must speak with Anarae Xanetia.*

A strange, detached lassitude came over Sparhawk, and he felt himself somehow separating, his awareness sliding away from his body.

"Attend to me, Xanetia." It was Sparhawk's altered voice, but he had no consciousness of having spoken.

"Most closely, World-Maker," the Anarae replied in her exhausted voice.

"Let the Child-Goddess assume the burden of supporting her sister. I have need of thy hands."

Aphrael slipped onto the bed and took Sephrenia from Xanetia's arms and held her in a tender embrace.

Take forth the box, Anakha, Bhelliom instructed, *and surrender it up unto Xanetia.*

Sparhawk's movements were jerky as he pulled the golden box out from under his tunic and lifted the thong upon which it was suspended up over his head.

"Gather about thee that serenity which the curse of Edaemus hath bestowed upon thee, Xanetia," Bhelliom instructed the Anarae in Sparhawk's voice, "and enfold the box—and mine essence—in thy hands, letting thy peace infuse that which thou dost hold."

Xanetia nodded and extended her glowing hands to take the box from Sparhawk's grasp.

"Very good. Now, take the Child-Goddess in thine arms. Embrace her and deliver me up unto her."

Xanetia clasped both Aphrael and Sephrenia in her arms.

"Excellent. Thy mind is quick, Xanetia. This is even better. Aphrael, open thou the box and draw me forth." Bhelliom paused. "No tricks," it admonished her with uncharacteristic colloquialism. "Seek not to ensnare me with thy wiles and thy soft touch."

"Don't be absurd, World-Maker."

"I know thee, Aphrael, and I know that thou art more dangerous than ever Azash was or Cyrgon could be. Let us both concentrate all our attention upon the cure of thy sister."

The Child-Goddess opened the lid of the box and lifted out the glowing sapphire rose. Sparhawk, all bemused, saw the steady white glow which emanated from Xanetia take on a faint bluish flush as Bhelliom's radiance joined her own.

"Apply me, poulticelike, to her wound, that I may heal that injury which Zalasta hath inflicted."

Sparhawk was a soldier and he knew a great deal about wounds. His stomach knotted when he saw the deep, seeping gash in the upper swell of Sephrenia's left breast.

Aphrael reached out with Bhelliom and gently touched it to the bleeding wound.

Sephrenia started to glow with an azure radiance. She half raised her head. "No," she said weakly, trying to push Aphrael's hand away.

Sparhawk took both her hands in his and held them. "It's all right, little mother," he lied softly. "Everything's been taken care of."

The wound in Sephrenia's breast had closed, leaving an ugly purple scar. Then, even as they watched, the sapphire rose continued its work. The scar shrank down to a thin white line that became fainter and fainter and finally disappeared entirely.

Sephrenia began to cough. It was a gurgling, liquid kind of cough such as a nearly drowned man might make.

"Hand me that basin, Sparhawk," Aphrael instructed. "She has to clear the blood out of her lungs."

Sparhawk reached out and took the large, shallow basin from the nightstand and handed it to her.

"Here," she said. "You can have this back now." She gave him the closed box, took the basin, and held it under Sephrenia's chin. "That's right," she said encouragingly to her sister as the small woman began coughing up chunks of clotted blood. "Get it all out."

Sparhawk looked away. The procedure was not pretty.

Put thy mind at rest, Anakha, Bhelliom's voice told him softly. *Thine enemies are unaware of what hath come to pass.* The jewel paused. *I have not given Edaemus his due, for he is very shrewd. Methinks none other could have perceived the true import of what he hath done. To curse his children as he hath was the only true way to conceal them. I shudder to imagine the pain it must have caused him.*

I do not understand, Sparhawk confessed.

A blessing rings and shimmers in the lucid air like bell-sound, Anakha, but a curse is dark and silent. Were the light which doth emanate from Anarae Xanetia a blessing, all the world would hear and feel its o'erwhelming love, but Edaemus hath made it a curse instead. Therein lay his wisdom. The accursèd are cast out and hidden, and no one—man or God—can hear or feel their comings and goings up and down in the land. When she did take the box in her hands, Anarae Xanetia did smother all sound and sense of my presence, and when she did embrace Aphrael and Sephrenia and enfold them in her luminous darkness, none living could detect me. Thy mate is safe—for now. Thine enemies have no knowledge of what hath come to pass.

Sparhawk's heart soared. *I do sorely repent my lack of trust, Blue-Rose,* he apologized.

Thou wert distraught, Anakha. I do freely forgive thee.

"Sparhawk." Sephrenia's voice was little more than a whisper.

"Yes, little mother?" He went quickly to the side of the bed.

"You shouldn't have agreed to this. You've put Ehlana in terrible danger. I thought you were stronger."

"Everything's all right, Sephrenia," he assured her. "Bhelliom just explained it to me. Nobody heard or felt a thing while you were being healed."

"How is that possible?"

"It was Xanetia's presence—and her touch. Bhelliom says she completely muffled what was going on. It has to do with the difference between a blessing and a curse, as I understand it. However it works, what just happened didn't put Ehlana in any danger. How are you feeling?"

"Like a half-drowned kitten, if you really want to know." She smiled weakly. Then she sighed. "I would never have believed that Zalasta could be capable of what he did."

"I'll make him wish he'd never thought of it," Sparhawk said grimly. "I'm going to tear out his heart, roast it on a spit, and then serve it up to Aphrael on a silver plate."

"Isn't he a nice boy?" Aphrael said fondly.

"No." Sephrenia's voice was surprisingly firm. "I appreciate the thought, dear ones, but I don't want either of you to do anything to Zalasta. I'm the one he stabbed, so I want to be the one who decides who gets him."

"I suppose that's fair," Sparhawk conceded.

"What have you got in mind, Sephrenia?" Aphrael asked.

"Vanion's going to be dreadfully upset when he hears about this. I don't want him raging and breaking up the furniture, so I'm going to give Zalasta to him—all tied up in a bright red ribbon."

"I still get his heart, though," Aphrael insisted.

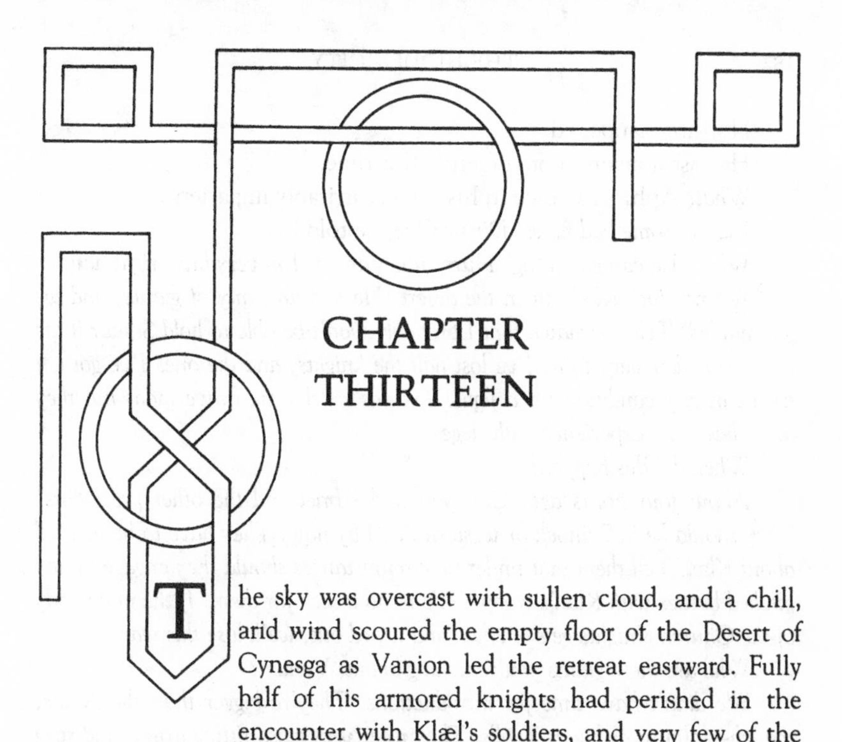

CHAPTER THIRTEEN

The sky was overcast with sullen cloud, and a chill, arid wind scoured the empty floor of the Desert of Cynesga as Vanion led the retreat eastward. Fully half of his armored knights had perished in the encounter with Klæl's soldiers, and very few of the survivors had escaped serious injury. Vanion had ridden forth from Sarna with an army. He was returning at the head of a column of groaning invalids, battered and dented, after what had really been no more than a skirmish.

Four Atans carried Engessa on a litter, and Queen Betuana strode along at his side, her face ravaged with grief. Vanion sighed. Engessa was still breathing, but only barely.

The preceptor straightened in his saddle, trying to shake off his shock and dismay and to think rationally. The fight with Klæl's warriors had decimated his force of Church Knights, and they had been central to the strategy of containment. Without those armored horsemen, the eastern frontier of Tamul proper was no longer secure.

Vanion muttered a sour oath. The only thing he could really do now was to warn the others about the change in the situation. "Sir Endrik," he called to the old veteran riding some distance behind, "take over here. I've got something to take care of."

Endrik came forward.

"Keep them going east," Vanion instructed. "I'll be back in a little bit." He spurred his tired horse into a loping canter and rode on ahead.

When he was about a mile ahead of the column, he reined in and cast the spell of summoning.

Nothing happened.

He cast it again, more urgently this time.

What? Aphrael's voice in his ear was irritably impatient.

I've got some bad news, Divine One, he told her.

What else can go wrong? Hurry up, Vanion. I'm very busy right now.

We ran into Klæl out in the desert. He had an army of giants, and we got mauled. Tell Sparhawk that I probably won't be able to hold Samar if the Cynesgans lay siege to it. I've lost half the knights, and the ones I've got left aren't in any condition for a fight. Tikume's Peloi are brave men, but they don't have any experience with sieges.

When did this happen?

About four hours ago. Can you find Abriel and the other preceptors? They should be in Zemoch or western Astel by now. They have to be warned about Klæl. Tell them that under no circumstances should they engage in any pitched battles with Klæl's troops. We're no match for them. If the main body of the Church Knights gets waylaid and wiped out, we'll lose this war.

Who are these giants you're talking about, Vanion?

We didn't have time for introductions. They're bigger than the Atans, though—almost as big as Trolls. They wear very close-fitting armor and steel face masks. Their weapons aren't like anything I've ever seen, and they've got yellow blood.

Yellow? That's impossible!

It's yellow all the same. You can come here and look at my sword-blade, if you'd like. I managed to kill a couple of them while I was covering Betuana's retreat.

Retreat? Betuana?

She was carrying Engessa.

What's wrong with Engessa?

He was out front a little ways, and Klæl's soldiers attacked him. He fought well, but they swarmed him under. We charged into them, and Betuana cut her way through to Engessa. I ordered a retreat and covered Betuana while she carried Engessa to the rear. We're taking him back to Sarna, but I think it's a waste of effort. The side of his head's been bashed in, and I'm afraid we're going to lose him.

Don't say that, Vanion. Don't ever say that. There's always hope.

Not much this time, Divine One. When somebody breaks into a man's brain, about all you can do for him is dig a grave.

I'm not going to lose him, Vanion! How fast can you get him back to Sarna?

Two days, Aphrael. It took us two days to get here, and two days out means two days back.

Can he hold on that long?

I doubt it.

She said a short, ugly word in Styric. *Where are you?*

Twenty leagues south of Sarna and about five leagues out into the desert.

Stay there. I'll come and find you.

Be a little careful when you approach Betuana. She's behaving very strangely.

Say what you mean, Vanion. I don't have time for riddles.

I'm not sure what I mean, Aphrael. Betuana's a soldier, and she knows that people sometimes get killed in battle. Her reaction to what's happened to Engessa is—well—excessive. She's broken down completely.

She's an Atan, Vanion. They're a very emotional people. Go back and halt your column. I'll be there in a little while.

Vanion nodded, although there was no one there to nod to, turned his horse, and rode back to rejoin his knights. "Any change?" he asked Queen Betuana.

She lifted her tear-streaked face. "He opened his eyes once, Vanion-Preceptor," she replied. "I don't think he saw me, though." She was holding Engessa's hand.

"I talked with Aphrael," he advised her. "She's coming here to have a look at him. Don't give up hope yet, Betuana. Aphrael cured *me*, and I was closer to being dead than Engessa is."

"He *is* fairly strong," she said. "If the Child-Goddess can heal his wound before it carries him off—" Her voice caught with an odd little note.

"He'll be all right, your Majesty," he said, trying to sound more certain than he really was. "Can you get word to your husband—about Klæl, I mean? He should know about those soldiers Klæl hides under his wings."

"I'll send a runner. Should I tell Androl to come to Sarna instead of going to Tosa? Klæl is here *now*, and Scarpa's army won't reach Tosa for quite some time—and that's only if they can evade the Trolls."

"Let's wait until I've had the chance to talk with the others first. Is King Androl already on the march?"

"He should be. Androl always jumps when I suggest something. He's a good man—and very, very brave." She said it almost as if defending her husband from some unspoken criticism, but Vanion noticed that she absently stroked Engessa's ashen face even as she spoke.

"He must have been in a hurry," Stragen said, still puzzling over Sparhawk's terse note.

"He's never been very good at writing letters—" Talen shrugged. "—except for that one time when he spent days composing lies about what we were supposedly doing on the Isle of Tega."

"Maybe that took it all out of him." Stragen folded the note and looked closely at it. "Parchment," he said. "Where did he get his hands on parchment?"

"Who knows? Maybe he'll tell us when he comes back. Let's go take a walk on the beach. I need some exercise."

"All right." Stragen picked up his cloak, and he and the younger thief went downstairs and out into the street.

The southern Tamul Sea was calm, and the moon-path across its dark surface was unbroken and very bright. "Pretty," Talen murmured when the two reached the damp sand at the edge of the water.

"Yes," Stragen agreed.

"I think I've come up with something," Talen said.

"So have I," Stragen replied.

"Go ahead."

"No, let's hear yours first."

"All right. The Cynesgans are massing on the border, right?"

"Yes."

"A good story could unmass them."

"I don't think there is such a word."

"Did we come here to discuss vocabulary? What will the Cynesgans do if they hear that the Church Knights are coming? Wouldn't they almost have to send an army to meet them?"

"I think Sparhawk and Vanion want to keep the fact that the knights are coming more or less a secret."

"Stragen, how are you going to keep a hundred thousand men a secret? Let's say that I tell Valash that I've picked up a very reliable report that a fleet of ships flying church banners has rounded the southern tip of Daconia bound for Kaftal. Wouldn't that cause the other side some concern? Even if they know about the knights coming across Zemoch, they'd *still* have to send troops to meet that fleet. They couldn't ignore the possibility that the knights are coming at them from two different directions."

Stragen suddenly laughed.

"What's so funny?"

"You and I have been running together for too long, Talen. We're starting to think alike. I came up with the idea of telling Valash that the Atans are going to cross the steppes of eastern Astel and strike down into northern Cynesga toward the capital."

"Nice plan," Talen said.

"So's yours." Stragen squinted out across the moon-bathed water. "Either story's strategically credible," he mused. "They're exactly the kind of moves a military man *would* come up with. What we're *really* planning is a simultaneous strike from the east and the west. If we can make Cyrgon believe that we're going to hit him from the north and south instead, we'll pull him so far out of position that he'll never be able to get his armies back to meet our real attacks."

"Not to mention the fact that we'll cut his army in two."

"We'll have to be careful, though," Stragen cautioned. "I don't think even Valash is gullible enough to swallow these stories if we drop them both on him at the same time. We'll have to spread them out and dribble them to him a bit at a time. What I'd *really* like to do is let the fairy tale about the Atans come from someone other than me."

"Sparhawk could probably get Aphrael to arrange that," Talen suggested.

"If he ever comes back. His note was a little vague. Let's get things rolling, though. We can modify your story a bit. Push your make-believe fleet back to Valesia. Give Cyrgon some time to worry about it before we pinpoint Kaftal as the final destination. I'll plant a couple of hints about the Atans massing up near their northwestern frontier. We'll let things stand that way until Sparhawk comes back."

Talen sighed.

"What's wrong?"

"This is almost legal, isn't it?"

"I suppose you could say so, yes. Is there some problem with that?"

"If it's legal, why am I having so much fun?"

"Nothing?" Ulath asked, opening the neck of his red uniform jacket.

"Not a peep," Tynian replied. "I cast the spell four times, and I still can't raise her."

"Maybe she's busy."

"It's possible, I guess."

Ulath rubbed at his cheek reflectively. "I definitely think I'll shave off Sir Gerda's beard," he muttered. "You know, it *could* be that it's because we're in No-Time. When we did this the first time—back in Pelosia—none of our spells worked."

"I think this spell's different, Ulath. I'm not really trying to *do* anything. I just want to talk with Aphrael."

"Yes, but you're mixing magic. You're trying to use a Styric spell when you're up to your ears in a Trollish one."

"Maybe that's it. I'll try again when we get to Arjun and go back into real time."

Bhlokw came shambling back through the grey light of Ghnomb's frozen moment, passing a flock of stationary birds hanging in the air. "There are some of the dens of the man-things in the next valley," he reported.

"Many or few?" Ulath asked him.

"Many," Bhlokw replied. "Will the man-things have dogs there?"

"There are always dogs near the dens of the man-things, Bhlokw."

"We should hurry, then." The shaggy Troll paused. "What do the man-things call this place?"

"It is the place Arjun—I think."

"That is the place where we want to go, is it not?"

"Yes."

"Why?"

"The wicked ones have told the one called Berit to go there. It is our thought that we should go there in Ghnomb's broken moment and listen to the bird-talk of the man-things. One of the wicked ones may say where the one called Berit is to go next. The next place may be the place where Anakha's mate is. It would be good to know this."

Bhlokw's shaggy brow furrowed as he struggled his way through that. "Are the hunts of the man-things always so not-simple?" he asked.

"It is the nature of our kind to be not-simple."

"Does it not make your head hurt?"

Ulath smiled, being careful not to show his teeth. "Sometimes it does," he admitted.

"It is my thought that a simple hunt is better than a not-simple hunt. The hunts of the man-things are so not-simple that sometimes I forget why I am hunting. Trolls hunt things-to-eat. The man-things hunt thought."

Ulath was a bit startled at the Troll's perception. "Your thought may be good," he admitted. "The man-things *do* hunt thought. We put much value on it."

"Thought is good, U-lat, but you can not eat it."

"We hunt thought after our bellies are full."

"That is how Trolls and the man-things are different, U-lat. I am a

Troll. My belly is never full. Let us hurry. It is my thought that it will be good to know if the dogs of this place are as good-to-eat as the dogs of the other place." He paused. "I do not wish to cause you anger, U-lat, but it is my thought that the dogs of the man-things are more good-to-eat than the man-things themselves." He scratched at his cheek with one shaggy paw. "I would still eat a man-thing if my belly was empty, but I would like a dog better."

"Let us go find you a dog, then."

"Your thought is good, U-lat." The huge beast reached out and affectionately patted Ulath on the head, nearly driving him to his knees.

The Child-Goddess touched her fingertips lightly to the sides of Engessa's broken head, and her eyes became distant.

"Well?" Vanion asked, his tone urgent.

"Don't rush me, Vanion. The brain is very complicated." She continued her gentle probing. "Impossible," she said finally, withdrawing her fingers.

Betuana groaned.

"Please don't do that, Betuana," Aphrael said. "All I meant was that I can't do it here. I'll have to take him someplace else to repair him."

"The island?" Vanion guessed.

She nodded. "I can control things there. This is still Cynesga—Cyrgon's place. I don't think he'd give me permission no matter how sweetly I asked him. Can you pray here, Betuana?"

The Atan queen shook her head. "Only in Atan itself."

"I'm going to talk to your God about that. It's really *very* inconvenient." She bent again and put her hand on Engessa's chest.

The Atan general appeared to stop breathing, and his face and body were suddenly covered with frost.

"You've killed him!" Betuana shrieked at her.

"Oh, hush! I just froze him to stop the bleeding until I can get him to the island. The injury itself isn't so bad, but the bleeding's tearing up the rest of his brain. The freezing slows it down to a trickle. That's all I can do for right now, but it should be enough to keep his body from doing any more damage to itself while you're taking him back to Sarna."

"There's no hope," Betuana said with a look of anguish.

"What are you talking about? I can have him back on his feet in a day or two—but I have to take him to the island where I can control time. The brain is easy. It's the heart that's so—well, never mind that. Listen closely, Betuana. As soon as you and Vanion get him to Sarna, I want you to go to the Atan border as fast as you can run. As soon as you get across that line, fall on your knees and start praying to your God. He'll be stubborn—he always is—but keep after him. Make a pest of yourself until he gives in. I need his permission to take Engessa to my island. If nothing else works, promise him that I'll do something nice for him someday. Don't be *too* specific, though. Keep bearing down on the fact that *I* can save Engessa, and *he* can't."

"I will do as you have commanded, Divine One," Betuana declared.

"I didn't *command*, Betuana. I only suggested. I don't have the authority to command you." The Child-Goddess turned to Vanion. "Let me see your sword," she said. "I want to have a look at this yellow blood."

Vanion drew his sword and offered it to her hilt-first.

She shuddered. "*You* hold it, dear one. Steel makes me nauseous." She squinted at the stains on the blade. "Astonishing," she murmured. "That isn't blood at all."

"It's what came out of them when we cut them."

"Perhaps, but it's still not blood. It's some kind of bile. Klæl's going a little far afield for allies. Those giants you ran across don't come from here, Vanion. They aren't like any creatures on *this* world."

"We noticed that almost immediately, Divine One."

"I'm not talking about their size or shape, Vanion. They don't even seem to have the same kind of internal organs as the humans and animals. I'd guess that they don't even have lungs."

"*Everything* has lungs, Aphrael—except maybe fish."

"That's *here*, dear one. If these creatures have bile in their veins instead of blood, then they're relying on their livers for—" she broke off, frowning. "I guess it *is* possible," she said a little dubiously. "I'd hate to smell the air on their world, though."

"You *do* know that I haven't got the foggiest idea of what you're talking about, don't you?"

She smiled. "That's all right, dear one. I love you anyway."

"Thank you."

"Don't mention it."

"It *could* be good country, friend Tikume," Kring said, adjusting his black leather jerkin and looking around at the rocky desert. "It's open and not too rugged. All it needs is water—and a few good people." The two of them rode at the front of their disorganized mob of Peloi.

Tikume grinned. "When you get right down to it, friend Kring, that's all Hell really needs."

Kring laughed. "How far is it to this Cynesgan camp?" he asked.

"Another five leagues. It's easy fighting, Domi Kring. The Cynesgans ride horses and carry curved swords much like your sabers, but their horses are scrubby and not very good, and the Cynesgans are too lazy to practice their swordsmanship. To make it even better, they wear flowing robes with big, floppy sleeves. Half the time they get tangled up in their own clothing."

Kring's grin was wolfish.

"They run fairly well, though," Tikume added, "but they always come back."

"To the same camps?" Kring asked incredulously.

Tikume nodded. "It makes it even easier. We don't even have to go looking for them."

"Incredible. Are they using rotten tree stumps for leaders?"

"From what I've heard, they're getting their orders from Cyrgon." Tikume rubbed his shaved scalp. "Do you think it might be heresy to suggest that even a God can be stupid?"

"As long as you don't say it about *our* God, I think you're safe."

"I wouldn't want to get in trouble with the Church."

"Patriarch Emban's a reasonable man, Domi Tikume. He won't denounce you if you say unflattering things about our enemy." Kring raised up in his stirrups to peer across the brown, gravel-strewn expanse of the Desert of Cynesga. "I'm looking forward to this," he said. "I haven't been in a real fight for a long time." He sank back into his saddle. "Oh, I almost forgot. I talked with friend Oscagne about the possibility of a bounty on Cynesgan ears. He said no."

"That's a shame. Men fight better if they've got an incentive of some kind."

"It even gets to be a habit. We had a fight with the Trolls up in northern Atan, and I had a dead Troll's ear half sawed off before I remembered nobody was around to buy it from me. That's a funny-looking hill up there, isn't it?" He pointed ahead at an almost perfectly shaped dome rearing up out of the desert floor.

"It *is* a little odd," Tikume agreed. "There aren't any rocks on its sides—just dust."

"Probably some kind of dust dune. They have sand dunes down in Rendor that look like that. The wind whirls the sand around and leaves it in round hills."

"Would dust behave like sand?"

"Evidently so. There's the proof just up ahead."

And then, even as they watched, the hill split down the middle and its sides fanned out. They stared at the triangular face of Klæl as he rose ponderously to his feet, shedding great waterfalls of dust from his gleaming black wings.

Kring reined in sharply. "I *knew* something wasn't right about that hill!" he exclaimed, cursing his own inattention, as their men surged around them.

"He didn't come alone this time!" Tikume shouted. "He had soldiers hidden under his wings! Hold!"

"Big devils, aren't they?" Kring squinted at the armored warriors rushing toward them. "Big or little, though, they're still infantry, and that's all the advantage we need, isn't it?"

"Right!" Tikume chortled. "This should be more fun than chasing Cynesgans."

"I wonder if they've got ears," Kring said, drawing his saber. "If they do, we might just want to gather them up. I still haven't given up on friend Oscagne yet."

"There's one way to find out," Tikume said, hefting his javelin and leading the charge.

The standard Peloi tactics seemed to baffle Klæl's soldiers. The superb horses of the nomads were as swift as deer, and the eastern Peloi's preference for the javelin over the saber was an additional advantage. The horsemen split up into small groups and began their attack. They slashed forward in long files, each group concentrating on one of the steel-masked monsters and each Peloi hurling his javelin into the huge bodies at close range and then swerving away to safety. After a few such attacks, the front ranks of the enemy warriors bristled like hedgehogs with the short spears protruding from their bodies.

The armored soldiers grew increasingly desperate, and they flailed ineffectually at their swift-charging tormentors with their brutal maces, savaging the unoffending air and almost never striking a solid blow.

"Good fight!" Kring panted to his friend after several charges. "They're big, but they're not quite fast enough."

"And not in very good condition either," Tikume added. "That last one I skewered was puffing and wheezing like a leaky bellows."

"They *do* seem to be having some trouble getting their breath, don't they?" Kring agreed. His eyes suddenly narrowed. "Wait a minute, let's try something. Tell your children to just ride in and then wheel and ride out again. Don't waste any more javelins."

"I don't quite follow, Domi."

"Have you ever gone up into the high mountains?"

"A few times. Why?"

"Do you remember how hard it was to get your breath?"

"Right at first, I suppose. I remember getting a little light-headed."

"Exactly. I don't know where Klæl went to recruit these soldiers, but it wasn't from around here. I think they're used to thicker air. Let's make them chase us. Why go to all the trouble of killing somebody if the air's going to do the job for you?"

"It's worth a try." Tikume shrugged. "It takes a lot of the fun out of it, though."

"We can have fun with the Cynesgans later," Kring told him. "Let's run Klæl's infantry to death first. *Then* we can go slaughter Cyrgon's cavalry."

"Sort of follow my lead on this," Stragen told Talen as the two mounted the rickety stairs leading up to the loft. "I've gotten to know Valash fairly well, so I can gauge his reactions a little better than you can."

"All right." Talen shrugged. "He's your fish. I'll let you play him."

Stragen opened the door to the stale-smelling loft, and the two of them threaded their way through the clutter to Valash's corner.

The bony Dacite in the brocade jacket was not alone. A gaunt Styric with open, seeping sores on his face slumped in a chair at the table. The Styric's right arm hung limply at his side, the right side of his ulcerated face sagged, and his right eyelid drooped down to almost totally cover the eye. He was mumbling to himself, evidently completely unaware of his surroundings.

"This isn't a good time, Vymer," Valash said.

"It's quite important, Master Valash," Stragen said quickly.

"All right, but don't take too long."

As they approached the table, Talen's stomach suddenly churned. An overpowering odor of putrefying flesh emanated from the comatose Styric.

"This is my master," Valash said shortly.

"Ogerajin?" Stragen asked.

"How did you know his name?"

"You mentioned it to me once, I think—or maybe it was one of your friends. Isn't he a little sick to be out and about?"

"That's none of your concern, Vymer. What's this important information you have for me?"

"Not me, Master Valash. Reldin here picked up something."

"Speak up, then, boy."

"Yes, Master Valash," Talen said, ducking his head in a sort of half bow. "I went into a waterfront tavern earlier today, and I heard a couple of Edomish sailors talking. They seemed excited about something, so I slipped a little closer to find out why they were so worked up. Well, you know how Edomishmen feel about the Church of Chyrellos."

"Get on with it, Reldin."

"Yes, sir. I was only trying to explain. Anyway, one of the sailors had just reached port, and he was telling the other one to get word to somebody in Edom—Rebal, I think his name is. It seems that the first sailor had just come in from Valesia, and when he'd been leaving port there, his ship passed a fleet coming into the harbor at Valles."

"What's so significant about that?" Valash demanded.

"I was just coming to that. What made the first sailor so excited was the fact that the ships he saw were all flying the banners of the Church of Chyrellos and the rails were lined with men wearing armor. He kept babbling something about Church Knights coming to impose heresies on the people of Tamuli."

Valash was staring at him in openmouthed horror.

"As soon as I heard that part, I slipped away. Vymer here thought you might want to know about it, but I wasn't so sure. What difference should it make to us that the Elenes are arguing about religion? It doesn't involve us, does it?"

"How many ships?" Valash demanded in a half-strangled tone. His eyes were bulging.

"The sailor wasn't too specific, Master Valash." Talen smiled. "I sort of got the impression that he ran out of the numbers that he knew the names of. I guess that fleet stretched from horizon to horizon. If those men in armor *are* Church Knights, I'd say that *all* of them are on board these ships. I've heard things about those people. *I* certainly wouldn't want to be the one they're coming after. How much would you say this information's worth, Master Valash?"

Valash reached for his purse without any protest.

"Have any messengers from those camps out in the woods come by lately, Master Valash?" Stragen asked suddenly.

"That's none of your concern, Vymer."

"Whatever you say, Master Valash. All I was getting at is that you ought to warn them about talking in public. I came across a couple of men who looked as if they've been living in the woods. One of them was telling the other that they couldn't do anything until Scarpa got instructions from Cyrga. Who's Cyrga? I've never heard of him."

"It's not a who, Vymer," Talen said. "It's a where. Cyrga's a town over in Cynesga."

"Really?" Stragen's expression grew curious. "This is the first time I've ever heard the name. Where is it? What route would you take to get to Cyrga?"

"The pathway lies close by the Well of Vigay," the diseased Ogerajin announced in a loud, declamatory voice.

Valash made a slightly strangled noise and ineffectually tried to wave his hands warningly in front of his master's face, but Ogerajin brushed him aside. "Keep morning at thy back," the Styric continued.

"Master Ogerajin," Valash protested in a squeaky tone.

"Silence, knave," Ogerajin thundered at him. "I will answer this traveler's question. If it is his intent to present himself and bow down to Cyrgon, he must know the way. Proceed, traveler, past the Well of Vigay and trek northwesterly into the desert. Thy destination shall be the Forbidden Mountains where none may go without Cyrgon's leave except at their peril. When thou dost reach those black, forbidding heights, seek ye the Pillars of Cyrgon, for without them to guide thee, Cyrga will remain forever hidden."

"Please, Master." Valash was helplessly wringing his hands as he stared in chagrin at the raving old lunatic.

"I have commanded thy silence, knave. Speak once more and thou shalt surely die." He turned back to fix Stragen with his single wild eye. "Be not dismayed, traveler, by the Plains of Salt which nomads fear to cross. Ride, boldly ride across the dead whiteness, empty of life save only where miscreants labor in the quarries to mine the precious salt.

"From the verge of the Plains of Salt wilt thou behold low on the horizon before thee the dark shapes of the Forbidden Mountains, and, if it please Cyrgon, his fiery white pillars will guide thee to his Hidden City.

"Let not the Plain of Bones disquiet thee. The bones are those of the nameless slaves who toil until death for Cyrgon's chosen, and, having served their purpose, are then given to the desert.

"Beyond the Plain of Bones wilt thou come to the Gates of Illusion behind which lies concealed the Hidden City of Cyrga. The eye of mortal man cannot perceive those gates. Stark they stand as a fractured wall at the verge of the Forbidden Mountains to bar thy way. Bend thine eye, however, upon Cyrgon's two white pillars and direct thy steps toward the emptiness which doth lie between them. Trust not the evidence which thine eye doth present unto thee, for the solid-seeming wall is as mist and will not bar thy way. Pass through it and proceed along the dark corridor to the Glen of Heroes where lie the unnumbered regiments of Cyrgon in restless sleep, awaiting the trumpet call of his mighty voice summoning them forth once more to smite his enemies."

Valash stepped back a pace and urgently beckoned to Talen to follow him.

Curious, Talen followed the Dacite. "Don't pay any attention to Master Ogerajin, boy," Valash said urgently. "He hasn't been well lately, and he has these spells quite often."

"I'd already guessed that, Master Valash. Shouldn't you get him to a physician? He's really raving, you know."

"There's nothing a physician could do for him." Valash shrugged. "Just make sure that Vymer understands that the old man doesn't know what he's talking about." Valash seemed unusually concerned about Ogerajin's ravings.

"He already knows, Master Valash. Anytime somebody starts throwing the 'thees' and 'thous' around, you can be fairly sure that his saddle's starting to slip."

The diseased Styric was still raving in that hollow, declamatory voice. "Beyond the Glen of Heroes wilt thou see the Well of Cyrgon, sparkling in the sun and sustaining the Hidden City.

"Close by the well in fields laced with channels thou wilt see black Cyrga rising like a mountain within its walls of night. Go boldly there and into the city of the Blessed Cyrgai. Mount the steep streets to the summit of that enclosèd peak, and there at the crown of the known world thou wilt find amid that blackness the white, where columns of chalk bear the lintels and roof of the Holy of Holies wherein Cyrgon burns eternal upon the sacred altar.

"Fall upon thy face in that awful presence, crying '*Vanet, tyek Alcor! Yala Cyrgon!*' and, should it please him, he will hear thee. And should it please him not, he will destroy thee.

"Thus, traveler, is the way to the Hidden City which lieth at the heart of Mighty Cyrgon, King and God of all that was, all that is, and all that shall ever be."

Then the crazed Styric's face contorted into a grotesque mask of glee, and he began to cackle in a shrill, meaningless giggle.

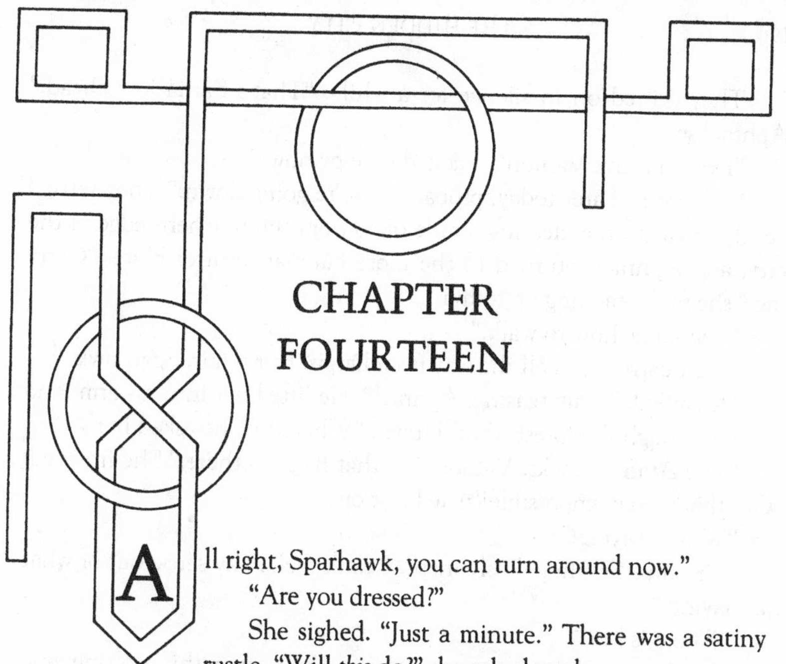

CHAPTER FOURTEEN

All right, Sparhawk, you can turn around now."

"Are you dressed?"

She sighed. "Just a minute." There was a satiny rustle. "Will *this* do?" she asked tartly.

He turned. The Goddess was wrapped in a shimmering white robe. "That's a little better," he told her.

"Prude. Give me your hand."

He took her slender hand in his and they drifted upward, rising out of the forested hills just east of Dirgis. "Sarna's somewhat to the west of due south," he told her.

"I know where it is." Her tone was crisp.

"I was just trying to be helpful."

The ground beneath them began to flow back as they sped southwesterly.

"Can people see us from the ground?" he asked curiously.

"Of course not. Why?"

"Just wondering. It occurred to me that if they can it might explain a lot of the wild stories that crop up in folklore."

"You humans are very creative. You can invent wild stories without any help from us."

"You're in a disagreeable frame of mind today. How long is it going to take us to get there?"

"Just a few minutes."

"It's an interesting way to travel."

"It's overrated."

They drifted on in silence for a while. "That's Sarna just ahead," Aphrael said.

"Do you think Vanion's reached here by now?"

"I doubt it. Later today, probably. We're going down." They settled gently to earth in a clearing a mile or so from the northern edge of the city, and Aphrael returned to the more familiar form of Flute. "Carry me," she said, reaching up to him.

"You know how to walk."

"I just carried you all the way from Dirgis. Fair *is* fair, Sparhawk."

He smiled. "Only teasing, Aphrael." He lifted her into his arms and started through the forest toward town. "Where to?" he asked her.

"The Atan barracks. Vanion says that Itagne's there." She frowned. "Oh, that's *really* impossible!" she burst out.

"What's wrong?"

"Sir Anosian's hopelessly inept. I can't make any sense out of what he's saying."

"Where is he?"

"At Samar. He's trying to tell me about something Kring and Tikume just discovered, but I'm only getting about every third word. Why *won't* the man concentrate on his studies?"

"Anosian's sort of—ah—"

"The word you're looking for is *lazy*, Sparhawk."

"He likes to conserve His energy," Sparhawk defended his fellow Pandion.

"Of *course* he does." She frowned. "Stop a minute," she said.

"What's the matter?"

"I just thought of something."

"What now?"

"It just occurred to me that Tynian may have been a little unselective when he was gathering those knights he brought back from Chyrellos."

"He brought the best men he could lay his hands on."

"I think that's the problem. I've been wondering why I haven't been getting any reports from Komier. I don't think Tynian left him a single Pandion who has any more skill than Anosian does. There aren't all that many of you who can reach out more than a few leagues, and Tynian seems to have inadvertently commandeered them all."

"Could you make any sense at all about what Anosian was trying to tell you?"

"It's something about breathing. Somebody's having problems with it. I'll run on down there after we talk with Itagne. Maybe Anosian can be coherent if I'm in the same room with him."

"Be nice."

They passed through the city gates and entered Sarna. Sparhawk carried the Child-Goddess through the narrow streets to the bleak stone fortress that housed the local Atan garrison.

They found the red-mantled Itagne in a large conference room examining the map that covered one entire wall. "Ah, Itagne," Sparhawk said, "there you are." He set Flute down on her feet.

"I'm afraid you have the advantage of me, Sir—?"

"It's me, Itagne—Sparhawk."

"I'll *never* get used to that," Itagne said. "I thought you were in Beresa."

"I *was*—until yesterday."

"How did you get here so fast?"

Sparhawk laid his hand on Flute's little shoulder. "Need you ask?"

"Oh. What brings you to Sarna?"

"Vanion ran into trouble out in the desert. He's coming back. He and Betuana are bringing Engessa in on a litter."

"Do you mean there's somebody in this world big enough to hurt Engessa?"

"Perhaps not in *this* world, Itagne," Aphrael told him. "Klæl's brought in an army from someplace else. They're very strange. Vanion and Betuana should get here this afternoon. Then Betuana has to go to Atan. How far is that?"

Itagne looked at the map. "Fifteen leagues."

"Good. It shouldn't take her long, then. She has to get her God's permission for me to take Engessa to the island. The side of his head's been bashed in, and I can't fix that here."

"Good God!" Itagne exclaimed.

"How nice of you to notice."

He smiled faintly. "What else is going on?" he asked.

"Quite a bit," Sparhawk told him. "Zalasta tried to kill Sephrenia."

"You're not serious!"

"I'm afraid so. We had to use Bhelliom to save her life."

"Sparhawk!" Itagne's eyes widened.

"It's all right Itagne," Aphrael assured him, going across the room to him and holding out her hands.

"Didn't that endanger Queen Ehlana?" he asked, lifting her into his lap.

Sparhawk shook his head. "Xanetia can muffle those telltale noises, I guess. Ehlana's still safe—or so Bhelliom tells me." His face, however, was worried.

"Thank God!"

"You're welcome," Aphrael said, "but it was really Bhelliom's idea. We still have some problems, though. Vanion's encounter with Klæl's army cost him about half of his knights."

"That's disastrous! We won't be able to hold Samar without those knights!"

"Don't be quite so sure, Itagne," she said. "I just received a garbled message from a Pandion named Anosian. He's in Samar, and Kring and Tikume have discovered something about Klæl's soldiers. I'll run down there and find out what's going on."

"Klæl's keeping an eye on Berit and Khalad," Sparhawk continued. "They saw him while they were crossing the Sea of Arjun." He rubbed at the side of his face. "Can you think of anything else, Aphrael?"

"Lots of things," she replied, "but they don't have much to do with what we're doing here." She kissed Itagne and slipped down out of his lap. "I shouldn't be too long," she told them. "If Vanion gets here before I come back, break the news about Sephrenia to him gently and tell him that she's all right now. Keep a grip on him, gentlemen. It's wintertime, and you need the roof on this building." She went to the door, opened it, and vanished as she stepped through.

Tiana lay on the north shore of the large lake known as the Sea of Arjun. It was a bustling Tamul town with an extensive harbor. As soon as the scruffy lake freighter docked, Berit and Khalad led their horses ashore and mounted. "What was the name of that inn again?" Khalad asked.

"The White Gull," Berit replied.

"Poetic," Khalad noted.

"The other names had probably already been used up. You can only have so many lions and dragons and boars in one town before people start to get confused."

"Krager's starting to give us more specific instructions in those notes," Khalad said. "When he sent us to Sopal, he just gave us the name of the town. Now he's picking our accommodations for us. That *might* mean that we're getting closer to the end of this little excursion."

"Sir Ulath said that they're going to send us to Arjuna from here."

"If I'd known we were going to spend so much time wandering around this lake, I'd have brought a fishing line."

"I'm not really all that fond of fish, myself."

"Who is? It's an excuse to get outside. My brothers and I have found that if we lay around the house too long, our mothers start finding things for us to do."

"You've got a strange family, Khalad. Most men only have one mother."

"It was Father's idea. There's the White Gull." Khalad pointed up the street.

The inn was surprisingly clean and substantial. It had a well-maintained stable, and the rooms were neat almost to the point of fussiness. The two young men saw to their horses, dropped their saddlebags off in their room, and took advantage of the bathhouse adjoining the rear of the inn. Then, feeling much improved, they adjourned to the taproom to pass the time until supper. Khalad rose and closely examined the porcelain stove. "It's an interesting idea," he told Berit. "I wonder if it'd catch on in Eosia."

"I sort of like looking at the fire myself," Berit replied.

"You can stare at the candles, if that's all you want. A fireplace isn't very efficient, and it makes an awful mess. A stove's a lot more practical—and you can cook on it. When we get home, I think I'll build one for my mothers."

Berit laughed. "If you start tearing up their kitchen, they'll take their brooms to you."

"I don't think so. The notion of a stew that doesn't have cinders floating in it might appeal to them."

The man who approached their table wore a hooded smock, and the hood partially concealed his face. "You don't mind if I join you, do you?" he asked, sitting down and pushing the hood back slightly.

It was the same Styric they had last seen on the shore of the Gulf of Micae.

"You made good time, neighbor," Berit said. "Of course, you knew where you were going, and we didn't."

"How long did it take you to get dry?" Khalad asked him.

"Shall we skip the pleasantries?" the Styric said coldly. "I have further instructions for you."

"You mean you didn't stop by just to renew our acquaintance?" Khalad said. "I'm crushed."

"Very funny." The Styric hesitated. "I'm going to reach into my pocket for the note, so don't start drawing your knives."

"Wouldn't dream of it, old boy," Khalad drawled.

"This is for you, Sparhawk." The Styric handed Berit the sealed parchment.

Berit took the parchment and broke the seal. He carefully lifted out the identifying lock of the queen's hair and read aloud, " 'Sparhawk. Go overland to Arjun. You'll receive further instructions there. Krager.' "

"He must have been drunker than usual," Khalad observed. "He didn't bother with all the snide little comments this time. Just out of curiosity, friend, why didn't he send us straight on to Arjun from Sopal? He could have saved everybody a great deal of time."

"That's really none of your business, Elene. Just do as you're told."

"I'm a peasant, Styric, so I'm used to doing that. Prince Sparhawk here might get a little impatient, though, and that makes him bad-tempered." Khalad squinted at the lumpy-faced messenger. "Since the subject's come up anyway, I've got a word of friendly advice for you, old boy. It's about twenty days on horseback from here to Arjun. He's going to be very unpleasant by the time he gets there. If you should happen to be the one who delivers the next message, I wouldn't get too close to him."

"I think we can come up with a way for him to work off his bad temper," the Styric sneered. "You don't *have* twenty days to get to Arjun. You have fourteen." He stood up. "Don't be late." He turned and started toward the door.

"Let's go," Khalad said.

"Where?"

"After him."

"What for?"

Khalad sighed. "To shake him down, Berit," he explained with exaggerated patience. "I want to strip him and go through his clothes. He just *might* have the next message on him."

"Are you mad? They'll kill the queen if we do that."

"Just because we rough up their messenger boy? Don't be silly. They want the Bhelliom, and the queen's the only thing they've got to trade for it. We could routinely kill every single one of their messengers, and they wouldn't do a thing to her. Let's go shake that Styric up a little bit and go through his pockets. If we can get hold of the next message, we might be able to get the jump on them."

"You know, I think you're right. They *won't* do anything to the queen, will they?"

"Not a chance, my Lord. Let's go teach that Styric some manners. It's exactly the sort of thing Sparhawk would do."

"He *would*, wouldn't he?" Berit looked closely at his friend. "That fellow really irritates you, doesn't he?"

"Yes, as a matter of fact, he does. I don't like his attitude."

"Well, let's go change it, then."

"I'm not going to do anything foolish," Kalten said. "I just want to have a look around." The three of them were sitting under their tree in Narstil's cluttered jungle camp. They had a fire going, and three stolen chickens were spitted over it, dripping grease into the flames.

"It won't hurt," Caalador said to Bevier. "If the time ever comes when we have to go in there, we should probably know the lay of the land."

"Are you sure you can keep a handle on your temper?" Bevier asked Kalten. "You'll be all alone there, you know."

"I'm all grown up now, Bevier," Kalten assured him. "I'm not going to do anything noisy until *after* things are back the way they should be. We may not get a chance like this again. Senga's invited me to go along to help him sell beer. It's the most natural thing in the world, and nobody's going to recognize me. I can pick up some very valuable information in Natayos, and if I happen to see somebody I recognize standing in a window or something, we'll know for sure exactly where those two friends of ours are located. Then the fellow with the broken nose can have a word with his blue friend and they can lift them out before anybody can even blink. Then we can all go down there and explain to certain people just how unhappy we are."

"I'm in favor of it, myself," Caalador said to Bevier.

"It's tactically sound," Bevier admitted, "but—uh—Col here doesn't have any way to call for help if he gets in trouble."

"I won't need any help, because I'm not going to do anything out of the ordinary. I'm going anyway, Shallag, so don't waste your breath trying to talk me out of it."

Senga came across the littered camp. "The cart's all loaded, Col," he called. "Are you about ready?"

Kalten stood up. "Any time you are, Senga," he replied, pulling his half-cooked chicken off the spit and going to join his newfound friend. "I'm getting bored just sitting here counting trees."

It took the two of them about three hours to reach Natayos, since there is no real way to hurry an ox. The trail was fairly well traveled, and it wound around through the jungle, following the course of least resistance.

"There it is," Senga said as the cart jolted through a ford that crossed a narrow stream. He pointed across the stump-dotted clearing at an ancient city, a ruin so old that the passage of centuries had rounded down the very stones. "Stay close to me when we get there, Col. There are a couple of places we have to keep away from. There's one building right near the gate that they *really* don't want anybody to go near."

"Oh?" Kalten said, squinting at the mossy ruin ahead. "What's inside that makes them so touchy."

"I haven't the faintest idea, and I'm not curious enough to risk my health by asking."

"Maybe it's their treasure house," Kalten speculated. "If this army's as big as you say, they've probably picked up quite a bit of loot."

Senga shrugged. "It could be, I suppose, but I'm not going to fight all those guards just to find out. We're here to sell beer, Col. We'll get a goodly share of their treasure that way, and it's not as risky."

"But it's so *honest*," Kalten objected, grinning. "Isn't honest work immoral for people like us?"

Senga laughed and tapped the ox's rump with the long, slender stick he carried. The creaking cart jolted over the uneven ground toward the moldering walls.

"Ho, Senga!" one of the slovenly guards at the gate greeted Kalten's friend. "What kept you? It's been as dry as a plate of sand since the last time you left."

"You fellows are overworking my brewer," Senga replied. "He can't keep up with the demand. We have to let the beer age a *little* while before you drink it. Green beer does funny things to a man's guts."

"You haven't raised your prices again, have you?"

"No. Same price as before."

"Ten times what you paid for the beer in the first place, I'll wager."

"Oh, not quite *that* much. Where do you want me to set up?"

"Same place as last time. I'll pass the word, and they'll start lining up."

"I want some guards this time, Mondra," Senga told him. "I don't want another riot when the last cask runs dry, the way there was last week."

"I'll see to it. Save some for me."

The oxcart clattered through the gate and into a wide street where most of the moss had been worn off the cobblestones. A great deal of work had clearly taken place here in Natayos in the past few years. The squared-off stones of the broken walls had been rather carelessly restacked and then shored up with peeled log braces. Long-vanished roofs had been replaced with crude thatching made of tree limbs, providing nesting sites for raucous tropical birds, and here and there blackened piles of half-burned trees and bushes marked the places where indifferent workmen had attempted to dispose of the mountains of brush that had been cleared from the streets and houses. The men living here lounged idly in the streets. There were Elenes from Astel, Edom, and Daconia, as well as Arjunis and Cynesgans. They were a roughly dressed, unshaven lot who showed no signs that they even knew the meaning of the word *discipline*.

"What price are you getting for this?" Kalten asked, patting one of the beer barrels in the cart.

"A penny a gill," Senga replied.

"That's outrageous!"

"They don't *have* to buy it." Senga shrugged. "Get the money *before* you start to pour. Don't take promises."

"You've put my moral qualms to rest, Senga." Kalten laughed. "At *that* price, this is hardly honest."

"There's that building I was telling you about."

Kalten tried to look casual as he turned to stare at the substantial-looking ruin. "They *really* don't want anybody to look into that place," he said. "Those bars on the windows make it look like a jail."

"Not quite, Col. Those bars are there to keep people *out*, not in."

Kalten grunted, still staring intently at the building. The barred windows had panes of glass in them, cheap, cloudy glass that had been poorly installed. Drapes on the inside cut off any possibility of seeing anything or anyone who might be in there. There were guards at the door, and other guards stationed at every corner. Kalten wanted to howl with frustration. The gentle girl who had become the center of his life was possibly no more than twenty yards away, but she might as well have been on the other side of the moon; and even if she were to look out through that clouded glass she would not recognize his altered features.

Senga paid the guards in the square with beer, and then he and his friend got down to work. Scarpa's rebels were rowdy, shouting and laughing, but they were generally in a good humor. They lined up in an orderly fashion and came to the rear of the cart two by two, where Senga and Kalten filled their containers with the amber beer. There were a few arguments about the capacity of the assorted tankards, jugs, and pails, but Senga's word on the subject was final, and anyone who objected too loudly was sent back to the end of the line to think things over for an hour or so while he worked his way back to the front again.

It was after the two entrepreneurs had drained the last barrel and sent the disappointed latecomers away that Kalten saw a familiar figure come weaving across the mossy square toward the oxcart. Krager was not wearing well. His head was shaved and as pale as a fish-belly, and his dissipated face was eroded by decades of hard drinking. His clothing, though obviously expensive, was wrinkled and filthy. He shook continually with a palsied tremor that ran through him in waves.

"I don't suppose you brought any wine," he asked Senga hopefully.

"Not much call for it," Senga told him, refastening the tailgate of the cart. "Most of these fellows want beer."

"Do you know any place where you can *get* wine?"

"I can ask around. What's your preference?"

"Arcian red, if you can find any."

Senga whistled. "*That* will cost you, my friend. I could probably chase down some of the local reds for you, but the imported stuff—that's going to take a *big* bite out of your purse."

Krager smirked at him. "It's no problem," he said in his slurred voice. "I'm what you might call independently wealthy at the moment. These local reds taste like pig swill. I want *real* wine."

"It might take a while," Senga told him dubiously. "I've got contacts in Delo that might be able to find some for you, but Delo's a long way off."

"When are you coming back?"

"A couple of days. The brewery where I buy this slop's running day and night, but I still can't keep up."

"Bring me a couple of barrels of the local pig swill then—enough to tide me over until you can find me some Arcian red."

"You can count on me," Senga assured him. He gave Krager a hard look. "I'll need something in advance, though. I'll have to *buy* the Arcian red before I can sell it to you. I'm doing fairly well, but I'm not *that* rich yet."

Krager fumbled for his purse.

Kalten was suddenly gripped by an almost intolerable impatience. He was sure now that Alean was here. Krager's presence virtually confirmed it. The prisoners were almost certainly being held in the building with barred windows. He absolutely *had* to get back to Narstil's camp so that Bevier could pass the word on to Aphrael. If Xanetia *could* enter

Natayos unseen, she could either penetrate the prison walls or reach into Krager's wine-sodden mind to verify what was almost a certainty now. If all went well, it would be no more than a few days until he and Sparhawk were reunited with the women they loved. *Then* they could all come here and do unpleasant things to the people responsible.

Vanion and Betuana reached Sarna late that afternoon, and the Atan queen scarcely paused before setting out for the border.

"It was ghastly, Sparhawk," Vanion said, leaning wearily back in his chair and putting his visored helmet on the table. "They're like no soldiers I've ever seen before. They're big, and they're fast, and their hides are so tough that most of the time my sword just bounced off them. I don't know where Klæl found them, but they've got yellow blood, and they made mincemeat out of my knights."

"Kring and Tikume ran into them as well, I guess," Sparhawk told him. "Anosian tried to pass word to Aphrael, but he garbled the spell so badly that she couldn't make any sense out of it. She's a little unhappy with Tynian. When he was gathering up the knights he brought back to Matherion, he accidentally picked every Pandion who has the least bit of skill with the spells. That's why she can't get any reports from Komier."

"We might have to send somebody to join him and handle communications—except that it'd take weeks for him to get there."

"Not if Aphrael takes him, it won't," Sparhawk disagreed. "She carried me from Beresa to Sopal—almost a thousand miles—in about a half an hour."

"You're not serious!"

"You'll *love* flying, Vanion."

"You're carrying tales, Sparhawk."

They turned quickly.

The Child-Goddess was sitting in a chair at the far end of the room with her grass-stained little feet up on the table.

"I *wish* you wouldn't do that," Sparhawk told her.

"Would you prefer some kind of announcement, Sparhawk? Multitudes of spirits bawling hymns of praise to introduce me? It's a little ostentatious, but I can arrange it."

"Just forget I said anything."

"I'll do that. I had a chat with Anosian, and he's practicing now—very hard. Kring and Tikume ran across Klæl and his soldiers out in the desert, and they discovered something you gentlemen should know. I was right, Vanion. Klæl's soldiers have bile in their veins instead of blood because they breathe with their livers. That means that the air where they come from isn't anything like the air here—probably something like marsh gas. There's something in it that they need, and they can't get it out of our air. The Peloi used their standard cut-and-run tactics, and after a little while those monsters started to collapse. Next time you come up against them, just turn around and run away. If they try to chase you, they'll choke to death. Did Betuana leave?"

"Yes, Divine One," Itagne replied.

"Good. The quicker I can get Engessa to my island, the quicker I'll have him back on his feet."

"I've been meaning to ask you about that," Sparhawk said. "You said that his brain's been injured."

"Yes."

"The brain's very complicated, isn't it?"

"Yours aren't quite as complex as ours, but they aren't simple, by any means."

"And you can heal Engessa's brain on your island?"

"Of course."

"If you can fix a brain, you should be able to fix somebody's heart. Why didn't you just take Sephrenia to your island and heal her there? Why did you come to Beresa and try to steal Bhelliom?"

"*What's this?*" Vanion exclaimed, coming to his feet.

"Wonderful, Sparhawk," Aphrael said dryly. "I'm awed by your subtlety. She's all right, Vanion. Bhelliom brought her back."

Vanion smashed his fist down on the table and then controlled himself with an obvious effort. "Would it inconvenience anybody to tell me what happened?" he asked them in an icy voice.

"We were in Dirgis." Aphrael shrugged. "Sephrenia was alone in the room, and Zalasta came in and stabbed her in the heart."

"Good God!"

"She's fine, Vanion. Bhelliom took care of it. She's coming along very well. Xanetia's with her."

Vanion started toward the door.

"Oh, come back here," the Child-Goddess told him. "As soon as I get Engessa to the island and deal with his injury, I'll take you to Dirgis. She's asleep now anyway, and you've seen her sleep before—lots of times."

Vanion flushed slightly and then looked a bit sheepish.

"You still haven't answered my question," Sparhawk said. "If you can fix a brain, why can't you fix a heart?"

"Because I can shut a brain down to work on it, Sparhawk," she replied in a long-suffering tone. "The heart has to keep on beating, and I can't work on it while it's jumping around like that."

"Oh, I guess that makes sense."

"Do you happen to know where I could find Zalasta?" Vanion asked in a dreadful voice.

"He's probably gone back to Natayos," Aphrael replied.

"After I visit Sephrenia, do you suppose you could take me there? I'd *really* like to have a talk with him."

"I get his heart," the Child-Goddess said.

Vanion gave her a strange look.

"It's an ongoing joke," Sparhawk told him.

"I'm not joking, Sparhawk," Aphrael said bleakly.

"We can't go to Natayos," Sparhawk said. "Ehlana might be there, and Scarpa will kill her if we come pounding on the gate. Besides, I think you'll have to talk with Khwaj before you do anything to Zalasta."

"Khwaj?" Vanion asked.

"Tynian told Aphrael that Khwaj has his own plans for our Styric friend. He wants to set him on fire."

"I've got some more interesting ideas," Vanion said grimly.

"I wouldn't be so sure, my Lord. Khwaj wants to set Zalasta on fire, but he doesn't want to burn him to death. He's talking about an eternal flame—with Zalasta screaming in the middle of it—forever."

Vanion considered that. "What a merry idea," he said finally.

"My lady," Alean whispered urgently, "come quickly. Zalasta's returned."

Ehlana drew the linen headcloth down over her forehead and joined her maid at the defective window. The wimple had been Alean's idea. It fit snugly over the queen's ravaged scalp, and covered her throat and the underside of her chin as well. It was uncomfortable, but it concealed the horror Krager's knife had made of her hair. She bent and looked out through the small triangular opening in the window.

Zalasta's gaunt face was twisted with grief, and his eyes were dead. Scarpa came hurrying up, his face eager. "Well?" he demanded.

"Go away, Scarpa," Zalasta told him.

"I only wanted to be sure you were all right, Father," Scarpa replied with obvious insincerity. Scarpa had fashioned a crude crown for himself out of a serving bowl made of hammered gold. He was evidently unaware of how absurd he looked with the lopsided adornment perched on his shaved head.

"Leave me!" Zalasta thundered. "Get out of my sight!"

"Is she dead?" Scarpa ignored the dreadful threat implicit in his father's voice.

Zalasta's face hardened. "Yes," he replied in a strangely neutral tone. "I drove my knife straight into her heart. I'm deciding right now whether or not I can live with what I've done. Please stay, Scarpa, by all means. This was *your* idea, after all. It was such a marvelous notion that I may want to reward you for it."

Scarpa backed away, his suddenly rational eyes now filled with fear.

Zalasta barked two words in Styric and reached out his hand, his fingers curved like hooks. Scarpa clutched at his belly and screeched. His makeshift crown fell unnoticed as Zalasta implacably dragged him back.

"You're pathetically obvious, Scarpa," Zalasta grated, his face only inches from his son's, "but your plan had one minor flaw. I may very well kill myself for what I did to Sephrenia, but I'll kill you first—just as unpleasantly as I possibly can. I may just kill you anyway. I don't really like you, Scarpa. I felt a certain responsibility for you, but that's a word you wouldn't understand." His eyes suddenly burned. "Your madness must be contagious, my son. I'm starting to lose my grip on sanity myself. You talked me into killing Sephrenia, and I loved her far more than I could ever love you." He unhooked his fingers. "Run away, Scarpa. Pick up your cheap toy crown and run. I'll be able to find you when I decide to kill you."

Scarpa fled, but Ehlana did not see him leave. Her eyes were filled with tears, and she turned from the window with a grief-stricken wail.

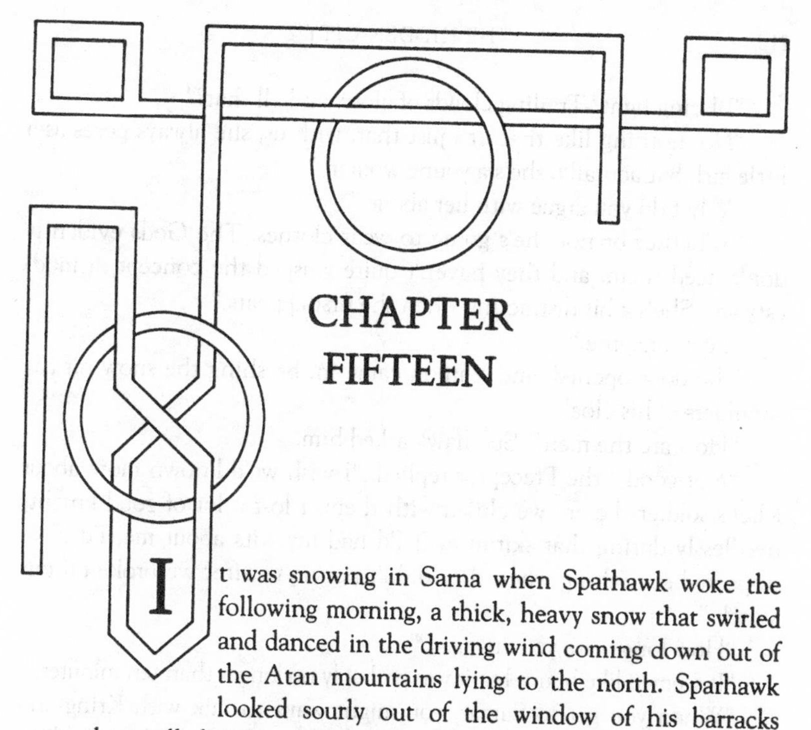

CHAPTER FIFTEEN

It was snowing in Sarna when Sparhawk woke the following morning, a thick, heavy snow that swirled and danced in the driving wind coming down out of the Atan mountains lying to the north. Sparhawk looked sourly out of the window of his barracks room, then pulled on his clothes and went looking for the others.

He found Itagne sitting by the stove in the war room with a sheaf of documents in his lap. "Something important?" he asked as he entered.

"Hardly," Itagne replied. He made a face and put the papers away. "I made a serious blunder last spring before Oscagne uprooted me and sent me to Cynestra. I was teaching a class in foreign relations at the university, and I slipped and said the fatal words, 'write a paper.' Now I've got a bale of these things to plow through." He shuddered.

"Bad?"

"Unbelievably so. Undergraduates should never be allowed to touch a quill pen. So far I've encountered fifteen different versions of my own lecture notes—all couched in graceless, semiliterate prose."

"Where's Vanion?"

"He's checking on his wounded. Have you seen Aphrael yet this morning?"

Sparhawk shook his head. "She could be anywhere."

"Did she actually fly you here from Dirgis?"

"Oh, yes—and up from Beresa before that. It's an unusual experience, and it always starts with the same argument."

Itagne gave him a questioning look.

"She has to revert to her real form when she does it."

"Blazing light? Trailing clouds of glory, and all that?"

"No, nothing like that. It's just that, with us, she always poses as a little girl, but actually, she's a young woman."

"What do you argue with her about?"

"Whether or not she's going to wear clothes. The Gods evidently don't need them, and they haven't quite grasped the concept of modesty yet. She's a bit distracting when she first appears."

"I can imagine."

The door opened, and Vanion came in, brushing the snow off the shoulders of his cloak.

"How are the men?" Sparhawk asked him.

"Not good," the Preceptor replied. "I wish we'd known more about Klæl's soldiers before we closed with them. I lost a lot of good knights needlessly during that skirmish. If I'd had my wits about me, I'd have suspected something when they didn't pursue us after we broke off our attack."

"How long were you engaged?"

"It seemed like hours, but it was probably no longer than ten minutes."

"When you get to Samar, you might want to talk with Kring and Tikume. We should try to get some idea of just how long those soldiers can function in our air before they start to collapse."

Vanion nodded.

There was really nothing for them to do, and the morning dragged sluggishly by.

It was shortly before noon when Betuana, clad in close-fitting otter-skin clothing, came running effortlessly out of the swirling snow. Her almost-inhuman stamina was somehow unnerving. She seemed hardly winded and not even flushed as she entered the room where they waited. "Invigorating," she noted absently as she peeled off her outer garment. She took one lock of her night-dark hair and stretched it out to look critically at its sodden length. "Does anyone have a comb?" she asked.

They all started at the sound of a blaring trumpet fanfare from the other end of the room. They spun around and saw the Child-Goddess. She was surrounded by a nimbus of pure light, she sat sedately in midair, and she was smiling sweetly at Sparhawk. "Is that sort of what you had in mind?" She asked him.

He cast his eyes upward. "Why me?" he groaned. Then he looked at her smiling little face. "I give up, Aphrael," he said. "You win."

"Of course. I always win." She gently settled to the floor, and her light dimmed. "Come here, Betuana. Let me comb that out for you." She held out her hands, and a comb appeared in one and a towel in the other.

The Queen of the Atans went to her and sat in a chair.

"What did he say?" Aphrael asked as she began to wrap Betuana's dripping hair in the length of cloth.

"He said 'no' right at first," the queen replied, "and 'no' the second and third times as well. He started to weaken about the twelfth time, as I remember it."

"I knew it would work." Aphrael smiled, working the towel through Betuana's locks.

"Are we missing something?" Vanion asked her.

"The Atans don't call on their God very often, so he almost *has* to respond when they do. He was probably concentrating on something else and each time Betuana called him, he had to put it down and go see what she wanted."

"I was very polite," Betuana smiled. "But I *did* keep asking. He's afraid of you, Divine One."

"I know." Aphrael laid down her towel and picked up the comb. "He thinks I'm going to steal his soul or something. He won't come anywhere near me."

"I let him know that I was going to keep on calling him until he gave me permission," Betuana went on, "and he finally gave in."

"They always do." Aphrael shrugged. "You'll get what you want eventually if you just keep asking."

"It's called *nagging*, Divine One," Sparhawk told her.

"How would you like to listen to a few days of trumpet fanfares, Sparhawk?" she asked.

"Ah—no, thanks. It was good of you to ask, though."

"He *definitely* gave his permission?" Aphrael asked the queen.

Betuana smiled. "Very definitely. He said, 'Tell her she can do anything she wants! Just leave me alone!' "

"Good. I'll take Engessa to the island, then." Aphrael pursed her lips. "Maybe you'd better send a runner to your husband. Tell him about Klæl's soldiers. I know your husband, so you'll have to *order* him not to attack them. I've never known *anyone* so totally incapable of turning around as he is."

"I'll *try* to explain it to him," Betuana said a little dubiously.

"Good luck. Here." Aphrael handed over the comb. "I'll take Engessa to the island, thaw him out, and get started."

Ulath called a halt on the outskirts of town, and Bhlokw summoned Ghnomb. The God of Eat appeared holding the half-eaten hindquarter of some large animal in one huge paw.

"We have reached the place where the one called Berit has been told to come," Ulath told the huge Troll-God. "It would be well now if we come out of No-Time and go into the time of broken moments."

Ghnomb gave him a baffled look, clearly not understanding what they were doing.

"U-lat and Tin-in hunt thought," Bhlokw explained. "The man-things have bellies in their minds as well as the bellies in their bellies. They have to fill both bellies. Their belly-bellies are full now. That is why they ask this. It is their wish to now fill their mind-bellies."

A slow look of comprehension began to dawn on Ghnomb's brutish face. "Why did you not say this before, Ulath-from-Thalesia?"

Ulath groped for an answer.

"It was Bhlokw who found that we have mind-bellies," Tynian stepped in. "We did not know this. We only knew that our minds were hungry. It is good that Ghworg sent Bhlokw to hunt with us. Bhlokw is a very good hunter."

Bhlokw beamed.

Ulath quickly expanded the metaphor. "Our mind-bellies hunger for thoughts about the wicked ones," he explained. "We can track those thoughts in the bird-noises the man-things make when they speak. We will stand on one side of the broken moment where they can not see us, and listen to the bird-noises they are making. We will follow those tracks to the ones we hunt, and they will not know we are there. Then we will listen to the bird-noises *they* make and learn where they have hidden Anakha's mate."

"You hunt well," Ghnomb approved. "I had not thought of this kind of hunting before. It is almost as good as hunting things-to-eat. I will help you in your hunt."

"It makes us glad that you will," Tynian thanked him.

Arjun was the capital of the Kingdom of Arjuna, a substantial city on the south shore of the lake. The royal palace and the stately homes of the noble families of the kingdom lay in the hills on the southern edge of town, and the commercial center was near the lakefront.

Ulath and Tynian concealed their horses and proceeded on foot through the grey half light of Ghnomb's broken moments into the city itself. Then they split up and began to search for the food their mind-bellies craved. Bhlokw went looking for dogs.

It was almost evening when Ulath came out of another of the seedy taverns near the docks on the east side of town. "This is going to take all month," he muttered to himself. The name *Scarpa* had cropped up in a few of the conversations he had overheard, and each time he heard it, he had eagerly drawn closer to listen. Unfortunately, however, Scarpa and his army were general topics of conversation here, and Ulath had not been able to pick up anything that was at all useful.

"Get out of my way!" the voice was harsh, peremptory. Ulath turned to see who was being so offensive.

The man was a richly dressed Dacite. He was riding a spirited black horse, and his face bore the marks of habitual dissipation.

Though he had never seen the fellow before, Ulath recognized him immediately. Talen's pencil had captured that face almost perfectly. Ulath smiled. "Well, now," he murmured, "that's a little better." He stepped out into the street and followed the prancing black horse.

Their destination was one of the grand houses near the royal palace. A liveried servant rushed from the house to greet the sneering Elene. "We've been eagerly awaiting your arrival, my Lord," he declared, bowing obsequiously.

"Get somebody to take care of my horse." The Elene snapped as he dismounted. "Is everybody here?"

"Yes, Baron Parok."

"Astonishing. Don't just stand there, fool. Take me to them at once."

"Yes, my Lord Baron."

Ulath smiled again and followed them into the house.

The room to which the servant led them appeared to be a study of some kind. The walls were lined with bookcases, though the books shelved there showed no signs of ever having been opened. There were about a dozen men in the room: some Elene, some Arjuni, and even one Styric.

"Let's get down to business," Baron Parok told them, negligently tossing his plumed hat and his gloves down on the table. "What have you to report?"

"Prince Sparhawk has reached Tiana, Baron Parok," the lone Styric told him.

"We expected that."

"We did not, however, expect his treatment of my kinsman. He and that brute he calls his squire followed our messenger and assaulted him. They tore off all his clothes and turned all his pockets inside out."

Parok laughed harshly. "I've met your cousin, Zorek," he said. "I'm sure he richly deserved it. What did he say to the prince to merit such treatment?"

"He gave them the note, my Lord, and that ruffian of a squire made some insulting remark about a twenty-day journey on horseback. My cousin took offense at that and told them that they only had fourteen days to make the journey."

"That was *not* in the instructions," Parok snapped. "Did Sparhawk kill him?"

"No, my lord." Zorek's tone was sullen.

"Pity," Parok said darkly. "Now I'll have to attend to it myself. You Styrics get above yourselves at times. When I have leisure, I'm going to run your cousin down and hang his guts on a fence as an example to the rest of you. You're being paid to do as you're told, not to get creative." He looked around. "Who's got the next note?" he asked.

"I have, my Lord," a rather prosperous-looking Edomishman replied.

"You'd better hold off on delivering it. Zorek's cousin upset our timetable with his excursion into constructive creativity. Let Sparhawk cool his heels here for a week or so. *Then* give him the note that tells him to go on to Derel. Lord Scarpa wants his army to start moving north before we send Sparhawk on to Natayos for the exchange."

"Baron Parok," a baggy-eyed Arjuni in a brocade doublet said arrogantly, "this delay—particularly here in the capital—poses some threat to my king. This Sparhawk person is notoriously irrational, and he *does* still have the jewel of power in his possession. His Majesty does *not* want that Elene barbarian lingering here in Arjun with spare time on his hands. Send him on to Derel immediately. If he's going to destroy some place, let it be Derel instead of Arjun."

"You have amazingly sharp ears, Duke Milanis," Parok said sardonically. "Can you *really* hear what King Rakya is saying when you're a mile from the palace?"

"I'm here to protect his Majesty's interests, Baron. I have full authority to speak for him. His Majesty's alliance with Lord Scarpa is *not* etched on a diamond. Keep Prince Sparhawk moving. We don't want him here in Arjun."

"And if I don't?"

Milanis shrugged. "His Majesty will abrogate the alliance and make a full report of what you people have been doing—and what you're planning to do—to the Tamul ambassador."

"I see that the old saw about the stupidity of trusting an Arjuni is still true."

"Just do as you're told, Parok," Milanis snapped. "Don't bore me with all these tedious protests and racial slurs. His Majesty's report to the ambassador has already been written. All he requires is an excuse to send it across town."

A servant entered with a flagon and a tray of wineglasses, and Ulath took advantage of the open door to slip from the room. It was going to take a while to round up Tynian and Bhlokw, and then they were going to have to compose a fairly extensive message to Aphrael.

After he had slipped out of the house, however, Sir Ulath very briefly indulged himself. He leapt high into the air with a triumphant bellow, smacking his hands together with glee. Then he composed himself and went looking for his friends.

The black-armored Sir Heldin returned to rejoin Patriarch Bergsten at the head of the column.

"Any luck?" Bergsten asked him.

Heldin shook his head. "Sir Tynian was very thorough," he rumbled in his deep basso. "He winnowed through the ranks of the Pandion Order like a man panning for gold. I think he took just about everybody who can even *pronounce* the Styric language."

"*You* know the spells."

"Yes, but Aphrael can't hear me. My voice is pitched too low for her ears."

"That raises some very interesting theological points," Bergsten mused.

"Could we ponder them some other time, your Grace? Right now we have to get word of what happened in Zemoch to Sparhawk and Vanion. The war could be over by the time Ambassador Fontan's messengers reach them."

"Talk with the other orders, Heldin," Bergsten suggested.

"I don't think it would work, your Grace. Each order works through the personal God of the Styric who taught them the secrets. We have to get word to Aphrael. *She's* the one who's perched on Sparhawk's shoulder."

"Heldin, you spent too much time practicing with your weapons during your novitiate. Theology *does* have a purpose, you know."

"Yes, your Grace," Heldin sighed, rolling his eyes upward and bracing himself for a sermon.

"Don't do that," Bergsten told him. "I'm not talking about *Elene* theology. I'm talking about the misguided beliefs of the Styrics. How many Styric Gods are there?"

"A thousand, your Grace," Heldin replied promptly. "Sephrenia always made some issue of that."

"Do these thousand Younger Gods exist independently of each other?"

"As I understand it, they're all related—sort of like a family."

"Amazing. You *did* listen when Sephrenia was talking to you. You Pandions all worship Aphrael, right?"

"*Worship* would be too strong a term, your Grace."

"I've heard stories about Aphrael, Heldin." Bergsten smiled. "She has a private agenda. She's trying to steal the whole of humankind. Now then, I'm a member of the Genidian Order." He paused. "I *was*," he corrected himself. "We make our appeals to Hanka; the Cyrinics work through Romalic; and the Alciones deal with Setras. Do you imagine that in their misty heaven somewhere above the clouds these Styric Gods might now and then talk with each other?"

"Please don't beat me over the head, Bergsten. I overlooked something, that's all. I'm not stupid."

"Never said you were, old boy." Bergsten smiled. "You just needed spiritual guidance, that's all. That's the purpose of our Holy Mother. Come to *me* with your spiritual problems, my son. I will gently guide you—and if guidance doesn't work, I'll take my ax and drive you."

"I see that your Grace adheres to the notion of the Church Muscular," Heldin said sourly.

"That's *my* spiritual problem, my son, not yours. Now go find an Alcione. Legend has it that Aphrael and Setras are particularly close. I think we can count on Setras to pass things along to his thieving little cousin."

"*Your Grace!*" Heldin protested.

"The Church has had her eye on Aphrael for centuries, Heldin. We know all about your precious little Child-Goddess and her tricks. Don't let her kiss you, my friend. If you do, she'll pinch your soul while you're not looking."

There were a dozen wobbly oxcarts this time, all heavily laden with beer barrels, and Senga had recruited several dozen of Narstil's shabby outlaws to assist him in guarding and dispensing his product. Kalten had rather smoothly insinuated Caalador and Bevier into the company.

"I still think you're making a mistake, Senga," Kalten told his good-natured employer as their rickety cart jolted along the rough jungle path toward Natayos. "You've got a complete lock on the market. Why lower your prices?"

"Because I'll make more money if I do."

"That doesn't make sense."

"Look, Col," Senga explained patiently, "when I came here before, I only had one cartload of beer. I could get any price I asked, because my beer was so scarce."

"I guess that makes sense."

"I've got an almost unlimited supply now, though, so I'm making my profit on volume instead of price."

"That's what doesn't make sense."

"Let me put it this way. Which would you rather do—steal ten crowns from one man or a penny from each of ten thousand men?"

Kalten did some quick counting on his fingers. "Oh," he said. "Now I see what you're driving at. Very shrewd, Senga."

Senga puffed himself up a little. "It never hurts to think long-range, Col. My *real* concern is the fact that it's not really all that hard to make beer. If some clever fellow's got a recipe, he could set up his own brewery right here. I don't want to get involved in a price war just when things are starting to go well for me."

They had left Narstil's camp at daybreak, and so it was midmorning when they reached Natayos. They passed unchallenged through the gates, rumbled by the house with barred windows, and set up shop again in the same square as before. As Senga's closest associate, Kalten had been promoted to the position of Chief of Security. The reputation for unpleasantness he had established early on in Narstil's camp ensured that none of the outlaws would question his orders, and the presence of Bevier, patch-eyed, lochaber-armed, and obviously homicidal, added to his authority.

"We ain't likely t' accomplish too much here, Col," Caalador muttered to Kalten as the two of them stood guard near one of the busy beer carts. "Ol' Senga's so worried 'bout some feller slippin' by 'thout payin' that me'n you is tied down tighter'n a couple o' dawgs on short leashes."

"Wait until later, Ezek," Kalten advised. "We'll be able to move around a little more freely after everybody gets drunk."

Bevier slouched over to join them, his short-handled lochaber in his fist. People automatically got out of his way for some reason. "I just had a thought," he said.

"You want to kill somebody?" Kalten suggested.

"Be serious, Col. Why don't you take your friend Senga aside and suggest that he set up a permanent establishment here in Natayos? It's the logical thing to do, and it'd give the three of us an excuse to stay here. If we cleaned out one of these ruined buildings and opened a tavern, we could stay here and run it. It makes more sense than selling beer off the tailgate of an oxcart."

"He's got hisself a point there, Col," Caalador said. "Ol' Shallag here, he *looks* like he drinks blood for breakfast, but his head's still a-workin' in back o' that there eye patch."

Kalten thought about it. "It *would* set us up right here in Natayos, wouldn't it? We'd be able to keep an eye on things." He looked around. "Senga's a little worried that somebody here might start his own brewery," he said for the benefit of nearby soldiers. "If the three of us are right here, we could probably persuade anybody who does that to take up another hobby. I'll go talk with Senga and see what he thinks of the notion."

He found his good-natured friend sitting at a makeshift table behind one of the oxcarts. The outlaw was counting money with an almost dreamy expression on his face. "Oh, this is just *fine*, Col," he almost crooned.

"They're only pennies."

"I know, but there are so *many* of them."

"Shallag came up with an idea."

"He wants to thin out the crowd by hacking the head off every third man in line?"

"Shallag's not really *that* bad."

"Oh, really? Every man in camp has nightmares about him."

"He hasn't killed a single man since he came to Arjuna."

"He's saving up. He's just biding his time until he can gather up a few dozen of us all together and kill all of us at once."

"Do you want to listen to his idea, or haven't you finished making bad jokes yet?"

"Sorry. Go ahead."

"He thinks we ought to clean out one of these empty ruins and set up a permanent tavern."

"You mean like a real business? With a counter and tables and chairs and all that?"

"Why not? Now that your brewer's working full time, you've got access to a steady supply, and this is where your customers are. If you set up shop here, you can sell beer all day every day instead of just coming here once a week. Then your customers would come to you in manageable numbers instead of by the regiment."

"I never thought of it," Senga admitted. "I just thought I'd make a quick profit and then run for the border. I could set up a real tavern here, Col—a real, honest-to-God legitimate business. I wouldn't have to steal any more."

"I've seen your price list, Senga. Don't worry. You're still stealing."

Senga ignored him. "Maybe I could call it 'Senga's Palace,' " he said in a dreamy tone of voice. He frowned. "No," he decided. "That's a little too flashy for a beer tavern. I think I'll just call it 'Senga's.' That'd definitely be a more lasting memorial than just a grave marker with the date when I got hung carved on it." Then he shook his head and sighed. "No, Col," he said regretfully. "It wouldn't work. If I took you and my other guards out of here, Scarpa's soldiers would just march in and drink up all my beer without paying."

"Why take us out, then? We can stay right here and make sure they pay."

"I'm not sure Narstil would like it if we didn't go back to camp at night."

"Senga," Kalten said gently, "do you really need Narstil any more? You're an honest businessman now. You shouldn't be associating with bandits."

Senga laughed. "You're coming at me a little too fast, Col. Give me some time to adjust my thinking." Then he suddenly swore.

"What's wrong?"

"It's a beautiful idea, Col, but it won't work."

"Why not?"

"Because I'll need Scarpa's permission to set up shop here, and I'm not going to go anywhere near him to ask for it."

"I don't think you'll have to, my friend. I went rummaging around through those heaps of trash in Narstil's camp yesterday, and guess what I found?"

"What?"

"A very fancy, silver-mounted cask of Arcian red. It's even equipped with a silver spigot. The fellow who stole it didn't know how much it was worth—he's a beer man. I got it off him for half a crown. I'll sell it to you, and you can make a present of it to that Krager fellow.

Why don't we let *him* persuade Scarpa to give you permission to go into business here?"

"Col, you're a genius! What'll you take for that cask of Arcian red?"

"Oh—five crowns, I guess."

"*Five crowns?* Ten times what you paid for it? That's robbery!"

"You ought to know, Senga. You're my friend, but business *is* business, after all."

They found the bleary-eyed Krager sitting on a broken wall watching the crowd of thirsty soldiers in the square without much interest. He held a tankard in one hand and he drank from it occasionally with obvious distaste.

"Ah, there you are, Master Krager," Senga said jovially. "Why don't you dump out that slop and try a sup of this?" He patted the ornate wine cask he was carrying under one arm.

"More local swill?" Krager asked.

"Try it and see what you think," Senga suggested.

Krager emptied his wine out on the ground and held out his pewter tankard. Senga turned the handle of the silver spigot and dribbled about a half cupful of Arcian red into it.

Krager squinted into his mug and sniffed at it suspiciously. Then his eyes rolled up ecstatically. "Oh, dearie, dearie me!" he breathed in a reverent tone of voice. He took a small sip and actually seemed to quiver with delight.

"I thought you might like it," Senga said. "Now that I've got your attention, I've got a business proposition for you. I'd like to set up a permanent tavern here in Natayos, but I'll need permission to do that. I'd take it as a real favor if you could see your way clear to put in a good word for me with Lord Scarpa. I'd be very grateful to you if you can get his approval."

"*How* grateful?" Krager asked quickly.

"Probably about *this* grateful." Senga patted the silver-mounted cask again. "Tell Lord Scarpa that I won't cause any problems. I'll pick one of these empty buildings a little way off from his main camp and clean it out and fix the roof my very own self. I'll provide my own security and make sure that none of his soldiers gets *too* drunk."

"Go ahead and get started, Master Senga," Krager said, eyeing the cask. "You've got my personal guarantee that Lord Scarpa will agree." He reached out for the wine.

Senga stepped back. "*After*, Master Krager," he said firmly. "At the moment, I'm filled with appreciation. The gratitude comes *after* Scarpa gives his permission."

Then Elron came hurrying across the crowded square. "Krager!" he said in a shrill voice. "Come at once! Lord Scarpa's in a rage! He's commanded us all to meet him at headquarters immediately!"

"What's the matter?" Krager rose to his feet.

"Cyzada just came in from Cynesga. He told Zalasta and Lord Scarpa that Klæl went to have a look at the fellow we've been following all this time! It's not Sparhawk, Krager! Whoever it is *looks* like Sparhawk, but Klæl knew immediately that it's somebody else!"

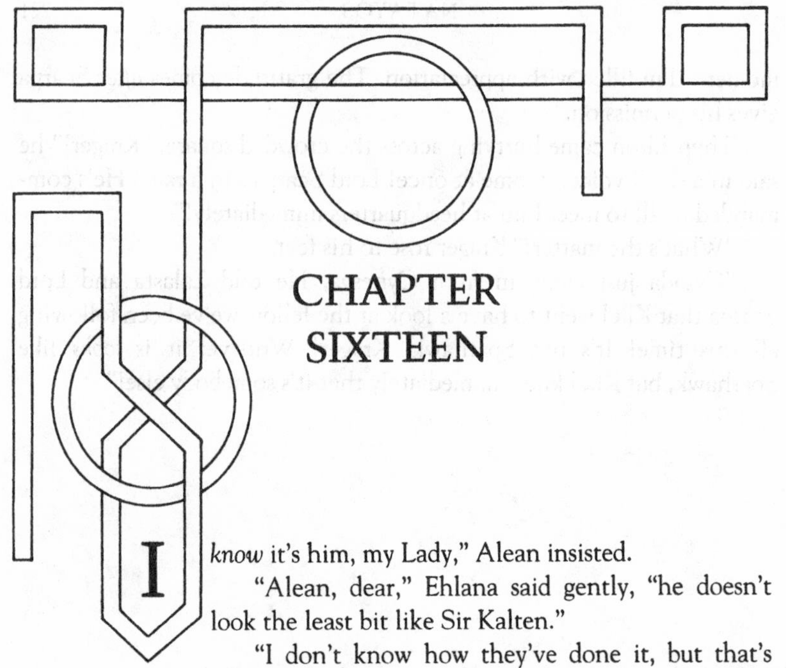

CHAPTER SIXTEEN

I *know* it's him, my Lady," Alean insisted.

"Alean, dear," Ehlana said gently, "he doesn't look the least bit like Sir Kalten."

"I don't know how they've done it, but that's Kalten out there in the street," the girl replied. "My heart sings every time he walks by."

Ehlana peered through the little opening in the window. The man *looked* like an Elene, there was no question about that, and Sephrenia *was* a magician, after all.

The thought of Sephrenia filled the queen's eyes with tears again. She straightened, quickly wiping her eyes. "He's gone by," she said. "What makes you so sure, dear?"

"A thousand things, my Lady—little things. It's the way he holds his head, that funny way he rolls his shoulders when he walks, his laugh, the way he hitches up his sword belt. They've changed his face somehow, but I know it's him."

"You *could* be right, Alean," Ehlana concluded a bit dubiously. "I could probably pick Sparhawk out of a crowd no matter *whose* face he happened to be wearing."

"Exactly, my Lady. Our hearts know the men we love."

Ehlana began to pace the floor, her fingers absently adjusting the wimple that covered her head. "It's not impossible," she conceded. "Sparhawk's told me about all the times he disguised himself when he was in Rendor, and Styric magic might very well be able to change people's faces. And of course, if Sephrenia hadn't been able to do it,

Bhelliom certainly could have. Let's trust your heart and say that it *is* Sir Kalten out there."

"I *know* it is, my Lady."

"It *does* stand to reason," Ehlana mused. "If Sparhawk's somehow found out that we're here, he'd most *definitely* want to have some of our friends close by when the rest of them come to rescue us." She frowned as a thought came to her. "Maybe he *doesn't* know for sure, though. Kalten *might* just be here to look around. We have to come up with some way to let him know that we're here before he gives up and moves on."

"But, my Lady," the girl with the huge eyes protested, "if we try to call out to him, we'll put him in terrible danger." She bent and looked out at the street again. "He's coming back," she said.

"Sing, Alean!" Ehlana exclaimed suddenly.

"What?"

"Sing! If anyone in the whole world would recognize your voice, Kalten would!"

Alean's eyes suddenly widened. "He *would*!" she exclaimed.

"Here. Let me watch his face. Sing your soul out, Alean! Break his heart!"

Alean's voice throbbed as her clear soprano reached effortlessly up in aching song. She sang "My Bonnie Blue-Eyed Boy," a very old ballad which Ehlana knew held special significance for her maid and the blond Pandion. The queen looked out the window again. The roughly dressed man in the street was standing stock still, frozen in place by Alean's soaring voice.

All doubt vanished from Ehlana's mind. It *was* Kalten! His eyes streamed tears, and his expression had become exalted, adoring.

And then he did something so unexpected that Ehlana was forced to revise her long-held opinion about his intelligence. He sat down on the mossy cobblestones, removed one shoe, and began to whistle an accompaniment to Alean's song. He *knew*! And he was whistling to let them know that he knew! Not even Sparhawk could have responded so quickly, or come up with so perfect a way to convey his understanding of the situation.

"That's enough, Alean," Ehlana hissed. "He got our message."

Alean stopped singing.

"What are you doing there?" one of the Arjunis who guarded the door demanded, coming into view.

"Stone in my shoe," Kalten explained, shaking the shoe he'd just removed. "It felt like a boulder."

"All right, move on."

Kalten's altered features took on a truculent look. He pulled his shoe back on and stood up. "Friend," he said in a pointed sort of way, "you'll be getting off duty before very long, and you might just decide to stop by Senga's tavern for a few tankards of beer. I'm in charge of security there, and if you start pushing me around *here*, I might just decide that you're too rowdy to be served when you get *there*. Understand?"

"I'm supposed to keep people away from this building," the guard explained, quickly modifying his tone.

"But politely, friend, politely. Every man in this whole place is armed to the teeth, so we all have to be polite to each other." Kalten threw a guarded glance at the barred window from which Ehlana watched. "I learned politeness when I took up with Shallag—you know him, don't you? The one-eyed fellow with the lochaber ax?"

The guarded shuddered. "Is he as bad as he looks?" he asked.

"Worse. He'll hack your head off if you even sneeze on him." Kalten squared his shoulders. "Well, I guess I'd better be getting back to the tavern. As my friend Ezek says, ' 'Tain't hordly likely that I'll make no profit lollygaggin' around in the street.' Come on by the tavern when you get off work, friend. I'll buy you a tankard of beer." And he went off down the street, still whistling "My Bonnie Blue-Eyed Boy."

"Treasure him, Alean," Ehlana said, her heart still soaring, "and don't let that face deceive you. He gave me more information in two minutes than Sparhawk could have in an hour."

"My Lady?" Alean looked baffled.

"He knows that we're here. He started to whistle along while you were singing. He also told me that Sir Bevier and Caalador are here with him."

"How did he do that?"

"He was talking with the guard. Bevier's probably the only man in Daresia right now with a lochaber ax, and his other friend sounds just like Caalador. They know we're here, Alean, and if they know, Sparhawk knows. We might as well start packing. We'll be leaving here shortly and going back to Matherion." She laughed delightedly and threw her arms around her maid.

Kalten tried very hard to keep his face expressionless as he walked back along the moss-covered streets toward Senga's tavern, but the excitement kept bubbling up in him, and it was very difficult to keep from laughing out loud.

Scarpa's army had cleared the northern quarters of Natayos and restored the buildings there to some degree of habitability when they had first arrived, but most of the city was still a vine-choked ruin. Senga had considered several possible sites for his tavern and had rather shrewdly decided to set up operations some distance deeper into the old city to avoid interference from officious sergeants or junior Elene officers with deep convictions and not much sense. He had chosen a low, squat building with thick walls but no roof, a deficiency easily overcome with tent canvas. He had considered hiring off-duty soldiers to clear the brush out of the street leading from Scarpa's main camp to the tavern door, but Caalador had persuaded him to save his money. "Ther ain't no need, Senga," the disguised Cammorian had told the harried businessman, reverting to his dialect. "Them thirsty soldiers'll clear the street fer us ther very own-selfs 'thout no money changin' hands a-tall." The tavern crouched in the ruins, indistinguishable from nearby buildings except for its canvas roof and the crudely lettered sign reading SENGA'S out front.

Kalten entered the tavern through the side door and paused to let his eyes adjust to the dimmer light. The place was moderately crowded, even at midday, and the six aproned outlaws from Narstil's camp hustled back and forth behind a rough plank counter, drawing foamy beer and collecting money.

Kalten pushed through the noisy crowd, looking for Bevier and Caalador. He found them sitting at a table on the near side of the room. Bevier's sawed-off lochaber and Caalador's stout cudgel lay in plain sight on the table as a sort of constant reminder to the assembled revelers that while having a good time was encouraged, there *were* strictly enforced limits.

Kalten carefully lowered himself onto the bench, keeping his exuberance tightly bottled in. He leaned forward, motioning his friends closer. "They're here," he said quietly.

Caalador looked around the tavern. "Wal," he drawled, "not quite *all* of 'em, but most likely ever'body who's off-duty."

"I'm not talking about this crowd, Ezek. I'm talking about the house with the barred windows. The people we've been looking for are definitely inside that house."

"How do you know?" Bevier demanded in an intense whisper. "Did you see them?"

"I didn't have to. One of them is a very special friend of mine, and this friend recognized me—even with this face. Don't ask me how."

"Are you sure?" Bevier pressed.

"Oh, yes. This friend started to sing in a voice I'd recognize in the middle of a thunderstorm. It was a very old song that has a personal meaning for the two of us. Our friends inside recognized me, there's no question about it. This friend I was just talking about only sings that song for me."

"I don't suppose there was any way you could let them know that you'd received their message?" Caalador asked. "Short of tearing down the door, I mean?"

"No, I didn't have to tear down the door. I whistled along. I've done that before, so my friend knew what I was trying to say. Then I struck up a conversation with one of the guards, and I slipped in enough hints to let our friends inside know the things they ought to be aware of."

Caalador leaned back in his chair. "Yer idee 'bout this yere tavern's workin' out real good, Shallag. We bin a-pickin' up all sorts o' useful infermation since we settled in."

Kalten looked around the tavern. "Things are quiet right now," he said quietly. "The fights probably won't start until the sun goes down. Why don't we take a stroll back into the ruins? I think we'd better have another chat with that certain little girl. This time we've got some *good* news for her."

"Let's get at it," Caalador said, rising to his feet. He pushed his way through to the counter, spoke briefly with one of the foam-soaked outlaws, and then led the way outside. They went around behind the tavern and pushed their way along a vine-choked side street that ran past some fallen buildings where bright-colored birds perched, squawking raucously. They went into a partially collapsed ruin, and Kalten and Caalador stood watch while Bevier cast the spell.

The Cyrinic was grinning when he came out. "You'd better brace yourself, Kalten," he said.

"What for?"

"Aphrael plans to kiss you into insensibility the next time she sees you."

"I suppose I can live with that. I gather she was pleased?"

"She almost ruptured my eardrums."

"Well, as she always says, 'We only live to please those we love.' "

Scarpa was screaming even before he came through the door. His voice was high and shrill, his eyes bulged, and his makeshift crown was askew.

He was clearly in the throes of hysterical rage. His lips and beard were flecked with foam as he burst into the room. "Your husband has betrayed you, woman!" he shrieked at Ehlana. "You will pay for his perfidy! I will have your life for this!" He started toward her, his hands extended like claws.

Then Zalasta was in the doorway. "No!" he barked in an icy tone.

Scarpa spun on his father. "Stay out of this!" he shrieked. "She is *my* prisoner! I will punish her for Sparhawk's treachery!"

"No, actually you won't. You'll do as I tell you to do." Zalasta spoke in Elenic, and all traces of his accent were gone now.

"He disobeyed my orders! I will make him pay!"

"Are you so stupid that you didn't expect this? I *told* you how devious the man was, but your mind's so clogged with cobwebs that you wouldn't listen."

"I gave him an *order*!" Scarpa's voice had risen to a squeal. He stamped his foot. Then he stamped the other. Then he began jumping up and down on the floor, quite literally dancing with fury. "I am the *emperor*! He *must* obey me!"

Zalasta did not even bother to use magic this time. He simply swung his staff and knocked his hysterical son to the floor, sending his crown rolling. "You sicken me," he said in a voice loaded with contempt. "I have no patience with these temper tantrums. You are *not* the emperor. When you're in this condition, you're not even meaningful." His face was unemotional, and his eyes were remote. "Have a care, Scarpa," he said in a dreadful voice. "There's nothing in this world that I love now. You have freed me from all human attachments. If you annoy me, I'll squash you like a bug."

Scarpa scrambled away from the terrible old man, flecks of foam speckling his face.

"What's happened?" Ehlana asked anxiously.

"One of my associates—Cyzada of Esos—just arrived from Cynesga," Zalasta replied calmly. "He brought us some news that we probably should have expected. Your husband's a devious man, Ehlana. We thought that we had him, but he managed to wriggle free."

"I don't understand."

"We left him instructions when we abducted you. He was supposed to take his squire and set out on horseback for the town of Beresa in southern Arjuna. We had people watching, and he *seemed* to be obeying. He was *not*, however. Evidently he's not as fond of you as we'd thought he was."

"He was simply following my orders, Zalasta. I told him that under no circumstances was he to give up the Bhelliom."

"How did you manage that?" Zalasta seemed actually startled.

"Your lunatic son here told Elron to kill Baroness Melidere. Elron's a hopeless incompetent, so Melidere was able to deflect his sword thrust. I have some remarkable people working for me, Zalasta. Melidere was able to play dead very convincingly. I feigned hysteria and managed to whisper instructions to her while I covered her with a blanket." She gave him a rather malicious sidelong glance. "Your mind must be slipping, Zalasta. You didn't even notice that I no longer had my ring. I left *that* with Melidere as well."

"Very resourceful, Ehlana," he murmured. "You and your husband are stimulating opponents."

"I'm so glad you approve. How did Sparhawk trick you?"

"We're not entirely sure. We had people watching him from the moment he left the imperial compound in Matherion, and he followed our orders to the letter. We even diverted him a couple of times to prevent any tricks. Then Klæl escaped again and went looking for Bhelliom. The man we *thought* was Sparhawk was on a ship crossing the Sea of Arjun with his squire, Khalad. Klæl took one look and instantly knew that the man who *appeared* to be your husband was *not* Anakha. That's the news that Cyzada just brought to us."

She smiled almost beatifically at him. "And so now Sparhawk's out there somewhere—with Bhelliom in his fist and murder in his heart—and you haven't the faintest idea of where he might be, and quite probably not even what he looks like. You've got a big problem, Zalasta."

"You're very quick, your Majesty. You think even faster than my colleagues."

"That isn't very difficult. You're surrounded with defectives. Which particular stroke of my genius is it that you admire?"

He smiled faintly. "I rather like you, Ehlana," he told her. "You have spirit. My assorted defectives haven't yet fully grasped the implications of your husband's ploy. If he's somehow managed to make someone resemble him, he's surely able to alter his own features as well."

"He does it all the time, Zalasta. He had a great deal of experience with disguises when he was in Rendor. It's all falling apart on you, isn't it? I'd suggest that you start running immediately."

"I'll be leaving shortly, right enough, but *you'll* be going with me. Tell your maid to start making preparations for a journey."

"What are you saying?" Scarpa scrambled to his feet. "She *can't* leave here!" he shrieked. "We're going to make the exchange here!"

"You imbecile," Zalasta sneered. "You didn't *really* think I was going to let you go through with that, did you? I never had any intention of letting you get within five miles of Bhelliom."

Scarpa gaped at him.

"It was a misguided attempt to save your life, idiot. Bhelliom would have destroyed you in the instant that you touched it."

"Not if I had the rings. They would have protected me." Scarpa's eyes were wild again.

"The rings are a fraud." Zalasta sneered. "They have no power over Bhelliom whatsoever."

"You're lying!"

"You desperately want to believe that, don't you, Scarpa? You thought that all you had to do to gain control of the most powerful force in the universe was to put on a pair of rings. Ghwerig the Troll-Dwarf made the rings at Bhelliom's instruction. They were designed to deceive a *Troll* into thinking he had some power over the jewel. *Bhelliom* induced Ghwerig to make the rings, and then it tricked Aphrael into stealing them. Everyone's attention was so fixed on the rings that we didn't even bother trying to steal Bhelliom from the royal crown of Thalesia."

Scarpa suddenly sneered. "You just outsmarted yourself, old man. If Bhelliom's so deadly, how is it that the kings of Thalesia could touch it and not die?"

"Because Bhelliom's *alive*, you dolt. It has an awareness. It kills only those it *wants* to kill—and that would certainly include you. You're my son, and even *I* want to kill you most of the time. You had some deranged, half-formed notion that you could just pick up Bhelliom and start giving it commands, didn't you?"

Scarpa flushed guiltily.

"Can't you get it through your sick head that only a God—or Anakha—can safely take up Bhelliom and start giving it orders? I realized that over a century ago. Why do you think I made an alliance with Azash—or with Cyrgon? Did you think I was having religious yearnings?" He smiled a cruel smile. "Did you really think Bhelliom would have made you a match for me, Scarpa? You were going to put on the rings, snatch up the Bhelliom, and order it to kill me, weren't you? I almost wish the situation were different. I'd have loved to have seen the expression on your face as Bhelliom slowly turned you to stone." Zalasta straightened. "Enough of this," he said. He went to the door. "Come in here," he barked, "all of you."

The men who entered were fearful and hesitant as they sidled through the door. Krager appeared to have been frightened to the point that he was sober, and Elron was actually cringing. The third man was a stringy-looking Styric with a long beard, shaggy eyebrows, and sunken, burning eyes.

"All right, gentlemen," Zalasta said, "this new development calls for a change of plans. My son and I have discussed the matter, and he's evidently decided that he wants to go on living, because he's agreed to follow my instructions. I'm going to take the queen and her maid to a safe place. Natayos is no longer secure. Sparhawk could literally be anywhere. For all I know, he's already here. I want you three to stay here with Scarpa. Keep sending those letters of instruction to this counterfeit Sparhawk. Don't let our enemies know that we're on to them. Give me a couple of days and then send instructions to Panem-Dea. Tell them to prepare suitable quarters for two very important ladies. Then wait two more days and send a closed carriage down there. Security's an alien concept to those cretins at Panem-Dea, so word of your message will be all over southern Arjuna almost before your messenger arrives. Cyzada, I want *you* to keep a close watch over my deranged son here. If he doesn't follow my instructions to the letter, I want you to summon one of the servants of Azash from the netherworld to kill him. Be creative, old boy. Pick the cruelest and most hideous demon you can find. If Scarpa disobeys me again, I want him to take a long, long time to die, and I want them to be able to hear him screaming all the way from here to Matherion."

Cyzada's dead eyes came alight with a sudden cruel anticipation. He fixed a ghastly smile on the now totally rational Scarpa. "I'll see to it, Zalasta," he promised in a hollow voice. "I know just the one to call on."

Scarpa shrank back fearfully.

"Where are you going to take the prisoners, Lord Zalasta?" Elron quavered. "Where can you be safe from that vengeful monster they call Anakha?"

"You don't need to know that, Elron," Zalastra replied. "The Pandions have a reputation for severity when they interrogate prisoners. You won't be able to tell them what you don't know—even when they start to torture you."

"Torture?" Elron's eyes widened, and his voice came out in a terrified squeak.

"This is the real world, Elron, not some romanticized daydream. The posturing and play-acting are over now, but I'm sure we'll all be impressed by how heroically you endure the agonies they'll surely inflict on you when they catch you."

Elron fell back in a near faint.

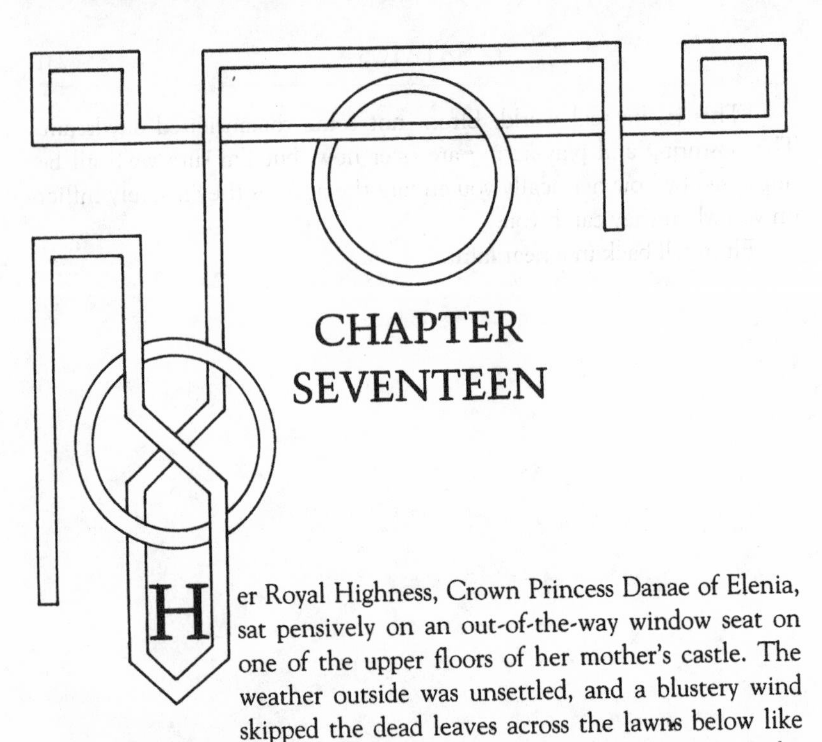

CHAPTER SEVENTEEN

Her Royal Highness, Crown Princess Danae of Elenia, sat pensively on an out-of-the-way window seat on one of the upper floors of her mother's castle. The weather outside was unsettled, and a blustery wind skipped the dead leaves across the lawns below like scurrying brown mice. Danae absently stroked her purring cat as she considered options, alternatives, and possibilities.

Mirtai, grim, implacable, and wearing an Atan breastplate of polished steel and black leather, stood several yards down the corridor, her face set in an expression of sullen obedience and her hand on her sword hilt.

"You're still angry with me, aren't you?" Danae asked the golden giantess, not even bothering to turn around.

"It's not my place to either approve or disapprove of my owner." Mirtai was being stubborn about it.

"Oh, stop that. Come here."

Mirtai marched up the hall to where her capricious little owner was sitting. "Yes?"

"I'm going to try again. Please listen to me this time."

"As your Majesty commands."

"That's getting very tiresome, you know. We love you, Mirtai."

"Is your Majesty speaking in the royal plural?"

"You're starting to make me cross. I've got a name, and you know what it is. We all love you, and it would have broken our hearts if you'd decided to kill yourself. I spoke to you the way I did to bring you to your senses, you ninny."

"I know why you did it, Danae, but did you have to humiliate me in front of the others?"

"I apologize."

"You can't do that. You're a queen, and queens *can't* apologize."

"I can if I want." Danae paused. "So there," she added.

Mirtai laughed and suddenly embraced the little girl. "You're never going to learn how to be a queen, Danae."

"Oh, I don't know. Being the queen just means that you get what you want. I do that all the time anyway. I don't need a crown or an army for something as simple as that."

"You're a very spoiled little girl, your Majesty."

"I know, and I love every minute of it."

Then the princess heard a faint, far-away murmur, a murmur that Mirtai could not, of course, even sense. "Why don't you go find Melidere?" she suggested. She sighed and rolled her eyes upward. "I'm sure she's looking for me anyway. It's probably time for another one of those girl lessons."

"She's giving you instruction in courtly manners and traditional courtesies, Danae," Mirtai reproved her. "If you're going to be a queen, you'll need to know those things."

"I think it's silly, myself. Go on ahead, Mirtai. I'll be along in a minute."

The giantess went off down the hall, and Princess Danae spoke very quietly. "What is it, Setras?" she asked the empty air.

"You already know the courtesies, Aphrael," her curly-haired cousin said, appearing suddenly beside her. "Why are you taking lessons?"

"It gives Melidere something to occupy her mind with and keeps her out of mischief. I spent a great deal of time and effort getting her and Stragen together. I don't want her to spoil it by getting bored and starting to look for outside entertainment."

"That's very important to you, isn't it?" Setras sounded a little puzzled. "Why should the things they do to perpetuate themselves interest you at all?"

"You probably wouldn't understand, Setras. You're too young."

"I'm as old as you are."

"Yes, but you don't pay any attention to what your worshippers are doing when they're alone together."

"I know what they're doing. It's ridiculous."

"*They* seem to like it."

"Flowers are much more dignified about it," he sniffed.

"Is this what you wanted to talk to me about?"

"Oh, I almost forgot. I have a message for you. There's an Alcione Knight—one of the ones who serve *me*. I think you know him. He's a moon-faced fellow named Tynian."

"Yes."

"He went back to Chyrellos to pick up some help, and it seems that he inadvertently chose every Pandion skilled enough to pass messages on to you and brought them all to this part of the world, so there wasn't anybody with the Church Knights to tell you what happened in Zemoch."

"Yes, I already know about that. Anakha's going to talk with Tynian about that. What happened in Zemoch?"

"The Church Knights had an encounter with Klæl. A third of them were killed."

Aphrael unleashed a blistering string of curses.

"Aphrael!" he gasped. "You're not supposed to talk that way!"

"Oh, go bury it, Setras! Why didn't you tell me about this as soon as you got here?"

"I was curious about the other thing," he confessed. "It's not as if they *all* got killed, Aphrael. There are still plenty of them left. In a little while there'll be as many as before. They're ferociously prolific."

"I love them *all*, you dolt! I don't want to lose any of them."

"You're greedy. That's one of your shortcomings, cousin. You can't keep them *all*, you know."

"Don't make any wagers on that, Setras. I'm only just getting started." She threw her hands in the air. "This is impossible! You don't even understand the message you're trying to give me. Where are the Church Knights now?"

"They're coming across the steppes of central Astel to invade Cynesga. They'll probably run into Klæl again when they get there. I hope they don't *all* get killed."

"Who's in command?"

"One of Romalic's servants—an old man called Abriel—*was* in charge when they left Chyrellos, but he got killed in Zemoch, so one of the high priests of the Church of the Elene God—a Thalesian named Bergsten—is giving orders now."

"I should have guessed," she said. "I have a few things to take care of first. Then I'll go find Bergsten and get a *true* account of what happened."

"I was *only* trying to help." Setras sounded a little injured.

"You did just fine, cousin." Aphrael forgave him. "It's not your fault that you haven't been keeping abreast of things here."

"I have important things on my mind, Aphrael," he said defensively. "Come by my studio sometime," he added brightly. "I made a sunset the other day that's probably one of the best pieces I've ever done. It's so lovely that I've decided to keep it."

"Setras! You can't just stop the sun that way!"

"There's nobody living there, Aphrael. They won't notice."

"Oh, dear!" She buried her face in her hands.

"You're disappointed in me, aren't you?" His lower lip trembled slightly, and his large, luminous eyes filled with sudden tears. "And I try so hard to make you and the others proud of me."

"No, Setras," she said. "I still love you."

He brightened. "Everything's all right, then, isn't it?"

"You're a dear, Setras." She kissed him. "Run along now. I have to talk with these others."

"You *will* come and look at my sunset, won't you?"

"Of course, cousin. Go along now." She lifted her drowsing cat and blew into the furry creature's ear. "Wake up, Mmrr," she said.

The yellow eyes opened.

"Go back to the place where we nest," the little princess said, speaking in cat. "I have to do something." She set Mmrr down on the floor, and the cat arched her back, hooking her tail into a sinuous question mark, and yawned. Then she padded off down the corridor.

Danae looked around, probing with eyes and mind to make certain she was alone. There were human males knocking around the halls of this castle, and the appearance of a naked Goddess always excited the males. It was flattering, of course, but it was also a little confusing for a being with a total lack of any reproductive urges. No matter how hard she tried, Aphrael had never been able to understand how the mating impulse of human males could be so indiscriminate.

The Child-Goddess briefly resumed her true person and then divided, becoming both little girls.

"You're starting to get older, Danae," Flute noted.

"Does it show? Already?"

"It's noticeable. You still have a way to go before you're fully mature, though. Are you really sure you want to go through with this?"

"It might help us all to understand them a little better. I don't think Setras even knows that it takes a male and a female to—well, you know." Danae blushed.

"Setras isn't overly bright. Can I borrow Mirtai?" Flute asked.

"What for?"

"You don't really need her here, and after what happened in Dirgis, I'd like to have somebody I trust to stand guard over Sephrenia."

"Good idea. Let's go talk with Sarabian and the others. They'll be able to send messengers to people we don't have any contacts with."

Flute nodded. "It would be *so* much more convenient if they were *all* ours."

Danae laughed. "I think Setras was right. We *are* greedy, aren't we?"

"We love them all, Danae. I don't see any reason why they can't love us."

The two little girls started off down the corridor hand in hand. "Danae," Flute said, "do you think Mirtai might be afraid of heights?"

"He *does* look a lot like that picture Talen drew, doesn't he?" Tynian murmured to Ulath.

"Very close," Ulath agreed. "That boy has a tremendous talent."

"Yes. He draws well, too."

Ulath laughed shortly. Then he looked at the men clustered around Parok and drew Tynian a little farther away from them. "Parok's giving all the orders," he whispered, "but the Arjuni in the flamboyant doublet speaks for King Rakya."

"Sarabian's going to be very put out with the King of Arjun."

Ulath nodded. "I wouldn't be at all surprised to see a new king on the throne before long."

"What exactly did Parok say about Natayos? You couldn't have mistaken his meaning, could you?"

"Not a chance, Tynian. Just before he got into the argument with Duke Milanis, Parok said that Scarpa wanted to move his army out of Natayos before they gave Sparhawk the last note. I almost started cheering when he said that they were going to tell Sparhawk to go to Natayos for the exchange."

"We'll have to be careful, though. They *could* be holding Ehlana someplace else. They may not take her to Natayos until the last minute."

"We'll find out for sure once Xanetia goes there." Ulath shrugged.

The door to the book-lined room opened, and a liveried servant hurried in. "An important message has arrived from Natayos, Baron," he told Parok. "The messenger rode his horse half to death."

"Horses are cheap. Send the fellow in."

"I could learn to dislike tnat man," Tynian murmured.

"I already do," Ulath replied. He looked up speculatively. "We're sort of invisible, aren't we?" he asked.

"That's what Ghnomb says."

"Can you imagine the expression Parok would get on his face if he suddenly got ripped up the front with an invisible knife?"

"Slowly," Tynian added. "Very, very slowly."

The messenger from Natayos was a shabbily dressed Dacite, and he was reeling with exhaustion as he staggered into the room. "Baron," he gasped. "Thank God I found you."

"Speak up, man!"

"Could I have a drink of water?"

"Talk first. Then you can drink anything you want."

"Lord Scarpa ordered me to tell you that the man you've been watching *isn't* Sparhawk."

"I see that Scarpa's finally gone completely mad."

"No, Baron. Zalasta confirmed it. Somebody they call Klæl went and had a look at this man you've been giving the notes to. They seemed to think you'd know who this Klæl fellow is. Anyway, he sent word that the man with the broken nose *looks* like Sparhawk, but it's not really him. This Klæl must have some way to know for sure."

Parok began to swear sulfurously.

"That tears it," Tynian growled. "I'll pass this on to Aphrael. We'd better get Berit and Khalad to safety."

"Did Scarpa kill Sparhawk's wife?" Baron Parok asked the messenger.

"No, my Lord Baron. He was going to, but Zalasta stopped him. I'm supposed to tell you not to do anything to let the imposter know that we're on to him. Zalasta needs some time to move the prisoners to someplace that's safe. He wants you to continue as if nothing had happened. After he has those two women clear, he'll get word to you that it's all right to kill the man who's posing as Sparhawk."

"Zalasta's in full command then?"

"Yes, Baron Parok. Lord Scarpa's a bit—ah—distraught, I suppose you might say."

"You might say crazy, too. That'd be more accurate." Parok started to pace the floor. "I wondered how much it would take to push Scarpa over the edge," he muttered. "It's probably better this way. Zalasta's a Styric, but at least his head's on straight. Go back and tell him that I've received his message and that I won't do anything to upset his plans.

Let him know that I have no real fondness for Scarpa and that I'll be completely loyal to him."

"I will, my Lord Baron."

Duke Milanis rose and crossed the room to close the window. "What in God's name is that awful smell?" he exclaimed.

Tynian turned and saw the hulking Troll standing just behind them. "Bhlokw," he said, "it is not good that you come into the dens of the man-things this way."

"I was sent by Khwaj, Tin-in," Bhlokw explained. "Khwaj grows tired of waiting. He wants to burn the wicked ones always."

Then their dim half moment suddenly filled with smoke, and the enormous presence of the Fire-God was there. "Your hunt takes too long, Ulath-from-Thalesia. Have you found any of the wicked ones yet? If you have, point out which one it is. I will make it burn forever."

Tynian and Ulath exchanged a long look. Then Tynian grinned wolfishly. "Let's," he said.

"Why don't we?" Ulath agreed. He looked at the flickering God of Fire. "Our hunt has been successful, Khwaj," he declared. "We have found one of the ones who stole Anakha's mate. You can make it burn forever now." He paused. "There are others we also hunt, though," he added. "We do not want to frighten them away so that they will be harder to hunt. Can Ghnomb put the one we have found into No-Time? You can burn it always there. When it burns in No-Time, the others of its herd will not smell the smoke or hear the crying-out with hurt, and so they will not run away."

"Your thought is good, Ulath-from-Thalesia," Khwaj agreed. "I will talk with Ghnomb about this. He will make it so that the one who burns always burns in the time which does not move. Which one of these should I burn?"

"That one," Ulath replied, pointing at Baron Parok.

Duke Milanis was turning from the window when he suddenly stopped, becoming a statue in midstride.

Baron Parok continued his restless pacing. "We're going to have to start taking extra precautions," he said, not yet realizing that the men around him were no longer moving. Then he turned and almost bumped into the exhausted messenger from Natayos. "Get out of my way, idiot!" he snapped.

The man did not move.

"I told you to take a message to Zalasta," Parok raged. "Why are you still here?" He struck the messenger across the face and cried out in pain as his hand hit something harder than stone. He looked around wildly. "What's the matter with all of you?" he demanded in a shrill voice.

"What did it say?" Khwaj's voice was dreadful.

Parok gaped at the vast Troll-God, shrieked, and ran for the door.

"It does not understand that it is now in No-Time," Ulath replied in Trollish.

"It should know why it is being punished," Khwaj decided. "Will it understand if you talk to it in the bird-noises of the man-things?"

"I will *make* it understand," Ulath promised.

"It is good that you will. Speak to it."

Parok was hammering futilely on the immovable door.

"That won't do you any good, old boy," Ulath urbanely advised the terrified Dacite nobleman. "Things have definitely taken a turn for the worse for you, Baron. This large fellow with the smoke coming out of his ears is the Troll-God Khwaj. He disapproves of your abduction of Queen Ehlana."

"Who are you?" Parok half screamed. "What's going on here?"

"You've been brought to the place of punishment, Baron," Tynian advised him. "As my friend here just explained, Khwaj is quite put out with you. Trolls are very moralistic. Things that we've come to take in stride—abductions, poisonings, and holding people for ransom—upset them enormously. There *is* one small advantage, though. You're going to live forever, Baron Parok. You'll never, ever die."

"What are you talking about?"

"You'll see."

"Does it understand now?" Khwaj demanded impatiently.

"It is our thought that it does," Ulath replied in Trollish.

"Good." Khwaj implacably advanced on the cringing Dacite, extending one vast paw. Then he clapped it down on top of Parok's head. "Burn!" he growled.

Baron Parok shrieked.

Then his face seemed to split, and incandescent fire came spurting out through his skin. His doublet smoked for an instant and then flashed into ashes.

He shrieked again.

His form was still the form of a man, but it was a form etched in flame. The baron burned, unconsumed, and he danced and howled in agony.

Khwaj struck the immovable door with one huge paw, and the door burst outward in flaming chunks. "Go!" he roared. "Run! Run forever, and burn always!"

The flaming Dacite fled shrieking.

The town of Arjun stood frozen in that eternal instant of perpetual now. The citizens, like statues, stood frozen stock-still, unaware of the burning wraith that ran through their silent streets. They did not hear its agonized screams. They did not see it flee toward the lakeshore.

Baron Parok ran, all ablaze, trailing greasy smoke. He reached the docks and fled in flames out a long pier stretching into the dark waters of the sea of Arjun. He did not pause when he reached the end of the pier, but plunged off, yearning toward the quenching water. But, like the moment itself, the surface of the lake was unyielding and as hard as diamond. The wraith of flame howled in frustration, kneeling on the glittering surface and hammering on it, pleading to be let in, begging to drown in the blessed coolness just beyond reach. Then Parok leapt to his feet, driven by the Troll-God's awful command. Shrieking still in agony, the man-shape of eternal flame ran out across the dark crystal surface, receding incandescent until it was no more than a single bright spark far out on the night-darkened lake. And its lost wail of pain and endless solitude came echoing back to the incurious shore.

"I wish Sparhawk would find his way home again," Talen muttered as he and Stragen once again climbed the rickety stairs to the loft. "We've got some fairly important information, and there's no way to pass it on to the others."

"There's nothing we can do about it right now," Stragen told him. "Let's see how Valash reacts to this story you cooked up. Keep it sort of vague until we see which way he jumps."

"And then will you teach me how to pick a pocket?" Talen asked with overly feigned enthusiasm.

"All right." Stragen sighed. "I apologize. I'll concede that you know what you're doing."

"Oh, *thank* you, Vymer!" Talen gushed. "Thank you, thank you!"

"You've been spending too much time with Princess Danae," Stragen muttered sourly. "I hope she *does* marry you. You deserve it."

"Bite your tongue, Stragen. I can still run faster than she can."

"Running doesn't always help, Reldin. I thought I could run, too, but Melidere cut my legs out from under me with a single word."

"Oh? Which word was that?"

"Profit, my young friend. She waved unlimited amounts of gold in front of my face."

"You sold out, Stragen," Talen accused. "You betrayed every bachelor in the world for money."

"Wouldn't you have? We're not talking about a few farthings here."

"It's the principle of the thing," Talen replied loftily. "*I* wouldn't sell out for money."

"I don't think it'll be money that Danae's going to offer you, my innocent young friend. If you start running right now, you *might* escape, but I sort of doubt it. I knew your father, and there's a certain weakness in your family. Danae's going to get you, Talen. You don't have a chance."

"Could we talk about something else? This is a very distressing sort of subject."

Stragen laughed, and they went through the patched door at the top of the stairs.

Valash sat in the faint light of his single candle, listening with a look of pained resignation on his face as Ogerajin babbled and drooled a long, strung-out series of disconnected phrases.

"He doesn't seem to be getting any better," Stragen observed quietly when he and Talen joined the two at the table.

"He won't *get* better, Vymer." Valash sighed. "I've seen this particular disease run its course before. Don't get too close to him. He's virulently infectious at this stage."

"I certainly wouldn't want to catch what he's got." Talen shuddered.

"Do you have something for me?" Valash asked.

"I'm not going to swear to this, Master Valash," Talen said cautiously. "The fellows I picked it up from weren't any too reliable. You might want to pass it on to Panem-Dea, though. It concerns them rather directly, so they might want to take a few extra precautions."

"Go on," Valash said.

"Well, I overheard a couple of Arjuni soldiers talking in a tavern down by the waterfront—*real* Arjuni soldiers, I mean, not the ones Lord Scarpa's recruited. They were talking about some orders that just came in from the capital of Arjuna. From what I was able to gather, they've been ordered to prepare for an extended campaign out in the jungle. They *think* they're going to be mounting an attack on Lord Scarpa's camp at Panem-Dea."

"Impossible!" Valash snorted.

"They were saying that the orders came from King Rakya himself. The message had been sent to their officers, of course, so they probably garbled it, but they're convinced that the Arjuni army's going to attack Scarpa's forces. I just thought you ought to know."

"Those soldiers were drunk, Reldin. King Rakya is our ally."

"Really? What an amazing thing. He ought to let his troops know about it, then. The two I was listening to were positively drooling about all the loot they thought they were going to carry out of Panem-Dea."

"The queen is coming to Panem-Dea," Ogerajin suddenly sang in a wheezy voice to the tune of an old nursery song, "the queen is coming to Panem-Dea." Then he began to cackle in a high-pitched laugh.

A look of sudden chagrin crossed Valash's face. "Calm yourself, Master Ogerajin," he said, giving Stragen and Talen a worried look.

"The queen is coming to Panem-Dea, riding in a carriage," Ogerajin sang in his cracked voice.

"Don't pay any attention to him," Valash said rather too quickly. "He's only babbling."

"His mind really *is* slipping, isn't it?" Stragen noted.

"Six white horses and silver wheels—" Ogerajin sang on.

"Have you ever *heard* such gibberish?" Valash asked with a weak laugh.

"Our presence must be disturbing him," Stragen said. "Does he generally drift off to sleep later in the evening?"

"Usually."

"Good. From now on, Reldin and I'll come by after midnight, when he's asleep."

"I'd appreciate it, Vymer." Valash looked at them, his face still worried. "He wasn't always like this, you know. It's the disease."

"I'm sure of it. He's probably not even aware of what he's saying."

"Exactly, exactly. He's completely out of his head. Why don't you two just forget his crazy singing?" Valash snatched his purse from his belt and dug out several coins. "Here. Come by again after he's gone to sleep."

The two thieves bowed and quietly left.

"Nervous, wasn't he?" Talen said as they went back down the stairs.

"You noticed. He even forgot himself and opened his purse."

They reached the bottom of the stairs. "Where to?" Talen asked.

"No place for the moment. Keep this to yourself, Talen."

"Keep what?"

But Stragen was already speaking in sonorous Styric, weaving his fingers intricately in the air in front of him.

Talen stared as Stragen opened his hands palm up and made a sort of tossing gesture rather like a man releasing a pigeon. His eyes became distant, and his lips moved silently for a time. Then he smiled. "Surprised her," he said. "Let's go."

"What's going on here?" Talen demanded.

"I passed the things we just discovered along to Aphrael." Stragen shrugged.

"*You?* When did you learn Styric magic?"

"It's not really all that difficult, Talen." Stragen grinned. "I've seen Sparhawk do it often enough, and I *do* speak Styric, after all. The gestures were a little tricky, but Aphrael gave me some instructions. I'll do it better next time."

"How did you know it would work?"

"I didn't. I thought it was time I gave it a try, though. Aphrael's very pleased with me."

"You *do* know that you just volunteered to serve her, don't you? I know *that* much about her. You're her slave now, Stragen. She's got you."

"Oh, well." Stragen shrugged. "I suppose a man could do worse. Aphrael's a thief herself, so I'm sure we'll get along." He squared his shoulders. "Shall we go?" he suggested.

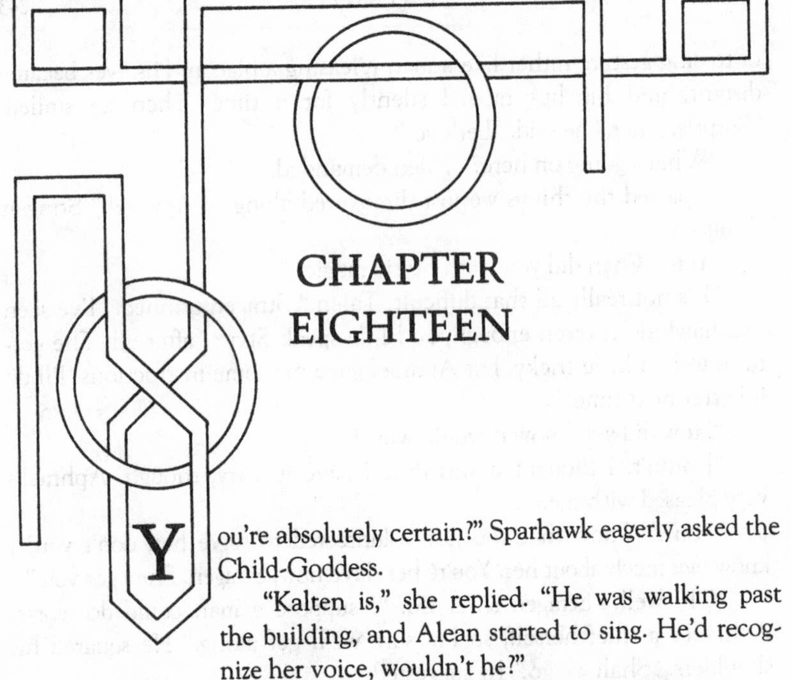

CHAPTER EIGHTEEN

"You're absolutely certain?" Sparhawk eagerly asked the Child-Goddess.

"Kalten is," she replied. "He was walking past the building, and Alean started to sing. He'd recognize her voice, wouldn't he?"

Sparhawk nodded. "She could raise him from the dead by singing to him. How fast can you get me to Natayos?"

"Let's take the others to Dirgis first. I want to fill Xanetia and Sephrenia in on what's been happening."

"I already know about all that. I need to get to Natayos, Aphrael."

"All in good time, Sparhawk. It's not going to take us long to get to Dirgis, and the others might have some useful ideas."

"Aphrael—" he began to protest.

"We'll do it my way, Sparhawk," she told him firmly. "It won't take all that long, and it might give you enough time to get your temper under control. The others are waiting in the room with the map on the wall. Let's get them and go to Dirgis."

There was one brief argument before they started. "I have no need of a horse," Betuana insisted, tightening the lace on one of her half boots.

Aphrael sighed. "Please do it my way, Betuana," she said.

"I can run faster than a horse. Why burden myself with one?"

"Because you know how far it is from here to Dirgis, and the horse doesn't. It's easier for me that way. Please, Betuana, just for me." The Child-Goddess looked appealingly at the armored Atan queen.

Betuana laughed and gave in.

And so they went out into the snowy courtyard, mounted, and rode out into the streets of Sarna. The sky was heavy with clouds that obscured the surrounding mountains, and it was spitting snow. They left town by way of the east gate and slogged their way up the steep slope to the top of the gorge. Sparhawk, Itagne, and Vanion rode in the lead, breaking trail for the Queen of Atan, who rode wrapped in her heavy cloak, with the Child-Goddess nestled in her arms. There was a strange dichotomy in the personality of the little divinity that troubled Sparhawk. He knew that she was wise beyond his ability to comprehend it, and yet she was still in most ways a little girl. Then he remembered the naked reality of the *true* Goddess, and all hope of ever understanding her vanished.

"Can't we go any faster?" Vanion demanded.

Sparhawk's friend had been in an agony of impatience ever since he had learned of the attack on Sephrenia, and Sparhawk had at times feared that he might have to physically restrain him. "Fast or slow doesn't matter, Vanion," he said. "We can run or crawl, and we'll still get there at just about the same time."

"How can you be so calm?"

"You get numb after a while," Sparhawk laughed wryly.

It was perhaps a quarter of an hour later when they crested the top of that long hill and looked down at the town of Dirgis—where the sun was shining brightly.

"That's incredible!" Itagne exclaimed. Then he turned to look back down the trail they had just climbed, and his eyes suddenly went very wide.

"I asked you not to do that, Itagne," Aphrael reminded him.

"It's still snowing there," he choked, "but—" He stared at the sun-drenched snowfield just ahead again.

"Why do people *always* want to stop right there?" the little girl said irritably. "Just move along, Itagne. Once you've passed the crossover between the two places, it won't bother you any more."

Itagne resolutely set his face forward and rode on into the bright sunlight. "Did you understand that, Sparhawk?" he asked in a strained voice.

"Sort of. Do you really want to hear about what happens to you when you step through the place where two hundred miles have just been abolished?"

Itagne shuddered.

They rode down the hill and entered the city.

"How much farther?" Vanion demanded.

"Just a little way," Sparhawk replied. "It's not all that big a town."

They rode through the narrow streets where the snow lay thickly piled against the sides of the buildings. They reached the inn, rode into the courtyard just behind it, and dismounted.

"Everything's been fixed now, Betuana," Aphrael was assuring the Atan queen. "I'm keeping him in a deep sleep so that everything has a chance to knit back together again."

"Who's watching over him? Perhaps I should go there."

"No, Betuana," Aphrael said firmly. "I don't have permission to take you there—yet."

"But he's alone."

"Of course he's not alone. I'm right there beside him."

"But—" Betuana stared at the little girl.

"Try not to think about it." The Child-Goddess pursed her lips thoughtfully. "Engessa-Atan's a deceptive man, you know—probably because he's so quiet. I didn't realize how remarkable he really is until I got into his mind."

"I have always known," Betuana said. "How long will it be necessary to keep him away from me—us."

Aphrael let the queen's slip pass without comment. "A few weeks. I want to be sure that everything's healed. Let's go inside before Vanion has apoplexy."

Sparhawk led them into the inn where the innkeeper seemed to be so engrossed in wiping off a table that he was totally oblivious to anything else. They went up the stairs, and Sparhawk was startled to see Mirtai standing guard at Sephrenia's door. "What are *you* doing here?" he asked her. "I thought you were back in Matherion."

"I've been lent out," she replied, "like an old cloak."

"You know that's not true, Mirtai," Aphrael said. "Danae's perfectly safe where she is, but I needed someone I could count on to guard Sephrenia. Let's go inside."

Sephrenia was sitting up in bed when they entered, and Xanetia was hovering protectively over her. The room was flooded with sunlight.

Vanion went directly to the woman he loved, knelt at her bedside, and gently put his arms around her. "I'm never going to let you out of my sight again," he told her in a thick voice.

Sephrenia took his face between her hands and kissed him.

"You'll hurt yourself."

"Hush, Vanion," she told him, embracing his head and holding his face fiercely against her body.

Aphrael's huge eyes were luminous with tears. Then she seemed to shake off her sudden emotion. "Let's get started," she said crisply. "A great deal has happened since the last time we were all together like this."

"And all of it bad," Itagne added in a gloomy voice.

"Not entirely," she said. "The worst of it is that Klæl ambushed the Church Knights in the mountains of Zemoch. He had those strange soldiers with him, and our friends lost almost half their number in killed and wounded."

"Good God!" Itagne groaned.

Since Sparhawk already knew the details of recent events, his mind turned to the mystery of Klæl's soldiers. He touched his fingertips to the bulge under his tunic. *Blue-Rose*, he said in the silence of his mind.

I hear thee, Anakha.

Our friends have encountered Klæl again. He hath brought warriors here from some other place.

It was not unexpected. Klæl is unsuited to direct engagement with humans by reason of his size.

We are like mice in his eyes? Sparhawk surmised.

Thou dost wrong thyself, Anakha.

Perhaps. These soldiers are not of this world, methinks. Their blood is yellow and their faces are much like Klæl's face.

Ah, the voice said. *Thou wilt recall that I once told thee that it is customary for Klæl and me to contest with each other for possession of the various worlds I have caused to be?*

Yes.

It pains me to admit this, Anakha, but I have not always prevailed in these contests. Klæl hath wrested some of my worlds from me. It is from one of those worlds—Arcera would be my surmise—that he hath brought these creatures which thou and thy companions have met.

They are fearsome, Blue-Rose, but not invincible. We have noted some evidence of distress in them during prolonged sojourns here.

I would be surprised hadst thou not. The air of Arcera would sear thy lungs shouldst thou take but one breath of it. The air of this *world is so sweet and wholesome that it may be most simply assimilated by thy kind and other creatures here. The creatures of Arcera are not so fortunate.* Their *means of assimilating the noxious miasmas of their home are far more complex than* thy *simple means of suspiration. Moreover, that which would be lethal to thee hath become necessary for them. I am certain that they find thine air thin and unsatisfying by comparison.*

And deadly? Sparhawk pressed.

In time, most certainly.

Wouldst thou venture a surmise as to how much *time it might take our air to kill them?*

Thou art savage, Anakha.

I am outnumbered, Blue-Rose. The warriors of Klæl put our cause in direst peril. We must *know how long they can survive here.*

That will vary from warrior to warrior. No more than a day, certainly, and exertion will hasten the process.

I thank thee, Blue-Rose. My *companions and I will devise tactics to use this information to best advantage.*

"Pay attention, Sparhawk," Aphrael told him.

"Sorry," he apologized. "I was conferring with our friend." He patted the bulge at his front. He looked at Vanion. "I picked up some more information about the weakness of Klæl's soldiers," he said. "You and I need to work out some tactics."

Vanion nodded.

"Are you sure Berit and Khalad are all right?" Sephrenia asked the little girl.

Aphrael nodded. "Zalasta doesn't want us to know that he's found out that we were deceiving him. He's given orders to everyone to behave as if nothing's happened." She thought a moment. "I guess that's about all," she said. "Bergsten's coming across the steppes; Kalten, Bevier, and Caalador are already in Natayos; and Ulath, Tynian, and their pet Troll will be there before long."

"Can you get word to the emperor?" Itagne asked her. "He should know that the King of Arjuna's in league with Scarpa."

"I'll take care of it," she promised. Then she frowned slightly. "Sephrenia," she said, "have you been giving Stragen instruction in the secrets?"

"No, why?"

"He cast the spell of the secret summoning. He didn't do it very well, but he got my attention."

"How in God's name did he learn that?" Vanion exclaimed, still holding Sephrenia in his arms.

"Probably from watching the rest of you. Stragen's very quick, and he *does* speak Styric. Stealing secrets is almost the same as picking pockets, I guess. Anyway, it was Stragen who told me about Scarpa's other forts. He and Talen are planting false stories with that Dacite in order to confuse the other side."

"Methinks it is time for me to go to Natayos," Xanetia said. "We must verify the presence there of Anakha's queen and make preparations for her rescue."

"*Before* Zalasta tries to move her," Sparhawk added. "I'd better go along as well. The others are there already, and Kalten might need a firm hand to keep him from doing anything rash. Besides, if Ehlana and Alean are there, we might just as well pull them out of danger. Then I'll disperse Scarpa's army and we'll go have a talk with Cyrgon."

"And Zalasta," Vanion added bleakly.

"Oh, by the way," Aphrael said, "is anybody keeping a list of the people we want to do things about? If you are, you can scratch off Baron Parok's name."

"Did Ulath kill him?" Sparhawk guessed.

"Oh, he isn't dead, Sparhawk. You see, when Khwaj started pushing Ulath and Tynian for information about the people who'd abducted Ehlana, they gave him Parok."

"What happened?" Itagne asked.

"Ghnomb froze time." She shrugged. "Then Khwaj set fire to Parok. He's completely engulfed in flame. He's still running, and he'll run—and burn—in that empty, unmoving instant for all eternity."

"Dear God!" Itagne choked in horror.

"I'll pass that on to Khwaj, Itagne," the Child-Goddess promised. "I'm sure he'll be pleased that you approve."

The air was cool and dry and the sky was peculiarly grey. Tynian and Ulath rode out of Arjun in frozen time with Bhlokw shambling along between their horses. "How long would you say it's going to take us to reach Natayos?" Tynian asked.

"Oh," Ulath replied, "I don't know—a couple of seconds, probably."

"Very funny."

"I rather liked it." Ulath looked up at the flock of birds hanging in midair overhead. "I wonder if a man ages at all when he's walking around in this No-Time."

"I don't know. You could go ask Baron Parok, I suppose."

"I doubt that he'd be very coherent." Ulath scratched at one bearded cheek. "I'm definitely going to shave this thing off, and if Gerda doesn't like it, that's just too bad." Then he thought of something he had been meaning to ask their shaggy friend. "Bhlokw," he said.

"Yes, U-lat?"

"It makes us sad that our hunt takes us to the lands of the sun where the heat causes hurt to you."

"It causes no hurt to me, U-lat. There is no heat or cold in No-Time."

Ulath stared at him. "You are sure?" he asked incredulously.

"Do you feel heat?" Bhlokw asked simply.

"No," Ulath admitted, "I do not. It had been my thought—" He broke off, frowning and trying to frame his next question in coherent Trollish. "We were far to the north when you and your pack-mates ate the children of Cyrgon who were both dead and not dead."

"Yes. It was north from where we are now."

"Then Ghnomb took you and your pack-mates into No-Time."

"Yes."

"Then Ghworg led you to the lands of the sun."

"Yes."

"There was no hurt caused to you when he did this?"

"No. The hurt was caused by the things that were not how they should be."

"Which things were not how they should be?"

"All of the Trolls were one pack. This is not how it should be. Troll-packs do not have so many. It is not a good way to hunt." Bhlokw rubbed at his shaggy face with one massive paw. "We did not hunt this way when we were in the Troll-range where we are supposed to be. My thought was that Ghworg's mind was sick when he came to us and told us to cross the ice-which-never-melts to come to this place. It was not Ghworg who did this. It was Cyrgon. Cyrgon had made himself to look like Ghworg and spoke in Ghworg's voice. It was my mind which was sick. My thought should have told me that it was not Ghworg."

"Does it cause hurt to you that the Trolls are all one pack?"

"Much hurt, U-lat. I do not like it when things are not how they should be. I have known Grek for many snows. His pack hunts near my pack in the Troll-range. I do not like Grek. It has been in my thought for the past two snows to kill him. Ghworg will not let me kill him. This causes hurt to me."

"It will not be this way always, Bhlokw," Ulath said consolingly. "After we have killed all of Cyrgon's children, the Gods will take the Trolls back to the Troll-range. Then things will be how they should be again."

"It will make me glad when they are. I would really like to kill Grek." Bhlokw shambled away mournfully.

"What was that all about?" Tynian asked.

"I'm not sure," Ulath admitted. "I'm groping around the edges of something here. I know it's right in front of me, but I can't put my finger on it."

"For the moment, let's just hope that the Troll-Gods can control the homicidal impulses of their children," Tynian said fervently.

"Trollicidal," Ulath corrected.

"What?"

"You said *homicidal.* Bhlokw wants to kill Grek. Grek's a Troll. The right word would be *Trollicidal.*"

"That's petty quibbling, Ulath."

"Right is right, Tynian," Ulath replied in a faintly injured tone.

It was still quite early the next morning when Aphrael returned from Sarna. The sky to the east was lighted with the pale approach of day, even though the moon still held sway above the western horizon.

Sparhawk and Xanetia had been waiting for no more than half an hour when they heard the familiar trill of Flute's pipes coming from back in the dark forest.

"That was quick," Sparhawk said as the Child-Goddess joined them.

"It's not as if Sarna were on the other side of the continent, Sparhawk," she replied. "I got them all settled in." She smiled. "Vanion's being a pest. He was trying to make Sephrenia go to bed when I left."

"She *has* been very weak Aphrael," he reminded her.

"But she isn't now. She needs to be up and moving about. Turn your backs."

Xanetia looked puzzled.

"It's one of her quirks," Sparhawk explained. "She doesn't want people watching while she changes." He looked at the Child-Goddess. "Don't forget the clothes this time, Aphrael," he told her. "Let's not offend the Anarae."

"You're so tiresome about that, Sparhawk. Now please turn around."

It only took a few moments. "All right," Aphrael said. They turned. Sparhawk noted the Goddess was once again garbed in that satiny white robe.

"Thou art fair beyond description, Divine One," Xanetia said.

Aphrael shrugged. "I cheat a lot. Do you trust me, Anarae?"

"With my life, Divine Aphrael."

"I hope you're taking notes, Sparhawk."

"Have you arranged for some noise to hide what you're doing from Zalasta?"

"I don't have to. Xanetia's coming along, and her presence will conceal everything."

"I suppose I hadn't thought of that," he admitted.

"Now then, Anarae," Aphrael explained, "We're all going to hold hands. Then we'll rise up into the air. It's really better if you don't look down. As soon as we get above the tops of these mountains, we'll start moving. You won't feel any wind or cold or sense of movement. Just hold onto my hand and try to think of something else. It won't take very long." She squinted toward the eastern horizon. "We'd better get started. I'd like to get us to Natayos and into a good hiding place before Scarpa's soldiers start stirring around." She held out her hands, and Sparhawk and Xanetia took them.

Sparhawk steeled himself and watched the ground rapidly receding as they rose swiftly toward the dawn sky.

"You're squeezing, Sparhawk," Aphrael told him.

"Sorry. I'm still not entirely used to this." He looked at Xanetia. The Anarae, all aglow, was a picture of absolute serenity as they rose higher and higher.

"The world is fair," she said softly with a note of wonder in her voice.

"*If* you get high so that you can't see the ugliness." Aphrael smiled. "I come up here to think now and then. It's one place where I can be fairly sure I won't be interrupted." She took a bearing on the newly risen sun, which had seemed almost to rush up into the sky as they rose, set her face resolutely toward the southeast, and gave a peculiar little nod.

The earth beneath began to flow smoothly, rushing toward them from the front and receding just as rapidly behind.

"It seemeth me a merry way to travel," Xanetia observed.

"I've always rather liked it," Aphrael agreed. "It's certainly faster than plodding along on horseback."

They fled southeasterly with an eerie kind of silence around them.

"The Sea of Arjun," Sparhawk said, pointing toward a large body of water off to the right.

"So small?" Xanetia said. "I had though it larger."

"We're up quite a ways," Aphrael explained. "Everything looks small from a distance."

They sped on and were soon over the dense green jungle that covered the southeastern coast of the continent.

"We'll go down a bit now," Aphrael warned. "I'll take a bearing on Delo, and then we'll swerve toward the southwest to reach Natayos."

"Will we not be seen from the ground?" Xanetia asked.

"No—although it's an interesting idea. Your light would definitely startle people. Whole new religions could be born if people on the ground started seeing angels flying over their heads. There's Delo."

The port city looked like a child's toy carelessly left on the shore of the deep blue Tamul Sea. They veered to the southwest, following the coastline and gradually descending.

Aphrael was peering intently down at the jungle rushing back beneath them. "There," she said triumphantly.

The ruin might have been more difficult to find had not the northern quarter been cleared of the brush and trees which covered the rest of the ancient city. The tumbled grey stones of the half-fallen buildings stood out sharply in the light of the sunrise, and the newly cleared road stretching toward the north was a yellow scar cut deeply into the face of the dark green of the jungle.

They settled gently to earth on the road about a quarter of a mile north of the ruins, and Sparhawk immediately led them back a hundred paces into the thick undergrowth. He was tense with excitement. If Kalten was right, he was less than a mile from the place where Ehlana was being held captive.

"Go ahead, Xanetia," Aphrael suggested. "I want to look you over before you go into the city. This is important, but I don't want to put you in any danger. Let's be sure nobody can see you."

"Thou art overly concerned, Divine One. Over the centuries, we of the Delphae have perfected this particular subterfuge." She straightened, and her face assumed an expression of almost unnatural calm. Her form seemed to shimmer, and little rainbow flickers of light seethed beneath her plain homespun robe. She blurred and wavered, her form becoming indistinct.

Then she was only an outline, and Sparhawk could clearly see the trunk of the tree behind her.

"How do you make the things on the other side of you visible?" Aphrael asked curiously.

"We bend the light, Divine One. That is at the core of this deception. The light flows around us like a swift-moving stream, carrying with it the images of such objects as our bodies would normally obscure."

"Very interesting," Aphrael mused. "I hadn't even thought of that possibility."

"We must be wary, however," Xanetia told the Goddess. "Our shadows, like telltale ghosts, can betray us."

"That's simple. Stay out of the sunlight."

Sparhawk concealed a faint smile. Even a Goddess could give blatantly obvious instructions sometimes.

"I shall most carefully adhere to thine advice, Divine One," Xanetia replied with exaggerated calm.

"You're making fun of me, aren't you, Xanetia?"

"Of course not, Divine Aphrael." Even the outline was gone now, and Xanetia's voice seemed to come out of nowhere. "To work, withal," she said, her sourceless voice receding in the direction of the road. "I shall return anon."

"I'll have to compliment Edaemus," Aphrael said. "That's a very clever means of concealment. Turn around, Sparhawk. I'm going to change back."

After the Child-Goddess had resumed the familiar form of Flute, she and Sparhawk made themselves comfortable and waited as the sun gradually rose. The jungle steamed, and the air was alive with the chattering of birds and the buzzing of insects. The moments seemed to drag. They were so close to Ehlana that Sparhawk almost imagined that he could smell her familiar fragrance. "Are Ulath and Tynian here yet?" he asked, more to get his mind away from his anxious concern than out of any real curiosity.

"Probably," Flute replied. "They set out from Arjun yesterday morning. It probably seemed like three weeks to them, but it was no more than a heartbeat for everybody else."

"I wonder if they stayed in No-Time or just merged into Scarpa's army."

"It's hard to say. Maybe I should have checked before Xanetia left."

Then they heard several men talking on the road. Sparhawk crept closer, with Aphrael just behind him.

"Because I don't trust these soldiers, Col," a rough-looking fellow was saying to a blond Elene.

"It's daytime, Senga. Nobody's going to ambush your beer wagons in broad daylight."

"You can't be too careful. Money's running short here in Natayos, and that beer's the lifeblood of my business. A thirsty man who's running short of money might do anything."

"Have you considered lowering your prices?" an evil-looking fellow with a black eye patch asked.

"Bite your tongue, Shallag," Senga replied.

"Just a suggestion." The patch-eyed man shrugged as the dozen or so heavily armed men moved on out of earshot.

"You recognized them, of course," Aphrael murmured to Sparhawk.

"Kalten and Bevier, yes. I didn't see Caalador, though." He thought for a moment. "Will you be all right here? Alone, I mean?"

"Well, it's *awfully* dangerous, Sparhawk—lions and tigers and bears, you know."

"It was a silly question, wasn't it?"

"I'd say so, yes. What have you got in mind?"

"Kalten and Bevier are obviously working for that fellow they called Senga. I think I can get them to vouch for me. They seem to have the run of Natayos, so hiring on as a beer guard would give me a way to get into the city without attracting attention."

"Will you be able to restrain yourself when you're that close to Mother?"

"I'm not going to do anything foolish, Aphrael."

"Well, I suppose it's all right. You have my permission."

"Oh, *thank* you, Divine Aphrael," he said. "Thank you, thank you, thank you."

"You have a very clever mouth, Sparhawk," she said tartly.

"It's probably the clever company I've been keeping lately." He shrugged.

"I have to run back to Sarna for a little while," Aphrael told him. "Try to stay out of trouble when you get into the city."

"I'll miss you desperately." He grinned.

"You're in an odd humor today."

"I feel good. If all goes well, I'll have your mother out of there before the sun goes down."

"We'll see."

They waited as the sun crept farther up in the eastern sky. Then from off to the north they heard the approach of several heavily laden wagons. "I'll keep you posted," Sparhawk promised, and he stepped out of the bushes to stand at the side of the muddy road.

The first wagon, drawn by four patient oxen, came creaking around a bend. The wagonbed was piled high with barrels, and the one known as Senga sat on the seat beside the villainous-looking driver. Kalten, his expression oddly familiar on his altered face, was perched on top of the barrels.

"Ho, Col," Sparhawk called from the roadside. "I *thought* I recognized your voice when you passed here a little while ago."

"Well, strike me blind if it isn't Fron!" Kalten exclaimed with a broad grin. Sparhawk suddenly wondered what might have happened if Kalten hadn't recognized him. Kalten was laughing now with genuine delight. "We all thought you'd run away to sea when things came apart on us back in Matherion."

"It didn't work out." Sparhawk shrugged. "There was a bo'sun on board who was a little too free with his whip. He decided to swim for shore one dark night. I can't imagine what came over him. We were twenty leagues out to sea when I helped him over the side."

"People do strange things sometimes. What are you doing here?"

"I heard about this army, and I thought it might be a good place to hide. Word's going about that this Scarpa fellow plans to attack Matherion. I've got a few old scores to settle there, so I decided to tag along for fun and profit."

"I think we can find a better spot for you than back in the rear ranks of Scarpa's army." Kalten nudged Senga's shoulder with his foot. "The fellow standing ankle-deep in the mud there is an old friend of ours from Matherion," he told the tavernkeeper. "His name's Fron, and he's a very good man in a fight. When the police jumped on us back in Matherion, he stood shoulder to shoulder with Shallag, holding them off while the rest of us got away. Do you think there might be a spot for him in your operation here in Natayos?"

"Do you vouch for him, Col?" Senga asked.

"I couldn't ask for better help if trouble crops up."

"You're in charge of security." Senga shrugged. "Hire anybody you want."

"I was hoping you'd see it that way." Kalten beckoned to Sparhawk. "Climb on up, Fron," he said. "I'll show you the wonders of Natayos."

"From the top of a beer wagon?"

"Can you think of a better place?"

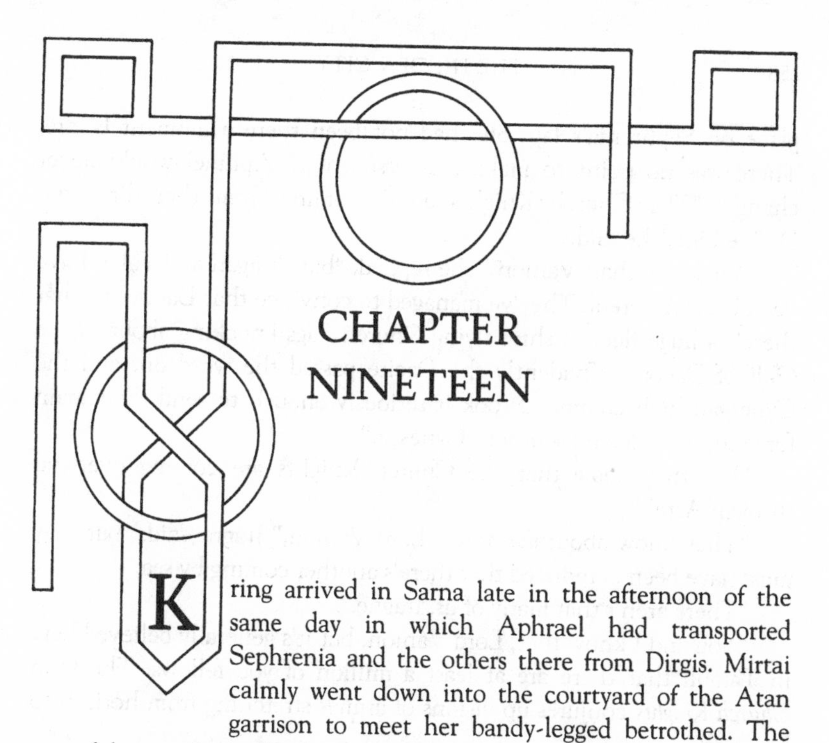

CHAPTER NINETEEN

Kring arrived in Sarna late in the afternoon of the same day in which Aphrael had transported Sephrenia and the others there from Dirgis. Mirtai calmly went down into the courtyard of the Atan garrison to meet her bandy-legged betrothed. The two of them embraced rather formally and then came into the building.

"She seems very restrained," Vanion observed quietly to Betuana as the two watched from the window of the conference room.

"It is not seemly to openly display affection in public, Vanion-Preceptor," the queen replied. "Decorum must be maintained, even though the heart might prefer it otherwise."

"Ah."

"Ho, friend Vanion," Kring said as he and his tall beloved entered, "you're just the man I was looking for."

"It's good to see you, too, friend Kring. How are things going in Samar?"

"It's quiet. The Cynesgans have pulled back from the border. Is there something going on to the south that I haven't been told about?"

"Not that I know of. Why do you ask?"

"The Cynesgans were massing just across the border, and we were expecting them to come across to lay siege to Samar almost any time. Then several days ago they pulled back and left only a few units in place. The rest of their army marched south."

"Why would they do that?" Vanion asked, frowning.

"Probably to meet the Church Knights," Aphrael replied.

Vanion turned to see the Child-Goddess calmly sitting in her usual place on Sephrenia's lap. She had not been there a moment before. There was no point to making an issue of it. Aphrael would never change. "The Church Knights aren't coming from that direction, Divine One," he said.

"*We* know that, Vanion," she replied, "but Stragen and Talen have been busy in Beresa. They've managed to convince that Dacite spy that there's a huge fleet of ships flying Church flags knocking about in the Gulf of Daconia. Evidently the Dacite passed the word on, and the Cynesgan high command took it seriously enough to send their main force south to defend southern Cynesga."

"But they *know* that the Church Knights are coming overland through Astel."

"They know about *that* force, Lord Vanion," Itagne said, "but they must have been convinced that there's another coming by sea."

"There aren't that many of us, Itagne."

"You and I know that, Lord Vanion, but it's generally believed here in Tamuli that there are at least a million of you fellows. The term *Church Knights* conjures up visions of armies stretching from horizon to horizon."

Vanion frowned. "Oh," he said finally. "I think I understand. During the Zemoch wars, we joined forces with the armies of the kings of Eosia. The Tamul observers must have thought that everyone in armor was a Church Knight."

"I think I'll have a talk with the emperor," Itagne mused. "Titles of nobility might be in order for your pair of thieves. This imaginary fleet of theirs seems to have pulled half the Cynesgan army off the border and most likely pinned down the Arjunis as well."

"It's a great little fleet—" Vanion grinned. "—and you don't even have to feed the sailors. Let's keep the stories alive." He looked at Aphrael. "Could you arrange some illusions, Divine One?"

"Dragons? Flights of angels?"

"How about a thousand ships hull-down on the horizon instead?"

"What do I get in return?"

"Stop teasing," Sephrenia told her with a gentle smile.

"Where would you like your make-believe boats, Vanion?"

He thought about it. "Why don't you just bounce them up and down the coastline of Daconia and western Arjuna?" he suggested. "Let's run the Cynesgans and Arjunis ragged trying to position themselves to defend against landings."

"I'll go take care of it right now," she said, slipping down from her sister's lap, "before I forget."

"When did you ever forget anything?" Sephrenia smiled.

"I don't know. I must have at some time, though. I've probably forgotten exactly when." She gave them all an impish little smile, and then she vanished.

Kring was sitting at Mirtai's side, and he had been squinting speculatively at the ceiling, absently running one hand over his stubbled scalp. He was not free to use the other, since Mirtai had taken possession of it. Her contented, almost placid, expression clearly said that she did not intend to release his hand in the foreseeable future.

"If Divine Aphrael can keep those Cynesgan troops more or less permanently distracted, Tikume and I'll be able to hold Samar without any help," the Domi said, "particularly now that we know how to deal with Klæl's soldiers." He rubbed even more briskly at his scalp.

"Quit worrying at it," Mirtai told him. "I'll shave you just as soon as we finish here."

"Yes, love," he agreed immediately.

"Oh, that reminds me," Vanion said. "Sparhawk had a talk with Bhelliom. Klæl's soldiers can only breathe our air for about a day before they start dying, and exertion speeds up the process. If you come across them again, keep them running."

Kring nodded.

A tall Atan came in and murmured something to Itagne.

"I'm really awfully busy right now, old boy," Itagne objected.

"He's most insistent, Itagne-Ambassador."

"Oh, very well." Itagne rose to his feet. "I'll be right back, Lord Vanion," he said, and followed the Atan from the room.

"Did Sparhawk find out what country Klæl's soldiers come from, friend Vanion?" Kring asked. "I'd sort of like to avoid that place."

"I don't think you need to worry, Domi Kring." Sephrenia smiled. "Klæl's soldiers were brought here from someplace beyond the stars."

Kring frowned. "You might want to have a talk with Sparhawk, friend Vanion," he said. "I enjoy a good fight as much as the next man, but if he's going to declare war on the whole universe, he ought to let the rest of us in on his plans."

"I'll definitely speak with him about it, Domi Kring." Vanion said. Then he sighed. "I wish we'd known more about Klæl's soldiers earlier.

The Church Knights encountered them in the mountains of Zemoch and lost half their number in killed and wounded."

"I'm sorry, friend Vanion. Did you lose many old comrades?"

"Many, Domi Kring," Vanion replied sadly, "many."

"How's friend Engessa coming along?" Kring asked Betuana.

"Aphrael says that he's recovering, Domi," she replied. "I'd like to see that for myself, though."

Itagne returned, accompanied by a Tamul wearing slightly out-of-date clothing. "Would you please see to it that we're not disturbed?" he said to the Atan guard in the hall. Then he closed and bolted the door. "I have some good news for a change," he said then. He put his hand on the stranger's shoulder. "This is my very dear—though newfound—friend, Ekrasios," he said.

Betuana frowned. "That is not a Tamul name," she said.

"No, your Majesty," Itagne agreed, "it's not. Actually, it's Dephaeic. The Delphae are such a musical people. It probably derives from the fact that they still speak classical Tamul. My friend here just stopped by to advise us that the Delphae have decided to come out of their splendid seclusion. Ekrasios, this is Preceptor Vanion, the close friend of Anakha. The regal lady is Betuana, Queen of the Atans. The short fellow is Domi Kring of the western Peloi. The tall, pretty girl with the death grip on his hand is Mirtai, his betrothed, and the exquisite Styric lady is Sephrenia, High Priestess of the Goddess Aphrael."

"Nobles all," Ekrasios greeted them with a formal bow. "I bring greetings from Beloved Edaemus. Divine Aphrael hath persuaded him that we have common cause in the current situation, and he hath thus relaxed his centuries-old prohibition upon us. I am sent to thee, Lord Vanion, to advise thee that I and diverse companions are at thine immediate disposal. Where might we best be deployed to further our cause?"

"If I may, Lord Vanion?" Itagne interposed. "It just occurred to me that the Delphae might be best suited to empty those ruins in the Arjuni jungles. If Ekrasios and his friends were to appear in all their glowing splendor at the gates of Scarpa's camps down there, the rebels would probably go back home and take up peaceful pursuits—just as fast as they possibly could."

"Well said," Mirtai murmured her agreement.

"He certainly moves around, doesn't he?" Ulath said to Tynian as the beer wagon with Sparhawk and Kalten perched atop the barrels rumbled past on the ancient street. "Last I heard, he was in Dirgis."

"The natcherl rules don't seem t' apply t' ol' Sporhawk," Tynian replied in a bad imitation of Caalador's dialect. "What do you think? Should we slip back into real time? Or should we stay where we are?"

"I think we'll be more useful if we stay out of sight," Ulath replied.

"That's fine with me, but how are we going to get word to Sparhawk and the others that we're here?"

"I'll slip a note in his pocket—or blow in his ear."

"That ought to get his attention."

Bhlowk came shambling back up the street with a mournful expression on his apelike face. "There are no dogs here," he reported in Trollish.

"Soldiers don't usually keep dogs, Bhlowk," Tynian explained.

"I have hunger, Tin-in. Would the man-things here miss one of their herd—a small one?"

"We might have a problem here," Tynian muttered to Ulath. "It's definitely in our best interests to keep our friend here well-fed."

Ulath scratched at his now-clean-shaven cheek. "We can't just turn him loose," he noted. "He'll attract attention if he starts grabbing people and jerking them into these broken moments."

"He's invisible, Ulath."

"Yes, but if some Arjuni suddenly vanishes and his bones start getting tossed back out of nowhere, it's bound to attract attention." He turned back to the Troll. "It is our thought that it would not be good for you to kill and eat the man-things here, Bhlokw. We hunt thought here, and if you kill and eat the man-things, you will frighten the thought away."

"I do not like this hunting of thought, U-lat," Bhlowk complained. "It makes things not-simple."

"The forest is near, Bhlokw," Tynian said. "There must be many good-to-eat things there."

"I am not an Ogre, Tin-in," Bhlokw protested in a slightly offended tone. "I do not eat trees."

"There should be creatures that are good-to-eat among the trees, Bhlokw," Ulath said. "That is what Tin-in was trying to say. It was not his thought to insult you."

Bhlokw glowered at Tynian for a moment. "I will go hunt now," he said abruptly. Then he turned and shambled off.

"You have to be careful, Tynian," Ulath warned his friend. "If you want to get into a fight almost immediately, all you have to do is suggest to a Troll that he might be an Ogre."

"They're actually prejudiced?" Tynian asked in amazement.

"You wouldn't *believe* how prejudiced," Ulath replied. "Trolls and Ogres have hated each other since the beginning of time."

"I thought that prejudice was a human failing."

"Some things are just too good to stay private, I guess. Let's follow Sparhawk and let him know that we're here. He might have something for us to do."

They trailed along behind the beer caravan winding through the cleared streets toward that part of Natayos that was still choked in brush and vines. The wagons trundled along a recently cleared street and then went around behind a canvas-roofed building identified by a crudely lettered sign that read "Senga's."

"Trust Kalten to get close to the beer," Tynian said.

"Truly," Ulath agreed. "Wait here. I'll go let Sparhawk know that we're in Natayos." He walked over to where Sparhawk, Kalten, and Bevier, looking strange with their altered features, stood off to one side while Senga supervised the unloading of the barrels. "Ramshorn," he said quietly. "Don't get excited and start looking around," he added. "You won't be able to see me."

"Ulath?" Kalten asked incredulously.

"Right. Tynian, Bhlokw, and I got here yesterday. We've been nosing around."

"How have you managed to become invisible?" the patch-eyed Bevier asked.

"We aren't actually. Ghnomb's breaking the seconds into two pieces. We're only present during the smaller piece. That's why you can't see us."

"But you can see *us*?"

"Yes."

"Ulath, that's logically inconsistent."

"I know, but Ghnomb *believes* that it works, and I guess his belief is strong enough to override logic. Tynian and I are here, and nobody can see us. Is there anything you want us to do?"

"Can you get into that building near the gate?" Sparhawk asked quickly. "The one with the barred windows?"

"Not a chance. We already looked into the possibility. Too many guards on the doors. Bhlokw even tried going in through the roof, but it's all sealed up."

"That's my *wife* in there, Ulath!" Sparhawk exclaimed. "Are you saying that you tried to send a *Troll* into the same building with her?"

"Bhlokw wouldn't have hurt her, Sparhawk—frightened her a little, maybe, but he wouldn't have hurt her. We sort of thought he might be able to go in through the roof, pick Ehlana and Alean up, and carry them out." Ulath paused. "It wasn't really our idea, Sparhawk. Bhlokw volunteered—well, actually he didn't even volunteer. He just started climbing up the wall before we could stop him. He said, 'I will go get them. I will bring Anakha's mate and her friend out so that we can kill all these children of Cyrgon and eat them.' Bhlokw's a little elemental, but his heart's in the right place. I hate to admit it, but I'm actually starting to like him."

Kalten looked around nervously. "Where is he now?" he asked.

"He's out hunting. When we were knocking around those cities by the lake, we persuaded him not to eat people. We got him started on dogs instead. He really likes them, but there aren't any dogs here in Natayos, so he's out in the woods—probably chasing elephants or something." Then something flickered at the corner of Ulath's eye. "What in God's name is that?" he exclaimed.

"What?" Kalten asked, looking around in bafflement.

"There's somebody made out of rainbows coming around the side of the building!" Ulath gaped at the clearly defined shape approaching. The many-colored light was dazzling.

"That's Xanetia," Sparhawk explained. "Can you actually *see* her?"

"Are you saying that you *can't*?"

"She's invisible, Ulath."

"Not to *me*, she isn't."

"It must have something to do with the peculiar time you're in, my friend," Bevier suggested. "You'd better let her know that you can see her. It might be important someday."

The shimmering rainbow stopped a few paces away. "Anakha," Xanetia said softly.

"I hear thee, Anarae," Sparhawk replied.

"It pains me to tell thee that I have failed," she confessed. "The mind of Scarpa is so twisted that I cannot wring coherence from his thought. I did gently probe the minds of some of his followers, however, and I must sadly advise thee that thy queen is no longer here in Natayos. When our enemies did discover the subterfuge involving young Sir Berit, Zalasta did spirit thy wife and her handmaiden away under cover of darkness. I shall endeavor to glean their destination from the thoughts of others here, an it please thee."

Ulath's heart twisted with sympathy at the look of sudden despair that came over Sparhawk's face.

They ran easily in their endless regiments, tall and lightly armored, with their bronze limbs glowing in the cool grey light. The towering King Androl ran smoothly at the front of his army. It was good to be on the move again, and the prospect of battle was exhilarating. Battle was meaningful, and one could actually *see* results. The absence of his wife had thrust a thousand petty administrative chores on Androl's unprepared shoulders. It was so frustrating to make decisions about things he didn't really understand and even more frustrating not to see any immediate results that would have told him whether or not his decisions had been correct. Once again the King of Atan thanked his God for giving him Betuana to wife. They made a good team, actually. The queen was very skilled with details. Her mind was quick, and she could pick out subtleties and nuances that frequently escaped her husband. Androl, on the other hand, was made for action. He gladly let his wife make all the tiresome decisions, and then, when it was all settled and they knew what they were going to do, *he* took charge of carrying her decisions out. It was better that way, actually. The King of Atan was fully aware of his limitations and he knew that his wife forgave him when he occasionally overlooked something. He hoped that he didn't disappoint her too much.

Her suggestion—she never gave him orders—that he take the bulk of their people to the south end of Lake Sarna in preparation for a grand battle at Tosa was exactly the sort of thing Androl truly loved. Here was action, simple and uncomplicated. The troublesome decisions had all been made, the enemy had been identified, and all the boring details had been swept out of the way. He smiled as he led his army into the last outcropping of mountains some fifty leagues to the southeast of Tualas. Betuana's message had hinted that the battle at Tosa would be a titanic one, a grand clash at arms with struggling armies stretching for miles and the ring of sword against sword reaching to the skies. He would make her proud of him.

The route through the outcropping mountains led up a long ridgeline, through a narrow notch, and then down into the deep gorge of a turbulent stream that had gnawed at the rock for eons.

King Androl was breathing a bit heavily when he crested the ridgeline and led his forces through the notch. The wasted hours spent conferring with Ambassador Norkan had taken off Androl's edge. A warrior should never permit himself to be lured away from the practice field or the exercise yard. He picked up the pace as he led his army down into the narrow gorge, running smoothly along the south bank of the rushing mountain river. If *he* was out of shape, his soldiers probably were as well. He hoped that he could find a suitable place for an encampment at Lake Sarna, a proper encampment with enough space for training and practice and those necessary calisthenics that honed warriors to the peak of fitness. Androl was sublimely confident that *any* opposing force could be overcome if only his army were fully trained and fit.

"Androl-King!" General Pemaas shouted over the sound of the turbulent stream. "Look!"

"Where?" Androl demanded, half-turning and reaching for his sword.

"At the top of the gorge—on the right!"

The Atan king craned his neck to peer up the sheer cliff-face to the rocky brink high above.

The King of Atan had seen many things in his life, but nothing to compare with the vast, monstrous form rearing suddenly above them on the rim of the gorge.

The thing was glossy black, like polished leather, and it had enormously outspreading wings, jointed and batlike. Its wedge-shaped head was accentuated by blazing eye-slits and a gaping mouth that dripped flame.

King Androl considered it. The problem, of course, was the fact that the towering creature was at the top of the gorge while he stood at the bottom. He could turn and retrace his steps, running back up the gorge to the notch and scrambling around the rocks to reach the rim; but that would give the thing plenty of opportunity to run away, and then he would have to chase it down in order to kill it. In his present less-than-perfect condition, that would be very tedious. He could always climb up the cliff, but that would still take time, and the creature might very well see him coming and try to flee.

Then, amazingly, the large being at the top of the gorge provided the solution. It raised its enormous arms and began to slash at the top of the cliff with what appeared to be fire of some kind.

Androl smiled as the cliff-face began to topple outward, tumbling and roaring down into the gorge. The silly beast was accommodatingly providing the means for its own destruction. How could it *be* so stupid?

King Androl adroitly dodged a tumbling, house-sized boulder, carefully assessing the rapidly growing slope of rubble piling up at the base of the cliff.

The beast actually intended to attack! Androl laughed with delight. The creature was stupid beyond imagining, but he *did* have to give it credit for courage—foolish courage, of course, but courage nonetheless. All the universe knew that Androl of Atan was invincible, and yet this poor dumb brute meant to pit its puny strength against the greatest warrior since the beginning of time.

Androl looked speculatively at the steep, growing slope of rubble, ignoring the cries of those of his soldiers not nimble enough to avoid being crushed in the avalanche rumbling down upon them. Almost high enough now. Just a few more feet.

And then he judged that the steep slope had grown high enough to give him access to the stupid creature roaring and flapping its wings high above. He dodged another boulder and began his rush, scrambling, dodging, leaping, as he swiftly mounted toward the doomed beast above him.

When he was almost to the top, he paused, drew his sword, and set himself.

And then with a savage war cry he rushed up the remaining slope, ignoring the momentary flicker of sympathy he felt for the brave, misguided creature he was about to kill.

"Where do you think you're going?" a burly Dacite wearing a shabby uniform tunic and holding a long pike demanded as Sparhawk and Kalten pulled the wobbly cart with two large barrels in it around the corner of the building.

"We've got a delivery from Senga for Master Krager," Kalten replied.

"Anybody could say that."

"Go ask him," Kalten suggested.

"I wouldn't want to disturb him."

"Then you'd better let us past. He's been waiting for this wine for quite some time now. If you keep us from delivering it, he'll *really* be disturbed. He might even be disturbed enough to take the matter to Lord Scarpa."

The guard's face grew apprehensive. "Wait here," he said, then turned and went along the back of the building to the heavy door.

"I'll stay in the background when we get inside," Sparhawk quietly told his friend. "If he asks, just tell him that I'm a strong back you commandeered to help pull the cart."

Kalten nodded.

"Are you here, Anarae?" Sparhawk asked, looking around in spite of the fact that he knew he wouldn't be able to see her.

"Right at thy side, Anakha," her voice replied softly.

"We'll keep him talking for as long as we can. He'll probably be a little drunk. Will that make it difficult for you?"

"I have shared the thoughts of this Krager before," she told him. "He is coherent unless he is far gone with drink. If it be convenient, direct his attention toward the house where thy queen was late held captive. That may prod his mind toward thoughts of interest to us."

"I'll see what I can do, Anarae," Kalten promised.

The Dacite guard came back. "He'll receive you," he announced.

"Somehow I was almost sure he would." Kalten smirked. "Master Krager's very fond of this particular wine." He and Sparhawk lifted the shafts of the cart and pulled it along over the rough, littered ground at the back of the semirestored ruin that appeared to be Scarpa's main headquarters.

Krager was eagerly waiting in the doorway. His head was shaved, but he still looked much the same. He was dishevelled and unshaven, his nearsighted, watery eyes were bloodshot, and his hands were visibly shaking. "Bring it inside," he ordered in his familiar, rusty-sounding voice.

Kalten and Sparhawk set the shafts of the cart down, untied the ropes that had held the two barrels in place, and carefully eased one of them out onto the ground. Kalten measured the height of the barrel with a length of the rope and then checked the width of the doorway. "Just barely," he said. "Tip it over, Fron. We'll be able to roll it in."

Sparhawk heaved the barrel over onto its side, and he and his friend rolled it through the doorway into the cluttered room beyond. There was an unmade bed against one wall, and clothes littered the floor. The place was permeated with the acrid smell of Krager's unwashed, wine-sodden body, and there was a heap of empty casks and broken earthenware bottles in one corner.

"Where did you want these, Master Krager?" Kalten asked.

"Anyplace," Krager said impatiently.

"That's not thinking ahead," Kalten said critically. "They're too heavy for you to move by yourself. Pick a spot that'll be convenient."

"You might be right." Krager squinted around the room. Then he went to a place near the head of the bed and kicked some clothes out of the way. "Put them right here," he instructed.

"Ah—before we go any further, why don't we settle up? These are very expensive, Master Krager."

"How much?"

"Senga told me that he had to have fifty crowns a barrel. Arcian red's very hard to come by this far away from Arcium."

"*Fifty crowns?*" Krager exclaimed.

"Each," Kalten insisted. "He told me to open the barrels for you, too."

"I know how to open a wine barrel, Col."

"I'm sure of it, but Senga's an honest businessman and he wants me to make sure you're satisfied before I take your money." He rolled the barrel over against the wall. "Help me set it up, Fron," he told Sparhawk. They righted the barrel, and Kalten took a pry-bar out from under his belt. "Beer's a lot easier to deal with," he noted. "Somebody ought to tell those Arcian vintners about the advantages of putting a bunghole in the side of a barrel." He carefully pried up the lid as Krager, cup in hand, eagerly waited at his elbow.

"Give it a try, Master Krager," Kalten said then, lifting off the lid and stepping aside.

Krager dipped his cup into the deep red liquid, lifted it with a trembling hand, and drank deeply. "Marvelous!" he sighed happily.

"I'll tell Senga that it meets with your approval," Kalten said. He laughed. "You wouldn't expect it of a highway robber, but Senga's very concerned about satisfying his customers. Would you believe that he even had us pour out a barrel of beer that had gone sour? Come on, Fron, let's get the other barrel. We'll have Master Krager test that one and then we'll settle accounts."

The two of them went back outside and manhandled the second barrel out of the cart.

"Ask him why they've taken the guards off the doors of the house where they were holding Ehlana and Alean," Sparhawk muttered.

"Right." Kalten grunted as they lowered the wine barrel to the ground.

They put the second barrel beside the first, Kalten pried open the lid, and Krager sampled it.

"Satisfactory?" Kalten asked.

"Just fine," Krager said. He dipped out another cup and sank back happily on his bed. "Absolutely splendid."

"That'll be a hundred crowns, then."

Krager pulled a heavy purse out from under his belt and negligently tossed it to Kalten. "Here," he said. "Count it out yourself. Don't steal too much."

"This is business, Master Krager," Kalten told him. "If I was robbing you, I'd have my knife against your throat." He swept some clothing and a few dried crusts of bread off the top of a table with his forearm, opened the purse, and started counting out coins. "We noticed that all the guards have been pulled away from the house with the bars on the windows," he said. "A couple of days ago a man couldn't get within twenty paces of that place, but this morning Fron and I wheeled that cart right past the front door, and nobody paid any attention to us. Has Lord Scarpa moved whatever was so valuable out of there?"

Krager's puffy face became suddenly alert. "That's none of your business, Col."

"I didn't say it was. You might just make a suggestion to Lord Scarpa, though. If he doesn't want people to notice things like that, he shouldn't change anything. He should have kept all the guards right where they were. Senga and the rest of us are all robbers, you know, and we all more or less believed that Lord Scarpa was keeping his treasure in that house. The word *treasure* makes men like us prick up our ears."

Krager stared at him and then he began to laugh.

"What's so funny?" Kalten looked up from his counting.

"It was a treasure all right, Col—" Krager smirked. "—but not the kind you can count."

"Like you say, it's none of my business, but every man who works in Senga's tavern knows that it's been moved. I'm sure they'll all be poking around in these ruins looking for the new storehouse."

"Let them look." Krager shrugged. "The treasure's a long, long way from here by now."

"I hope you've still got guards on it. Those woods out there are crawling with fellows like Fron and me. Would you come here and check my count?"

"I trust you, Col."

"You're a fool, then."

"Take another ten crowns for yourself and your man," Krager said expansively, "and then if you don't mind, I'd like to be alone with my two new friends here."

"You're very generous, Master Krager." Kalten took some more coins from the purse, scooped up all the ones he had previously counted out, and dumped them into the side pocket of his smock. "Let's go, Fron," he said to Sparhawk. "Master Krager wants to be alone."

"Tell Senga that I'm grateful to him," Krager said, dipping out more wine, "and tell him to keep his eye out for more of this excellent vintage. I'll buy all he can find."

"I'll tell him, Master Krager. Enjoy yourself." And Kalten led the way out of the reeking room.

Sparhawk closed the door and held out his hand.

"What?" Kalten asked.

"My five crowns, if you don't mind," Sparhawk said firmly. "Let's keep accounts current, shall we?"

"Thou art shrewd, Sir Kalten," Xanetia's whispered voice came to them. "Thou didst most skillfully guide his thought in precisely the direction most useful to us."

Kalten made some show of counting coins into Sparhawk's hand. "What did you find out, Anarae?" he asked in a tense voice.

"Some day or two ago, a closed carriage did depart from this place after making some show of stopping—under heavy guard—at the door to the house upon which all our attention hath been fixed. The carriage, which was but a ploy, is bound for Panem-Dea. Those we seek are not inside, however. They had long since departed from Natayos with Zalasta."

"Did Krager know where Zalasta was taking them?" Sparhawk asked.

"It was evidently in Zalasta's mind that none here should know," Xanetia replied, "but Krager, ever alert to the main chance, was well aware that news of Zalasta's destination might well save his life should things go awry, and he did strive most assiduously to learn the Styric's plans. By feigning drunken stupor, he was able to be present when Zalasta did speak with his comrade, Cyzada. The twain spake in Styric, but Krager, unbeknownst to us all, hath a smattering of that tongue, and he was thus able to glean from their hurried conversation the very information which he—and we—are most curious about."

"That's a surprise," Kalten muttered. "Drunk or sober, Krager's a shrewd one, all right. Where's Zalasta taking the ladies, Anarae?"

Xanetia sighed. "The information is melancholy, Sir Kalten," she told him. "I do fear me that it is Zalasta's intent to take the queen and her handmaiden to the Hidden City of Cyrga, where Cyrgon himself doth hold sway, and by his power there can deny us all access to those we love."

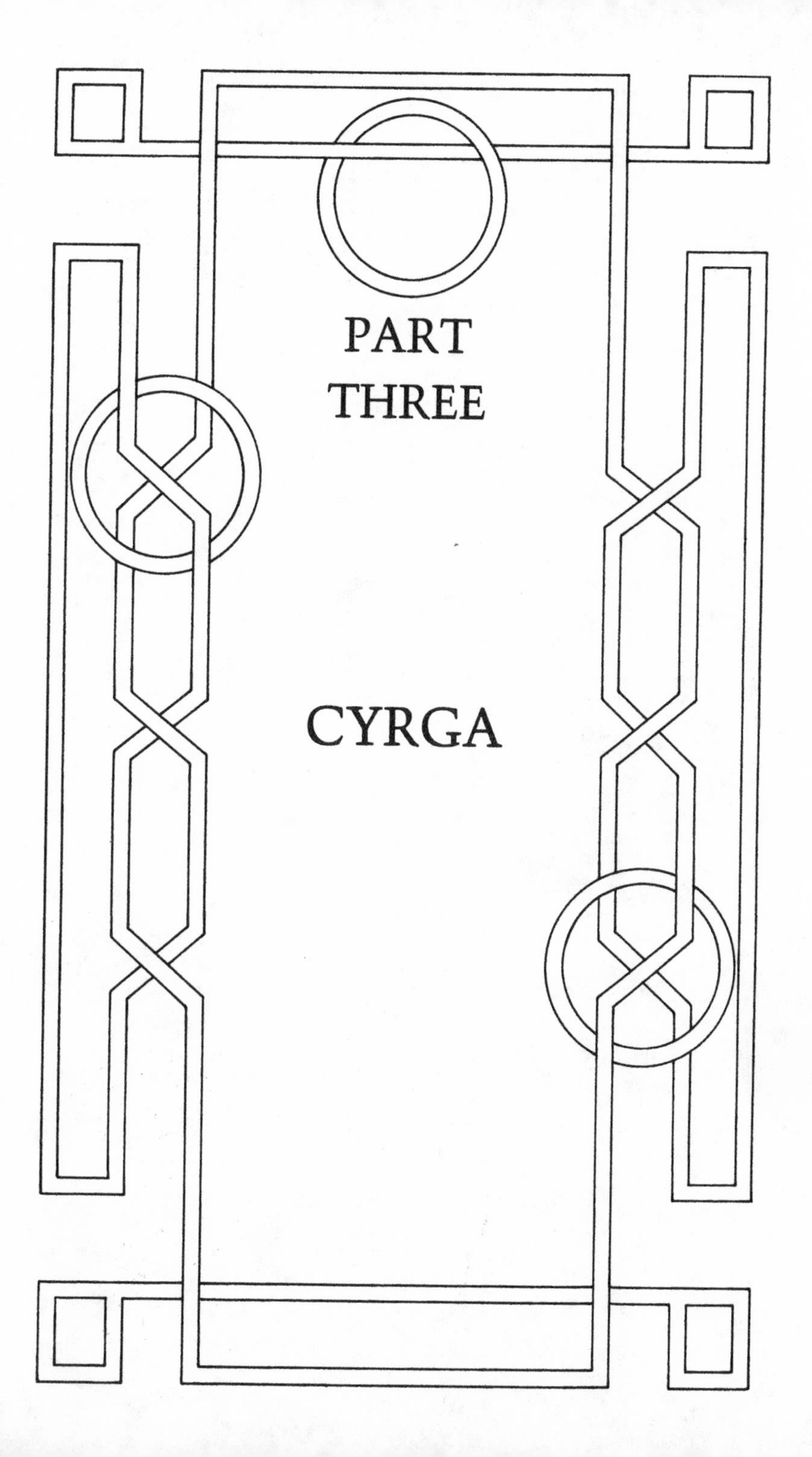

PART THREE

CYRGA

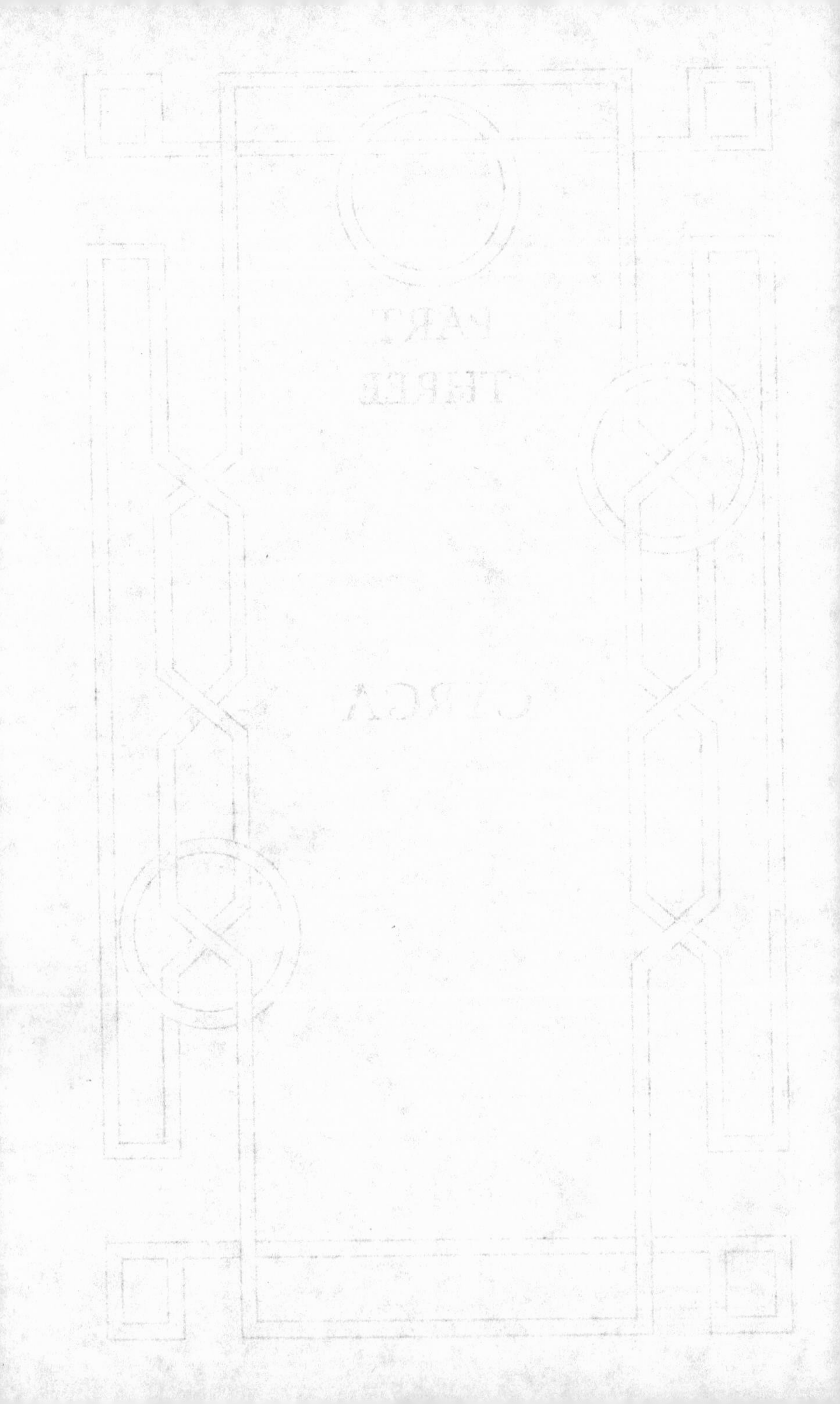

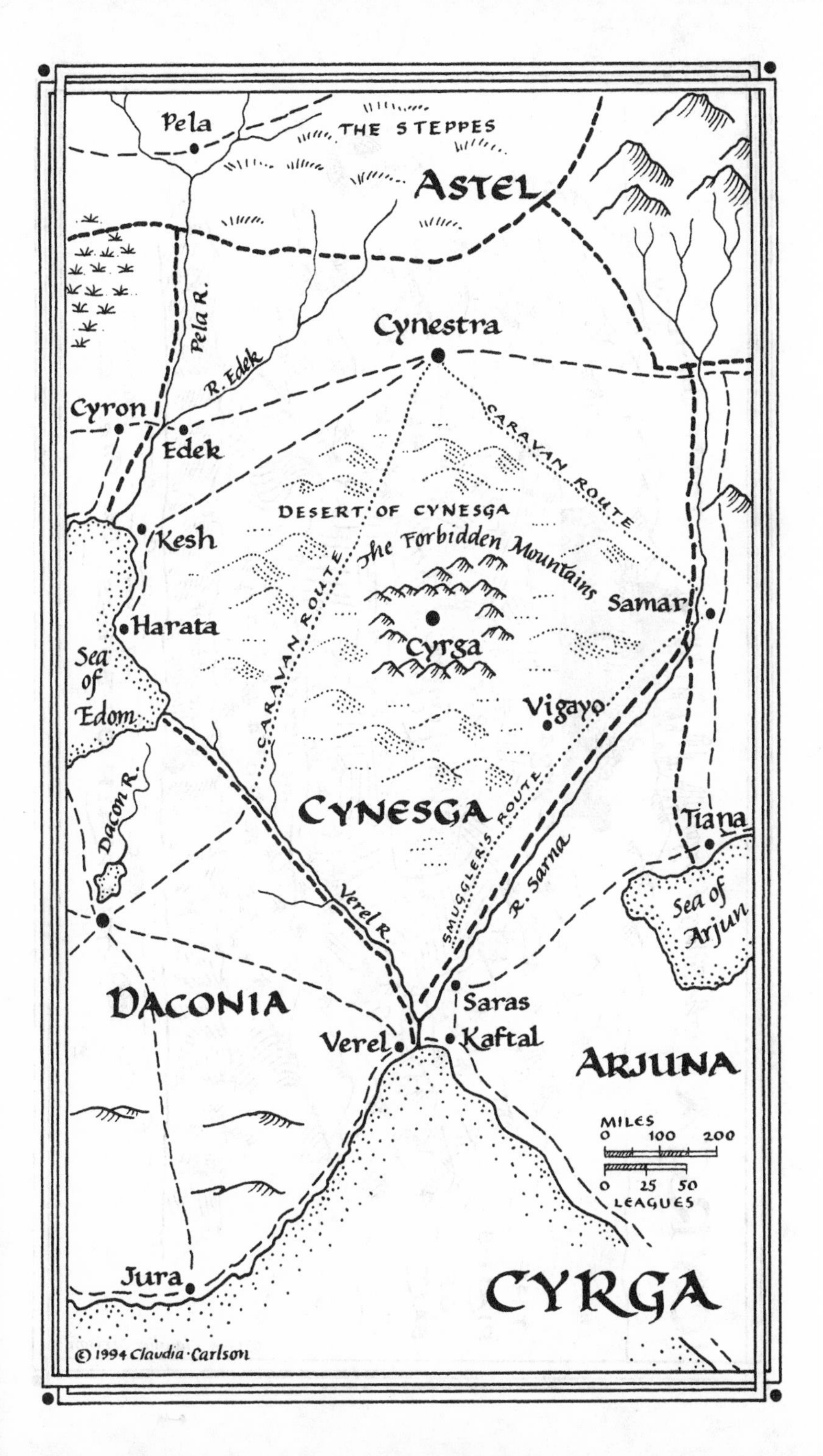
Pela
THE STEPPES
ASTEL
Pela R.
R. Edek
Cynestra
Cyron
Edek
CARAVAN ROUTE
DESERT OF CYNESGA
Kesh
The Forbidden Mountains
Samar
Harata
Cyrga
Sea of Edom
CARAVAN ROUTE
Vigayo
Dacon R.
CYNESGA
SMUGGLERS ROUTE
R. Sarna
Tiana
Sea of Arjun
Verel R.
DACONIA
Saras
Verel
Kaftal
ARJUNA
MILES
0 100 200
0 25 50
LEAGUES
Jura
CYRGA

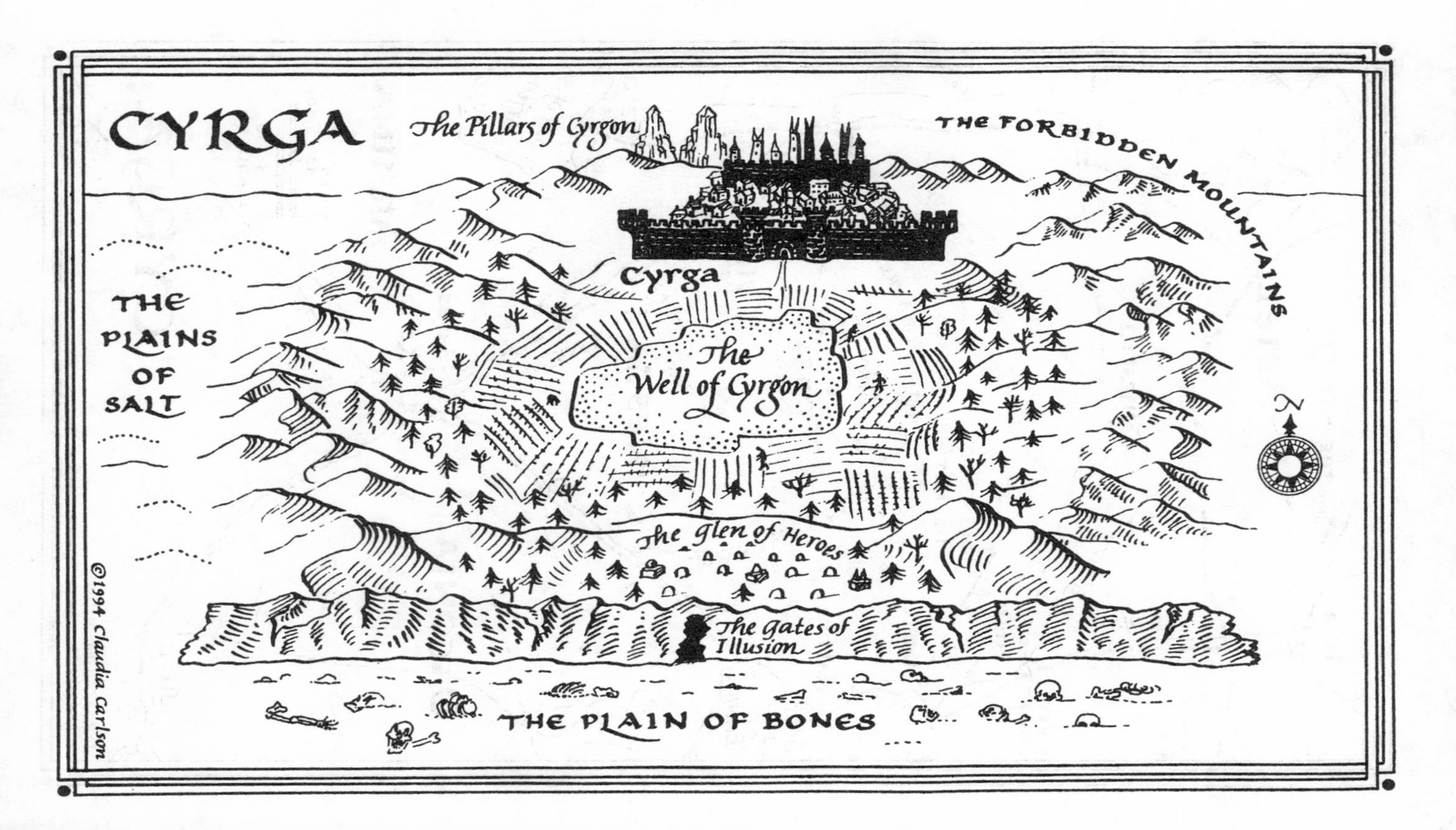
CYRGA
The Pillars of Cygon
THE FORBIDDEN MOUNTAINS
Cyrga
THE PLAINS OF SALT
The Well of Cyrgon
N
The Glen of Heroes
The Gates of Illusion
THE PLAIN OF BONES
©1994 Claudia Carlson

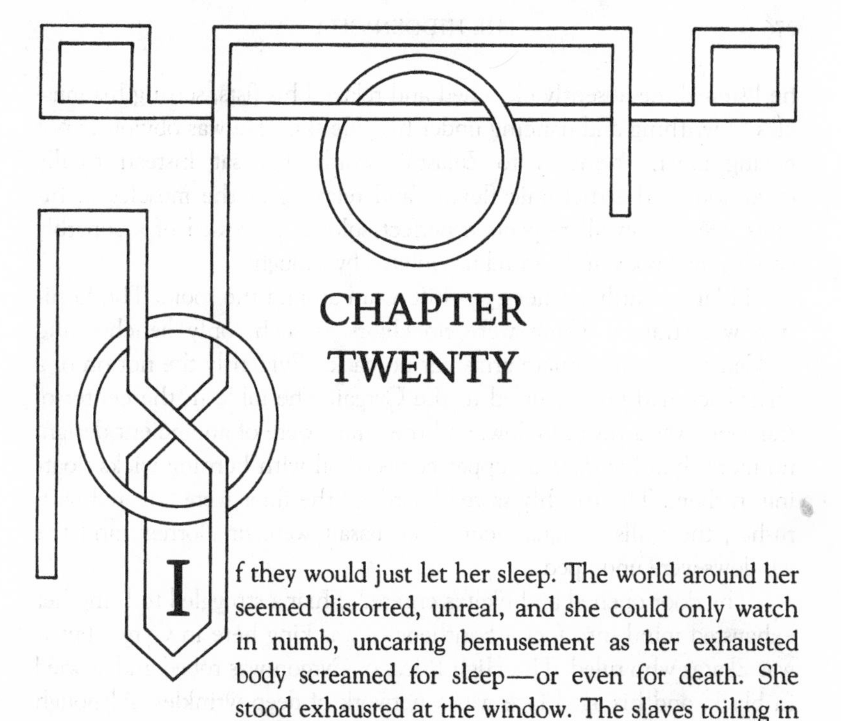

CHAPTER TWENTY

If they would just let her sleep. The world around her seemed distorted, unreal, and she could only watch in numb, uncaring bemusement as her exhausted body screamed for sleep—or even for death. She stood exhausted at the window. The slaves toiling in the fields around the lake below looked almost like ants crawling across the winter-fallow fields as they grubbed at the soil with crude implements. Other slaves gathered firewood among the trees on the sloping sides of the basin, and the puny sounds of their axes drifted up to the dark tower from which she watched.

Alean lay on an unpadded bench—sleeping or dead, Ehlana could no longer tell which, but she envied her gentle maid in either case.

They were not alone, of course. They were never alone. Zalasta, his own face gaunt with weariness, talked on and on with King Santheocles. Ehlana was too tired to make any sense of the haggard Styric's droning words. She absently looked at the King of the Cyrgai, a man in a close-fitting steel breastplate, a short leather kirtle, and ornate steel wristguards. Santheocles was of a race apart, and generations of selective breeding had heightened those features most admired by his people. He was tall and superbly muscled. His skin was very fair, although his carefully curled and oiled hair and beard were glossy black. His nose was straight, continuing the unbroken line of his forehead. His eyes were very large and very dark—and totally empty. His expression was haughty, cruel. His was the face of a stupid, arrogant man devoid of compassion or even simple decency.

His ornate breastplate left his upper arms and shoulders bare, and as he listened, he absently clenched and relaxed his fists, setting his muscles to writhing and dancing under his pale skin. He was obviously not paying much attention to Zalasta's words, but sat instead totally engrossed in the rhythmic flexing and relaxing of the muscles in his arms. He was in all respects a perfect soldier, possessed of a superbly conditioned body and a mind unviolated by thought.

Ehlana wearily let her eyes drift again around the room. The furniture was strange. There were no chairs as such, only benches and padded stools with ornate arms but no backs. Evidently the notion of a chair-back had not occurred to the Cyrgai. The table in the center of the room was awkwardly low, and the lamps were of an ancient design, no more than hammered copper bowls of oil with burning wicks floating in them. The roughly sawed boards of the floor were covered with rushes, the walls of square-cut black basalt were unadorned, and the windows were undraped.

The door opened and Ekatas entered. Ehlana struggled to bring her exhausted mind into focus. Santheocles was king here in Cyrga, but it was Ekatas who ruled. The High Priest of Cyrgon was robed and cowled in black, and his aged face was a network of deep wrinkles. Although his expression was every bit as cruel and arrogant as that of his king, *his* eyes were shrewd and ruthless. The front of his black robe was adorned with the symbol that seemed to be everywhere here in the Hidden City, a white square surmounted by a stylized golden flame. There was some significance to it, certainly, but Ehlana was too tired to even wonder what it might be. "Come with me," he commanded abruptly. "Bring the women."

"The servant girl is of no moment," Zalasta replied in a slightly challenging tone. "Let her sleep."

"I am not accustomed to having my commands questioned, Styric."

"*Get* accustomed, Cyrg. The women are *my* prisoners. My arrangement is with Cyrgon, and you're no more than an appendage to that arrangement. Your arrogance is beginning to annoy me. Leave the girl alone."

Their eyes locked, and a sudden tension filled the room. "Well, Ekatas?" Zalasta said very quietly, "has the time come? Have you finally worked up enough courage to challenge me? Any time, Ekatas. Any time at all."

Ehlana, now fully alert, saw the flicker of fear in the eyes of Cyrgon's priest. "Bring the queen, then," he said sullenly. "It is *she* whom Cyrgon would behold."

"Wise decision, Ekatas," Zalasta said sardonically. "If you keep making the right choices, you might even live for a little while longer."

Ehlana took her cloak and gently covered Alean with it. Then she turned to face the three men. "Let's get on with this," she told them, mustering some remnant of her royal manner.

Santheocles rose woodenly to his feet and put on his high-crested helmet, taking great paints to avoid mussing his carefully arranged hair. He spent several moments buckling on his large round shield, and then he drew his sword.

"What an ass," Ehlana noted scornfully. "Are you really sure you should trust his Majesty with anything sharp? He might hurt himself with it, you know."

"It is customary, woman," Ekatas replied stiffly. "Prisoners are always kept under close guard."

"Ah," she murmured, "and we *must* obey the dictates of custom, mustn't we, Ekatas? When custom rules, thought is unnecessary."

Zalasta smiled faintly. "I believe you wanted to take us to the temple, Ekatas. Let's not keep Cyrgon waiting."

Ekatas choked back a retort, jerked the door open, and led them out into the chilly hallway.

The stairs that descended from the topmost tower of the royal palace were narrow and steep, endless stairs winding down and down. Ehlana was trembling by the time they reached the courtyard below.

The winter sun was very bright in that broad courtyard, but there was not much heat to it.

They crossed the flagstoned courtyard to the pale temple, a building constructed not of marble but of chalky limestone. Unlike marble, the limestone had a dull, unreflective surface, and the temple looked somehow diseased, leprous.

They mounted the stairs to the portico and entered through a wide doorway. Ehlana had expected it to be dark inside this Holy of Holies, but it was not. She stared with a certain apprehensive astonishment at the source of the light even as Ekatas and Santheocles prostrated themselves, crying in unison, "*Vanet, tyek Alcor! Yala Cyrgon!*"

And then it was that the queen understood the significance of that ubiquitous emblem that marked virtually everything here in the Hidden City. The white square represented the blocky altar set in the precise center of the temple, but the flame that burned atop that altar was no stylized representation. It was instead an actual fire that twisted and flared, reaching hungrily upward.

Ehlana was suddenly afraid. The fire burning on the altar was not some votive offering, but a living flame, conscious, aware, and possessed of an unquenchable will. Bright as the sun, Cyrgon himself burned eternal on his pale altar.

"No," Sparhawk decided, "we'd better not. Let's just sit tight—at least until Xanetia has the chance to winnow through a few minds. We can always come back and deal with Scarpa and his friends later. Right now we need to know where Zalasta's taking Ehlana and Alean."

"We already know," Kalten said. "They're going to Cyrga."

"That's the whole point," the now-visible Ulath told him. "We don't know where Cyrga is."

They had gone back into the vine-choked ruins and had gathered on the second floor of a semi-intact palace to consider options.

"Aphrael has a general idea," Kalten said. "Can't we just start out for central Cynesga and do some poking around when we get there?"

"I don't think that'd do much good," Bevier pointed out. "Cyrgon's been concealing the place with illusions for the past ten eons. We could probably walk right through the streets of the city and not even see it."

"He's not hiding it from *everybody*," Caalador mused. "There *are* messages going back and forth, so *somebody* here in Natayos has to know the way. Sparhawk's right. Why don't we let Xanetia do the poking around *here*, instead of the lot of us going off into the desert to dodge scorpions and snakes while we turn over pebbles and grains of sand?"

"We stay here, then?" Tynian asked.

"For the time being," Sparhawk replied. "Let's not do anything to attract attention until we find out what Xanetia can discover. That's our best option at the moment."

"We were so *close*!" Kalten fumed. "If we'd just gotten here a day or two earlier."

"Well, we didn't," Sparhawk said flatly, forcing back his own disappointment and frustration, "so let's salvage what we can."

"With Zalasta getting farther and father away with every minute," Kalten added bitterly.

"Don't worry, Kalten," Sparhawk told him in a tone as cold as death. "Zalasta can't run far enough or fast enough to get away from me when I decide to go after him."

"Are you busy, Sarabian?" Empress Elysoun asked tentatively from the doorway of the blue-draped room.

"Not really, Elysoun," he sighed, "just brooding. I've had a great deal of bad news in the last day or so."

"I'll come back some other time. You're not much fun when you've got things on your mind."

"Is that all there is in the world, Elysoun?" he asked her sadly. "Only fun?"

Her sunny expression tightened slightly, and she stepped into the room. "That's what you married us for in the first place, wasn't it, Sarabian?" She spoke in crisp Tamul that was not at all like her usual relaxed Valesian dialect. "Our marriages to you were to cement political alliances, so we're here as symbols, playthings, and ornaments. We're certainly not a part of the government."

He was rather startled by her perception and by the sudden change in her. It was easy to underestimate Elysoun. Her single-minded pursuit of pleasure and the aggressively revealing nature of her native dress proclaimed her to be an empty-headed sensualist, but this was a completely different Elysoun. He looked at her with new interest. "What have you been up to lately, my love?" he asked her fondly.

"The usual." She shrugged.

He averted his eyes. "Please don't do that."

"Do what?"

"Bounce that way. It's very distracting."

"It's supposed to be. You didn't think I dress this way because I'm too lazy to put on clothes, did you?"

"Is that why you came by, for fun? Or was there something more tedious?" They had never talked this way before, and her sudden frankness intrigued him.

"Let's talk about the tedious things first," she said. She looked at him critically. "You need to get more sleep," she chided.

"I wish I could. I've got too much on my mind."

"I'll have to see what I can do about that." She paused. "There's something going on in the women's palace, Sarabian."

"Oh?"

"A lot of strangers have been mingling with the assorted lap dogs and toadies that litter the halls."

He laughed. "That's a blunt way to describe courtiers."

"Aren't they? There's not a real man among them. They're in the palace to help us with our schemes. You *did* know that we spend our days plotting against each other, didn't you?"

He shrugged. "It gives you all something to do in your spare time."

"That's the only kind of time we have, my husband. *All* of our time is spare time, Sarabian, that's what's wrong with us. Anyway, these strangers aren't attached to any of the established courts."

"Are you sure?"

Her answering smile was wicked. "Trust me. I've had dealings with all the regular ones. They're all little more than butterflies. These strangers are wasps."

He gave her an amused look. "Have you actually winnowed your way through *all* the courtiers in the women's palace?"

"More or less." She shrugged again—quite deliberately, he thought. "Actually it was rather boring. Courtiers are a tepid lot, but it was a way to keep track of what was going on."

"Then it wasn't entirely—?"

"A little, perhaps, but I have to take steps to protect myself. Our politics are subtle, but they're savage."

"Are these strangers Tamuls?"

"Some are. Some aren't."

"How long has this been going on?"

"Since we all moved back to the women's palace. I didn't see any of these wasps when we were all living here with the Elenes."

"Just the past few weeks, then?"

She nodded. "I thought you should know. It could be just more of the same kind of thing that's been going on for years, but I don't really think so. It *feels* different somehow. Our politics are more indirect than yours, and what's happening in the women's palace is men's politics."

"Do you suppose you could keep an eye on it for me? I'd be grateful."

"Of course, my husband. I *am* loyal, after all."

"Oh, really?"

"Don't make that mistake, Sarabian. Loyalty shouldn't be confused with that other business. That doesn't mean anything. Loyalty does."

"There's a lot more to you than meets the eye, Elysoun."

"Oh? I've never tried to conceal anything." She inhaled deeply.

He laughed again. "Do you have plans for this evening?"

"Nothing that can't be put off until some other time. What did you have in mind?"

"I thought we might talk awhile."

"Talk?"

"Among other things."

"Let me send a message first. Then we can talk for as long as you like—among those other things you mentioned."

They were two days out of Tiana on their way around the west end of the lake on the road to Arjuna. They had camped on the lakeshore some distance from the road, and Khalad had shot a deer with his crossbow. "Camp meat," he explained to Berit as he skinned the animal. "It saves time and money."

"You're really very good with that crossbow," Berit said.

Khalad shrugged. "Practice," he replied. Then his head came up sharply. "Company coming." He pointed toward the road with his knife.

"Arjuni," Berit noted, squinting at the approaching riders.

"Not all of them," Khalad disagreed. "The one in front's an Elene—an Edomishman, judging from his clothes." Khalad wiped his bloody hands on the long grass, picked up his crossbow, and recocked it. "Just to be on the safe side," he explained. "They *do* know who we really are, after all."

Berit nodded bleakly and loosened his sword in its scabbard.

The riders reined in about fifty yards away. "Sir Sparhawk?" the Edomishman called out in Elenic.

"Maybe," Berit called back. "What can I do for you, neighbor?"

"I have a message for you."

"I'm touched. Bring it on in."

"Come alone," Khalad added. "You won't need your bodyguards."

"I've heard about what you did to the last messenger."

"Good," Khalad replied. "We sort of intended for word of that to get around. The fellow had a little trouble being civil, but I'm sure you have better manners. Come ahead. You're safe—as long as you're polite."

The Edomishman still hesitated.

"Friend," Khalad said pointedly, "you're well within range of my crossbow, so you'd better do as I tell you. Just come on in alone. We'll conduct our business, and then you and your Arjuni friends can be on your way. Otherwise, this might turn unpleasant."

The Edomishman conferred briefly with his bodyguards and then rode cautiously forward, holding a folded parchment above his head. "I'm not armed," he announced.

"That's not very prudent, neighbor," Berit told him. "These are troubled times. Let's have the note."

The messenger lowered his arm slowly and extended the parchment. "The plans have changed, Sir Sparhawk," he said politely.

"Astonishing." Berit opened the parchment and gently took out the lock of identifying hair. "This is only about the third time. You fellows seem to be having some difficulty making up your minds." He looked at the parchment. "That's accommodating. Somebody even drew a map this time."

"The village isn't really very well known," the Edomishman explained. "It's a tiny place that wouldn't even be there if it weren't for the slave trade."

"You're a very good messenger, friend," Khalad told him. "Would you like to carry a word back to Krager for me?"

"I'll try, young Master."

"Good. Tell him that I'm coming after him. He should probably start looking back over his shoulder, because no matter how this turns out, one day I'll be there."

The Edomishman swallowed hard. "I'll tell him, young Master."

"I'd appreciate it."

The messenger carefully backed his horse off a few yards and then rode back to rejoin his Arjuni escort.

"Well?" Khalad asked.

"Vigayo—over in Cynesga."

"It's not much of a town."

"You've been there?"

"Briefly. Bhelliom took us there by mistake when Sparhawk was practicing with it."

"How far is it from here?"

"About a hundred leagues. It's in the right direction, though. Aphrael said that Zalasta's taking the queen to Cyrga, so Vigayo's got to be closer than Arjun. Pass the word, Berit. Tell Aphrael that we'll start out first thing in the morning. Then you can come and help me cut up this deer. It's ten days to Vigayo, so we're probably going to need the meat."

"He hath been there," Xanetia told them. "His memories of the Hidden City are vivid, but his recollection of the route is imprecise. I could glean no more than disconnected impressions of the journey. His madness hath bereft his thought of coherence, and his mind doth flit from reality to illusion and back without purpose or direction."

"I'd say we got us a problem," Caalador drawled. "Ol' Krager, he don't know th' way on accounta he wuz too drunk t' pay attention when Zalasta wuz a-talkin' 'bout how t' git t' Cyrga, an' Scorpa's too crazy t' remember how he got thar." His eyes narrowed, and he discarded the dialect. "What about Cyzada?" he asked Xanetia.

She shuddered. "It is not madness nor drunkenness which doth bar my way into the thought of Cyzada of Esos," she replied in a voice filled with revulsion. "Deeply hath he reached into the darkness that was Azash, and the creatures of the netherworld have possessed him so utterly that his thought is no longer human. His spells at first did in some measure control those horrid demons, but then he did summon Klæl, and in that act was all unloosed. Prithee, do not send me again into that seething chaos. He doth indeed know a route to Cyrga, but we could in no wise follow *that* path, for it doth lie through the realm of flame and darkness and unspeakable horror."

"That more or less exhausts the possibilities of this place, then, doesn't it?" They all turned quickly at the sound of the familiar voice. The Child-Goddess sat demurely on a windowledge holding her pipes in her hands.

"Is this wise, Divine One?" Bevier asked her. "Won't our enemies sense your presence?"

"There's no one left here who can do that, Bevier," she replied. "Zalasta's gone. I just stopped by to tell you that Berit's received new instructions. He and Khalad are going to Vigayo, a village just on the other side of the Cynesgan border. As soon as you're ready, I'll take you there."

"What good will that do?" Kalten asked.

"I need to get Xanetia close to the next messenger," she replied. "Cyrga's completely concealed—even from me. There's a key to that illusion and *that's* what we have to find. Without that key, we could all grow old wandering around out in that wasteland and still not find the city."

"I suppose you're right," Sparhawk conceded. He looked directly at her. "Can you arrange another meeting? We're getting close to the end of this, and I need to talk with the others—Vanion and Bergsten in particular, and probably with Betuana and Kring as well. We've got armies at our disposal, but they won't be much use if they're running off in three different directions or attacking Cyrga piecemeal. We've got a general idea of where the place is, and I'd like to put a ring of steel around it, but I *don't* want anybody to go blundering in there until we get Ehlana and Alean safely out."

"You're going to get me in trouble, Sparhawk," she said tartly. "Do you have any idea of the kinds of promises I'll have to make to get permission for that kind of gathering? And I'll have to *keep* all those promises, too."

"It's really very important, Aphrael."

She stuck her tongue out at him, and then she wavered and vanished.

"Domi Tikume sent orders, your Reverence," the shaved-headed Peloi advised Patriarch Bergsten when they met in the churchman's tent just outside the town of Pela in central Astel. "We're to provide whatever assistance we can."

"Your Domi's a good man, friend Daiya," the armored Patriarch replied.

"His orders stirred up a hornet's nest," Daiya said wryly. "The idea of an alliance with the Church Knights set off a theological debate that went on for days. Most people here in Astel believe that the Church Knights were born and raised in Hell. A fair number of the debaters are currently taking the matter up with God in person."

"I gather that religious disputes among the Peloi are quite spirited."

"Oh, yes," Daiya agreed. "The message from Archimandrite Monsel helped to quiet things, though. Peloi religious thought isn't really all that profound, your Reverence. We trust God and leave the theology to the churchmen. If the Archimandrite approves, that's good enough for us. If he's wrong, *he's* the one who'll burn in Hell for it."

"How far is it from here to Cynestra?" Bergsten asked him.

"About a hundred and seventy-five leagues, your Reverence."

"Three weeks," Bergsten muttered sourly. "Well, there's not much we can do about that, I suppose. We'll start out first thing in the morning. Tell your men to get some sleep, friend Daiya. It's probably going to be in short supply for the next month or so."

"Bergsten." The voice crooning his name was light and musical.

The Thalesian Patriarch sat up quickly, reaching for his ax.

"Oh, don't do that, Bergsten. I'm not going to hurt you."

"Who's there?" he demanded, fumbling for his candle and his flint and steel.

"Here." A small hand emerged from the darkness with a tongue of flame dancing on its palm.

Bergsten blinked. His midnight visitor was a little girl—Styric, he guessed. She was a beautiful child with long hair and large eyes as dark as night. Bergsten's hands started to tremble. "You're Aphrael, aren't you?" he choked.

"Keen observation, your Grace. Sparhawk wants to see you."

He drew back from this personage that standard Church doctrine told him did not—could not—exist.

"You're being silly, your Grace," she told him. "You know that I couldn't even be talking to you if I didn't have permission from your God, don't you? I can't even come near you without permission."

"Well, theoretically," he reluctantly conceded. "You *could* be a demon, though, and the rules don't apply to them."

"Do I *look* like a demon?"

"Appearance and reality are two different things," he insisted.

She looked into his eyes and pronounced the true name of the Elene God, one of the most closely kept secrets of the Church. "A demon couldn't say that name, could it, your Grace?"

"Well, I suppose not."

"We'll get along well, Bergsten." She smiled, kissing him lightly on the cheek. "Ortzel would have argued that point for weeks. Leave your ax here, please. Steel makes my flesh crawl."

"Where are we going?"

"To meet with Sparhawk. I already told you that."

"Is it far?"

"Not really." She smiled, opening the tent flap.

It was still night in Pela, but it was broad daylight beyond the tent flap—a strange sort of daylight. A pristine white beach stretched down to a sapphire sea all under a rainbow-colored sky, and a small green eyot surmounted by a gleaming alabaster temple rose from that incredibly blue sea about a half mile from the beach.

"What place is this?" Bergsten asked, poking his head out of the tent and looking around in amazement.

"I suppose you could call it Heaven, your Grace," the Child-Goddess replied, blowing out the flame dancing on her palm. "It's mine, anyway. There are others, but this one's mine."

"Where is it?"

"Everywhere and anywhere. All the Heavens are everyplace all at once. So are all the Hells, of course—but that's another story. Shall we go?"

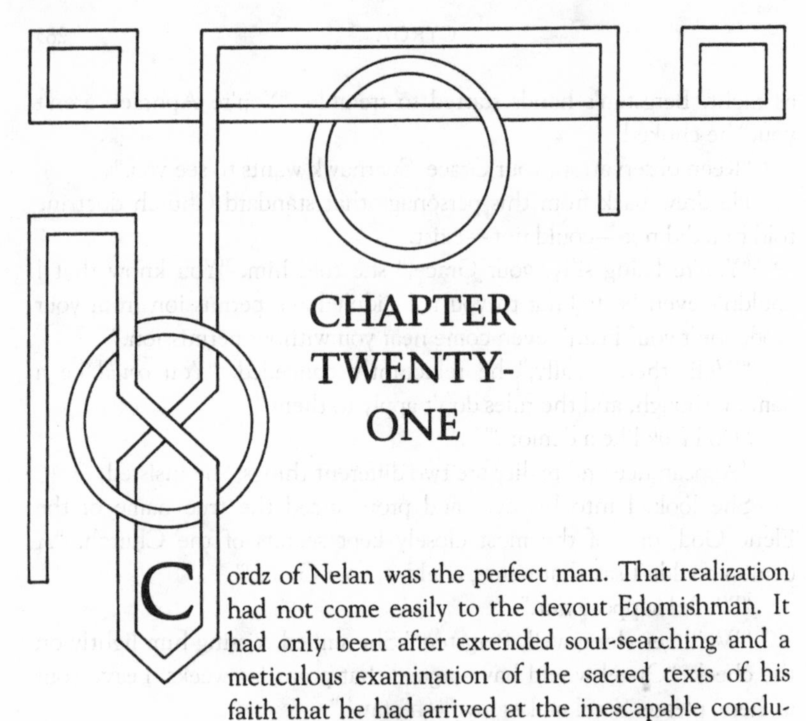

CHAPTER TWENTY-ONE

Cordz of Nelan was the perfect man. That realization had not come easily to the devout Edomishman. It had only been after extended soul-searching and a meticulous examination of the sacred texts of his faith that he had arrived at the inescapable conclusion. He was perfect. He obeyed all of God's commandments, he did what he was supposed to do, and he did not do the things that were forbidden. Isn't that what perfection is all about?

It was a comfort to be perfect, but Cordz was not one to rest on his laurels. Now that *he* had achieved perfection in the eyes of God, it was time to turn his attention to the faults of his neighbors. Sinners, however, seldom sin openly, so Cordz was obliged to resort to subterfuge. He peeked through windows late at night; he eavesdropped on private conversations; and, when his sinful neighbors cleverly concealed their wrongdoing from him, he imagined the sins they *might* be committing. The Sabbath was a very special day for Cordz, but not for the sermons. After all, what need had a perfect man for sermons? It was on the Sabbath that he was able to rise to his feet and denounce the sins of his neighbors, both the sins they *had* committed and the sins they *might* be committing.

He probably irritated the Devil. God knows he irritated his neighbors.

But then a crisis had arisen in Edom. The debauched and heretical Church of Chyrellos, after two eons of plotting and scheming, was finally preparing to make her move against the righteous. The Church Knights were on the march, and horrors beyond imagining marched with them.

Cordz was among the first to enlist in Rebal's army; the perfect man abandoned his neighbors to their sinful ways to join a holier cause. He became Rebal's most trusted messenger, killing horses by the dozen as he rushed about the Elene kingdoms of western Tamuli carrying the dispatches so vital to the cause.

On this particular day Cordz was flogging his exhausted horse southward toward the corrupt cities of southern Daconia, cesspools of sin and licentiousness, if the truth were to be known, where the citizens not only did not *know* that they were sinners, they did not even *care*. Worse yet, an obscure and probably heretical tradition of the Dacite Church prevented laymen from speaking aloud during Sabbath services. Thus, God's very own spokesman, the perfect man, was not permitted to expose and denounce the sins he saw all around him. The frustration of it sometimes made him want to scream.

He had been riding hard for the past week and he was very tired. Thus it was with some relief that he finally crested the hill that overlooked the port city of Melek.

Then all thoughts of the sins of others vanished. Cordz reined in his staggering horse and gaped in horror at what he saw.

There on a sea sparkling in the winter sun was a vast armada, ships beyond counting, sailing majestically down the coast under the red and gold banners of the Church of Chyrellos!

The perfect man was so overcome with horror that he did not even hear the plaintive sound of a shepherd's rude pipe playing a Styric air in a minor key somewhere off to his left. He gaped for a time at his worst nightmare, and then he desperately drove his spurs into his horses's flanks, rushing to spread the alarm.

General Sirada was the younger brother of Duke Milanis, and he commanded the rebel forces in Panem-Dea. King Rakya had so arranged it that most of Scarpa's generals were Arjuni. Sirada knew that there were risks involved, but the younger sons of noble families were obliged to take risks if they wanted to get ahead in the world. For them, rank and position had to be won. Sirada had endured the years of association with the crazy bastard son of a tavern wench and the discomfort of camping out in the jungle waiting for his chance.

And now it had come. The madman in Natayos had finally sent the order to march. The campaign had begun. There was no sleep in Panem-Dea that night. The preparations for the march went on through the hours of darkness, and the undisciplined rabble Sirada commanded was incapable of doing *anything* quietly. The general spent the night poring over his maps.

The strategy was sound; he was forced to admit that. He was to join forces with Scarpa and the other rebels near Derel. Then they would march north to the Tamul Mountains to be reinforced by Cynesgans. From there, they would march on Tosa in preparation for the final assault on Matherion.

General Sirada's own strategy was much simpler. Scarpa would crush any resistance at Tosa, but he would not live to see the gleaming domes of the imperial capital. Sirada smiled thinly and patted the little vial of poison he carried in his inside pocket. The army would capture Matherion, but it would be General Sirada who would lead the final assault and personally run his sword through Emperor Sarabian. The younger brother of Duke Milanis expected an earldom at the very least to come out of this campaign.

The door banged open, and his adjutant burst into the room, his eyes starting from his head and his face a pasty white. "Good God, my General!" he shrieked.

"What do you think you're doing?" Sirada demanded. "How *dare* you? I'll have you flogged for this!"

"We're being attacked, my General!"

Sirada could hear the squeals of terror now. He rose quickly and went out the door.

It was not yet daylight, and a clinging mist had crept out of the tangled forest to blur the ruined walls and houses of Panem-Dea. There were fires and flaring torches pushing back the darkness with their ruddy light, but there were other lights in the weed-choked streets as well: pale, cold lights that did not burn or flicker. Creatures of light, pale as wandering moons, stalked the streets of Panem-Dea. The general's heart filled with terror. It was impossible! The Shining Ones were a myth! There were no such creatures!

Sirada shook off his fright and drew his sword. "Stand fast!" he roared at his demoralized men. "Form up! Pikemen to the front!" He bulled his way into the milling mob of terrified troops, flailing about him with the flat of his sword. "Form up! Make a line!"

But there was no rationality nor fear of authority in the panic-stricken faces of his poorly trained men. The screaming mob simply diverged and bypassed him on either side. He ran at them again, swinging great strokes with his sword, cutting down his own men.

He was so desperate to restore order that he did not even feel the knife-stroke that went in just below his ribs on the left side. He could not even understand why his knees buckled or why he fell under the trampling feet of his soldiers as they fled screaming into the trackless forest.

"Are you sure this map's accurate, Tynian?" Patriarch Bergsten demanded, peering at the miniature world under his feet.

"It's the most accurate map you'll ever see, your Grace," Tynian assured him. "Bhlokw cast the spell, and the Troll-Gods put their hands into the ground and felt the shape of the continent. This is it—down to the last tree and bush. Everything's here."

"Except for Cyrga, Tynian-Knight," Engessa amended. The Atan general was completely healed now, and he looked as fit as ever. His face, however, was troubled. His queen had greeted him almost abruptly when she had first arrived, and she was quite obviously avoiding him.

Sephrenia was seated on one of the benches in Aphrael's alabaster temple with the rainbow light from the impossible sky playing over her face. "We'd hoped that Schlee might be able to feel Cyrga when he recreated the continent, your Grace," she said, "but Cyrgon's illusion seems to be absolute. Not even a Trollish spell can break it."

"What's the best guess we can come up with?" Bergsten asked.

Aphrael walked lightly across the tiny world Bhlokw had conjured up for them. She stepped over the minuscule city of Cynestra and continued south to a mountainous region in the center of the desert. "It used to be somewhere in this general vicinity," she said, gesturing vaguely over the mountains.

"Used to be?" Bergsten asked her sharply.

She shrugged. "Sometimes we move things."

"Whole cities?"

"It's possible—but it's a reflection of bad planning."

Bergsten shuddered and began marking off distances on the miniature continent with a long piece of string. "I'm up here at Pela," he told them, pointing at a spot in central Astel. "That's almost three hundred leagues from the general vicinity of Cyrga, and I'll have to stop to capture Cynestra along the way. The rest of you are much closer, so you're going to have to hold off a bit if we all want to get there at approximately the same time."

Aphrael shrugged. "I'll tamper," she said.

Bergsten gave her a puzzled look.

"Divine Aphrael has ways of compressing time and distance, your Grace," Sparhawk explained. "She can—"

"I don't want to hear about it, Sparhawk!" Bergsten said sharply, putting his hands over his ears. "You've already put my soul in danger just by bringing me here. Please don't make it any worse by telling me things I don't need to know about."

"Whatever you say, your Grace," Sparhawk agreed.

Emban was pacing around the cluster of upthrusting mountains in the center of the Cynesgan desert. "We're all going to be converging on these mountains," he said. "I'm no expert, but wouldn't our best move be just to stop in the foothills and wait until everyone's in place before we make the final assault?"

"No, your Grace," Vanion said firmly. "Let's stay out a bit from the foothills—at least a day's ride. If we run into Klæl's creatures, we'll need room to maneuver. I want a lot of flat ground around me when that happens."

The fat little churchman shrugged. "You're the soldier, Vanion." He pointed toward the south. "There's our weakness," he said. "We've got a good concentration of forces coming out of the east, the north-east, and the north, but we don't have anybody covering the south."

"Or the west," Sarabian added.

"I'll cover the west, your Majesty," Bergsten told him. "I can position my knights and the Peloi to block off that entire quadrant."

"That still leaves the south," Emban mused.

"It's already been taken care of, Emban," Aphrael assured him. "Stragen's been spinning stories about a vast Church fleet off the southern coast, and I've been weaving illusions to back him up. How long is it going to take the Trolls to get into position north of Zhubay, Ulath?"

"Just as long as it takes to persuade the Troll-Gods that we need their children there instead of in the Tamul Mountains," the big Thalesian replied, "—a day or so probably. Once they're convinced, they'll put their children into No-Time. If we didn't have to stop now and then to feed the Trolls, we could be in Zhubay before you could even blink. If I knew where Cyrga was, I could have fifteen hundred Trolls on the doorstep by morning."

"There's no need to rush." The Child-Goddess looked around with steely eyes. "Nobody—and I mean *nobody*—is going to move on Cyrga until I know that Ehlana and Alean are safe. If I have to, I can keep you running around in circles out there in that desert for generations, so don't try to get creative on me."

"Is the Queen of Elenia so very important to you, Divine One?" Betuana asked mildly. "War is hard, and we must accept our losses."

"It's a personal matter, Betuana," Aphrael said shortly. "These are your positions." She gestured over the miniature continent. "Bergsten will come in from the north and west to cover that side of the city; Ulath, Tynian, and Bhlokw will bring the Trolls down from Zhubay and join with Betuana's Atans on their left flank; Vanion will come in from the east and be joined on *his* left by Kring and the Peloi; Stragen's persuaded that disgusting Dacite in Beresa that there are a million or so Church Knights landing on the coast around Verel and Kaftal, and that should divert most of the armies of Cynesga. We'll all converge on Cyrga. There are some discrepancies in the distances, but I'll take care of those. When the time comes, you *will* all be in place—even if I have to pick you up one by one and carry you." She stopped abruptly. "What *is* your problem, Bergsten? Don't laugh at me, or I'll take you by the nose and shake you."

"I wasn't laughing, Divine One," he assured her. "I was only smiling in approval. Where *did* you learn so much about strategy and tactics?"

"I've been watching you Elenes make war since shortly after you discovered fire, your Grace. I was bound to learn a *few* of the tricks of the trade." She turned suddenly on Bhlokw. "What?" she asked irritably in Trollish.

"U-lat has said to me what you have said, Child-Goddess. Why are we doing this?"

"To punish the wicked ones, Priest of the Troll-Gods."

"*What?*" Sparhawk said to Ulath in stunned amazement. "What did she call him?"

"Oh?" Ulath said mildly. "Didn't you know? Our shaggy friend has a certain eminence."

"They actually have priests?"

"Of course. Doesn't everybody?"

"It is good to punish the wicked ones who have taken Anakha's mate away," Bhlokw was saying, "but do we need to take so many? Khwaj will punish the wicked ones. This is the season of Schlee, and we should be following the way of the hunt. The young must be fed or they will die, and that is not a good thing."

"Oh, dear," Aphrael murmured.

"What's happening here, Sir Ulath?" Sarabian asked.

"The Trolls are hunters, your Majesty," Ulath explained, "not warriors. They have no real understanding of warfare. They eat what they kill."

Sarabian shuddered.

"It *is* very moral, your Majesty," Ulath pointed out. "From a Troll's point of view, wasting the meat is criminal."

Aphrael was squinting at the priest of the Troll-Gods. "It is a good thing to do that which follows the way of the hunt *and* punishes the wicked ones at the same time," she said. "If we hunt this way, we will cause hurt to the wicked ones *and* bring much meat to the young during the season of Schlee."

Bhlokw considered that. "The hunts of the man-things are not-simple," he said dubiously, "but it is my thought that the hunts of the God-things are even *more* not-simple." He reflected on it. "It is good, though. A hunt that gathers more than meat is a good hunt. You hunt very well, Child-Goddess. Sometime we might take eat together and talk of old hunts. It is good to do this. It makes pack-mates closer so that they hunt together better."

"It would make me glad if we did this, Bhlokw."

"Then we will do it. I will kill a dog for us to eat. Dog is even more good-to-eat than pig."

Aphrael made a slight gagging sound.

"Will it cause anger to you if I speak to our pack-mates in bird-noises, Bhlokw?" Sparhawk stepped in. "It will soon be time for the hunt to begin, and all must be made ready."

"It will not cause anger to me, Anakha. U-lat can say to me what you are saying."

"All right, then," Sparhawk said to the rest of them. "We all know how we're going to converge on Cyrga, but there are several of us who have to go in first. Please hold off on your attack until we're in position. Don't crowd us by trampling on our heels."

"Who are you taking in with you, Sparhawk?" Vanion asked.

"Kalten, Bevier, Talen, Xanetia, and Mirtai."

"I don't quite—"

Sparhawk held up one hand. "Aphrael made the choices, my Lord," he said. "If there are any objections, take them up with her."

"You have to have those people with you, Sparhawk," Aphrael explained patiently. "If you don't, you'll fail."

"Whatever you say, Divine One," he surrendered.

"You'll be out in front of Berit and me then?" Khalad asked.

Sparhawk nodded. "The people on the other side will expect us to trail along behind you. If we're in front, it might confuse them—at least that's what we're hoping. Aphrael will take us directly to Vigayo and we'll nose around a bit. If the fellow with the next message is already there, Xanetia should be able to pick up your next destination. Sooner or later, somebody's going to have to give you the key to the illusion that's hiding Cyrga, and *that's* the one piece of information we have to have. Once we've got that, the rest is easy."

"I like his definition of easy," Caalador murmured to Stragen.

Emban jotted another note on his inevitable list. Then he cleared his throat.

"*Must* you, Emban?" Bergsten sighed.

"It helps me to think, Bergsten, and it makes sure that we haven't left anything out. If it bores you so much, don't listen."

"The man-things talk much when they decide how they will hunt, U-lat," Bhlokw complained.

"It is the nature of the man-things to do this."

"It is because the hunts of the man-things are too much not-simple. It is my thought that their hunts are not-simple because they do not eat the ones they kill. They hunt and kill for reasons which I do not understand. It is my thought that this thing the man-things call 'war' is a very great wickedness."

"It is not in our thought to cause anger to the priest of the Troll-Gods," Patriarch Bergsten said in flawless Trollish. "The thing which the man-things call 'war' is like the thing which happens when two Troll-packs come to hunt on the same range."

Bhlokw considered that. Then he grunted as comprehension came over his shaggy face. "Now it is clear to me," he said. "This thing the man-things call 'war' is like the hunting of thought. That is why it is not-simple. But you still talk much." The Troll squinted at Emban. "That one is the worst," he added. "His mind-belly is as big as his belly-belly."

"What did he say?" Emban asked curiously.

"It wouldn't translate very well, your Grace," Ulath replied blandly.

Patriarch Emban gave him a slightly suspicious look and then meticulously laid out their deployment once again, checking items off his list as he went. When he had finished, he looked around. "Can anybody think of anything else?"

"Perhaps," Sephrenia said, frowning slightly. "Our enemies know that Berit's not really Sparhawk, but they're going to think that Sparhawk won't have any choice but to follow along behind. It might help to confirm that belief. I think I know a way to duplicate the sound and sense of Bhelliom. If it works, our enemies will think that Sparhawk's somewhere in the column of knights Vanion's going to lead out into the desert. They'll concentrate on us rather than looking for him."

"You're putting yourself in danger, Sephrenia," Aphrael objected.

"There's nothing particularly new about that." Sephrenia smiled. "And when you consider what we're trying to do, no place is really safe."

"Is that it, then?" Engessa asked, standing up.

"Probably, friend Engessa," Kring replied, "except for the hour or so we'll all spend telling each other to be careful."

Engessa squared his shoulders, turned, and faced his queen directly. "What are your orders, Betuana-Queen," he asked her with military formality.

She drew herself up with a regal stiffness. "It is our instruction that you return with us to Sarna, Engessa-Atan. There you will resume command of our armies."

"It shall be as you say, Betuana-Queen."

"Directly upon our return, you will send runners to my husband, the king. Tell him that there is no longer a threat to Tosa. The Shining Ones will deal with Scarpa."

He nodded stiffly.

"Further, tell him that I have need of his forces in Sarna. That is where we will prepare for the main battle, and he should be there to take command." She paused. "This is not because we are dissatisfied with *your* leadership, Engessa-Atan, but Androl *is* the king. You have served well. The royal house of Atan is grateful."

"It is my duty, Betuana-Queen," he replied, clashing his fist against his breastplate in salute. "No gratitude is necessary."

"Oh, dear," Aphrael murmured.

"What's wrong?" Sephrenia asked her.

"Nothing."

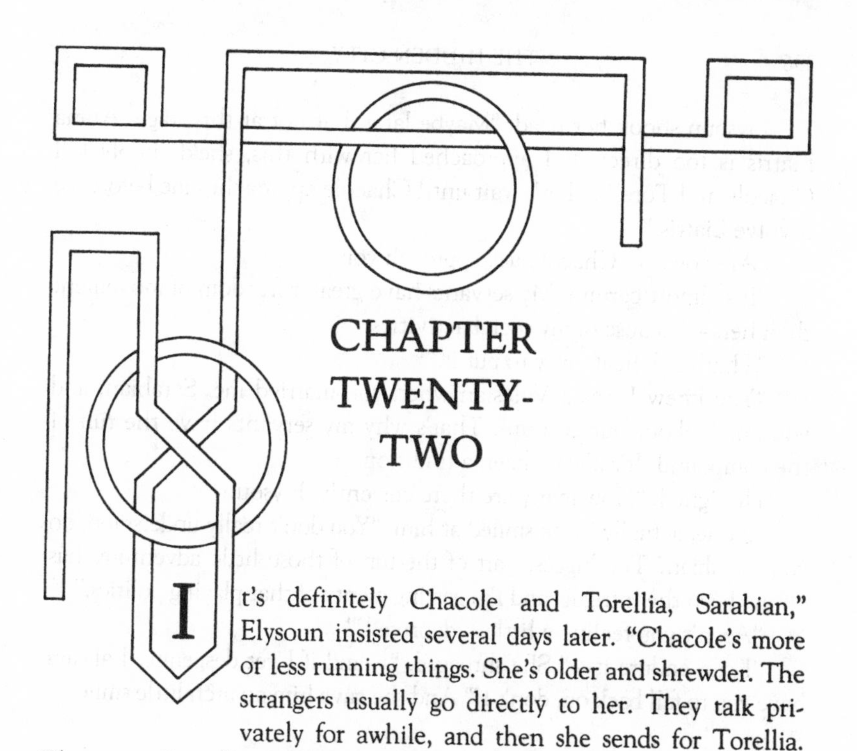

CHAPTER TWENTY-TWO

It's definitely Chacole and Torellia, Sarabian," Elysoun insisted several days later. "Chacole's more or less running things. She's older and shrewder. The strangers usually go directly to her. They talk privately for awhile, and then she sends for Torellia. They weren't really all that fond of each other before, but now they've got their heads together all the time."

"They're probably getting orders from home," Sarabian mused. "King Jaluah of Cynesga is Chacole's brother, and Torellia's the daughter of King Rakya of Arjuna. Can you get any sense at all of what they might be up to?"

She shook her head. "It's too early."

"Early?"

"Women's politics again. We're more devious than men. Chacole will want everything in place before she starts to form other alliances. She's got Torellia under control, but she's not quite ready to start trying to expand yet."

"You're sure that Torellia's the subordinate one?"

She nodded. "Chacole's servants are lording it over hers. That's the first sign of dominance in the women's palace. Cieronna's servants are all insufferable because she's the first wife, and we're all subordinate to her—except for Liatris, of course."

"Of course." Sarabian smiled. "No one in his right mind is impertinent to Liatris. Has she killed anybody lately?"

"Not since she butchered Cieronna's footman last year."

"There's a thought. Should we bring Liatris into this?"

Elysoun shook her head. "Maybe later, but not at this stage. Atana Liatris is too direct. If I approached her with this, she'd simply kill Chacole and Torellia. Let's wait until Chacole approaches me before we involve Liatris."

"Are you sure Chacole *will* approach you?"

"It's almost certain. My servants have greater freedom of movement than hers—because of my social activities."

"That's a delicate way to put it."

"You knew I was a Valesian when you married me, Sarabian, and you know about our customs. That's why my servants have the run of the compound. It's always been a tradition."

He sighed. "How many are there currently, Elysoun?"

"None, actually." She smiled at him. "You don't really understand, do you, Sarabian? The biggest part of the fun of those little adventures has always been the intrigue, and I'm getting plenty of that playing politics."

"Aren't you feeling a little—deprived?"

"I can endure it—" She shrugged. "—and if I get desperate, I always have you to fall back on, don't I?" And she gave him an arch little smile.

"Wal, sir, Master Valash," Caalador drawled, leaning back in his chair in the cluttered loft, "Ol' Vymer here, he done tole me that yer a' willin' t' pay good money fer infermation, an' he sorta figgered ez how y' might want t' hear 'bout the stuff I seen in southwest Atan fer yer very ownself."

"You two have known each other for quite some time then?" Valash asked.

"Oh, gorsh yes, Master Valash. Me'n Vymer goes way back. We wuz all t'gether durin' that fracas in Matherion—him an' me an' Fron an' Reldin—along with a couple others—when the fellers from Interior come a-bustin' in on us. They wuz hull *bunches* o' excitement that night, let me tell yew. Anyway, after we shuck off the po-lice, we all split up an' scattered t' th' winds. 'Tain't a *real* good idee t' stay all bunched up whin yer a-runnin' from th' law."

Stragen sat back from the table out of the circle of light from the single candle, carefully watching Valash's face. Caalador had just arrived to replace Sparhawk and Talen in the ongoing deception of Valash, and Stragen was once again impressed by how smooth his friend really was. Valash seemed lulled by the easy, folksy charm of Caalador's dialect. Stragen despised the slovenly speech, but he was forced to admit its utility. It always seemed so genuine, so innocently artless.

"Where *is* Fron, anyway?" Valash asked.

"Him an' Reldin tuk off 'bout a week ago." Caalador shrugged. "I happened t' stop off in a tavern up in Delo whilst I wuz a-comin' on down yere, an' they wuz a feller what had *policeman* wrote all over him who wuz describin' ol' Fron an' the boy right down t' th' warts. Soon's I got yere, I tole 'em 'bout it, an' they figgered that it might just be time t' move on. Anyhow, Vymer here sez as how yer innerested in whut's a-goin' on here an' thar, an' I seen a few things after we all got run outta Matherion that he's a-thankin' might be worth somethin' to ya."

"I'll certainly listen, Ezek." Valash raised his head sharply as the comatose Ogerajin began to mumble in his sleep.

"Is he all right?" Stragen asked.

"It's nothing," Valash said shortly. "He does that all the time. Go ahead, Ezek."

"Wal, sir, she wuz a couple weeks ago, I guess, an' I wuz a-hot-footin' it across Atan, figgerin' t' make m' way on acrost Astel t' Darsos—on accounta the law bein' hot on m' heels an' all. I wuz a-comin' on down outten th' mountings when I pult up short, cuz I seen more gol-dang Atans than I thought they wuz in the hull world—I mean, they wint on fer *miles*! They wuz *multitudes* o' them big rascals—all geared up fer war an a-lookin' real mean an' on-friendly-like."

"The entire Atan army?" Valash exclaimed.

"It lookt t' me more like a gineral my-grashun of the hull dang race, Master Valash. Y' ain't niver *seen* s' miny of 'em!"

"Where exactly were they?" Valash asked excitedly.

"Wal, sir, close ez I could make out, they wuz right close t' the Cynesgan border—up thar close by a little town calt Zhubay. Iff'n y' happen t' have a map handy, I could point out th' egg-zact spot fer ya." Caalador squinted at the Dacite. "Whut would y' say this infermaytion's worth, Master Valash?"

Valash didn't even hesitate when he reached for his purse.

"It was very strange, Domi Tikume," Kring told his friend as they rode at the head of their massed tribesmen out into the Cynesgan desert the morning after the conference on Aphrael's island. "The Child-Goddess said that we were all dreaming, but everything seemed so real. I could actually smell the flowers and the grass. I've never smelled anything in a dream before."

Tikume looked dubious. "Are you *sure* it wasn't heresy to go there, Domi Kring?"

Kring laughed wryly. "Well, if it was, I was in good company. Patriarch Emban was there, and so was Patriarch Bergsten. Anyway, you and I are supposed to continue making these raids into Cynesga. Then we're supposed to go ahead and ride in toward those mountains out in the middle of the desert. We're hoping that Prince Sparhawk will have pinpointed the exact location of Cyrga by the time we get there."

One of the scouts who had been ranging the burnt brown desert ahead came galloping back. "Domi Tikume," he said as he reined in. "We've found them."

"Where?" Tikume demanded.

"There's a dry watercourse about two miles ahead, Domi. They're crouched down in there. I'd say they're planning to ambush us."

"What sort of soldiers are they?" Kring asked.

"There was Cynesgan cavalry and more of those big ones with the steel masks that we've been running to death lately. There was some other infantry as well, but I didn't recognize them."

"Breastplates? Short kirtles? Helmets with high crests, and big round shields?"

"Those are the ones, Domi Kring."

Kring rubbed one hand across his shaved scalp. "How wide is the watercourse?" he asked.

"Fifty paces or so, Domi."

"Crooked? Fairly deep?"

The scout nodded.

"It's an ambush, all right," Kring said. "The cavalry probably intends to let us see them and then retreat into the gully. If we follow them, we'll run right into the infantry. We've been running Klæl's soldiers to death in open country, so they want to get us into tight quarters."

"What do we do?" Tikume asked.

"We stay out of that streambed, friend Tikume. Send out flankers to cut off their cavalry after they ride out. We'll slaughter them, and that should bring Klæl's soldiers out into the open."

"What about the Cyrgai? Are they more of those ones out of the past that we keep coming across?"

"I don't think so. This is inside the borders of Cynesga, so they're probably live ones from Cyrga itself." Kring stopped suddenly, and a slow grin crossed his face. "I just thought of something. Send out your flankers, friend Tikume. Give me some time to think my way through this."

"That's a particularly nasty grin there, friend Kring."

"I'm a particularly nasty fellow sometimes, friend Tikume," Kring replied, his grin growing even wider.

"Slavers," Mirtai said shortly after she had peered down the rocky hill at the column creeping slowly across the barren brown gravel toward the village clustered around the oasis. The almost instantaneous change from the humidity of the Arjuni jungle to the arid Cynesgan desert had given Sparhawk a slight headache.

"How can you tell at this distance?" Bevier asked her.

"Those hooded black robes," she replied peering again over the boulder which concealed them. "Slavers wear them when they come into Cynesga so that the local authorities won't interfere with them. Cynesga's about the only place left where slavery's openly legal. The other kingdoms frown on it."

"There's a thought, Sparhawk," Bevier said. "If we could get our hands on some of those black robes, we'd be able to move around out in the desert without attracting attention."

"We don't look very much like Arjuni, Bevier," Kalten objected.

"We don't have to," Talen told him. "From what I heard back in Beresa, there are bands of raiders out in the desert who ambush the caravans in order to steal the slaves, so the Arjuni slavers hire lots of fighting men of all races to help protect the merchandise."

"Oh," Kalten said. "I wonder where we could lay our hands on black robes."

"I see a hundred or so of them right out there," Bevier said, pointing at the caravan.

"Elenes," Xanetia sighed, rolling her eyes upward.

"You're even starting to *sound* like Sephrenia, Anarae," Sparhawk said with a faint smile. "What are we overlooking?"

"Robes of any shade or hue will serve, Anakha," she explained patiently, "and doubtless may be obtained in Vigayo close by yon oasis."

"They have to be black, Anarae," Bevier objected.

"Color is an aspect of light, Sir Bevier, and I am most skilled at controlling light."

"Oh," he said. "I guess I didn't think of that."

"I had noticed that myself—almost immediately."

"Be nice," he murmured.

Bergsten's knights and their Peloi allies crossed the Cynesgan border on a cloudy, chill afternoon after what *seemed* to be several days of hard riding, and headed southeasterly toward the capital at Cynestra. Peloi scouts ranged out in front, but they encountered no resistance that day. They made camp, put out guards, and bedded down early.

It was not long after they had broken camp and set out on what was ostensibly the next morning that Daiya came riding back to join Bergsten and Heldin at the head of the column. "My scouts report that there are soldiers massing about a mile ahead, your Reverence," he reported.

"Cynesgans?" Bergsten asked quickly.

"It does not appear so, your Reverence."

"Go have a look, Heldin," Bergsten ordered.

The Pandion nodded and spurred his horse to the top of a rocky hill a quarter mile to the front. His face was bleak when he returned. "We've got trouble, your Grace," he rumbled. "They're more of those monsters we came up against in eastern Zemoch."

Bergsten muttered a fairly savage oath. "I *knew* things were going too well."

"Domi Tikume has warned us about these foreign soldiers," Daiya said. "Would it offend your Reverence if I suggested that you let *us* deal with them? Domi Tikume and Domi Kring have devised certain tactics that seem to work."

"I'm not offended in the slightest, friend Daiya," Bergsten replied. "*We* didn't exactly cover ourselves with glory the last time we encountered those brutes, so I'd be very interested in seeing something that's a little more effective than *our* tactics were."

Daiya conferred briefly with his clan-chiefs, and then he led Bergsten, Heldin, and several other knights up to the top of the hill to watch.

Bergsten immediately saw the advantages of light cavalry as opposed to armored knights mounted on heavy war horses. The huge soldiers in their tight-fitting armor seemed baffled by the slashing attacks of the Peloi armed with javelins. They floundered forward, desperately trying to close with their tormentors, but the cat-footed horses of the Peloi were simply too quick. The javelins began to take their toll, and more and more of the hulking monsters fell in that deadly rain.

"The idea is to force them to run, your Reverence," Daiya explained. "They're very dangerous in close quarters, but they don't seem to have much endurance, so they aren't nearly as much a threat in a running fight."

"Vanion told me about that," Bergsten said. "Did Domi Tikume give you any idea of how long it takes them to run out of breath?"

"Nothing very specific, your Reverence."

Bergsten shrugged. "That's all right, friend Daiya. We've got plenty of open ground, and it's still morning. We can run them all day if we have to."

Stung by the repeated attacks, the huge soldiers began to lumber forward in a kind of shuffling trot, brandishing their horrid weapons and bellowing hoarse war cries.

The Peloi, however, refused those challenges and continued their slash-and-run tactics.

Then, driven and stung beyond endurance, the creatures broke into a shambling run.

"It's feasible," Sir Heldin mused in his deep, rumbling basso. "We'd need different equipment, though."

"What are you talking about, Heldin?" Bergsten demanded.

"Looking to the future, your Grace," Heldin replied. "If those beasts become a standard fixture, we'll have to modify a few things. It might not be a bad idea to train and equip a few squadrons of Church Knights to serve as light cavalry."

"Heldin," Bergsten said acidly, "if those things become a standard fixture, it'll be because we've lost this war. What makes you think there'll *be* any Church Knights at that point?"

"They're breaking off, your Reverence!" Daiya cried excitedly. "They're running away!"

"But where are they running to, Daiya?" Bergsten demanded. "It's the air that's killing them, and the air's everywhere. Where can they go, Daiya? Where can they go?"

"Where can they go?" Kring asked in bafflement as Klæl's soldiers broke off from their clumsy pursuit of the Peloi horsemen and fled into the desert.

"Who cares?" Tikume laughed. "Let them run. We've still got those Cyrgai penned up in that gully. We'd better get them to moving before some clever subaltern in the rear ranks has time to take his bearings."

The Cyrgai were following a strategy from the dawn of time. They advanced steadily, marching in step, with their large round shields protecting their bodies and with their long spears leveled to the front. As the Peloi slashed in on them, they would stop and close ranks. The front rank would kneel with overlapping shields and leveled spears. The ranks behind would close up, their shields also overlapping and spears also to the front.

It was absolutely beautiful—but it didn't accomplish anything at all against cavalry.

"We have to get them to run, Domi Tikume!" Kring shouted to his friend as they galloped clear of the massed Cyrgai regiments again. "Pull your children back a little farther after the next attack! This won't work if those antiques just keep plodding! Make them run!"

Tikume shouted some orders, and his horsemen altered their tactics, pulling back several hundred yards and forcing the Cyrgai to come to them.

A brazen trumpet sounded from the center of one of the advancing regimental squares, and the Cyrgai broke into a jingling trot, their ranks still perfectly straight.

"They look good, don't they?" Tikume laughed.

"They would if this was a parade ground," Kring replied. "Let's sting them again and then pull back even farther."

"How far is it to the border?" Tikume asked.

"Who knows? Nobody I've talked with is really sure. We're close, though. Make them run, Tikume! Make them run!"

Tikume rose in his stirrups. "Pass the word!" he bellowed. "Full retreat!"

The Peloi turned tail and galloped to the east across the rattling brown gravel.

A thin cheer went up from the massed regiments of the Cyrgai, and the trumpet sounded again. The ancient soldiers, still in perfect step and with their ranks still perfectly straight, broke into a running charge. Sergeants barked the staccato cadence, and the sound of the half boots of the Cyrgai beating on the barren ground was like the pounding of some huge drum.

And then the full light of a winter midday dimmed as if some giant, silent wings had somehow blotted out the sun. A chill wind swept across the desert, and there was a wailing sound like the sum of human woe.

The suddenly stricken Cyrgai, rank upon rank, died soundlessly in midstride, falling limply to earth to be trampled by their blindly advancing comrades, who also fell, astonished, on top of them.

Kring and Tikume, both pale and trembling, watched in awestruck wonder as the ancient Styric curse did its dreadful work. Then, sickened, they wheeled and rode back eastward, turning their backs on the heaped reminder of those perfect soldiers rushing blindly into chill, wailing obliteration.

"These clothes are good enough for Arjuna and Tamul proper, neighbor," Sparhawk told the shopkeeper later that same day, "but they don't exactly turn the trick in a dust storm. I think that last one put about four pounds of dirt down my back."

The shopkeeper nodded sagely. "Other races laugh at our customary garb, good Master," he observed. "They usually keep laughing right up until the time when they ride through their first dust storm."

"Does the wind blow all the time out there?" Talen asked him.

"Not quite *all* the time, young Master. The afternoons are usually the worst." He looked at Sparhawk. "How many robes will you be needing, good Master?"

"There are six of us, neighbor, and none of us are so fond of each other that we'd care to share a robe."

"Have you any preferences in colors?"

"Does one color keep the dust out better than the others?"

"Not that I've noticed."

"Then any color will do, I guess."

The shopkeeper hustled into his storeroom and returned with a pile of neatly folded garments. Then he smiled, rubbed his hands together, and broached the subject of the price.

"He overcharged you, you know," Talen said as they emerged from the cluttered shop into the dusty street.

Sparhawk shrugged. "Perhaps," he said.

"Someday I'm going to have to teach you about the finer points of haggling."

"Does it really matter?" Sparhawk asked, tying the bundle of Cynesgan robes to the back of his saddle. He looked around. "Anarae?"

"I am here, Anakha," her whispered voice responded.

"Were you able to find anything?"

"Nay, Anakha. Clearly the messenger hath not yet arrived."

"Berit and Khalad are still several days away, Sparhawk," Talen said quietly, "and this isn't such an attractive place that the messenger would want to get here early to enjoy the scenery." He looked around at the winter-dispirited palm trees and the muddy pond that lay at the center of the cluster of white houses.

"Attractive or not, we're going to have to come up with some reason for staying," Sparhawk said. "We can't leave until the messenger gets here and Anarae Xanetia can listen to what he's thinking."

"I can remain here alone, Anakha," Xanetia told him. "None here can detect my presence, so I do not need protection."

"We'll stay all the same, Anarae," Sparhawk told her. "Courtesy and all that, you understand. An Elene gentleman will *not* permit a lady to go about unescorted."

An argument had broken out on the shaded porch of what appeared to be a tavern or a wineshop of some kind. "You don't know what you're talking about, Echon!" a wheezy-voiced old man in a patched and filthy robe declared loudly. "It's a good hundred miles from here to the River Sarna, and there's no water at all between here and there."

"You either drink too much or you've been out in the sun too long, Zagorri," Echon, a thin, sun-dried man in a dark blue robe, scoffed. "My map says that it's sixty miles—no more."

"How well do you know the man who drew the map? I've been here all my life, and I know how far it is to the Sarna. Go ahead, though. Take only enough water for sixty miles. Your mules will die, and you'll be drinking sand for that last forty miles. It's all right with me, though, because I've never liked you all that much anyway. But, mark my words, Echon. It's one hundred miles from the Well of Vigay there to the banks of the Sarna." And the old man spat in the direction of the pale brown pond.

Talen suddenly began to laugh.

"What's so funny?" Sparhawk asked him.

"We just had a stroke of luck, revered leader," the boy replied gaily. "If we're all finished up here, why don't we go back to where the others are waiting? We'll all want to get a good night's sleep—since we'll probably be leaving first thing in the morning."

"Oh? For where?"

"Cyrga, of course. Wasn't that where we wanted to go?"

"Yes, but we don't know where Cyrga is."

"That's where you're wrong, Sparhawk. We *do* know the way to Cyrga—at least *I* do."

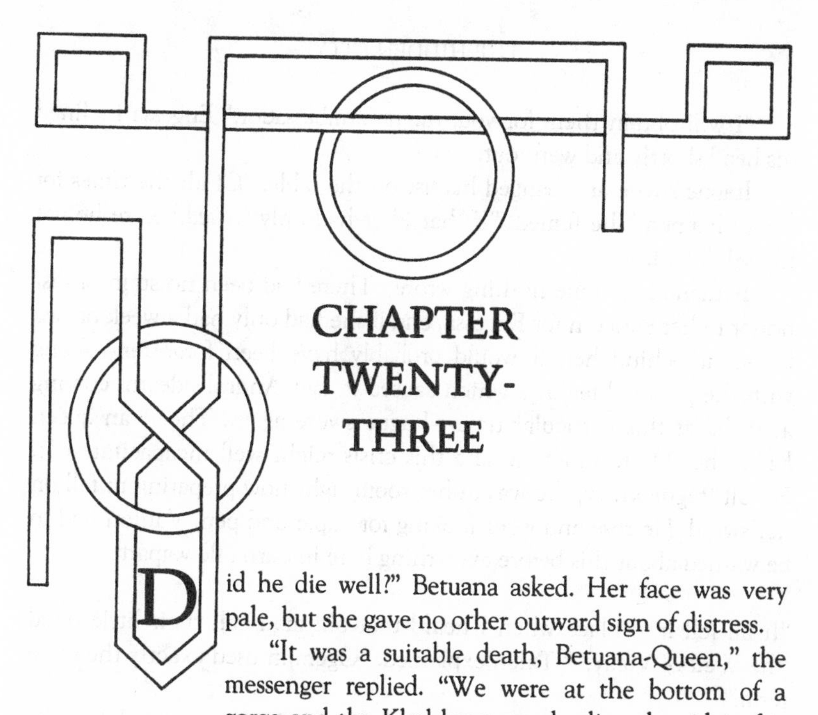

CHAPTER TWENTY-THREE

"Did he die well?" Betuana asked. Her face was very pale, but she gave no other outward sign of distress.

"It was a suitable death, Betuana-Queen," the messenger replied. "We were at the bottom of a gorge and the Klæl-beast was hurling the sides of it down upon us. Androl-King attacked the beast, and many escaped that would have died if he had not."

She considered it. "Yes," she agreed finally. "It was suitable. It will be remembered. Is the army fit to travel?"

"We have many injured, Betuana-Queen, and thousands are buried in the gorge. We withdrew to Tualas to await your commands."

"Leave some few to care for the injured, and bring the army here," she told him. "Tosa is no longer in danger. The danger is here."

"It shall be as you say, my Queen." He clashed his fist against his breastplate in salute.

The Queen of Atan rose to her feet, her still-pale face betraying no emotion. "I must go apart and consider this, Itagne-Ambassador," she said formally.

"It is proper, Betuana-Queen," he responded. "I share your grief."

"But not my guilt." She turned and slowly left the room.

Itagne looked at the stony-faced Engessa. "I'd better pass the word to the others," he said.

Engessa nodded shortly.

"Could you speak with the messenger before he leaves, Engessa?" Itagne asked. "Lord Vanion will need casualty figures before he can change his strategy."

"I will obtain them for you, It'agne-Ambassador." Engessa inclined his head shortly and went out.

Itagne swore and banged his fist on the table. "Of all the times for *this* to happen!" he fumed. "If that idiot had only *waited* before he got himself killed!"

Betuana had done nothing wrong. There had been no stain of dishonor in her concern for Engessa, and if she had only had a week or two to put it behind her, it would probably have been forgotten—along with the personal feelings which caused it. But Androl's death, coming as it did at this particular time—Itagne swore again. The Atan queen *had* to be able to function, and this crisis might well incapacitate her. For all Itagne knew, she was in her room right now preparing to fall on her sword. He rose and went looking for paper and pen. Vanion had to be warned about this before everything here in Sarna flew apart.

"It all fell into place when I heard that old man call their little pond 'the Well of Vigay,' " Talen explained. "Ogerajin used exactly the same term."

"I don't know that it means very much," Mirtai said dubiously. "Cynesgans call all these desert springs wells. Vigay was probably the one who discovered it."

"But the important thing is that *this* is one of the landmarks Ogerajin mentioned," Bevier said. "How did the subject come up?" he asked Talen.

"Stragen and I were spinning moonbeams for Valash," the boy replied. "Ogerajin had just arrived from Verel, and he was sitting in a chair with his brains quietly rotting. Stragen was telling Valash about something he'd supposedly overheard—some fellow telling another that Scarpa was waiting for instructions from Cyrga. He was fishing for information, and he casually asked Valash what route a man would have to follow to get to Cyrga. That's when Ogerajin jumped in. He started rambling about the 'Well of Vigay' and the 'Plains of Salt' and other places with names that sounded as if they'd come right out of a storybook. I thought he was just raving, but Valash got really excited and tried to hush him up. That's what made me pay attention—I got the feeling that Ogerajin was giving Stragen very specific directions to Cyrga, but that the directions were all clouded over with those storybook names. This 'Well of Vigay' business makes me start to wonder if the directions were as cloudy and garbled as I thought they were right at first."

"What were his exact words, young Talen?" Xanetia asked.

"He said, 'The pathway lies close by the Well of Vigay.' That's when Valash tried to shut him up, but he kept right on. He said something about wanting to give Stragen directions so that he could go to Cyrga and bow down to Cyrgon. He told him to go northwest from the 'Well of Vigay' to the 'Forbidden Mountains.' "

Sparhawk checked over his map. "There *are* several clusters of mountains in central Cynesga, and that's the general region Aphrael pointed out back on the island. What else did he say, Talen?"

"He sort of jumped around. He talked about the 'Forbidden Mountains' and the 'Pillars of Cyrgon.' Then he doubled back on himself and started talking about the 'Plains of Salt.' From what he told Stragen, you're supposed to be able to see these 'Forbidden Mountains' from those salt plains. Then there was something about 'Fiery White Pillars' and 'The Plain of Bones.' He said that the bones are 'the nameless slaves who toil until death for Cyrgon's Chosen.' Evidently when a slave dies in Cyrga, he's taken out and dumped in the desert."

"That boneyard wouldn't be very far from the city, then," Kalten mused.

"It *does* all sort of fit together, Sparhawk," Bevier said seriously. "The Cynesgans themselves are largely nomads, so they wouldn't have any real need for large numbers of slaves. Ogerajin spoke of 'Cyrgon's Chosen.' That would be the Cyrgai, and *they're* probably the ones who buy slaves."

"And that would mean that the caravan of slavers we saw is going to Cyrga, wouldn't it?" Talen added excitedly.

"*And* they were going northwest," Mirtai said, "the exact direction Ogerajin was raving about."

Sparhawk went to his saddlebags and took out his map. He sat down again and opened it, holding it firmly as the desert wind started to flap its corners. "We know that Cyrga's somewhere in these mountains in central Cynesga," he mused, "so we'll be going in that direction anyway. If Ogerajin was just raving and his directions don't go anyplace, we'll still be in the right vicinity if we follow them."

"It's better than just sitting here waiting for Berit and Khalad," Kalten said impatiently. "I have to be doing *something*—even if it's only riding around in circles out there in the desert."

Sparhawk wordlessly put a comforting hand on his old friend's shoulder. His own desperate concern was at least as driving as Kalten's, but he knew that he had to keep it separate, remote. Desperate men make mistakes, and a mistake here could put Ehlana in even greater peril. His emotions screamed at him, but he grimly, implacably, pushed them into a separate compartment of his mind and firmly closed the door.

"Anakha would be made glad if we would do this," Ulath said in Trollish to the enormous presences.

Ghworg, God of Kill, rumbled ominously. "Anakha's thought is like the wind," he complained. "One time he said to us, 'Go to the place the man-things call the Tamul Mountains to kill the children of Cyrgon.' Now he says to us, 'Go to the place the man-things call Zhubay to kill the children of Cyrgon.' Can he not decide which children of Cyrgon he wants us to kill?"

"It is the way of the hunt, Ghworg," Tynian explained. "The children of Cyrgon are not like the red-deer, which feed always in the same range. The children of Cyrgon are like the reindeer, which go from this place to that place as the seasons change to find better food. Before, they were going to this place, Tamul Mountains, to feed, but now they go to the place Zhubay to feed. If we hunt in the Tamul Mountains, we will find no game to kill and eat."

"It speaks well," Ghnomb, God of Eat, said. "It is not Anakha's thought which changes, it is the path of the creatures we hunt which changes. The way of the hunt tells us that we must go where they graze if we would find them and kill them and eat them."

"This hunt becomes more and more not-simple," Ghworg grumbled.

"That is because the man-things are more not-simple than the deer-things," Khwaj, God of Fire, told him. "The thought of Tynian-from-Deira is good. The one who hunts where there is no game does not eat."

Ghworg pondered it. "We must follow the way of the hunt," he decided. "We will take our children to the place Zhubay to hunt the children of Cyrgon. When they come there to graze, our children will kill them and eat them."

"It would make us glad if you would," Tynian said politely.

"I will take our children into the Time-Which-Does-Not-Move," Ghnomb said. "They will be in the place Zhubay before the children of Cyrgon come there."

Schlee, God of Ice, stuck his huge fingers into the dirt. The earth shuddered slightly and contorted itself into his picture of the continent.

"Show us where, Ulath-from-Thalesia," he said. "Where is the place Zhubay?"

Ulath walked some distance along the southwestern edge of the tiny mountains of Atan, peering intently at the ground. Then he stopped, bent, and touched a spot a short way out into the northern end of the Desert of Cynesga. "It is here, Schlee," he said.

Ghworg, God of Kill, stood up. "We will take our children there," he declared. "Let us make Anakha glad."

"They're watching us, Vanion," Sephrenia said quietly.

He pulled his horse in closer to hers. "Styrics?" he asked quietly.

"One of them is," she replied. "He's not particularly skilled." She smiled faintly. "I may have to hit him over the head to get his attention."

"Whatever it takes, love," he said. He glanced back over his shoulder at the column of knights and then on ahead. They were coming down out of the mountains, and the Valley of the Sarna was beginning to broaden. "We should reach that bridge tomorrow," he told her. "After we cross the river, we'll be in Cynesga."

"Yes, dear one," she said, "I've seen the map."

"Why don't you cast the spell?" he suggested. "Let's give our inept Styric out there a chance of earn his keep." He looked at her gravely. "I'm having some second thoughts about this, Sephrenia. Klæl's still out there, and if he thinks Sparhawk's somewhere in this column with Bhelliom, he'll be all over us."

"You can't have it both ways, Vanion," she said with a fond smile. "You said that you were never going to let me out of your sight, so if you insist on going into dangerous places, I'm sort of obliged to go along. Now if you'll excuse me, I'll wake up that Styric." She began to speak softly in Styric, her fingers weaving the spell as she did so.

Vanion was puzzled. He took a certain pride in his familiarity with most of the spells, but this was one he had never seen or heard before. He watched more closely.

"Never mind," she told him crisply, breaking off the spell. "You don't need to know this one."

"But—"

"Just look over there, Vanion," she said. "I can do this without any help." She paused. "Humor me, dear one. A girl needs a *few* secrets, after all."

He smiled and turned his head.

There was a kind of vague blurring in the air about ten yards away, and then, as surely as if he were really there, Vanion saw Sparhawk appear, mounted as always on his evil-tempered roan. So real was the image that flies were attracted to the horse. "Brilliant!" Vanion exclaimed. He sent out a probing thought and even encountered the familiar sense of Sparhawk's presence. "If I didn't know better, I'd swear that he was really here. Can you sustain this illusion?"

"Naturally," she said in an infuriatingly offhand way. And then she laughed, reached out, and fondly touched his cheek.

"What took you so long?" Talen asked the Child-Goddess when she appeared on the edge of their camp outside Vigayo the following morning.

"I've been busy," she replied with a little shrug. "This is a fairly complex business, you know. We all *do* want to get there at approximately the same time, don't we? What's the problem here, Sparhawk?"

"We might have just had a bit of good luck for a change, Divine One," he replied. "Talen and I were in the village yesterday, and we heard one of the villagers refer to their oasis as 'the Well of Vigay.' "

"So?"

"Why don't you tell her about it, Talen?"

The young thief quickly repeated the conversations between Ogerajin and Stragen back in Beresa.

"What do you think?" Kalten asked the Child-Goddess.

"Does somebody have a map?" she asked.

Sparhawk went to his saddlebags, took out his tightly rolled map, and brought it to her.

She spread it out on the ground, knelt in front of it, and studied it for several moments. "There *are* some salt flats out there," she conceded.

"And they *are* in the right direction," Bevier pointed out.

"Ogerajin's been there," Talen added, "at least he *says* he has, so he'd almost have to know the way, wouldn't he?"

"There's also a slaver's route that runs off to the northwest," Mirtai said. "We saw a caravan following it when we first got here, and Ogerajin mentioned the fact that the Cyrgai keep slaves. It sort of stands to reason that the slave caravan's bound for Cyrga, doesn't it?"

"You're hanging all this speculation on the ravings of a madman, you know," Flute said critically.

"You said yourself that Cyrga's somewhere in central Cynesga," Kalten reminded her, "and that's where all of this points. Even if Ogerajin left some things out, we'll still end up in the general vicinity of Cyrga. We'll be a lot closer than we are right now, anyway."

"Since you've all made up your minds, why did you bother me with it?" Her tone was just a bit petulant.

Talen grinned at her. "We didn't think it'd be polite to run off without telling you, Divine One."

"I'll get you for that, Talen," she threatened.

"How far ahead of us would you say that caravan is by now?" Sparhawk asked Mirtai.

"Ten leagues," she replied, "twelve at the most. Slave caravans don't move very fast."

"I think that's our best bet, then," he decided. "Let's put on those black robes and get started. We'll trail along a couple of leagues behind that caravan, and anybody who happens to see us will think we're stragglers."

"Anything's better than just sitting still," Kalten said.

"Somehow I was sure you'd feel that way about it," Sparhawk replied.

"We're little more than prisoners here," Empress Chacole declared, waving her hand at the luxurious furnishings of the women's palace. Chacole was a ripe-figured Cynesgan lady in her thirties. Her tone was one of only idle discontent, but her eyes were hard and shrewd as she looked at Elysoun.

Elysoun shrugged. "*I've* never had any trouble coming and going as I choose."

"That's because you're a Valesian," Empress Torellia told her with just a touch of resentment. "They make allowances for you they don't make for the rest of us. I don't think it's very fair."

Elysoun shrugged again. "Fair or not, it's the custom."

"Why should you have more freedom than the rest of us?"

"Because I have a more active social life."

"Aren't there enough men in the women's palace for you?"

"Don't be catty, Torellia. You're not old enough to make it convincing." Elysoun looked appraisingly at the Arjuni empress. Torellia was a slender girl in her midtwenties, and, like all Arjuni women, she was quite subservient. Chacole was obviously taking advantage of that.

"You don't see anybody restricting Cieronna's movements," Chacole said.

"Cieronna's the first wife," Elysoun replied, "and she's the oldest. We should respect her age if nothing else."

"I will *not* be a servant to an aging Tamul hag!" Chacole flared.

"She doesn't *want* you as a servant, Chacole," Elysoun told her. "She already has more servants than she can count—unless Liatris has thinned them out some more. All Cieronna really wants is a fancier crown than the rest of us have and the right to walk in front of us in formal processions. It doesn't take much to make her happy. She's not the brightest person in Matherion."

Torellia giggled.

"Here comes Gahenas," Chacole hissed.

The jug-eared Tegan empress, covered to the chin in scratchy wool, approached them with a disapproving expression, an expression that came over her face every time she so much as looked at the barely dressed Elysoun. "Ladies," she greeted them with a stiff little nod.

"Join us, Gahenas," Chacole invited. "We're discussing politics."

Gahenas' bulging eyes brightened. Tegans lived and breathed politics.

"Chacole and Torellia want to get up a petition to our husband," Elysoun said. She raised her arms and yawned deeply, stretching back and literally thrusting her bare breasts at Gahenas.

Gahenas quickly averted her eyes.

"I'm sorry, ladies," Elysoun apologized. "I didn't get much sleep last night."

"How do you find enough hours in the day?" Gahenas asked spitefully.

"It's only a matter of scheduling, Gahenas." Elysoun shrugged. "You can get all sorts of things accomplished if you budget your time. Why don't we just drop it, dear? You don't approve of me, and I don't really care. We'll never understand each other, so why waste our time trying?"

"You can go anywhere in the imperial compound you want to, can't you, Elysoun?" Chacole asked rather tentatively.

Elysoun feigned another yawn to conceal her smile. Chacole had finally gotten to the point. Elysoun had wondered how long it was going to take. "I can come and go more or less as I choose," she replied. "I guess all the spies got tired of trying to keep up with me."

"Do you suppose I could ask a favor of you?"

"Of course, dear. What do you need?"

"Cieronna doesn't like me, and her spies follow me everywhere I go. I'm involved in something at the moment I'd rather she didn't find out about."

"Why, Chacole! Are you saying that you've finally decided to go a little farther afield for entertainment?"

The Cynesgan empress gave her a blank stare, obviously missing her point.

"Oh, come now, dear," Elysoun said slyly. "We all have our little private amusements here inside the women's palace—even Gahenas here."

"I most certainly do *not*!" the Tegan protested.

"Oh, *really*, Gahenas? I've seen that new page boy of yours. He's absolutely luscious. Who's *your* new lover, Chacole? Some husky young lieutenant in the guards? Did you want me to smuggle him into the palace for you?"

"It's nothing like that, Elysoun."

"Of *course* it isn't," Elysoun agreed with heavy sarcasm. "All right, Chacole. I'll carry your love notes for you—if you're really sure you trust me that close to him. But why go so far afield, sister dear? Gahenas has this lovely young page boy, and I'm sure she's trained him very well—haven't you, Gahenas?" She raised one mocking eyebrow. "Tell me, dear," she added, "was he a virgin? Before you got your hands on him, I mean?"

Gahenas fled with Elysoun's mocking laughter following after her.

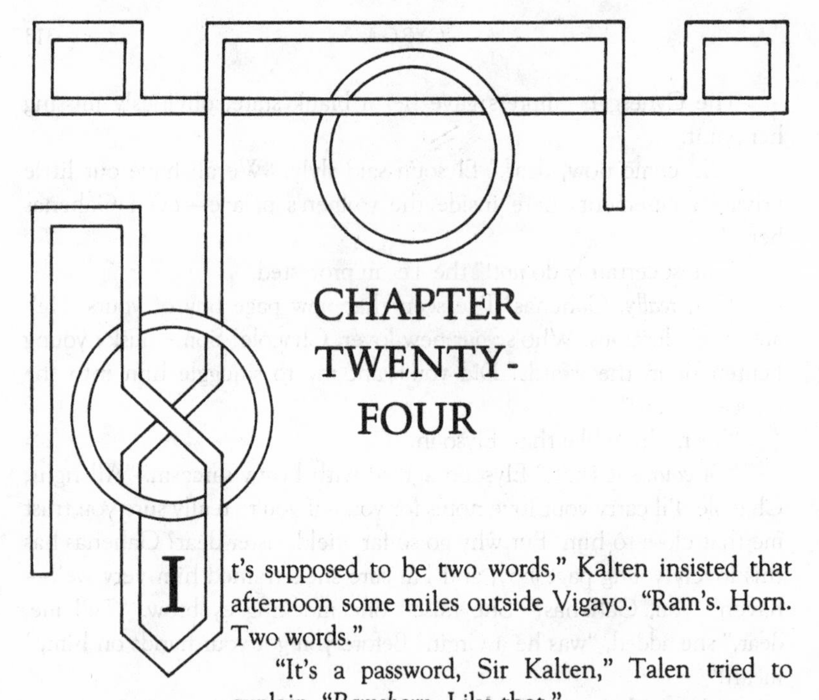

CHAPTER TWENTY-FOUR

"It's supposed to be two words," Kalten insisted that afternoon some miles outside Vigayo. "Ram's. Horn. Two words."

"It's a password, Sir Kalten," Talen tried to explain. "*Ramshorn*. Like that."

"What do *you* say, Sparhawk?" Kalten asked his friend. "Is it one word or two?" The three of them had just finished piling rocks in a rough approximation of a grave at the side of the trail, and Talen and Kalten were arguing about the crude marker the boy had prepared.

"What difference does it make?" Sparhawk shrugged.

"If it's spelled wrong, Berit might not recognize it when he rides by," Talen said.

"He'll recognize it," Sparhawk disagreed. "Berit's quick. Just don't disturb the arrangement of those yellow rocks on the top of the grave."

"Are you sure Khalad will understand what those rocks mean?" Talen asked skeptically.

"Your father would have," Sparhawk replied, "and I'm sure he taught Khalad all the usual signals."

"I still say it's supposed to be two words," Kalten insisted.

"Bevier!" Sparhawk called.

The Cyrinic Knight walked back to the imitation grave with an inquiring expression.

"These two are arguing about how to spell *ramshorn*," Sparhawk told him. "You're the scholar. *You* settle it."

"I say he spelled it wrong," Kalten said truculently. "It's supposed to be two words, isn't it?"

"Ah—" Bevier said evasively, "there are two schools of thought on that."

"Why don't you tell them about it as we ride along?" Mirtai suggested.

Sparhawk looked at Xanetia. "Don't," he warned her quietly.

"What wouldst thou not have me do, Anakha?" she asked innocently.

"Don't laugh. Don't even smile. You'll only make it worse."

It may or may not have been three weeks later. Patriarch Bergsten had given up on trying to keep track of actual time. Instead he glared in sullen theological discontent at the mud-walled city of Cynestra and at the disgustingly young and well-conditioned person coming toward him. Bergsten believed in an orderly world, and violations of order made him nervous.

She was very tall and she had golden skin and night-dark hair, she was also extremely pretty and superbly muscled. She emerged from the main gate of Cynestra under a flag of truce, running easily out to meet them. She stopped some distance to their front, and Bergsten, Sir Heldin, Daiya, and Neran, their Tamul translator, rode forward to confer with her. She spoke at some length with Neran.

"Keep your eyes where they belong, Heldin," Bergsten muttered.

"I was just—"

"I know what you were doing. Stop it." Bergsten paused. "I wonder why they sent a woman."

Neran, a slender Tamul who had been sent along by Ambassador Fontan, returned. "She's Atana Maris," he told them, "commander of the Atan garrison here in Cynestra."

"A *woman*?" Bergsten was startled.

"It's not uncommon among the Atans, your Grace. She's been expecting us. Foreign Minister Oscagne sent word that we were coming."

"What's the situation in the city?" Heldin asked.

"King Jaluah's been quietly dribbling troops into Cynestra for the past month or so," Neran replied. "Atana Maris has a thousand Atans in her garrison, and the Cynesgans have been trying to restrict their movements. She's been growing impatient with all of that. She probably would have moved against the royal palace a week ago, but Oscagne instructed her to wait until we arrived."

"How did she get out of the city?" Heldin rumbled.

"I didn't ask her, Sir Heldin. I didn't want to insult her."

"What I meant was, didn't they try to stop her?"

"They're dead if they did."

"But she's a *woman*!" Bergsten objected.

"You're not really familiar with the Atans, are you, your Reverence?" Daiya asked.

"I've heard of them, friend Daiya. The stories all seem wildly exaggerated to me."

"No, your Reverence, they aren't," Daiya said firmly. "I know of this girl's reputation. She's the youngest garrison commander in the entire Atan army, and she didn't get to where she is by being sweet and ladylike. From what I've heard, she's an absolute savage."

"But she's so pretty," Heldin protested.

"Sir Heldin," Neran said firmly to him, "while you're admiring her, pay particular attention to the development of her arms and shoulders. She's as strong as a bull, and if you offend her in any way at all, she'll tear you to pieces. She almost killed Itagne—or so the rumor has it."

"The foreign minister's brother?" Bergsten asked.

Neran nodded. "He was here on a mission and he decided to place the city under martial law. He needed Atana Maris' help with that, so he seduced her. Her response was enthusiastic—but very muscular. Be very careful around her, gentlemen. She's almost as dangerous to have as a friend as an enemy. She asked me to give you your instructions."

"*Instructions?*" Bergsten erupted. "I don't take orders from women!"

"Your Grace," Neran said, "Cynestra's technically still under martial law, and that puts Atana Maris in charge. She's been ordered to deliver the city to you, but she's instructed you to wait outside the walls until she's crushed all the resistance. She wants to present the city to you as a gift—all neat and tidy. Please don't spoil it for her. Smile at her, thank her politely, and wait right here until she's finished cleaning the streets. After she's got all the bodies stacked in neat piles, she'll invite you in and turn the city over to you—along with King Jaluah's head, more than likely. I know that the situation seems unnatural to you, but for God's sake don't do anything to offend her. She'll go to war with you just as quickly as with anybody else."

"But she's so pretty," Heldin objected again.

Berit and Khalad dismounted and led their horses down to the oasis to water them. In theory, they *might* have reached Vigayo this soon. "Can you tell if he's here?" Khalad muttered.

Berit shook his head. "I *think* that means that he's not a Styric. We'll just have to wait for him to come to us." He looked around at the few white-walled houses shaded by low palm trees. "Is there any kind of inn here?"

"Not very likely. I see a lot of tents on the other side of the oasis. I'll ask around, but don't get your hopes up."

Berit shrugged. "Oh, well. We've lived in tents before. Find out where we're permitted to set up."

The village of Vigayo itself was clustered along the eastern side of the oasis, and the informal encampment of nomads and merchants stretched along the west shore of what was actually a fair-sized pool of artesian water. Berit and Khalad picketed their horses, erected their tent near the water, and sat down in the shade to wait. "Can you tell if Sparhawk's around anyplace?" Khalad asked.

Berit shook his head. "He may have already passed through. Or he could be watching from one of the hills outside of town. He might not want people to know that he's here."

It was an hour or so past sunset, and twilight was descending when a Cynesgan in a loose-fitting striped robe approached their tent. "I'm supposed to ask if one of you might be named Sparhawk," he said in a slightly accented voice.

Berit rose to his feet. "I might be named Sparhawk, neighbor."

"Might be?"

"That's the way you phrased your question, friend. You've got a note for me. Why don't you just hand it over and be on your way? We don't really have anything else to talk about, do we?"

The messenger's face hardened. He reached inside his robe, took out a folded and sealed parchment, and negligently tossed it at Berit's feet. Then he turned and walked away.

"You know, Berit," Khalad said mildly, "sometimes you're even more abrasive than Sparhawk himself."

Berit grinned. "I know. I'm trying to maintain his reputation." He bent, picked up the parchment, and broke the seal. He removed the identifying lock of hair and quickly read the brief message.

"Well?" Khalad asked.

"Nothing very specific. It says that there's a caravan route running off to the northwest. We're supposed to follow that. We'll get further instructions along the way."

"Will it be safe to use the spell and talk with Aphrael once we get out of town?"

"I think so. I'm sure she'd have told me if I wasn't supposed to use it here in Cynesga."

"We don't have much choice," Khalad said. "We can't tell if

Sparhawk's already been here, if he's here now, or if he's still on the way, and we've got to let him know about these new instructions."

"Do you think we ought to start out tonight?"

"No, let's not start floundering around in the dark. We might miss the trail, and there's nothing out in that desert but empty."

"I won't do anything to put Berit in any kind of danger," Elysoun insisted a few days later. "I'm very fond of him."

"They found out that he was posing as Sparhawk quite some time ago, Elysoun," Baroness Melidere told her. "You won't be putting him in any more danger than he's already in. Telling Chacole about his disguise will convince her that you've gone over to her side—*and* that you have access to important information."

"You might want to make them believe that your husband's totally smitten with you, Empress Elysoun," Patriarch Emban added. "Let them think that he tells you everything."

"*Are* you smitten with me, Sarabian?" Elysoun asked archly.

"Oh, absolutely, my dear." He smiled. "I adore you."

"What a nice thing to say." She smiled warmly.

"Later, children," Melidere told them absently, her forehead furrowed with concentration. "At the same time you tell Chacole about Berit's disguise, drop a few hints about a fleet of Church ships in the Gulf of Daconia. Stragen's been very carefully planting that particular lie, so let's give them some confirmation. After you tell them about Berit, they'll be inclined to believe your story about the fleet." She looked at the emperor. "Is there anything else we can give them that won't hurt us? Something they can verify?"

"Does it have to be important?"

"Not really, just something that's true. We need another truth to get the mix right."

"The mix?"

"It's like a recipe, your Majesty." She smiled. "Two parts truth to one part lie; stir well and serve. If you get the mix right, they'll swallow the whole thing."

They had set out at first light, and the sun had not yet risen when they topped a low ridge and saw a vast, flat expanse of dead whiteness lying ahead. Time, like climate, had lost all meaning.

"I'd hate to have to cross *that* in the summertime," Kalten said.

"Truly," Sparhawk agreed.

"The slavers' trail swings north here," Bevier noted, "probably to go around those flats. If a Cynesgan patrol stumbles across us out there, we might have trouble convincing them that we're attached to that caravan we've been following."

"We'll just say that we got lost," Kalten said with a shrug. "Let me do the talking, Bevier. I get lost all the time anyway, so I can be fairly convincing. How far is it to the other side, Sparhawk?"

"About twenty-five leagues, according to my map."

"Two days—even if we push," Kalten calculated.

"And no cover," Bevier added. "You couldn't hide a spider out—" He broke off. "What's that?" he asked, pointing at an intensely bright spot of light on the mountainous western horizon.

Talen squinted at the light. "I think it might be the landmark we've been looking for," he said.

"How did you arrive at that?" Kalten asked skeptically.

"It's in the right direction, isn't it? Ogerajin said that we were supposed to go northwest from Vigayo to the Plains of Salt. Then he said, 'From the verge of the Plains of Salt wilt thou behold low on the horizon before thee the dark shapes of the Forbidden Mountains, and, if it please Cyrgon, his fiery white pillars will guide thee to his Hidden City.' There *are* mountains there, and that light's coming from right in the middle of them. Wouldn't it almost *have* to be coming from the pillars?"

"The man was crazy, Talen," Kalten objected.

"Maybe," Sparhawk disagreed, "but so far, everything he described is right where he said it would be. Let's chance it. It's still the right direction."

"About the only thing that might cause us any trouble would be if we stumbled across a helpful Cynesgan patrol and they decided to escort us back to that caravan we've been following for the last few days," Mirtai observed.

"Logically, our chances of coming across a patrol out there on the flats are very slim," Bevier suggested. "Cynesgans would normally avoid that waste in the first place, and the war's probably pulled almost everybody off patrol duty in the second."

"And any patrols unlucky enough to cross us won't be making any reports in the third," Mirtai added, her hand on her sword hilt.

"We've tentatively located the pillars," Sparhawk said, "and if Ogerajin knew what he was talking about, we'll have to take a line of sight on them to penetrate the illusion. Now that we've found them, let's not lose them. We'll just have to take our chances out there on the flats. If we're lucky, nobody will even notice us. If not, we'll try lying to them, and if that doesn't work, we still have our swords." He looked around at them. "Does anybody have anything else to add?"

"I think that covers it," Kalten said, still somewhat dubious.

"Let's get started, then."

"They just broke off and ran away, friend Vanion," Kring said a day or so later. Kring's face was baffled. "We were using those tactics Tikume and I came up with, and everything was going more or less the way we expected, and then somebody blew a horn or something, and they turned tail and ran—but where? If what we've been told is true, there's no place in the whole world they can go to catch their breath."

"Did you have anybody follow them?" Vanion asked.

"I probably should have, I suppose, but I was concentrating on luring the Cyrgai across the border." Kring smiled at Sephrenia. "That Styric curse doesn't seem to have worn thin in the last ten thousand years, Lady. Three full regiments of Cyrgai went down like newly mown wheat when they crossed the border." He paused. "They're not really very bright, are they?"

"The Cyrgai? No. It's against their religion."

"You'd think that at least a *few* of them would have realized that something was wrong, but they just kept running across the border and falling over dead."

"Independent thinking isn't encouraged among them. They're trained to follow orders—even bad ones."

Kring looked at the bridge crossing the Sarna. "You'll be operating from here, friend Vanion?" he asked.

"I'll put a force on the other side of the bridge," Vanion replied, "but our main camp will be on this side. The river marks the boundary between Tamul proper and Cynesga, doesn't it?"

"Technically, I suppose." The Domi shrugged. "The curse line's a couple of miles farther west, though."

"The boundary's changed several times over the years," Sephrenia explained.

"Tikume thought I should come up here and talk things over with you, friend Vanion," Kring said then. "We don't want to interfere with Sparhawk, so we haven't been going too far into Cynesga, but we're running out of people to chase."

"How far in have you been going?" Vanion asked.

"Six or seven leagues," Kring replied. "We come back to Samar every night—although there's no real reason for it now. I don't think there's any danger of a siege any more."

"No," Vanion agreed. "We've pushed them enough so that they can't really concentrate on Samar now." He opened his map and frowned at it for a few moments, then he dropped to one knee and spread it out on the winter-brown grass. "Step on that corner, please," he said to Sephrenia. "I don't want to have to chase it again."

Kring looked puzzled.

"Household joke," Sephrenia explained, putting one small foot on the corner of Vanion's map. "Vanion's fond of maps, and an errant breeze turned his current favorite into a kite two days ago."

Vanion let that pass. "I'll agree that we don't want to crowd Sparhawk, Domi, but I think we'll want to build some fortified positions out there in the desert. They'll give us jumping-off places when we start our advance on Cyrga."

"I had the same thought, friend Vanion."

"Let's establish a presence across that border," Vanion decided. "I'll send word to Betuana, and she'll do the same."

"How deep in should we go?" Kring asked.

Vanion looked at Sephrenia. "Ten leagues?" he suggested. "That's not so deep that we'll be stepping on Sparhawk's heels, but we'll have room to maneuver, and it'll give you some elbow room for that spell of yours."

"Using the spell's a good plan, friend Vanion," Kring said a bit dubiously, "but you're deliberately drawing the best our enemies can throw at us to yourself—and to Lady Sephrenia. Is that what you want? I don't mean to be offensive, but your fight with Klæl's soldiers seriously reduced your ranks."

"That's one of the reasons I want forts out there in the desert, Domi," Vanion said wryly. "If worse comes to worst, I'll pull back into those positions. I'm almost sure I can count on some dear friends on my flanks to come to my rescue."

"Well said," Sephrenia murmured.

"Stop," Khalad said sharply, reining in his horse when they were perhaps five miles outside Vigayo.

"What is it?" Berit asked tensely.

"Somebody named Ramshorn died," Khalad said, pointing. "I think we should stop and pay our respects."

Berit looked at the crude grave beside the trail. "I looked right through it," he confessed. "Sorry, Khalad."

"Pay attention, my Lord."

"It seems you've said that before."

They dismounted and approached the rude "grave."

"Clever," Berit murmured quietly. It was probably not necessary to lower his voice, but it had gotten to be a habit.

"Talen's idea, probably," Khalad said as they both knelt beside the mound. "It's a little subtle for Sparhawk."

"Isn't that supposed to be two words?" Berit asked, pointing at the weathered plank with *Ramshorn* roughly carved into its face.

"You're the educated one, my Lord. Don't touch those rocks."

"Which rocks?"

"The yellow ones. We'll mix them up as soon as I read them."

"You read rocks? Is that like reading sea gulls?"

"Not exactly. It's a message from Sparhawk. He and my father worked this out a long time ago." The short-bearded young man leaned first this way and then that, squinting at the mound. "Naturally," he said finally with a certain resignation. He rose and moved to the head of the grave.

"What?"

"Sparhawk wrote it upside down. Now it makes sense." Khalad studied the apparently random placement of the yellowish rocks on the top of the predominantly brown mound. "Pray, Berit," he said. "Offer up a prayer for the soul of our departed brother, Ramshorn."

"You're not making any sense, Khalad."

"Somebody might be watching. Act religious." The husky young squire took the reins of their horses and led them several yards away from the ill-defined trail. Then he bent, took Faran's left foreleg in both hands, and carefully inspected the hoof.

Faran gave him an unfriendly stare.

"Sorry," Khalad apologized to the bad-tempered brute, "it's nothing important." He lowered the hoof to the gravel again. "All right, Berit," he said then, "say 'Amen,' and we'll get going again."

"What was that all about?" Berit's tone was surly as he remounted.

"Sparhawk left a message for us," Khalad replied, swinging up into his saddle. "The arrangement of the yellow rocks told me where to find it."

"Where is it?" Berit asked eagerly.

"Right now? It's in my left boot. I picked it up when I was checking Faran's hoof."

"I didn't see you pick up a thing."

"You weren't supposed to, my Lord."

Krager awoke with the horrors to the sound of distant screaming. Days and nights had long since blurred in Krager's awareness, but the sun shattering against his eyes told him that it was full and awful morning. He had certainly not intended to drink so much the previous night, but the knowledge that he was reaching the bottom of his last cask of Arcian red had somehow worried at him as he had grown progressively drunker, and the knowledge that it would soon be all gone had somehow translated itself in his fuddled mind into a compulsion to drink it all before it somehow got away from him.

Now he was paying for that foolishness. His head was throbbing, his stomach was on fire, and his mouth tasted as if something had crawled in there and died. He was shaking violently, and there were sharp stabbing pains in his liver. He sat on the edge of his tangled bed with his head in his hands. There was a sense of dread hanging over him, a shadowy feeling of horror. He kept his burning eyes closed and groped under the bed with one shaking hand for the emergency bottle he always kept there. The liquid it contained was neither wine nor beer but a dreadful concoction of Lamork origin that was obtained by setting certain inferior wines out in the winter and allowing them to freeze. The liquid that rose to the top and remained unfrozen was almost pure spirits. It tasted foul, and it burned like fire going down, but it put the horrors to sleep. Shuddering, Krager drank off about a pint of the awful stuff and lurched to his feet.

The sun was painfully bright when he stumbled out into the streets of Natayos and went looking for the source of the screams that had awakened him. He reached a central square and recoiled in horror. Several men were being systematically tortured to death while Scarpa, dressed in his shabby imitation royal robe and his makeshift crown, sat in an ornate chair watching with approval.

"What's going on?" Krager asked Cabah, a shabby Dacite brigand with whom he had frequently gotten drunk.

Cabah turned quickly. "Oh, it's you, Krager," he said. "As closely as I can gather, the Shining Ones descended on Panem-Dea."

"That's impossible," Krager said shortly. "Ptaga's dead. There aren't any more of those illusions to keep the Tamuls running around in circles."

"If we can believe what some of those dying fellows said, the ones who went into Panem-Dea weren't illusions," Cabah replied. "A fair number of the officers there got themselves dissolved when they tried to stand and fight."

"What's happening here?" Krager asked, pointing at the screaming men bound to poles set up in the middle of the square.

"Scarpa's making examples of the ones who ran away. He's having them cut to pieces. Here comes Cyzada." Cabah pointed at the Styric hurrying out of Scarpa's headquarters.

"What are you *doing*?" the hollow-eyed Cyzada bellowed at the madman sitting on his cheap throne.

"They deserted their posts," Scarpa replied. "They're being punished."

"You need every man, you idiot!"

"I ordered them to march to the north to join my loyal armies." Scarpa shrugged. "They concocted lies to excuse their failure to obey. They must be punished. I *will* have obedience!"

"You will *not* kill your own soldiers! Order your butchers to stop!"

"That's quite impossible, Cyzada. An imperial order, once given, cannot be rescinded. I have commanded that every deserter from Panem-Dea be tortured to death. It's out of my hands now."

"You maniac! You won't have a soldier left by tomorrow morning! They'll *all* desert!"

"Then I will recruit more and hunt them all down. I *will* be obeyed!"

Cyzada of Esos controlled his fury with an obvious effort. Krager saw his lips moving and his fingers weaving intricate patterns in the air. "Let's get out of here, Cabah!" he said urgently.

"What? The crazy man ordered us all to watch."

"You don't want to watch what's going to happen next," Krager told him. "Cyzada's casting a spell—Zemoch, most likely. He's summoning a demon to teach our 'emperor' the real meaning of the word *obedience*."

"He can't do that. Zalasta left his son in charge here."

"No, actually Cyzada's in charge. I personally heard Zalasta tell that Styric who's wriggling his fingers right now to kill Scarpa the minute he stepped out of line. 'Course Cyzada might have something else in mind, but either way, it won't be pretty. I don't know about you, my friend, but *I'm* going to find someplace to hide. I've seen the kind of creatures that were subject to Azash before, and I'm feeling a little delicate this morning, so I don't want to see one again."

"We'll get into trouble, Krager."

"Not if the demon Cyzada's summoning right now eats Scarpa alive, we won't." Krager drew in a deep breath. "It's up to you, Cabah. Stay if you want, but I think I've seen as much as I want to of Natayos."

"You're going to desert?" Cabah was aghast.

"The situation's changed. If Sparhawk's allied himself with the Delphae, I want to be a long way from here when they come glowing out of that jungle. I find that I'm suddenly homesick for Eosia. Come or stay, Cabah, but *I'm* leaving—now."

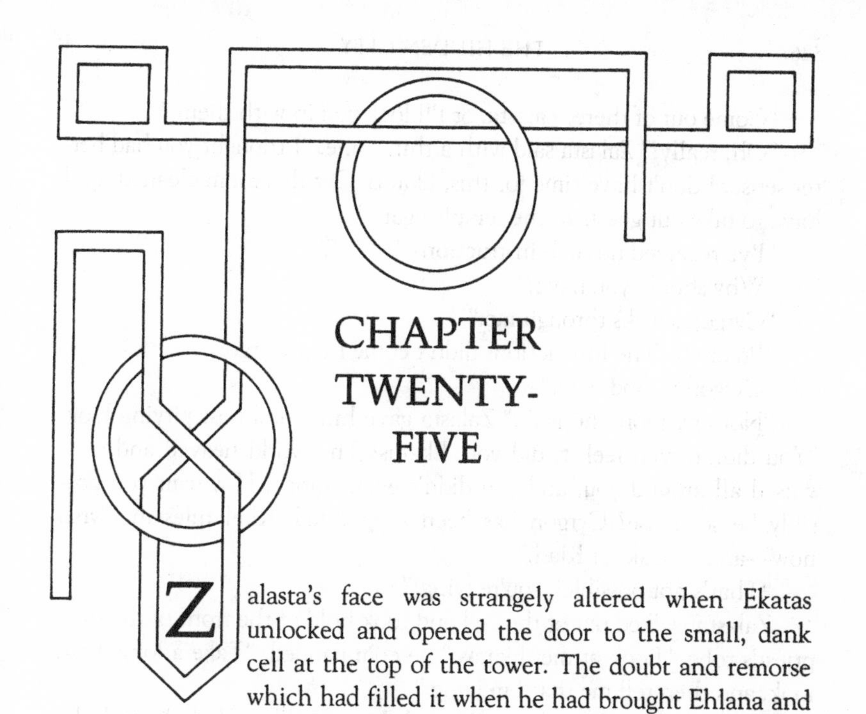

CHAPTER TWENTY-FIVE

Zalasta's face was strangely altered when Ekatas unlocked and opened the door to the small, dank cell at the top of the tower. The doubt and remorse which had filled it when he had brought Ehlana and Alean to Cyrga were gone, and the Styric's expression was now one of calm detachment. He took in the horrid little room at a glance. Ehlana and Alean were chained to the wall, and they were sitting on heaps of moldy straw that were supposed to serve as beds. Crude earthenware bowls filled with cold gruel sat untouched on the floor. "This won't do, Ekatas," Zalasta said in a remote kind of voice.

"It's really none of your concern," the high priest replied. "Prisoners are kept closely confined here in Cyrga." As always, Ekatas sneered when he spoke to Zalasta.

"Not *these* prisoners." Zalasta stepped into the cell and took up the chains that bound the two women to the wall. Then, showing no emotion, he crushed them into powdery rust. "The situation here has changed, Ekatas," he snapped, helping Ehlana to her feet. "Get this mess cleaned up."

Ekatas drew himself up. "I don't take orders from Styrics. I am the High Priest of Cyrgon."

"I'm truly sorry about this, your Majesty," Zalasta apologized to Ehlana. "My attention's been diverted for the past week or so. Evidently I didn't make my wishes clear to the Cyrgai. Please excuse me for a moment, and I'll correct that oversight." He turned back to Ekatas. "I told you to do something," he said in a dreadful voice. "Why haven't you started?"

"Come out of there, Zalasta, or I'll lock you in with them."

"Oh, really?" Zalasta said with a thin smile. "I thought you had better sense. I don't have time for this, Ekatas. Get this room cleaned up. I have to take our guests to the temple again."

"I've received no such instructions."

"Why should you have?"

"Cyrgon speaks through me."

"Precisely. The instructions didn't come from Cyrgon."

"Cyrgon is God here."

"Not any more, he isn't." Zalasta gave him an almost pitying look. "You didn't even feel it, did you, Ekatas? The world heaved and convulsed all around you, and you didn't even notice. How can you possibly be so dense? Cyrgon has been supplanted. Klæl rules in Cyrga now—and I speak for Klæl."

"That's not possible! You're lying!"

Zalasta walked out of the cell and took hold of the front of the high priest's robe. "Look at me, Ekatas," he commanded. "Take a long, hard look, and then tell me that I'm lying."

Ekatas struggled momentarily, and then, unable to help himself, he looked into Zalasta's eyes. The blood slowly drained from his face, and then he screamed. He screamed again, trying to tear himself free from the Styric's iron grasp. "I beg of you!" he cried out in a voice filled with horror, "No more! No more!" Then he sagged, covering his eyes with his hands.

Zalasta contemptuously let go of the front of his black robe, and he fell to the floor, weeping uncontrollably.

"Now do you understand?" Zalasta asked him, almost gently. "Cyzada and I tried to warn you and our petty Godling about the dangers involved in summoning Klæl, but you wouldn't listen. Cyrgon wanted to enslave Bhelliom, and now he's the slave of Bhelliom's opposite. And, since I speak for Klæl, I guess that makes you *my* slave." He prodded the weeping priest with one foot. "Get up, Ekatas! Get on your feet when your master speaks!"

The groveling priest scrambled to his feet, his tear-streaked face still filled with unspeakable horror.

"Say it, Ekatas," Zalasta said in a cruel voice. "I want to hear you say it—or would you like to witness the death of another star?"

"M-M-Master," the high priest choked.

"Again—a little louder, if you don't mind."

"Master!" It came out almost as a shriek.

"Much better, Ekatas. Now wake up those lazy cretins in the guard-room next door and put them to work cleaning this cell. We have preparations to make when I come back from the temple. Anakha's bringing Bhelliom to Cyrga, and we'll want to be ready when he arrives." He turned. "Bring your maid, Ehlana. Klæl wants to look at you." Zalasta paused, surveying her critically. "I know that we've treated you badly," he half apologized, "but don't let our bad manners break your spirit. Remember who you are and draw that about you. Klæl respects power and those who wield it."

"What do I say to him?"

"Nothing. He'll find out what he wants to know just by looking at you. He doesn't understand your husband, and seeing you will give him some hints about Anakha's nature. Anakha's the unknown element in this business. He always has been, I suppose. Klæl understands Bhelliom. It's Bhelliom's creature who baffles him."

"You've changed, Zalasta."

"I suppose I have," he admitted. "I have a feeling that I won't live much longer. Klæl's touch does peculiar things to people. We'd better not keep him waiting." He looked at Ekatas, who stood trembling violently. "I want this room clean when we come back."

"I'll see to it, Master," Ekatas promised in a grotesquely servile tone.

"How do you find them again?" Itagne asked curiously. "What I'm trying to get at is that the Trolls are in this 'No-Time,' but you and Tynian had to come out into real time in order to come into Sarna, so time started moving for you. How do you get back to the moment when you left the Trolls?"

"Please don't ask metaphysical questions, Itagne," Ulath replied with a pained expression. "We just go back to the spot where we left the Trolls, and there they are. We deal with *where* and let the Troll-Gods deal with *when*. They seem to be able to jump around in time without paying much attention to the rules."

"Where are the Trolls right now?"

"Just outside of town," Tynian replied. "We didn't think it was a good idea to bring them into Sarna with us. They're starting to get a little out of hand."

"Is it something we should know about, Tynian-Knight?" Engessa asked.

Ulath leaned back in his chair. "Cyrgon disrupted Trollish behavior rather profoundly when he went to Thalesia and posed as Ghworg," he explained somberly. "Zalasta told him about the Trolls, but Cyrgon's been a little out of touch, so he mistook the Trolls for the Dawn-men. The Dawn-men were herd animals, but the Trolls sort of run in packs. Herd animals will accept any member of their species, but pack animals are a little more selective. It's to our advantage right now to have the Trolls behave like a herd. At least we can keep them all going in the same direction, but some problems are starting to crop up. The packs are beginning to separate, and there's a great deal of snapping and snarling going on."

Tynian glanced at Queen Betuana, who, gowned all in black, was sitting somewhat apart from them. He motioned Engessa slightly to one side. "Is she all right?" he asked very quietly.

"Betuana-Queen is in ritual mourning," Engessa replied, also in a half whisper. "The loss of her husband has touched her very deeply."

"Were they really that close?"

"It did not seem so," Engessa admitted. His eyes were troubled as he looked at his melancholy queen. "The mourning ritual is seldom observed now. I am keeping careful watch over her. She must not be allowed to do herself injury." Engessa's shoulder muscles bunched.

Tynian was startled. "Is there any real danger of that?"

"It was not uncommon a few centuries ago," Engessa replied.

"We'd been expecting you earlier," Itagne was saying to Ulath. "As I understand it, *No-Time* means that the Trolls can go from one place to another almost instantaneously."

"Not quite instantaneously, Itagne. We've been a week or so getting here from the Tamul Mountains. We have to stop and go back into real time every so often so that they can hunt. Hungry Trolls aren't the best of traveling companions. So now, tell us, what's been happing? We can't make contact with Aphrael when we're in No-Time."

"Sparhawk's found some clues about the location of Cyrga," Itagne replied. "They aren't too precise, but he's going to try to follow them."

"How's Patriarch Bergsten coming?"

"He's captured Cynestra—had it handed to him on a plate, actually."

"Oh."

"Do you remember Atana Maris?"

"The pretty girl who commanded the garrison in Cynestra? The one who liked you?"

Itagne smiled. "That's the one. She's an abrupt sort of girl, and I'm quite fond of her, and when she saw Bergsten and the Church Knights approaching, she decided to present him with the city. She swept the streets clean of Cynesgan troops and opened the gates for Bergsten. She was going to give him King Jaluah's head as well, but he persuaded her not to."

"Pity," Ulath murmured, "but that's the sort of thing you have to expect when a good man gets religion."

"Vanion's in place," Itagne continued, "and he and Kring are establishing strongholds about a day's ride out into Cynesga. We're going to do the same here, but we thought we'd wait until you arrived first."

"Is anybody encountering any significant opposition?" Tynian asked.

"It's hard to say exactly," Itagne mused. "We're moving on central Cynesga, but Klæl's soldiers pop out of every crack between two rocks. The farther back we push them, the tighter they'll be concentrated. If we don't come up with a way to neutralize them, we'll have to carve our way through them, and from what Vanion tells me, they don't carve very well. Kring's tactics are working smoothly enough now, but when we get closer to Cyrga . . ." He spread his hands helplessly.

"We'll work something out," Ulath said. "Anything else?"

"It's all still sort of up in the air, Sir Ulath," Itagne replied. "The fairy stories Stragen and Caalador are hatching in Beressa are diverting most of the Cynesgan cavalry away from the eastern border. Half of them are running south toward the coast around Kaftal, and the other half are running north toward a little village called Zhubay. Caalador added an imaginary massing of the Atans up there to Stragen's illusory fleet off the southern coast. Between them, they've split the entire Cynesgan army in two and sent them off to chase moonbeams."

"You say that half of them are going north?" Tynian asked innocently.

"Toward Zhubay, yes. They seem to think the Atans are massing there for some reason."

"What an amazing thing," Ulath said with a straight face. "It just so happens that Tynian and I have been sort of drifting in that general direction anyway. Do you think the Cynesgans would be *too* disappointed if they came up against Trolls instead of Atans?"

"You could go up there and ask them, I suppose," Itagne replied, also with no hint of a smile. They all knew what was going to happen at Zhubay.

"Convey our apologies to them, Ulath-Knight," Betuana said with a sad little smile.

"Oh, we *will*, your Majesty," Ulath assured her, "*if* we can find any of them still in one piece after they've frolicked around with the Trolls for a couple of hours."

"Get out of there!" Kalten shouted, galloping his horse toward the doglike creatures clustered around something lying on the gravel floor of the desert. The beasts scampered away, hooting with soulless laughter.

"Are they dogs?" Talen asked in a sick voice.

"No," Mirtai replied shortly. "Hyenas."

Kalten rode back. "It's a man," he reported bleakly, "or what's left of one."

"We must bury him," Bevier said.

"They'd only dig him up again," Sparhawk told him. "Besides," he added, "if you start trying to bury them all, we'll be here for several lifetimes." He gestured at the bone-littered plain stretching off to the low range of black mountains lying to the west. He looked at Xanetia. "It was a mistake to bring you along, Anarae," he apologized. "This is going to get worse before it gets any better."

"It was not unexpected, Anakha," she replied.

Kalten looked up at the flock of vultures circling overhead. "Filthy brutes," he muttered.

Sparhawk raised up in his stirrups to peer ahead. "We've got a couple more hours until the sun goes down, but maybe we'd better pull back a mile or two and set up camp a little early. We'll have to spend *one* night out there. Let's not spend two."

"We need those pillars for landmarks anyway," Talen added, "and they're a lot brighter when the sun first comes up."

"That's *if* that bright spot we've been following really comes from those pillars," Kalten said dubiously.

"They got us here, didn't they? This *has* to be what Ogerajin called 'the Plain of Bones,' doesn't it? I admit, I had my own doubts right at first. Ogerajin was raving so much of the time that I was sure that he'd garbled at least some of the directions, but he hasn't led us astray yet."

"We still haven't seen the city, Talen," Kalten reminded him, "so I'd sort of hold off on composing the letter of thanks."

"I've got all the money I'll ever need, Orden," Krager said expansively, leaning back in his chair and looking out through the window at the buildings and the harbor of the port city of Delo. He took another drink of wine.

"I wouldn't go around announcing that, Krager," the burly Orden advised, "particularly not here on the waterfront."

"I've hired some bodyguards, Orden. Can you ask around and find out if there's a fast ship leaving for Zenga in Cammoria in the next week or so?"

"Why would anybody want to go to Zenga?"

"I grew up there, and I'm homesick," Krager replied with a shrug. "Besides, I'd sort of like to grind a few faces—all the people who said that I'd come to no good end while I was growing up."

"Did you happen to come across a fellow named Ezek while you were in Natayos?" Orden asked. "I think he's a Deiran."

"The name rings a bell. I think he was working for the fellow who ran the tavern."

"I sent him down there," Orden explained, "him and the other two—Col and Shallag. They were going to see if they could join Narstil's band of outlaws."

"They may have, but they were working in the tavern when I left."

"It's none of my business, but if you were doing so well in Natayos, why did you leave?"

"Instincts, Orden," Krager replied owlishly. "I get this cold little feeling at the base of my skull, and I know that it's time to run. Have you ever heard of a man named Sparhawk?"

"You mean Prince Sparhawk? Everybody's heard of him. He's got quite a reputation."

"Oh, yes. That he does. Anyway, Sparhawk's been looking for an opportunity to kill me for twenty years or so, and that's the sort of thing that puts a very fine edge on a man's instincts." Krager took another long drink.

"You might want to give some thought to drying out for a while," Orden advised, looking meaningfully at Krager's tankard of Arcian red. "I run a tavern, and I've learned to recognize the signs. Your liver's starting to go on you, my friend. Your eyeballs are turning yellow."

"I'll cut down once I get out to sea."

"I think you'll have to do more than just cut down, Krager. You're going to have to give it up entirely if you want to go on living. Believe me, you *don't* want to die the way most drunkards do. I knew one who screamed for three straight weeks before he finally died. It was awful."

"There's nothing wrong with my liver," Krager said truculently. "It's just the funny light in here. When I get out to sea, I'll space out my drinks. I'll be all right." His face had a haunted expression, however, and the mere mention of giving up strong drink had set his hands to trembling violently.

Orden shrugged. He *had* tried to warn the man. "It's up to you, Krager," he said. "I'll ask around and see if I can find a ship that'll get you out of Prince Sparhawk's reach."

"Soon, Orden. Soon." Krager held out his tankard. "In the meantime, why don't we have another?"

Ekrasios and his party of Delphae reached Norenja late in the afternoon on a murky day when heavy clouds hung low over the treetops and there was not a breath of air moving. Ekrasios took his boyhood friend, Adras, and crept forward through the tangle of brush and vines to the edge of the clearing to survey the ruin.

"Thinkest thou that they will offer resistance?" Adras asked quietly.

"That is difficult to predict," Ekrasios replied. "Anakha and his companions have advised that these rebels are but poorly trained. Methinks their response to our sudden appearance will depend on the character of their officers. Better that we leave them a clear path to the surrounding forest. Should we encircle them, desperation will impel them to fight."

Adras nodded. "They have made some effort to repair the gates," he said, pointing at the entrance to the city.

"The gates will pose no problem. I will instruct thee and our companions in the spell which doth modify the curse of Edaemus. Those newly made gates are constructed of wood, and wood is as susceptible to decay as is flesh." He looked up at the dirty grey clouds. "Canst thou make any estimate as to the time of day?"

"No more than two hours until dusk," Adras replied.

"Let us proceed, then. We must find yet another gate to provide means of escape for those whom we would confront this night."

"And if there be none other?"

"Then those who would escape must find their own way. I am reluctant to unleash the full force of the curse of Edaemus. Should necessity compel me to it, however, I will not shrink from that stern duty. Should they flee, well and good. Should they choose to stay and fight, we will do what we must. I do assure thee, Adras, that when tomorrow's sun rises, none living shall remain within the walls of Norenja."

"Good God!" Berit exclaimed, peering over the edge of the dry gully at the huge soldiers in close-fitting armor running westward across the sun-baked gravel. "They're *monsters*!"

"Keep your voice down," Khalad cautioned. "There's no way of knowing how good their ears are."

The strange, bestial soldiers were larger than Atans, and their burnished steel breastplates fit their torsos snugly, outlining each muscle. They wore helmets adorned with fanciful horns or wings, and the visors of those helmets were individualized, evidently forged to fit each warrior's face. They ran westward in a sort of ragged formation, and their hoarse gasping was clearly audible even at this distance.

"Where are they going?" Berit demanded. "The border's off in the other direction."

"That one who's trailing along behind the others has a broken-off javelin sticking out of him," Khalad replied. "I'd say that means that they've come up against Tikume's Peloi. They've already been to the border, and now they're coming back."

"Back to where?" Berit was baffled. "Where can they go? They can't breathe here."

Khalad cautiously poked his head above the rim of the gully and squinted out across the rocky desert. "They seem to be going toward that cluster of hills about a mile to the west." He paused. "Just how curious are we feeling today, Berit?"

"What have you got in mind?"

"This gully comes down out of those hills, and if we follow it and keep our heads down, they won't see us. Why don't we drift off toward the west? We might find out something useful if we tag along behind those fellows."

Berit shrugged. "Why not?"

"That's really not a very logical answer, Berit. I can think of a half-dozen reasons why not." Khalad squinted at the panting soldiers lurching across the desert. "Let's do it anyway, though."

They slid back down into the gully and led their horses along the dry watercourse toward the west.

They moved quietly along the bottom of the wash for about a quarter of an hour. "Are they still out there?" Berit whispered.

"I'll look." Khalad carefully climbed back up the steep bank to the rim of the gully and eased his head up far enough to look. Then he slid back down again. "They're still staggering toward the hills," he reported. "This gully starts getting shallower up ahead. Let's leave the horses here."

They crept along, crouched over to stay out of sight, and as the gully started to run uphill, they found that they were forced to crawl on their hands and knees.

Khalad rose slightly to look again. "They seem to be swinging around behind that other hill," he said quietly. "Let's slip up to the top of this ridge and see what's back there."

The two of them crawled out of the now-shallow wash and slanted their way up to the ridgeline to a point from which they could see what lay behind the hill Khalad had pointed out.

It was a kind of shallow basin nestled down among the three hills that heaved up out of the surrounding desert. The basin was empty.

"Where did they go?" Berit whispered.

"That basin was the place they were making for," Khalad insisted with a puzzled frown. "Wait. Here comes that one with the javelin in his belly."

They watched the wounded soldier stumble into the basin, half falling, then rising again to drag himself along. He raised his masked face and bellowed something.

Khalad and Berit waited tensely.

Then two other soldiers emerged from a narrow opening in the side of one of the hills, descended to the floor of the basin, and half dragged their injured comrade back up the hill and through the mouth of the cave.

"That answers that," Khalad said. "They ran across miles of open desert to get to that cave."

"Why? What good will it do them?"

"I haven't got a clue, Berit, but I think it's important." Khalad stood up. "Let's go back to where we left the horses. We can still cover a few more miles before the sun goes down."

Ekrasios crouched at the edge of the forest waiting for the torches inside the walls of Norenja to burn down and for the sounds of human activity to subside. The events at Panem-Dea had confirmed the assessment of these rebels Lord Vanion had given him at Sarna. Given the slightest opportunity, these poorly trained soldiers would flee, and that suited Ekrasios very well. He was still somewhat reluctant to unleash the curse of Edaemus, and people who ran away did not have to be destroyed.

Adras returned, ghosting back to the edge of the jungle through the night mist. "All is in readiness, Ekrasios," he reported quietly. "The gates will crumble at the merest touch."

"Let us then proceed," Ekrasios replied, standing up and relaxing the rigid control that dimmed his inner light. "Let us pray that all within yon walls may flee."

"And if they do not?"

"Then they must surely die. Our promise to Anakha binds us. We *will* empty yon ruin—in one fashion or the other."

"It's not so bad here," Kalten said as they dismounted. "The bones are older, for one thing." Necessity had compelled them to camp in the hideous boneyard the previous night, and they were all eager to reach the end of the horror.

Sparhawk grunted, looking across the intervening stretch of desert at the fractured basalt cliff that seemed to mark the eastern edge of the Forbidden Mountains. The sun had just come up above the eastern horizon, and its brilliant light reflected back from the pair of quartz-laced peaks rearing up out of the rusty black mountains just to the west.

"Why are we stopping here?" Mirtai asked. "That cliff's still a quarter of a mile away."

"I think we're supposed to line up on those two peaks," Sparhawk replied. "Talen, can you remember Ogerajin's exact words?"

"Let's see." The boy frowned in concentration. Then he nodded shortly. "I've got it now," he said.

"How do you do that?" Bevier asked him curiously.

Talen shrugged. "There's a trick to it. You don't think about the words. You just concentrate on where you were when you heard them." He lifted his face slightly, closed his eyes, and began to recite. " 'Beyond the Plain of Bones wilt thou come to the Gates of Illusion behind which lies concealed the Hidden City of Cyrga. The eye of mortal man cannot perceive those gates. Stark they stand as a fractured wall at the verge of the Forbidden Mountains to bar thy way. Bend thine eye, however, upon Cyrgon's two white pillars and direct thy steps toward the emptiness which doth lie between them. Trust not the evidence which thine eye doth present unto thee, for the solid-seeming wall is as mist and will not bar thy way.' "

"That didn't even sound like your own voice," Bevier said.

"That's part of the trick," Talen explained. "That was Ogerajin's voice—sort of."

"All right, then," Sparhawk said. "Let's see if he really knew what he was talking about." He squinted at the two brilliant points of reflected light. "There are the pillars." He took a few steps to the right and shook his head. "From here they merge into one light." Then he walked to the left. "It does the same thing here." Then he went back to his original location. "This is the spot," he said with a certain amount of excitement. "Those two peaks are very close together. If you move a few feet either way, you can't even see that gap between them. Unless you're really looking for it, you could miss it altogether."

"Oh, that's just fine, Talen," Kalten said sarcastically. "If we go any closer, the cliff will block off our view of the peaks."

Talen rolled his eyes upward.

"What?" Kalten asked.

"Just start walking toward the cliff, Kalten. Sparhawk can stand here and keep his eyes on the gap. He'll tell you whether to go to the right or the left."

"Oh." Kalten looked around at the others. "Don't make an issue of it," he told them. Then he started off toward the cliff.

"Veer to the right," Sparhawk told him.

Kalten nodded and changed direction.

"Too far. Back to the left a little."

The blond Pandion continued toward the cliff, altering his direction in response to Sparhawk's shouted commands. When he reached the cliff, he went along slapping his hands on the face of the rock. Then he drew his heavy dagger, stuck it into the ground, and started back.

"Well?" Sparhawk called when he had covered half the distance.

"Ogerajin didn't know what he was talking about," Kalten shouted.

Sparhawk swore.

"Do you mean there's no opening?" Talen called.

"Oh, the opening's there, all right," Kalten replied, "but it's at least five feet to the left of where your crazy man said it would be."

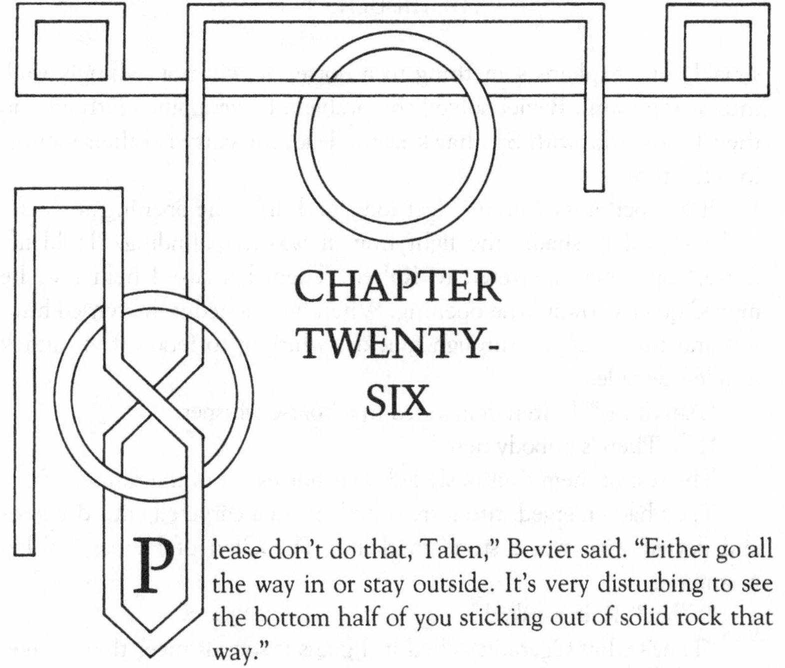

CHAPTER TWENTY-SIX

Please don't do that, Talen," Bevier said. "Either go all the way in or stay outside. It's very disturbing to see the bottom half of you sticking out of solid rock that way."

"It's not solid, Bevier." The boy stuck his hand into the rock and pulled it out again to demonstrate.

"Well, it *looks* solid. Please, Talen, in or out. Don't hover in between."

"Can you feel anything at all when you poke your head through?" Mirtai asked.

"It's a little cooler in there," Talen replied. "It's a sort of cave or tunnel. There's a light at the far end."

"Can we get the horses through?" Sparhawk asked.

Talen nodded. "It's big enough for that—if we go through in single file. I guess Cyrgon wanted to keep down the chances of anybody accidentally discovering the opening."

"You'd better let me go first," Sparhawk said. "There might be guards at the other end."

"I'll be right behind you," Kalten said, retrieving his dagger and drawing his sword.

" 'Tis a most clever illusion," Xanetia observed, touching the rock face on the left of the gate. "Seamless and indistinguishable from reality."

"It's been good enough to hide Cyrga for ten thousand years, I guess," Talen said.

"Let's go in," Sparhawk said. "I want to have a look at this place."

There was difficulty with the horses, of course. No matter how reasonably one explains something to a horse, he will not willingly walk into a stone wall. Bevier solved the problem by wrapping cloth around their heads, and, with Sparhawk in the lead, the party led their mounts into the tunnel.

It was perhaps a hundred feet long, and since the opening at the far end was still in shade, the light from it was not blinding. "Hold my horse," Sparhawk muttered to Kalten. Then, his sword held low, he moved quietly toward the opening. When he reached it, he tensed himself and then stepped through quickly, whirling to fend off an attack from either side.

"Anything?" Kalten demanded in a hoarse whisper.

"No. There's nobody here."

The rest of them cautiously led their horses out of the tunnel.

They had emerged into a tree-shaded swale carpeted with dry grass and dotted with white stone markers. "The Glen of Heroes," Talen murmured.

"What?" Kalten asked.

"That's what Ogerajin called it. I guess it sounds nicer than 'graveyard.' The Cyrgai seem to treat their own dead a little better than they do the slaves."

Sparhawk looked across the extensive cemetery. He pointed to the western side where a slight rise marked the edge of the burial ground. "Let's go," he told his friends. "I want to see just exactly what we're up against."

They crossed the cemetery to the bottom of the rise, tied their horses to the trees growing there, and carefully crept to the top.

The basin was significantly lower than the floor of the surrounding desert, and there was a fair-sized lake nestled in the center, dark and unreflective in the morning shadows. The lake was surrounded by winter-fallow fields, and a forest of dark trees stretched up the slopes of the basin. There was a sort of rigid tidiness about it all, as if nature itself had been coerced into straight lines and precise angles. Centuries of brutal labor had been devoted to hammering what might have been a place of beauty into a stern reflection of the mind of Cyrgon himself.

The hidden valley was perhaps five miles across, and on the far side stood the city that had remained concealed for ten eons. The surrounding mountains had provided the building materials, and the city wall and the buildings within were constructed of that same brownish-black volcanic basalt. The exterior walls were high and massive, and a steep, conelike hill, its sides thickly covered with buildings, rose inside those walls. Surmounting that hill was yet another walled enclosure with black spires rising on one side and, in startling contrast to the rest of the city, white spires on the other.

"It's not particularly creative," Bevier observed critically. "The architect doesn't seem to have had much imagination."

"Imagination was not a trait encouraged amongst the Cyrgai, Sir Knight," Xanetia told him.

"We could swing around the sides of the basin and get closer," Kalten suggested. "The trees would hide us. The ground around the lake doesn't offer much concealment."

"We've got some time," Sparhawk said. "Let's get away from the mouth of this tunnel. If it's the only way in or out of the valley, there's bound to be traffic going through here. I can see people working in those fields down there—slaves, most likely. There'll be Cyrgai watching them, and there may be patrols as well. Let's see if we can pick up some kind of routine before we blunder into anything."

Berit and Khalad made a dry camp in another cluster of jumbled boulders two days west of the place where they had seen the strange soldiers. They watered their horses sparingly, built no fire, and ate cold rations. Khalad spoke very little, but sat instead staring moodily out at the desert.

"Quit worrying at it, Khalad," Berit told him.

"It's right in front of my face, Berit. I know it is, but I just can't put my finger on it."

"Do you want to talk it out? Neither one of us is going to get any sleep if you spend the whole night wrestling with it."

"I can brood quietly."

"No, actually you can't. We've been together too long, my friend. I can hear you thinking."

Khalad smiled faintly. "It has to do with those creatures," he said.

"Really? I never would have guessed. That's all you've been thinking about for the past two days. What did you want to know about them—aside from the fact that they're big, ugly, savage, and they've got yellow blood?"

"That's the part that's nagging at me—that yellow blood. Aphrael says that it's because they breathe with their livers. They do that because what they're used to breathing isn't air. They can get along here for a little while, but when they start exerting themselves, they start to fall apart. The ones we saw the other day weren't just running around aimlessly out there in the desert. They had a specific destination in mind."

"That cave? You think it might be a haven for them?"

"*Now* we're starting to get somewhere," Khalad said, his face growing intent. "The Peloi are probably the best light cavalry in the world, but Klæl's soldiers are almost as big as Trolls, and they seem to be able to ignore wounds that would kill one of us. I don't think they're running from the Peloi."

"No. They're trying to run away from the air."

Khalad snapped his fingers. "*That's it!*" he exclaimed. "*That's* why they break off and run back to those caves. They aren't hiding from the Peloi. They're hiding from the air."

"Air is air, Khalad—whether it's out in the open or inside a cave."

"I don't think so, Berit. I think Klæl has filled that cave with the kind of air his soldiers are used to breathing. He can't change all the air on the whole world, because it would kill the Cyrgai as well as all the rest of us, and Cyrgon won't let him do that. He *can* fill a cave with that other kind of air, though. It'd be the perfect place. It's closed-in and more or less airtight. It gives those monsters a place to go when they start to get winded. They can rest up in there and then come back out and fight some more. You'd better pass this on, Berit. Aphrael can let the others know that Klæl's soldiers are hiding out in caves because they can breathe there."

"I'll tell her," Berit said dubiously. "I'm not sure what good it's going to do us, but I'll tell her."

Khalad leaned back on his elbows with a broad grin. "You're not thinking, Berit. If something's giving you problems, and it's hiding out in a cave, you don't have to go in after it. All you have to do is collapse the entrance. Once it's trapped inside, you can forget about it. Why don't you pass this on to Aphrael? Suggest that she tell the others to collapse every cave they come across. She won't even have to do it herself." Then he frowned again.

"What's wrong now?"

"That was too easy," Khalad told him, "and it doesn't really help all that much. As big as those beasts are, you could collapse a whole mountain on them, and they could still dig their way out. There's something else that hasn't quite come together yet." He held up one hand. "I'll get it," he promised. "I'll get it if it takes me all night."

Berit groaned.

"I have decided to go with you, Bergsten-Priest," Atana Maris replied haltingly in heavily accented Elenic. She had come up from behind their column when they were five days south of Cynestra.

Bergsten suppressed an oath. "We're an army on the move, Atana Maris," he tried to explain diplomatically. "We wouldn't be able to make suitable arrangements for your comfort or safety when we stop for the night."

"Arrangements?" She looked at Neran, the translator, with a puzzled expression.

Neran spoke at some length in Tamul, and the tall girl burst out laughing.

"What's so funny, Atana?" Bergsten asked suspiciously.

"That you would worry about *that*, Bergsten-Priest. I am a soldier. I can defend myself against any of your men who admire me too much."

"Why have you decided to come along with us, Atana Maris?" Heldin stepped in.

"I had a thought after you left Cynestra, Heldin-Knight," she replied. "It has been in my mind for much weeks now to go find Itagne-Ambassador. You are going to the place where he will be, so I will go with you."

"We could carry a message to him for you, Atana. You don't really have to go along."

She shook her head. "No, Heldin-Knight. It is a personal matter between Itagne-Ambassador and me. He was friendly to me when he was in Cynestra. Then he had to go away, but he said to me that he would write letters to me. He did not do that. Now I must go find him to make sure that he is well." Her eyes went hard. "If he *is* well, I must know if he does not want to be friendly to me any more." She sighed. "I hope much that his feelings have not changed. I would not want to have to kill him."

"I want no part of this," Gahenas said abruptly, standing up and giving the rest of them a reproving look. "I was willing to join with you if it meant tweaking Cieronna's nose, but I'm not going to involve myself in treason."

"Who said anything about treason, Gahenas?" Chacole asked her. "There won't be any *real* danger to our husband. We're just going to make it *appear* that there's a plot against him—and we're going to plant enough evidence to lay the plot at Cieronna's door. If something *were* to happen to Sarabian, the crown prince would be elevated to the imperial throne, and Cieronna would be regent—which none of us want to happen. No, we'll expose her plot before anything really happens, so she'll be discredited—probably imprisoned—and we won't have to kowtow to her any more."

"I don't care what you say, Chacole," the jug-eared Tegan empress declared flatly. "You're putting something in motion that's treasonous, and I won't be a party to it. I'm going to keep an eye on you, Chacole. Dismiss your spies and drop this wild scheme at once, because if you don't . . ." Gahenas left it hanging ominously in the air as she turned on her heel and stalked away.

"That was very clumsy, Chacole," Elysoun drawled, carefully selecting a piece of fruit from the silver platter on the table. "She might have gone along if you hadn't gone into such detail. She didn't *have* to know that you were actually going to send out your assassins. You weren't really sure of her yet, and you went too fast."

"I'm running out of time, Elysoun." Chacole's tone was desperate.

"I don't see the need for all this urgency," Elysoun replied, "and how much time did you save today? That Tegan hag's going to be watching your every move now. You blundered, Chacole. Now you're going to have to kill her."

"*Kill?*" Chacole's face went white.

"Unless you don't mind losing your head. One word from Gahenas can send you to the block. You aren't really cut out for men's politics, dear. You talk too much." Elysoun rose lazily to her feet. "We can discuss this later," she said. "I have an enthusiastic young guardsman waiting for me, and I wouldn't want him to cool off." She sauntered away.

Elysoun's casual attitude concealed a great deal of urgency. Chacole's Cynesgan upbringing had made her painfully obvious. She had drawn on the hatred of Sarabian's other wives for Empress Cieronna. That part was clever enough, but the elaborate, involved story of staging an imitation assassination attempt was ridiculously excessive. Very clearly the attempt was *not* designed to fail, as Chacole and Torellia so piously proclaimed. Elysoun began to walk faster. She had to get to her husband in order to warn him that his life was in immediate danger.

"Xanetia!" Kalten said, starting back in surprise as the Anarae suddenly appeared in their midst that evening, "can't you cough or something before you do that?"

"It was not mine intent to startle thee, my protector," she apologized.

"My nerves are strung a little tight right now," he said.

"Did you have any luck?" Mirtai asked.

"I gleaned much, Atana Mirtai." Xanetia paused, collecting her thoughts. "The slaves are not closely watched," she began, "and their supervision is given over to Cynesgan overseers, for such menial tasks are beneath the dignity of the Cyrgai. The desert itself doth confine the slaves. Those foolish enough to attempt escape inevitably perish in that barren waste."

"What's the customary routine, Anarae," Bevier asked her.

"The slaves emerge from their pens at dawn," she replied, "and, unbidden and unguarded, leave the city to take up their tasks. Then, at sunset, still uncommanded and scarce noticed, they return to the city and to the slave pens for feeding. They are then chained and locked in their pens for the night, to be released again at first light of day."

"Some of them are up here in these woods," Mirtai noted, peering out through the trees that concealed them. "What are they supposed to be doing?"

"They cut firewood for their masters in this extensive forest. The Cyrgai warm themselves with fires in the chill of winter. The kenneled slaves must endure the weather."

"Were you able to get any sense of how the city's laid out, Anarae?" Bevier asked her.

"Some, Sir Knight." She beckoned them to the edge of the trees so that they could look across the valley at the black-walled city. "The Cyrgai themselves live on the slopes of the hill which doth rise within the walls," she explained, "and they do hold themselves aloof from the more mundane portion of the city below. There is yet another wall within the outer one, and that inner wall doth protect Cyrgon's Chosen from contact with inferior races. The lower city doth contain the slave pens, the warehouses for foodstuffs, and the barracks of the Cynesgans who oversee the slaves and man the outer wall. As thou canst see, there is yet that final wall which doth enclose the summit of the hill. Within *that* ultimate wall lieth the palace of King Santheocles and the Temple of Cyrgon."

Bevier nodded. "It's fairly standard for a fortified town, then."

"If thou wert aware of all this, why didst thou ask, Sir Knight?" she asked tartly.

"Confirmation, dear lady," he replied, smiling. "The city's ten thousand years old. They might have had different ideas about how to build a fort before the invention of modern weapons." He squinted across the valley at walled Cyrga. "They're obviously willing to sacrifice the lower city," he said. "Otherwise that outer wall would be defended by Cyrgai. The fact that they've turned that chore over to the Cynesgans means that they don't place much value on those warehouses and slave pens. The wall at the foot of 'Mount Cyrgon' will be more fiercely defended, and if necessary, they'll pull back up the hill to that last wall that encloses the palace and the temple."

"All of this is well and good, Bevier," Kalten interrupted him, "but where are Ehlana and Alean?"

Bevier gave him a surprised look. "Up on top, of course," he replied, "either in the palace or in the temple."

"How did you arrive at that?"

"They're hostages, Kalten. When you're holding hostages, you have to keep them close enough to threaten them when your enemies get too close. *Our* problem is how to get into the city."

"We'll come up with something," Sparhawk said confidently. "Let's go back into the woods a ways and set up for the night."

They moved back among the trees and ate cold rations, since a fire was out of the question.

"The problem's still there, Sparhawk," Kalten said as evening settled over the hidden valley. "How are we going to get inside all those walls?"

"The first wall's easy," Talen said. "We just walk in through the gate."

"How do you propose to do that without being challenged?" Kalten demanded.

"People walk out of the city every morning and back again every evening, don't they?"

"Those are slaves."

"Exactly."

Kalten stared at him.

"We want to get into the city, don't we? That's the easiest way."

"What about the other walls?" Bevier objected.

"One wall at a time, Sir Knight," Talen said gaily, "one wall at a time. Let's get through the outer one first. *Then* we'll worry about the other two."

Daiya the Peloi came riding hard back across the gravelly desert about midmorning the next day. "We've found them, your Reverence," he reported to Bergsten as he reined in. "The Cynesgan cavalry tried to lead us away from where they're hiding, but we found them anyway. They're in those hills just ahead of us."

"More of those big ones with masks on their faces?" Heldin asked.

"Some of those, friend Heldin," Daiya replied, "but there are others as well—wearing old-fashioned helmets and carrying spears."

"Cyrgai," Bergsten grunted. "Vanion mentioned them. Their tactics are so archaic that they won't be much of a problem."

"Where exactly are they, friend Daiya?" Heldin asked.

"They're in a large canyon on the east side of those hills, friend Heldin. My scouts saw them from the canyon rim."

"We definitely don't want to go into that canyon after them, your Grace," Heldin cautioned. "They're infantry, and close quarters are made to order for their tactics. We'll have to devise some way to get them to come out into the open."

Atana Maris asked Neran a question in Tamul, and he replied at some length. She nodded, spoke briefly to him, and then she ran off toward the south.

"Where's she going?" Bergsten demanded.

"She said that your enemies have laid a trap for you, your Grace," Neran replied with a shrug. "She's going to go spring it."

"Stop her, Heldin!" Bergsten said sharply.

It must be said in Sir Heldin's defense that he *did* try to catch up to the lithe, fleet-footed Atan girl, but she merely glanced back over her shoulder, laughed, and ran even faster, leaving him far behind, flogging at his horse and muttering curses.

Bergsten's curses were *not* muttered. He blistered the air around him. "What is she *doing*?" he demanded of Neran.

"They're planning an ambush, your Grace," Neran replied calmly. "It won't work if somebody sees them hiding in that canyon. Atana Maris is going to run into the canyon, let them see her, and then run out again. They'll have to try to catch her. That'll bring them out into the open. You might want to give some thought to picking up your pace just a bit. She'll be terribly disappointed in you if you're not in position when she leads them out."

Patriarch Bergsten looked out across the desert at the golden Atana running smoothly to the south with her long black hair flying behind her. Then he swore again, rose up in his stirrups, and bellowed, "Charge!"

Ekrasios and his comrades reached Synaqua late in the afternoon just as the sun broke through the heavy cloud cover that had obscured the sky for the past several days.

The ruins of Synaqua were in much greater disrepair than had been the case with Panem-Dea and Norenja. The entire east wall had been undercut by one of the numerous streams that flowed sluggishly through the soggy delta of the Arjun River, and it had collapsed at some unknown time in the past. When Scarpa's rebels had moved in to occupy the ruin, they had replaced it with a log palisade. The construction was shoddy, and the palisade was not particularly imposing.

Ekrasios considered that as he sat alone moodily watching the sun sinking into a cloud bank off to the west. A serious problem had arisen following their disastrous assault on Norenja. It had *seemed* that there were many gates through which the panic-stricken rebels could flee, but their commander had blocked off those gates with heaps of rubble as a part of his defenses. The terrified soldiers had been trapped inside the walls, and had therefore had no choice but to turn and fight. Hundreds had died in unspeakable agony before Ekrasios had been able to divert his men into the uninhabited parts of the ruin so that the escape route through the main gate was open. Many of the Delphae had wept openly at the horror they had been forced to inflict on men who were essentially no more than misguided peasants. It had taken Ekrasios two days and all of his eloquence to keep half his men from abandoning the cause and returning immediately to Delphaeus.

Adras, Ekrasios' boyhood friend and his second-in-command, was among the most profoundly disturbed. Adras now avoided his leader whenever possible, and what few communications that passed between them were abrupt and official. And so it was that Ekrasios was somewhat surprised when Adras came to him unsummoned in the ruddy glow of that fiery sunset.

"A word with thee, Ekrasios?" he asked tentatively.

"Of course, Adras. Thou knowest that it is not needful for thee to ask."

"I must advise thee that I will not participate in this night's work."

"We are bound by our pledge to Anakha, Adras," Ekrasios reminded him. "Our Anari hath sworn to this, and we are obliged to honor his oath."

"I cannot, Ekrasios!" Adras cried, sudden tears streaming down his face. "I cannot *bear* what I have done and must do again should I enter yon city. Surely Edaemus did not intend for us so to use his dreadful gift."

There were a dozen arguments Ekrasios might have raised, but he knew in his heart that they were all spurious. "I will not insist, Adras. That would not be the act of a friend." He sighed. "I am no less unquiet than thou, I do confess. We are not suited for war, Adras, and the curse of Edaemus makes *our* way of making war more horrible than the casual bloodletting of other races. Since we are not fiends, the horror doth tear at our souls." He paused. "Thou art not alone in this resolve, art thou, Adras? There are others as well, are there not?"

Adras nodded mutely.

"How many?"

"Close on to an hundred and fifty, my friend."

Ekrasios was shaken. Quite nearly a third of his force had literally defected. "You trouble me, Adras," he said. "I *will* not command thee to forswear the dictates of thy conscience, but thine absence and that of they who feel similarly constrained do raise doubts about our possible success this night. Let me think on't." He began to pace up and down in the muddy forest clearing, considering various possibilities. "We may yet salvage some measure of victory this night," he said finally. "Let me probe the extent of thy reluctance, my friend. I do concede that thou canst not in conscience enter the ruin which doth lie before us, but wilt thou abandon me utterly?"

"Never, Ekrasios."

"I thank thee, Adras. Yet mayest thou and thy fellows further our design without injury to thy sensibilities. As we discovered at Norenja, the curse of Edaemus extends its effects to things other than flesh."

"Truly," Adras agreed. "The gates of that mournful ruin did collapse in decay at our merest touch."

"The east wall of Synaqua is constructed of logs. Might I prevail upon thee and thy fellows to pull it down whilst I and the remainer of our force do enter the city?"

The mind of Adras was quick. His sudden grin erased the estrangement that had marred their friendship for the past several days. "Thou wert born to command, Ekrasios," he said warmly. "My friends and I will most happily perform this task. Do thou and thy cohorts enter Synaqua by the front gate whilst I and mine do open a huge back gate to the east, that they who reside within yon city may freely depart. Both ends are thus served."

"Well said, Adras," Ekrasios approved. "Well said."

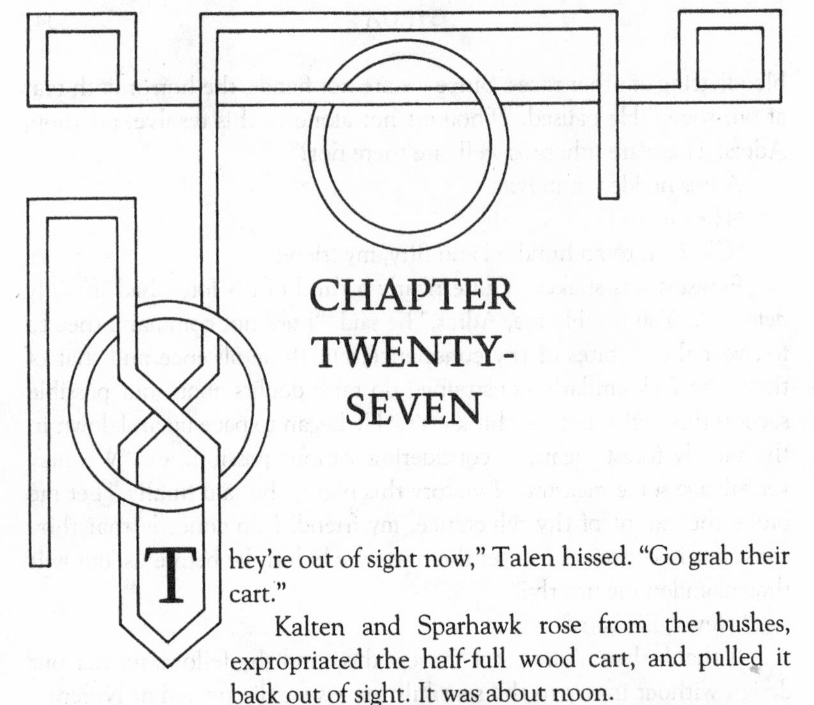

CHAPTER TWENTY-SEVEN

They're out of sight now," Talen hissed. "Go grab their cart."

Kalten and Sparhawk rose from the bushes, expropriated the half-full wood cart, and pulled it back out of sight. It was about noon.

"I still think this is a really stupid idea," Kalten grumbled. "Assuming that we don't get stopped when we try to go through the gate, how are we going to unload our weapons and mail shirts without being seen? And how are we going to get out of the slave pen to pick them up?"

"Trust me."

"This boy's making me old, Sparhawk," Kalten complained.

"We might be able to pull it off, Kalten," Bevier said. "Xanetia told us that the Cynesgan overseers don't pay much attention to the slaves. Right now, though, we'd better get this cart away from here before the fellows it belongs to come back and find that it's gone."

They pulled the wobbly, two-wheeled cart along the narrow track toward the spot where Xanetia and Mirtai were concealed in the bushes. "Lo," Mirtai said dryly from her hiding place, "our heroes return with the spoils of war."

"I love you, little sister," Sparhawk retorted, "but you've got an overly clever mouth. Kalten's got a point, Talen. The Cynesgan overseers themselves might be too stupid to notice what we're doing, but the other slaves probably will, and the first one to open his mouth about it will probably get a lot of attention."

"I'm a-workin' on that port, Sporhawk," the boy replied. He dropped to his knees and scrutinized the underside of the cart. "No problem," he said confidently, rising and brushing dirt off his bare knees. They had modified the Cynesgan robes they had bought in Vigayo by removing the sleeves and hoods and cutting the tails off just above the knees. The resulting garments now resembled the smocks worn by the slaves who labored in the fields and woods surrounding Cyrga.

While the rest of them fanned out through the woods to pilfer firewood from the stacks cut by the slaves, Talen remained behind, working at something on the underside of the cart. They had amassed a sizable pile by the time he had finished. Sparhawk returned once more with an armload of wood to find the boy just finishing up. "Do you want to take a look at this, Sparhawk?" he asked from under the cart.

Sparhawk knelt to examine the young thief's handiwork. Talen had wedged the ends of slender tree limbs between the floorboards of the cart, then had woven them into a shallow basket that fit snugly under the bottom of the stolen conveyance. "Are you sure it won't come apart if we hit a bump?" he asked dubiously. "It might be a little embarrassing to have all our weapons and our mail come spilling out just as we're passing through the gate."

"I'll ride in it myself, if you want," Talen replied.

Sparhawk grunted. "Tie the swords together so that they won't rattle, and stuff grass in around the shirts to muffle the clinking."

"Yes, O Glorious Leader. And how many other things that I already know did you want to tell me?"

"Just do it, Talen. Don't make clever speeches."

"I'm not trying to be offensive, Mirtai," Kalten was saying. "It's just that your legs are prettier than mine."

Mirtai lifted the bottom of her smock a little and looked critically at her long, golden legs. Then she squinted at Kalten's. "They are rather, aren't they?"

"What I'm getting at is that they won't be quite as noticeable if you smear some mud on them. I don't think the gate guards are blind, and if one of them sees the dimples on your knees, he'll probably realize that you aren't a man, and he might decide to investigate further."

"He'd better not," she replied in a chill tone.

"There are not so many dens of the man-things in this place as there were in the place Sopal or the place Arjun," Bhlokw noted as he and Ulath looked down at the village at Zhubay. It had *seemed* that they had been traveling for several days, but they all knew better.

"No," Ulath agreed. "It is a smaller place, with fewer of the man-things."

"But there are many of the dens-of-cloth on the other side of the water hole," the Troll added, pointing at the large tent city on the far side of the oasis.

"Those are the ones we hunt," Ulath told him.

"Are you certain that we are permitted to kill and eat those?" Bhlokw asked. "You and Tin-in would not let me do that in the place Sopal or the place Arjun or even in the place Nat-os."

"It is permitted here. We have put bait out to bring them to this place so that we can hunt them for food."

"What bait do you use to lure the man-things?" Bhlokw asked curiously. "If the minds of the Gods ever get well again and they let us go back to hunting the man-things, it would be good to know this."

"The bait is thought, Bhlokw. The man-things in the dens-of-cloth have come to this place because certain of our pack-mates put it in their thought that the tall man-things with the yellow skin will be here. The ones in the dens-of-cloth have come here to fight with the tall ones with yellow skin."

Bhlokw's face contorted into a hideous approximation of a grin. "That is good bait, U-lat," he said. "I will summon Ghworg and Ghnomb and tell them that we will hunt now. How many of them may we kill and eat?"

"All, Bhlokw. All."

"That is not a good thought, U-lat. If we kill and eat them all, they will not breed, and there will not be new ones to hunt in the next season. The good thought is always to let enough run away so that they can breed to keep the numbers of their herd the same. If we eat them all now, there will be none to eat by-and-by."

Ulath considered that as Bhlokw cast the brief Troll-spell that summoned Ghworg and the others. He decided not to make an issue of it. The Trolls were hunters, not warriors, and it would take far too long to explain the concept of total war to them.

Bhlokw conferred at some length with the enormous presences of his Gods in the grey light of No-Time, and then he raised his brutish face and bellowed his summons to the Trolls.

The great shaggy mass flowed down the hill toward the village and the forest of tents beyond the oasis in the steely light of frozen time as Ulath and Tynian watched from the hilltop. The Trolls divided, went around the village, and moved in among the Cynesgan tents, fanning out as each of the great beasts selected its prey. Then, evidently at a signal from Bhlokw, the chill light flickered and the sunlight returned.

There were screams, of course, but that was to be expected. Scarcely a man in the entire world would *not* scream when a full-grown Troll suddenly stepped out of nowhere immediately in front of him.

The carnage in that vast slaughtering ground beyond the oasis was ghastly, since the Trolls were bent not on fighting the Cynesgans but on tearing them to pieces in preparation for the feast to follow.

"Some of them are getting away," Tynian observed, pointing at a sizable number of panic-stricken Cynesgans desperately flogging their horses southward.

Ulath shrugged. "Breeding stock," he said.

"What?"

"It's a Trollish concept, Tynian. It's a way to guarantee a continuing food supply. If the Trolls eat them all today, there won't be any left when suppertime rolls around tomorrow."

Tynian shuddered with revulsion. "That's a *horrible* thought, Ulath!" he exclaimed.

"Yes," Ulath agreed, "moderately horrible, but one should always respect the customs and traditions of one's allies, wouldn't you say?"

At the end of a half hour, the tents were all flattened, the breeding stock had been permitted to escape, and the Trolls settled down to eat. The Cynesgan threat in the north had been effectively eliminated, and now the Trolls were free to join the march on Cyrga.

Khalad sat up suddenly, throwing off his blankets. "Berit," he said sharply.

Berit came awake instantly, reaching for his sword.

"No," Khalad told him. "It's nothing like that. Do you know what firedamp is?"

"I've never heard of it." Berit yawned and rubbed at his eyes.

"I'm going to have to talk with Aphrael, then—personally. How long will it take you to teach me the spell?"

"That depends, I guess. Can't you pass what you have to tell her through me?"

"No. I need to ask her some questions, and you wouldn't understand what I'm talking about. I've got to talk with her myself. It's very important, Berit. I don't have to understand the language to just repeat the words, do I?"

Berit frowned. "I'm not sure. Sephrenia and the Styric who replaced her at Demos wouldn't let us do it that way, because they said we had to think in Styric."

"That could just be *their* peculiarity, not Aphrael's. Let's try it and find out if I can reach her."

It took them almost two hours, and Berit, sandy-eyed and definitely in need of more sleep, began to grow grouchy toward the end.

"I'm going to be mispronouncing words," Khalad said finally. "There's no way I'll ever be able to twist my mouth around to make some of those sounds. Let's try it and see what happens."

"You'll make her angry," Berit warned.

"She'll get over it. Here goes." Khalad began haltingly to pronounce the spell, and his fingers faltered as he moved them in the accompanying gestures.

"What on *earth* are you doing, Khalad?" Her voice almost crackled in his ears.

"I'm sorry, Flute," he apologized, "but this is urgent."

"Berit's not hurt, is he?" she demanded with a note of concern.

"No. He's fine. It's just that I need to talk with you personally. Do you know what firedamp is?"

"Yes. It sometimes kills coal miners."

"You said that Klæl's soldiers breathe something like marsh gas."

"Yes. Where are we going with this? I'm sort of busy just now."

"Please be patient, Divine One. I'm still groping my way toward this. Berit told you that we saw some of those aliens run into a cave, didn't he?"

"Yes, but I still don't—"

"I thought that Klæl might have filled the cave with marsh gas so that his soldiers could go there to breathe, but now I'm not so sure. Maybe the gas was already there."

"Would you *please* get to the point?"

"Is it possible that firedamp and marsh gas are anything at all alike?"

She sighed one of those infuriating, long-suffering sighs. "Very much alike, Khalad—which sort of stands to reason, since they're the same thing."

"I *do* love you, Aphrael," he said with a delighted laugh.

"What brought that on?"

"I *knew* there had to be a connection of some kind. This is a desert, and there aren't any swamps here. I couldn't for the life of me figure out where Klæl might be getting marsh gas to fill that cave. But he didn't

have to, did he? If marsh gas is the same thing as firedamp, all he had to do was find a cave with a seam of coal in it."

"All right, now that I've answered your question and satisfied your scientific curiosity, can I go?"

"In a minute, Divine Aphrael," he said, rubbing his hands together gleefully. "Is there some way that you can blow some of *our* air into that cave so that it'll mix with the firedamp those soldiers are breathing?"

There was another of those long pauses. "That's *dreadful*, Khalad!" she exclaimed.

"And what happened to Lord Abriel and Lord Vanion's knights *wasn't*?" he demanded. "This is war, Aphrael, and it's a war we absolutely *have* to win. If Klæl's soldiers can run into those caves to catch their breath, they'll be coming out and attacking our friends every time we turn around. We have to come up with a way to neutralize them, and I think this is it. Can you take us back to that cave where we saw those soldiers?"

"All right." Her tone was a little sulky.

"What were you talking with her about?" Berit asked.

"A way to win the war, Berit. Let's gather up our things. Aphrael's going to take us back to that cave."

"Are they still coming?" Vanion called back to Sir Endrik, who was trailing behind the other knights.

"Yes, my Lord," Endrik shouted. "Some of them are starting to fall behind, though."

"Good. They're starting to weaken." Vanion looked out across the rocky barrens lying ahead. "We've got plenty of room," he told Sephrenia. "We'll lead them out onto those flats and run them around for a while."

"This is cruel, Vanion," she reproved him.

"They don't *have* to follow us, love." He rose up in his stirrups. "Let's pick up the pace, gentlemen," he called to his knights. "I want those monsters to really run."

The knights pushed their horses into a gallop and moved out onto the barren flats with a vast, steely jingling sound.

"They're breaking off!" Endrik called from behind after about a half an hour.

Vanion raised his steel-clad arm to call a halt. Then he reined in and looked back.

The masked giants had given up their pursuit and were running due

west now, staggering toward an outcropping of rocky hills several miles away.

"*That's* the part that has everybody baffled," he told Sephrenia. "From what Aphrael told me, the others have encountered the same thing. Klæl's soldiers chase after us for a while, and then they break off and run toward the nearest cluster of hills. What can they possibly hope to find that's going to do them any good?"

"I have no idea, dear one," she replied.

"This is all very fine, I suppose," Vanion said with a worried frown, "but when we begin our final advance on Cyrga, we won't have time to run those brutes into exhaustion. Not only that, Klæl will probably start massing them in units larger than these regiments we've been coming across out here in the open. If we don't come up with some way to neutralize them permanently, our chances of getting to Cyrga alive aren't very good."

"Lord Vanion!" one of the knights cried out in alarm. "There are more of them coming!"

"Where?" Vanion looked around.

"From the west!"

Vanion peered after the fleeing monsters. And then he saw them. There were *two* regiments of Klæl's soldiers out there on the flats. The one they had encountered earlier was reeling and staggering toward the hills jutting up from the horizon. The other was coming toward them *from* the hills, and the second regiment showed no signs of the exhaustion which had incapacitated their fellows.

"This is ridiculous," Talen muttered, examining the lock on his chain with sensitive fingertips.

"You said you could unlock them," Kalten accused in a hoarse whisper.

"Kalten, *you* could unlock these. They're the worst locks I've ever seen."

"Just open them, Talen," Sparhawk told him quietly. "Don't give lectures. We still have to get out of this pen."

They had merged with the other woodcutters and had passed unchallenged through the gates of Cyrga just as the sun was setting. Then they had followed the slaves to an open square near the gate, unloaded their cart onto one of the stacks of wood piled there, and leaned the cart against a rough stone wall with the others. Then, like docile cattle, they had gone into the large slave pen and allowed the

Cynesgan overseers to chain them to rusty iron rings protruding from the rear wall of the pen.

They had been fed a thin, watery soup and had then bedded down in piles of filthy straw heaped against the wall to wait for nightfall. Xanetia was not with them. Silent and unseen, she roamed the streets outside the pen instead.

"Hold your leg still, Kalten," Talen hissed. "I can't get the chain off when you're flopping around like that."

"Sorry."

The boy concentrated for a moment, and the lock snapped open. Then he moved on, crawling through the rustling straw.

"Don't get so familiar," Mirtai's voice muttered in the darkness.

"Sorry. I was looking for your ankle."

"It's on the other end of the leg."

"Yes. I noticed that myself. It's dark, Atana. I can't see what I'm doing."

"What are you men doing there?" It was a whining, servile kind of voice coming from somewhere in the straw beyond where Kalten lay.

"It's none of your business," Kalten rasped. "Go back to sleep."

"I want to know what you're doing. If you don't tell me, I'll call the overseers."

"You'd better shut him up, Kalten," Mirtai muttered. "He's an informer."

"I'll deal with it," Kalten replied darkly. He slipped away through the rustling straw.

"What are you doing?" the slave with the whining voice demanded. "How did you—" The voice broke off, and there was a sudden thrashing in the straw and a kind of wheezy gurgling.

"What's gong on out there?" A harsh voice called from the overseer's barracks. The barracks doorway poured light out into the yard.

There was no answer, only a few spasmodic rustles in the straw. Kalten was breathing a little hard when he returned to his place, quickly wrapped his chain around his ankle again, and covered it with straw.

They waited tensely, but the Cynesgan overseer evidently decided not to investigate. He went back inside, closing the door behind him and plunging the yard into darkness again.

"Does that happen often—among slaves, I mean?" Beavier whispered to Mirtai as Talen was unchaining him.

"All the time," she murmured. "There's no loyalty among slaves. One slave will betray another for an extra crust of bread."

"How sad."

"Slavery? I could find harsher words than sad."

"Let's go," Sparhawk told them.

"How are we going to find Xanetia?" Kalten whispered as they crossed the pen.

"We can't. She's going to have to find us."

It took Talen only a moment to unlock the gate, and they all slipped out into the dark street beyond. They crept along that street to the large square where the firewood was stacked and stopped before stepping out into the open.

"Take a look, Talen," Sparhawk suggested.

"Right." The young thief melted away into the darkness. The rest of them waited tensely.

"It's all clear," Talen's whisper came to them after a few minutes. "The carts are over here."

They followed the sound of his hushed voice and soon reached the line of wood carts leaning against the wall.

"Did you see any guards?" Kalten asked.

"Who's going to stay up all night to guard a woodpile?" Talen dropped down onto his stomach and wormed his way under the cart. There was a faint creaking of the tightly woven limbs of the makeshift basket. "Here," Talen said. A sword-tip banged against Sparhawk's shin.

Sparhawk took the sword, handed it to Kalten, and then leaned down. "Pass them out hilt-first," he instructed. "Don't poke me with the sharp end of a sword that way."

"Sorry." Talen continued to pass out weapons and then followed them with their mail shirts and tunics. They all felt better once they were armed again.

"Anakha?" The voice was soft and very light.

"Is that you, Xanetia?" Sparhawk realized how foolish the question was almost before it left his lips.

"Verily," she replied. "Come away, I prithee. The whisper is the natural voice of stealth, and it doth carry far by night. Let us away 'ere they who watch this sleeping city come hither in search of the source of our incautious conversation."

"We're going to have to wait a bit," Khalad said. "Aphrael has to blow air into that cave."

"Are you sure this is going to work?" Berit asked dubiously.

"No, not really, but it's worth a try, isn't it?"

"You don't even know for sure that they're still inside the cave."

"That doesn't really matter. Either way they won't be able to hide in the cave any more." Khalad began to carefully wrap a length of oil-soaked rag around one of his crossbow bolts. Then, being careful to conceal the sparks with his body, he began striking his flint and steel together. After a moment, his tinder caught; he lit his stub of a candle and brushed the fire out of his tinder. Then he carefully put the candle behind a fair-sized rock.

"Aphrael seems to be unhappy about this, Khalad," Berit said as a chill breeze came up.

"I wasn't too happy about what happened to Lord Abriel," Khalad replied bleakly. "I had a good deal of respect for that old man, and these monsters with yellow blood tore him to pieces."

"Then you're doing this for revenge?"

"No. Not really. This is just the most practical way to get rid of them. Ask Aphrael to let me know when there's enough air in the cave."

"How long is that likely to take?"

"I have no idea. All the coal miners who've ever seen it up close are dead." Khalad scratched at his beard. "I'm not entirely sure what's going to happen here, Berit. When marsh gas catches on fire, it just burns off and goes out. Firedamp's a little more spectacular."

"What's all this business about blowing air into the cave?" Berit demanded.

Khalad shrugged. "Fire's a living thing. It has to be able to breathe."

"You're just guessing about this, aren't you? You don't have any idea at all whether or not it's going to work—or if it does, what's going to happen."

Khalad gave him a tight grin. "I've got a good working theory."

"I think you're insane. You could set the whole desert on fire with this silly experiment of yours."

"Oh, that probably won't happen."

"*Probably?*"

"It's very unlikely. I can just make out that cave mouth. Why don't I try it?"

"What happens if you miss?"

Khalad shrugged. "I'll shoot again."

"That's not what I meant. I was—" Berit broke off, listening intently. "Aphrael says that the mixture's right now. You can shoot whenever you're ready."

Khalad held the point of his crossbow bolt in the candle flame, turning it slowly to make certain that the oily rag was evenly ablaze. Then he set the burning bolt in place, laid the forestock of his crossbow on a rock, and took careful aim. "Here goes," he said, slowly pressing the lever.

The crossbow gave a ringing thud, and the burning arrow streaked through the darkness and disappeared into the narrow cave mouth.

Nothing happened.

"So much for your good working theory," Berit said sardonically.

Khalad swore, banging his fist on the gravel. "It *has* to work, Berit. I did everything exactly—"

The sound was beyond noise when the hill exploded, and a ball of fire hundreds of feet across seethed skyward out of the crater that had suddenly replaced the hill. Without thinking, Khalad threw himself across Berit's head, covering the back of his own neck with his hands.

Fortunately, what fell on them was small gravel for the most part. The larger rocks fell much farther out into the desert.

It continued to rain gravel for several minutes, and the two young men, battered and shaken, lay tensely clenched, enduring the cataclysmic results of Khalad's experiment.

Gradually, the stinging rain subsided.

"*You idiot!*" Berit screamed. "You could have killed us both!"

"I must have miscalculated just a little," Khalad conceded, shaking the dirt out of his hair. "I'll have to work on it a bit before we try it again."

"*Try it again? What are you talking about?*"

"It *does* work, Berit," Khalad said in his most reasonable tone of voice. "All I have to do is fine-tune it a little bit. Every experiment's got a few rough places around the edges." He stood up, banging the side of his head with the heel of his hand to shake the ringing out of his ears. "I'll get it perfected, my Lord," he promised, helping Berit to his feet. "The next time won't be nearly so bad. Now, why don't you ask Aphrael to take us back to camp? We're probably being watched, so let's not arouse any suspicions."

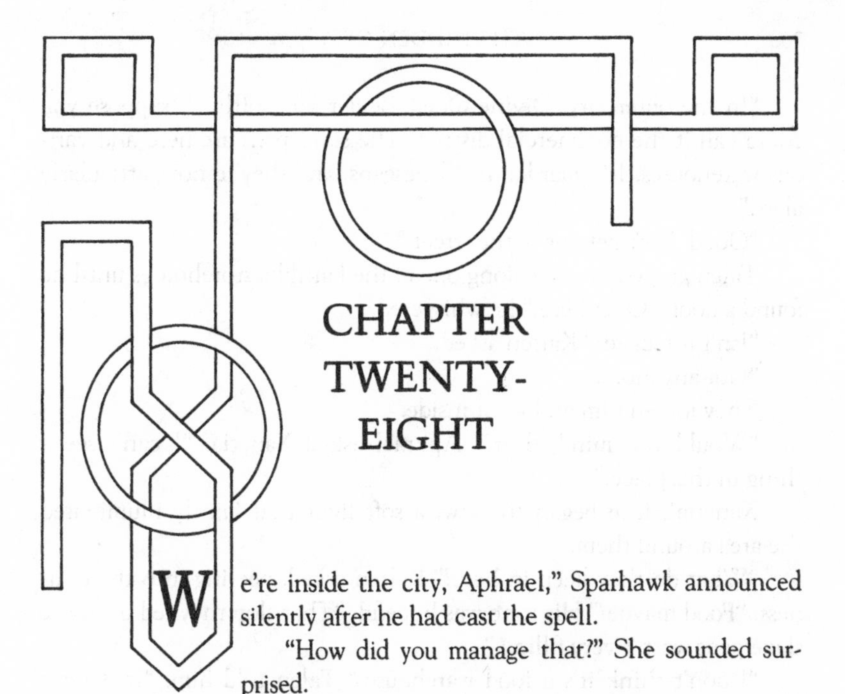

CHAPTER TWENTY-EIGHT

"We're inside the city, Aphrael," Sparhawk announced silently after he had cast the spell.

"How did you manage that?" She sounded surprised.

"It's a long story. Tell Khalad that I've marked the passageway that leads into the valley. He'll know what to look for."

"Have you found out where they're keeping Mother yet?"

"Speculatively."

There was a long pause. "I'd better come there," she decided.

"How will you find us?"

"I'll use you as a beacon. Just keep talking to me."

"I don't think it's a good idea. We're right in Cyrgon's lap here. Won't he be able to sense you?"

"Xanetia's there, isn't she?"

"Yes."

"Then Cyrgon won't feel a thing. That's why I sent her along." She paused again. "Who came up with a way to get you inside the city?"

"It was Talen's idea."

"You see? And you wanted to argue with me about taking him with you. When *will* you learn to trust me, Father? Keep talking. I've almost got you located. Tell me how Talen managed to get you inside the walls of Cyrga."

He described the subterfuge at some length.

"All right," she said from just behind him. "That's enough. I get the general drift." He turned and saw her in Xanetia's arms. She looked around. "I see that the Cyrgai haven't discovered fire yet. It's darker than the inside of an old boot here. Exactly where are we?"

"In the outer city, Divine One," Bevier said softly. "I suppose you could call it the commercial district. The slave pens are here and various warehouses. It's guarded by Cynesgans, and they're not particularly alert."

"Good. Let's get out of the street."

Talen groped his way along one of the barnlike storehouses until he found a door. "Over here," he whispered.

"Isn't it locked?" Kalten asked.

"Not any more."

They joined him and went inside.

"Would you mind, dear?" Aphrael asked Xanetia. "I can't see a thing in this place."

Xanetia's face began to glow, a soft light that faintly illuminated the area around them.

"What do they keep in here?" Kalten asked, peering into the dimness. "Food maybe?" His tone was hopeful. "That slop they fed us in the slave pens wasn't very filling."

"I don't think it's a food warehouse," Talen told him. "It doesn't smell quite right."

"You can go exploring some other time," Aphrael told him crisply. "We have other things to do now."

"How are the others making out?" Sparhawk asked her.

"Bergsten's captured Cynestra," she reported, "and he's coming south with the Church Knights. Ulath and Tynian took the Trolls to Zhubay, and the Trolls ate about half of the Cynesgan cavalry. Betuana and Engessa are marching southwest with the Atans. Vanion and Sephrenia are out in the desert laying down false hints that you're with them. Kring and Tikume are allowing themselves to be chased all over the desert west of Sarna by Cyrgai, Cynesgan calvary, and Klæl's overgrown soldiers—although I don't think *those* brutes are going to be a problem for much longer; Khalad's devised a way to neutralize them."

"All by himself?" Talen sounded surprised.

"Klæl outsmarted himself. He found caves where his soldiers could breathe, and they were hiding in the caves and then coming out to attack us. Khalad's come up with a way to set the caves on fire. The results are fairly noisy."

"That's my brother for you," Talen said proudly.

"Yes," the Child-Goddess said critically. "He's inventing new horrors at every turn. Stragen and Caalador have managed to convince that Dacite in Beresa that we've got an invasion force off the south coast and—" She stopped. "You know about all this already, Sparhawk. Why am I wasting time describing it to you?"

"It's all going according to plan, then?" he asked her. "No setbacks? No new surprises?"

"Not for *us*. Crygon's not having such a good time, though. The Delphae have almost completely dispersed Scarpa's army, so the danger to Matherion's pretty much evaporated. I've enlisted some of my family to lend a hand. They're compressing time and distance. As soon as Ehlana's safe, I'll pass the word, and we'll have whole armies knocking at the gates of Cyrga."

"Did you get word of Khalad's invention to the others?" Talen asked her.

"My cousin Setras is taking care of it for me. Setras is a little vague sometimes, but I went over it with him several times. I don't think he'll garble it *too* badly. Everything's in place. The others are simply waiting for word from us to start moving, so let's get down to business. Has anyone had a chance to look around here at all?"

"I have explored the outer city to some degree, Divine Aphrael," Xanetia replied. "Anakha deemed it unwise for me to share their captivity in the slave pens."

The Child-Goddess handed Talen a large sheet of stiff, crackling parchment and a pencil. "Here," she said to him, "earn your keep."

"Where did you get these?" he asked curiously.

"I had them in one of my pockets."

"You don't *have* any pockets, Flute."

She gave him one of those long-suffering looks.

"Oh," he said. "I keep forgetting that for some reason. All right, Anarae, you describe the city, and I'll draw it."

The sketch that emerged was fairly detailed—as far as it went. "I was not able to penetrate the wall which doth encircle the inner city," Xanetia apologized. "The gates are perpetually locked, for the Cyrgai do hold themselves aloof from their Cynesgan hirelings and from the slaves whose toil supports them."

"This should be enough to work with for now," Flute said, pursing her lips as she examined Talen's drawing. "All right, Bevier, you're the expert on fortifications. Where's the weak spot?"

The Cyrinic studied the sketch for several minutes. "Did you see any wells, Anarae?" he asked.

"Nay, Sir Knight."

"They've got a lake right outside the front gate, Bevier," Kalten reminded him.

"That wouldn't do much good if the city were under siege," Bevier replied. "There has to be some source of water inside the walls—either a well or some kind of a cistern. A siege ends rather quickly when the defenders run out of water."

"What makes you think that the place was built to hold off a siege?" Mirtai asked. "Nobody's supposed to be able to find it."

"The walls are a little too high and thick to be purely ornamental, Atana. Cyrga's a fortified city, and that means that it was built to withstand a siege. The Cyrgai aren't very bright, but *nobody's* stupid enough to build a fort without water inside. That's my best guess, Divine Aphrael. Find out how they're getting water—both here in the outer city and in the inner city as well. There might be a weakness there. If not, we may have to tunnel under the inner wall or try to scale it."

"Let's hope it doesn't come to that," Aphrael said. "We're inside the enemy city, and the longer we putter around, the more chance there is of being discovered. If it's in any way possible, we want to free Ehlana and Alean tonight. I'll send out word and start the others moving. Nobody's going to get much sleep tonight, but that can't be helped. All right, then, Xanetia, let's go look for water. The rest of you stay here. We don't want to have to go looking for you when we come back."

"Are you mad, Gardas?" Bergsten demanded of the massively armored Alcione Knight. The Thalesian Patriarch refused to look at the pleasant-faced young man standing beside the knight. "I'm not even supposed to admit that he exists, much less sit down and talk with him."

"Aphrael said you might be tedious about this, Bergsten," noted the person whom Gardas had escorted into the Patriarch's tent. "Would it help at all if I did something miraculous?"

"God!" Bergsten said. "Please don't do that! I'm probably in trouble already!"

"Dolmant had some problems when I visited him, too," Aphrael's cousin observed. "You servants of the Elene God have some strange ideas. *He* doesn't get excited about us, so why should you? Anyway, the normal rules are all more or less suspended until this crisis is over. We've even enlisted Edaemus and the Atan God—and they haven't spoken to any of the rest of us for eons. Aphrael wants me to tell you about something having to do with the soldiers Klæl brought with him. Somebody named Khalad has devised a means of destroying them."

"Tell Gardas about it," Bergsten suggested. "He can pass it on to me, and I won't get into trouble."

"I'm sorry, Bergsten, but Aphrael insisted that I say it directly to you. Just pretend that I'm a dream or something." Setras' face grew slightly puzzled, and his large, luminous eyes revealed a frightening lack of comprehension. "I don't entirely understand this," he confessed. "Aphrael's much more clever than I am—but we love each other, so she doesn't throw my stupidity into my face very often. She's terribly polite. She's even nice to *your* God, and he can be terribly tedious sometimes—where was I?"

"Ah," Sir Gardas said gently, "you were going to tell his Grace about Klæl's soldiers, Divine Setras."

"I was?" The large eyes were blank. "Oh, yes. I was, wasn't I? You mustn't let me ramble on like that, Gardas. You *know* how easily I get distracted."

"Yes, Divine Setras. That *had* occurred to me."

"Anyway," Setras pushed on, "this Khalad person—a frightfully clever young man, I gather—realized that there might be some similarity between the awful stuff Klæl's soldiers breathe and something he calls 'firedamp.' Have you any idea at all of what he was talking about, Bergsten?" Setras hesitated. "Am I supposed to call you 'your Grace' the way Gardas did? Are you really that graceful? You look awfully large and clumsy to me."

"It's a formal mode of address, Divine One," Sir Gardas explained.

"Oh. We don't have to be formal with each other, do we, Bergsten? We're almost old friends now, aren't we?"

The Patriarch of Emsat swallowed very hard. Then he sighed. "Yes, Divine Setras," he said. "I suppose we are. Why don't you go ahead and tell me about this strategy Sparhawk's squire has devised?"

"Of course. Oh, there's one other thing, too. We have to be at the gates of Cyrga by morning."

"Please, Atana Liatris," Baroness Melidere said patiently to Sarabian's Atan wife, "we *want* them to make the attempt."

"It is too dangerous," Liatris said stubbornly. "If I go ahead and kill Chacole and Torellia, the others will run away and that will be the end of it."

"Except that we'll never find out who else is involved," Patriarch

Emban explained, "and we won't know for certain that they won't try again."

Princess Danae sat a little apart from them with Mmrr curled up in her lap. Her vision was strangely doubled with one image superimposed on the other. It seemed that the dark streets of Cyrga lay just behind the people speaking here in the sitting room.

"I'm touched by your concern, Liatris," Sarabian was saying, "but I'm not nearly as helpless as I seem." He flourished his rapier.

"And we *will* have guards nearby," Foreign Minister Oscagne added. "Chacole and Torellia almost *have* to be getting help from somebody inside the government—some leftover from that coup attempt, most likely."

"I will wring his identity from them before I kill them," Liatris declared.

Sarabian winced at the word *wring*.

"We are near, Divine Aphrael," Xanetia's voice seemed at once a long way away and very close. "Methinks I do smell water." The dark, narrow street they followed opened out into some kind of square a hundred feet farther on.

"Let's catch them all, Liatris," Elysoun urged her sister-empress. "You might be able to beat one or two names out of Chacole and Torellia, but if we can catch the assassins in the actual attempt, we'll be able to sweep the palace compound clean. If we don't, our husband's going to have to go through the rest of his life with a drawn rapier."

"Hark!" Xanetia whispered in that other city. "I do hear the sound of running water."

Danae concentrated very hard. It was exhausting to keep things separate.

"I really hate to have to put it this way, Liatris," Sarabian said regretfully, "but I forbid you to kill either Chacole or Torellia. We'll deal with them *after* their assassins try to kill me."

"As my husband commands," Liatris responded automatically.

"What I want you to do is to protect Elysoun and Gahenas," he continued. "Gahenas is probably in the greater danger right now. Elysoun's still useful to the people involved in this, but Gahenas knows more than they want her to. I'm sure they'll try to kill her, so let's get her out of the women's palace tonight."

"It is beneath the street, Divine One," Xanetia said. "Methinks there is some volume of water passing under our feet."

"Truly," the Child-Goddess replied. "Let's follow the sound back to its source. There has to be *some* way to get to the water here in the outer city."

"How did you become involved in this, Elysoun?" Liatris was asking.

Elysoun shrugged. "I have more freedom of movement than the rest of you," she replied. "Chacole needed somebody she trusted to carry messages out of the women's palace. I pretended to fall in with her plan. It wasn't too hard to deceive Chacole. She *is* a Cynesgan, after all."

"It is here, Divine One," Xanetia whispered, laying her hand on a large iron plate set into the cobblestones. "Thou canst feel the urgent rush of water through the very iron."

"I'll take your word for it, Anarae," Aphrael replied, cringing back from the notion of touching iron. "How do they get it open?"

"These rings do suggest that the plate can be lifted."

"Let's go back and get the others. I think this might be the weakness Bevier was looking for."

Danae yawned. Everything seemed to be under control here, so she curled up in her chair, nestled Mmrr in her arms, and promptly fell asleep.

"Couldn't you have just—well—?" Talen wiggled his fingers.

"It's iron, Talen," Flute said with exaggerated patience.

"So? What's that got to do with it?"

She shuddered. "I can't bear the touch of iron."

Bevier looked intently at her. "Bhelliom suffers from the same affliction," he observed.

"Yes. So what?"

"That would suggest a certain kinship."

"Your grasp of the obvious is positively dazzling, Bevier."

"Behave yourself," Sparhawk chided.

"What's so unpleasant about iron?" Talen asked. "It's cold, it's hard, you can pound it into various shapes, and it gets rusty."

"That's a nice scholarly description. Do you know what a lodestone is?"

"It's a piece of iron ore that sticks to other iron, isn't it? I seem to remember Platime talking about something called magnetism once."

"And you actually listened? Amazing."

"*That's* why Bhelliom had to congeal itself into a sapphire!" Bevier exclaimed. "It's the magnetism of iron, isn't it? Bhelliom can't bear it—and neither can *you*, can you?"

"Please, Bevier," Aphrael said weakly. "Just thinking about it makes my flesh crawl. Right now we don't want to talk about iron. We want to talk about water. There's a stream or river of some kind running under the streets here in the outer city, and it's flowing in the direction of the inner wall. There's a large iron plate set in the middle of the street not far from here, and you can hear the water running beneath it. I think that's the weakness you were looking for. The water's running through a tunnel of some kind, and that tunnel goes under the wall of the inner fortress—at least I hope so. I'll go find out as soon as you gentlemen lift off that iron plate for me."

"Did you see any patrols in the streets?" Kalten asked.

"Nay, Sir Knight," Xanetia replied. "Centuries of custom have clearly dulled the alertness of the Cynesgans responsible for the defense of the outer city."

"A burglar's dream," Talen murmured. "I could get rich in this town."

"What would you steal?" Aphrael asked him. "The Cyrgai don't believe in gold and silver."

"What do they use for money?"

"They don't. They don't need money. The Cynesgans provide them with everything they need, so they don't even think about money."

"That's monstrous!"

"We can discuss economics some other time. Right now I want to investigate their water supply."

"You idiot!" Queen Betuana raged at her general.

"We had to find out, Betuana-Queen," Engessa explained, "and I will not send another where I will not go."

"I am most displeased with you, Engessa-Atan!" Betuana's retreat into ritualized mourning had vanished. "Did your last encounter with the Klæl-beasts teach you nothing? They could have been lurking just inside the cave, and you would have faced them alone again."

"It is not reasonable to suppose that they would have," he replied stiffly. "Aphrael's messenger told us that the Klæl-beasts take shelter in caves that they might breathe a different air. The air at the entrance to this cave will be the same as the air outside. It is of no moment, however. It is done, and no harm came from it."

She controlled her anger with an obvious effort. "And what did you prove by your foolish venture, Engessa-Atan?"

"The Klæl-beasts have sealed the cave, Betuana-Queen," he replied. "Some hundred paces within stands a steel wall. It is reasonable to suppose that it may in some fashion be opened. The Klæl-beasts retreat beyond the barrier, close it behind them, and are then able to breathe freely for a time. Then they emerge again and attack us once more."

"Was this information worth the risk of your life?"

"We have yet to discover that, my Queen. The tactics devised by Kring-Domi keep us out of the reach of the Klæl-beasts, but I do not like this running away."

Betuana's eyes hardened. "Nor do I," she conceded. "I dishonor my husband's memory each time I turn and flee."

"Aphrael's cousin told us that Khalad-squire had found that the air which the Klæl-beasts breathe will burn when it mixes with *our* air."

"I have not seen air burn before."

"Nor have I. If the trap that I have set for the Klæl-beasts works, we may both see it happen."

"What sort of trap, Engessa-Atan?"

"A lantern, my Queen—well hidden."

"A lantern? That's all?"

"If Khalad-squire was right, it should be enough. I closed the lantern so that the Klæl-beasts will see no light when they open their steel door to come out again. All unseen, their air will join with ours and the mix will find its way to the candle burning inside my lantern. Then we will discover if Khalad-squire was right."

"Then we must wait until they open that door. I will not leave them behind us until I know without any doubt that this burning of air will kill them. As Ulath-Knight says, only a fool leaves live enemies behind him."

They concealed themselves behind an outcropping of rock and waited, intently watching the cave mouth faintly visible in the light of the stars. "It may be some time before they open their door, my Queen," Engessa noted.

"Engessa-Atan," Betuana said firmly, "I have long thought that this formality of yours is out of place. We are soldiers, and comrades. Please address me as such."

"As you wish, Betuana-Atan."

They waited patiently, watching the sizable peak and the dark mouth of the cave. Then, like a deep, subterranean thunder, a stunning sound shattered the silence, shaking the ground, and a great billow of boiling fire blasted out of the cave mouth, searing the few scrubby thornbushes growing nearby. The fire spewed out of the cave, roaring on and on, until it gradually subsided.

Engessa and his queen, shocked by that violent eruption, could only stare in wonder. Finally, Betuana rose to her feet. "Now I have seen air burn," she noted in a cool sort of way. "It was worth the wait, I suppose." Then she smiled at her still-shaken comrade "You lay good traps, Engessa-Atan, but now we must hurry to rejoin the Trolls. Ulath-Knight says that we must reach Cyrga by morning."

"Whatever you say, Betuana-Atan," he replied.

"All together, when I say, 'lift,' " Sparhawk instructed, settling his hands into place around the ring, "and don't let it clank when we set it down. All right, lift."

Kalten, Bevier, Mirtai, and Sparhawk all rose slowly, straining to lift the rusty iron plate up out of its place among the worn cobblestones.

"Be careful," Talen said to Mirtai. "Don't fall in."

"Do you want to do this?" she asked.

The four of them shuffled around slightly and moved the ponderous weight to one side so that the large square hole was partially uncovered. "Set it down," Sparhawk said from between his clenched teeth. "Easy," he added.

They slowly lowered the cover to the stones.

"It'd be easier to pick up a house," Kalten wheezed.

"Turn your backs," Flute instructed.

"Do you have to do that?" Talen asked. "Is it like flying?"

"Just turn around, Talen."

"Don't forget the clothes," Sparhawk told her.

"They'd just be in my way. If you don't like it, don't look." Her voice was already richer.

Bevier had his eyes tightly closed, and his lips were moving. He obviously was praying—very hard.

"I'll be right back," the Goddess promised. "Don't go away."

They waited for what seemed to be hours. Then they heard a faint splashing down below. The splashing was accompanied by muffled laughter.

Talen knelt at the edge of the rectangular shaft. "Are you all right?" he whispered.

"I'm fine."

"What's so funny?"

"The Cyrgai. You wouldn't *believe* how stupid they are."

"What did they do now?"

"The water comes from a large artesian spring right near the outer wall. The Cyrgai built a sort of cistern around it. Then they built a tunnel that goes under the inner wall to carry water to a very large pool that lies underneath the mountain they've built their main city on."

"What's wrong with that?"

"Nothing—as far as it goes. They seem to have realized the same thing that Bevier did. Their water source is a weakness. They very carefully built a stone lattice at the mouth of the tunnel. Nobody can get into the tunnel from the cistern."

"I still don't see anything to laugh about."

"I'm just coming to that. This shaft that leads down to the tunnel seems to have been added later—probably so that they could get into the tunnel to clean it."

"That doesn't sound like such a bad idea. It *is* supposed to be drinking water, after all."

"Yes, but when they dug the shaft, they forgot something. The other end of the tunnel—the one that's inside their second wall—is completely open. There aren't any bars, no lattice, no chains, nothing."

"You're not serious!"

"May muh tongue turn green iff'n I ain't."

"This is going to be easier than I thought," Kalten said. He leaned over and peered down into the darkness. "Is that current very swift?" he called down softly.

"Swift enough," Aphrael replied. "But that's all right. It speeds you right straight through, so you won't have to hold your breath so long."

"Do what?" His voice was choked.

"Hold your breath. You have to swim underwater."

"Not me," he said flatly.

"You *do* know how to swim, don't you?"

"I can swim in full armor if I have to."

"What's the problem, then?"

"I *don't* swim underwater. It sends me into a panic."

"He's right, Aphrael," Sparhawk called down softly. "As soon as Kalten's head goes underwater, he starts screaming."

"He can't do that. He'll drown."

"Exactly. I used to have to stand on his chest to squeeze the water out of him. It happened all the time when we were boys."

"Oh, dear," she said. "I hadn't counted on this."

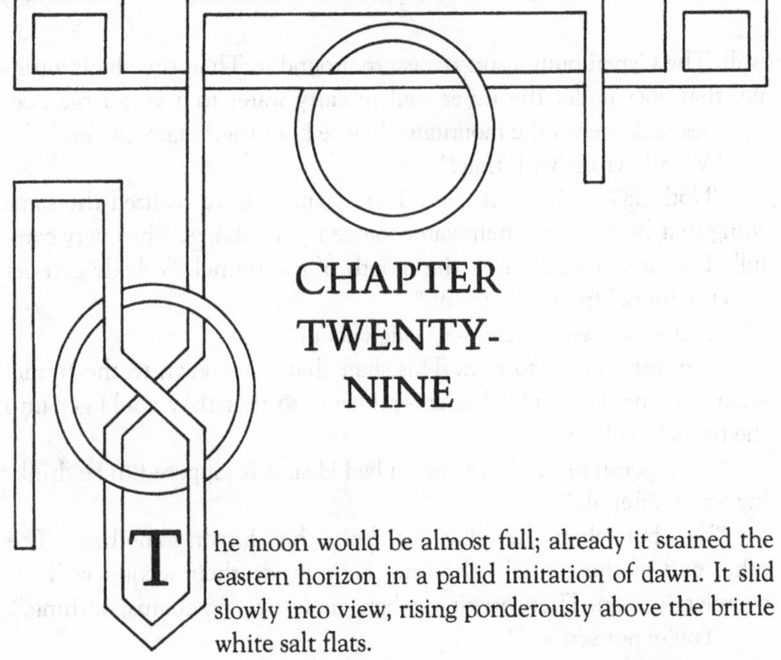

CHAPTER TWENTY-NINE

The moon would be almost full; already it stained the eastern horizon in a pallid imitation of dawn. It slid slowly into view, rising ponderously above the brittle white salt flats.

"Good God!" Berit exclaimed, staring at the horror all around them. What had seemed to be round white rocks by the faint light of the stars were revealed as bleached skulls, nesting in jumbles of bones and staring in mute accusation at the heavens.

"It looks as if we've come to the right place," Khalad observed. "The note Sparhawk left us talked about a 'Plain of Bones.' "

"It goes on forever!" Berit gasped, looking off toward the west.

"Let's hope not. We have to cross it." Khalad stopped, peering intently toward the west. "There it is," he said, pointing toward a gleaming spot of reflected light in the center of a low range of dark hills some distance beyond the ghastly plain.

"There what is?"

"Our landmark. Sparhawk called it the 'Pillars of Cyrgon.' Something out there's catching the moonlight. We're supposed to ride toward that spot."

"Who's that?" Berit hissed, pointing at a figure walking toward them out of the bone-littered desert.

Khalad loosened his sword in its sheath. "Another note from Krager, maybe," he muttered. "Let's start being a little careful, my Lord. I think we're getting very close to the place where we'll have outlived our usefulness."

The figure coming out of the desert seemed to be moving at no more than a casual stroll, and as he came closer, they were able to make out his features.

"Watch yourself, Khalad!" Berit hissed sharply. "He's not human!"

Khalad felt it as well. It was nothing really definable, just an overpowering sense of presence, an aura that no human had. The figure appeared to be that of an extraordinarily handsome young man. He had tightly curled hair, classic features, and very large, almost luminous eyes. "Ah, there you are, gentlemen," he said urbanely in flawless Elenic. "I've been looking all over for you." He glanced around. "This is a really *wretched* place, don't you think? Exactly the sort of place you'd expect the Cyrgai to inhabit. Cyrgon's terribly warped. He adores ugliness. Have you ever met him? Frightful fellow. No sense of beauty whatsoever." He smiled, a radiant, slightly vague smile. "My cousin Aphrael sent me. She'd have come herself, but she's a little busy right now—but then, Aphrael's *always* busy, isn't she? She can't stand to sit quietly." He frowned. "She wanted me to tell you something." His frown intensified. "What was it, now? I have the worst memory lately." He held up one hand. "No," he said, "don't tell me. It'll come to me in a moment. It's terribly important, though, and we're supposed to hurry. I'll probably think of it as we go along." He looked around. "Do you gentlemen by any chance happen to know which way we're supposed to go?"

"It won't work, Aphrael," Kalten said morosely. "I've tried it when I was dead drunk and the same thing happens. I go crazy when I feel the water closing over my head."

"Just try it, Kalten," the minimally dressed Goddess urged. "It really will relax you." She pushed the tankard into his hand.

He sniffed suspiciously. "It *smells* good. What is it?"

"We drink it at parties."

"The beer of the Gods?" His eyes brightened. "Well, now." He took a cautious sip. "*Well* now," he said enthusiastically. "That's the way it's *supposed* to taste."

"Drink it all," she instructed, watching him intently.

"Gladly." He drained the tankard and wiped his lips. "That's *really* good. If a man had the recipe for *that*, he could—" He broke off, his eyes glazed.

"Lay him down," Aphrael instructed, "quickly, before he stiffens up. I don't want him all twisted into a pretzel when I drag him through the tunnel."

Talen was doubled over with both hands tightly over his mouth to stifle his laughter.

"What's *your* problem?" the Goddess demanded tartly.

"Nothing," he gasped. "Nothing at all."

"I've got a long way to go with that one," Aphrael muttered to Sparhawk.

"Is this going to work?" Sparhawk asked her. "Kalten, I mean? Can you really drag an unconscious man underwater for any distance without drowning him?"

"I'll stop his breathing." She looked around at the others. "I don't want any of you to try to help me," she cautioned. "You just concentrate on getting through yourselves. I don't have to breathe, but you do, and I don't want to have to spend an hour fishing you out of that pool one by one after we get there. Now, does anybody *else* have any problems you haven't told me about? This is the time to talk about them—*before* we're all underwater." She looked pointedly at Bevier. "Is there something *you'd* like to tell me, Sir Knight? You seem to be having a crisis of some sort."

"It's nothing, Divine One," he mumbled. "I'll be fine. I swim like a fish." He deliberately avoided looking at her.

"What's bothering you, then?"

"I'd really rather not say."

She sighed. "Men." Then she climbed into the shaft leading down toward the unseen water rushing toward the inner wall. "Bring Kalten," she ordered, "and let's get at this."

"I'd really like to do something about that," Sephrenia murmured to Vanion as they peered over the top of the gravel mound at the encampment of the slavers.

"So would I, love," Vanion replied, "but I think we'd better wait until later. If everything goes the way it's supposed to, we'll be waiting for them when they reach Cyrga." He raised himself a bit higher. "I think that's the salt flats just beyond that trail they're following."

"We'll be able to tell for certain when the moon rises," she replied.

"Have you heard anything at all from Aphrael?"

"Nothing I can make any sense of. The echoes are very confusing when she's in two places at the same time. I gather that things are coming to a head in Matherion, and she and Sparhawk are swimming."

"Swimming? This is a desert, Sephrenia."

"Yes, I noticed that. They've found *something* to swim in, though." She paused. "Does Kalten know how to swim?" she asked.

"He splashes a great deal, but he manages to drag himself through the water. I wouldn't call him graceful, by any means. Why do you ask?"

"She's having some sort of problem with him, and it has to do with the swimming. Let's go back and join the others, dear one. Just the sight of those slavers is setting my blood to boiling."

They slid back down the gravel-strewn mound and walked along a shallow gully toward their armored soldiers.

The Cyrinic knight, Sir Launesse, stood somewhat diffidently beside a burly, intricately curled, and massively eyebrowed personage with heavy shoulders and a classical demeanor. "Sephrenia!" the clearly nonhuman being said in a voice that could probably have been heard in Thalesia. "Well met!"

"Well met indeed, Divine Romalic," she replied with just a trace of a weary sigh.

"Please, dear," Vanion murmured, "ask him to lower his voice."

"Nobody else can hear him," she assured him. "The Gods speak loudly—but only to certain ears."

"Thy sister bids me give thee greetings," Romalic announced in a voice of thunder.

"Thou art kind to bear those greetings, Divine One."

"Kindness and courtesy aside, Sephrenia," the huge God declaimed, combing his beard with enormous fingers, "are thou yet prepared to serve us all and to assume thy proper place?"

"I am unworthy, Divine One," she replied modestly. "Surely there are others wiser and better suited."

"What's this?" Vanion asked.

"It's been going on for a long time, dear one," she explained. "I've been avoiding it for centuries. Romalic always has to bring it up, though."

It all fell into place in Vanion's mind. "Sephrenia!" he gasped. "They want you to be Over-Priestess, don't they?"

"It's Aphrael, Vanion, not me. They think they can get around her by offering this to me. I don't really want it, and they don't really want to give it to me, but they're afraid of her, and this is their way to placate her."

"Aphrael bids thee to make haste," Romalic proclaimed. "Ye must all be at the gates of Cyrga 'ere dawn, for this is the night of decision, when Cyrgon and, yea, even Klæl, must be confronted and, we may hope, confounded. E'en now doth Anakha move ghostlike through the streets of the Hidden City toward his design. Let us hasten." He lifted his voice and thundered, "On to Cyrga!"

"Is he always like this?" Vanion murmured.

"Romalic?" Sephrenia said. "Oh, yes. He's perfectly suited to the Cyrinic Knights. Come along, dear one. Let's go to Cyrga."

There were dim, flickering lights far above, but the pool was sunk in inky blackness when Sparhawk surfaced and explosively blew out the breath he had been holding.

"Kalten," he heard Aphrael saying, "wake up."

There was a startled cry and a great deal of splashing.

"Oh, stop that," the Goddess told Sparhawk's friend. "It's all over, and you came through it just fine. Xanetia, dear, could we have a little light?"

"Of a certainty, Divine One," the Anarae replied, and her face began to glow.

"Are we all here?" Aphrael asked quietly, looking around. As Xanetia's light gradually increased, Sparhawk saw that the Goddess appeared to be no more than waist-deep in the pool, and she was holding Kalten up by the back of his tunic.

"Do you want to give me a hand with this, Sparhawk?" Bevier said.

"Right." Sparhawk swam over to join the Cyrinic, and together they hauled in the slender rope Bevier had trailed behind him as they had come through the tunnel. At the other end of the rope were their tightly bundled mail shirts and swords.

"Wait a minute," Bevier said when the rope suddenly went taut. "It's caught on something." He drew in several deep breaths, plunged under the surface, and went hand-over-hand back along the rope.

Sparhawk waited, unconsciously holding his own breath. Then the rope came free, and he hauled it in quickly. Bevier popped to the surface again, blowing out air.

"Are you sure you aren't part fish?" Sparhawk asked him.

"I've always had good lungs," Bevier replied. "Do you think we should get out our swords?"

"Let's see what Aphrael says first," Sparhawk decided, peering around. "I don't see any place to climb up out of the water yet."

"Now what?" Talen was asking the Goddess. "We're swimming around at the bottom of a well here." He looked up at the sheer sides of the shaft rising from the pool. "There are some openings up there, but there's no way to get to them."

"Did you bring it, Mirtai?" Aphrael asked.

The giantess nodded. "Excuse me a moment," she said, and she sank beneath the surface and began to pull off her tunic.

"What's she doing?" Talen asked, peering down through the clear water.

"She's taking off her clothes," Aphrael replied, "and she doesn't need any help from you. Keep your eyes where they belong."

"*You* run around naked all the time," he protested. "Why should you care if we watch Mirtai get undressed?"

"It's entirely different," she replied in a lofty tone. "Now do as you're told."

Talen thrust himself around in the water until he had his back to Mirtai. "I'm never going to understand her," he grumbled.

"Oh, yes you will, Talen," she told him in a mysterious little voice, "but not quite yet. I'll explain it all to you in a few more years."

Then Mirtai rose to the surface holding the coil of rope that had been slung over her shoulder under her tunic. "I'll need something to stand on, Aphrael," she said, hefting the grappling hook attached to one end of the rope. "I won't be able to throw this while I'm treading water."

"All right, gentlemen," Aphrael said primly, "eyes front."

Sparhawk's smile was concealed in the dimness. Talen was right. Aphrael seemed almost unaware of her own nakedness, but Mirtai's was an entirely different matter. He heard the sound of water trickling off the sleek limbs of the golden giantess as she rose to stand, he surmised, on its very surface.

Then he heard the whistling sound of the grappling hook as Mirtai swung it in wider and wider circles. Then the whistling stopped for an interminable, breathless moment. There was the clink of steel on stone high above, followed by a grating sound as the points dug in.

"Good cast," Aphrael said.

"Lucky," Mirtai replied. "It usually takes two or three throws."

Sparhawk felt a touch on his shoulder. "Here," Mirtai said, handing him the rope. "Hold this while I get dressed. Then we'll climb up and go find your wife."

"What on *earth* are you doing, Bergsten?"

The Patriarch of Emsat started violently and jerked his head around to stare at the God who had just walked up behind him.

"You're supposed to be hurrying, you know," Setras chided him. "Aphrael wants everybody to be in place by morning."

"We came across some of Klæl's soldiers, Divine One," Sir Heldin rumbled. "They're inside that cave." He pointed at a barely visible opening in the hillside across the shallow gully.

"Why didn't you deal with them? I told you how to do it."

"We put a lantern in there, but there's a door inside the cave, Setras-God," Atana Maris advised him.

"Well, *open* it, dear lady," Setras said. "We really *must* reach Cyrga by morning. Aphrael will be terribly vexed with me if we're late."

"We'd gladly open it if we knew how, Divine One," Bergsten told him, "but late or not, I *won't* ride away from here and leave those monsters behind me, and if that vexes Aphrael, that's just too bad." The handsome, stupid God irritated Bergsten for some reason.

"Why do I have to do everything myself?" Setras sighed. "Wait here. I'll deal with this, and then we'll be able to move on. We're terribly behind schedule, you know. We'll have to get cracking if we're going to make it by morning." He strolled on across the rocky gully and entered the cave.

"That young fellow's *really* trying my patience," Bergsten muttered. "Trying to explain something to him is like talking to a brick. How *can* he be so—" Bergsten pulled up short just this side of heresy.

"He's coming back out," Atana Maris said.

"I thought he might," Bergsten said with some satisfaction. "Apparently he didn't have any better luck with that door than we did."

Setras was strolling toward them humming a Styric melody when the entire hill vanished in a great, fiery explosion that shook the very earth. The fire billowed out with a dreadful, seething roar, hurling Bergsten and the others to the ground and engulfing Aphrael's cousin.

"Dear God!" Bergsten gasped, staring at the boiling fire.

Then Setras, with not so much as a hair out of place, came sauntering out of the fire. "There now," he said mildly, "that wasn't so difficult, was it?"

"How did you get the door open, Divine One?" Heldin asked curiously.

"I didn't, old boy." Setras smiled. "Actually, they opened it for me."

"Why would they do that?"

"I knocked, dear boy. I knocked. Even creatures like that have *some* manners. Shall we be going, then?"

"They are much feared by the other Cyrgai," Xanetia reported, "and all do give way to them."

"That would be useful—if it weren't for the racial differences," Bevier noted.

"Such differences do not pose an insurmountable obstacle, Sir Knight," Xanetia assured him. "Should it prove needful, thy features and those of thy companions may once more be altered. Divine Aphrael can doubtless serve in her sister's stead in the combining of the two spells which do yet disguise ye."

"We can talk about that in a moment," Flute said. "First, though, I think we should all get some idea of how this part of the city's laid out." The Goddess had resumed her more familiar form, and Bevier for one seemed much relieved.

"Methinks this mount is not of natural origin, Divine One," Xanetia told her. "The sides are of uniform steepness, and the avenues which do ascend to the top are more stairways than streets. Cross-streets, however, do encircle the hill at regular intervals."

"Unimaginative, aren't they?" Mirtai observed. "Are there many of them wandering around out there?"

"Nay, Atana. 'Tis late, and most have long since sought their beds."

"We *could* chance it," Kalten mused. "If Flute and Xanetia can make us look like Cyrgai, we could just march right up the hill."

"Not in *these* clothes we can't," Sparhawk disagreed.

Talen slipped out of the shadows to reenter the passageway leading back to the central shaft of the well. In many ways the agile young thief could be nearly as invisible as Xanetia. "More soldiers coming," he whispered.

"Those patrols could get to be a nuisance," Kalten said.

"These aren't like those others," Talen told him. "They aren't patrolling the side streets. They're just climbing the stairs toward the top of the city. They aren't wearing the same kind of armor either."

"Describe them, young master Talen," Xanetia said intently.

"They're wearing cloaks, for one thing," Talen replied, "and they've got a sort of emblem on their breastplates. Their helmets are different, too."

"Temple Guards, then," Xanetia said, "the ones of which I spake earlier. I did glean from the thought of such few as I encountered that other Cyrgai do avoid them insofar as they might, and that all are obliged to bow down when they pass."

Sparhawk and Bevier exchanged a long look. "There are the clothes you wanted, Sparhawk." Bevier said.

"How many are there?" Sparhawk asked Talen.

"I counted ten."

Sparhawk considered it. "Let's do it," he decided, "but try to keep the noise down." And he led them out of the passageway into the street.

"Good God, Ulath!" Itagne exclaimed, "don't do that! My heart almost stopped!"

"Sorry, Itagne," the big Thalesian apologized. "There's no really graceful way to come out of No-Time. Let's go talk with Betuana and Engessa."

They rode back to join the queen and her general.

"Sir Ulath just arrived with news, your Majesty," Itagne said politely.

"Ah," she said. "Good news or bad news, Ulath-Knight?"

"A little of each, your Majesty," he replied. "The Trolls are a couple of miles east of here."

"And what's the good news?"

He smiled slightly. "That *is* the good news. The bad news is that there's another large force of Klæl's soldiers waiting in ambush just south of here. They'll probably hit you within the hour. They're in our way, and we have to hurry. Sparhawk and the others are going to rescue Ehlana and her maid tonight, and he wants us all to converge on the city by morning."

"We must fight the Klæl-beasts then," she said.

"That could be troublesome," Itagne murmured.

"Tynian and I have worked out a solution of sorts," Ulath continued, "but we don't want to offend you, your Majesty, so we thought I should stop by and talk it over first. Klæl's troops are preparing to ambush *you*. I know you'd prefer to deal with that yourself, but in the interests of expediency, would you be willing to forgo the pleasure?"

"I'd be willing to *listen*, Ulath-Knight," she said.

"There are ways we could just slip around that ambush, but Klæl can probably do the same kinds of things to time and distance that Aphrael and her cousins can, and I don't think we want those brutes coming up behind us."

"What's your solution then, Ulath-Knight?"

"I've got a sizable force at my disposal, your Majesty," he replied, "and they're hungry. Since we're too busy right now for an extended romp through the desert, why don't we just let the Trolls have Klæl's soldiers for breakfast?"

Sir Anosian looked a little shaken as he rode forward to speak with Kring and Tikume.

"What's the matter, friend Anosian?" Tikume asked the black-armored Pandion. "You look as if you just saw a ghost."

"Worse, friend Tikume," Anosian replied. "I've just been reprimanded by a God. Most men don't survive that experience."

"Aphrael again?" Kring guessed.

"No, friend Kring. This time it was her cousin Hanka. He's very abrupt. The Genidian Knights rely on him for assistance with their spells."

"He was unhappy with you?" Tikume asked. "What did you do this time?"

Anosian made a sour face. "Sometimes my spells are a little sloppy," he admitted. "Aphrael's generous enough to forgive me. Her cousin isn't." He shuddered. "Divine Hanka's going to hurry us along just a bit."

"Oh?"

"We have to be at the gates of Cyrga by morning."

"How far is it?" Kring asked him.

"I have no idea," Anosian admitted, "and under the circumstances, I didn't think it would be prudent to ask. Hanka wants us to ride west from here."

Tikume frowned. "If we don't know how far it is, how can we be sure we'll get there by morning?"

"Oh, we'll get there all right, friend Tikume," Anosian assured him. "I think we'd better start moving, though. Divine Hanka's notoriously short-tempered. If we don't start riding west very soon, he might just decide to pick us up and *throw* us from here to Cyrga."

The Temple Guardsman assumed a warlike posture—a rather stiff, formalized pose such as one occasionally sees on a frieze carved by an indifferently talented sculptor. Kalten brushed the man's sword aside and slammed his fist against the side of his helmet. The guardsman reeled away and fell heavily onto the cobblestones. He was struggling to rise again when Kalten kicked him solidly in the face.

"Quietly, Kalten!" Sparhawk said in a hoarse whisper.

"Sorry. I guess I got carried away." Kalten bent and peeled back the fallen guardsman's eyelid. "He'll sleep till noon," he said. He straightened and looked around. "Is that all of them?"

"That was the last," Bevier whispered. "Let's get them out of the middle of the street. The moon's going to make it up over those mountains soon, and it'll be as bright as day down in this basin in just a little while."

It had been a short, ugly little fight. Sparhawk and his friends had rushed out of a dark side street and had fallen on the detachment from the rear. Surprise had accounted for much of their success, and what surprise had not accomplished had been more than made up for by the ineptitude of the ceremonial troops. Sparhawk concluded that the Cyrgai looked impressive, but that their training over the centuries had grown so formalized and detached from reality that it had almost become more a form of dance than a preparation for real combat. Since the Cyrgai could not cross the Styric curse line, they had not been involved in any real fights for ten thousand years, and so they were hopelessly unprepared for all the nasty little tricks that crop up from time to time in close, hand-to-hand fighting.

"I still don't see how we're going to pull this off," Talen puffed as he dragged an inert guardsman back into the shadows. "One look will tell the gate guards that we're not Cyrgai."

"We've already discussed that," Sparhawk told him, "while you were out scouting. Xanetia and Aphrael are going to mix spells again—the way the Anarae and Sephrenia did back in Matherion. We'll look enough like Cyrgai to get us through the gate—particularly if the rest of the Cyrgai are as much afraid of these Temple Guardsmen as Xanetia says they are."

"As long as the subject's come up," Kalten said, "after we've bluffed our way past those gate guards, I want my own face back. We stand a fair chance of getting killed tonight, and I'd like to have my own name on my tombstone. Besides, if by some remote chance we succeed, I don't want to startle Alean by coming at her with a stranger's face. After what she's been through, she's entitled to see the real me."

"I don't have any problem with that," Sparhawk agreed.

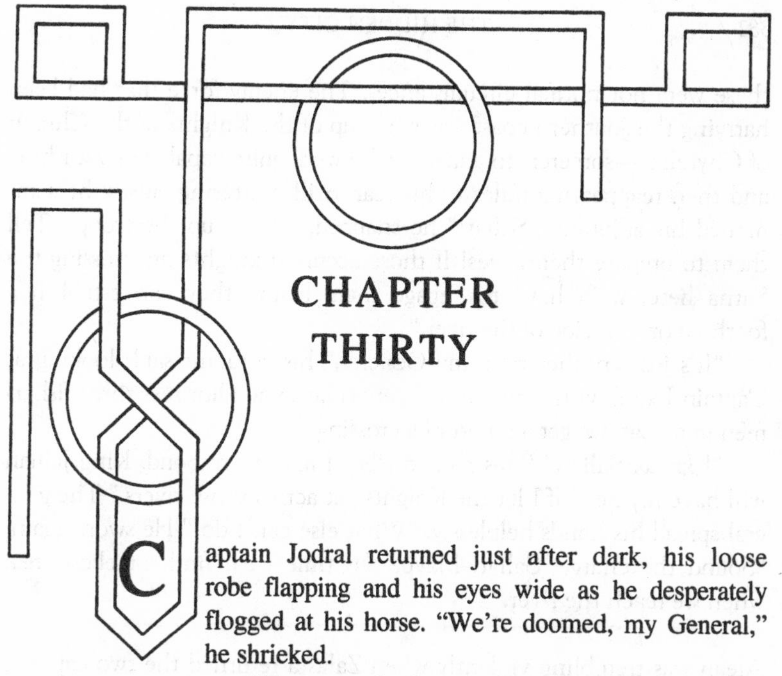

CHAPTER THIRTY

Captain Jodral returned just after dark, his loose robe flapping and his eyes wide as he desperately flogged at his horse. "We're doomed, my General," he shrieked.

"Get control of yourself, Jodral!" General Piras snapped. "What did you see?"

"There are millions of them, General!" Jodral was still on the verge of hysteria.

"Jodral, you've never seen a million of anything! Now, what's out there?"

"They're coming across the Sarna, General," Jodral replied, trying his best to control his quavering voice. "The reports about that fleet are true. I saw the ships."

"Where? We're ten leagues from the coast."

"They've sailed up the River Sarna, General Piras, and they've lashed their ships together side by side to form bridges."

"Absurd! The Sarna's five miles wide down here! Talk sense, man!"

"I know what I saw, General. The other scouts will be along shortly to confirm it. Kaftal's in flames. You can see the light of the fire from here." Jodral turned and pointed south toward a huge, flickering orange glow in the sky above the low coastal hills standing between the Cynesgan forces and the sea.

General Piras swore. This was the third time this week that his scouts had reported a crossing of the lower Sarna or the Verel River, and he had not thus far seen any sign of hostile forces. Under normal circumstances, he'd have simply had his scouts flogged or worse, but these were not normal circumstances. The enemy force that had been harrying the southern coast was made up of the Knights of the Church of Chyrellos—sorcerers to a man—who were quite capable of vanishing and then reappearing miles to his rear. Still muttering curses, he summoned his adjutant. "Sallat!" he snapped, "Wake up the troops. Tell them to prepare themselves! If those accursed knights *are* crossing the Sarna here, we'll have to engage them before they can establish a foothold on this side of the river."

"It's just another ruse, my General," his adjutant said, looking at Captain Jodral with contempt. "Every time some idiot sees three fishermen in a boat, we get a report of a crossing."

"I *know*, Sallat," Piras replied, "but I *have* to respond. King Jaluah will have my head if I let the Knights get across those rivers." The general spread his hands helplessly. "What else can I do?" He swore again. "Sound the charge, Sallat. Maybe *this* time we'll find somebody real when we reach the river."

Alean was trembling violently when Zalasta returned the two captives to the small but now scrupulously clean cell following yet another of those hideous, silent interviews with the bat-winged Klæl, but Ehlana felt drained of all emotion. There was a perverse seductiveness to the strangely gentle probing of that infinite mind, and Ehlana always felt violated and befouled when it was over.

"That will be the last time, Ehlana," Zalasta told her apologetically. "If it's any comfort to you, he's still baffled by your husband. He cannot understand how any creature with such power would willingly subordinate himself to—" He hesitated.

"To a mere woman, Zalasta?" she suggested wearily.

"No, Ehlana, that's not it. Some of the worlds Klæl dominates are wholly ruled by females, and males are kept for breeding purposes only. No, Klæl simply cannot understand the relationship between you and Sparhawk."

"You might explain the meaning of love to him, Zalasta." She paused. "But you don't understand it yourself, do you?"

His face went cold. "Good night, your Majesty," he said in an unemotional tone. Then he turned and left the cell, closing and locking the door behind him.

Ehlana had her ear pressed to the door before the clanging echo of its closing had subsided.

"I do not fear them," she heard King Santheocles declare.

"Then you're a bigger fool than I thought," Zalasta told him bluntly. "All of your allies have been systematically neutralized, and your enemies have you surrounded."

"We are Cyrgai," Santheocles insisted. "No one can stand against us."

"That may have been true ten thousand years ago when your enemies dressed in furs and charged your lines with flint-tipped spears. Now you face Church Knights armed with steel; you face Atan warriors who can kill your soldiers with their fingertips; you face Peloi who ride through your ranks like the wind; you face Trolls, who not only kill your soldiers, but also eat them. If that weren't bad enough, you face Aphrael, who can stop the sun or turn you to stone. Worst of all, you face Anakha and Bhelliom, and that means that you face obliteration."

"Mighty Cyrgon will protect us." Santheocles' voice was set in a willful note of stubborn imbecility.

"Why don't you go talk with Otha of Zemoch, Santheocles?" There was a sneer in Zalasta's voice. "He'll tell you how the Elder God Azash squealed when Anakha destroyed him." Zalasta suddenly broke off. "*He comes!*" he choked. "Closer than we'd ever thought possible!"

"What are you talking about?" Ekatas demanded.

"Anakha is here!" Zalasta exclaimed. "Go to your generals, Santheocles! Tell them to call out their troops and order them to scour the streets of Cyrga, for Anakha is within your walls! Hurry, man! Anakha is here, and our deaths stalk the streets with him! Come with me, Ekatas! Cyrgon must be warned, and eternal Klæl! The night of decision is upon us!"

And thou, O Blue, all cares and griefs shall ban
And lift our hearts to heights unknown to mortal man

Elron ticked off the count on his fingers and swore. No matter how he slurred or compressed the words of that last line, it still had one beat too many. He hurled his quill pen across the room and sank his face into his hands in an artful pose of poetic despair. Elron did that frequently when composing verse.

Then he hopefully raised his face as a thought came to him. He *was* nearing the final stanzas of his masterpiece, after all, and an alexandrine *would* add emphasis. What would the critics say?

Elron agonized over the decision. He cursed the day when he had chosen to cast the most important work of his career in heroic couplets.

He hated iambics. They were so mercilessly regular and unforgiving, and pentameter was like a chain around his neck, jerking him up short at the end of every line. "Ode to Blue" hung in the balance while her creator struggled with the sullen intransigences of form and meter.

Elron could not be sure how long the screaming had been going on or exactly when it had started. His mind, caught up in a creative frenzy, had blotted out everything external to that one maddeningly recalcitrant line. The poet rose irritably to his feet and went to the window to look out at the torchlit streets of Natayos. What were they screaming about?

Scarpa's soldiers—ignorant, unwashed serfs for the most part—were running, bawling in terror like so many bleating sheep. What had set them off this time?

Elron leaned slightly out to look up the street. There seemed to be a different kind of light coming from the part of the ruined city that was still buried in tangled brush and creeping vines. Elron frowned. It was most definitely not torchlight. It seemed to be a pale white glow instead, steady, unwavering, and coming from dozens of places at the same time.

Then Elron heard Scarpa's voice rising over the screams. The crazy charlatan was shouting orders of some kind in his most imperial voice. The rabble in the streets, however, were ignoring him. The army was streaming along the cobbled streets of ruined Natayos toward the main gate, pushing, howling, jamming together and struggling to get through that hopelessly clogged gateway. Beyond the gate, Elron saw winking torches streaming off into the surrounding jungle. What in God's name was going on here?

Then his blood suddenly froze. He gaped in horror at the glowing figures emerging from the side streets of the ruin to stalk implacably along the broad avenue that led to the gate. The Shining Ones who had depopulated Panem-Dea, Norenja, and Synaqua had finally descended on Natayos!

The poet stood frozen for only a moment, and then his mind moved more quickly than he'd have thought possible. Flight was clearly out of the question. The gate was so completely jammed that even those who had already reached it had little chance of forcing their way through. Elron dashed to his writing table and swatted his candle with the flat of his hand, plunging the room into darkness. If there were no lights in the windows of this upper floor, the horrors that stalked the streets would have no reason to search. Frantically, stumbling in the darkness, he ran from room to room, desperately searching for any other burning candles that might betray his location.

Then, certain that he was safe for the moment at least, the one known throughout Astel as Sabre crept back to his room to peer fearfully around the edge of the windowframe at the street below.

Scarpa stood atop a partially collapsed wall issuing contradictory commands to regiments that evidently only he could see. His threadbare velvet cloak was draped over his shoulders and his makeshift crown was slightly askew.

Not far from where he stood, Cyzada was saying something in his hollow voice—an incantation of some kind, Elron guessed—and his fingers were weaving intricate designs in the air. Louder and louder he spoke in guttural Styric, summoning God only knew what horrors to face the silent, glowing figures advancing on him. His voice rose to a screech, and he pawed at the air, frantically exaggerating the gestures.

And then one of the incandescent intruders reached him. Cyzada screamed and flinched back violently, but it was too late. The glowing hand had already touched him. He reeled back as if that almost gentle touch had been some massive blow. Staggering, he turned as if to flee, and Elron saw his face.

The poet retched, clamping his hands over his mouth to hold in any sound that might give away his presence. Cyzada of Esos was dissolving. His already unrecognizable face was sliding down the front of his head as if it were melted wax, and a rapidly spreading stain was discoloring the front of his white Styric robe. He staggered a few steps toward the still-raving Scarpa, his arms reaching hungrily out toward the madman even as the flesh slid away from those skeletal, outstretched hands. Then the Styric slowly collapsed to the stones, bubbling and seething, his decaying body oozing out through the fabric of his robe.

"Archers to the front!" Scarpa commanded in his rich, theatrical voice. "Sweep them with arrows!"

Elron fell to the floor and scrambled away from the window.

"Cavalry to the flanks!" he heard Scarpa command. "Sabers at the ready!"

Elron crawled toward his writing table, groping in the dark.

"Imperial guardsmen!" Scarpa bellowed. "Quicktime, march!"

Elron found the leg of the table, reached up, and frantically began grabbing at the sheets of paper lying on the tabletop.

"First Regiment—charge!" Scarpa commanded in a great voice.

Elron knocked over the table, whimpering in his desperate haste.

"Second Regiment—" Scarpa's voice broke off suddenly, and Elron heard him scream.

The poet spread his arms, trying to gather the priceless pages of "Ode to Blue" out of the darkness.

Scarpa's voice was shrill now. "Mother!" he shrieked. "Pleaseplease please!" The resonant voice had become a kind of liquid screech. "Pleasepleaseplease!" It sounded almost like a man trying to cry out from underwater. "Pleasepleaseplease!" And then the voice wheezed off into a dreadful gurgling silence.

Clutching the pages he had found, Sabre abandoned his search for any others, scurried across the room on his hands and knees, and hid under the bed.

Bhlokw's expression was reproachful as he shambled back across the night-shrouded gravel. "Wickedness, U-lat," he accused. "We are pack-mates, and you said a thing to me that was not so."

"I would not do that, Bhlokw," Ulath protested.

"You put the thought into my mind-belly that the big things with iron on their faces were good-to-eat. They are *not* good-to-eat."

"Were they bad-to-eat, Bhlokw?" Tynian asked sympathetically.

"*Very* bad-to-eat, Tin-in. I have not tasted anything so bad-to-eat before."

"I did not know this, Bhlokw," Ulath tried to apologize. "It was my thought that they were big enough that one or two might fill your belly."

"I only ate one," Bhlokw replied. "It was so bad-to-eat that I did not want to eat another. Not even Ogres would eat those, and Ogres will eat anything. It makes me not-glad that you said the thing that was not so to me, U-lat."

"It makes me not-glad as well," Ulath confessed. "I said a thing which I did not know. It was wicked of me to do this."

Queen Betuana drew Tynian aside. "How long will it take us to reach the Hidden City, Tynian-Knight?" she asked.

"Is your Majesty talking about how long it's really going to take or how long it's going to seem."

"Both."

"It's going to *seem* like weeks, Betuana-Queen, but in actual time, it'll be instantaneous. Ulath and I left Matherion just a few weeks ago in real time, but it seems that we've been on the road for nearly a year. It's very strange, but you get used to it after a while."

"We must start soon if we are to reach Cyrga by morning."

"Ulath and I'll have to talk with Ghnomb about that. He's the one who stops time, but he's also the God of Eat. He may not be happy with us. The idea of letting the Trolls kill Klæl's soldiers was a good one, but Ghnomb expects them to eat what they kill, and they don't like the taste."

She shuddered. "How can you stand to be around the Troll-beasts, Tynian-Knight? They're horrible creatures."

"They aren't really so bad, your Majesty," Tynian defended them. "They're very moral, you know. They're fiercely loyal to their own packs; they don't even know how to lie; and they won't kill anything unless they intend to eat it—or unless it attacks them. As soon as Ulath finishes apologizing to Bhlokw, we'll summon Ghnomb and talk with him about stopping time so that we can get to Cyrga." Tynian made a face. "*That's* what's going to take a while. You have to be patient when you're trying to explain something to the Troll-Gods."

"Is that what Ulath-Knight is doing?" she asked curiously, "Apologizing?"

Tynian nodded. "It's not as easy as it sounds, your Majesty. There's nothing in Trollish that even comes close to 'I'm sorry,' probably because Trolls never do anything that they're ashamed of."

"*Will* you be still?" Liatris hissed at the protesting Gahenas. "They're in the next room right now."

The three empresses were hiding in a dark antechamber adjoining the Tegan's private quarters. Liatris stood at the door with her dagger in her hand.

They waited in tense apprehension.

"They're gone now," Liatris said. "We'd better wait for a little while, though."

"Will you *please* tell me what's going on?" Gahenas asked.

"Chacole sent some people to kill you," Elysoun told her. "Liatris and I found out about it, and came to rescue you."

"Why would Chacole do that?"

"Because you know too much about what she's planning."

"That silly plan to implicate Cieronna in a spurious assassination plot?"

"The plot wasn't spurious, and Cieronna wasn't even remotely connected with it. Chacole and Torellia are planning to kill our husband."

"Treason!" Gahenas gasped.

"Probably not. Chacole and Torellia are members of royal houses currently at war with the Tamul Empire, and they're getting orders from home. The assassination of Sarabian could technically be called an act of war." Elysoun stopped as a wave of nausea swept over her. "Oh, dear," she said in a sick little voice.

"What's wrong?" Liatris demanded.

"It's nothing. It'll pass."

"Are you sick?"

"Sort of. It's nothing to worry about. I should have eaten something when you woke me up, that's all."

"You're white as a sheet. What's wrong with you?"

"I'm pregnant, if you really have to know."

"It was bound to happen eventually, Elysoun," Gahenas said smugly. "I'm surprised it didn't happen earlier, the way you carry on. Have you any idea at all of who the father is?"

"Sarabian," Elysoun replied with a shrug of her shoulders. "Do you think it's safe to leave now, Liatris? I think we'd better get to our husband as quickly as we can. Chacole wouldn't have sent people to kill Gahenas unless this was the night when she was planning her attempt on Sarabian."

"She'll have people watching all the doors," Liatris said.

"Not all the doors, dear." Elysoun smiled. "I know of at least three that she's not aware of. You see, Gahenas, there are some advantages to having an active social life. Check the hallway, Liatris. Let's get Gahenas out of here before Chacole's assassins come back."

The Cyrgai at the bronze gate stood back fearfully as Sparhawk led the others up the last few steps. "Yala Cyrgon!" the officer in charge said, smashing his fist against his breastplate in a kind of formal salute.

"Respond, Anakha," Xanetia's voice murmured in Sparhawk's ear. " 'Tis customary."

"Yala Cyrgon!" Sparhawk said, also banging on his chest and being careful not to allow the cloak he'd removed from the unconscious Temple Guardsman to open and reveal the fact that he was wearing his mail shirt rather than an ornate breastplate.

The officer seemed not to notice. Sparhawk and the others marched through the gate and moved along a broad street toward a kind of central square. "Is he still watching?" Sparhawk muttered.

"Nay, Anakha," Xanetia replied. "He and his men have returned to the guardroom beside the gate."

It had appeared from below that the only buildings within the walls at the summit of Cyrga were the fortress-palace and the temple, but that was not entirely true. There were other structures as well, low, utilitarian-looking buildings—storehouses for the most part, Sparhawk guessed. "Talen," he said over his shoulder, "ease over to the side of the street. Find a door you can get open in a hurry. Let's get out of sight while Xanetia scouts around."

"Right," Talen replied. He ducked into the shadows, and a moment later they heard his whisper and quickly moved to the door he was holding open for them.

"Now what?" Kalten asked.

"Xanetia and I go looking for Ehlana and Alean," Aphrael's voice replied out of the darkness.

"Where were you?" Talen asked curiously, "when we were coming up the hill, I mean?"

"Here and there," she replied. "My family's moving all the others into position, and I wanted to be sure everything's going according to schedule."

"Is it?"

"It is now. There were a couple of problems, but I took care of them. Let's get at this, Xanetia. We still have a lot to do before morning."

"Ah, there they are," Setras said. "I wasn't really all that far off, now was I?"

"Are you sure this time?" Bergsten demanded.

"You're cross with me, aren't you, Bergsten?"

Bergsten sighed, and decided to let it pass. "No, Divine One," he replied. "We all make mistakes, I guess."

"That's frightfully decent of you, old boy," Setras thanked him. "We were moving in generally the right direction. I was just off a few degrees, that's all."

"Are you certain those are the right peaks this time, Divine One?" Heldin rumbled.

"Oh, absolutely," Setras said happily. "They're exactly as Aphrael described them. You notice how they glow in the moonlight?"

Heldin squinted across the desert at the two glowing spires rearing up out of the dark jumble of broken rock. "They look about right," he said dubiously.

"I have to go find the gate," Setras told them. "It's supposed to be exactly on a line from the gap between the two peaks."

"Are you sure, Divine One?" Bergsten asked. "It's that way on the south side, but do we know for certain that it's the same here on the north?"

"You've never met Cyrgon, have you, old boy? He's the most rigid creature you've ever seen. If there's a gate on the south, there'll be one on the north as well, believe me. Don't go away. I'll be right back." He turned and strolled off across the desert toward the two peaks glowing in the moonlight.

Atana Maris was standing to one side of Bergsten and Heldin with a slightly troubled look on her face.

"What's the matter, Atana?" Heldin asked her.

"I think there is something I do not understand, Heldin-Knight," she replied, struggling to put her thought into Elenic. "The Setras person is a God?"

"A Styric God, yes."

"If he is a God, how did he get lost?"

"We're not certain, Atana Maris."

"That is what I do not understand. If Setras-God were a human, I would say that he is stupid. But he is a God, so he cannot be stupid, can he?"

"I think you'd better take that up with his Grace here," Heldin replied. "I'm only a soldier. He's the expert on theology."

"Thanks, Heldin," Bergsten said in a flat tone of voice.

"If he *is* stupid, Bergsten-Priest, how can we be certain that he's brought us to the right place?"

"We have to trust Aphrael, Atana. Setras may be a little uncertain about things, but Aphrael isn't, and she talked with him for quite some time, as I recall."

"Speaking slowly," Heldin added, "and using short, simple words."

"Is it possible, Bergsten-Priest?" Maris asked insistently. "*Can* a God be stupid?"

Bergsten looked at her helplessly. "*Ours* isn't," he evaded, "and I'm sure yours isn't either."

"You didn't answer my question, Bergsten."

"You're right, Atana," he replied, "I didn't—and I'm not going to. If you're really curious, I'll take you to Chyrellos when this is all over, and you can ask Dolmant."

"Bravely spoken, Lord Bergsten," Heldin murmured.

"Shut up, Heldin."

"Yes, your Grace."

Sparhawk, Bevier, and Kalten stood at a small, barred window in the musty-smelling warehouse looking out at the fortresslike palace rearing above the rest of the city. "That's really archaic," Bevier said critically.

"It looks strong enough to me," Kalten said.

"They've built the main structure of the palace right up against the outer wall, Kalten. It saves building two walls, but it compromises the structural integrity of the fortress. Give me a couple of months and some good catapults, and I could pound the whole thing to pieces."

"I don't think catapults had been invented when they built it, Bevier," Sparhawk said. "It was probably the strongest fort in the world ten thousand years ago." He looked out at the gloomy, rearing pile. As Bevier had noted, the main structure was backed up against the wall that separated this part of Cyrga from the rest of the city. Shorter towers stair-stepped up to the large central tower that shouldered high above the rest of the palace and grew, or so it seemed, out of the wall itself. It appeared that the palace had not been built to look out over the city, but rather to face the white limestone temple. The Cyrgai clearly looked at their God, and turned their backs on the rest of the world.

The door that Talen had unlocked to provide them entry into this storehouse creaked as it opened and then closed again. Then the soft glow of Xanetia's face once again dimly illuminated the area around her.

"We've found them," the Child-Goddess said as the Anarae set her down on the flagstoned floor.

Sparhawk's heart leaped. "Are they all right?"

"They haven't been treated very well. They're tired and hungry and very much afraid. Zalasta took them to see Klæl, and that's enough to frighten anybody."

"Where are they?" Mirtai demanded intently.

"At the very top of that highest tower at the back of the palace."

"Did you talk with them?" Kalten asked intently.

Aphrael shook her head. "I didn't think it was a good idea. What they don't know about, they can't talk about."

"Anarae," Bevier said thoughtfully, "would the soldiers in the palace let Temple Guardsmen move around freely in there?"

"Nay, Sir Knight. The Cyrgai are much driven by custom, and Temple Guardsmen have little cause to enter the palace."

"I guess we can discard these, then," Kalten said, pulling off the ornate bronze helmet and dark cloak he had purloined in the lower city. He touched his cheek. "We still look like Cyrgai. We could steal some different uniforms and then just march in, couldn't we?"

Xanetia shook her head. "The soldiers within the palace are all kinsmen, members of the royal clan, and are all known to one another. Subterfuge would be far too perilous."

"We've got to come up with a way to get into that tower!" Kalten said desperately.

"I already have," Mirtai told him calmly. "It's dangerous, but I think it's the only way."

"Go ahead," Sparhawk told her.

"We might be able to sneak up through the palace, but if we're discovered, we'd have to fight, and that'd put Ehlana and Alean in immediate danger."

Sparhawk nodded bleakly. "It's just too dangerous to risk," he agreed.

"All right, then. If we can't go through the palace, we'll have to go up the outside."

"You mean climb the tower?" Kalten asked incredulously.

"It's not as difficult as it sounds, Kalten. Those walls aren't built of marble, so they aren't smooth. They're rough stone blocks, and there are plenty of handholds and places to put your feet. I could climb that back wall like a ladder, if I had to."

"I'm not really very graceful, Mirtai," he said dubiously. "I'll do anything at all to rescue Alean, but I won't be much good to her if I make a misstep and fall five hundred feet into the lower city."

"We have ropes, Kalten. I'll keep you from falling. Talen can scamper up a wall like a squirrel, and I can climb almost as well. If we had Stragen and Caalador along, they'd be halfway up the side of that tower by now."

"Mirtai," Bevier said in a pained voice, "we're wearing mail shirts. Climbing a sheer wall with seventy pounds of steel hanging from your shoulders might be a little challenging."

"Then take it off, Bevier."

"I might need it when I get up on top."

"No problem," Talen assured him. "We'll bundle them all together and pull them up behind us. I do sort of like it, Sparhawk. It's quiet; it's fairly fast; and there probably won't be any guards going hand-over-hand around the outside of the tower looking for intruders. Mirtai's had training from Stragen and Caalador, and I was born for burglary. She and I can do the real climbing. We'll drop ropes down to the rest of you at various stages along the way, and you can haul up the mail and swords behind you. We can get to the top of that tower in no time at all. We can do it, Sparhawk. It'll be easy."

"I can't really think of any alternatives," Sparhawk conceded dubiously.

"Let's do it, then," Mirtai said abruptly. "Let's get Ehlana and Alean out of there, and once they're safe, we can start to take this place apart."

"After I get my real face back," Kalten added adamantly. "Alean's entitled to that much consideration."

"Let's do that right now, Xanetia," Aphrael said. "Kalten will nag us about it all night if we don't."

"Nag?" Kalten objected.

"What color was your hair again, Kalten? Purple, wasn't it?" she asked him with an impish little smile.

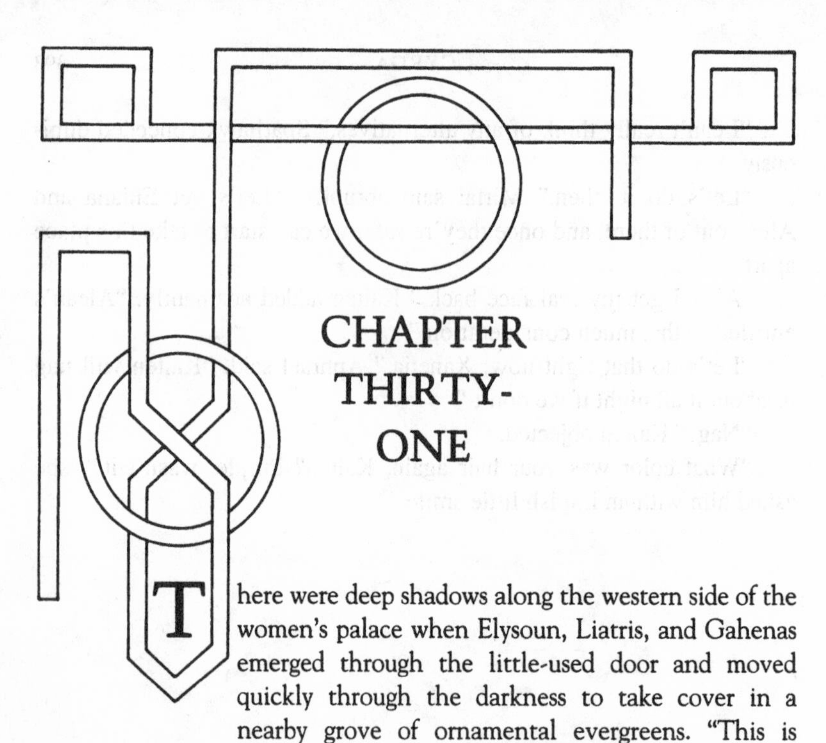

CHAPTER THIRTY-ONE

There were deep shadows along the western side of the women's palace when Elysoun, Liatris, and Gahenas emerged through the little-used door and moved quickly through the darkness to take cover in a nearby grove of ornamental evergreens. "This is going to be the dangerous part," Liatris cautioned in a low voice. "Chacole knows by now that her assassins weren't able to find Gahenas, and she's certain to have her people out to try to prevent us from reaching Ehlana's castle."

Elysoun looked out at the moon-drenched lawn. "That's impossible," she said. "It's just too bright. There's a path that goes on through this grove. It comes out near the Ministry of the Interior."

"That's the wrong direction, Elysoun," Gahenas protested. "The Elene castle's the other way."

"Yes, I know, but there's no cover. There's nothing between here and the castle but open lawn. We'd better stick to the shadows. If we go around on the other side of Interior, we'll be able to go through the grounds of the Foreign Ministry. It's only about fifty yards from there to the drawbridge of the castle."

"What if the drawbridge has been raised?"

"We'll worry about that when we get there, Gahenas. Let's get into the gardens around the Foreign Ministry first."

"Let's go, then, ladies," Liatris said abruptly. "We're not accomplishing anything by standing around talking. Let's go find out what we're up against."

"Back here," Talen whispered to them, coming out of a narrow alleyway. "The palace wall runs back to the place where it joins the outer fortifications at the end of this alley. The right angle where the two walls meet is perfect for climbing."

"Will you need this?" Mirtai asked, holding her grappling hook out to him.

"No. I can make it to the top without it, and we'd better not risk having some sentry up there hear the hook banging on the stones." He led them back along the alley to the cul-de-sac where the palace wall butted up against the imposing fortifications separating the compound from the rest of the city.

"How high would you say it is?" Kalten asked, squinting upward. It was strange to see Kalten's face again after all the weeks it had been disguised. Sparhawk tentatively touched his own face and immediately recognized the familiar contours of his broken nose.

"Thirty feet or so," Bevier replied softly to Kalten's question.

Mirtai was examining the angle formed by the joining of the two walls. "This won't be very difficult," she whispered.

"The whole structure's poorly designed," Bevier agreed critically.

"I'll go up first," Talen said.

"Don't do anything foolish up there," Mirtai cautioned.

"Trust me." He set his foot up on one of the protruding stones of the outer wall and reached for a handhold on the palace wall. He went up quickly.

"We'll check for sentries when we get up there," Mirtai quietly told the others. "Then we'll drop a rope down to you." She reached up and began to follow the young thief up the angle between the two walls.

Bevier leaned back and looked upward. "The moon's up now," he said.

"Thinkest thou that it might reveal us?" Xanetia asked him.

"No, Anarae. We'll be climbing the north side of the tower, so we'll be in shadow the whole way to the top."

They waited tensely, craning their necks to watch the climbers creeping upward.

"Somebody's coming!" Kalten hissed, "Up there—along the battlements!"

The climbers stopped, pulling back into the shadows of the sharp angle between the two walls.

"He's got a torch," Kalten whispered. "If he holds it out over those battlements . . ." he left it hanging.

Sparhawk held his breath.

"It's all right now," Bevier said. "He's going back."

"We might want to deal with him when we get up there," Kalten noted.

"Not if we can avoid it," Sparhawk disagreed. "We don't want somebody else to come looking for him."

Talen had reached the battlements. He clung to the rough stones for a moment, listening. Then he slipped over the top and out of sight. After several interminable moments, Mirtai followed him.

Sparhawk and the others waited in the darkness.

Then Mirtai's rope came slithering down the wall.

"Let's go," Sparhawk said tensely, "one at a time."

The building blocks were of rough, square-fractured basalt, and they protruded unevenly from the walls, making climbing much simpler than it appeared. Sparhawk didn't even bother to use the rope. He reached the top and clambered over the battlements. "Do the sentries have any kind of set routine up here?" he asked Mirtai.

"It seems that each one has his own section of wall," she replied. "The one at this end doesn't walk very fast. I'm guessing, but I'd say that it'll be a quarter of an hour before he comes back."

"Is there any place where we can take cover before then?"

"There's a door in that first tower," Talen said, pointing at the squat structure rising at the end of the parapet. "It opens onto a stairwell."

"Have you taken a look at the back wall yet?"

Talen nodded. "There's no parapet along that side, but there's a ledge a couple of feet wide where the outer wall joins the back of the palace. We'll be able to make our way along that until we get on that central tower. Then we get to start climbing."

"Does the sentry look back there when he reaches this end of the parapet?"

"He didn't last time," Mirtai said.

"Let's look at that stairwell, then," Sparhawk decided. "As soon as the others are up, we'll hide in there until the sentry reaches this end and starts back. That should give us a half hour to crawl along that ledge to the central tower. Even if he looks around the corner next time, we should be out of the range of his torch by then."

"He's right on top of these things, isn't he?" Talen said gaily to Mirtai.

"What *is* this boy's problem?" Sparhawk demanded of the golden giantess.

"There's a certain kind of excitement involved in this, Dorlin'" Mirtai replied. "It sets the blood to pounding."

"Dorlin'?"

"Professional joke, Sparhawk. You probably wouldn't understand."

Vanion's scouts had returned about sunset to report contact with Kring to the south and Queen Betuana's Atans to the north. The ring of steel around the Forbidden Mountains was drawing inexorably tighter. The moon was rising over the desert when Betuana and Engessa came running in from Vanion's right flank and Kring and Tikume rode in from the left.

"Tynian-Knight will be along soon, Vanion-Preceptor," Engessa reported. "He and Ulath-Knight have spoken with Bergsten-Priest on *their* right. Ulath-Knight has remained with the Trolls to try to prevent incidents."

"Incidents?" Sephrenia asked.

"The Trolls are hungry. Ulath-Knight gave them a regiment of the Klæl-beasts to eat, but the flavor did not please the Trolls. Ulath-Knight tried to apologize, but I am not sure if the Trolls understood."

"Have you seen Berit and Khalad yet, friend Vanion?" Kring asked.

"No, but Aphrael said that they're just ahead of us. Her cousin guided them to the spot where that hidden gate's supposed to be."

"If they know where the gate is, we could go on in," Betuana suggested.

"We'd better wait, dear," Sephrenia replied. "Aphrael will let me know as soon as Sparhawk rescues Ehlana and Alean."

Tynian came riding across the vast open graveyard. "Bergsten's in place," he reported, swinging down out of his saddle. He looked at Itagne. "I have a message for you, your Excellency."

"Oh? From whom?"

"Atana Maris is with Bergsten. She wants to talk with you."

Itagne's eyes widened. "What's *she* doing here?" he exclaimed.

"She said that your letters must have gone astray. Not a single one of them reached her. You *did* write to her, didn't you, your Excellency?"

"Well—I was intending to." Itagne looked slightly embarrassed. "Something always seemed to come up, though."

"I'm sure she'll understand." Tynian's face was blandly expressionless. "Anyway, after she handed the city of Cynestra over to Bergsten, she decided to come looking for you."

Itagne's expression was sightly worried. "I hadn't counted on that," he confessed.

"What's this?" Betuana asked curiously.

"Ambassador Itagne and Atana Maris became good friends while he was in Cynestra, your Majesty," Sephrenia explained, "*very* good friends, actually."

"Ah," Betuana said. "It's a little unusual, but it's not unheard of, and Maris has always been an impulsive girl." Although the Atan queen still wore deep mourning, she seemed to have abandoned her ritual silence. "A word of advice, Itagne-Ambassador—if you'd care to hear it."

"Of course, your Majesty."

"It's not at all wise to toy with the affections of an Atan woman. It might not seem so, but we're very emotional. Sometimes we form attachments that aren't really appropriate." She did not look at Engessa as she said it. "Appropriate or not, however, those emotions are extremely powerful, and once the attachment is formed, there's very little we can do about it."

"I see," he said. "I'll definitely keep that in mind, your Majesty."

"Do you want me to go find Berit and Khalad and bring them back here, friend Vanion?" Kring asked.

Vanion considered it. "We'd better stay away from that gate," he decided. "The Cyrgai might be watching. Berit and Khalad are *supposed* to be there, but we aren't. Let's not stir anything up until Sparhawk sends word that his wife's safe. Then we'll *all* go in. There are a number of accounts that are long past due, and I think the time's coming when we'll want to settle up."

The ledge that ran along the back of the palace made reaching the central tower a matter of hardly more than a casual stroll. It still took time, however, and Sparhawk was acutely aware of the fact that the night was already more than half over. Mirtai and Talen moved up the side of the tower quickly, but the rest of them, roped together for safety, made much slower progress.

Sparhawk was peering upward when Kalten joined him. "Sparhawk, where's Aphrael?" the blond Pandion asked quietly.

"Everywhere. Didn't she tell you?"

"Very funny." Kalten looked off toward the east. "Are we going to make it before it starts getting light?"

"It could be close. There seems to be some kind of balcony just above us—and lighted windows."

"Are we going around them?"

"I'll have Talen take a look. If there aren't too many Cyrgai in the room, we might be able to finish this climb inside."

"Let's not take chances, Sparhawk. I'll climb all the way to the moon if I have to. Go ahead on up. I've got the rope tied off."

"Right." Sparhawk started to climb again. A slight breeze had come up, brushing the basalt wall with tenuous fingers. It was not strong enough to pose any dangers as yet, but Sparhawk definitely didn't want it getting any stronger.

"You're out of condition, Sparhawk," Mirtai told him critically when he reached the spot just below where she and Talen clung to the wall.

"Nobody's perfect. Can you make out any details of that balcony yet?"

"I was just going to swing over and have a look," Talen replied. He untied the rope from about his waist and began working his way across the wall toward the balcony.

You're making me cross, Sparhawk. Aphrael's voice seemed very loud in the silence of his mind. *I have plans for that young man, and they don't include scraping him up off a street five hundred feet below.*

He knows what he's doing. You worry too much. As long as you're here, could you give me a few details about the top of this tower?

There's a separate building up there—probably an afterthought of some kind. It's got the three rooms, a guardroom for the platoon or so of ceremonial troops, the cell where Mother and Alean are being held, and a large room across the front. Santheocles spends most of his time there.

Santheocles?

The King of the Cyrgai. He's an idiot. They all are, but he's worse than most.

Is there a window in Ehlana's cell?

A small one. It's barred, but you couldn't get through it anyway. The building up there is smaller than the rest of this tower, so there's a kind of parapet that runs all the way around it.

Do those guards patrol it?

No. There's no real need for that. It's the highest place in the city, and the notion that somebody might scale the tower has never occurred to the Cyrgai.

Is Santheocles up there right now?

He was, *but I think he might have left since I looked in through the window. Zalasta was with him—and Ekatas. There was some sort of gathering they were planning to attend.*

There was a low whistle, and Sparhawk looked toward the balcony. Talen was motioning to him. "I'm going to go have a look," Sparhawk told Mirtai.

"Don't be too long," she cautioned. "The night's starting to run out on us."

He grunted and started across toward the balcony.

The drawbridge was down, and no one was standing watch. "How very convenient," Elysoun said as she, Liatris, and Gahenas crossed the bridge into the courtyard of the castle. "Chacole thinks of everything, doesn't she?"

"I thought there were supposed to be Church Knights on guard here," Gahenas said. "Chacole couldn't bribe *them*, could she?"

"Lord Vanion took his knights with him," Liatris replied. "The responsibility for guarding the castle's been turned over to ceremonial troops from the main garrison. Some officer is probably quite a bit richer than he was yesterday. You've been here before, Elysoun. Where can we find our husband?"

"He's usually up on the second floor. There are royal apartments there."

"We'd better get up there in a hurry. That unguarded gate makes me very nervous. I doubt that we'd be able to find a guard anywhere in the castle, and that means that Chacole's assassins have free access to Sarabian."

The balcony appeared not to have been used for at least a generation. Dust lay deep in the corners, and the thick crust of bird droppings on the floor was undisturbed. Talen was crouched beside the window, peering around the edge, when Sparhawk came up over the stone balustrade. "Is there anybody in there?" the big Pandion whispered.

"A whole crowd," Talen whispered back. "Zalasta just came in with a couple of Cyrgai."

Sparhawk joined his young friend and looked in.

The room appeared to be some kind of torchlit throne room. The balcony where Sparhawk and Talen crouched was above the level of the floor and was reached from the inside by a flight of stone stairs. There was a slightly raised dais at the far end of the room with a throne carved from a single rock at the back of it. A well-muscled, handsome man in an ornate breastplate and a short leather kirtle sat there, surveying the men around him with an imperious expression. Zalasta stood to one side of the man on the throne, and a wrinkled man in an ornamented black robe was at the front of the dais speaking in his own language. Sparhawk swore and quickly cast the spell that would attract the notice of the Child-Goddess.

Now what? Aphrael's voice sounded in his mind.

Can you translate for me?

I can do better than that.

He seemed to hear a faint buzzing sound and felt a momentary giddiness.

"—and even now those forces do surround the sacred city," the wrinkled man was saying in a language Sparhawk now understood.

A man with iron-grey hair and powerfully muscled arms stepped forward from the gathering before the dais. "What is there to fear, Ekatas?" he asked in a booming voice. "Mighty Cyrgon clouds the eyes of our enemies as he has for a hundred centuries. Let them crouch among the bones beyond our valley and seek vainly the Gates of Illusion. They are as blind men and pose no danger to the Hidden City."

There was a murmur of agreement from the others standing before the dais.

"General Ospados speaks truth," another armored man declared, also stepping forward. "Let us, as we have always, ignore these puny foreigners at our gates."

"Shameful!" another bellowed, stepping to the front some distance from the two who had already spoken. "Will we hide from inferior races? Their presence at our gates is an affront that must be punished!"

"Can you make out what they're saying?" Talen whispered.

"They're arguing," Sparhawk replied.

"Really?" Talen's tone was sardonic. "Could you be a little more specific, Sparhawk?"

"Evidently Aphrael's cousins have managed to get everybody here. From what the fellow in the black robe was saying, the city's surrounded."

"It's a comfort to have friends nearby. What do these people plan to do about it?"

"That's what they're arguing about. Some of them want to just sit tight. Others want to attack."

Then Zalasta came to the front of the dais. "Thus says Eternal

Klæl," he declared. "The forces beyond the Gates of Illusion are as nothing. The danger is here within the walls of the Hidden City. Anakha is even now within the sound of my voice."

Sparhawk swore.

"What's wrong?" Talen demanded.

"Zalasta knows we're here."

"How did he find *that* out?"

"I have no idea. He says that he's speaking for Klæl, and Klæl can probably feel Bhelliom."

"Even through the gold?"

"The gold might hide Bhelliom from Cyrgon, but Bhelliom and Klæl are brothers. They can probably feel each other halfway across the universe—even when there are whole suns burning between them." Sparhawk held up his hand. "He's saying something else." He leaned closer to the window.

"I know you can hear me, Sparhawk!" Zalasta said in a loud voice, speaking in Elenic. "You're Bhelliom's creature, and that gives you a certain amount of power. But I am Klæl's now, and that gives me just as much as you have." Zalasta sneered. "The disguises were very clever, but Klæl saw through them immediately. You should have done as you were told, Sparhawk. You've doomed your two young friends, and there's not a single thing you can do about it."

There were a half-dozen men in nondescript clothing in the hallway outside the door to the room where the emperor had been the last time Elysoun had visited him. Elysoun did not even think. "Sarabian!" she shouted. "Lock your door!"

The emperor, of course, did not. After a momentary shocked pause while the assassins froze in their tracks and Liatris blistered the air around her with curses even as she drew her daggers, the door burst open and Sarabian, dressed in Elene hose, a full-sleeved linen shirt, and with his long black hair tied back, lunged out into the hallway, rapier in hand.

Sarabian was tall for a Tamul, and his first lunge pinned an assassin to the wall opposite the door. The emperor whipped his sword free of the suddenly collapsing body with a dramatic flourish.

"Quit showing off!" Liatris snapped at her husband as she neatly ripped one of the assassins up the middle. "Pay attention!"

"Yes, my love," Sarabian said gaily, crouching again into *en guarde*.

Elysoun had only a small, neat dagger with a five-inch blade. It was long enough, though. An Arjuni assassin with a foot-long poniard parried Sarabian's next thrust and, snarling spitefully, plunged his needle-like dagger at the emperor's very eyes. Then he arched back with a choked cry. Elysoun's little knife, sharp as any razor, had plunged smoothly into the small of his back, ripping into his kidneys.

It was Gahenas, however, who shocked them all. Her weapon was a slim curved knife. With a shrill scream, the jug-eared Tegan empress flew into the middle of the fray, slashing at the faces of Chacole's hired killers. Screeching, Gahenas hacked at the startled assailants, and Sarabian took advantage of every lapse. His thin blade whistled as he danced the deadly dance of thrust and recover. This is not to say that the Emperor of Tamuli was a master swordsman. He *was* fairly skilled, but Stragen might have found room for criticism. In truth, it was the wives who carried the day—or night, in this case.

"Inside, my dear ones," Sarabian said, thrusting his savage women toward the door while he slashed at the empty air over the fallen assassins. "I'll cover your backs."

"Oh, dear," Liatris murmured to Elysoun and Gahenas, "he's such a baby."

"Yes, Liatris," Elysoun replied, wrapping one arm affectionately about her ugly Tegan sister, "but he's ours."

"Kring's coming," Khalad said quietly, pointing at the shadowy horseman galloping across the bone-littered gravel in the moonlight.

"That's not a good idea," Berit said, frowning. "Somebody might be watching."

The Domi reached them and reined in sharply. "Come away!" he urged.

"What's wrong?" Berit demanded.

"The Child-Goddess says for you to come back to where the others are! The Cyrgai are coming out to kill you."

"I was wondering how long it was going to take them to decide to try that," Khalad said, swinging up into his saddle. "Let's go, Berit."

Berit nodded, reaching for Faran's reins. "Is Lord Vanion going to do anything when the Cyrgai come out?" he asked Kring.

Kring's answering grin was wolfish. "Friend Ulath has a little surprise for them when they come through the gate," he replied.

Berit looked around. "Where is he?" he asked. "I don't see him."

"Neither will the Cyrgai—until it's too late. Let's get back away from this cliff. We'll let them see us when they come out. They've been ordered to kill you, so they'll come running after us. Friend Ulath has six or eight very hungry Trolls with him, and they'll be right on top of the Cyrgai when they come out."

"Did he know where you were?" Kalten asked tensely as they clung to the wall.

"I don't think so," Sparhawk replied. "He knows that I'm somewhere in the city, but there are several ways I could be listening to him. I don't think he realized just how close I was when he started making threats."

"Are Berit and Khalad going to be all right?"

Sparhawk nodded. "Aphrael was with me when Zalasta made his little speech. She's taking care of it."

"All right, Sparhawk," Mirtai called from above them, "here comes the rope."

The free end of the rope came slithering down out of the dimness above them, and Sparhawk quickly climbed up. "How much farther?" he asked quietly when he reached Mirtai's side.

"About one more climb," she replied. "Talen's already up there."

"He should have waited," Sparhawk fumed. "I'm going to have a talk with that boy."

"It won't do any good. Talen likes to take chances. Is Kalten still dragging our equipment behind him? I'd hate to get up there and have to deal with things with just my fingernails."

"He's hauling it up—stage by stage." Sparhawk peered up the wall. "Why don't you let me go on ahead this time? Get the others up there as quickly as you can. We've still got a lot left to do, and this night won't last forever."

She gestured up the rough stone wall. "Feel free," she said.

"I don't know if I've ever said this," he told her, "but I'm glad you came along. You're probably the best soldier I've ever known."

"Don't get emotional, Sparhawk. It's embarrassing. Are you going to go up the wall? Or did you want to wait for the sun to come up?"

He started up, moving carefully. It was to their advantage that the north side of the tower was in shade, but the deep shadows made it necessary to feel for each handhold and to probe carefully with his toes for places to put his feet. He concentrated on the climbing and resisted the impulse to lean back to look at the wall above and the sharp line of the edge of the parapet some fifty feet farther up.

"What kept you?" Talen whispered as the big Pandion clambered over the top of the balustrade marking the edge of the parapet.

"I stopped to smell the flowers," Sparhawk replied acidly. He looked quickly toward the east and saw the faint light of false dawn outlining the mountains. They had at most one more hour of darkness left. "No sentries, I gather?" he whispered.

"No," Talen replied quietly. "The Cyrgai evidently feel that they need their sleep."

"Sparhawk?" Kalten's whisper came from below.

"Up here."

"Take the baggage." A coil of rope came unwinding up out of the darkness.

"Give me a hand with this, Talen." He leaned over the stone railing. "Get clear of it," he called down softly to Kalten. "We're going to pull it up."

Kalten grunted, and they could hear him moving across the wall to one side. Then Sparhawk and Talen slowly pulled the awkward, bulky bundle up to the top of the tower, being careful not to let it bang against the stones of the wall. Sparhawk quickly retrieved his sword and then fumbled through the mail shirts, searching for his own.

Kalten was puffing as he climbed up over the railing. "Why did you let me get so badly out of shape, Sparhawk?" he asked accusingly.

Sparhawk shrugged. "Careless, I guess. Ah, here it is." He lifted his own shirt free of the others.

"How can you tell?" Talen asked curiously. "In the dark, I mean?"

"I've worn it for over twenty years. Believe me, I recognize it. See how the others are coming."

Talen went to the rail and helped Xanetia onto the parapet while Bevier and Mirtai clambered over on their own.

It took only a couple of minutes for the knights to re-arm themselves. "Where did Talen go?" Kalten whispered, looking around.

"He's snooping," Mirtai replied, settling her sword belt into place.

"I think it's called scouting," Bevier corrected her.

She shrugged. "Whatever."

Then Talen came back. "I think I found what we're looking for," he said softly. "There's a small window with a sort of iron grate over it. It's up high, so I didn't look in."

"Is Aphrael coming back?" Bevier asked. "Should we wait for her?"

Sparhawk shook his head. "It's going to start getting light before long. Aphrael knows what we're doing. She's making sure the others are all in place."

Talen led them around to the east side of the tower. "Up there," he whispered, pointing at a small, barred window about ten feet up the side of the rough wall.

"Do any of the windows on the front side have bars?" Sparhawk asked him.

"No, and they're bigger and closer to the floor."

"That's it, then." Sparhawk fought back an urge to shout with exultation. "Aphrael described that window to me."

Kalten squinted up at the iron-grated window high in the wall. "Let's make sure of this before we start to celebrate." He braced his hands on the wall and set his feet wide apart. "Climb up and take a look, Sparhawk."

"Right." Sparhawk put his hands on his friend's arms and climbed up his broad back. He set his feet carefully on Kalten's shoulders and slowly straightened, reaching up to grasp the rusty grating that covered the window. He pulled his face up and peered into the darkness. "Ehlana?" he called softly.

"*Sparhawk?*" Her voice was startled.

"Please keep your voice down. Are you all right?"

"I am now. How did you get here?"

"It's a long story. Is Alean there, too?"

"Right here, Prince Sparhawk," the girl's silvery voice replied. "Is Kalten with you?"

"I'm standing on his shoulders right now. Can you make a light of any kind?"

"Absolutely not!" Ehlana's voice was stricken.

"What's wrong?"

"They've cut off all my hair, Sparhawk!" she moaned. "I don't want you to look at me!"

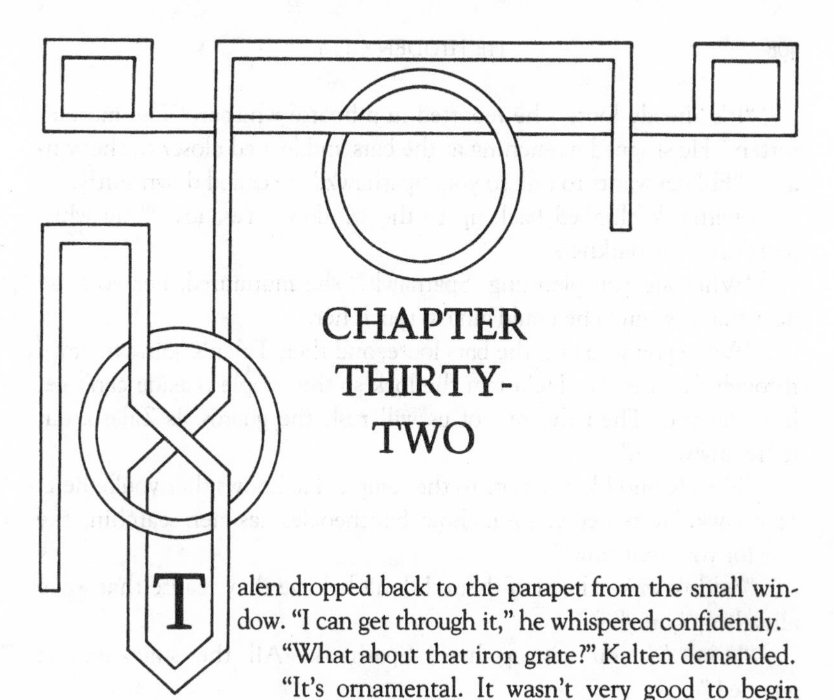

CHAPTER THIRTY-TWO

Talen dropped back to the parapet from the small window. "I can get through it," he whispered confidently.

"What about that iron grate?" Kalten demanded.

"It's ornamental. It wasn't very good to begin with, and it's been there for at least a couple of centuries. It won't take long to work it loose."

"Let's hold off until Xanetia gets back," Sparhawk decided. "I want to know what we're up against before we start crashing around."

"I'm not trying to be offensive," Mirtai said softly to Talen, "but I don't see what good it's going to do us to have you inside the cell when the fighting starts and a half-dozen Cyrgai rush into the cell to kill Ehlana and Alean."

"It's on accounta the fact that they ain't a-gonna *git* in the cell, Dorlin'," he said with an outrageous grin. "The door's locked."

"They've got a key."

"Give me about a half a minute with the lock, and their key won't fit. They won't get in; trust me."

"Are there alternatives?" Bevier asked.

"Not in the amount of time we've got left before it starts getting light," Sparhawk replied with a worried glance at the eastern horizon. "Kalten, go up and have a look at that grating."

"Right." The blond Pandion climbed up to the small window, took hold of the ancient iron lattice in both hands, and began to heave on it. Crumbs and fragments of mortar began to shower down on the rest of them.

"Quietly!" Mirtai whispered urgently at him.

"It's already loose," he reported in a hoarse whisper. "The mortar's rotten." He stopped wrenching at the bars and leaned closer to the window. "Ehlana wants to talk to you, Sparhawk," he called down softly.

Sparhawk climbed back up to the window. "Yes, love?" he whispered into the darkness.

"What are you planning, Sparhawk?" she murmured, her voice so near that it seemed he could almost touch her.

"We're going to pull the bars loose, and then Talen's going to crawl through the window. He'll jam the lock so the people outside can't get into the cell. Then the rest of us will rush the guards. Is Zalasta out there anywhere?"

"No. He and Ekatas went to the temple. He knows that you're here, Sparhawk. He sensed you somehow. Santheocles has men searching the city for you right now."

"I think we're ahead of them. I don't believe they realize that we're already up here."

"How *did* you get up here, Sparhawk? All the stairways are guarded."

"We climbed up the outside of the tower. When do those guards out there start stirring around?"

"When it begins to get light, usually. They cook what passes for food around here in the guardroom. Then a couple of them bring breakfast to Alean and me."

"Your breakfast might be a little late this morning, love," he whispered with a tight grin. "I think the cooks might have other things on their minds before long."

"Be careful, Sparhawk."

"Of course, my Queen."

"Sparhawk," Mirtai called up softly. "Xanetia's back."

"I have to run now, dear," he whispered into the darkness. "We'll have you out of there shortly. I love you."

"What a lovely thing to say."

Sparhawk quickly climbed back down to the parapet. "Welcome back, Anarae," he greeted Xanetia.

"Thou art in a peculiar humor, Anakha," she replied in a slightly puzzled tone.

"I just had a chat with my wife, Anarae," he said. "That always brightens my day. How many guards will we have to deal with?"

"I do fear me that they number some score or more, Anakha."

"That could be a problem, Sparhawk," Bevier noted. "They're

Cyrgai and none too bright, but twenty of them might give us some trouble."

"Maybe not," Sparhawk disagreed. "Aphrael said that there are only three rooms up here—the main room, the cell where Ehlana and Alean are, and the guardroom. Was she right, Anarae?"

"Indeed," she replied. "The cell and the guardroom are here on this north side. The main room is on the south, overlooking the Temple of Cyrgon. I did glean from the sleepy thought of such Cyrgai who were awake that this ultimate tower is the customary retreat of King Santheocles, for he doth take some pleasure in surveying his domain from the parapet—and above all in receiving the adulation of his subjects in the city below."

"Stupid," Mirtai muttered. "Doesn't he have anything better to do?"

Xanetia smiled faintly. "Much else would be quite beyond him, Atana. His guardsmen, limited though they themselves are, do hold their king's understanding in low regard. But his wits, or lack thereof, are of little moment. Santheocles is the descendant of the royal house, and his sole function is to wear the crown."

"A hat rack could do that," Talen noted.

"Truly."

"Do the guardsmen have any kind of set routine?" Bevier asked.

"Nay, Sir Knight. They do but hold themselves in readiness to respond to the commands of their king, nothing more. In truth, they are trumpeteers rather than warriors. Their primary duty is to announce with brazen notes to their fellow citizens that Santheocles will appear on the parapet to accept the adulation of the Cyrgai."

"And they do their waiting in the guardroom?" Sparhawk pressed.

"Save only for the pair who stand guard at the door to thy queen's prison and the other pair who bar the stairway which doth lead down into the lower levels of this tower."

"Can they get into the queen's cell from the guardroom?" Bevier asked intently.

"Nay. There is but one door."

"And how wide is the doorway between the guardroom and the main room?"

"Wide enough for one man only, Sir Bevier."

"Kalten and I can hold that one, Sparhawk."

"Are there any other doors to the guardroom?" Kalten asked.

Xanetia shook her head.

"Any large windows?"

"One window only—the mate to this one above us—though it is not barred."

"That narrows the opposition down to just those four guards in the main room," Kalten said. "Bevier and I can keep the rest of them penned in for a week, if we have to."

"And Sparhawk and I can deal with the ones at the cell door and the top of the stairs," Mirtai added.

"Let's get Talen inside that cell," Sparhawk said, looking again toward the east where a faint lessening of the darkness had begun.

Kalten scrambled back up the wall to the window and began digging at the mortar with his heavy dagger.

"Slip around and keep watch, Anarae," Sparhawk whispered. "Let us know if anybody comes up those stairs."

She nodded and went back around the corner of the tower.

Sparhawk climbed up and attacked the mortar on the left side of the iron lattice while his friend continued to dig at the right. After a few moments Kalten took hold of the rusty iron and pulled. "The bottom's loose," he muttered. "Let's get the top."

"Right." The two of them went to the top of the window and began to chip away the mortar there. "Be careful when it breaks away," Sparhawk cautioned. "We don't want it clanging down on that parapet."

"This side's free," Kalten whispered. "I'll hold it while you dig your side loose." He reached inside, found a secure handhold with his right hand, and grasped the grating with his left.

Sparhawk dug harder, sending a shower of chunks and dust to the parapet below. "I think that's got it," he whispered.

"We'll see." Kalten's shoulders heaved and there was a grinding sound as the ancient grate tore loose from the wall. Then, with the same movement, Sparhawk's burly friend hurled the heavy obstruction out beyond the balustrade.

"What are you *doing*?" Sparhawk choked.

"Getting rid of it."

"Do you know how much noise that thing's going to make when it hits the ground?"

"So what? It's five hundred feet down. Let it make all the noise it wants to. If some Cyrgai or Cynesgan slave driver's standing under it, he's in for a nasty surprise, but we can live with that, can't we?"

Sparhawk pushed his head through the now-unobstructed opening. "Ehlana?" he whispered, "are you there?"

"Where else *would* I be, Sparhawk?"

"Sorry. Stupid question, I suppose. The bars are out of the way now. We're sending Talen in. Shout or something as soon as he gets the lock jammed so that the guards can't get through the door."

"Get out of the way, Sparhawk," Talen said abruptly from just below. "I can't get in there with you filling up the whole window."

Sparhawk swung himself clear of the opening, and the agile boy began to wriggle his way through. Suddenly he stopped. "It's not working," he muttered. "Pull me back out."

"What's wrong?" Kalten demanded.

"Just pull me back out, Kalten. I don't have time to explain."

Sparhawk's heart sank as he and Kalten hauled the young thief back.

"Hold on for a minute." Talen turned until he was on his side, and then he extended his arms until they were stretched out above his head. "All right, push."

"You'll just get stuck again," Kalten objected.

"Then you'll have to push harder. This is what comes of all that wholesome food, exercise, and clean living you keep pushing on me, Sparhawk. I've grown so much that I can't get my shoulders through." He began to wriggle through the opening again. "Push, gentlemen!" he instructed.

The two of them pushed their hands against the soles of his feet.

"Harder!" he grunted.

"You'll tear all your skin off," Kalten warned.

"I'm young. I heal fast. Push!"

The two shoved at his feet, and, with a great deal of squirming and a few muttered oaths, he was through.

"Is he all right?" Sparhawk whispered hoarsely through the window.

"I'm fine, Sparhawk," Talen whispered back. "You'd better get moving. This won't take me very long."

Sparhawk and Kalten dropped back to the parapet. "Let's go," Sparhawk said shortly, and the three knights and the Atan giantess moved quickly around the narrow parapet to the south side of the tower.

"Quietly, Anakha." Xanetia's voice seemed to come out of nowhere.

"Are they stirring yet, Anarae?" Bevier whispered.

"Some few sounds do emanate from the guardroom," her voice replied.

There were two large unglazed windows at the front of the tower, one on each side of the broad door. Sparhawk cautiously raised his head above the lower edge of one of them and peered inside. The room, as Aphrael had reported, was fairly large. It was sparsely furnished with benches, a few backless chairs, and a couple of low tables, and it was lighted with primitive oil lamps. There was a narrow door on the right side of the rear wall with two statuelike Cyrgai, one on each side, guarding it. The stairway on the left side of the room, also guarded, was enclosed on three sides by a low wall. The second doorway, the one leading into the guardroom, was also on the left side, not far from the top of the stairs.

Sparhawk looked intently at the guards, closely studying their weapons and equipment. They were well-muscled men in archaic breastplates, crested helmets, and short leather kilts. Each had a large round shield strapped to his left arm, and each grasped an eight-foot spear in his right. They all had swords and heavy daggers belted at their waists.

Sparhawk moved his head away from the window. "You'd all better take a look," he whispered to his friends.

One by one, Kalten, Bevier, and Mirtai raised up slightly to peer into the room.

"Is this locked, Anarae?" Sparhawk whispered, pointing at the door leading out onto the parapet.

"I did not think it wise to try it, Anakha. Cyrgai construction is crude, and me thinks no doorlatch in the city may be attempted soundlessly."

"You're probably right," he breathed. "Let's pull back around the corner," he told the others, leading them around to the east side.

"It's getting lighter," Kalten noted, pointing toward the horizon.

Sparhawk grunted. "We'll go in through the windows," he told them. "We'd just jam up if we tried to go through the doorway anyhow. Bevier, you and Mirtai go through the one on the far side of the door. Kalten and I'll go through the one on this side. Be careful. Those spears seem to be their primary weapon, so they've probably had lots of training with them. Get in close and fast. Take them down in a hurry and then block that door to the guardroom. We're going to have to hold those stairs, too."

"I'll do that, Sparhawk," Mirtai assured him. "You concentrate on getting our friends out of that cell."

"Right," he agreed. "As soon as they're free, I'll unleash the Bhelliom. That should change the odds up here significantly."

And then there was a clear voice raised in aching song that soared out above the sleeping city.

"That's the signal!" Kalten told them. "That's Alean! Talen's finished up! Let's go!"

"You heard him!" Sparhawk said, stepping back so that Bevier and Mirtai could get past. "I'll give the word, and we'll all go in at the same time!"

Bevier and Mirtai crouched low as they ran past the window on the near side to take positions under the window beyond the door. "Stay clear of this, Anarae," Sparhawk murmured to the invisible Xanetia. "It's not your kind of fight." He frowned. There was no sense of her presence nearby. "All right, Kalten," he said then, "let's get to work."

The two of them silently crept forward, swords in hand, to crouch beneath the broad window. Sparhawk raised slightly to look along the parapet. Bevier and Mirtai waited tensely under the far window. He drew in a deep breath and set himself. "Now!" he shouted, setting his hand on the windowledge and vaulting through into the room.

There had been four Cyrgai inside before. Now there were ten.

"They're changing the guard, Sparhawk!" Bevier shouted, swinging his deadly lochaber in both hands.

They still had the element of surprise, but the situation had drastically changed. Sparhawk swore and cut down a Cyrgai carrying a pail of some kind—the captives' breakfast, most likely. Then he rushed the four confused guards milling in front of the cell door. One of them was fighting with the lock while the other three tried to get into position. They were disciplined, there was no question about that, and their long spears *did* raise deadly problems.

Sparhawk swore a savage oath and swung his heavy broadsword, chopping at the spears. Kalten had moved to one side, and he was also swinging massive blows at the spears. There were sounds of fighting coming from the other side of the room, but Sparhawk was too intent on breaking through to the guard who was trying to force the cell door to turn and look.

Two of the spears were broken now, and the Cyrgai had discarded them and drawn their swords. The third soldier, his spear still intact, had stepped back to protect the one still feverishly struggling with the lock.

Sparhawk risked a quick glance at the other side of the room, just in time to see Mirtai lift a struggling guard over her head and hurl him bodily down the stairs with a great clattering sound. Two other Cyrgai lay dead or dying nearby. Bevier, even as he had in Otha's throne room in Zemoch, held the door to the guardroom while Mirtai, like some great, golden cat, savaged the remaining guards at the top of the stairs. Sparhawk quickly turned his attention back to the men he faced.

The Cyrgai were indifferent swordsmen, and their oversized shields seriously hindered their movements. Sparhawk made a quick feint at the head of one, and the man instinctively raised his shield. Sparhawk instantly recovered and, ducking low, drove his sword up into the gleaming breastplate. The Cyrgai cried out and fell back with blood gushing from the sheared gash in his armor.

It was not enough. The Cyrgai at the cell door had abandoned his efforts to unlock it and had begun slamming his shoulder against it. Sparhawk could clearly hear the splintering of wood. Desperately, he renewed his attack. Once the Cyrgai broke through that door—

And then, without even being forced, the door swung inward. With a triumphant shout, the Cyrgai who had been battering at the door drew his sword.

And then he screamed as a new light flooded the room.

Xanetia, blazing like the sun, stood in the doorway with one deadly hand extended.

The Cyrgai screamed again, falling back, tangling himself in the struggles of his two comrades. Then he broke free, ran to the window, and plunged through.

He was still running when he went over the balustrade with a long despairing scream.

The two other Cyrgai at the cell door also fled, scurrying around the room like frightened mice. "Mirtai!" Sparhawk roared. "Stand clear! Let them go!"

The Atana had just raised another struggling warrior over her head. She threw him down the stairs and turned sharply. Then she dodged clear to allow the demoralized Cyrgai to escape.

"Stand aside, Sir Knight!" Xanetia commanded Bevier. "*I* will bar that door, and I do vouchsafe that none shall pass!"

Bevier took one look at her glowing face and stepped away from the guardroom door.

The Cyrgai inside the room also looked at her, and then they slammed the door shut.

"It's all right now, Ehlana," Sparhawk called.

Talen came out first, and his face was pale and shaken. The boy's tunic was ripped in several places, and a long, bleeding scrape on one arm spoke of his struggle to get through the narrow window. He was staring in awe at Xanetia. "She came through the window in a puff of smoke, Sparhawk!" he choked.

"Mist, young Talen," Xanetia corrected in a clinical tone. She was still all aglow and facing the guardroom door. "Smoke would be impractical for human flesh."

There was a great deal of noise coming from the guardroom. "They seem to be moving furniture in there, Sparhawk," Bevier laughed. "Piling it against the door, I think."

Then Alean came running out of the cell to hurl herself into Kalten's arms, and, immediately behind her, Ehlana emerged from her prison. She was even more pale than usual, and there were dark circles under her eyes. Her clothing was tattered, and her head was tightly bound in a bandagelike wimple. "Oh, Sparhawk!" she cried in a low voice, holding her arms out to him. He went to her and enfolded her in a rough embrace.

From far below there came a savage bellow.

"Anakha!" Bhelliom's voice roared in Sparhawk's mind. "Cyrgon hath awakened to his peril! Release me."

Sparhawk jerked the pouch out from under his tunic and fumbled with the drawstring.

"What's that shouting?" Talen demanded.

"Cyrgon knows that we've released Ehlana!" Sparhawk replied tensely, drawing Kurik's box out of the pouch. "Open!" he commanded.

The lid raised, and the blue radiance of the Bhelliom blazed forth. Sparhawk carefully lifted out the jewel.

"They're coming up the stairs, Sparhawk!" Mirtai warned.

"Get clear!" he said sharply. "Blue-Rose!" he said then, "canst thou bar the way to our enemies, who even now rush up yon stairway?"

The Bhelliom did not answer, but the waist-high wall surrounding the head of the stairs collapsed, crashing down into the stairwell with a great clattering and a billowing cloud of dust.

Advise Aphrael that her mother is safe. Bhelliom's voice was crisp. *Let the attack begin*.

Sparhawk cast the spell. *Aphrael!* he said sharply. *We've got Ehlana! Tell the others to move in!*

Can Bhelliom break Cyrgon's illusion? she asked in a tone every bit as crisp as the sapphire rose's had been.

Blue-Rose, Sparhawk said silently, *the illusion of Cyrgon doth still impede the advance of our friends upon the city. Canst thou dispel it that they may bring their forces to bear upon this accursed place?*

It shall be as thou wouldst have it, my son.

There was a momentary pause, and then the earth seemed to shudder slightly, and a vast shimmer ran in waves across the sky.

From the leprous white temple far below there came a shrill screech of pain.

"My goodness," Flute said mildly as she suddenly appeared in the center of the room. "I've never had a ten-thousand-year-old spell broken. I'll bet it hurts like anything. Poor Cyrgon's having an absolutely *dreadful* night."

"The night is not yet over, Child-Goddess," Bhelliom spoke through Kalten's lips. "Save thine unseemly gloating until all danger is past."

"Well, *really*!"

"Hush, Aphrael. We must look to our defenses, Anakha. What Cyrgon knoweth, Klæl doth also know. The contest is at hand. We must make ready."

"Truly," Sparhawk agreed. He looked around at his friends. "Let's go," he told them. "We'll spread out along the parapet, and keep your eyes open. Klæl's coming, and I don't want him creeping up behind me. Is that stairway completely blocked?"

"A mouse couldn't get through all that rubble," Mirtai told him.

"We can forget about the guards," Bevier announced, removing his ear from the guardroom door. "They're still rearranging the furniture."

"Good." Sparhawk went to the door leading out to the parapet. It opened with a shrill protest of rusty hinges. "Don't start getting brave," he cautioned his friends. "The fight's between Bhelliom and Klæl. Spread out and keep watch."

The eastern sky was pale with the approach of day as they came out onto the parapet, and Cyrgon's agonized shrieking still echoed through the Hidden City.

"There," Talen said, pointing toward the basalt escarpment beyond the lake to the south.

A mass of figures, tiny in the distance and still dark in the dawn light, were streaming out of 'the Glen of Heroes,' moving into the basin before the gates of Cyrga.

"Who are they?" Ehlana cried, suddenly gripping Sparhawk's arm.

"Vanion," Sparhawk told her, "along with just about everybody else—Betuana, Kring, Ulath and the Trolls, Sephrenia—"

"*Sephrenia?*" Ehlana exclaimed. "She's dead!"

"You didn't really think I'd let Zalasta kill my sister, did you, Ehlana?" Flute said.

"But, he said that he'd stabbed her in the heart!"

The Child-Goddess shrugged. "He did, but Bhelliom cured it. And don't worry, Vanion's going to take steps."

Talen came running around the parapet from the back of the tower. "Bergsten's coming in from the other side," he reported. "His knights just trampled about three regiments of Cyrgai underfoot without even slowing down."

"Are we going to be caught in the middle of a siege here?" Kalten asked with a worried expression.

"Not too likely," Bevier replied. "The defenses of this place are pitifully inadequate, and Patriarch Bergsten tends to be a very abrupt sort of man."

There was a sudden eruption far below, and the roof of the pale temple exploded, hurling chunks of limestone in all directions as the infinite darkness of Klæl shouldered his way up out of the House of Cyrgon. His vast, leathery wings spread wide, and his blazing, slitted eyes looked about wildly.

"Prithee, Anakha, hold me aloft that my brother may behold me." The voice coming from Kalten's lips was detached.

Sparhawk's hand was shaking as he raised the sapphire rose over his head.

Kalten, moving somewhat woodenly, gently put Alean's clinging arms aside and stepped to the stone rail at the front of the parapet. He spoke in a tongue no human mouth could have produced, and his words could quite probably have been heard in Chyrellos, half a world away.

Enormous Klæl, waist-deep in the ruins of Cyrgon's Temple, raised his triangular face and roared his reply, his fanged mouth dripping flame.

Attend closely, Anakha. Bhelliom's voice in Sparhawk's mind was very quiet. *I will continue to taunt mine errant brother, and, all enraged, will he come to do battle with me. Be thou steadfast in the face of that approaching horror, for our success or failure does hang entire upon thy courage and the strength of thine arm.*

I do not take thy meaning, Blue-Rose. Am I to smite Klæl?

Nay, Anakha. Thy task is to free me.

The beast of darkness below savagely kicked aside the limestone rubble and advanced on the palace with hungry arms outstretched. When he reached the massive gates, he brushed them from his path with a whip of lightning clutched in one enormous fist.

Kalten continued his deafening taunts, and Klæl continued to howl his fury as he crushed his way through the lower wings of the palace, destroying everything that lay in the path of his relentless drive toward the tower.

And then he reached it, and, seizing its rough stones in his two huge hands, he began to climb, his wings clawing at the morning air as he mounted up and up.

How am I to free thee, Blue-Rose? Sparhawk asked urgently.

My brother and I must be briefly recombined, my son, Bhelliom replied, *to become one again, as we once were, else must I forever be imprisoned within this azure crystal—even as Klæl must remain in his present monstrous form. In our temporary combination will we both be freed.*

Combine? How?

When he doth reach this not-inconsiderable height and doth exult with resounding bellow of victory, must thou hurl me straightway into his gaping maw.

Do what?

He would with all his soul devour me. Make it so. In the moment of our union shall Klæl and I both be freed of our present forms, and then shall our contest begin. Fail not, my son, for this *is thy purpose and the destiny for which I made thee.*

Sparhawk drew in a deep breath. *I* will *not fail thee, Father,* he pledged with all his heart.

Still raging and with his leathery wings straining for purchase on the wind, Klæl mounted higher and higher up the front of the palace tower. Sparhawk felt a sense of odd, undismayed detachment come over him. He looked full into the face of the King of Hell and felt no fear. His task was simplicity in itself. He had only to hurl the sapphire rose into that gaping maw and, should a suitable opportunity for that not present itself, to hurl himself—with Bhelliom in his outstretched fist instead. He felt no regret nor even sadness as the unalterable resolve settled over him. Better this than to die in a meaningless, unremembered skirmish on some disputed frontier as so many of his friends had. This had significance, and for a soldier, that was the best one could hope for.

And still Klæl came, climbing higher and higher, reaching hungrily for his hated brother. No more than a few yards below now, his slitted eyes blazed in cruel triumph and his jagged fangs dripped fire as he roared his challenge.

And then Sparhawk leapt atop the ancient battlement to stand poised with Bhelliom aloft in his fist. "For God and my Queen!" He bellowed his defiance.

Klæl reached up with one awesome hand.

Then, like the sudden uncoiling of some tight-wound spring, Sparhawk struck. His arm snapped down like a whip. "Go!" he shouted as he released the blazing jewel.

As true as an arrow the sapphire rose flew from his hand even as Klæl's mouth gaped wider. Straight it went to vanish in the flaming maw.

The tower trembled as a shudder ran through the glossy blackness of the enormity clinging to its side, and Sparhawk struggled to keep his balance on his precarious perch even as Kalten fell backward to the parapet.

Klæl's wings stiffened to their fullest extent, quivering with awful tension. The great beast swelled, growing even more enormous. Then he contracted, shriveling.

And then he exploded.

The detonation shook the very earth, and Sparhawk was hurled back from the battlement to fall heavily on the parapet. He rolled quickly, came to his feet, and rushed back to the battlements.

Two beings of light, one a glowing blue, the other sooty red, grappled with each other on insubstantial air not ten feet away. Their struggle was elemental, a savage contesting of will and strength. They were featureless beings, and their shapes were only vaguely human. Heaving back and forth, they clung to each other like wrestlers in some rude village square, each bending all his will and force to subdue his perfectly matched opponent.

Sparhawk and his friends lined the battlements, frozen, awed, able only to watch that primeval struggle.

And then the two broke free of each other and stood, backs bowed and arms half-extended, each facing his immortal brother in some inconceivable communion.

It falls to thee, Anakha, Bhelliom's voice in Sparhawk's mind was calm. *Should Klæl and I continue, this world shall surely be destroyed, as hath oft-time come to pass before. Thou art of this world and must therefore be my champion. Constraints are upon thee which do not limit me. Klæl's champion is also of this world and is similarly constrained.*

It shall be even as thou hath said, my father, Sparhawk replied. *I will serve as thy champion if need be. With whom must I contend?*

A great roar of rage came from far below, and a living flame surged up out of the shattered ruins of the chalk-white temple.

There is thine opponent, my son, the azure spirit replied. *Klæl hath called him forth to do battle with thee.*

Cyrgon!

Even so.

But he is a God!

And art thou not?

Sparhawk's mind reeled.

Look within thyself, Anakha. Thou art my son, and I made thee to be the receptacle of my will. I now release that will to thee that thou mayest be the champion of this world. Feel its power infuse thee.

It was like the opening of a door that had always been closed. Sparhawk felt his mind and will expanding infinitely as the barrier went down, and with that expansion there came an unutterable calm.

Now art thou truly *Anakha, my son!* Bhelliom exulted. *Thy will is now* my *will.* All *things are now possible for thee. It was* thy *will which vanquished Azash. I was but thine instrument.* In this *occasion, however, shalt thou be* mine. *Bend thine invincible will to the task. Seize it in thine hands and mold it. Forge weapons with thy mind and confront* Cyrgon. *If thine heart be true, he cannot prevail against thee. Now go. Cyrgon awaits thee.*

Sparhawk drew in a deep breath and looked down at the rubble-littered square far below. The flame which had emerged from the ruins had coalesced into a blazing man-shape standing before the wreck of the temple. "Come, Anakha!" it roared. "Our meeting hath been foretold since before time began! *This* is thy destiny! Thou art honored above all others to fall by *my* hand."

Sparhawk deliberately pushed aside the windy pomposity of archaic expression. "Don't start celebrating until after you've won, Cyrgon!" he shouted his reply. "Don't go away! I'll be right down!" Then he set one hand atop the battlement and lightly vaulted over it.

He stopped, hanging in midair. "Let go, Aphrael," he said.

"What are you *doing*?" she exclaimed.

"Just do as you're told. Let me go."

"You'll fall."

"No, I won't. I can handle this. Don't interfere. Cyrgon's waiting for me, so please let go."

It was not actually flying, although Sparhawk was certain that he *could* fly if he needed to. He felt a peculiar lightness as he drifted down toward the ruins of the House of Cyrgon. It was not that he had no weight; it was more that his weight had no meaning. His will was somehow stronger than gravity. Sword in hand, he settled down and down like a fearsome, drifting feather.

Cyrgon waited below. The burning figure of the ancient God drew his fire about him, congealing the incandescent flame into the antique armor customarily worn by those who worshiped him—a burnished steel cuirass, a crested helmet, a large round shield, and a sword in his fist.

A peculiar insight came to Sparhawk as he slid down through the dawn-cool air. Cyrgon was not so much stupid as he was conservative. It was change that he hated, change that he feared. Thus he had frozen his Cyrgai eternally in time and had erased any potential for change or innovation from their minds. The Cyrgai, unmoved by the winds of time, would remain forever as they had been when their God had first conceived of them. He had wrought an ideal and fenced it all about with law and custom and an innate hatred of change, and frozen thus, they were doomed—and had been since the first of them had placed one sandaled foot on the face of the ever-changing world.

Sparhawk smiled faintly. Cyrgon, it appeared, needed instruction in the benefits of change, and his first lesson would be in the advantages of modern equipment, weaponry, and tactics. Sparhawk thought, *Armor*, and he was immediately encased in black-enameled steel. He almost casually discarded his plain working sword and filled his hand with his heavier and longer ceremonial blade. Now he was a fully armed Pandion Knight, a soldier of God—*of several Gods*, he rather ruefully amended that thought. And he was, almost by default, the champion not only of his queen, his Church, and his God, but also, if he read Bhelliom's thought correctly, of his fair and sometimes vain sister, the world.

He drifted down and settled to earth amidst the wreck of the destroyed temple. "Well met, Cyrgon," he said with profoundest formality.

"Well met, Anakha," the God replied. "I had misjudged thee. Thou art suitable now. I had despaired of thee, fearing that thou wouldst never have realized thy true significance. Thine apprenticeship hath been long and methinks, hindered by thine inappropriate affiliation with Aphrael."

"We're wasting time, Cyrgon," Sparhawk cut through the flowery courtesies. "Let's get at this. I'm already late for breakfast."

"So be it, Anakha!" Cyrgon's classic features were set in an expression of approval. "Defend thyself!" And he swung a huge sword-stroke at Sparhawk's head.

But Sparhawk had already begun his stroke, and so their swords clashed harmlessly in the air between them.

It was good to be fighting again. There were no politics here, no confusion of dissembling words or false promises, just the clean, sharp ring of steel on steel and the smooth flow of muscle and sinew over bone.

Cyrgon was quick, as quick as Martel had been in his youth, and, despite his hatred of innovation, he learned quickly. The intricate moves of wrist and arm and shoulder that marked the master swordsman seemed to come unbidden, almost in spite of himself, to the ancient God. "Invigorating, isn't it?" Sparhawk panted through a wolflike grin, lashing a stinging cut at the God's shoulder. "Open your mind, Cyrgon. Nothing is set in stone—not even something as simple as this." And he lashed out with his sword again, flicking another cut onto Cyrgon's sword arm.

The immortal rushed at him, forcing the oversized round shield against him, trying with will and main strength to overcome his better-trained opponent.

Sparhawk looked into that flawless face and saw regret and desperation there. He bunched his shoulder, as Kurik had taught him, and locked his shield arm, forming an impenetrable barrier against the ineffectual flailing of his opponent. He parried only with his lightly held sword. "Yield, Cyrgon," he said, "and live. Yield, and Klæl will be banished. We are of *this* world, Cyrgon. Let Klæl and Bhelliom contend for other worlds. Take thy life and thy people and go. I would not slay even thee."

"I spurn thine insulting offer, Anakha!" Cyrgon half shrieked.

"I guess that satisfies the demands of knightly honor," Sparhawk muttered to himself with a certain amount of relief. "God knows what I'd have done if you'd accepted." He raised his sword again. "So be it, then, brother," he said. "We weren't meant to live in the same world together anyway." He felt his body and will seem to swell inside his armor. "Watch, brother," he grated through clenched teeth. "Watch and learn."

And then he unleashed five hundred years of training, coupled with his towering anger, at this poor, impotent Godling, who had ripped asunder the peace of the world, a peace toward which Sparhawk had yearned since his return from exile in Rendor. He ripped Cyrgon's thigh with the classic *pas-four*. He slashed that perfect face with Martel's innovative *parry-pas-nine*. He cut away the upper half of Cyrgon's oversized round shield with Vanion's third-feint-and-slash. Of all the Church Knights, the Pandions were the most skilled swordsmen, and of all the Pandions, Sparhawk stood supreme. Bhelliom had called him the equal of a God, but Sparhawk fought as a man—superbly trained, a little out of condition, and really too old for this kind of thing—but with an absolute confidence that if the fate of the world rested in his hands, he was good for at least one more fight.

His sword blurred in the light of the new-risen sun, flickering, weaving, darting. Baffled, the ancient Cyrgon tried to respond.

The opportunity presented itself, and Sparhawk felt the perfect symmetry of it. Cyrgon, untaught, had provided the black-armored Pandion precisely the same opening Martel had given him in the Temple of Azash. Martel had fully understood the significance of the series of strokes. Cyrgon, however, did not. And so it was that the thrust which pierced him through came as an absolute surprise. The God stiffened and his sword fell from his nerveless fingers as he lurched back from that fatal thrust.

Sparhawk recovered from the thrust and swept his bloody sword up in front of his face in salute. "An innovation, Cyrgon," he said in a detached sort of voice. "You're really very good, you know, but you ought to try to stay abreast of things."

Cyrgon sagged to the flagstoned court, his immortal life spilling out through the gash in his breastplate. "And wilt thou take the world now, Anakha?" he gasped.

Sparhawk dropped to his haunches beside the stricken God. "No, Cyrgon," he replied wearily. "I don't want the world—just a quiet little corner of it."

"Then why camest thou against me?"

"I didn't want you to have it either, because if you had, my little part wouldn't have been safe." He reached out and took the pallid hand. "You fought well, Cyrgon. I have respect for you. Hail and farewell."

Cyrgon's voice was only a whisper as he replied, "Hail and farewell, Anakha."

There was a great despairing howl of frustration and rage. Sparhawk looked up and saw a man-shape of sooty red streaking upward into the dawn sky as Klæl resumed his endless journey toward and beyond the farthest star.

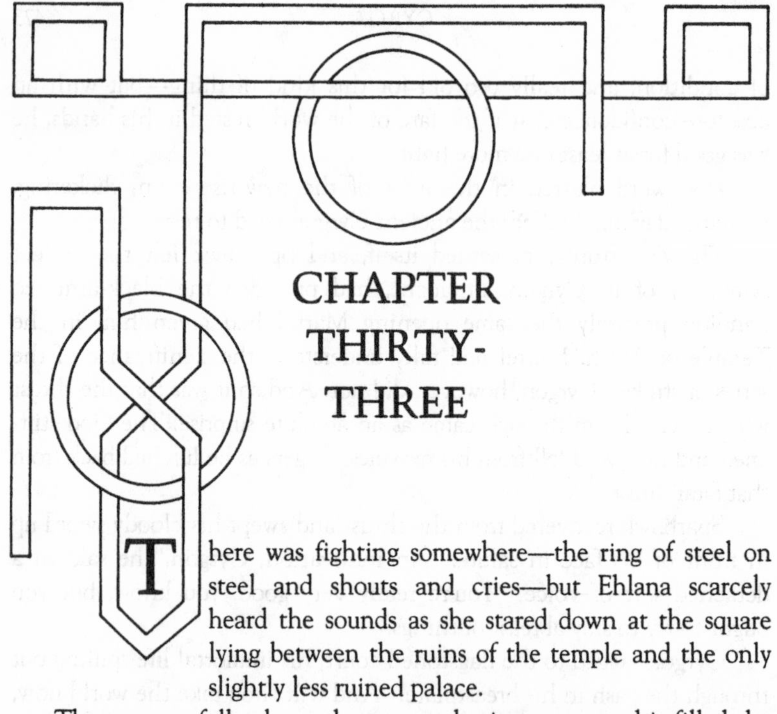

CHAPTER THIRTY-THREE

There was fighting somewhere—the ring of steel on steel and shouts and cries—but Ehlana scarcely heard the sounds as she stared down at the square lying between the ruins of the temple and the only slightly less ruined palace.

The sun was fully above the eastern horizon now, and it filled the ancient streets of Cyrga with harsh, unforgiving light. The Queen of Elenia was exhausted, but the ordeal of her captivity was over, and she yearned only to lose herself in her husband's embrace. She did not understand much of what she had just witnessed, but that was not really important. She stood at the battlements holding the Child-Goddess in her arms, gazing down at her invincible champion far below.

"Do you think it might be safe for us to go down?" she asked the small divinity in her arms.

"The stairway's blocked, Ehlana," Mirtai reminded her.

"I can take care of that," Flute said.

"Maybe we'd better stay up here," Bevier said with a worried frown. "Cyrgon and Klæl are gone, but Zalasta's still out there somewhere. He might try to seize the queen again so that he can use her to bargain his way out of here."

"He'd better not," the Child-Goddess said ominously. "Ehlana's right. Let's go down."

They went back inside, reached the head of the stairs, and peered down through billowing clouds of dust. "What did you do?" Talen asked Flute. "Where did all the rocks go?"

She shrugged. "I turned them into sand," she replied.

The stairway wound downward along the inside of the tower walls. Kalten and Bevier, swords in hand, led the way, prudently investigating each level as they reached it. The top three or four levels were empty, but as they began the descent to a level about midway down the inside of the tower, Xanetia hissed sharply. "Someone approaches!"

"Where?" Kalten demanded. "How many?"

"Two, and they do mount the stairs toward us."

"I'll deal with them," he muttered, gripping his sword hilt even more tightly.

"Don't do anything foolish," Alean cautioned.

"It's the fellows coming up the stairs who are being foolish, love. Stay with the queen." He started on ahead.

"I'll go with him," Mirtai said. "Bevier, it's your turn to guard Ehlana."

"But—"

"Hush!" she commanded. "Do as you're told."

"Yes, ma'am," he surrendered with a faint smile.

A murmured sound of voices came echoing up the stairs.

"Santheocles!" Ehlana identified one of the speakers in a short, urgent whisper.

"And the other?" Xanetia asked.

"Ekatas."

"Ah," Xanetia said. Her pale brow furrowed in concentration. "This is not exact," she apologized, "but it seemeth me that they are unaware of thy release, Queen of Elenia, and they do rush to thy former prison, hoping that by threatening thy life might they gain safe conduct through the ranks of their enemies."

There was a landing perhaps twenty steps down the narrow stairway, and Kalten and Mirtai stopped there, stepping somewhat apart to give themselves room.

Santheocles, wearing his gleaming breastplate and crested helmet, came bounding up the stairs two at a time with his sword in his hand. He stopped suddenly when he reached the landing, staring at Kalten and Mirtai in stupefied disbelief. He waved his sword at them and issued a peremptory command in his own language.

"What did he say?" Talen demanded.

"He ordered them to get out of his way," Aphrael replied.

"Doesn't he realize that they're his enemies?"

"*Enemy* is a difficult concept for someone like Santheocles," Ehlana told him. "He's never been outside the walls of Cyrga, and I doubt that he's seen more than ten people who weren't Cyrgai in his entire life. The Cyrgai obey him automatically, so he hasn't had much experience with open hostility."

Ekatas came puffing up the stairs behind Santheocles. His eyes were wide with shock and his wrinkled face ashen. He spoke sharply to his king, and Santheocles placidly stepped aside. Ekatas drew himself up and began speaking sonorously, his hands moving in the air before him.

"Stop him!" Bevier cried. "He's casting a spell!"

"He's *trying* to cast a spell," Aphrael corrected. "I think he's in for a nasty surprise."

The high priest's voice rose in a long, slow crescendo and he suddenly leveled one arm at Kalten and Mirtai.

Nothing happened.

Ekatas held his empty hand up in front of his face, gaping at it in utter astonishment.

"Ekatas," Aphrael called sweetly to him, "I hate to be the bearer of bad tidings, but now that Cyrgon's dead, your spells won't work anymore."

He stared up at her, comprehension and recognition slowly dawning on his face. Then he spun and bolted through the door on the left side of the landing and slammed it behind him.

Mirtai moved quickly after him. She briefly tried the door, then stepped back and kicked it to pieces.

Kalten advanced on the sneering King of the Cyrgai. Santheocles struck a heroic pose, his oversized shield extended, his sword raised, and his head held high.

"He's no match for Kalten," Bevier said. "Why doesn't he run?"

"He doth believe himself invincible, Sir Bevier," Xanetia replied. "He hath slain many of his own soldiers on the practice field, and thus considers himself the paramount warrior in all the world. In truth, however, his subordinates would not strike back or even defend themselves, because he was their king."

Kalten, grim-faced and vengeful, fell on the feebleminded monarch like an avalanche. The face of Santheocles was filled with shock and outrage as, for the first time in his life, someone actually raised a weapon against him.

It was a short, ugly fight, and the outcome was quite predictable. Kalten battered down the oversized shield, parried a couple of stiffly formal swings at his head, and then buried his sword up to the hilt in the precise center of the burnished breastplate. Santheocles stared at him in sheer astonishment. Then he sighed, toppled backward off the blade, and clattered limply down the stairs.

"*Yes!*" Ehlana exulted in a savage voice as the most offensive of her persecutors died.

From beyond the splintered door came a long, despairing scream fading horribly away, and Mirtai emerged with an expression of bleak satisfaction.

"What did you do to him?" Kalten asked curiously.

"I defenestrated him," she replied with a shrug.

"*Mirtai!*" he gasped. "That's *awful*!"

She gave him a baffled look. "What are you talking about?"

"That's a *terrible* thing to do to a man!"

"Throw him out a window? I can think of much worse things to do to somebody."

"Is *that* what that word means?"

"Of course. Stragen used to talk about it back in Matherion."

"Oh." Kalten flushed slightly.

"What did you think it meant?"

"Ah—never mind, Mirtai. Just forget I said anything."

"You must have thought it meant *something*."

"Let's just drop it, shall we? I misunderstood, that's all." He looked up at the others. "Let's go on down," he suggested. "I don't think there'll be anybody else in our way."

Ehlana suddenly burst into tears. "I *can't*!" she wailed. "I can't face Sparhawk like this!" She put one hand on the wimple that covered her violated scalp.

"Are you still worrying about that?" Aphrael asked.

"I look so *awful*!"

Aphrael rolled her eyes upward. "Let's go into that room," she suggested. "I'll fix it for you—if it's so important."

"Could you?" Ehlana asked eagerly.

"Of course." The Child-Goddess squinted at her. "Would you like to have me change the color?" she asked. "Or maybe make it curly?"

The queen pursed her lips. "Why don't we talk about that a little?" she said.

The Cynesgans who manned the outer wall of the Hidden City were not particularly good troops in the first place, and when the Trolls came leaping out of No-Time to scramble up the walls toward them, they broke and ran.

"Did you tell the Trolls to open the gates for us?" Vanion asked Ulath.

"Yes, my Lord," the Genidian replied, "but it might be a little while before they remember. They're hungry right now. They'll eat breakfast first."

"We *have* to get inside, Ulath," Sephrenia said urgently. "We have to protect the slave pens."

"Oh, Lord," he said. "I forgot about that. The Trolls won't be able to distinguish slaves from Cynesgans."

"I'll go have a look," Khalad volunteered. He swung down from his horse and ran forward to the massively timbered gates. After a couple moments he came back. "It's no particular problem, Lady Sephrenia," he reported. "Those gates would fall apart if you sneezed on them."

"What?"

"The timbers are very old, my Lady, and they're riddled with dry rot. With your permission, Lord Vanion, I'll take some men and rig up a battering ram. We'll knock down the gate so that we can get inside."

"Of course," Vanion replied.

"Come along, then, Berit," Khalad told his friend.

"That young man always manages to make me feel inadequate," Vanion muttered as they watched the pair ride back to rejoin the knights massed some yards to the rear.

"As I remember, his father had the same effect on you," Sephrenia said.

Kring came galloping back around the wall. "Friend Bergsten's preparing to assault the north gate," he reported.

"Send word to him to be careful, friend Kring," Betuana advised. "The Trolls are already inside the city—and they're hungry. It might be better if he delayed his attack just a little."

Kring nodded his agreement. "Working with Trolls changes the complexion of things, doesn't it, Betuana-Queen? They're very good allies in a fight, but you don't want to let them get hungry."

About ten minutes later, Khalad and a few dozen knights dragged a large log into place before the gate, suspended it on ropes attached to several makeshift tripods, and began to pound on the rotting timbers. The gate shuddered out billows of powdery red dust and began to crumble and fall apart.

"Let's go!" Vanion called tersely to his oddly assorted army, and led the way into the city. At Sephrenia's insistence, the knights went straight to the pens, freed the shackled slaves, and escorted them to safety outside the walls. Then Vanion's force moved directly to the inner wall that protected the steep hill rising in the middle of Cyrga.

"How long is that likely to last, Sir Ulath?" Vanion said, gesturing toward a cluster of ravening Trolls.

"It's a little hard to say, Lord Vanion," Ulath replied. "I don't think we'll get much cooperation from them as long as there are still Cynesgans running up and down the streets here in the outer city, though."

"Maybe it's just as well," Vanion decided. "I think *we* want to get to Sparhawk and the others before the Trolls do." He looked around. "Khalad," he called, "tell your men to drag that battering ram up here. Let's pound down the gate to the inner city and go find Sparhawk."

"Yes, my lord," Khalad replied.

The gates to the inner wall were more substantial, and Khalad's ram was pounding out great booming sounds when Patriarch Bergsten came riding along the wall, accompanied by the veteran Pandion Sir Heldin, a Peloi whom Vanion did not recognize, and a tall, lithe Atan girl. Vanion was a bit startled to see that the Styric God Setras was also with them. "What do you think you're doing, Vanion?" Bergsten roared.

"Knocking down this gate, your Grace," Vanion replied.

"That's not what I'm talking about. What in God's name possessed you to let the Trolls make the initial assault?"

"It wasn't really a question of *let*, your Grace. They didn't exactly ask for permission."

"We've got absolute chaos here in the outer city. My knights can't concentrate on this inner wall because they keep running into Trolls. They're in a feeding frenzy, you know. Right now they'll eat anything that moves."

"Must you?" Sephrenia murmured with a shudder.

"Hello, Sephrenia," Bergsten said. "You're looking well. How much longer are you going to be with this gate, Vanion? Let's get our people into the inner city where all we have to worry about are the Cyrgai. Your allies are making my men very nervous." He looked up at the top of the inner wall, sharply outlined against the dawn sky. "I thought the Cyrgai were supposed to be soldiers. Why aren't they manning this wall?"

"They're a little demoralized right now," Sephrenia explained. "Sparhawk just killed their God."

"He *did*? I thought Bhelliom was going to do that."

She sighed. "In a certain sense it did," she said. "It's a little hard to separate the two of them at this point. Aphrael isn't entirely sure where Bhelliom leaves off and Sparhawk begins right now."

Bergsten shuddered. "I don't think I want to know about that," he confessed. "I'm in enough theological trouble already. What about Klæl?"

"He's gone. He was banished as soon as Sparhawk killed Cyrgon."

"Oh, fine, Vanion," Bergsten said with heavy sarcasm. "You make me ride a thousand leagues in the dead of winter, and the fighting's all over before I even get here."

"The exercise was probably good for you, your Grace." Vanion raised his voice. "How much longer, Khalad?" he called.

"Just a few more minutes, my Lord," Sparhawk's squire replied. "The timbers are starting to crack."

"Good," Vanion said bleakly. "I want to locate Zalasta. He and I have some things to talk about—at great length."

"They've all bolted, Sparhawk," Talen reported, returning from his quick survey of the ruined palace. "The gates are standing wide open, and we're the only people up here."

Sparhawk nodded wearily. It had been a long night, and he was emotionally as well as physically drained. He could still, however, feel that enormous calm that had settled over him when he had at last understood the true significance of his strange relationship with Bhelliom. There were some fleeting temptations—curiosity perhaps more than anything else—the desire to experiment and test the limits of newly recognized capabilities. He deliberately repressed them.

Go ahead, Sparhawk, Flute's voice in his mind had a slight challenge in it. He turned his head slightly to look quizzically at the ageless child standing beside his wife. Ehlana's face was serene as she ran her fingers through her long pale-blonde hair. *What did you want me to do?* he sent the thought back.

Anything that comes into your mind.

Why?

Aren't you just the least bit curious? Wouldn't you like to find out if you can turn a mountain inside out?

I can, he replied, *I don't see any reason to do something like that, though.*

You're hateful, Sparhawk! she suddenly flared.

What's your problem, Aphrael?

You're such a lump!

He smiled gently at her. *I know, but you love me anyway, don't you?*

"Sparhawk," Kalten called from the ornate bronze gate, "Vanion's coming up the hill. He's got Bergsten with him."

Vanion had known Sparhawk since his novitiate, but the weary-looking man in black armor seemed to be almost a stranger. There was something about his face and in his eyes that had never been there before. The preceptor approached his old friend with Patriarch Bergsten and Sephrenia with a sense of something very close to awe.

As soon as Ehlana saw Sephrenia, she ran to her with a low cry and embraced her fiercely.

"I see that you've wrecked another city, Sparhawk," Bergsten said with a broad grin. "That's getting to be a habit, you know."

"Good morning, your Grace," Sparhawk replied. "It's good to see you again."

"Did you do all this?" Bergsten gestured at the ruined temple and the half-collapsed palace.

"Klæl did most of it, your Grace."

The hulking churchman squared his shoulders. "I've got orders for you from Dolmant," he said. "You're supposed to turn the Bhelliom over to me. Why don't you do that now—before we both forget?"

"I'm afraid that isn't possible, your Grace," Sparhawk sighed. "I don't have it anymore."

"What did you do with it?"

"It no longer exists—at least not in the shape it was before. It's been freed from its confinement to continue its journey."

"You released it without consulting the Church? You're in trouble, Sparhawk."

"Oh, *do* be serious, Bergsten," Aphrael told him. "Sparhawk did what had to be done. I'll explain to Dolmant later."

Vanion, however, had something else on his mind. "This is all very interesting," he said bleakly, "but right now I'm far more concerned about finding Zalasta. Does anybody have any idea of where he went?"

"He might be under all that, Vanion," Ehlana told him, pointing at the ruined temple. "He and Ekatas were going there when they discovered that Sparhawk was here inside the walls of Cyrga. Ekatas escaped, and Mirtai killed him, but Zalasta might have been crushed when Klæl exploded the place."

"No," Aphrael said shortly. "He's nowhere in the city."

"I *really* want to find him, Divine One," Vanion said.

"Setras, dear," Aphrael said sweetly to her cousin, "would you see if you can find Zalasta for me? He has a great deal to answer for."

"I'll see what I can do, Aphrael," the handsome God promised, "but I really ought to get back to my studio. I've been letting my own work slide during all this."

"Please, Setras," she wheedled, unleashing that devastating little smile.

He laughed helplessly. "Do you see what I was talking about, Bergsten?" he said to the towering patriarch. "She's the most dangerous creature in the universe."

"So I've heard," Bergsten replied. "You'd probably better go ahead and do as she asks, Setras. You'll do it in the end anyway."

"Ah, there you are, Itagne-Ambassador," Vanion heard Atana Maris say in a deceptively pleasant tone of voice. He turned and saw the lithe young commander of the garrison at Cynestra descending on the clearly apprehensive Tamul diplomat. "I've been looking all over for you," she continued. "We have a great deal to talk about. Somehow, not one of your letters reached me. I think you should reprimand your messenger."

Itagne's face took on a trapped expression.

Betuana dispatched runners to Matherion just before noon, when the last of the demoralized Cyrgai capitulated. Sir Ulath made some issue of the fact that what had happened to the Cynesgans in the outer city might have influenced their decision to surrender to some degree. Patriarch Bergsten had taken to looking at his countryman with a critical and speculative eye. Bergsten was a rough-and-ready churchman, willing to bend all sorts of rules in the name of expediency, but he choked just a bit on Ulath's unbridled ecumenicism. "He's just a little too enthusiastic, Sparhawk," the huge Patriarch declared. "All right, I'll grant you that the Trolls were sort of useful, but—" He groped for a way to express his innate prejudices.

"There's a rather special kinship between Ulath and Bhlokw, your Grace." Sparhawk sidestepped the issue. "How much have we got left to do here? I'd sort of like to get my wife back to civilization."

"You can leave now, Sparhawk," Bergsten said with a shrug. "We can take care of cleaning up here. You didn't leave very much for the rest of us to worry about. I'll stay here with the knights to finish rounding up the Cyrgai; Tikume will take his Peloi back to Cynestra to help Itagne and Atana Maris set up the occupation; and Betuana's going to send her Atans into Arjuna to reestablish imperial authority." He made a sour face. "There's nothing really left but all the niggling little administrative details. You've robbed me of a very good fight, Sparhawk."

"I can send for more of Klæl's soldiers if you want, your Grace."

"No. That's all right, Sparhawk," Bergsten replied quickly. "I can live without any more of *those* fights. You'll be going straight back to Matherion?"

"Not straight back, your Grace. Courtesy obliges us to escort Anarae Xanetia back to Delphaeus."

"She's a very strange lady," Bergsten mused. "I keep catching myself just on the verge of genuflection every time she enters a room."

"She has that effect on people, your Grace. If you really don't need us here, I'll talk with the others, and we'll get ready to leave."

"What actually happened, Sparhawk?" Bergsten asked directly. "I have to make a report to Dolmant, and I can't make much sense out of what the others have been telling me."

"I'm not sure I can explain it, your Grace," Sparhawk replied. "Bhelliom and I were sort of combined for a while. It needed my arm, I guess." It was an easy answer, and it evaded a central issue that Sparhawk was not yet fully prepared to even think about.

"You were just a tool, then?" Bergsten's look was intent.

Sparhawk shrugged. "Aren't we all, your Grace? We're the instruments of God. That's what we get paid for."

"Sparhawk, you're right on the verge of heresy here. Don't throw the word *God* around like that."

"No, your Grace," Sparhawk agreed. "It's just a reflection of the limitations of language. There are things that we don't understand and don't have names for. We just lump them all together, call it *God*, and let it go at that. You and I are soldiers, Patriarch Bergsten. We get paid to hit the ground running when somebody blows a trumpet. Let Dolmant sort it out. That's what *he* gets paid for."

Sparhawk and his friends, accompanied by Kring, Betuana, and Engessa, rode out of shattered Cyrga shortly after dawn the following morning, bound for Sarna. Sparhawk had neither seen nor heard from Bhelliom since his encounter with Cyrgon, and he felt a peculiar sense of disappointment about that. The Troll-Gods had also departed with their children—all except for Bhlokw, who shambled along between Ulath and Tynian. Bhlokw was evasive about his reasons for accompanying them.

They rode northeast across the barren wastes of Cynesga, traveling in easy stages. The urgent need for haste was gone now. Sephrenia and Xanetia, once again working in concert, had returned all the faces to their rightful owners, and things were slowly settling back to normal.

It was about midmorning ten days after they had left Cyrga and when they were but a few leagues from Sarna that Vanion rode forward to join Sparhawk at the head of the column. "A word with you, Sparhawk?" he said.

"Of course."

"It's sort of private."

Sparhawk nodded, turned the column over to Bevier, and nudged Faran into a rolling canter. He and Vanion slowed again when they were about a quarter of a mile ahead of the others. "Sephrenia wants us to get married," Vanion said, cutting past any preamble.

"You're asking my permission?"

Vanion gave him a long, steady look.

"Sorry," Sparhawk apologized. "You took me by surprise. There are problems with that, you know. The Church will never approve, and neither will the Thousand of Styricum. We're not quite as hidebound as we used to be, but the notion of interracial or interfaith marriage still raises some hackles."

"I know," Vanion said glumly. "Dolmant probably wouldn't have any personal objections, but his hands are tied by Church law and doctrine."

"Who are you going to get to officiate, then?"

"Sephrenia's already solved that problem. Xanetia's going to perform the ceremony."

Sparhawk nearly choked on that.

"She *is* a priestess, Sparhawk."

"Well—technically, I suppose." Then Sparhawk suddenly broke out laughing.

"What's so funny?" Vanion demanded truculently.

"Can you imagine the look on Ortzel's face when he hears that a preceptor of one of the four orders, a Patriarch of the Church, has been married to one of the Thousand of Styricum by a Delphaeic priestess?"

"It *does* violate a few rules, doesn't it?" Vanion conceded with a wry smile.

"A *few*? Vanion, I doubt that you could find any single act that'd violate more."

"Do you object, too?"

"Not me, old friend. If this is what you and Sephrenia want, I'll back the two of you all the way up to the Hierocracy."

"Would you stand up with me, then? During the ceremony, I mean?"

Sparhawk clapped him on the shoulder. "I'd be honored, my friend."

"Good. That'll keep it all in the family. Sephrenia's already spoken to your wife about it. Ehlana's going to stand with her."

"Somehow I almost knew that was coming." Sparhawk laughed.

They passed through Sarna and proceeded north along a snow-clogged mountain trail toward Dirgis in southern Atan. After they left Dirgis, they turned westward again and rode higher into the mountains.

"We're leaving a very wide trail behind us, Sparhawk," Bevier said late one snowy afternoon, "and the trail's leading directly to Delphaeus."

Sparhawk turned and looked back. "You've got a point," he conceded. "Maybe I'd better have a talk with Aphrael. Things have changed a bit, but I don't think the Delphae are *quite* ready to welcome crowds of sightseers." He turned Faran around and rode back to join the ladies. Aphrael, as usual, rode with Sephrenia. "A suggestion, Divine One?" Sparhawk said tentatively.

"You sound just like Tynian."

He ignored that. "How good are you with weather?" he asked.

"Did you want it to be summer?"

"No. Actually I want a moderate-sized blizzard. We're leaving tracks in the snow behind us, and the tracks are pointing right straight at Delphaeus."

"What difference does that make?"

"The Delphae might not want unannounced visitors."

"There won't be any—announced or otherwise. You promised to seal their valley, didn't you?"

"Oh, God!" he said. "I'd forgotten about that! This is going to be a problem. I don't have Bhelliom anymore."

"Then you'd better try to get in touch with it, Sparhawk. A promise is a promise, after all. Xanetia's kept her part of the bargain, so you're morally obliged to keep yours."

Sparhawk was troubled. He rode off some distance into a thick grove of spindly sapling pines and dismounted. "Blue-Rose," he said aloud, not really expecting an answer. "Blue-Rose."

I hear thee, Anakha, the voice in his mind responded immediately. *I had thought thou might be in some way discontent with me.*

Never that, Blue-Rose. Thou hast fulfilled—or exceeded—all that I did require of thee. Our enemies are overthrown, and I am content. I did, however, pledge mine honor to the Delphae in exchange for their aid. I am obliged to seal up their valley that none of this world may come upon them.

I do recall thy pledge, Anakha. It was well-given. Soon, however, it will not be needful.

Thy meaning escapes me.

Watch then, my son, and learn. There was a lengthy pause. *It is not mine intent to offend, but why hast thou brought this to me?*

I gave my word that I would seal their valley, Father.

Then seal it.

I was not certain that I could still speak with thee to entreat thine aid.

Thou hast no need of aid, Anakha—not mine nor that of any other. Did not thine encounter with Cyrgon convince thee that all *things are possible for thee? Thou are Anakha and my son, and there is none other like thee in all the starry universe. It was needful to make thee so, that my design might be accomplished. Whatsoever thou couldst do through me, thou couldst as easily have done with thine own hand.* The voice paused. *I am, however, somewhat pleased that thou wert unaware of thine ability, for it did give me some opportunity to come to know thee. I shall think often of thee in my continuing journey. Let us then proceed to Delphaeus, where thy comrade Vanion and our dearly loved Sephrenia will be joined, and where thou wilt behold a wonder.*

Which particular wonder is that, Blue-Rose?

'Twould hardly be a wonder for thee shouldst thou know of it in advance, my son. There were faint traces of amusement in the voice as the sense of Bhelliom's presence faded.

It was early on a snowy evening when they crested a ridge and looked down into the valley where the glowing lake, misty in the swirling snowflakes, shone with a light almost like that of the moon. Ancient Cedon awaited them at the rude gate to this other hidden city, and standing beside him was Itagne's friend, Ekrasios.

They talked until quite late, for there was much to share. It was midmorning of the following day before Sparhawk awoke in the oddly sunken bedroom he shared with his wife. It was one of the peculiarities of Delphaeic construction that the floors of most of their rooms were below ground-level. Sparhawk didn't give it much thought, but Khalad had seemed quite intrigued by the notion.

Sparhawk gently kissed his still-sleeping wife, slipped quietly from their bed, and went looking for Vanion. He remembered his own wedding day, and he was quite sure that his friend was going to need some support.

He found the silvery-haired preceptor talking with Talen and Khalad in the makeshift stable. Khalad's face was bleak. "What's the problem?" Sparhawk asked as he joined them.

"My brother's a little unhappy," Talen explained. "He talked with Ekrasios and the other Delphae who dispersed Scarpa's army down in Arjuna, and nobody could tell him one way or the other about what happened to Krager."

"I'm going to operate on the theory that he's still alive," Khalad declared. "He's just too slippery not to have escaped."

"We have plans for you, Khalad," Vanion told him. "You're too valuable to spend your whole life trying to chase down a weaselly drunkard who may or may not have gotten out of Natayos alive."

"It won't take him all that long, Lord Vanion," Talen said. "As soon as Stragen and I get back to Cimmura, we'll talk with Platime, and he'll put out the word. If Krager's still alive—anywhere in the world—we'll find out about it."

"What are the ladies doing?" Vanion asked nervously.

"Ehlana's still asleep," Sparhawk replied. "Are you and Sephrenia going back to Matherion with us when we leave here?"

"Briefly," Vanion replied. "Sephrenia wants to speak with Sarabian about a few things. Then we'll go back to Atan with Betuana and Engessa. It's only a short trip from there to Sarsos. Have you noticed what's going on between Betuana and Engessa, by the way?"

Sparhawk nodded. "Evidently Betuana's decided that the Atans need a king. Engessa's suitable, and he's probably a great deal more intelligent than Androl was."

"That's not saying too much for him, Sparhawk," Talen said with a broad grin. "Androl was hardly any more intelligent than a brick."

The day wore on. The ladies, of course, made extended preparations. The knights, on the other hand, did what they could to keep Vanion's mind occupied.

An obscure tenet of the Delphaeic faith dictated that the ceremony take place on the shore of the glowing lake just at dusk. Sparhawk dimly perceived why this might be appropriate for the Shining Ones, but the wedding of Vanion and Sephrenia had little if anything to do with the covenant between the Delphae and their God. Courtesy, however, dictated that he keep his opinions to himself. He *did* offer to clothe Vanion in traditional black Pandion armor, but the preceptor chose instead to wear a white Styric robe. "I've fought my last war, Sparhawk," he said a bit sadly. "Dolmant won't have any choice but to excommunicate me and strip me of my knighthood after this. That makes me a civilian again. I never really enjoyed wearing armor all that much anyway." He looked curiously at Ulath and Tynian, who were talking earnestly with Bhlokw just outside the stable door. "What's going on there?"

"They're trying to explain the concept of a wedding to their friend. They aren't making very much headway."

"I don't imagine that Trolls set much store in ceremonies."

"Not really. When a male feels that way about a female, he takes her something—or somebody—to eat. If she eats it, they're married."

"And if she doesn't?"

Sparhawk shrugged. "They usually try to kill each other."

"Do you have any idea of why Bhlokw didn't go off with the rest of the Trolls?"

"Not a clue, Vanion. We haven't been able to get a straight answer out of him. Evidently there's something the Troll-Gods want him to do."

The afternoon dragged on, and Vanion grew more and more edgy with each passing moment. Inevitably, however, the grey day slid into a greyer evening, and dusk settled over the hidden valley of Delphaeus.

The path from the city gate to the edge of the lake had been carefully cleared, and Aphrael, who was not above cheating on occasion, had strewn it with flower petals. The Delphae, all aglow and singing an ancient hymn, lined the sides of the path. Vanion waited at the edge of the lake with Sparhawk, and the other members of their party stood in smiling anticipation as Sephrenia, with Ehlana at her side, emerged from the city to walk down to the shore.

"Courage, my son," Sparhawk murmured to his old friend.

"Are you trying to be funny?"

"Getting married doesn't really hurt, Vanion."

It happened when the bride and her attendant were perhaps halfway to the lakeshore. A sudden cloud of inky darkness appeared at the edge of the snow-covered meadow, and a great voice bellowed, "*NO!*" Then a spark of incandescent light emerged from the center of the cloud and began to swell ominously, surging and surrounded by a blazing halo of purplish light. Sparhawk recognized the phenomenon.

"I forbid this abomination!" the great voice roared.

"Zalasta!" Kalten exclaimed, staring at the rapidly expanding sphere.

The Styric was haggard and his hair and beard were matted. He wore his customary white robe and held his polished staff in his trembling hands. He stood inside the glowing sphere, surrounded by its protective nimbus. Sparhawk felt an icy calm descending over him as he prepared his mind and spirit for the inevitable confrontation.

"I have lost you, Sephrenia!" Zalasta declared, "but I *will* not permit you to wed this Elene!"

Aphrael dashed to her sister, her long black hair flying and a look of implacable determination on her small face.

"Fear not, Aphrael," Zalasta said, speaking in formal Styric. "I have not come to this accursed place to pit myself against thee or thine errant sister. I speak for Styricum in this matter, and I have come to prevent this obscene sham of a ceremony which will befoul our entire race." He straightened and pointed an accusing finger at Sephrenia. "I abjure thee, woman. Turn away from this unnatural act! Go out from here, Sephrenia of Ylara! This wedding shall not take place!"

"It *will*!" Sephrenia's voice rang out. "You cannot prevent it! Go away, Zalasta! You lost all claim on me when you tried to kill me!" She raised her chin. "And have you come to try again?"

"No, Sephrenia of Ylara. That was the result of a madness that came over me. There is yet another way to prevent this abomination." And he quickly turned, leveling his deadly staff at Vanion. A brilliant spark shot from the tip of the staff, sizzling in the pale evening light, straight as an arrow it flew, carrying death and all Zalasta's hatred.

But vigilant Anakha was ready, having already surmised at whom Zalasta would direct his attack. The deadly bolt flew straight, but agile Anakha stretched forth his hand to subdue it. He grasped the spark and saw its fury spurting out between his fingers. Then, like a small boy throwing a stone at a bird, he hurled it back to explode against the surface of the blazing sphere.

Well done, my son, Bhelliom's voice applauded.

Zalasta flinched violently within his protective sphere. Pale and shaken, he stared at the dreadful form of Bhelliom's Child.

Methodical Anakha raised his hand, palm outward, and began to chip away at the blazing envelope that protected the desperate Styric with bolt after bolt of the kind of force that creates suns, noting almost absently as he did that the wedding guests were scattering and that Sephrenia was rushing to Vanion's side. As he whipped out that force again and again, curious Anakha studied it, testing its power, probing for its limits.

He found none.

Implacable Anakha advanced on the deceitful Styric who had been ultimately the cause of a lifetime of suffering and woe. He knew that he could obliterate the now-terrified sorcerer with a single thought.

He chose not to.

Vengeful Anakha moved forward, savaging the Styric's last desperately erected defenses, cutting them away bit by bit and brushing aside Zalasta's pitiful efforts to respond.

"Anakha! It is not right!" The voice spoke in Trollish.

Puzzled Anakha turned to look.

It was Bhlokw, and Bhelliom's Child had respect for the shaggy priest of the Troll-Gods.

"This is the last of the wicked ones!" Bhlokw declared. "It is the wish of Khwaj to cause hurt to it! Will the Child of the flower-gem hear the words of Khwaj?"

Troubled Anakha considered the words of the priest of the Troll-Gods. "I will hear the words of Khwaj," he said. "It is right that I should do this, for Khwaj and I are pack-mates."

The enormity of the Fire-God appeared, steaming away the snow covering the meadow around him. "Will Bhelliom's Child be bound by the word of his pack-mate, Ulath-from-Thalesia?" he demanded in a voice that roared like a furnace.

"The word of Ulath-from-Thalesia is my word, Khwaj," honorable Anakha conceded.

"Then the wicked one is mine!"

Regretful Anakha curbed his wrath. "The words of Khwaj are right words," he agreed. "If Ulath-from-Thalesia has given the wicked one to Khwaj, then I will not say that it shall not be so." He looked at the terrified Styric, who was struggling desperately to retain some small measure of defense. "It is yours, Khwaj. It has caused me much hurt, and I would cause hurt to it in return, but if Ulath-from-Thalesia has said that it is the place of Khwaj to cause hurt to it, then so be it."

"Bhelliom's Child speaks well. You have honor, Anakha." The Fire-God looked accusingly at Zalasta. "You have done great wickedness, one-called-Zalasta."

Zalasta stared at Khwaj in terrified incomprehension.

"Say to it what I have said, Anakha," Khwaj requested. "It must know why it is being punished."

Courteous Anakha said, "I will, Khwaj." He looked sternly at the disheveled Styric. "You have caused me much pain, Zalasta," he said in a dreadful voice, speaking in Styric. "I was going to repay you for all those friends of mine you destroyed or corrupted, but Khwaj here has laid claim to you, and I'm going to honor his claim. You should have stayed away, Zalasta. Vanion would have hunted you down eventually, but death is a little thing, and once it over, it's over. What Khwaj is going to do to you will last for eternity."

"Does it understand?" Khwaj demanded.

"In some measure, Khwaj."

"In time it will understand more, and it has much time. It has always." And the dreadful Fire-God moved forward, blew away Zalasta's last pitiful defenses, and laid a strangely gentle hand on the cringing Styric's head. "Burn!" he commanded. "Run and burn until the end of days!"

And, all aflame, Zalasta of Styricum went out from that place shrieking and engulfed in endless fire.

Compassionate Anakha sighed as he watched the burning man run out across the snowy meadow, growing smaller and smaller in the distance and with his cries of agony and woe and unspeakable loneliness receding with him as he began the first hour of his eternal punishment.

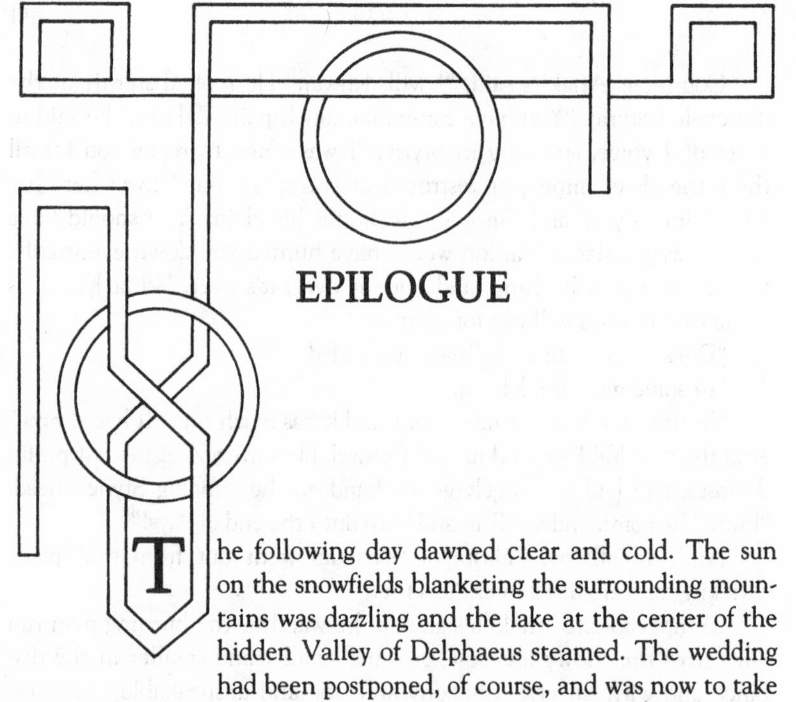

EPILOGUE

The following day dawned clear and cold. The sun on the snowfields blanketing the surrounding mountains was dazzling and the lake at the center of the hidden Valley of Delphaeus steamed. The wedding had been postponed, of course, and was now to take place this evening.

There had been questions, naturally, but Sparhawk had put them to rest by explaining that everything that had happened had been Bhelliom's doing, and that he had only been its instrument—which was not *exactly* a lie.

They spent the day quietly and gathered again as the sun went down and the shadows of evening settled over the valley. A strange sense of anticipation had nagged at Sparhawk all afternoon. Something was going to happen here. Bhelliom had told him that he would behold a wonder, and that was not the kind of word Bhelliom would use lightly.

The shadows of evening deepened, and Sparhawk and the other men escorted Vanion down to the shore of the glowing lake to await the bride's party while the Shining Ones once again sang the ancient hymn which had been so abruptly broken off the previous evening.

Then the bride appeared at the gate with the Queen of Elenia at her side and the other ladies close behind them. The Child-Goddess, whirling and dancing in the air and with her clear voice raised in flute-song, preceded them, again strewing their path with flower petals.

Sephrenia's face was serene as she came down the path to the lake. As the small Styric bride approached the man whom two major religions had forbidden her to marry, her personal Goddess provided a visible symbol that *she*, at least, approved. The stars had just begun to appear overhead, and one of them seemed to have lost its way. Like a tiny comet, a brilliant spark of light descended over the radiant Sephrenia and settled gently on her head as a glowing garland of spring flowers.

Sparhawk smiled gently. The similarity to the crowning of Mirtai during her rite of passage was a little too obvious to miss.

Critic, Aphrael's voice accused.

I didn't say anything.

Well, don't.

Sephrenia and Vanion joined hands as the Delphaeic hymn swelled to a climax. And then Xanetia, all aglow and accompanied by two other glowing forms, one white and the other blue, came walking across the lake. A yearning kind of murmur passed through the Delphae, and, as one, they sank reverently to their knees.

The Anarae tenderly embraced her Styric sister and kissed Vanion chastely on the cheek. "I have entreated Beloved Edaemus to join with us here and to bless this most happy union," she told the assemblage, "and he hath brought with him this other guest, who also hath some interest in our ceremony."

"Is that blue one who I think it is?" Kalten muttered to Sparhawk.

"Oh, yes," Sparhawk replied. "That's the form it took back in Cyrga—remember?—after I stuffed it down Klæl's throat."

"I was a little distracted at that point. Is that what it *really* looks like? After you peel off all the layers of sapphire, I mean?"

"I don't really think so. Bhelliom's a spirit, not a form. I think this particular shape is just a courtesy—for our benefit."

"I thought it had already left."

"No, not quite yet."

The glowing form of Edaemus straightened, somehow managing to look uncomfortable. Xanetia's face hardened and her eyes narrowed.

"I had thought ill of thee, Sephrenia of Ylara," the God of the Delphae admitted. "Mine Anarae hath persuaded me that my thought was in error. I do entreat thee to forgive me." Gentle Xanetia, it appeared, was not above a certain amount of bullying.

Sephrenia smiled benignly. "Of course I forgive thee, Divine Edaemus. I was not entirely blameless myself, I do confess."

"Let us all then pray to our separate Gods to bless the union of this man and this woman," Xanetia said in formal tones, "for methinks it doth presage a new birth of understanding and trust for all of mankind."

Sparhawk was a little dubious about that, but like the others, he bowed his head. He did not, however, direct his words to his Elene God. *Blue-Rose,* he sent out his thought.

Art thou praying, my son? The answering voice sounded slightly amused.

Consulting, Blue-Rose, Sparhawk corrected. *Others will direct our entreaty to our Elene God, and I do perceive that the time fast approaches when thou and I must part.*

Truly.

I thought to take this opportunity to ask a boon of thee.

If it be within my power.

I have seen the extent of thy power, Blue-Rose—and in some measure shared it. It is uncandid of thee to suggest that there are any *limits to what thou canst do.*

Be nice, Bhelliom murmured. It seemed to have become quite fond of that particular phrase. *What is this boon, my son?*

I do entreat thee to take all *thy power with thee when thou dost depart. It is a burden I am unprepared to accept. I am thy son, Blue-Rose, but I am also a man. I have neither the patience nor the wisdom to accept responsibility for what thou hast bestowed upon me. This world which thou hast made hath Gods in plenty. She doth not need another.*

Think, my son. Think of what thou dost propose to surrender.

I have, my father. I have been Anakha, for it was needful. Sparhawk struggled for a way to put his feelings into archaic Elenic. *When I did as Anakha confront the Styric Zalasta, I did feel a great detachment within myself, and that detachment abideth within me still. It seemeth me that thy gift hath altered me, making me more—or less—than a man. I would, an it please thee, no longer be 'patient Anakha' or 'curious Anakha' or 'implacable Anakha.' Anakha's task is finished. Now, with all my heart, I would be Sparhawk again. To be 'loving Sparhawk' or even 'irritated Sparhawk' would please me far more than the dreadful emptiness which is Anakha.*

There was a long pause. *Know that I am well-pleased with thee, my son.* There was pride in the silent voice in Sparhawk's mind. *I find more merit in thee in this moment than in any other. Be well, Sparhawk.* And the voice was gone.

The wedding ceremony was strange in some ways and very familiar in others. The celebration of the love that existed between Vanion and Sephrenia was there, but the preaching that distinguished the Elene ritual was not. At the conclusion, Xanetia gently laid her hands in loving benediction upon the heads of the two she had just joined. The gesture seemed to proclaim that the ceremony was at an end.

But it was not.

The second of the two figures that had accompanied Xanetia across the luminous waters of the lake stepped forward, all glowing blue, to add its own benediction. It raised its hands over the man and the woman, and for a brief moment they shared its azure incandescence. And when the light faded, Sephrenia had subtly changed. The cares and weariness which had marked her face in a dozen tiny ways were gone, and she appeared to be no older than Alean. The changes Bhelliom's glowing touch had wrought on Vanion were more visible and pronounced. His shoulders, which had imperceptibly slumped over the years, were straight again. His face was unlined, and his silvery hair and beard were now the dark auburn Sparhawk dimly remembered from the days of his novitiate. It was Bhelliom's final gift, and nothing could have pleased Sparhawk more.

Aphrael clapped her hands together with a squeal of delight and flew into the arms of the nebulous, glowing figure that had just rejuvenated her sister and Vanion.

Sparhawk rather carefully concealed a smile. The Child-Goddess had finally maneuvered Bhelliom into a position where she could unleash the devastating effects of her kisses upon it. The kisses *could*, of course, have been pure, effusive gratitude—but they probably weren't.

The wedding was at an end, but the glowing Delphae did not return to their empty city. Xanetia placed one supporting arm around Anari Cedon's frail old shoulders and guided him instead out onto the radiant surface of the lake, and the Shining Ones followed, raising a different hymn as incandescent Edaemus hovered in the air above them. The light of the lake grew brighter and brighter, and the ethereal glow of the Delphae seemed to merge, and individual figures were no longer distinguishable. Then, like the point of a spear, Edaemus streaked skyward, and all of his children streamed upward behind him. When Sparhawk and his friends had first come to Delphaeus, Anari Cedon had told them that the Delphae journeyed toward the light and that they would *become* the light, but that there were yet impediments. Bhelliom had evidently removed those barriers. The Delphae marked the starry sky like a comet as they rose together on the first step of their inconceivable journey.

The pale, clear radiance of the lake was gone, but it was not dark. An azure spark hung over it as Bhelliom surveyed what it had wrought and found that it was good. Then it, too, rose from the earth to rejoin the eternal stars.

They stayed that night in deserted Delphaeus, and Sparhawk awoke early as usual. He dressed himself quietly and left the simple bedroom and his tousled, sleeping wife to go outside to check the weather.

Flute joined him when he reached the city gate. "Why don't you put some shoes on?" he asked her, noting that her bare, grass-stained little feet were sunk in the snow.

"What do I need with shoes, Father?" She held out her arms, and he picked her up.

"It was quite a night, wasn't it?" he said, looking up at the cloudy sky.

"Why did you do that, Sparhawk?"

"Do what?"

"You know what I mean. Do you realize what you could have done? You could have turned this world into a paradise, but you threw it all away."

"I don't think that would have been a good idea, Aphrael. My idea of paradise would probably have been different from other people's." He sniffed at the chill air. "I think we've got weather coming," he observed.

"Don't change the subject. You had ultimate power. Why did you give it up?"

He sighed. "I didn't really like it all that much. There wasn't any effort involved in it, and when you get something without working for it, it doesn't really have any value. Besides, there are people who have claims on me."

"What's that got to do with it?"

"What could I have done if Ehlana had decided that she wanted Arcium? Or if Dolmant had decided that he wanted to convert Styricum, or all of Tamuli? I have loyalties and obligations, Aphrael, and sooner or later, I'd have made bad decisions because of them. Trust me. I made the right choice."

"I think you're going to regret it."

"I've regretted lots of things. You learn to live with it. Can you get us to Matherion?"

"You could have done it yourself, you know."

"Don't beat it into the ground, Aphrael. If you don't want to, then we'll just plow our way through the snow. We've done it before."

"You're hateful, Sparhawk. You *know* I won't let you do that."

"*Now* do you see what I mean about the power of loyalties and obligations?"

"Don't start lecturing me. I'm in no mood for it. Go wake up the others, and let's get started."

"Whatever you say, Divine One."

They located the rather large communal kitchen in which the Delphae had prepared all their meals and the storerooms where the food was kept. Despite their eons of enmity, the dietary prejudices of the Styrics and Delphae were remarkably similar. Sephrenia found the breakfast much to her liking, but Kalten grumbled a great deal. He *did* eat three helpings, however.

"Whatever happened to friend Bhlokw?" Kring asked, pushing back his plate. "I just realized that I haven't seen him since Zalasta took fire."

"He went off with his Gods, Domi," Tynian replied. "He did what they sent him to do, and now he and the rest of the Trolls are on their way back to Thalesia. He wished us all good hunting. That's about as close as a Troll can come to saying good-bye."

"It might sound a little strange," Kring admitted, "but I liked him."

"He's a good pack-mate," Ulath said. "He hunts well, and he's willing to share what he kills with the others in the pack."

"Oh, yes," Tynian agreed with a shudder. "If it wasn't a freshly killed dog, it was a haunch of raw Cyrgai."

"It was what he had, Tynian," Ulath defended his shaggy friend, "and he was ready to share it. You can't ask more than that, can you?"

"Sir Ulath," Talen said, "I've just eaten. Do you suppose we could talk about something else?"

They saddled their horses and rode out of Delphaeus.

As he left, Khalad reined in, dismounted, and closed the gate. "Why did you do that?" Talen asked him. "The Delphae aren't coming back, you know."

"It's the proper thing to do," Khalad said as he remounted. "Leaving it open would have been disrespectful."

Since they all knew who she really was, Flute made no attempt to conceal her tampering this time. The horses plodded along, as horses will if they aren't being pushed, but every few minutes the horizon flickered and changed. Once, somewhat east of Dirgis, Sparhawk rose in his stirrups to look to the rear. Their clearly visible trail stretched back to the middle of an open meadow where it stopped abruptly, almost as if the horses and riders had been dropped there out of the sky.

They reached the now-familiar hilltop overlooking fire-domed Matherion and its harbor just as evening was approaching, and they rode down to the city gratefully. They had all been long on the road, and it was good to be home again. Sparhawk rather quickly amended that thought in his mind. Matherion was not really home. Home was a dank, unlovely city on the Cimmura River, half a world away.

There were some startled looks at the gate of the imperial compound, and some that were even more startled at the drawbridge to Ehlana's castle. Vanion had stubbornly rejected his wife's urgings to conceal his head and face with the hood of his cloak and quite literally flaunted the fact that thirty-odd years had somehow fallen away. Vanion was like that sometimes.

There were some visible changes inside the castle as well. They found the emperor in the blue-draped sitting room on the second floor, and in addition to Baroness Melidere, Emban, and Oscagne, three of his wives, Elysoun, Gahenas, and Liatris, were also present. Elysoun was probably the most notable, since she was now modestly dressed.

"Good God, Vanion!" Emban exclaimed when he saw the Pandion Preceptor, "what's happened to you?"

"I got married, your Grace," Vanion replied. He smoothed back his mahogany-colored hair. "This was one of the wedding presents. Do you like it?"

"You look ridiculous!"

"Oh, I wouldn't say that," Sephrenia disagreed. "I rather like it."

"I gather that congratulations are in order," Sarabian said urbanely. There was a marked difference in the Tamul emperor. He had a self-confidence and a commanding presence that had not been there before. "Considering the enormous religious barriers, who performed the ceremony?"

"Xanetia did, your Majesty," Vanion replied. "Delphaeic doctrine didn't have any objections."

Sarabian looked around. "Where *is* Xanetia?" he asked.

Sephrenia pointed upward with one finger. "Out there," she replied rather sadly, "with the rest of the Delphae."

"What?" The emperor's expression was baffled.

"Edaemus took them, Sarabian," Flute explained. "Evidently he and Bhelliom made some sort of arrangement." She looked around. "Where's Danae?"

"She's in her room, Divine One," Baroness Melidere said. "She was a little tired, so she went to bed early."

"I'd better go tell her that her mother's home," the Child-Goddess said, going toward the door leading back into the rest of the apartment.

"We've received any number of reports," Foreign Minister Oscagne said, "but they were all couched in generalities—'the war's over, and we won,' that sort of thing. No offense intended, Queen Betuana. Your Atans are excellent messengers, but it's hard to get details out of them."

She shrugged. "Perhaps it's a racial flaw, Oscagne-Excellency." As she always did now, Betuana stood very close to the silent Engessa. She seemed reluctant to let him get very far away from her side.

"The thing that puzzles me the most is the rather garbled message I got from my brother," Oscagne confessed.

"Itagne-Ambassador has a great deal on his mind just now," Betuana said blandly.

"Oh?"

"He and Atana Maris became quite friendly when he was posted to Cynestra last fall. *He* didn't take it too seriously, but *she* did. She came looking for him. She found him in Cyrga and took him back with her to Cynestra."

"Really?" Oscagne said, his face betraying no hint of a smile. Then he shrugged. "Oh, well," he added, "it's time that Itagne settled down anyway. As I recall, Atana Maris is a very vigorous young woman."

"Yes, Oscagne-Excellency, and very determined. I think your clever brother's days as a bachelor are numbered."

"What a shame," Oscagne sighed. "Pardon me a moment." He went rather quickly into the next room, and they all heard the sounds of muffled laughter coming from there.

And then Danae, her black hair flying, came running into the room to hurl herself into her mother's arms.

Sarabian's face went bleak. "Who finally killed Zalasta?" he asked. "He was at the bottom of all this, when you get right down to it."

"Zalasta isn't dead," Sephrenia said sorrowfully, lifting Flute into her lap.

"He *isn't*? How did he manage to get away?"

"We let him go, your Majesty," Ulath replied.

"Are you mad? You *know* the kind of trouble he can stir up."

"He won't be causing any more trouble, your Majesty," Vanion said, "unless he happens to start a few grass fires."

"He won't do that, Vanion," Flute said. "It's a spiritual fire, not a real one."

"Will somebody *please* tell me what happened?" Sarabian said.

"Zalasta showed up at Sephrenia's wedding, your Majesty," Ulath told him. "He tried to kill Vanion, but Sparhawk stopped him. Then our friend here was just about to do something fairly permanent about Zalasta, but Khwaj asserted a prior claim. Sparhawk considered the politics of the situation and agreed. Then Khwaj set Zalasta on fire."

"What a gruesome idea," Sarabian shuddered. Then he looked at

Sephrenia. "I thought you said that he isn't dead. But Sir Ulath just told me that he'd been burned to death."

"No, your Majesty," Ulath corrected. "I just said that Khwaj set fire to him. The same thing happened to Baron Parok."

"The Trollish notion of justice sort of appeals to me," Sarabian said with a bleak smile. "How long will they burn?"

"Forever, your Majesty," Tynian replied somberly. "The fire is eternal."

"Good God!"

"It's further than I'd have gone," Sparhawk conceded, "but as Ulath said, there were political considerations involved."

They talked until quite late, providing details of the campaign, the rescue of Ehlana and Alean, the freeing of Bhelliom, and the final confrontation between Sparhawk and Cyrgon. Sparhawk rather carefully stressed his surrogacy in that particular event and made some issue of the fact that he was no longer Anakha. He wanted that particular book permanently closed with no doubts remaining in anyone's mind that there was absolutely no way to reopen it.

Also during the course of that long conversation, Sarabian told them of the attempt on his life by Chacole and Torellia. "They might have actually pulled it off if it hadn't been for Elysoun," he concluded, looking fondly at his now-demure Valesian wife.

Mirtai looked at Elysoun with one questioningly raised eyebrow. "Why the change of costume?" she asked bluntly.

Elysoun shrugged. "I'm with child," she replied. "I guess my days of adventuring are over." She looked at Mirtai's puzzled expression. "It's a Valesian custom," she explained. "We're allowed a certain amount of freedom until our first pregnancy. After that, we're supposed to behave ourselves." She smiled. "I'd more or less exhausted the potentials of the imperial compound anyway," she added. "Now it's time to settle down—and catch up on my sleep."

"Has anybody heard from Stragen and Caalador?" Talen asked.

"Viscount Stragen and Duke Caalador came back to Matherion a week ago," Sarabian replied.

"New embellishments?" Ehlana asked with some surprise.

"Rewards for services rendered, Ehlana." Sarabian smiled. "It seemed appropriate. Duke Caalador's accepted a position in the Ministry of the Interior, so he's gone back to Lebas to settle up his affairs there."

"And Stragen?"

"He's on his way to Astel, your Majesty," Baroness Melidere replied with a bleak smile. "He said that he wants to have a few words with Elron."

"Did Elron manage to get out of Natayos alive?" Kalten sounded surprised. "Ekrasios said that the Shining Ones had obliterated the place."

"The word Caalador picked up was that Elron hid out somewhere while the Shining Ones were dissolving Scarpa and Cyzada. Then, after they were gone, he crept out of the ruins and bolted for home. Stragen's going to look him up." The Baroness looked at Khalad. "Krager got out as well," she told him. "Caalador found out that he was bound for Zenga in eastern Cammoria. There's something you should know about Krager, though."

"Oh?"

"Do you remember how King Wargun died?"

"His liver finally gave out on him, didn't it?"

She nodded. "The same thing's happening to Krager. Caalador talked with a man named Orden in the town of Delo. Krager was completely out of his head when they put him on the ship bound for Zenga."

"He's still alive, though, isn't he?" Khalad asked bleakly.

"If you can call it that." She sighed. "Let it go, Khalad. He wouldn't even feel it if you ran your sword through him. He wouldn't know who you were or why you were killing him."

"Thank you, Baroness," Khalad said, "but I think that when we get back to Eosia, Berit and I'll run on down to Zenga just to make sure. Krager's gotten away from us just a few too many times to take any chances. I want to see him in the ground."

"Can I come, too?" Talen asked eagerly.

"No," Khalad replied.

"What do you mean, no?"

"It's time for you to start your novitiate."

"That can wait."

"No, it can't. You're already a half a year late. If you don't start training now, you'll never become proficient."

Vanion looked approvingly at Sparhawk's squire. "Don't forget what we talked about earlier, Sparhawk," he said. "And pass my recommendation on to Dolmant."

"What's this?" Khalad asked.

"I'll tell you about it later," Sparhawk replied.

"Oh, by the way, Ehlana," Sarabian said, "as long as the subject's come up anyway, would you be put out with me if I bestowed a title on your little songbird here?" He smiled fondly at Alean. "I certainly hope not, dear heart, because I'm going to do it anyway—for outstanding service to the empire, if nothing else."

"What a splendid idea, Sarabian!" Ehlana exclaimed.

"I can't really take much credit for the notion of the titles, I'm afraid," he admitted a bit ruefully. "Actually, they were your daughter's idea. Her Royal Highness is a very strong-minded little girl."

Sparhawk glanced briefly at his daughter and then at Flute. They wore identical expressions of smug self-satisfaction. Divine Aphrael clearly would not let anything stand in the way of her matchmaking. Sparhawk smiled briefly and then cleared his throat. "Ah—your Majesty," he said to the emperor, "it's growing rather late, and we're all tired. I'd suggest that we continue this tomorrow."

"Of course, Prince Sparhawk," Sarabian agreed, rising to his feet.

"A word with you, Sparhawk?" Patriarch Emban said as the others started to file out.

"Of course." They waited until they were alone in the room.

"What are we going to do about Vanion and Sephrenia?" Emban asked.

"I don't exactly follow you, your Grace."

"This so-called marriage is going to put Dolmant in a very difficult position, you know."

"It's not a 'so-called marriage,' Emban," Sparhawk said firmly, cutting across the formalities.

"You know what I mean. The conservatives in the Hierocracy will probably try to use it to weaken Sarathi's position."

"Why tell them, then? It's none of their business. A lot of things that our theology can't explain have happened here in Tamuli, your Grace. The empire's outside the jurisdiction of our Church, so why tell the Hierocracy anything about them?"

"I can't just lie to them, Sparhawk."

"I didn't suggest that. Just don't talk about it."

"I *have* to report to Dolmant."

"That's all right. He's flexible." Sparhawk considered it. "That's probably your best course anyway. We'll take Dolmant off to one side and tell him about everything that's happened here. We'll let *him* decide how much to tell the Hierocracy."

"You're putting an awful burden on him, Sparhawk."

Sparhawk shrugged. "That's what he gets paid for, isn't it? Now if you'll excuse me, your Grace, there's a family reunion going on that I should probably attend."

There was a melancholy sense of endings for the next several weeks. They were all fully aware of the fact that once the weather broke, most of them would be leaving Matherion. The likelihood that they would ever gather again was very slight. They savored their moments together, and there were frequent private little interludes when two or perhaps three of them would gather in out-of-the way places, ostensibly to talk at great length about inconsequential matters, but in fact to try to cement faces, the sounds of voices, and very personal connections forever in their memories.

Sparhawk entered the sitting room one blustery morning to find Sarabian and Oscagne with their heads together over a bound book of some kind. There was a certain outrage in their expressions. "Trouble?" Sparhawk asked.

"Politics," Sarabian said sourly. "That's always trouble."

"The Contemporary History Department at the university has just published their version of recent events, Prince Sparhawk," Oscagne explained. "There's very little truth in it—particularly in light of the fact that Pondia Subat, our esteemed prime minister, turns out to be a hero."

"I should have deleted Subat as soon as I found out about his activities," Sarabian said moodily. "Who would be the best one to answer this tripe, Oscagne?"

"My brother, your Majesty," the foreign minister replied promptly. "He *is* a member of the faculty, and he has a certain reputation. Unfortunately, he's in Cynestra just now."

"Send for him, Oscagne. Get him back here before Contemporary History contaminates the thinking of a whole generation."

"Maris will want to come, too, your Majesty."

"Fine. Your brother's too clever by half. Let's keep Atana Maris nice and close to him. She might be able to teach him humility."

"What are we going to do with the Cyrgai, your Majesty?" Sparhawk asked. "Sephrenia says that the curse that confined them was lifted when Cyrgon died, and even though it's not actually their fault, there really isn't any place for them in the modern world."

"I've been brooding about that myself," the emperor admitted. "I think we'll want to keep them away from normal human beings. There's an island about five hundred leagues east of Tega. It's fairly fertile and it has a more or less acceptable climate. Since the Cyrgai are so fond of isolation, it should turn the trick. How long do you think it might take them to invent boats?"

"Several thousand years, your Majesty. The Cyrgai aren't very creative."

Sarabian grinned at him. "I'd say that's the perfect place, then."

Sparhawk grinned back. "Sounds good to me," he agreed.

Spring came to eastern Tamuli in a rush that year. A sudden warm, wet wind blew in off the Tamul Sea, cutting the snow off the sides of nearby mountains in a single night. The streams ran bank-full, of course, so it was still too early for travel. Sparhawk's impatience grew with each lingering day. It was not so much that he had anything pressing to attend to, but more that this prolonged farewell was extremely painful.

There *was* one fairly extended argument. Ehlana insisted at first that they should all journey to Atan to celebrate the wedding of Mirtai and Kring.

"You're being ignorant again, Ehlana," Mirtai finally told her with characteristic bluntness. "You've seen weddings before, and you've got a kingdom to run. Go back to Cimmura where you belong."

"Don't you want me to be present?" Ehlana's eyes filled with tears.

Mirtai embraced her. "You *will* be, Ehlana," she said. "You're in my heart forever now. Go back to Cimmura. I'll come by after Kring and I get settled in Pela—or wherever we decide to live."

Vanion and Sephrenia decided to accompany Queen Betuana's party as far as Atana and then to proceed on to Sarsos. "It's probably the best place for us, dear one," Sephrenia told Sparhawk. "I have a certain status there, and I can shout down the fanatics who'll try to object to the fact that Vanion and I are married now."

"Well put," Sparhawk said. Then he sighed. "I'm going to miss you, little mother," he told her. "You and Vanion won't ever be able to come back to Eosia, you know."

"Don't be absurd, Sparhawk." She laughed. "I've always gone anyplace I wanted to go, and I always will. There are ways I can disguise Vanion's face—and mine—so we'll stop by from time to time. I want to keep an eye on your daughter, if nothing else." Then she kissed him. "Run along now, dear one. I have to go talk with Sarabian about Betuana."

"Oh?"

"She's been muttering some nonsense about abdicating so that she can marry Engessa. The Atans are subject to the imperial crown, so I have to persuade Sarabian to keep her from doing something foolish. Engessa will make a very good co-ruler, and Sarabian needs stability in Atan."

As the spring runoff began to recede and the soggy fields around the capital began to dry out, Sparhawk went down to the harbor looking for Captain Sorgi. There were less battered and more luxurious ships swinging at anchor in the crowded harbor, but Sparhawk trusted Sorgi, and to sail home with him would provide a comforting sense of continuity to the conclusion of this whole business. He found the curly-haired sea captain in a neat, well-lighted wharfside tavern that was quite obviously run by an Elene proprietor.

"There'll be thirteen of us, Captain," Sparhawk said, "and seven horses."

"We'll be a bit crowded, Master Cluff," Sorgi replied, squinting at the ceiling, "but I think we can manage. Are you going to be covering the cost of the passage yourself?"

Sparhawk grinned. "The emperor has graciously offered to defray the expense," he said. "He's a friend, so please don't bankrupt him."

Sorgi grinned back. "I wouldn't think of it, Master Cluff." He leaned back in his chair. "It's been an interesting time, and the Tamul Empire's an interesting place, but it'll be good to get back home again."

"Yes," Sparhawk agreed. "Sometimes it seems that I've spent my whole life trying to get back home."

"I'll reckon up the cost of the voyage and have my bo'sun bring it up to the imperial compound to you. I almost lost him down in Beresa, you know."

"Your bo'sun?"

Sorgi nodded. "A couple of rascals waylaid him in an alleyway. He barely got out alive."

"Imagine that," Sparhawk said blandly. Evidently Valash had tried to cut some corners on the hiring of assassins as well as on everything else.

"When exactly did you want to sail, Master Cluff?"

"We haven't quite decided yet—sometime in the next week or so. I'll let you know. Some of our friends are leaving to go overland to Atan. It might be best if we sailed on the same day."

"Good idea," Sorgi approved. "It's always best not to drag out the farewells. Sailors have learned how to say good-bye in a hurry. When the time comes to leave, we always have to catch the tide, and it won't wait."

"Well put, Sorgi." Sparhawk smiled.

Not surprisingly it was Betuana who made the decision. "We'll leave tomorrow," she declared flatly at the dinner table a week later.

"So soon?" Sarabian's voice sounded slightly stricken.

"The streams are down and the fields are dry, Sarabian-Emperor," she pointed out. "Why should we linger?"

"Well . . ." he let it trail off.

"You're too sentimental, Sarabian," she told him bluntly. "You know that we're going to leave. Why prolong it? Come to Atan next fall, and we'll go boar hunting. You spend too much time penned up here in Matherion."

"It's pretty hard for me to get away," he said dubiously. "Somebody has to stay here and mind the store."

"Let Oscagne do it. He's honorable, so he won't steal too much."

"Your Majesty!" Oscagne protested.

She smiled at him. "I was only teasing you, Oscagne," she told him. "Friends can do that without giving offense."

There was little sleep for any of them that night. There was packing, of course, and a myriad of other preparations, but the bulk of the night was spent running up and down the hallways with urgent messages that were all basically the same: "Promise that we'll keep in touch."

And they all did promise, of course, and they all really meant it. The fading of that resolve would not begin for at least a year—or maybe even two.

They gathered in the castle courtyard just as dawn was breaking over the Tamul Sea. There were all the customary kisses and embraces and gruff handshakes.

It was finally Khalad, good, solid, dependable Khalad, who looked appraisingly at the eastern sky, cleared his throat, and said, "We'd better get started, Sparhawk. Sorgi'll charge you for an extra day if you make him miss the morning tide."

"Right," Sparhawk agreed. He lifted Ehlana up into the open carriage Sarabian had provided and in which Emban, Talen, Alean, and Melidere were already seated. Then he looked around and saw Danae and Flute speaking quietly together. "Danae," he called his daughter, "time to go."

The Crown Princess of Elenia kissed the Child-Goddess of Styricum one last time and obediently came across the courtyard to her father.

"Thanks for stopping by, Sparhawk," Sarabian said simply, holding out his hand.

Sparhawk took the hand in his own. "My pleasure, Sarabian," he replied. Then he swung himself up into Faran's saddle and led the way across the drawbridge and out onto the still-shadowy lawns.

It took perhaps a quarter of an hour to reach the harbor, and another half hour to load the horses in the forward hold. Sparhawk came back up on deck where the others waited and looked toward the east, where the sun had not yet risen.

"All ready, Master Cluff?" Sorgi called from the quarterdeck at the stern of his ship.

"That's it, Captain Sorgi," Sparhawk called back. "We've done what we came to do. Let's go home."

The self-important bo'sun strutted up and down the deck unnecessarily supervising the casting off of all lines and the raising of the sails.

The tide was moving quite rapidly, and there was a good following breeze. Sorgi skillfully maneuvered his battered old ship out through the harbor to the open sea.

Sparhawk lifted Danae in one arm and put the other about Ehlana's shoulders, and they stood at the port rail looking back at the city the Tamuls called the center of the world. Sorgi swung his tiller over to take a southeasterly course to round the peninsula, and just as the sails bellied out in the breeze, the sun slid above the eastern horizon.

Matherion had been pale in the shadows of dawn, but as the sun rose, the opalescent domes took fire, and shimmering, rainbow-colored light played across the gleaming surfaces. Sparhawk and his wife and daughter stood at the rail, their eyes filled with the wonder of the glowing city that seemed somehow to be bidding them its own farewell and wishing them a safe voyage home.

Here ends the tale of Sparhawk's adventures in the Tamul Empire.

But further magic awaits.
Follow David Eddings back to the world of The Belgariad *and* The Malloreon.
Follow him back to the very beginning, for the story behind the legend of
BELGARATH THE SORCERER!

ABOUT THE AUTHOR

DAVID EDDINGS was born in Spokane, Washington, in 1931, and was raised in the Puget Sound area north of Seattle. He received a Bachelor of Arts degree from Reed College in Portland, Oregon, in 1954 and a Master of Arts degree from the University of Washington in 1961. He has served in the United States Army, worked as a buyer for the Boeing Company, has been a grocery clerk, and has taught college English. He has lived in many parts of the United States.

His first novel, *High Hunt* (published by Putnam in 1973), was a contemporary adventure story. The field of fantasy has always been of interest to him, however, and he turned to THE BELGARIAD in an effort to develop certain technical and philosophical ideas concerning the genre.

Eddings and his wife, Leigh, currently reside in the Southwest.